The One F

by

Jake Lewin

1.

A New Beginning

"Here he comes, Richard!"

"You're the last man!"

"Don't foul him!"

Richard was playing for his village youth team against another local side. He was running alongside their left winger Nathan, who had just managed to dribble past the two players in front of him. He pulled out his extravagant party trick of multiple scissors feints, as he pushed into the penalty area.

He'll cut inside after three rounds, Richard remembered what he wrote on his pre-match notes and stuck out his left foot once Nathan completed his latest step overs. He took the ball away from the winger cleanly and after he calmly cleared the danger, the referee blew the whistle to signal half time.

"Another great tackle, Richard! You're truly unbeatable today!"

I wonder what he thinks, Richard acknowledged the praise from his coach Simon but couldn't help glancing over at David, who was jotting something down in his pocket-sized notebook.

It was just another Saturday morning in September. Richard's youth football team were playing their third game of what was his second full season with the club, since his family's return from Munich in southern Germany after eight years.

He had his ten-minute walk to the village green with all the usual essentials in his bag – a new pair of boots for the season, a pair of slip-on shin pads, a bottle of orange flavoured energy drink, a ten pound note and his mobile phone. He never packed more and he never packed less.

When he arrived at the ground covered by a sea of fiery-red leaves, his coach Simon was having a friendly chat with another man at the other end of the pitch. He gave them a wave before going into the dressing room to put his boots and shin pads on.

Looking good for action! He thought after checking the mirror to see if his short brown hair was still as neatly styled to the right as he intended.

"How can your boots look brand new after the mud bath last week?" his friend Mark the left back asked.

"I cleaned them with a toothbrush as soon as I got home," he explained.

"I guess that's what I'll do with such an expensive pair of boots..." Mark muttered.

"I treat them all the same, but I do love these. All black with a little bit of gold sprinkles, the perfect combination. They are so much lighter than the other ones, too."

"Didn't you win them from a side bet with your dad?"

"That's the best part. Are you ready? Let's go."

The two boys joined their teammates for their warm up on the pitch. Simon was there waiting with the man he was talking to a moment ago.

"Hey Richard, can you come and meet this gentleman here please?" Simon said as he waved Richard over.

Richard had a look at this man. He was in his forties, a couple of inches taller than him at about five foot eleven, looked physically fit with barely any unnecessary fat, had a head full of curly chestnut hair and a slightly patchy beard. He seemed friendly but his eyes told Richard that he was a deep thinker, and he was probably analysing him at the same time.

"Hi, I'm Richard. Nice to meet you."

"Hi Richard, how are you doing? My name is David Norman, Head of Under 18's from Thames Ditton Football Club."

2

"The Black Dragons that were promoted to the Championship last season?" Mark overheard and got excited. "Are you here to scout Richard?"

"It's not a big deal – Simon and I used to play here when we were young," David said with a warm, gentle smile. "We're meeting up for dinner today and he asked me to come early to see you play. Are you nervous?"

"Nerves are for the unprepared."

"That's good, I like your confidence. What's your full name Richard?"

"It's Richard Lucas, sir. I'll see you later."

"Well done boys," Simon said as he handed out the water bottles at half time. "Nice work in defence. Just need to spread the ball wide a bit quicker to get those crosses in."

"So I see that you're well prepared, Richard," David referred to his previous remark.

"The way his body moves, it's a giveaway really," Richard said in his usual emotion-less tone, while he downed the second half of his energy drink.

David smiled and pulled Simon away for a chat that was inaudible. They came back and Simon announced, "I want you to play in centre midfield for the second half, Richard. Can you swap with him please, Jordan?"

"How does that work? Richard's only a right back and never played there before?" Jordan asked.

"Just do as I said. I want you to take care of that Nathan as well as Richard did," Simon responded.

For the first time in his football journey, Richard was playing in centre midfield for a full-sized team. He always believed that was his best position but was never persistent enough to fight over all the other kids for it.

Is that David's idea? They were dangerous playing through us in the middle during the first half so he wants me to stop them? Then they'll go wide and put crosses it... oh I get it, their strikers can't beat our big centre backs. Cunning plan... is that normal for a youth team in the Championship? Anyway, I guess I need to carry out my

3

side of the bargain for that to work. Richard analysed the new arrangement in his head.

The second half started. The away side continued to attack through the middle but they immediately faced a wall in the shape of Richard in front of them, as he energetically pressed the players in possession and either dispossessed them or cut out their passes. He was like a magnet to the ball as he accurately predicted the movements and passing lines of his opponents.

Just as David planned, they ended up avoiding the middle and played on the wings instead. But their crosses were easily dealt with by the home team's centre backs. They tried cutting back from the byline but they were cut out by the well-positioned Richard. On one such occasion he found Mark in space on the left and his cross was headed in by the centre forward.

Frustrated by Richard's constant blockage of their advances, the away side's big centre midfielder took matters into his own hands and tried to take the defender on. He brought the ball to one side and when Richard approached him, he gave him a legitimate but forceful shoulder charge. Richard saw that coming and while there was a huge difference in weight, he countered the challenge with a small jump and maintained his balance when he landed. And while the big midfielder was stunned by his resistance, he slid in and kicked the ball away.

The pattern continued as no matter what the midfielder threw at Richard, he had a way to bounce back and tackled him. There was simply no way through and the 1-0 score line remained for the rest of the match.

"That was well executed, boys!" Simon gave his post-match speech in the dressing room. "The key in the second half is to make their play predictable by forcing them wide, to play around us and not through. They ended up crossing it into the heads of big Joe and Tony and the rest was easy. Good counter attacking and a lovely finish too, Tyler."

"That was way more tactical then the normal Simon," Mark whispered.

4

"Of course it wasn't his idea," Richard said. "It was David the coach from the Championship."

"Do you think he likes you? You look so cool in midfield today."

"I don't know the level he's looking for... I've done what I can. I love playing in the middle, even though I've never been this tired before."

"Well, good luck!"

Simon asked Richard to stay behind and they met David outside after all the other kids had left.

"Hey Richard, you had a good game there. How did you feel about the second half?" he asked.

"It's the first time I played as a centre mid. That was challenging but enjoyable."

"Did this man not play you there before?" David said while pointing at Simon. "He's missing a trick here – I think you will be a great number six."

"Was it your intention to use me as a road block to direct their play wide? How did you know they'll do it?"

"After your brilliant first half and the way you started the second, of course they'd avoid going against you in the middle. But they didn't know it was a plan all along to nullify their attack."

"Are all these analyses and plans what you do ahead of every single youth game?"

"Yes, it is. Do you want to come and see it yourself?" David asked with a smile.

"Does it mean-"

"Yes. Come and have a trial with us next week. Come Friday after lunch and stay until Sunday, is that okay?"

"I'll arrange with the school. I'm sure they'll let me do it given it's only September."

"Good, I'll see you then. Simon will drop your parents a message to confirm."

"See you next week, David."

"Good luck with that Richard, you're the best I have," Simon said. "Time for a beer at the local, David?"

"You know I'll never say no to that!" David said with a satisfying smile.

5

Richard turned up at the Thames Ditton academy in Surrey for a trial a week later. David and his assistant met him at the reception.

"Here you are Richard," David opened up the conversation. "Thanks for making the journey. This is Nick Easter, one of our youth coaches here. He will be looking after you over these three days."

"Pleased to meet you, Richard. Are you ready for your stay here?"

Richard learnt from his online research that Nick used to play for the club and only retired at the end of last season. He was in his mid-thirties, about six foot two in height with a body full of muscles. But he had a warm and gentle smile on his face.

"Yes, I am, what will we be doing?"

"We'll have some medical checks and individual assessments after you settle down, then a full schedule with practice matches on both Saturday and Sunday. We have double sessions whenever we don't have a league match and for these days we are mixing the under 18's and under 21's. Does that work with you? How would you like to be called, are you Richard or Rich?"

"Thanks for the detail. You can call me Rich, I don't really mind."

"Well then, Rich. I'll take you to your room and we'll go from there," Nick said as he grabbed Richard's bag. "That's some heavy bag, what have you got with you there?"

"Just a couple of books I've been reading."

"That's interesting – what are they?"

"The life & theory of Évariste Galois."

"Who is that?"

"A French mathematician."

"Oh… what did he do?" Nick stuttered. He looked a little in awe with what he heard.

"He solved some 350-year-old problem then got killed in a duel, all before he was twenty-one."

"That's… quite different," Nick chose not to follow up on that topic and switched to showing Richard the various rooms instead.

"Here you are. Trainees that aren't local are normally accommodated by a host family, but as you are a trialist you'll get to stay in one of our guest rooms here. You'll find the training gear in the wardrobe. Meet me at the medical centre when you're ready, it's at the end of the long corridor we only just walked past."

"Thanks Nick, I'll see you soon," Richard said with a polite smile. He specifically trained himself this just for these occasions.

The first day went painlessly. Nick and the team acknowledged that Richard had a good level of basic skills with both feet but also highlighted that he was rather weak on the physical side – definitely something to work on. Nick accompanied him to the players' canteen for dinner and he had an early night.

Richard arrived at the training ground the next day to a rather cold reception by the other players.

"Are you the trialist of the day? You look a little skinny for us here, are you sure you're not with the under 16's?" one of the boys asked.

"Hey you'd never know, he may be the next Lionel Messi!" another one said before they all laughed.

For them, I may just be another trialist who comes and goes, but that suits me fine – I'm not here to please anyone. He thought.

Just as he tried to move away to find some space for his usual stretches, another boy came over and said, "Hi there, welcome to the Black Dragons. I'm Tom, I hope you get to stay here."

He was just over six feet tall and his upper body was much stronger than Richard, with his broad chest pumping with muscles and arms that were more suited to rugby players. He had light brown eyes, a thick pair of eyebrows and his mid-length brown hair was neatly combed backwards. He seemed a friendly character.

7

"Hi Tom, nice to meet you," Richard responded with his standard polite smile.

The two had a short exchange and Richard learnt that Tom had been training at the club since he was very young.

"Why are you only stretching? Warm up should be dynamic, follow me," he said.

Richard went after Tom as he jogged across the pitch for about two minutes, followed by ten minutes of stretching while moving – knee raises, lunges, squats and some leg swings. They then gathered around Nick with the other players when he called them over to make an announcement.

"Boys, we have Richard with us today and tomorrow. Let's make him feel welcome and train well!"

After some further fast drills to complete the warm up, there were some rather intensive HIIT training before several pass and move practices using plenty of tools. Richard was fit and skilful enough to manage those without any pain and he noticed a number of players who impressed. Tom was one of them with his accurate passing and ball protection, and there was also a lean, serious looking boy with spiky ash brown hair who moved and shot with an agility that was eye-catching.

This isn't any ordinary academy, it's exactly where I want to be, he thought.

The second half of training was a full-sized match with thirty-minute halves. Nick put Richard and that lean boy in the same team and Tom in the other. Richard learnt from the other players that the boy's name was Danny. He noticed that David had also arrived to watch from the side line.

Richard started as a right back in a 4-3-3 formation. He could see that the other side was in a similar shape, with a very tall right winger called Peter and a mobile looking one with short dark braided hair on the left called Rob. Tom was in centre midfield and Danny was playing as a left winger, but his posture suggested he preferred to cut in from wide instead of hugging the touch line.

The game started and after a few passes, the right-footed Rob received the ball and immediately ran with it. To have a gauge of his speed, Richard let him run along the touch line, restricting his space to cut in. He was quicker than most players he encountered before but he was able to keep up to a degree. Believing that he had run clear, Rob pushed the ball inwards towards goal with his right foot just passed the edge of the box.

Okay, you're in the trap, Richard thought as he slid in.

The black boot with gold sprinkles appeared from Rob's right and the ball went out for a corner. Richard had timed his tackle inside the penalty area perfectly to stop Rob on his track.

"That's pretty good, bro," Rob said to Richard.

"You are very fast," Richard returned the compliment as he helped Rob up from the ground.

The game went on. Now that he was aware of his speed, Richard gave Rob a couple of yards and when he initiated another foot race, Richard came out on top with the head start he gave himself.

Rob's close control was not as amazing as his speed and he found no way past Richard on a one against one situation, no matter which trick he brought out. Towards the end of the first half, he gave it another go with a quick double touch but just when he thought he succeeded, that annoying black boot of Richard's was there again, taking the ball away from underneath him cleanly.

Release all you have if you see players at the right level, Richard remembered what Simon told him the last time they spoke.

From the corner of his eye, Richard could see Danny on the left with space in front of him and decided to give it a go – he sent the ball there with a massive cross field pass.

Danny seemed to have read his mind and was already sprinting towards it. He made the rest look like formalities as he comfortably controlled the ball, cut inside the centre half and sent it to the bottom corner. All executed smoothly.

9

While still bearing his dead serious impression, he pointed his finger at Richard before clapping his hands twice to acknowledge the assist. Richard replied with a couple of claps.

After the break, Richard noticed that Nick had swapped the wingers of the other team and thought he must have passed the speed test with Rob and it was going to be all aerial with Peter.

As he noticed during the first half, Peter the giant was not a good dribbler and whenever he had the ball on the ground, Richard managed to dispossess him rather easily. However, the challenge came when the ball was crossed in by Rob from the other side. With a height disadvantage of at least six inches, there was no match at the far post. All Richard could do was to hold firm to his position and disturb Peter as much as he could by jumping in front of him. He did manage to put Peter off a few times but it was looking dangerous.

After a couple of scares from such aerial attacks, the right-sided centre back named Les came across to Richard and asked him to leave Peter to him in those situations. Les was one of those from the under 21 team and was certainly big enough for an aerial battle with Peter.

"Make sure you tell me and Stevie his whereabouts and win the second ball, alright?" he asked, with Stevie being the younger centre back on his left.

"Sure and thank you."

With Peter's threat mitigated, Richard's side managed to win the game 2-0, with the skilful centre forward Owen scoring the second goal after some good work between him and Danny late in the second half.

"How do you think about the game, Rich?" David asked a visually tired Richard.

"You have some great players here, and thanks for putting me through the challenges. I enjoyed them," Richard said as he was catching his breath, "Do you like what you've seen?"

"I expect nothing less, boy," it sounded like David was trying to mimic Richard's usual cold and dry tone.

"Glad you are not disappointed then," Richard gave him a matching reply.

"Now have a shower and some rest. I'll see you tomorrow," David said, before giving Richard a pat on the back.

"Thanks," said Richard with a slightly more genuine smile as he headed to the changing room.

How did I do? Richard tried to remember details of the match during his shower. *I definitely dealt with Rob well, even though he was seriously fast. But I could only do so much with Peter when the cross came from the other side, I hope I don't get marked down for that. I want to stay here. I want to play with these good players – Les, Tom, Danny and Owen were some of the greatest I've played with or against.*

"Hey newbie, how long do you want to stay in the shower for?"

That voice sounded like Tom.

"Sorry I'll be out soon. I was just thinking."

"I hope it is about the match? Come and we can talk about it."

"We as in?"

"Just me, Danny, Owen and Ollie."

"Who is Ollie?"

"He didn't play today, that wimp pulled his hammy during the week."

"Okay, I'll meet you guys outside."

Richard got changed and went to the players' restaurant to meet his teammates.

"Hey this way, newbie!" someone with black spiky hair whom he hadn't met before was waving, but as he sat next to Danny he must be Ollie.

"You did some good today, I'll definitely remind my stupid cousin that you had him in your pocket!"

"How did you find Danny with that ball?"

"Where did you come from?"

"How did you know David?"

"Why did you…?"

11

Richard now knew that Ollie could talk.

"Give him a chance, Wally," Tom arrived with Owen and their trays of food. "Go help yourself Richard, you must be starving after that."

Richard went to the counter and got himself a big portion of pasta and roast chicken. *How am I going to communicate with the other players? Maybe if I stay busy eating they will just talk amongst themselves? And why did Tom call Ollie a Wally?*

"Hey Richie are you sure you can eat all those?" Ollie started again.

"You can call me Rich or Richard, and yes I am very hungry."

"Are you always this cool? That'll make you a good pair with our Danny here – you two can run the greatest silent movie ever."

Richard looked over to Danny, who had been staring at his phone for the whole time he was here, he seemed to be watching some clips, but Richard couldn't tell what they were.

"What are you watching Danny?" he asked.

"It's just some skills compilations online," Danny coolly responded as he put his phone away, "Your plate needs more vegetables than that."

"Here he is with his lecture on healthy diet again!" Ollie said.

"It's important if you want to be a proper footballer," Danny continued in his ice-cold manner.

"We're athletes at the end of the day. If you don't look after your body you'll soon be eliminated," said Owen.

Richard finally got a chance to have a good look at Owen, who was playing for the under 21 team despite only being seventeen. He was just under six feet tall, lean and had very short dark hair. His dark brown eyes sparkled – he looked like an ambitious and determined person. And his football skills backed him up.

Ollie went on and on about all sort of topics and the rest gave him the odd response – Richard actually found it enjoyable, being able to talk about football with other fanatics.

The young players were going to watch the first team play at the stadium that afternoon and Tom invited Richard along, "Do you fancy a game at the Dragons? We can sneak you in – just keep the team tracksuit on."

"Are you sure it will be okay?"

"Yes – we're regulars at the ground and the youth team never used up the allocations."

"That will be great, thanks Tom."

The stadium was located on the other side of the motorway. Tom led Richard to a public tunnel decorated with club colours to give him the "fans' experience" instead of using the one for staff. The modern stadium appeared in front of their eyes at the end of it – it was a complete bowl with one slightly taller side, giving it a sloped roof. The stadium had four stands: the main one in the north was the Ditton End, which housed the executive boxes, club offices, changing rooms, press facilities and corporate hospitality suites. The opposite was the dedicated Family Stand for younger supporters. The taller stand behind the west goal was simply named the West Stand and the one to the east was naturally the East Stand. The more vocal home supporters were seated in the West Stand and its corner with the Ditton End, with the visiting fans in the opposite corner.

The boys made it to the stadium fifteen minutes before kick off. The staff at the Ditton End turnstiles opened the gate as soon as she saw Tom – she didn't even bat an eyelid on Richard.

It wasn't the biggest stadium that Richard had been to but it was full and there was a good atmosphere – the stands were close to the pitch and the shape of the roof above the home end must have been carefully designed as it seemed to amplify the volume generated by the fans.

The players were back to the dressing rooms after their warm up when Richard arrived and the stadium was playing the club's theme song, which was "I Want It Now" by Queen, the British rock band from the seventies. It was chosen by the fans a few seasons ago.

The players returned to the pitch to a massive welcome from the home supporters. It was only their third home game in their maiden season in the Championship and they were still waiting for their first victory after drawing three and losing one of their previous four games.

Tom gave Richard a brief introduction to the first team as the announcer read out their names to cheers from the crowd. He was full of admiration for the team's long-serving captain and midfield general Michael as well as the regular starters of the team that clinched promotion, such as left back Youssef, centre back Keith, defensive midfielder Kalim and striker Kalifa. Wingers George and Andrés were making their first starts for the first team after graduating from the under 21 team.

"We could become them in a few years' time," said an excited Tom.

The away team from the Midlands were a regular in the division and they started the game on the front foot, trying to destabilise the Black Dragons with a focus on wing play. The home side weathered the storm well with some solid defending. Kalim and Michael were busy but composed in midfield and they slowly started the dictate the game with Ross the Welsh attacking player in front of them. The passing was assured and movements from the rest of the team were good. However, the teams couldn't find a breakthrough and the half ended goalless.

Richard went to the stall with Tom for some refreshments and they discussed the half in detail on the way and back. Richard could tell that Tom was very enthusiastic about the team – by far the most in this group of players. Danny and Owen were watching the match calmly while Ollie was on his phone all the time.

The second half was end-to-end as the teams fought for the three points. Bob Warner, the home team's manager, brought right winger Luciano, his new recruit from Argentina, on at the hour mark and he changed the dynamics of the game with his mesmerising skills. He glided past players with ease and created plenty of chances from his crosses. The home side eventually edged it right at the death from one of these, as captain Michael smashed the ball into the back of the net in front of the West Stand.

The crowd was ecstatic – everyone was up on their feet with their hands in the air, screaming at the top of their voices. Tom was hugging the supporter sitting next to him on the other side, who seemed to be a complete stranger. Richard was happy for the team.

The match ended 1-0. The home fans sang another song from Queen, "We are the Champions", after the final whistle, with the word "Champions" replaced by "Dragons". Apparently it was what they did after every victory. Tom joined in and was very proud.

The young players decided to go separate ways afterwards and Tom walked Richard back to the training ground. They had such a good chat about the game that Tom ended up having an early dinner with Richard at the players' restaurant.

What a day. Tom seems to be a really nice person. What is going to happen tomorrow? Whatever it is, I just need to continue being me and give it my best shot. I'd love to stay here, Richard thought before he fell asleep.

It was day three of the trial and Richard got to the training ground earlier than most players. Danny was already jogging in the far side and he was approached by a tall boy with dark blonde curly hair. He looked a bit older than the other academy players, even those from the under 21's.

"Hi, I'm Thomas. You must be the trialist Richard," he said as he offered a handshake.

"Yes I am, how are you doing? I didn't see you here yesterday?"

"I was away for a few days. How are you finding it so far?" he sounded like a nice person.

"Pretty good, I guess. Should I call you Tom or Thomas?"

"We've agreed that Nelson is Tom and I'm Thomas."

15

"Okay I get it. Where do you play?"

"I'm a centre back for most of the time but sometimes I play defensive mid, you?"

"I'm a right back, but I'd love to play in centre midfield," Richard made a conscious effort to tell others he was not just a right back.

"Maybe you'll get the chance if you speak to the boss?"

"I'll let him decide. I'm sure he knows what is best for the team."

"Are you sure about that? If you don't ask, you don't get."

More players arrived at this point so Richard and Thomas moved away and started their warm ups. Thomas did it in exactly the same way as Tom the day before – they must have been taught together.

Should I ask David about playing in the middle? What if I perform badly and never get another chance? But what if I play badly at right back and never get a chance? Richard thought.

Training was more focused on the physical side, with David demanding the youngsters to have plenty of running and jumping, sometimes with weights and one section using those parachutes on the back, as seen on some professional training online.

This is proper training, isn't it? It started to sink in a bit for Richard. *It's now or never, Rich.*

At the drinks break, Richard went over to have a word with David.

"David, can I play in centre mid if there is a match later today?" Richard asked directly. "I like how it went last week."

"It's good that you asked, Richard. I'll let you know later," David kept his cards close to him.

It was practice match time.

"Okay boys. I want Josh, Ollie, Lewis, Thomas, Les, Tom, Danny, Mitchell, Peter, Owen and Richard on red and the rest on black please," David announced. "Richard, I want you, Tom and Danny in midfield today. You focus on breaking up play, Danny does the creative and Tom

16

does a bit of both. Support each other and make the most of these sixty minutes. All the best."

"Thanks sir," Richard with the game face on.

"Have you played in the middle before, Rich? I thought you said you're a right back?" Ollie asked.

"Well you are our regular right back Wally, where else will Richard play?" one of the boys said.

"I've only played there once, but I always want to give that a go," Richard had a deep breath before he continued. "I'll need your support to make this work, will you help me?"

"I'm glad you asked the gaffer for this, I'll do what I can and I'm sure the others will too, how are we thinking?" Thomas offered his support.

"Of course, we want you to succeed and stay here, what do you want us to do?" said the giant Peter.

"Thank you. We need to provide options to each other at all times, wherever you are, if you make a run I'll be able to find you. We can also do these…" Richard told the team what he had been planning.

"Leave that to us. Let's win this, reds!" Les with the final rallying cry.

The match began. The other team seemed to have been instructed to attack through the middle to test Richard's ability. But he was able to repel waves and waves of challenges in unbeatable form. He won all individual battles on the ground and forced plenty of opponents to lose the ball to his midfield partner Tom. The two seemed to have developed a strong understanding between them already, as if they had been playing together for years.

They also recycled the ball well with the hard-working Danny in front of them and the highly mobile Lewis and Ollie at full backs. After some fifteen minutes into the half, Richard intercepted a pass, played a quick one two with Tom and hit a curling high ball to send Lewis into space. His cross was met by a towering Peter at the far post for the opening goal.

"That was just brilliant Rich, I start to love playing with you," Tom said during half time.

17

"The feeling is mutual," Richard said with a genuine smile. "It was enjoyable."

Seeing as they could not penetrate the centre, team black altered their play and focused on the wings instead in the second half. Their crosses were handled well by Thomas, Les and Tom who dropped deep to help. Richard marshalled the edge of the area in such situations and were spraying the ball left and right smoothly, with the attackers interchanging positions regularly to confuse the black's defence.

As the blacks pushed for an equaliser, Tom won the ball in midfield and Richard sent a quick and powerful low ball to Owen on the right, who expertly laid it off with a flick for Danny to score with a spectacular long-range effort.

The reds won the match 2-0 in rather comfortable fashion.

"Well done for your win reds," David congratulated the team. "Where did all these movements in attack and defensive shape come from? I know we coach you guys well but we haven't looked at those in this level of detail yet."

"It's all from this lad," Les said as he pointed at Richard. "He described all these scenarios and gave us simple instructions to carry out. I just didn't know it'd work such a treat."

"Is that so, Richard?" David asked with a satisfying smile.

"Yes I thought they would work in my head so I wanted to test them out for real," Richard replied as his face blushed. "I'm glad we did it."

"That's very good. Don't be embarrassed by it," David said as he nodded his head. "Go and have a shower and come to my office afterwards please."

"I'm sure you'll be alright, bro, that was so cool!" Ollie started talking again.

"Stop piling on the pressure, just let him relax before he sees the boss," said Tom. "Saying that, I'm sure you'll be fine."

Richard arrived at David's office at the end of his three-day trial.

"Thanks for coming Richard. How do you feel about these three days?" David asked.

"I have to thank you for the invitation. I've played some of the best football ever. I enjoyed it very much," Richard had finally warmed up to David.

"That is very good. At the end of the day, if we don't enjoy playing the game, why should we even bother? I think the team and staff enjoyed your presence too, well done!"

"Will I get to stay?"

"Are you nervous, Richard?"

"I knew that comment would come back to bite me," Richard said with a little blush on his face. "I am prepared for the worst, but I really want to stay so yes I am nervous."

"Well then," David started talking with a serious face and a horrible pause. "We don't normally sign sixteen-year-olds to our academy, let alone someone turning seventeen soon, as in your case. It is a bit late for a lot of our desired developments to happen."

Richard was stunned. He did put his best efforts into the trial but they seemed pointless if he couldn't even meet the pre-conditions.

David broke out a gentle smile and continued, "but I think there are things we would like to work with you. We would offer you a scholarship contract to join us for a year and a bit, until your eighteenth birthday. How does that sound?"

Richard was still there sitting motionlessly. He couldn't believe what he heard.

"Richard? Are you okay?" David asked.

"Yes, David, yes. Yes! Please!" Richard woke up from being spaced out.

"That's great news. Congratulations, Nick and Carla will be in contact once the paperwork is ready."

"Wait," the sensible part of Richard had also returned, "how about my A-Levels?"

19

"I've heard that you're a bit of a scholar. Training will be in the evenings and weekends so you will just go to school as normal. We actually encourage our players to take some form of further education and the younger players are doing their GCSE's with our partner school ten minutes' walk from here, which was classified as outstanding by Ofsted."

"I guess that's all good then!"

"Indeed, I'll see you when you join us officially," David offered a handshake.

"Thank you so much David, I'm looking forward to that day."

Richard' parents were in the living room when he got home.

"Richard," his father said, with his eyes focused on his newspaper, "how's your trip to London?"

"It went well," Richard said. "They are offering me a scholarship contract at their academy."

"I never doubted your football abilities, but how is it going to work with your studies with the club being miles away?"

"I'll be staying with a local host family. Training will be in the evenings and weekends so studies will just continue normally. They have a partnership with an outstanding school for their players."

"Oh my God you're going to live away from home?" asked his mother, who sounded concerned.

"Mum I'm seventeen in three months, I can handle this. I would move out when I go to University in less than two years' time anyway."

"I'm not too worried about that. What is going to happen after your A-Levels? Will you go to University or continue playing?" his dad switched the topic back into his studies.

"There's no guarantee I'll become a professional football player so I will be studying as hard as before."

"Only if you keep up with it. You promised us to get four A's. You've already failed your GCSE's," his father said.

"I wouldn't call six A's and three B's a failure, dad."

"It was for us. Nothing less than a hundred percent would do."

"That's what happens all the time. You just can't do encouragements, can you?"

"You won't need any if you are mature enough."

"Fine. I don't need any. I'm old enough to make the decision and I am joining the Black Dragons."

"Well if you say so we won't stand in the way, just remember your side of the deal."

Why does it always end like this? Is it me or him? Richard thought as he lay on his bed afterwards. *Well, no one can stop me doing what I want now.*

"Welcome back Richard and hello Mrs Lucas. How did you do in the last two weeks?" Nick warmly welcomed Richard and his mum back at the academy. "We have the contract for you in the office after your medicals. Are you ready? Will Mr Lucas join us later?"

"We can proceed," Richard said with a stone-cold face. "he won't be here."

Nick took Richard in for a full medical before meeting David at his office for the contract.

"Okay, Richard. That's all the paperwork done, welcome to our academy. As you have requested accommodation, we have assigned you to stay with the Stevenson's, one of our long-serving host families. They have two spare rooms so you'll house share with Thomas Bond."

"The old centre back?"

"Don't be rude – he's only a year older than you. He'll be a fine pal."

The club staff took Richard, his mum and his belongings to the host family half a mile away from the training complex. Thomas was there at the door along with

Mr and Mrs Stevenson, who looked to be in their fifties and seemed very nice.

"Hey Richard, I knew you'd come back – welcome to the Black Dragons!" said Thomas with a big smile on his face.

"Thanks for your help in that last game, Thomas. This won't happen without that," Richard remembered that Thomas was the first player to support his ideas.

"Well here you are, the hard work starts now. We're struggling a bit in the league, but we'll be better when the full team is back from international games."

"Oh we have players called up to international games?"

"Yeah Les went to the under 21s and Charlie, Owen and Adam were with the under 17s."

"I've met Les and Owen during my trial but never knew Charlie and Adam."

"You'll know them in due course. Charlie is one of our mates. We're having an under 18 team dinner tonight so you'll get to meet everyone else."

"Is that arranged specifically for me?"

"Don't be silly, we have one every other month. It just happened to be on the day you join."

Mrs Lucas had a brief conversation with the Stevenson's and she said her goodbye once she learnt about the team dinner.

"Here's the new chapter for you Richie, I'm sure you'll do well," she said with tears in her eyes.

"Thanks mum," Richard was still angry with his father but when his mum was leaving he suddenly felt a little emotional. "I'll be fine, don't worry."

He held on to his mum tightly but eventually let go.

"Open the big suitcase later tonight, I have something for you," Mrs Lucas said before she turned away towards the train station.

"Are you going to miss your parents?" Thomas asked.

"I guess… I'll miss mum a little bit."

"You'll be too busy once you start training. You're doing A-Levels as well, right?"

"Yes, do you know about the school?"

"Lots of us went there back in the days, you'll be fine."
Richard and Thomas arrived the nicely decorated bar on the first floor of the Ditton End. It was where the VIPs gathered before every match and David, the coaches and lots of players were already there. They were offered some juice in champagne glasses as they mingled with the others.

"Hey everybody," David tried to get everyone's attention by clicking his glass with a pen. "Today we officially welcome Richard Lucas to our academy. I don't need to say much to those who played with him during his excellent trial, but for those who didn't, Richard came from the same youth team I played for when I was young. He'll be playing in defence or midfield. Let's all give him a round of applause!"

"Your turn to say something," Thomas gave Richard a nudge.

"Err... hi everyone, my name is Richard," he said as his face and ears turned boiling hot. "I look forward to playing with you all."

"Welcome to the Black Dragons, Rich," said Tom. "After your awesome performance a couple of weeks ago I don't think there was any doubt that you'll join us. Shall we go round the room and introduce ourselves? I'm Tom Nelson, captain of the under 18s and hopefully your future midfield partner."

"Danny Westwood, attacking mid."

"I'm Ollie Wallace, people called me Wally."

"Steve Fraser, centre back."

"Kevin Black, left back."

"Paul Newman, striker."

"Rob Daniels, the very fast winger."

"Peter Knight, the very tall winger."

"Jack Simpson, goalkeeper."

"Harry Smith, centre mid."

"James Barton, defensive mid."

"Caden Cox, keeper."

"Mason Brown, centre back."

"Liam Paterson, right back."

"Billy McCarthy, centre back."

"Bradley Jones, centre mid."

"Finley Long, striker"

"We are missing our star players Charlie Ranger our left winger and Adam Jenkinson our number ten," concluded Tom.

"Now I know why you are called Wally," Richard said to Ollie.

"Well yeah, don't you think for a second that I am an actual Wally! Anyway, are you ready for your initiation?" Ollie was clearly excited.

"Initiation? What... do I need to do?" Richard started to worry.

"Well, the rule is that the newbie has to run around the pitch completely naked," Tom said to an absolutely horrified Richard, "but seeing that you look like the shy type, we won't be pushing you for that, just the one simple initiation song then! Do you have any favourites?"

"I really don't know where to start..." Richard's face had turned red again. "What do you do normally?"

"How about 'We are the Champions'? It's the song the fans sing every time the team win so let's do that one? Make sure you swap the word 'Champions' to 'Dragons'!" Tom said.

"O...kay..." Richard did know that song well.

"Can we have that on the karaoke machine please?" Tom asked Ollie who was next to it.

"Yep, got it!"

"Okay Rich, off you go!!"

However reluctant and embarrassed he was, when the music was on Richard started singing seriously. Unlike most, he actually knew his lyrics and sang pretty well. He just couldn't do half a job – he went for all the high notes and managed to complete the whole song.

The team weren't expecting to see a proper performance and were a little bit in awe to start, but they soon sang along and had a good time. One thing they had definitely learnt was that their new teammate was serious on just about everything.

There was a buffet after the initiation and it was a real treat to the teenagers who trained every other day. The food was on the healthy side with lots of unprocessed meat, pasta, vegetables and fruits.

"Did you sing for a band or something? That was more than decent!" Thomas told Richard when they walked back to the host family.

"I thought everyone can at least sing the right notes, is that not true?" Richard was a little surprised by Thomas's comment, as he always thought that was the minimum requirement, just like passing exams being a basic requirement for every student.

"I can assure you that isn't normal, Rich. Try listening to Charlie's singing when you have the chance, you won't be able to 'un-hear' it!"

"Charlie's family name is Ranger, right? Is he…?"

"Yes, his dad is the legendary Miles Ranger, who captained the team all the way from Conference South to League One. He's our Director of Football these days so he's in charge of player transfers."

"The way the club promoted through the league is really something."

"True, while the history of the club may trace back sixty-five years, it only took off when Dr Edwards bought it eighteen years ago. Look where we are now!"

"I've read about Dr Phillip Edwards. He is a pioneer in information security, the encryption algorithm he jointly developed is renowned in the world and his company is one of the most successful in security software."

"How do you know so much about the chairman?"

"I like reading about mathematicians and Dr Edwards is one of my favourites. Do we get to see him normally?"

"You are quite… different to a typical footballer, Richard. But no, we don't see the chairman that often."

Richard opened his mum's suitcase back in his room. It had some new clothes and two pairs of new football boots – exactly the same as his current ones, in black with gold sprinkles. There was a handwritten note with "Go for it Richie" on it – Richard felt really touched and he regretted not being a nicer son when he was living at home, but he promised to give everything he had to fulfil his dream of becoming a professional footballer.

2.

The Ranger

Richard was shown around the club the next day, including their home ground, named The Dragons Stadium, which was recently expanded to have a capacity of just over eight thousand seats. He had lessons on the club's history and philosophy: the club was found by a group of Welsh residences after the Second World War and played in the regional leagues until Dr Edwards took over eighteen years ago. It continued its first ten years under his ownership as a semi-professional club and turned professional when they were promoted to the National League, which was the fifth tier of English football. It took them three years to break into the English Football League and another five for the Championship. Residents in the local area were more interested in cricket traditionally but the club gradually built its fanbase through their community projects and successes on the pitch.

Dr Edwards's philosophy was to grow the club sustainably. The Welsh multi-millionaire invested in the club's infrastructure, youth development and scouting networks to ensure the club could operate on its own. They aimed to develop their own young talents and look for players with potential from all over Europe to avoid getting dragged into over-spending on transfer fees and salaries. The club's ethos was "Never beaten on efforts", which Richard believed was correctly reflected in the training intensity and the players' fitness level.

The club was known as the Black Dragons because it started as Ditton Dragons in its formative years and they wore an all-black outfit. Their logo, which was a variation of the historic flag of Surrey, featured the traditional blue and golden yellow checks of the county, the sprig of oak that symbolised the extensive rural areas nearby, a river pattern that represented River Thames and the Welsh dragon in the four segments.

The youth academy was given category two status in the Football Association's four-step classification. It meant that their under 18 and under 21 teams played in the Professional Development League. Both teams were in the second division of their respective level and mainly competed with other Championship clubs.

Richard had an interesting session with the fitness coaches afterwards – he never knew much about all the muscles and joints but it was good to know that they were all functioning well.

He had dinner with Mr and Mrs Stevenson for the first time that evening, while Thomas had his Friday date night with his girlfriend Elle. He learnt that Mr Stevenson worked at the local hospital as an x-ray technician and Mrs Stevenson was an office worker. The couple had been hosting youth players since her redundancy five years ago and they planned to retire in a few years to move back to their home town in Shropshire. Mrs Stevenson made a chicken casserole with plenty of vegetables to go with some mashed potatoes. It was simply delicious. She seemed very happy with the way Richard cleaned up his portion and promised to make him her "signature" fish pie one day.

Richard turned up to his first training session as an academy player the following morning. He felt proud changing into the club's kits – they wore a black shirt with thin, dark grey stripes, black shorts and golden yellow socks at home and a white shirt with blue and golden yellow patterns away, with the two colours coming from the flag of Surrey. The training gear came in light grey and red. It was so good that he was given clothes that fit – at his old club everyone was given a large shirt which was far too big for him.

"Good morning Rich," Ollie met him on the pitch with a cheesy grin. "How are you feeling? Ready for the big day?"

"Yes, I feel good to go."

"You know what, I've made some connections with your old team on Insta last night. They said you were known as 'The Unbeatable' there, why didn't you tell us that before?"

"It's... not a big deal. Just a defender doing some defending."

"Don't be shy about it – we've decided to put you to the test today. We'll challenge you to some one on ones."

"Do we really have to do that?"

"Yes, we absolutely do!"

The format of the challenge was for the attacker to approach Richard from the final third and they won if they dribbled past Richard and scored.

"Don't worry Richard, I'll back you up," Jack volunteered to be the keeper, "but it doesn't mean I can't take you on in a one on one!"

"I'm having my revenge today, buddy," the first challenger was Rob the fast winger. "Let's do this."

Rob started by taking the ball a little towards his left, with some cautious small touches with the outside of his right foot.

His main strength is his pace so he would find a gap to open up a chance to run, Richard was analysing his opponent in his head. *He'll want to cut in and curl one... as his left foot isn't that strong. Let's sell him that.*

Richard made a move once Rob crossed into the penalty area. He shifted a little bit towards his right while secretly switching his weight onto his right foot. Rob saw the space and pushed the ball to Richard's left, as he expected. The black boot with gold sprinkles struck, and Rob lost the ball again.

"I told you he got you in his pocket, cous. My turn!" said Ollie as he picked up the ball.

I guess he's trickier with his strong upper body, he'll protect his ball well. Richard had not seen Ollie play so was reading him carefully.

Instead of Rob's push and run style, Ollie was indeed slower in his build-up, with a couple of step overs and arms reaching out to protect his space. Richard engaged him higher up the pitch as he was confident in winning a foot race if it ended up that way but he kept his defensive shape from a yard away and held Ollie off.

He needs to do the attacking, so he'll look for a little touch pass my side or through my legs.

To temp Ollie into playing, Richard appeared to be moving a little bit forward towards him. His prey responded with a little touch towards Richard's left, and the ball was swiftly poked away.

"Don't make it look so easy, man," said Ollie as he walked away.

The next one up was Finley the young striker with light brown curly hair. Richard won a few duels against him in his second practice match and knew that while he had a great right foot for shots, he wasn't too skilful in terms of dribbling.

He's very confident in his shooting so he'll take one from afar, but he can't beat Jack that way.

Richard engaged Finley some thirty yards away from goal and gave him some space to tempt him into a long shot, while signalling to Jack behind his back to indicate where the shot was going. Finley did pull the trigger and hit a curling shot but it was saved comfortably by the keeper. Richard gave big Jack the thumb ups.

"I'm next, I'm next," said a high pitch voice. It was Harry the young left-footed midfielder who the rest of team called the "Wizz Kid".

He looks like a tricky player – and tricky players like a nutmeg, Richard had an idea.

As expected, Harry possessed a lot of skills and two very quick feet. Richard approached him with a slightly wider gap between his legs but secretly left his right foot behind.

Seeing a chance for glory, Harry sent the ball through, but it was blocked by that trailing foot of Richard's. Luckily for Harry, the ball bounced back to him. Richard stuck to his approach and Harry went for it again after a few more shimmies. This time Richard kicked the ball away.

"How did you block it?" Harry was frustrated. "The gap was clearly there."

"There's a lot for you to learn, kid," up came Tom. "I'll have a go. I'm not a great dribbler but I want to try coming up against 'The Unbeatable'."

Tom has good control over the ball but he doesn't have quick feet, he'll be a good protector of the ball and he'll switch direction if I make a move, so I'd better let him take the initiatives.

Richard decided to simply hold Tom up and wear him down. Whatever tricks Tom could think of, he just followed him with a matching defensive move while keeping his body shape intact to avoid being overpowered. Without the acceleration to lose Richard, Tom was running out of ideas and more importantly, patience.

He's tired of this now. He'll find half an opening and take a shot. Okay, show me what your left foot has.

Richard sold Tom some space to his right. Delighted to finally see an opening, Tom didn't hesitate and shifted his body there to take a left foot shot, but it went off target by some distance.

"You're lucky, Rich, I nearly beat you there," Tom said.

"Don't be daft Nelson, he sold you down your rubbish left peg," said the next challenger. "It won't be that easy with me, Richard."

That was the mighty Danny.

He and Owen are the ones I worry about most. He must have read my moves by now. There'll be no point setting up traps against him.

Richard played it safe this time, holding his position but expecting Danny to pull out something special.

He's nimble but his weight is all on his left, so if anything it will come from his right foot.

So it did. Danny rolled the ball onto the top of his right boot, flipped it slightly leftwards before changing it to the right sharply, all in one move when the ball was in the

31

air – a so-called Flip Flap, a trick that the great Brazilian player Ronaldinho was famous for.

Richard was a little shocked that Danny managed to pull that move off, but with his steady position he was able to close Danny down before he took a shot. Seeing that the gap was narrowed, Danny cut the ball back with his right foot, before quickly pushing it right again with his left foot to open up a bigger gap. This one looked too good for Richard to close and Danny put his shot away.

"Is he finally beaten?" the on-watching players wondered.

But the ball did not hit the target.

"Great block, Richard," Danny said respectfully. "You won."

"It's lucky my studs got in the way," Richard with a little smile. "You were amazing with those two tricks in quick succession."

"Oh so it was defected wide by Rich?" Ollie is a little confused. "I didn't see that."

"It was on target from my angle here," said Jack, "but of course I had it covered."

"Alright… anyone else wants to have a go at Richie?" Ollie with a raised voice.

"Let's end this madness and have some proper training," said a deep voice. "Welcome to the Black Dragons, Richard. You've done well here, the boys have worked you hard."

It was the towering centre back Les Hailey.

"Thanks for saving me Les. How was England under 21s?"

"I was only on the bench, but Sweden was good. Let's start training and have a proper catch up later."

The under 18 team had a practice game at the end of another intensive training session.

Nick put Danny, Paul, Peter, Steve, James and others on the black side and Richard, Tom, Ollie, Thomas and the rest on the red. One of the returnees from international games Charlie joined in and was one of the blacks. Adam the other one picked up an injury during the call-up and won't be playing for some time.

"Hey you must be the Richard the boys talked about?" Charlie came over for a handshake. "I'm Charlie Ranger, good luck with the game, you'll need it."

Richard had a look at Charlie. He was about six foot one, he had a strong upper body with wide shoulders. His two dark brown eyebrows nearly connected in the middle and had short dark ginger hair. He looked like an ox with an angst, his eyes carried the stare of an assassin.

"He has his eyes on you Rich, be careful," Thomas whispered.

"Sounds fun. I can't wait for more one on ones," Richard said with a sarcastic smile.

Richard was playing in centre midfield with Tom, Harry played in front of them with Rob and Mitchell on the wings supporting Finley. Charlie started the game as a left winger.

The match began. Charlie demanded the ball and had his wish granted swiftly by James. He ran straight towards the middle, where Richard was stationed. He was going for a take on.

He is a tough one with that strong upper body. Once he is running at pace he'll be difficult to stop. Let's surprise him and get into his mind! Richard did his usual analysis.

Contrary to the calm and safe style he demonstrated so far, Richard launched into a sliding tackle straight away and took the ball off Charlie, who clearly was not expecting it and had over-run it slightly.

"You mean business, matey," Charlie with an intimidating look on his face.

"There's no holding back," Richard was unfazed as usual.

Charlie retrieved the ball from his teammates and was approaching Richard again. This time he had the ball under close control – Richard's strategy seemed to have worked as he was not opening up for the bigger and more dangerous strides.

To be fair, Charlie was a very skilful player, with two very good feet and a well-balanced body shape, but his insistence on going alone against Richard made it easy for the reds as they teamed up to deal with him. They were not treating this as the duels earlier and quickly scored two goals from counter attacks after taking the ball off him.

"Stop being a dick and play properly, Charles," Danny was getting angry. "You can't get pass both Tom and Richard."

"Just give me one more chance, I've figured out a way."

Charlie demanded the ball from Danny and brought it to the left, where he normally excelled in. As he started running with the space available, there was no stopping him. Tom came over to cover the beaten Ollie and was pushed aside by Charlie's strength as his balance wasn't quite ready for the challenge.

The next opponent in front of Charlie was Richard. Charlie's momentum was slowed down by Tom's challenge and had to face Richard on another one against one. He had the ball controlled with both feet as he shifted his body weight freely to change directions. He pushed the ball into one side, cut it back, had another feint to shoot, and cut it back again. Richard had been forced to stretch out his legs to block and so an inevitable gap appeared between his legs. Charlie tipped the ball through it with the outside of his right boot.

However, as Charlie ran after the ball with a satisfactory smile, a wall appeared in front of him. Thomas was there and he simply cleared the ball into touch.

"It doesn't work like this, Charlie, this isn't no one-man show," he said.

And it was time for a break.

"Why did you insist on going through the middle?" Richard walked over to ask Charlie.

"Err…" Charlie was a bit perplexed by his visit. "I just want to break this unbeatable nonsense."

"It is indeed nonsense. Every player is beatable and numerous players have done that against me. You did it just there but then you lost the ball to Thomas straight away, what did you gain from that? Football is about scoring goals and we should go for the most probable way to do it. My role is to stop that from happening and if me getting beaten in a take on means you lose the ball to my teammates, I'm more than happy."

"He is right," Danny joined in. "If he and Tom make it hard in the middle for us we'll just attack elsewhere. It's not like there are eleven Richard's in the side."

Charlie nodded before pulling Danny to one side to talk so Richard returned to his team.

The game resumed. Charlie demanded the ball from his teammates, seemingly to run with it again.

"It feels different this time," Richard said to Tom. "Keep an eye on Danny."

By this time, Charlie had already dribbled past Rob and Ollie. Richard came across to hold his progress but Charlie made a sharp turn in-field with his left foot and released the ball immediately to the on-coming Danny with his right, who played a return pass to the left again before Tom could close him down.

It became a foot race between Charlie and Richard. There was only going to be one out come as Richard could not match Charlie's pace and momentum. A simple one-two had created a chance for Charlie to cross. He hit one towards the near post beautifully with his left foot and Paul sneaked in front of Thomas to poke it home. 2-1.

"See how easy it can be," Danny said as he celebrated the goal with Charlie and Paul.

"Yeah I got it – don't try to break the wall but find the cracks," Charlie acknowledged. "Let's win this now."

The reds kicked off and the ball was with Finley, who brought it forward looking for a pass to Rob on the right wing. He was quickly closed down by the aggressive James and his weak lay off to Harry was cut out by the back-tracking Danny.

Danny turned and chipped the ball to Peter on the right, who headed it straight into Paul's path on the edge of the area. His low pass to the middle was emphatically finished by Charlie, who held off Thomas's challenge with his superior strengths.

All that happened with the midfield duo of Tom and Richard completely by-passed.

"We need to do something here," Richard discussed their next moves with Thomas and Tom. "I'll sit deeper to protect that area. Can you make sure Danny doesn't have time on the ball please, Tom? Let's ride out the storm."

As the reds re-organised their defence, they managed to hold out against the blacks for the rest of the game for it to finish 2-2. Richard was extremely busy with numerous tackles and interceptions deep in midfield. At the end it was a good chess game with both teams looking to outsmart the other.

"That was good fun, cheers for the game, Richard," said Charlie as he approached him to offer a handshake. "...Richard?"

Richard wasn't responding. He was catching his breath before everything turned dark and he collapsed to the ground.

"Hey Richard? Oi, we need a medic here!"

Richard heard lots of shouting when he was in the dark and felt someone putting him on a stretcher and moving him. He eventually felt well enough and he woke up in the medical room. The nurse Sue was by his side.

"Hey you are up. How are you feeling?" she had one of the most caring voices.

"What happened?"

"You passed out after the training match. You should be okay, just need more fluid and rest."

"The team must have laughed their socks off then, how embarrassing."

"No they were worried," Sue said as she completed her checks. "You can go back to your host family when you are ready, but before you go, I want you to finish this glass of water. I've heard that you only have energy drinks."

Richard prepared to head back to the Stevenson's but he realised he had not eaten anything for a while so he stopped by the players' canteen. He saw a number of players there, and they were delighted to see his return.

"Hey Rich are you better now?" asked Tom. "You were a bit pale earlier."

"Yes I feel fine now, the nurse said I was just exhausted."

"So you are mortal after all, matey," Charlie came across. "You need more training on your fitness."

"I'm normally fine but maybe today was a bit much with all those one-v-one's. They took me out both physically and mentally."

"You must be hungry, let's go and get some food. They must have something left in the kitchen," said Thomas who always seemed to know what the real problem was.

"I can do with eating a lot right now."

The under 18 team had no games that weekend and the coaches had arranged an additional fitness session for the players on the Sunday. It was the first time for Richard to go into the gym alongside his teammates and his weaknesses were plain for all to see, as his upper body strength was amongst the lowest of the team, only ahead of little Harry who was nearby a year younger than him.

"Oh Rich, I'm 70kg more than you in chest press!" laughed Charlie. "I know what I'll do next time I'm up against you, I'll just push you away!"

"You have plenty of work to do here," Tom added. "Even Danny can do 30kg more!"

"I know, I'll train more," an embarrassed Richard said.

"Let's see how good your legs are," said Thomas who just came off the machine.

Richard moved across to the leg press machine and he kept going until Stuart the Fitness Coach stopped adding more weights into it.

"That's about too much for players your size and age, well done!" he said.

"150kg? Isn't that higher than all of us?" Ollie was shocked.

"Wow that's some strength Rich!" Tom said.

37

"That explains your crazy cross field pass," Danny commented, "but you need to address this serious imbalance."

"Yes he definitely does," said Stuart. "I'll set up a schedule for you and you'll be fine in a few months if you work hard."

With the senior team away for their game the youth players were allowed to use the heated swimming pool in the training complex in the afternoon. Richard had a fair amount of fun with his teammates as they dived into the pool repeatedly and played water polo. They had some soft drinks in the players' lounge afterwards and watched the late afternoon match live.

I'm seriously enjoying this. There is such a great group of players here. I need to keep working hard to make sure I get to stay long term!

3.

The Orphan

It had been two weeks since Richard joined the Thames Ditton academy. He had enrolled into the club's partner school for his A-levels but whenever he had free time he would go to the academy for some extra training on his strengths and stamina. Most of his work was done in the gym but he would go to the ground for a run on the grass every now and then.

Every time he was there, he saw the same familiar face – it was Danny the lean attacking midfielder. He was fittingly known as "The Machine" by the rest of the team.

One late afternoon when there was no scheduled training, Richard noticed Danny was practising his long shots and decided to join in.

"Hey Danny," Richard waved as he moved towards him, "taking some shots from distance?"

"Hey Rich," Danny turned around and had another shot, this time flying over the bar. "How're things? You're not studying tonight?"

"I wanted to take a little break, got a bit fed up with all those differential equations."

"Are they physics or chemistry? I'm rubbish at school."

"It's maths. I'm not taking any science subjects."

"I've no idea what it is," Danny retrieved the ball and had another go, which also flew harmlessly over.

"What are you trying to do with this technique?" asked a curious Richard. "The lift you put on at the very end will surely send it skywards."

"You have good eyes there," Danny said when he came back with a few balls. "I'm trying to put some spin on it to make it dip."

"Oh like Tsubasa's Drive Shot?" Richard made reference to the popular Japanese animation.

"Yes, do you watch Captain Tsubasa too?" Danny responded with an odd piece of excitement on his face.

"Every episode of the original series, maybe a couple of times each, plus the manga," Richard was thrilled as he had finally found another fan. "Who's your favourite player?"

"Jun Misugi, the Ace of Glass," Danny said with admiration. "I'd wear number 14 in the future when I get to choose."

"I wish you have better luck with injuries than him," Richard said as he picked up one of the balls. "My favourite player is Hikaru Matsuyama, the Wild Eagle from Furano. What a warrior."

Richard rolled the ball forward with his foot before racing up to hit it. Danny watched on as the ball propelled down into the goal after making a huge arc in the air, just like Tsubasa's Drive Shot.

"How the hell did you do that?" Danny was clearly shocked. "You have to show me, Richard!"

"I've done some research into this. You were right when you said you need to generate some top spin to get it down," Richard explained slowly, "but it is too hard to get enough from standing still. So I rolled it forward to get some help."

"I see, let me try," Danny quickly picked up another ball and had a go with this new method. The ball went up and down in his desired fashion but landed just over the bar. "Oh this feels really good, I can sense a lot more dip in it."

The two young footballers spent the next hour or so practicing their dipping shots, until they thought they had mastered it to some degree, as well as being knackered.

"You surprised me every time you appeared," Danny recalled as he sat on the ground with Richard. "That cross field ball, the tactics, the one on ones, and then this. What other things can you do?"

"I still haven't managed to take free kicks like Ronaldo, have you?" said Richard after downing half a bottle of his favourite orange-flavoured energy drink.

"Oh the knuckle ball?" Danny sounded surprised. "That's just hitting the ball dead in the middle, isn't it?

"It's easier said than done," Richard with a sigh. "I haven't made it work yet."

"What other techniques from Captain Tsubasa do you know?" Danny took it back to the anime.

"My favourite is Taro's Green-Cut Pass," said Richard as he used his hands to demonstrate. "The one with heavy back spin to stop the ball bouncing away from the forward."

"That's the first time ball you hit to Charlie the other day, isn't it? He did say to me that ball was different to other passes he's seen."

"Yeah the way Tom rolled the ball back to me exaggerated the effect, together with the longer grass in that part of the pitch."

"It's funny how you are able to explain so many football things with science," said Danny as he stood up. "Do you fancy dinner tonight? We can carry on talking."

"Sure – just let me text Mrs Stevenson."

"Oh is that your host family? Where about is that?"

"It's just a few minutes' walk from here towards the station."

"That's good, I'm the other side of the railways. Do you fancy a burger? There's a new one in Kingston, just twenty minutes on the bus."

"Thomas talked about it but I haven't been there yet. Is it good?"

"Oh yeah – I'll treat you for teaching me the Drive Shot."

Richard and Danny sat down at the American restaurant. Danny ordered a double chicken burger while Richard fancied a half pounder with jalapeno and chilli sauce. They asked for a large milkshake each too.

"After all that talk about burgers and you ordered a chicken one?" Richard was curious.

"Chicken meat is lean," said Danny. "My body is a temple. I can't let my diet affect my football."

"But the milkshake…" Richard felt a little shameful for his choice and wanted to bring Danny down to his level.

"It's just protein. It'll help me build my muscles; I've asked for no syrup on mine."

"Let's not talk about food," Richard shifted away from the topic quickly. "When did you join the academy?"

"I only joined last year when I got offered a scholarship and left the children's home," Danny said slowly.

Richard knew Danny's background would be complicated given how he interacted with others, but he didn't think as far as him being an orphan.

"I've never met my parents," Danny continued. "my mum left me at the hospital where I was born and I was sent to various foster families, before they decided to put me in that place in Slough."

Richard was nodding as Danny carried on. He didn't think he should interrupt when someone was talking about their past, especially the one unfolding in front of him now.

"I think one of the families bought me a football and showed me a few games on tele. I was hooked since and I started bringing a ball everywhere I went," Danny said as he had a sip of his rather bland looking milkshake, "then Nick watched me play for the school team and asked if I would join the Dragons. Of course I said yes and the rest is history."

"How do you get on with your host family?" Richard was trying to know if Danny ever lived well with others.

"Paolo and Maria are quite nice to me but we only see each other during the meals, we don't talk much. I've probably talked more during our time here."

The food arrived at this point and the boys tucked in. The burgers were good – the two talked more about the other football related animations and mangas before heading back to their host families.

"See you tomorrow, buddy. You'll need to show me that double heel trick from 'Shoot!' that you talked about."

"I haven't really learnt it yet – it'll be embarrassing."

"That'll be fun then."

Richard got back to the Stevenson's. As he headed back to his room upstairs, a topless Thomas came out from the bathroom, probably just after a shower.

"Hey Rich, you're a bit late back from school?" Thomas asked as he was drying his hair with a towel.

"I had some shooting practice with Danny and then went to dinner with him."

"Wow that's impressive – I thought that boy does everything on his own. When did you get close to him?"

"Just today when we talked about dipping shots and Captain Tsubasa, you know what, he's also watched them all!"

"That's nice you can find someone to talk about that, I haven't got a clue."

"Do you know his background?"

"I don't really, all I've heard is that he doesn't have any family to go to during the holidays, so he would just stay and train through them. He's like hardcore."

"That sounds a little crazy."

"Oh yeah, but I guess it'll help him build a career out of football," said Thomas with a big sigh.

"Is something bothering you?" Richard noticed a couple of wrinkles appearing on Thomas's forehead.

"You probably haven't really thought about it as you study well," Thomas said as he walked into his room and made a gesture to suggest Richard to come with him, "but for us, if we don't get a professional contract at the end of academy life we won't know what to do for a living.

"I'm turning eighteen in November and this year will be make or break, as my scholarship contract runs out at the end of this season. I'll need to find a proper job and somewhere to live with Elle. I don't have a family home to go back to."

"I thought your mum called you the other day?" Richard asked.

"Well, she can't afford to have me with her new family," Thomas explained. "I grew up in a council estate near

43

Battersea Park and we were always skint – mum used to spend all her cash on booze and me and my little sister didn't have much to eat. It wasn't until I got the scholarship at the academy that I started to get some decent meals. Life wasn't good back then."

"I'm sure it'll work out for you and Elle, you'll be fine," Richard didn't know what else to say.

Richard wasn't used to these deep conversations but he had to face two in the same night. He understood Thomas's worry about not making it in football – like Thomas said, he never thought it would be a problem for him as he knew he could always study and do well in the real world, but for those with less fortune, it might be the end of it.

He then thought about his own family. Although there was always a barrier between them, his father was never short on providing everything he needed – books, clothes, gadgets, his beloved football boots etc. He would have to ask for them through mum but they always turned up. And the house he lived in back in the village wasn't shabby either.

Maybe I should be more grateful? Let's see where we get to next time we talk... he thought during his shower.

The under 18 team started the season in the Professional Development League 2 with one win, two draws and two defeats. Since Richard joined there had been two games but he was not deemed physically ready by David, and the team drew 2-2 and lost 3-2 in those games.

Richard was again named on the bench in match six, which was an away game to Bristol. David started with Jack in goal, Kevin, Thomas, Steve and Ollie in defence, the usual centre midfield pairing of James and Tom, then the fit-again Adam supporting Charlie, Danny and Paul upfront.

He noted from training that Adam was another top player with admirable skills and a special sense of moving into great attacking positions at the right time. He seemed to be good friends with James and Kevin, who weren't the most friendly towards him.

"We beat them 2-0 here last year," said Peter as he sat next to Richard on the bench. "Charlie and Darren scored the goals."

"Darren?" asked Richard as he didn't know anyone in the team with that name.

"Oh yeah he moved to a Premier League club in the midlands during the summer on a professional deal," Peter recalled. "He used to start ahead of Paul and scored lots of goals. Charlie was a bit upset when he said he was going."

"Did anyone else change clubs in the summer?" Richard was curious to know more about the history of this group.

"A few others," Peter said. "Most of them went to lower league teams when they were released by the club."

How many youth players does the club normally retain at the end of season? How many dreams were smashed? Richard wondered.

Back on the pitch, Charlie sent a cross in from the left for Danny, who was pushed in the back and the referee pointed at the spot for a penalty. Paul stepped up to take the kick.

"Bottom left," Richard whispered to himself as he watched Paul's run up and saw him put it into the bottom left corner for 1-0.

"How did you know that?" asked Peter.

"The way he runs," Richard pointed out. "The keeper knew it too but the kick was too good."

"Do you analyse everything you see?" Peter must have felt like he was talking to some human-shaped computer.

"Isn't that how our brains function?" Richard didn't know what he said sounded a bit condescending, but the gentle giant knew he was just being honest after getting to know him for a few weeks.

"Not really for everyone, Richard," he said. "At least mine doesn't do that."

The game resumed and after a series of passes, Danny whipped the ball in from deep and Charlie was there to head it in. 2-0 and the game looked comfortable. Then Danny made it three after a one-two with Paul.

"Nice work boys," said David at half time. "I expect the other team to come out strongly in the second half as they have nothing more to lose now. Be ready and follow your players."

He made one change at half time, replacing Adam with Rob. The other team had switched to a more direct style with their full backs taking a lot more risk and pushing up at every opportunity. Charlie and Rob were not tracking back much to help the onslaught happening to Ollie and Kevin.

The home team soon pulled one back. Ten minutes into the second half they doubled up on Ollie and the cross was converted by one of their strikers. Two minutes later, James was caught in possession and he pulled the opponent down just outside the area. He was given a yellow card for the professional foul.

The free kick was taken quickly towards their other striker who pull away from the under-prepared Steve to head it in.

"You're coming on, Rich," David called Richard back from his warm ups. "Are you nervous?"

"I thought you know me by now," said Richard as he took his bib off.

"Good, you'll go into right midfield and don't let them face Ollie alone," David gave him a pat at the back. "Protect what we have."

Paul was the player coming off as David moved Rob up front and swapped Danny and Charlie to offer Kevin a bit more protection on the left.

"Who's that new boy?" the other players said amongst themselves. "Isn't he a bit skinny at this level?"

They quickly passed the ball to their left winger to continue their attack. He had a look at Richard and thought he could take him on, but he didn't realise who he was facing – before he knew it the ball had already gone away from him.

The home side kept trying but they were not able to go through their left as Richard either won the ball from the attackers or cut out the pass before it even reached them. In short, no one was getting pass him – he was true to form.

The attackers switched to the other side late in the game but Danny was equally relentless and time was running out. The game ended 3-2.

"That was good," David told the team as they came off the pitch. "Great covering work for you Danny and well done, Richard, that was an impressive debut."

"Thanks boss," Richard replied. "That felt good. Glad I could help."

"Back to winning ways," Tom came over and put his arm around Richard's shoulder, clearly over the moon. "Wouldn't happen without you there, Rich. You made our lives easier. Did you see how that left footer looked after you took the ball off him time and time again? That was priceless."

"I hope the boss thinks you're ready from now on," said Danny as he was having some warm down stretches.

"I hope so too," said Richard as he had another sip of his energy drink.

David invited Richard and Tom to watch a live Champions League game at his house after training the following Tuesday. A top Italian team was playing and he wanted the youngsters to focus on their defensive midfielder.

"We'll use the player cam function to look at how the number six operates," he said. "You'll have to keep your noise down – my boys are sleeping and I'll be in trouble with the wife if we wake them up!"

David used the movements and actions of the player to teach Richard and Tom the art of playing defensive midfielder throughout the match. He emphasized the need to be aware of the space available and the whereabouts of the other players – in both teams.

"It's a little bit like driving – the more aware you are of everyone's position, the more time and space you have on the ball. Then you can, and need to, demand the ball from your teammates so that you can spread it around."

Richard was amazed at how much David knew the little details and learnt a lot from the experience. The player being watched was playing short and safe passes most of the time but he hit a delicious long through ball near the end of the game to set up the only goal of the match.

"Look at his decision making and vision – one lapse of concentration at the back and he opened them up for the goal. That's what you call a world class number six," David concluded. "Try to watch him and other players using this function – yes it is less entertaining but it'll be useful for your development."

Tom had been working part time at a hotel near Kingston and he asked Richard if he would join him and the others for a poker night there on Wednesday the following week, as he picked up a bonus in the form of a free suite. Richard used to play the game with his family friends and he agreed to join after his gym session in the afternoon.

"Walk straight into the lift and hit the fourth floor, we're in 405. Do not talk to the receptionist!" said Tom's text message.

Richard followed the instructions and knocked lightly on the door of the hotel room. Tom was there to open it and he waved Richard in with a shh gesture. Charlie, Rob, Ollie, Paul, Steve and Danny were already there having drinks and playing cards.

"Have you finished your gym work today?" Charlie asked. "Are you any better on your chest press?"

"I can do 20kg more now, getting there slowly."

"That's good! Fancy a drink? Or do you need some protein shakes?"

Richard had a look at what everyone was having and noticed that apart from Danny they were all having alcohol. He opted for the only soft drink left in the mini fridge.

"Where's Thomas? I thought he was coming?" he asked.

"He's gone over to Elle's. She texted him saying her parents are out so I'm sure they are having fun now!" Tom said with a pervy smile.

"Bondi is so obsessed with Elle. Do you remember the first time he saw her at school? He was completely hooked since!" said Rob.

"Yeah he just followed her around until she gave in," laughed Charlie.

"I'm surprise you're using your free night on us and not Mihara!" Paul added.

"Mates first, babes second!" Tom claimed with his fist up in the air.

"Of course you'll say that, your folks were never in so you two can just make out at home," Ollie highlighted the key point.

"There's that too!" Tom laughed.

"How long have you guys known each other?" Richard asked.

"All of us here apart from Danny have been together since junior school. We met Owen, Jack, and good old Darren since year seven. The others were recruited at various times. For those you know well, Big Peter and Bondi joined us at year nine and Danny only last year," Tom answered.

"It's so cool being able to play together for so long. I was with three different youth teams in Germany before the last one in Surrey so couldn't really develop a bond like yours," Richard said.

"It's never too late, as long as you work hard for the team and know your football. Danny doesn't say much but he's an integral part of the group now," Steve said.

"I'd say you're one of the gang already," said Tom. "I prefer having you in centre mid with me. Just don't tell James!"

"Oh where did James and Adam come from? Are they good friends?"

"Those two and Kevin are from the same school in the other side of town," Tom explained.

"Be careful with them, it's pretty rough where there are from," Charlie added.

"That's… great to know."

"They're fine. Don't make little Rich worry," said Danny.

"Well, let's see how good you are with poker first! Everyone chips in a tenner and the winner takes all!" Rob explained the rules.

The boys made room for one extra player to sit in and the game started. Richard knew how to play the game but always found it hard when he needed to bluff. So a win for him largely depended on having good hands. But it wasn't his lucky day – all his chips were gone within an hour. He was only better than Ollie, who lost first and had to be the dealer for the rest of the night.

From his observations, Paul was the most aggressive person around with some brave but probably not the best calls; Charlie was similar but a little more calculated; Steve and Tom were calm and well balanced; Rob was really good at deceiving others; while Danny was completely unpredictable with his never-changing impression.

The game eventually ended with Steve beating Charlie in the final showdown. Having finished second and third from bottom, the penalty for Richard and Tom was to pick up some pizzas (and a healthy chicken pasta for Danny) from Surbiton town centre.

"How long have you been working at this hotel?" Richard asked as they got outside.

"It's been about a year. I helped out in the kitchen for a few evenings a week," Tom said.

"Is it hard work?"

"Not really, just some lifting and cleaning."

"Don't you get to cook?"

"Sometimes they let me fry some chips and chop some vegetables, but most of it was just labour."

"Why do you do it?"

"Why? I need to earn my own money, Rich!"

"Sorry I didn't mean to be patronising."

"It's okay. Not everyone is as lucky as you though."

Richard didn't carry on with the conversation to have a think about it. He had his fair amount of ups and downs in the last few years, but they seemed minor when compared with those his teammates faced. He really needed to make the most of his privileged position and leave no efforts behind.

The boys night resumed after the rather late dinner when Ollie set up a private screening of his playlist of X-rated videos. Richard wasn't too keen on those but he went along with the group. Some of them were real "eye-openers" – he didn't understand why some people would go the distance in making them, and why some people would enjoy watching them.

"Did you enjoy that last one Rich?" Ollie asked.

"They are a little bit... too much," Richard hesitated but gave Ollie his honest view.

"Really? What's your preference?"

Richard didn't know what to say. It wasn't that he didn't like watching the actions but he wanted to see more romance in the build-up, which would probably sound too weird to the boys.

"Leave him alone, Wally!" Charlie came to the rescue.

"I just want to understand my future customer better," Ollie joked before playing his next selection.

Richard had two bottles of beer during the evening and that always made him very sleepy. Added to the fact that it was two in the morning, he felt asleep during one of the clips. By the time he woke up, he found himself surrounded by the feet of Danny and Tom either side of him. The group ended up having three sleeping head to toe on each double bed while Rob and Ollie crashed on the sofa. He couldn't fall back asleep straight away but he stayed very still in case he woke the others up. He eventually dozed away until Tom gave him a little nudge in the morning.

"Time to wake up buddy," he said.

"Good morning, how's everybody?"

"They're all getting ready, do you want to join us for breakfast at the local cafe?"

"Sure, I'm always up for a full English!"

"Mind you, you're now known as the one who fell asleep watching porn!"

"Oh my… it was the alcohol, honest!"

"It'll take you a while to recover from that!"

4.

The Difference

There was a two-week gap between games six and seven and Charlie, Thomas, Steve and Tom joined Danny and Richard for some additional training one day. Nick was also there to help. It all started from a conversation between the group a few days before that.

"Do you guys think we don't score enough goals from corners?" Charlie asked. "When's the last time we scored one?"

"Maybe April at the back end of last season?" Tom said. "What can we do about it though? Now that Darren's gone, we are not a tall side apart from Peter, and he doesn't start most games."

"But Steve, Thomas and I can head the ball well," replied Charlie. "Surely we should score one every now and then? What do you think, Rich?"

"You guys can head indeed," Richard said in his analytical mode, "but you need to go for a running jump as you are not taller than most defenders. So we need to come up with some moves to create the space for you to run. Let me think about it – we can have some extra training when we're ready."

"That sounds like a reasonable thing to do, guys," Nick overheard and joined in. "Let's put something together one day after the regular training."

Back in the training, Richard was explaining his plan to his teammates.

"We need the three of you to all run from outside the area together," Richard pointing at Charlie, Thomas and Steve. "Two of you will probably just be running aimlessly through the crowd, but we should see a gap for the third one to aim for the spot."

"Where is the spot?" asked Thomas. Charlie found it hilarious for some reasons but no one knew why.

"It'll be the point where it is easiest to score from," said Nick as he walked into an area between the penalty spot and the six-yard box. "About here, maybe a bit to the left for a corner from the right and vice versa. This is where the keeper is unlikely to reach. You can decide amongst yourselves who attack it in each kick."

"For you guys to get to maximum height from your running jump, you'll need to do this," said Nick before he ran and jumped, with his feet about a metre off the ground.

"How the hell did you jump this high?" Charlie was amazed.

"I was a centre back by trade," Nick explained. "The key is in the last step of your run – turn it a little sideways to transfer your forward momentum upwards. Try it."

Charlie, Steve, Thomas and Tom took in turns to make a running jump. Nick stood close to them to correct their run-ups.

"How are we going to get the ball to them?" asked Danny while he watched his friends practicing their jumps. "Even with a running jump, these guys may still get beaten by those really tall centre halves?"

"Have you seen corners by the old German international Sebastian Deisler?" asked Richard. "I used to watch him play when I was in Munich and if we can replicate the way he hit them, the ball will reach the guys from a higher point by-passing the defenders. They only need to put their heads in the right place to direct the ball in, no extra power needed."

"Oh I remember him – that'll need a lot of whip! It'll be fun to get it working though."

The two groups practiced their respectively parts and reconvened after about half an hour.

"Are you guys ready for the real thing? Let's get started," asked Tom. "What do I do anyway? I suppose I'm not one of the three attackers?"

"You can help by defending the spot with a standing jump," Nick said.

The group spent the whole evening on it, to the point where Nick felt it was good enough to be taken back to the larger group for some proper training – with defenders and goalkeeper etc.

"Remember how to run together without tripping over," said Nick jokingly. "If we have Peter in the team, he'll replace you in this move, Charlie, so make sure you'll show him what you've practiced tonight."

The team's next game was at home against a team from south Wales. Richard got his first start as James was injured during training after a collision with Rob.

"This is your chance to impress," Tom said.

David told the team that the opponents were well known for their ability with the ball and their movements, so everyone needed to be on alert and stick to their game plan of a low block combined with counter attack.

A low block was the term for defending with two banks of four (five in midfield for the 4-3-3 formation that the Black Dragons employed). The team sat deep in their area to restrict the space available for the team with the ball. David preferred a narrow and compact block which gave the opponent time and space in the wings, as the team had two good centre backs in Thomas and Steve, a commanding keeper in Jack to deal with crosses and a solid defensive midfield in Richard and Tom to combat any attempt to break through the middle. When they got the ball, they would counter using the ball holding ability of Adam, the pace and movement of Charlie and Danny, and the finishing of Paul.

Richard was playing in a competitive match with Adam for the first time. The wonderfully gifted player rarely talked to him and didn't seem overly keen to pass him the ball during training. He hoped it would be different in a real match.

The game started and as David predicted, the away team passed the ball around neatly. They didn't seem to be in a hurry to score so the home side were doing lots of running around without the ball, which was contrary to the idea of a low block.

Richard's tackling ability wasn't required as his excellent positioning prevented the opponent's advance in the middle. He intercepted a few passes but the team lost the ball soon after as they were tired with the chasing and couldn't build any momentum. The first half ended frustratingly goalless.

"We need to stop chasing the ball and let them approach us. You'll run out of steam soon if you carry on like this," David said to the team in the dressing room.

"Let them come to us? Will that be too dangerous?" Thomas asked.

"Not if you concentrate on keeping the shape of the block. By forcing them into a smaller area we'll have a better chance of winning the ball back. Paul, can you shut their path to pass back to the centre backs please?" David said.

"What do we do when we get the ball back?" Tom asked.

"Hit the wings. As we are going to invite them into our pitch, they'll be short at the back if and when we win the ball. Pass it the Charlie and Danny and support them," David said. "Charlie and Danny, when you get the ball, run at the defence and force whatever you can – throw ins, corners, free kicks. Of course if the chance is there you can go all the way and score."

The second half started with the Black Dragons retreating to their own half, inviting the away side to enter with the ball. The visitors were a little surprised by the move but they started spreading the ball in the final third, looking for a chance to score. However, they found it difficult to break through the compact shape of the home team. Tom picked up a stray pass outside the area and sent the ball wide to Danny on the right. He ran all the way to the byline with the ball and forced a corner off the centre back.

"Here we go, Rich," said Steve as he jogged up to join the attack.

It was agreed that Richard would take the out-swinging corners from the right and Danny would be responsible for those from the other side. Richard put the ball down at the corner and he could see Charlie, Thomas and Steve in position outside the area together, ready for the run up. He hit a dipping corner towards the area between the penalty spot and the six-yard box as per his training. The keeper didn't come out to punch or catch it and Steve was there jumping higher than the defenders – but his powerful header went just over the bar.

"That felt really good – I never thought I could jump that much higher than those centre backs," he said as he and Richard moved back into positions.

With the same tactic, the home team won a few more corner kicks from Charlie and Danny's adventurous runs. Richard took two more from the right, both were met by his teammates but one went wide and the other saved by the keeper. But the Black Dragons scored with the next one – Danny's in-swinging corner was headed in by Steve as he yet again jumped high above the defenders and put the ball into the net.

Steve celebrated his goal with a roar towards the bench – Nick was visibly happy as the team's efforts in training paid off.

The away side pressed for an equaliser but the home team held strong in their half, with Richard and Tom blocking a number of passes through the middle and creating dangerous counter attacks with Adam, Charlie and substitutes Rob and Finley in front of them. The match finished 1-0 to the Black Dragons.

"Good win that. We've got our new weapon!" Charlie was particularly proud as it was his idea to practice on corners.

The Black Dragons first team were travelling to Greenwich in east London the following Wednesday evening and Richard went to the match with Tom and

Charlie, the two most diehard supporters of the club in the youth teams. It was a hugely important game as the Dragons were fourth from bottom after fourteen games while their opponents were one place above them. It was a true six-pointer.

The youngsters arrived ahead for the 7:45pm kick off thanked to Richard's insistence on setting off early, as they encountered several delays with the train journey.

"Great call to leave early Rich, we would've missed the first half had we stuck to Charlie's plan," Tom said when they finally left the overcrowded train station.

"They never make it easy to travel across town!" Charlie moaned.

"Well, now we have another ten minutes before kick off, shall we get some food outside the stadium? It should be cheaper?" Richard suggested after spotting some fast food stalls.

"Yeah I've heard that it's a bit overpriced inside," said Tom.

"Of course! You can't watch a football game without having a burger from the van!" Charlie agreed.

The boys had a double cheese burger each before going through the traditional turnstiles. They timed it to perfection as the teams were lining up for the formalities. Contrary to most other venues, the view at the south stand that hosted the three thousand away fans was very decent.

"Good to see you again, Miles's boy," one of the travelling fans greeted Charlie. "Who have we got today?"

"Hey Geoff! You've met Tom before, this is Richard, our latest recruit in the under 18s," said Charlie.

"Welcome to the club, Richard. Hope to see you on the pitch one day!"

"Thank you. Do you go to lots of matches?"

"Every single one this season and last, only missed one the year before for my son's wedding!"

"That's really amazing! It's so good that the club has supporters like you!"

"We have a solid group of two thousand or so fans that would go anywhere with the club. We need to repay the way Dr Edwards invested in the community, he's such a great man."

"You're talking to the right person then! Dr Edwards is his idol!" Tom added.

"Really? Let me tell you more about him. I still remember the club's first ever match after he purchased the club. I was about thirty eight back then and Dr Edwards walked around town inviting everybody in. It ended as a defeat but the dream lived on, and what a dream it was…"

Richard ended up spending most of the first half listening to Geoff's stories. On the pitch, the home team took the lead in the middle of the half and the Black Dragons struggled to create any significant chances.

Tom dragged Richard with him to the food outlets to give him a break.

"Last time he kept talking for the full ninety minutes," he told Richard.

"Some of his stories were interesting," Richard said with a smile.

"Remember David set us a task for today."

"Yes, we need to compare the centre midfielders. I've been watching them."

"You must be good with multitasking!"

"Well, I wasn't fully listening…"

"I never know you can be naughty, Rich!"

"Let's use this as my get out of jail card when we get back."

Richard swapped seats with Charlie on his return and managed to watch the game closely. It was a worthy game as well – George equalised early from a low cross, only for the team to fall behind again soon after, then Kalifa levelled once more from the penalty spot. The midfield three of Michael, Ross and Kalim slowly took control of the game with their endless movements and tracking. They had a wonderful understanding between them and they initiated a quick counter attack to send Luciano through, who finally swung the match to the Black Dragons' favour with his third goal of the season. The comeback was completed.

The three thousand jubilant travelling fans took over the stadium with their singing for the remaining ten minutes while plenty of disappointed home fans made their exit. But there was another twist in stoppage time. A seemingly harmless long ball somehow found the home team's right winger, who was bundled over by Alain the centre back inside the area and the referee whistled for a penalty!

Richard and the others couldn't believe it – there was less a minute to go and the team were at risk of dropping two vital points!

The remaining home fans were all excited as they backed their main striker for the spot kick. He positioned himself for a long run up in front of the away end.

"He's going for a Panenka! Panenka!!" Richard shouted all of a sudden.

The Panenka penalty is a gently chipped kick, aimed at the middle of the goal, executed after a purposeful run and a fake that sends the goalkeeper diving to either side of the net. It is named after the former Czech footballer, Antonin Panenka, who first attempted this cheeky kick in the Euro 1976 final against West Germany.

Before anyone noticed what Richard said, the striker had taken his kick and it was indeed a cheeky little chip. Matt the veteran keeper was off balance trying to dive to his right but he miraculously managed to push his left hand up onto the ball and tipped it over the bar!

The away fans went absolutely wild for the turn of events and Tom was jumping onto Richard like he had just scored a goal himself.

"How did you know that? You're such a genius!" Tom shouted as he kissed Richard's cheek in excitement.

Richard wasn't able to respond so he just stood there and nodded repeatedly.

The referee blew the full time whistle when the resulting corner came to nothing and a match to remember was sealed.

Richard joined the away fans and sang the club's victory song at the top of his voice.

We are the Dragons, my friends.

And we'll keep on fighting till the end.

We are the Dragons!

We are the Dragons!

No time for losers,

Cause we are the Dragons, of Ditton!

The players went over to appreciate their supporters and Matt asked the crowd who the boy screaming Panenka earlier was. Geoff and Charlie duly gave the blushed Richard away.

"I heard you, son. How did you know he was going for it?" Matt asked.

"Err… the overly confident look on his face and the way he set his run up…" Richard said sheepishly.

"Don't be shy. It's a great call – you are the difference between one and three points today!" Matt said before taking his shirt off and handed it over to Richard as a reward.

The crowd gave Richard a good cheer as he walked back to where Tom and Charlie were.

"You stole the show today buddy!" Tom said.

"Well done Rich. I'll be telling my old man what you did tonight," said Charlie.

"That'll be embarrassing," Richard said quietly.

"Don't be, you'd never know how important those two points will be at the end of the season!" Tom said. "Let's pray now that the train is going to take us home!"

Well, they sort of did eventually. Richard was finally home at midnight, having travelled the twenty four miles in another two and a half hours.

The news did reach David quickly and he sent Richard a text to commend his actions when he was on the train.

The under 18 team went on an unbeaten run for the next four games with one win and three draws. Richard started every one of them and he formed a formidable partnership with Tom in the middle of the park with some impressive defending and passing, and the new set piece routine paid further dividends as they scored two more goals from corner kicks during those games.

James was available for selection in three of those games but was overlooked. He wasn't impressed with that and he vented it out on Richard when they were alone in the gym one day.

"Are you done here?" he asked when Richard was working out on the bench.

"Not yet, but those two benches over there are free."

"I know, but I only want to use THIS ONE!"

"I don't get it, what's the difference?"

"Because I want to. You need to respect your senior players, fucking rock star!"

"I was never told that there is seniority within the team?"

"There fucking is, and don't you think you'll keep me out of the team for long!"

"That's the boss's decision."

"That's because you're his fucking pet!"

"This is getting out of hand," Richard stood up and said, "maybe you should seek some help."

"Are you saying I'm fucking mental? I'll sort you out right here!"

He gave Richard a hefty shove and sent him crashing into the weights behind him. His back hurt but he swiftly and firmly stood back up. He might not be an aggressive person but he wouldn't run away from a fight. He looked James in his eyes and he saw lots of hatred, but also a piece of insecurity and despair.

The staff and other players in the gym came over to intervene and James quickly made his way out.

"Are you okay Richard?" asked Les the under 21 captain.

"I'm fine thanks. Is he always like this?"

"He's known to be a little hot-headed, but none more so than most of us footie players."

"It's sad that I'm affecting the harmony of the team…"

62

"Listen, Richard. Everyone here is working towards the same goal of playing professionally and there's no time to pity those who can't make it. You'll be the best of yourself and leave no regrets. James and any others can choose to do the same and give the gaffer a headache. If they can't do it, they go. It's as simple as that."

"I think I get it," Richard said after taking some time to think it through. "Thanks Les, I know what I need to do."

Game twelve was away at one of the teams in the northern section. The Professional Development League was split geographically into north and south sections and teams would play others in the same section twice and those in the other section once, making it a 29-game season. Richard had always suffered from travel sickness and the four-hour coach journey up north didn't do him a lot of favours. He had his tablets for it and had a nap during the trip but he needed a couple more hours after it to settle himself. Fortunately the team set off early in the morning so there was plenty of time for him to recover.

The home team were known for playing long balls and crosses towards their two big strikers. David had opted for a defensive 5-4-1 formation with Richard starting ahead of James again. The plan was to defend the aerial bombardments with the three centre halves and used the passing ability of Adam and Danny to initiate quick counter attacks with the lone striker Charlie, supported by either or both full backs.

It worked as the teams were cancelling each other out for most of the first half. However, a pass back by Kevin near the end was cut out by one of the strikers, who rounded Jack and scored. It was the worst time to concede a goal and the team were devastated.

With the team chasing a goal, David decided to change the shape back to the normal 4-3-3 at half time. The team will have to press high to stop the other team in possession then use their numerical advantage in midfield to attack.

But it got worse before it got better as the home team scored another goal from a corner through one of their centre backs. Now they were really up against it.

The other team attacked again with a high ball towards one of the strikers who drifted wide to their right. Kevin jumped up to challenge him but he landed awkwardly on his back and had to be taken off.

David was ready to replace him with Liam the substitute full back, but Richard came across and asked if he could bring James on to play in centre midfield and he would play at left back. He had an idea and he let his teammates know quietly.

The home side continued to attack down their right but Thomas was able to pick up the loose ball. He passed the ball to Danny, who exchanged a glance with Richard and quickly rolled the ball towards him. At the same time, Charlie began running towards his own goal, pulling one of the centre backs out with him.

Richard ran up to Danny's ball and hit it diagonally first time, with the ball flying towards the space behind the other team's central defenders, which was made bigger by Charlie's movement. Rob was running after it at full speed and the goalkeeper was also coming out to meet it. The ball landed between the two but just when the keeper thought the ball would simply bounce onto his hands, it didn't – it slowed down!

It was a perfect "Green-Cut Pass" that Danny and Richard had been practising. Rob controlled the ball ahead of the stranded keeper and squared it for Adam to make it 2-1.

It was Richard's plan all along – Danny's roll back to create the backspin, Charlie's movement to pull one centre back out, Rob's run from deep and his very long pass, all designed to catch the other team out, and it worked.

Stunned by such an extraordinary goal, the other team seemed to have lost its composure and they consistently hit the ball up field in hope for a favourable outcome. They nearly got it, as a bouncing ball ended up with the left winger, whose cross was met by an unmarked striker at the far post – he had completely lost his marker Richard, who misjudged the flight of the ball and was unable to offer any pressure. Fortunately for him, the lopping header to the far

64

post was cleared off the line by Thomas who didn't give up chasing.

His clearance was picked up by Ollie. He sent it forward towards Adam, who was fouled in the air by the centre back. The free kick was about thirty yards out, being slightly right to the goal.

The ball was put down by Danny, the regular taker who had a reasonable reputation in the league. Richard was standing behind him when Danny turned around and whispered.

"You take it, Rich. I know what you can do from this distance."

For everyone's surprise, Danny ran over the ball and Richard curled it with his right foot towards the top right corner... and it went in despite the best efforts from the keeper!

"I didn't know you have that in your locker too!" shouted Tom as he ran across to celebrate.

Richard was surrounded by his ecstatic teammates and all he did was pointing his finger at Danny, who was a few yards away, and clapped his hands twice.

Danny did the return gesture but with an added wink.

The game ended 2-2.

"Well done boys!" David was delighted. "That was a good come back!!"

"Good to see all those extra training paid off," he turned to Richard and said. "That ball was exquisite – well done! Saying that, the way the striker lost you in the far post needs some work, if we are going to put you into left back again."

"Yes sir," said Richard as he walked towards the changing room.

"Yes sir~~~ I'll do everything you ask me to sir~~~" James said to Adam behind them, mimicking what Richard said with a feminine tone.

David turned round and gave him a stare, but he carried on "I'll be careful if I were you Adam, he'll be after your number ten role soon."

"I'll say bring it on. Sucking up won't suddenly make someone a good player," Adam responded.

"You never know mate. It depends on how hard someone does it and if they swallow it afterwards!"

"Enough of this disgusting chat!" David warned and James finally ended his offensive.

The team were on their coach, ready for the return trip to London. Richard sat in his favourite spot – the second last row on the left. He read a study online that it was the safest seat on a coach that size.

"Hey Rich, do you mind if I sit next to you for the trip home?"

Richard looked up and was glad that it was a friendly face asking the question, "Of course not, be my guest, Thomas."

Thomas sat down and had a few exchanges with Richard about the match, his pass, and his goal.

"Your ability to spot and hit a first time through ball was quite something," he said.

"Thanks. I don't know why but I seem to be able to see where someone is going to run to and send the ball there, if they were running. Ask me to hit a static object and I'm more than likely to fail."

"That's a strange talent but a good one to have surely!"

"What is the moustache thing about? Why are you guys all having one?" Richard spotted it on Tom, Charlie and now Thomas.

"It's for Movember. It's a charity that raises awareness on men's mental health and suicide prevention, prostate cancer and testicular cancer. Do you want to join?" Thomas explained.

"Oh I didn't know about that, what do you need to do? Just grow a mo?"

"Yes that's all it is. Of course you can help with donating money too."

"I don't have much facial hair anyway but I'll give it a go, just don't laugh."

"I'm looking forward to it!" Thomas said before he moved on to a serious topic. "By the way, I'm moving out next week. I've rented a flat in Walton to live with Elle."

"That's good. Does it mean you've got a contract extension?" Richard remembered their conversation the other night well.

"Yes I have a three-year deal," Thomas said with his voice down. "Don't tell the others yet – some of them may not be getting theirs."

"Okay I won't. The two of you must be over the moon?"

"Oh yeah, we get the freedom to do whatever we want, whenever we want," Thomas with a smile, one of those that teenagers brought on whenever they thought about a certain subject, "Don't you want that?"

Richard had a look at Thomas's face and realised that with the threat of being released gone, he didn't look that old and was still a teenager. A good looking one as well, maybe one of the best in the team, alongside Finley and Chris, who played for the under 21.

"Rich? Are you still there?" Thomas noticed Richard was in his thinking mode again.

"Oh, yes..." Richard woke up. "No, relationships are just distractions."

"Don't be such a robot. That's one of Danny's favourite quotes."

"We'll see what life brings, really. Right now it is all about the football."

Richard closed the conversation and started his nap for the long journey as the effect of the travel sickness tablets kicked in.

It's kind of good that I've been so busy with training since coming to the academy. I'd rather not think about relationships for now, he thought.

67

5.

A New Left Back

It had been two months since Richard started training with the Thames Ditton academy and he knew who he would go to for everything: Charlie and Steve for gym sessions, Danny for skills training, Tom and Finley for food and Ollie for a random chat, if he ever needed one like that.

One day, Richard arrived at the academy early for training and saw a youngster waiting at the reception area with a couple of suitcases, looking a little lost.

"Hey, are you okay there?" asked Richard.

"Hi, I'm expecting to meet Miss Carla Robertson," the boy replied in a rather formal manner. "Is this where she would be?"

Richard had a good look at this boy in front of him as they made eye contact. He was a couple of inches shorter than him with a slim build, which was quite typical for a teenager. His dark brown hair was neat and clean; the longer top was brushed forward and had just enough products on it to make it look well maintained. His big brown eyes, hiding behind his pair of round glasses with dark metal frames, gave away his innocence but Richard felt there was a piece of sadness in them, they looked incomplete for some reason.

He was wearing a dark pair of jeans, a camouflage hoodie inside an orange down jacket from the famous French brand and a pair of limited edition basketball trainers. He didn't seem to belong here; he looked far too noble for the likes of Paul and Ollie, and even to Richard himself, who was considered to be wealthy by his mates. The boy in front should be heading to his skiing trip in the Alps or his weekly polo match at the country club.

"Excuse me," the boy continued in his lovely manner in his recently broken voice. "Is this the right place to meet Miss Robertson?"

"I'm sorry," Richard woke up from his analysis. "I've seen Carla earlier today so maybe she's just off for a break, she should be back here soon."

"Thank you," the boy said with a sweet smile. "Are you a player here? My name is Layne Moore, Layne as in L-a-y-n-e."

"Nice to meet you, Layne," Richard tried to up his level of elegance. "I'm Richard Lucas; I joined the club about two months ago."

"It looks like you're already making friends here," Richard turned around to see Carla walking towards them. "Are you Layne or Andrew? I'm Carla Robertson, Head of Football Operations."

"Hi Carla, I'll leave him in your capable hands," said Richard before he turned back to Layne and offered a handshake. "I'll see you around here."

"Thank you," Layne continued with his smile. "I'm looking forward to playing with you."

His hand was warm and soft. Richard felt as if a shockwave had just hit his body, a feeling of familiarity and peacefulness.

What a lovely boy! Who is he? Have I met him before? Richard thought as he headed to the changing room.

Don't even think about it, Richard, no, not here.

Richard completed the evening's training and returned to the host family for dinner. Mrs Stevenson told him that a new academy player had moved into Thomas's old room. Just as he walked upstairs, the door of the room opened and the new housemate came out to meet him.

"Hello Richard, it's nice to see you again," it was Layne, with his innocent smile.

"So you are my new housemate?" Richard tried hard not to show his delight. "That's very nice."

"I'll let you get back to your room first, shall we catch up during dinner?"

"Sure!"

Mrs Stevenson made Richard's favourite fish pie for dinner that night. Mr Stevenson had a night shift at the hospital so it was just the three of them.

Richard learnt from Layne during dinner that he joined the academy from his local side in Bath, a historic city in the western county of Somerset, where he was studying in a private school. His mother worked in the City so he qualified for the catchment area through her address in Richmond. He could have lived there and commute to training everyday but his mum wanted him to stay with a host family as she travelled out of the country for work most of the time. He was fifteen years old, left-footed and played as a left back.

Richard also heard that there was another young player named Andrew who joined the academy with Layne that day.

At the end of the meal, Layne invited Richard to his room to continue their conversation.

"So you'll be training with the under 16's tomorrow?" asked Richard.

"Probably the one after that. I'll have some inductions tomorrow."

"Oh yes I did them when I joined. Are you going to the school on the other side of the railways? I'm doing my A-Levels there. The schools here can't be better than your old one if it is a private school, why don't you join the likes of Bristol for football?"

"Yes I'm going to that school to complete my GCSE's. I came here because I want to be closer to my mum – she may travel a lot but she's based in London," said Layne before his face turned slightly downwards. "My dad passed away when I was four so I was only living with my aunt while I was in Bath."

"Oh I'm so sorry to hear that, it must be painful."

"It's okay now, I don't remember much about him apart from that he was crazy about football."

"Is that why you play?"

"That's how I started."

They talked more about football, their favourite players and teams. Like talking to any other teammates for the first time, Richard asked if Layne had seen the Captain Tsubasa series, and to his delight Layne was another fan. They then spent another good part of an hour talking about that before Layne asked a question.

"I hope you don't mind me asking," Layne said politely. "Is that a moustache that you're growing?"

"Err... yes, it's for Movember," Richard felt a little embarrassed for his rather weak attempt.

"I know that's for charity... but is that all you can do?" Layne couldn't stop giggling.

Richard found that sort of conversation refreshing, as he grew up alone in a rather serious and mature environment he couldn't remember being young much. *Is it what it's like to have a brother?* He wondered when he went back to his room.

The next evening Richard heard Layne described what he did during that day over dinner – visiting the stadium, learning about the history and heritage of the club etc. He also mentioned that he was in the same class at school with Danny and the other new joiner Andrew. He seemed easily excited and was always cheerful. He did notice the constantly thinking face of Richard and asked if he could relax a bit. Richard gave him a thankful smile, which was probably the best he could do. He had too much to think about – football, studies, his parents and of course himself, sometimes he wanted to just focus on the others to forget it, but there were times when he couldn't help it.

The next day was a Saturday and that was when all age groups trained at the same time on adjacent pitches, so Richard and Layne walked to the academy together.

"Hey Rich!" said a smiley Thomas as he approached the pair from behind. "Let me see how your mo is growing today... oh who's our new player here?"

"Hey," Richard walked across and gave Thomas a fist pump. He got used to his teammates making fun out of his effort.

"This is Layne, your successor at the Stevenson's. He's in the under 16 team."

"Ah you're the lucky one to taste all Mrs Stevenson's cooking then," said Thomas as he shook Layne's hand.

"Yes I'm only a couple of nights in and am giving her full marks already," said Layne with his usual youthful smile.

The three of them carried on walking and talked about which positions they played, the latest round of the Premier League, their fantasy teams and the next match in the league for the under 18's, which was against a local rival.

"How do you think we'll line up against the team from Shepherd's Bush next Sunday?" Thomas asked the tactician Richard.

"I guess we'll switch back to 4-3-3 after how we began the last match?" Richard said with his thinking hat and face on. "Charlie wasn't really at it in that formation, I suppose he needs to be on the wings rather than upfront on his own?"

"True, who's going to play left back? Kevin isn't back yet."

"I don't mind playing there as long as you are there to clean up the mess I made," Richard with a rare joke, "but I think it'll be either Mason or Liam, because I can offer a bit more in the middle."

"I think you're right – let's see what the boss says later," said Thomas as they arrived the training ground.

"I'm actually a left back, does it help?" Layne asked.

"No offence but I think you're a little light for the under 18's?" Richard said.

"Only kidding!"

"Shall we show you around or is someone meeting you?" Thomas asked.

"I am supposed to meet coach Bryan, do you know who he is?"

"That's okay we'll bring you to him."

After dropping Layne off with coach Bryan, Thomas and Richard walked to their pitch for training.

"I think he'll be a good housemate for you," said Thomas.

"What... what do you mean?" Richard turned around and asked, a little nervously.

"He'll bring you some childish or teenager things, something less serious to your mind. At this rate you'll look older than me in no time."

"Elle must be treating you well, you look so much more cheerful these days."

"I wouldn't swap her for anyone."

Richard looked at the sweet smile on Thomas's face and wondered, *Will I ever find someone that gives me this sort of satisfaction in life?*

After the usual training on stamina, passes and movements, David gathered the team together to talk about the game plan for the derby next Sunday.

"As you know," David raised his voice, "next Sunday's game is against one of our local rivals. We must win. Saying that, I want us to win using our efforts and skills, and not just by any means. At this level, and in fact any levels, we expect our players to be proper sportsmen. We respect our opponents. Is that understood?

"We'll attack this game using our strengths, so we'll go with our usual 4-3-3 formation with Adam supporting the front three of Charlie, Paul and Danny. That means Richard and Tom behind him to protect the back four. Steve and Thomas are the centre backs, Mason will play at left back with Ollie on the right. Jack will be in goal."

Thomas turned to Richard and gave him a wink, which he replied with a nod.

"I've lined up the under 16's for a practice match today. They have a couple of new kids so please don't bully them," said David as he turned to Charlie.

"They shouldn't be on the pitch if they aren't good enough!" Charlie said with a fake scary face, "Don't worry, I really love kids. My two little brothers can testify."

The coaches split the two teams into four and Layne was on the under 16 side that faced the under 18's that

Richard was in. He was wearing a long-sleeve under layer when he waved at Richard from the left back position and Richard gave him a nod, as he already had his game face on.

Soon after the game started Richard saw Danny with some space on the right and chipped to ball towards him, expecting him to have enough time to control it. But a defender appeared out of nowhere to cut it out, controlling the ball elegantly with his chest in the air. He then played the ball to the attacking midfielder Dillon, one of Charlie's younger brothers, and continued his run. Dillon's return ball to the space behind Ollie looked a little over hit but the steaming defender got to it in time and managed to cross the ball first time in a sliding motion. The ball found the striker but he headed it over under the challenge of Steve.

Richard looked absolutely amazed – that was Layne his new young housemate. He didn't assume Layne to be a bad player but he certainly did not expect him to be this good. His pace was extraordinary.

"Careful with your passes Rich, you nearly gifted them a goal!" Tom said quietly.

"I know. It's not going to be an easy game," Richard switched back to his competitive mode.

The other new player, Andrew, also took part in this practice game and played as a right-footed left winger. He had a much better build than Layne – Richard wouldn't be surprised if he was one of those kids who won everything at the school track and field events, and he looked to be just under six foot tall.

Ten minutes into the first half, Andrew picked up the ball in left midfield with his right foot. He brought the ball up slowly to face Ollie, as Layne galloped on the outside. He was much quicker than the tracking Danny so the two of them doubled up on Ollie momentarily. The defender hesitated for a second and that was enough for Andrew to find the space to shift inside and curl a shot into the far corner, making it 1-0 to the younger side.

A frustrated Tom summoned Ollie over for his lack of tackling, "You can't let a right-footer come inside like that, you have to show him the outside!"

"My bad. I'll close that path from now," Ollie held his hand up and apologised.

"There's something we can do about that, Tom," Richard came across and whispered to Tom and Danny, who nodded and moved back to their positions. Danny had a word with Adam and Paul on his way back to pass on the message.

The older boys kicked off and the ball was passed back to Richard. He had a look to his right and duly hit another low ball towards Danny on the wing.

As expected, Layne came out quickly to cut out the pass. And like before, he tried to play a one-two with Dillon inside him and ran forward at full speed for the return ball. However, they didn't realise that both Tom and Richard were closing Dillon down very quickly from behind and possession was swiftly lost. The ball was then sent by Richard to Adam with acres of space ahead of him, with Layne all the way up at the wrong end. Adam pulled the centre backs towards him and rolled the ball into the path for the lethal Danny. There could only be one outcome when he connected with the ball, and that's 1-1.

"Good plan, Rich, you pulled that young left back out well," Tom celebrated with Richard with a high five. "Shall we do it again though?"

Richard nodded and said, "I don't think they know it was a trap yet."

And they probably didn't. Soon after kick off, the young left back was caught out of position again by his housemate. This time he was running with the ball at Ollie but he didn't know Richard was tracking him discreetly. He slid in from his blind spot to tackle the ball off him, sending him tumbling out the touch line in the process.

"I'm not the one bullying the kids!" Charlie was shouting from afar for a laugh.

Danny was already on the run as Richard steadied himself for another long pass with his right foot. However, Dillon moved in to block him.

"Don't you think the same trick will work twice," he said.

"You're right, it won't," said Richard as he cut the ball back onto his left foot and hit a low pass forward for Adam instead. His left foot wasn't as proficient as his right and hence he could only hit it low, but it was a good through ball. Instead of cutting in for Danny, the midfielder crossed beautifully to the far post instead, where a towering Charlie was waiting and he scored with a powerful downward header.

It was 2-1 at half time.

The second half was completely dominated by the older team as their superior physical strengths and tactical knowledge shone through. They came out easy winners with a 5-1 score line.

"Great start to the game mate," Richard said as he offered Layne a handshake.

"You made it difficult for us, Mr Lucas," Layne answered as he walked past him with an angry impression, one that Richard wasn't expecting.

"Have I somehow offended him?" Richard asked Thomas, who was next to him.

"Of course you did buddy. David said don't bully the kids and you stitched him up a few times as well as sending him flying with that tackle. He'll hate you for a little while," Thomas said with a cheeky smile.

"I was just playing the game!" Richard felt he was unfairly criticised.

"Stop winding him up, Bondi," Tom chipped in, "but you did make him look bad, Rich. It hurts as it was his first game here. I'm sure he'll get over it. He looks more than a decent player."

"I hope so," Richard said quietly, as he felt a bit guilty for what he did to the youngster.

Layne didn't go home with Richard after training as the younger team were invited to watch the first team play at home in the afternoon. During dinner, Layne was back to his cheerful self when he gave a detailed description of the game and mocked Richard for his fantasy team's poor performance. Richard was relieved that Layne wasn't hurt by the humiliation that morning.

Later that night, Richard overheard from his room that Layne was on the phone with someone. He didn't hear any of the lengthy conversation apart from the end bit where Layne shouted "You don't have to come!" before ending the call. He then heard noises that suggested the boy next door might be weeping a little bit.

"Hey Layne," Richard walked into his room after a couple of knocks. "Are you alright?"

Layne looked up and Richard could see two lines of tears coming down from his eyes. He gave them a quick wipe and said, "I'm okay Richard, don't worry."

"I'm not sure if you really are," Richard said as he sat down next to him. "Come on, it feels better to say it out loud, try me."

Layne went quiet for a while before he started speaking, "That was my mum. We were talking about my new start here, the call was okay, it just ended badly."

"Was it about the practice match?" Richard was worried that he might have been the culprit. "It wasn't that bad, was it? I can apologise if you feel hard done by?"

"No, don't be silly. I didn't like the way I was exposed but I don't get hurt by that sort of things," Layne seemed to have calmed down a little as he smiled at Richard's reaction.

"My mum is in New York for work at the moment and she just told me she couldn't come back in time to watch my first proper match next week. That's all.

"She works in legal and in recent years she keeps flying to different conferences and is rarely at home. That's why she moved to London and left me with my aunt. I just wish I can spend more time with her."

"I suppose sometimes that's unavoidable?" Richard can't remember the last time his dad watched him play.

"I get that, but she's been away for two months now, even though I gave up everything in Bath just to be closer to her. It's not like I have anyone else to go to. She's all I have."

Richard could sense the tears coming down again. He didn't know what to do or say in these situations. He was the only child in the family and he wasn't really allowed to cry after he entered school. He naturally put his arm around Layne to console him, but that seemed to have the opposite effect, Layne felt the touch and was now curling up in Richard arms for a full breakdown. Richard had never been this close with anyone other than his parents and somehow felt he was responsible to help this boy from his misery. He'd been imagining what Layne must have gone through with the loss of his dad since he heard his story and now he thought how much he had underestimated it. Something really was immeasurable.

However distant my parents are, at least I have them. Looking at Layne, Thomas and Danny, it really isn't a given to everyone. Richard thought.

Layne calmed down after a while. He wiped his eyes with the sleeves of his t-shirt and looked up to Richard.

"Thanks for being here, I'm alright now," he said before trying to sound more mature. "I'm not normally like that."

"It's okay, everyone has their moment. Glad I could help."

"Are you free the Friday after next?"

"I think I am, why?"

"Can you have dinner with me? I've already booked a table for me and mum."

"I guess I can, but you may want to know that it is my seventeenth birthday the Wednesday before so in return you'll have to celebrate with me. I'm going out with the boys for a Brazilian barbecue."

"That will be nice. Won't your parents come around?"

"No they won't. They don't really like me choosing football over studies."

"But you haven't stopped studying though?"

"They didn't think that way."

"That makes us the perfect pair then. I'll definitely join you on Wednesday," Layne sat up and checked the time on his phone. "Do you want to go for a run? I like doing that when I'm stressed."

"At this sort of time?"

"Yes, are you up for it? I dare you."

"You may be faster on a sprint, but you can't beat me over long distance," Richard was glad that Layne had recovered.

And the boys went out for a run.

It was Richard's seventeenth birthday the following Wednesday. Some of his teammates knew and they bought him a little cake from a supermarket at training the night before. Charlie and Rob suggested he should go drinking with them at their mates but Richard declined the offer. Like Danny, he was not into drinking. However, contrary to Danny, Richard was very much into food. He had wanted to try a churrascaria, or Brazilian barbecue, for ages and he invited his friends to one in Kingston. As agreed the week before, Layne came along and joined Tom, Charlie, Steve, Jack, Danny and Thomas for the small trip.

None of the young footballers had a churrascaria before. They learnt at arrival that the barbecued meat would be served by the roving waiters from their large skewers directly onto the seated diners' plates. All they needed to do was to flip their coasters to the green side if they wanted that particular cut or to red otherwise.

For a bunch of teenagers, the concept of unlimited cuts of beef, pork, lamb, chicken, duck and fish sounded like heaven. They started by going to the counter for their appetisers. The likes of Charlie and Tom went straight for the chips, while Danny and Layne had plates full of salad. Then the waiters with large skewers started to appear and soon the boys were having pieces after pieces of delicious barbecue. Charlie was particularly fond of the picanha, which was a cut of beef top sirloin cap, and Richard was pleasantly surprised by the texture of the chicken hearts.

Layne seemed very keen to find out more about the team and was asking questions non-stop during the meal. He was interested in knowing what the team did during the day, and he learnt that everyone apart from Charlie, who worked as a lifeguard in the local swimming pool, was still in some sort of full time education: Tom and Thomas were having some vocational training at college, while the rest were still in school. The team were amazed to hear Richard's GCSE results. They knew he was bright but didn't expect their teammate to have six A's on his books and was targeting all four at A-Levels.

Layne also asked the team how they called each other on the pitch and if they were different to their nicknames. Tom said most of them were just known by their surnames or a variation of them but they also created some random ones. Layne couldn't stop laughing when he heard that Charlie's nickname was "Figo". Tom insisted it was a reference to his build and running style, and definitely not for his skills.

Near the end of the dinner when the whole party was literally full, Charlie ordered another round of drinks and challenged everyone to drink them in one go. But he secretly added two shots of whiskey in Richard's Coca-Cola for fun. Without knowing the difference until too late, Richard downed his drink in one.

Richard was a light weight in terms of both his physical weight and his drinking ability. Charlie soon found out he made a mistake in getting Richard drunk, as he simply passed out on the table.

"Oh well, he's done it again," Tom sighed. "Now who's going to take him home? He's too heavy for little Layne to handle on his own."

"I'll take him," said Thomas. "I know where they live, you know."

So the birthday celebration ended with the birthday boy unconscious.

Richard woke up from his slumber when the taxi arrived at the Stevenson's. He walked inside with the help of Layne and waved goodbye to Thomas.

"Did you have a good night, Layney boy?" he asked his young housemate cheerfully.

"That was fun, did you enjoy your birthday?"

"It was great having you guys around, I've never had anything like it."

"Why not? Did you not have friends back in Windlesham?"

"We only moved there when I was in year ten and I didn't mix with the others well," said Richard with a wry smile. "I was too serious on everything, I suppose."

"Being serious is a good thing," Layne said quietly. "I think it makes you trustworthy and dependable. I like it."

The last three words touched Richard's heart string and he turned round to look at the youngster. His big round eyes were full of admirations.

"This boy is so adorable!" he thought.

Richard didn't know where he found the courage from, as he moved forward to give Layne a kiss. Layne looked shell-shocked and froze on the spot. Richard realised what he was doing at the very last moment and pulled away, ending up with kissing Layne on his cheek.

"You... you must be drunk, Rich, you'd better go to bed," said a blushed Layne as he pushed Richard onto his bed and ran back to his own room.

Why did you do that Richard? You may have ruined everything! Richard was angry with himself. *But that may also be the only chance I'd ever have... his face is so smooth and warm, and he smells so nice...*

Richard woke up the next morning to find a little present and a card on his desk. Layne must have left them there the day before, but he was too occupied to notice. The card had a nice drawing of a foot kicking a football on the front, with the hand-written message "Wish you have a memorable 17th birthday" inside. He carefully opened the nicely wrapped present next – it was a small bottle of fragrance by an luxury Italian designer brand. He had a little try and really loved the casual and breezy, sparkling fruity-floral scent. He felt really sweet.

He thanked Layne when they had breakfast but he pretended to have zero knowledge of what he did the night before. He focused on talking about the highlights of all the Champions League games that they missed instead. He intentionally came home late after training so that he could have some time to cool down before spending the next evening with Layne.

Layne had originally booked a table for two at a nice steak house by the river in Richmond for him and his mum, but he cancelled it after having the meat feast on Wednesday with the team. He decided to go to the Winter Wonderland at Hyde Park with Richard instead.

It was one of the biggest Christmas markets in the country and there were all the festive stalls, rides, carousels, an ice rink, frozen sculptures and most importantly for Richard, numerous food outlets. Layne knew Richard spent eight years of his youth in Germany and was a super fan of sausages so he thought it would be a good idea.

Richard knocked on Layne's bedroom door when he was ready to go, in his usual grey hoodie, charcoal jeans and black bomber jacket. A few minutes later the youngster came out and Richard's heart stopped for a second. He styled his hair upwards with a neat side part, wearing a white turtleneck top, a pair of black smart trousers and a grey scarf inside his orange puffer jacket.

"Wow you look cool tonight!" he commented.

"Don't you laugh at me now," Layne replied with a little blush on his cheeks.

"Okay I won't, shall we go?"

Did he dress up for me? Or maybe he does that all the time? Richard thought when they were on the way.

The two had a lot of fun taking on the various game stalls. Layne took his revenge on Richard for the practice match in the dodgem while Richard won a giant Polar Bear soft toy for Layne at the "Beat the Goalie" challenge by hitting all his three shots into the top corner. They had a go at the ice rink as well – Richard had no idea what he was doing pushing a support device in the shape of a penguin while watching Layne spinning around performing his fancy moves.

They ended up having dinner at the Bavarian Village. Richard ordered a massive plate of mixed sausages: bratwurst, würstchen and currywurst on a bed of sauerkraut and mash. Layne didn't understand how he could eat so much when he only had room for some schnitzel vom schwein.

During the meal, Layne found an opportunity to bring Richard back to Wednesday night.

"Do you normally pass out when you had a drink?" he asked.

"Sometimes, especially if I drink too quickly," Richard could sense where this conversation was leading to.

"Do you remember what you did when you were drunk on Wednesday?"

"Nope, I was in the restaurant and the next second I was in bed," Richard had to lie. "What happened?"

"Nothing worth remembering," Layne said with a blushed cheek.

Richard was relieved that he didn't ask anything further and left it at that. He liked Layne's company and didn't want to ruin his relationship with him this early.

Once Richard's rather large appetite was fully satisfied, the two visited a few more Christmas stalls before heading back to the digs, considering that they had training early the next morning.

6.

The Derby

It was Sunday and the team were due to play their derby game against the team from Shepherd's Bush. It was a miserable day as rain was pouring down heavily. Kick off was at noon but the sky was already quite dark due to the thick grey clouds above.

It was an away game so the players gathered at the academy for their short coach trip. Kevin was still injured but the rest of the team were all fit and raring to go. Layne, Andrew and Dillon asked if they could come along to watch the game. David and Nick were fine as there were seats available on the coach anyway.

The coach journey was only about thirty minutes and the team arrived at the home team's training ground when the hosts were already on the pitch having a team talk. Richard had a look at the players and could see that most of the players were taller and stronger than him.

"It'll be a tough game," he told Thomas who sat next to him as usual.

"Football isn't just about strengths. We play our game and we'll be fine," Thomas was confident.

David stuck to his plan and started with the eleven players announced the week before. He noticed the opponents were playing with a 3-4-3 formation and warned Richard and Tom of the potential overload in midfield if the wide attackers come inside. He asked Charlie and Danny to pay more attention and help out if they saw the midfielders struggle but otherwise they should try to utilise the space behind the wing backs.

"We need to be quick on the ball then," Tom whispered to Richard. "Let's remind each other where the space is. Two touches max?"

"If we do get the ball that is," said Richard. "I think we'll be busy chasing shadows."

The home side kicked off. After a few rounds of head tennis, the ball fell to Adam on the right. Just as he controlled the ball, the opposing left back came in with a heavy challenge. He caught Adam's ankle quite badly, to the point that he had to be substituted and replaced by Rob. The referee showed the defender a yellow card, but the intention was clear – it was going to be a proper battle.

Richard was up against a tall midfielder named Leon, who also wasted no time in joining his teammate onto the referee's notebook, as he arrived late for a challenge and stamped on the young Dragon's right foot. It didn't cause any serious injuries but it was a sore one.

If anyone in the Thames Ditton team fancied a physical battle, it would be Charlie. He asked for the ball over the top into space from Richard, and as he was chasing it alongside the opposing right back, he gave him a strong shoulder charge and sent him to the ground. He then held off the right sided centre back and cut it back with his left foot. The ball rolled towards the penalty spot, where Danny was approaching. As he pulled the trigger, he was hacked down from behind by a returning midfielder. That was a penalty to the Black Dragons, and another yellow card for the team from Shepherd's Bush.

Richard, having been appointed as the team's second penalty taker behind Adam the week before, stepped up, gave the keeper an eye to the left and sent the ball into the bottom right corner. He ran to the bench to celebrate with David and he gave everyone there, including Layne, a high five.

The goal seemed to have given the home team the wake-up call they needed. They started passing the ball and pressed well without committing fouls. The Black Dragons couldn't get their balls out and kept being pegged back. As David expected, Richard and Tom had a hard time holding the line in front of the defence as the wide attackers took in turns to come in field for passes. The opposing players were not trying to take on the pair but they were passing the ball around them. From Richard's position they seemed to be everywhere, but as he and Tom were holding their grounds with Danny in the middle the attack had to go wide and crosses were being dealt with by the centre backs. The low block was doing its job.

The Black Dragons managed to hold on to their lead to finish 1-0 at half time.

"Great defending boys," David said, "but that isn't going to be sustainable. Rich and Tom will run out of steam soon and they'll find a break through. We need to go on the front foot and score another goal if we are to win this derby."

"Attack as the best form of defence?" Ollie asked. "Where shall we go for?"

"I guess we can do this…" Richard had an idea.

"Sounds like a plan. I like it," David concluded.

The second half started. The Black Dragons tried to slow the tempo down by keeping possession in their own half. The home players were pressing higher and higher up the pitch as they were desperate to get the ball back to attack. The ball was passed to Tom in midfield, and suddenly he gave the team a signal before rolling it across to Richard. He hit the ball first time to the right into the space behind the left wing back for Rob. For the first time in the match, Ollie made a run from his position and he picked up his cousin's through ball before the byline. He crossed the ball low towards Danny at the near post, who flicked it back first time to the edge of the box. The ball landed at the foot of the unmarked Tom, and he smashed the ball pass the hapless keeper to make it 2-0. He didn't score that often and he celebrated doing so in a local derby with a passionate knee slide near the corner flag.

That was Richard's plan all along: lured the defence out slowly, doubled up on the cautioned left wing back, occupied the centre backs with the three attackers and set Tom free to score. Plan well executed.

With the game at 2-0 with thirty-five minutes to go, the team from Shepherd's Bush had to throw everything at the young Dragons. Crosses were coming in and the home team's taller players were winning most of the first and second balls. With caution out of the window, the players were flying in with their tackles too, they were made more dangerous by the pouring rain. There were some lucky escapes for the players and the home team were picking up more yellow cards.

Another cross came in from the Black Dragons' left and was headed out by Thomas. The ball was in the air around the edge of the area and Richard jumped up to flick it out. Before he made contact with the ball, he felt a massive bang to the back of his head and crashed into the muddy ground. Things turned dark all of a sudden until he saw David pouring some ice-cold water onto his face. He felt really dizzy and there was some severe pain from the back of his head.

"Are you alright Rich? Can you see me?" David asked.

"Yeah... what's going on?" his voice was weak.

"You had a nasty clash of heads and passed out for a few seconds. We have to take you off and send you to the hospital."

"Wait, I can play on..."

"No chance, you suffered from a concussion and the back of your head is bleeding a fair bit. Just calm down and wait for the stretcher."

The medics came around to give Richard a thick layer of bandage round his head before putting him on a stretcher and took him off the pitch. He saw Layne amongst the other players when they walked past the bench, and his young housemate looked very concerned.

"How are you feeling, Richard? Does it hurt?" he asked.

"It does a fair bit but I'll be fine."

"Are you sure? It looks pretty bad."

"It's okay, I get to look like the classic Terry Butcher!" Richard joked with a rather painful grin.

"It's not funny, but I guess you're okay if you can make fun out of it."

The ambulance arrived and the paramedics moved Richard into it. Nick was going to escort him to the hospital alone but Layne got into the ambulance as well.

His eyes couldn't leave Richard at all and he kept asking if he was okay throughout the short trip.

Richard arrived at West Middlesex Hospital and had the necessary procedure done to stop the bleeding. He had a few stitches on the back of his head and was given some very strong painkillers. It was a good few hours before he was given a bed to rest in. Minutes later he saw Nick and Layne coming into the ward. Nick told him before he left that he had arranged everything with the hospital and Richard would have to stay in for at least a night for observation.

Layne wanted to stay and keep Richard company. Richard could clearly see that Layne had been crying and he must have said he was okay ten times before his young housemate was half convinced.

"How did the game go?" Richard realised he left the game with a good fifteen minutes remaining and he was desperate to talk about something else.

"We won 2-1. They pulled one back very late on," Layne checked his phone and read out a text from Thomas. "The team sent their best wishes."

"Good that. It would have been a massive waste if we didn't win after all this," said Richard with a forced smile. "What actually happened? Did you see it?"

"I was screaming from the bench," Layne recalled. "That Leon was charging in at full speed towards the ball and I didn't think he had any intention to stop. He was given a second yellow for dangerous play."

"I did hear someone's screaming before the impact, so I guess it was you," said Richard with a thankful impression. "That was some derby. I knew it's important but I didn't know players put that much more into it."

"It was just madness! Winning by injuring your opponents is not winning! Are you sure you'll be alright? I've read that concussion could have long-lasting impacts!"

"I wouldn't really know about that now…"

"Does it still hurt after you had those painkillers?"

"It's better but I wouldn't say it's good."

"Oh do you need to speak to the doctor?"

"Don't be silly!"

The boys continued chatting away until Richard noticed a familiar figure entering the ward.

It was his mum.

"How are you doing, Richie? Where did you get hurt?" she asked, looking clearly worried.

"It's at the back of my head, I'm alright now. Only you coming? Where's dad?" he asked the obvious.

"He's busy with work…"

"Of course he is. His son having a little head injury is not worth troubling him with," Richard was being sarcastic.

"Don't say that. You know he cares about you too."

"I can only see what I can see, I'm not going to second guess others' feelings," Richard acted like a teenager for once.

His mum ignored that last comment and examined his injury carefully. Her caring touch calmed Richard down a little. They had a more peaceful chat until the nurse came in and asked if the guests could leave as the visiting hours had passed. Richard could see that Layne was rather reluctant but he accepted he had to go eventually.

He said before he left, "Have some rest after dinner. Text me if you're bored."

"Will do, let the Stevensons know for me."

Watching Layne and his mum leave the ward, Richard had a lot to think about.

Layne clearly cares a lot about me, way more than normal friends. Is he seeing me as a family member? Is it something else? Maybe he's just being a kid? I am the adult here, and I should be able to control the situation. How should I handle this? It won't do us any good, definitely not if we want to progress in the football world… but I really like spending time with him… is this what it is? Oh God what should I do?

He continued to debate against himself in his head but as the second dose of painkillers kicked in, he fell into a well-earned sleep.

89

Richard was discharged from hospital the next day after some further checks. As he suffered from concussion David told him that he was not allowed to train at all for a week and then couldn't take part in contact training for a further two. By that point it would be Christmas so he would not play for five weeks altogether.

In his absence the team played three league matches, an unlucky 1-0 defeat away with a late penalty for the other team, followed by two 1-1 draws at home. Kevin was back in the team and David had put Bradley into Richard's position in midfield ahead of James after he played poorly and gave away the penalty in the first game. Richard heard from Tom that James didn't take it well.

He went to watch Layne and the under 16's train the day after he was discharged, as he was bored of sitting at home. There was a 5-a-side practice game and Layne was on the side that lost heavily to the team with Dillon and Elliot, both younger brothers of Charlie. They were toying with Layne with their mesmerising skills on the ball.

"My defending was so bad, I was dribbled past time and time again in the mini-game," said a disheartened Layne as he walked home with Richard. "The Rangers said I'm all pace and nothing else."

"Don't say that," Richard said to calm his young housemate. "They are good but there are ways to defend against them."

"Are you sure? Can you teach me please, Richard?"

"Mm... how do I put this... To start, you need to understand your opponents' strengths and preferences: while his control and footwork are great, Dillon is heavily right-footed and his balance isn't as well developed as Charlie. He'll struggle if you force him into his left foot and give him a little nudge.

"Elliot is really good with moving the ball about with the bottom of his feet. If you make a move first he'll change direction and move the other way. You have to be patient against him, keep your shape, literally do nothing and let him make a move – you may not get the ball off him but he can't take it pass you either."

"Wow! How do you know all these? Did you play against them before?"

"Only once against Dillon, but what I said was from watching them earlier."

"That's crazy! I'll try them on Thursday. Any tips on my positioning?"

"Oh, I'm sorry to say it but that does need some work."

"I know! Stop pointing out the obvious!"

"Positioning is about awareness of your whereabouts on the pitch. Understanding what the passing lines are would help. For example, you would normally stand between the passer and the receiver, but you'll need to be aware of where the potential through balls are and if anyone is covering them.

"I would say that if you don't have to gamble and win the ball, as in when the team have enough numbers back, you should cover the passing lines. If you are out-numbered and have to take some risks, pretend to leave one line open to tempt the pass and intercept.

"Have a think about these next time you're in a match and you'll see the difference."

"Oh my God you're so good with these!"

Layne's eyes were as big as humanly possible when he sounded his admiration – Richard found that very satisfying.

He went to see Layne train again two days later and he could see the difference – Layne had clearly given his advice some thoughts. The young Rangers were shocked as they kept being tackled by the pacy left back, and coach Bryan gave Layne plenty of praise at the end of the night.

"Did you see my tackling tonight? Your tips are amazing!" said a delighted Layne.

"You've put them to good use," Richard gave Layne the credit he deserved.

"Bryan was impressed by my positioning too, but he said there're still plenty to work on."

"Yes I saw that too, you're a fast learner."

"I want to know more about tactics, can you teach me those as well?"

"I'm not an expert in them… how about playing the football manager game together? We can try them out there."

"That's a great idea! Let's do that when we get back!"

As a result, Richard spent a lot of time with Layne in the next three weeks. He continued to watch him train before his own training and showed him all he knew on the art of defending. In the evenings they played the football management game on the laptop together, often discussing tactics until late. He found that they also shared a similar taste in music and were both fond of singing in private, so a game night with music on was like the perfect treat. And of course they walked to and back from school together.

As Richard did not have any siblings and Thomas was out with Elle until late most of the time he was at the house, it was the first time that he lived with someone of a similar age. He very much enjoyed their time together and he liked Layne's innocence and openness. When he was with his parents he had to behave in a mature manner and he would have to think everything through before saying it, if at all. However, when he was with Layne he could open up and say whatever on the top of his head, even if it was a silly comment or an illogical thought. In short, he was far less tensed as he used to be, which made him happy.

Richard noticed one night that Layne's toes were inflamed. His toe nails were all cramped and he appeared to be in a bit of discomfort.

"Look at your toes. They need some proper looking after if you want to be a proper footballer," Richard said.

"What am I supposed to do?"

"There are methods, just give me your clipper."

Richard carefully clipped Layne's toe nails one by one, making sure that the edges didn't cause any friction with the skin and also got rid of any dead skin for him.

When he turned round he noticed Layne was staring at him quietly. Richard's cheek went blushed as he felt the urge to get closer to Layne again – but this time he managed to control himself.

"How are you feeling now?" he asked in order to break the silence.

"... It's so much better! Where did you learn all that from?" Layne woke up and asked.

"That's from experience, I used to have the same problem. Why are you looking at me like that? Is there something on my face?"

"Oh, I was looking at your eyes. The way they reflected under the lights make them look like sparks in a deep blue sea... it's beautiful."

"Really?" Richard didn't know how to react, especially as Layne said it in such an innocent way.

"I didn't realise you have blue eyes before."

"It's quite normal, isn't it?"

"It is, but yours are different."

"Well, do you need your fingernails done too? I may as well."

"If you don't mind?"

"It's okay, just give me your hand... You seem to have the same issues here, let's take care of them."

Richard held Layne's hands and applied his expertise to them. He had a strange feeling – the two of them seemed to be connected in some ways and he felt so relaxed and comfortable – was it what it was?

"Thanks Richie, it feels so good!"

"Look at your legs. You made fun of my moustache last month while this is all you have? You're just like a little kid!" Richard couldn't help himself from making the comment.

"Oh, I've just turned fifteen! Not that you have much either, Mr Grown Up!" Layne said as he stroked Richard's leg with his soft hand.

"Okay okay... let's see where you are in two years' time," Richard called time on the conversation as he felt a little uncomfortable. "Give me a shout the next time you need to do this, I'll show you again."

"Thanks Richie," said Layne with a lovely smile. He started saying Richie after hearing how Richard's mum

93

called him at the hospital. Richard was happy with it – he wouldn't if it was anybody else.

The academy players were given a two-week break between Christmas and New Year. The trainees housed in host families returned home for the holiday. Layne went back to his family home in Bath as his mum managed to take the time off. Richard returned to Windlesham to a worried mother and the standard, ice cold father. It was kind of good to be back to his own room but he felt strange to be without his new found friends – he had built a very strong sense of belonging with the team during the last four months away.

Richard did a fair bit of exercise during the holiday as he felt his fitness was behind after three weeks of rest and light training only. He watched all the available football games on television, whichever division or wherever they were from, and studied all the players in his position. Layne had been contacting him regularly for all sorts of reasons and when they returned to the Stevenson's it was like they had never been apart. Layne had forgiven his mum and came back in a very good mood. He got Richard a bun from a famous bakery in Bath and the two were as close as ever.

The young players returned to the news that Adam had left Thames Ditton for the big Premier League side in west London. Due to the fact that he didn't sign a professional contract with the Black Dragons, the club would only receive a nominal fee decided by a tribunal. James kept bragging about his friend's achievement and claimed that he would follow suit one day.

The club played six matches during January and February and had some decent results, picking three wins and two draws. Following Adam's departure, Danny was given the opportunity to play in his favourite position as an attacking midfielder and he grabbed it with both hands with his performance. He was less creative than the former incumbent but he offered a different type of threat with his direct running and endless energy. Rob was the other benefited player as he became the regular starter on the right.

Richard was heavily involved in all six games as he cemented his place in the starting line-up. His main focus was to marshal the area in front of the back four with Tom but his superior defensive capability enabled his partner to make lung-busting runs forward to support Danny and the front three when the opportunity arose. His accurate passing also gave the team the important variation in play, as they managed their stamina with controlled possessions and stretched opponent defences with his occasional long, first time passes.

James was used sporadically as a result and he did not take it well. He whinged about it whenever he had the opportunity and became more and more aggressive during training. Nick had a word with him following some poorly timed tackles but the effect was yet to be seen.

The under 16 team won all their six games in the same period by some considerable margin. Layne was on fire as he provided an astonishing nine assists and scored two goals in those. Richard was at some of the matches and witnessed first-hand the awesome performances. The two housemates continued to spend plenty of time together in the evenings, either gaming, jogging, reading manga or watching anime. Layne led Richard into a few highly popular titles and the two could easily discuss them all night long.

One day, Richard went home alone after college. There was no training that day and Layne was staying late for some track and field event. Just as he went into his bedroom for some rest, he received a text on his phone.

It was from Sarah, a girl that he went to history classes with. He rarely talked to his classmates as he was seen as too studious for them but Sarah always had time for him. She was intelligent, knowledgeable and she was capable of giving Richard ideas on the subject that he hadn't thought of. But the quality that Richard liked most was her confidence – she knew what she wanted and she could explain it very well. They exchanged numbers as they paired up for the forthcoming project.

"I've seen that you've injured your head again. I hope it is not serious," she said in her text message.

"It was just a cut, nothing like last time."

"Did it hurt?"

"Not really, I'm used to it."

"That's a relief. You need to look after that brain of yours. It's too good to be wasted for kicking a bag of air."

"Don't be silly – you're better than me."

"Maybe only in history... Do you want a catch up on the project today?"

"I can do I suppose. How do you want to do it? Online?"

"I fancy a face to face discussion, how about the chain coffee shop near Surbiton station?"

"Sure, I'll be there in half an hour."

On top of getting a great plan for the project, Richard had a good time with Sarah at the cafe. He got to know her a lot more and he found her various philosophies and concepts very interesting. There was not a dull moment, even though other people would consider what they talked about as dull. They agreed to meet up more regularly to work on the project.

After a few meetings at the cafe, Sarah asked if Richard would join her for a walk in the nearby parks. Richard agreed, and they spent a lovely spring afternoon in the Royal Botanic Gardens in Kew. They walked up to the treetop, stood still to feel the hive, went inside the tropical glass house and up the pagoda. They continued their never-ending intellectual topics, be it in science, history, politics or whatever random concepts they could think of.

In short, Richard liked her company. She seemed to have unlimited topics to talk about and all Richard needed to do was to think of a response in an equally intelligent manner, something he loved doing.

Being his housemate, Layne noticed how much time Richard had been spending on his phone and he asked Richard about it one night.

96

"Who is this person that you've been texting every night? Is it Tom?"

"No, it's a girl from school."

"Oh how exciting! Are you two dating?"

"Not quite…"

"You must like her if you can spend this much time chatting with her?"

"She's alright I suppose. What do you think?"

"It… doesn't matter what I think, right? You're already a sixth former… it's only natural to get yourself a girlfriend!"

"You may be right… let's see how it develops."

From how easy and supportive Layne was in that conversation, Richard was more convinced that he only saw him as a brother. He became more willing to try if he could live an ordinary life by being with Sarah. He didn't want to repeat the painful experience of being brutally rejected and the risk of being exposed in the football world.

One evening, Sarah invited Richard to a West End theatre together. At the end of the night, she gave Richard a kiss, and they officially started dating.

Richard found he liked her, she was easy company and he didn't have any other options. He'd started now, so he was going to make the most of it. Even if he thought it might not be the best thing to do, his resolve settled as he walked home.

It was Charlie's eighteenth birthday a couple of weeks later. He was offered a new three-year contract by the club (well, by his father) and to celebrate, he invited Richard and the others to a house party at his friend's. Richard showed up with Sarah for the first time and they arrived at around five. Plenty of his teammates were already there, together with Charlie, his girlfriend Claire and some other friends of his. Tom said he would come around after work. Layne and the younger players were not invited as they were just too young. Similar to Richard, a number of players were not quite eighteen but the host didn't really care when he served them alcoholic drinks.

"So you must be Sarah, the lady who conquered 'The Unbeatable'? We thought he would just be another machine like that one over here," Thomas welcomed the pair with a cheeky smile while pointing at Danny, who was having some water at the other side of the room.

"Nice to meet you. I'm Sarah. He never told me about his moniker. You can tell me more about him."

The pair joined in with the rest and had some drinks. Paul, whose own eighteenth birthday pre-dated Charlie's by only a few days, brought out a round of shots to celebrate. Richard sensed the reluctance on Sarah's face and downed both of them.

"Good man, Richard!" Charlie was impressed. "You can't be a light weight all the time."

However, courage and ability were two different things. Richard's head started feeling dizzy and after a few minutes fighting it, he gave up and passed out on the sofa.

"Oh dear are you okay Richard?" Sarah asked.

"Don't worry he's always like that," Danny, who also took one of the shots, said in his monotone. "He'll be fine after a while, just leave him there."

While he was down on the sofa, Richard heard some of the conversations alongside his rapid heartbeat but none of them registered on his mind. His brain kept bringing him back to what he did the last time he was that drunk – when he kissed Layne on his birthday. That shock on Layne's face, how his cheek turned pink within seconds, and his pleasant scent…

He was feeling fine again after about half an hour. Sarah was sitting not far away having a chat with Claire, she noticed Richard's recovery and gave him a wave.

"Have some water mate," Thomas walked over with a glass of ice water. "Don't try to be a hero next time."

"I'm fine, it's just a bit of fun," Richard squeezed out a smile for him. "It's good that Charlie got offered a new contract, isn't it? Who's the next in line to get one?"

"James and Kevin turn eighteen in the next few weeks and then it'll be Tom in August, I'll sure he'll be fine. He'll be playing in the Prem one day. He's that good."

"That's true. What time are we going to have some food?" Richard started to feel hungry.

"Soon, I suppose," Thomas had a look at his watch. "Where's Charlie anyway?"

Just when the two of them looked around to find him, they heard a woman's scream – it was from Claire. Richard turned over to where she was looking at, and he saw Charlie having a kiss with another girl, one of his other friends that he couldn't remember the name for.

"What... are you doing?" Claire was shaking when she asked.

Charlie noticed what he had done, but was just standing there, probably didn't know what to do.

"I'm going home!" Claire must have felt extremely embarrassed.

"I'll keep her company," said Sarah as she chased after Claire. "I'll call you later."

On the other side, Paul escorted Charlie away.

So suddenly the party had lost its hosts and Richard had lost his partner.

"What should we do now?" he said.

"Err... Have a curry down town?" Ollie still had time for a joke.

Everyone looked at him with an accusatory stare, but he defended, "The party is literally over and we are hungry, right? What else would we do?"

He was actually right. The idea was supported by most so they ended up going to a local Indian restaurant. Tom and his girlfriend Mihara got the call and were already there.

"What time do you call this? Where the hell is Figo?" he had lots of questions after his team asked him to switch venue and then turned up half an hour late.

"Long story, Nelson," said Thomas. "Let's get our table first."

Tom was shocked but not exactly surprised by what happened at the house party, if anyone was going to do something stupid like that, it would have to be Charlie. He just felt for Claire. He was also disappointed that he didn't get to meet Sarah.

The team had a nice dinner anyway. Sarah texted Richard during it to say Claire had calmed down and she had gone home. When he got back to the Stevenson's, he was keen to tell Layne about what happened but he seemed to be asleep already.

His thoughts wandered to Charlie as he began to doze off, how was he going to resolve this?

7.

Pain

One day after training, Richard asked David if he would consider calling Layne up to the under 18's to improve the attacking threat on the left. Having turned fifteen the day before the end of August, he was eligible to play for the under 18's and Richard believed he could combine well with Charlie. His overlap could create room for the powerful winger to attack the goal from wide, and he also thought his crossing ability would be useful for the strikers. David understood Richard's points but he hesitated previously due to Layne's lack of positional sense. Richard reassured him that he had been training Layne in private and he could cover the space he left behind together with Thomas. David agreed to give it a go.

David asked Layne to join the next training section and announced it to the team. James wasn't impressed.

"Are we a nursery these days?" he asked.

"If they are good enough, they are old enough," David said. "Danny and Harry joined us when they were sixteen, Layne may look young but he is only a few months younger. I don't see a problem. We need more options at full back positions as they are the single most effective weapon to unlock low blocks by other teams."

"You only listen to your darling Richard these days anyway!" James revealed where his true hump was.

"How dare you suggest that?" David put up a serious face. "I made decisions with what I see and what I know, and it is entirely my call. Yes you guys are welcomed to come up with tactics on the pitch according to the situations, and Richard is pretty good with that, but it is always my call on who plays and who doesn't. Do you understand that, Mr Barton?"

"Of course you'd say that," James said before he murmured the rest, "coz he's the one you slept with all the time…"

James was referring to the times when David took Richard (and sometimes Tom and others) home to study live football games.

"This is way out of order! Go away now and come to my office tomorrow!"

David was always calm and polite and that was the angriest that Richard had seen. That exchange made him feel uneasy. He had a glance at Layne and there he was looking at him, wondering. Richard quickly shook his head and waved his hands to suggest what James said wasn't true, and the young one giggled – he probably found Richard's panic funny.

So what Tom said about James was true – he didn't take losing his position to Richard well. But he could only be the best he could be in training and leave the rest to the coaching team.

Training started after that and David took aside Richard, Charlie, Danny, Tom, Thomas and Layne to explain his vision on how this group could work together, while the other players followed Nick for the standard training.

"It's all about movements and timings," David explained. "We need to pick the right moment to execute these moves to maximise our impact and minimise the risks."

"Before we go there David, are you sure you don't want to clarify to the team about our visits to yours?" Richard was keen to clear his name.

"What do I need to explain?" David said with a smile.

"Oh Rich, remember rule number one on Champions League nights: no one talks about Champions League nights…" Tom tried to add more fuel to the fire.

"Yeah Rich, we get you," Danny chipped in with a wink.

"I'm too young to hear all these!" Layne pretended to cover his ears.

"Alright that's enough on poor Richard," David finally closed the topic. "Just for clarity for those who don't know, I invited players home every now and then to watch the big European games together for their tactical knowledge. We may have some pizzas but nothing more. I'll remind the rest of the team later. Now let's discuss our new move."

His plan was for the team to start with finding Charlie in the left wing position. He would hold the ball up using his strengths and skills when Layne ran up at speed on the outside. His pace should be able to either pull away Charlie's marker or be able to run free into space for a cross. At the same time Danny would run into the area to either pick up that cross or play some quick exchanges with Charlie to create a shooting chance for either of them. Tom would be slightly behind them to offer an escape route. The other attackers would operate in their normal positions.

When all these were going on, Richard and Thomas would have to be vigilant for the space Layne left behind. Richard to marshal the midfield while Thomas moved a little bit more towards the left in defence. David specifically mentioned to Richard that if he had to, he should commit a professional foul to stop the other side from counter attacking.

"So we are overloading the left," Richard had a question. "How often would we do it?"

"Good question. I want this to be one of our main routes to attack in the future, but until you're fully trained on it, we should only use it once or twice in a match."

The group spent the first half of the evening mastering the timing of the move before David expanded it to the wider group so everyone knew what the plan was. He did end the session clarifying the "Champions League nights", to Richard's relief.

The team kept practicing their new tactic for the rest of that week in the hope of being ready for the away game on Sunday. The attackers seemed to have familiarised their movements to create the overload so David decided to push them to the test in a mini game against his best defenders.

Richard was in the defending team and his role was to cover Layne's movement as a right midfielder. He experienced first-hand the youngster's scintillating pace: he adjusted his positioning to compensate for the difference but he still only succeeded in stopping around half of the attacks. One slight lapse of concentration would grant his young housemate the licence to run away, and once he was off it was near impossible to catch.

David was satisfied with the trial – the crossing and finishing could do with some refinements, but the movement and understanding were there, and if his strongest defence needed a good few attacks to figure out how to counter a move that they knew in advance, other teams would have conceded at least once by then.

"You're very difficult to defend against," Richard said as he walked home with Layne. "Once you start running it's so hard to keep pace."

"Really? We only managed three goals from my side, out of however many attempts though!"

"The key was that you created the space – once you master your crossing you'll be unstoppable. You've already pushed me to the limit, I'm not sure if I can carry on like that for ninety minutes."

"How did you block so many of my crosses?"

"It's to do with the trajectory. I can see where your balls are going by looking at your technique."

"Now I understand why Rob keeps saying you're very annoying! How can I get past you?"

"You can change the way you hit the ball. Instead of the standard way, add some swerve into it. It'll change the ball to a higher angle while hitting the same target."

"Like how you and Danny take corner kicks?"

"Yes, just like that. The extra height will probably take the first defender out too."

"Wow, let me try that tomorrow!"

104

Soon it was Sunday and the team made their coach journey to Yorkshire, where they faced one of the top teams in the northern section of the Professional Development League.

Layne was part of the squad but David decided to name him on the bench and start the game with Kevin. He thought it would be better to ease Layne into this level slowly.

The rest of the team was the same as usual, apart from Danny who fell ill and had to stay home – shame he wasn't a real robot. Harry started in his place.

The first half ended goalless. The young Black Dragons lacked creativity in the final third as they only managed to create two half chances during the forty five minutes, one from Charlie's solo effort and the other from Richard's dipping corner. The other team managed Rob's pace well and limited the options of Richard and Tom to just sideway passes.

David sent Layne out to warm up during half time but chose to continue with Kevin in the second half after he had a lengthy chat with him. He then called Richard, Tom, Charlie and Harry over.

"Let's try the move with Kevin in left back," David told the players. "He's confident with it."

"Sure. Kevin and Harry, just look at my signal," Tom said as he demonstrated it.

Richard thought the move wouldn't work with Kevin – while he appreciated many attributes of him, he just didn't have the necessary pace to open up that space. But he would rather not say it out loud to alienate another regular starter. He had nothing against Kevin and aimed to make the most of it for the team.

The second half started. It took the team nearly ten minutes to find an opening to pass the ball to Charlie on the left. Just as he controlled the ball, Tom gave the signal. Kevin started sprinting forward at full speed from his position on the halfway line and the other players shifting to the left to create the overload.

But the space did not appear as planned. The right midfielder tracked Kevin well and blocked that path off. By that point Charlie was struggling with pressure from two players and his desperate pass to Harry was intercepted by the centre back, who saw the gap behind Tom and passed it over him to their attacking midfielder. It became four against four in a counter attack.

Fortunately, the attacking midfielder with the ball chose to take on Richard, who managed to poke the ball away. But unfortunately, the loose ball fell to the supporting left back. He sent the ball long to the right sided forward, who lost Thomas and went through on goal. He finished the attack by lifting the ball over Jack into the empty net. 1-0.

"It was worth the try," David said to Nick. "That proved the point on why we need more pace down that end to make it work."

"Layne, you're going on," he then turned to the youngster. "Are you nervous?"

"Nerves are for the unprepared," Layne replied with a familiar phrase, be it in a much more innocent tone.

"Good. Go and show them!" David said after a few chuckles.

Layne and Peter came on for Kevin and Paul with roughly half an hour to go. Tom asked the team to keep it easy and settle down for five minutes first. Richard played a few easy balls to Layne to make sure he got a few good touches under his belt. The fifteen-year-old was making his debut at this level after all.

With about ten minutes to go, Tom gave the signal to initiate the move again. Richard chipped the ball forward to Charlie while Layne set off at full speed down the outside. Being late in the game, the opposing right midfielder simply couldn't keep up with his superior raw pace. The two on one against the right back was set, and he chose to stay tight on Charlie, whom he considered to be the main threat. Charlie laid the ball back to Tom and he swiftly sent it down the left for Layne.

The left back crossed it towards the near post, where the giant Peter was. He did it the way Richard suggested and it bypassed the centre back and found his target. Peter flicked it towards the edge of the goal area, and Harry was there to tap it home for 1-1.

The move worked. Harry was over the moon to have scored his first goal for the under 18's and he raced across to celebrate with Layne and the rest.

The other team, being near the top of their respective table, had to push again for their three points. That fell perfectly into the game plan for the Black Dragons. Ollie won the ball at the edge of the area and he passed it forward to Tom, who played a quick exchange with Richard before giving the signal for another move.

Charlie held the ball up as planned, as Layne galloped down the line. The right midfielder had been substituted and his replacement was trying hard to track back. After a feint to pass to Layne down the line, Charlie sent the ball through to Finley in the far side and he was one on one with the goalkeeper. He evaded him by taking the ball wide and he took a shot at the empty goal.

But the ball hit the outside of the post and went out!

Finley couldn't believe it. Neither could any of his teammates. But it was what it was, and the game soon reached full time.

"That was a good half of football," David said in the dressing room. "It's a shame we couldn't finish it off but you've done a great job out there. I'm proud of you all."

Richard was gutted at not winning the game, but he wouldn't blame Finley for not finishing the chance, it was such a fine line and he did his best. He was happy that Layne made the difference to the attacking play. He was also a little worried about how Kevin would react to being replaced in this fashion but as that was out of his control, he wouldn't think too much about it.

"Congratulations for making your debut! You brought us a new dimension with your pace and movement," Richard sat next to Layne back in the changing room. "That cross was exquisite!"

"Thanks for suggesting it to David in the first place," Layne said as he took his top off and wrapped himself in a towel before he fully undressed. "Are you coming for a shower?"

"You go ahead. I'll finish my drink and be there later."

Richard didn't fancy it – it was one of those communal showers and he would rather not get in with the others, especially his young housemate, however much he wanted to. He didn't want to embarrass himself in front of everyone.

The next game was at home against a mid-table team. After another week of training with the new move, David decided to start with Layne at left back. Kevin was visually not happy but David seemed to have made up his mind – even though he acknowledged that the youngster still had a lot to learn on his defending, he believed his potential contribution to the attacking side would outweigh that as the rest of the team was solid in defence. He also wanted to see if Layne could sustain this level for a full game.

Danny was back after his illness and he massively improved the fluidity of the team with his touch and movement. Tom was getting better with the timing of his signals and the team were more natural with carrying out the move. It became a serious threat to the opposing team.

David's worry about Layne's stamina was right, he couldn't keep bombing up and down the touch line for the full ninety minutes and his influence waned after the hour mark. David replaced him with Kevin but the team were already 2-0 up by that point, with both goals coming from the young left back's crosses.

No further goals were scored and the game ended comfortably.

"You guys are getting better with this, soon you won't need signals from Tom – it'll become one of the regular attacks," David told the team in the dressing room.

"To do that we need the defence to be disciplined," Nick added as he looked at Richard, "especially in your position, Richard."

Richard and Layne went to central London on Saturday afternoon after Layne tore his boots during training that morning. The team had an FA Youth Cup quarter final the next day so he desperately needed a new pair.

"Do you have any ideas what you're going for?" Richard asked during their journey on the train. "Are you going to change to a different brand?"

"I'd love to have another pair of my red ones with dragon scales, but they've stopped producing them already. I guess I'll just have to get whatever their new speed line model is."

"So there's no point going to the big multistorey shop on Oxford Street then," Richard was planning ahead. "We can go straight to Carnaby Street."

"We can still visit that big one," Layne seemed to know what Richard really wanted. "They've released the new generation of yours in black and gold again. You'll like them!"

"Have they? That'll be great if you don't mind," Richard was delighted. "Then we can go to that burger place we talked about for dinner."

"Sounds good, I want to try their milkshakes after seeing pictures of them online," Layne had slowly been influenced by Richard on his choice of food.

The pair visited all the football stores in Soho and Layne bought his new red boots. Richard loved the new editions but decided not to fork out for a new pair while his current ones were still going strong. They then stopped at a cafe for drinks. Just after they picked up their coffees and sat down, a familiar face showed up in front of them.

"Hey, what's the chance of meeting you here?" It was Sarah.

"Hey," Richard stood up and gave her a hug and kiss. "I thought you're off to the West End?"

"My friend had to leave early," she sat down next to Richard before turning to Layne. "You must be his young housemate Layne? I've seen you in school before. He talks about you a lot. Nice to meet you."

"Hi, nice to meet you," Layne replied.

"We were shopping around for a new pair of boots for him," said Richard.

Sarah had a glance at the bag containing the new boots next to Layne and asked, "Does it mean you're done with your shopping? Do you fancy seeing Les Mis with me? My friend has left me a spare ticket."

Richard was caught in two minds right there. It was one of the musicals that he really wanted to see and in theory he should go with his girlfriend, but he felt bad to leave Layne on his own after saying he'd have dinner with him.

"What do you think, Richie? I don't really mind," Layne noticed he was in thinking mode and asked.

"Are you sure?" Richard sensed his disappointment and part of him didn't want him to say yes.

"Yeah I'm a little tired so I'd better head back," Layne sounded determined.

"That's fine then. Take care on your way back, stick to the same route and text me when you arrive, okay?" asked Richard before he switched to Sarah. "Shall we go then? It's starting soon right?"

The pair said their goodbye and left for the theatre.

Richard turned round to have a look at the youngster from outside the cafe as he knew he was sitting by the window.

The boy was crying.

His head was buried between his arms but it was clear to Richard that he was sobbing badly.

All of a sudden Richard felt his heart was broken. There was this piercing pain in his chest that he hadn't experienced for a few years.

Part of him wanted to forget everything, run inside and hold Layne in his arms, but the other part thought it would be inappropriate – he chose to be with Sarah and he had to be responsible.

"Are you alright?" Sarah asked. "Let's go, we're up against it if you want something to eat beforehand."

Richard turned back with a very heavy heart and went with Sarah, leaving the distraught youngster behind. He couldn't really concentrate during the musical – his head was full of what-ifs and it was a real mess.

The pair returned to Surbiton after the theatre and Richard walked Sarah home as he always did.

"My parents and sister are away tonight, do you want to come in?" Sarah asked.

"Err... yes?" Richard was feeling nervous as he recognised what the situation meant potentially.

Sarah lived in a nice three-storey townhouse opposite a park. She led Richard into her room on the second floor and started kissing him as he came through the door.

The action escalated quickly and the pair were half naked when Sarah wanted to visit the Jack-and-Jill bathroom she shared with her younger sister.

Richard lay on Sarah's bed and thoughts were going through his head.

Is this something I should go ahead with? It feels natural and it'll be good to have the experience, but is this really what I want? I would have to be fair and responsible to Sarah and stay with her for the foreseeable future.

Deep down, the event that afternoon troubled him. He didn't know what he should do. He was comfortable with Sarah but he was beginning to find out what his true desire was – and if there was a chance that the feeling was mutual he couldn't afford to let it pass by.

"What are you doing, Mr Deep Thinker?" Sarah was back and she started touching and kissing Richard again.

They continued and when Sarah tried to take Richard's pants off he suddenly backtracked and said, "Sorry Sarah I'm not quite ready for this."

"What makes you think that? I have some condoms if that's what you're worrying about?"

"No it's not just that."

"Your body is clearly ready..."

"It's something in my head, I'm so sorry."

"That's okay. You have your reasons and I'll respect you for that."

111

He quickly put all his clothes back on and left the house after a goodbye kiss.

I'm in such a mess. She must be mad at me now. But it won't be fair to her if I went through it just for the experience, would it? I can't be so selfish.

I just can't stop thinking about… him, what should I do? He was keen to find out what happened to Layne after the cafe but he seemed to be resting already, so he had to leave it and went to bed instead – not that he would be able to fall asleep with his head full of thoughts, but he did have a cup game the next morning.

The Black Dragons won their FA Youth Cup quarter final 3-1 the next day. Layne was on fire and was involved in all three goals, scoring a sensational solo effort between setting up two with his crosses. The other team scored a consolation goal near the end of the game after a few players had been withdrawn.

Richard didn't manage to speak with Layne. He left early to the ground and he didn't make any eye contact during the game. He didn't even celebrate his first goal for the team. Richard tried to talk to him after the match but he only got some short answers back. He didn't know what to do.

Two weeks had passed and it was time for the FA Youth Cup semi-final. The team were away at the top west London club from the Premier League. It was held at their secondary stadium filled with over two thousand spectators, which was the biggest crowd for a lot of the young Black Dragons. With plenty of families in the stands, the atmosphere was quite festive, instead of any hostility that the players might expect. The weather had been poor for a few days but the pitch seemed to be holding up fine.

David decided to stick to their own game and played his strongest eleven with Jack, Ollie, Layne, Thomas, Steve, Richard, Tom, Danny, Rob, Charlie and Paul. The hosts had a team of multi-national youngsters that included Adam Jenkinson, the former Thames Ditton player, who welcomed his former teammates and coaches ahead of kick off.

Richard didn't have a lot of interactions with Layne in the two weeks apart from the odd hello and goodbye. He hadn't been seeing Sarah either, he told her he needed to focus on his studies and training but in truth he just wanted to have some time alone. He still hadn't figured out what he really wanted and what to do if he did.

The game against the Blues started with the Black Dragons on the front foot. Layne continued to play aggressively and he quickly established a lead for the team with another brilliant solo effort. Other teams were finding his pace and direct running from deep difficult to defend against. It was supported by good movements of the other players as well.

Soon one became two. Layne was running into space on the left again but Danny used him a decoy and curled the ball into the far corner instead.

The first half ended 2-0 to the dominant visitors. They defended really well, with Steve being the stand-out player, as he impressively won all his aerial duels and tackles.

The second half started in pretty much the same fashion until the seventh minute. A long ball was sent to the Black Dragons' box and was punched clear by the commanding Jack. The ball fell to Tom outside the area and he tried to cushion the ball down for Steve to collect. But the ball was a bit off and as Steve stretched to control it, he left foot slipped and he landed heavily on his left knee. He groaned instantly and looked to be in real pain. Thomas was nearest to him and all he did was screaming "medics" repeatedly towards the bench, in an obvious panic. Richard ran across and saw something he never thought he would – Steve's knee cap seemed to have popped out of the flesh at a strange angle. He was horrified.

Gary the physio ran over with David and Nick to check on Steve and decided to call for an ambulance straight away. There was nothing they could do. Steve was in such an agony that his teammates were all stunned. Nobody knew what to do or say, they were just frozen, standing there with no other feelings.

It took the paramedics a good twenty minutes to transfer Steve into the ambulance. The teams had to warm themselves up again for the remaining thirty-eight minutes of the game.

Richard didn't know about the others but his brain was empty, he couldn't think of anything other than Steve's knee cap, and he couldn't hear anything but Steve's screams in anguish.

The match resumed but the Thames Ditton players were nowhere near in the game. They couldn't pass the ball to each other; they weren't running and there was no shape in them. Their minds were miles away.

The other team weren't having any joy over Steve's misfortune but they were focused enough to play. They soon scored two goals to level the game up and there were still another twenty minutes to go. Tom tried to get the team together but when he saw the faces of his teammates, he knew the game was gone. However good these players were, they were just teenagers and they couldn't deal with what they had experienced.

David had to replace Richard and Thomas, who seemed to be suffering the most. But the team couldn't pick themselves up and conceded two more goals to lose the semi-final 4-2.

The manner they lost the game was unprofessional, but David didn't blame his young players. He probably felt as bad as them. The dressing room was dreadfully quiet.

Richard was distressed. The logical mind of him had already worked out what would happen to Steve – he would never play again – and he thought about how fragile they footballers could be and how things could all change in a second. Layne sat next to him and asked if he was okay. He nodded but when he looked up to him, he crashed into his shoulders and started crying.

And he was not alone.

Lots of the boys were crying. Some were weeping quietly, some were doing so forcefully, and some were repeatedly asking the question "why?".

David had to do something to settle the team. He moved to the centre of the dressing room and said, "Boys, I know you feel bad about Steve, we do too. But these things happen in football and you have to be strong, for yourselves and for him. He doesn't want us to be crybabies. We don't know how bad the injury is yet, stay strong and support each other. Okay?"

The boys calmed down eventually and picked themselves up for their showers. On the coach back, Thomas was sitting next to Richard as usual.

"Don't worry too much. It's out of our control," he said.

"I know, but I'm fearing the worst," Richard was back from being emotional. "How fragile is the whole thing? One second he was playing the game of his life, and the next he could be gone forever."

"Yeah, that's life, sometimes," Thomas really felt for his partner in defence. "That's why we need to live to the max and leave no regrets."

Live to the max and leave no regrets, Thomas's words went deep into Richard's thoughts. They hit him hard. He was stunned.

The coach completed the short journey back to the training ground, where the team were dismissed. Richard and Layne walked back to the Stevenson's together.

They talked briefly about Steve's injury and the conversation ended. There was something in Richard's chest that he had to say, following what Thomas said in the coach.

"Have you been avoiding me lately?" he asked.

"No, I'm just trying to give myself some space. I do have exams coming up," Layne replied calmly.

"But we were closer than this before?"

"We have always been housemates."

"No, we were closer."

"Like what?"

"We... we were more like... brothers?"

115

"Brothers?" Layne paused, took a deep breath and said, without turning round. "I can be the best little brother in this world for you if... if... that's what you want?"

If that's what you want?

Layne's question echoed repeatedly in Richard's head. He didn't know what to say. He couldn't decide. It wasn't a contest between Layne and Sarah. It was the dream of being a footballer – for both of them. He didn't want to ruin it because of his selfish desire. He didn't want either of them to regret in the future, especially when Layne was only young – he may not know what he really wanted.

The boys didn't say anything else and they went back to their separate rooms, quietly, maybe painfully.

8.

Summer

Richard's first season with the Black Dragons finished with the team seventh in the U18 Professional Development League 2, as they lost all of their five remaining matches of the season. The players were scarred mentally from their painful exit from the FA Youth Cup and couldn't gather themselves. The spark from Layne's introduction waned as the team's movement slowed down and even Richard had a dip in form – the defending was still watertight, but his vision and range of passing had been poor. The team needed a break and maybe a reset.

After the last game of the season for both the development teams, David and Ron, his counterpart in the under 21's, called for a team meeting at the training ground on a Tuesday evening as they announced the next steps for the youngsters. It was normally the time for the club to decide which players would progress to the next level, and which ones would sadly be released. The process was known by the players as "the cull", but this year's edition brought more surprises.

David informed the team that the FA had changed the age limit of the current under 21 league to twenty-three for the next season and as a result, the club had decided to abolish the reserve team and merge that with the new under 23's. At the same time, they wanted all under 23 players to sign professional contracts to prevent losing them to rival academies on the cheap. Training would become full-time to bring their standard closer to the first team.

A number of Richard's teammates grasped in shock – he wasn't too nervous as he was young enough to play for the under 18's next season but there were players on the cliff edge that meant this was make or break for them.

"With the focus on the first team and the forthcoming project on expanding our stadium further, we need to consider our budget carefully and we absolutely have to pick the right players for the new under 23 team. These players will be expected to step up to the first team when necessary and that implies a much higher standard – physically, technically and mentally, from the current academy teams.

"Inevitably, not every academy player will make the transition but we will discuss that in our one to one sessions. Is that clear?" said David as he closed off the announcement.

Having listened carefully, Richard understood why the club decided to take on this restructure but he feared for his friends. What would happen to them? What would happen to Layne who was just fifteen? Will they just continue in the under 18s?

David and Ron separated the two groups of players and handed out a timetable for the players' individual meetings. It was in alphabetical order so Richard would be in the middle, with Layne right after him.

They hadn't spoken to each other much in the weeks since their chat after Steve's injury, but with the uncertainties surrounding them they opened up a little as they walked around the training complex while waiting for their appointments.

"How are you feeling?" Layne asked.

"I think we'll be okay as we are still young. I fear for Tom and the others who are on the edge."

"What would you do if you are released?"

"It's not going to happen as my scholarship contract runs for another season, but I suppose I'll carry on studying and go to university. You?"

"I haven't thought about it yet, maybe I'll go back to Bath…"

Richard noticed the sadness on Layne's face. He shared the same feelings as that meant their time together at the Stevenson's would come to an end.

Will they stay connected?

Will they still be friends?

Will the feeling... go?

He didn't know what to say. He stared at his young housemate and remained speechless, biting his lips instead. Layne must have realised what went through his mind and emotions got the better of him – tears began to fall from his innocent eyes.

Richard felt this pain in his chest again and he naturally put his hands on Layne's shoulders to comfort him. The youngster crashed into him and had a proper breakdown.

"It's going to be okay. We're not really part of the selection process this time."

"I know... but I can't help thinking about what would happen when that time comes..."

Richard didn't respond. He just held Layne tight to him, with his eyes shut to stay at the moment. He didn't know what the future holds but he only wanted to take care of the boy in his arms right there.

He didn't know how long had passed when Layne eventually recovered. He wiped his tears and thanked Richard.

"Like you said, we'll be fine for at least another year. Let's not think too far ahead!" he said with a fake smile.

Richard was glad that Layne settled down but the thought of being separated from him lingered in his head. He really didn't want it to happen.

The two met James and Kevin on their way back to the office.

"Get out of my way!" James shouted.

"What's the matter with you?" Layne asked.

"None of your fucking business, kid!"

"I guess someone's not happy after meeting David?"

"I'm leaving this hell hole anyway! You can keep licking his muddy boots!"

"That's sad. How about you, Kev?" Richard asked.

"Don't pretend you bloody care. I bet you can't wait to see the back of your rivals!" James jumped in.

By the looks on Kevin's face, Richard was convinced that he shared the same fate as his friend. He wished him luck and pulled Layne away from the scene. James was still mumbling about something but he was only thinking about one thing.

The cull was really happening. Plenty of dreams were to be quashed. Today.

The pair were waiting outside David's room for their appointments when Peter the giant came out, looking relieved.

"It's your turn, Rich. I'm sure you'll be fine."

Richard knocked on the door and went in.

"Hi David," Richard said nervously. He really couldn't prepare for this.

"Hey Rich, come in and make yourself comfortable," said David with his usual gentle smile.

Once Richard had settled down, David asked him a question.

"Do you understand the concept of the new under 23 team?"

"Yes and no, can you elaborate a bit more please?"

"Sure. The main reason for the change is to raise the level of the team, who will become the reserve to the senior team from now on. We want to sign up the right players and develop them all the way through, from about sixteen to twenty-three years old, with the hope of turning them into first team players."

"Okay I get that. It makes sense," Richard nodded, "but I suppose I'm just staying with the under 18's anyway?"

"Well, no Richard," David smiled, "we are going to take you and a number of younger players into the under 23 team too. We think you are good enough and we want you to continue your development alongside your current teammates such as Tom and Charlie."

"Does that mean that..." Richard caught the last sentence.

"Yes," said David as he put some documents on his desk, "we would like to offer you a three-year professional contract, Mr Lucas. You don't have to sign it right away, take it home and have a good read. I'm looking forward to a positive response though, you are one of my key players."

"That's great, but how will I continue my A-Levels when training becomes full time?"

"We would arrange for you and others who want to continue education to have a combination of school lessons and private tuitions, but that is of course up to you and your parents."

"Sounds like a workable solution, thank you!" Richard was relieved, delighted, excited, everything in one go. "What would happen to Layne... and the other youngsters?"

"I can't tell you about anyone else before they know, but generally they will continue with their schoolboy contracts before they turn seventeen, and we risk losing them to category A academies cheaply as before, like how we lost Adam."

Richard opened the door and Layne and Tom were having a chat. Tom's meeting was after Layne's.

"How did it go?" Layne asked.

"They're offering me a professional contract!" said Richard with a big grin on his face.

"That's good buddy. I'm sure I'll join you too," said Tom as he and Richard shook hands.

Tom and Richard had a chat as Layne went in with David. His meeting was much shorter and he was out in just about five minutes.

"Hey Richie I'm moving to the under 23 team too!" the delighted youngster threw himself into Richard for a hug.

"That's wonderful!" Richard held onto Layne passionately. Even though it was expected, he was genuinely relieved that their time together would last a little longer.

"Ahem," Tom pretended to clear his throat, "I'll leave you two lovebirds here. See you later."

121

Richard and Layne looked at each other, smiled embarrassingly and slowly pulled apart.

"We should really celebrate this, shall we eat out tonight?" Richard asked.

"Sounds cool, how about...?"

They left the club house together, discussing their choice of food, chatting along as they were a few months ago.

Richard had a look at his first professional contract that night. He couldn't believe that he was a step closer to becoming a proper player in his favourite football management game. He used to edit himself and Layne into the game but they could soon become real. He signed it after a lengthy phone conversation with his parents, who sought assurance from him that he would be able to keep up with his studies.

Richard later found out that a good number of players in Tom's age group were going to the under 23 team, after promotions into the first team, transfer activities and releases of the current under 21 players, but there were no place for the likes of Liam, James and Kevin. Similar to Richard and Layne, Danny was also registered to the under 23 squad despite being eligible to play for the under 18's.

There was also the sad news that Steve the centre back would not be coming back to the team. His knee would recover well enough to not affect his daily life, but he would no longer be able to play competitively.

The new under 23 team would have between twenty-two to twenty-five players. Richard thought it would be an interesting challenge to be playing with the former under 21's such as Les, Lewis and their top scorer Owen. It would be an even bigger one to be ready for the first team, which sounded so far away less than a year ago, when he was merely playing for the village youth team.

Layne told Richard that he would stay on his current schoolboy contract with the club until he turned seventeen, by which time he might be offered a professional one. He could also in theory sign for other clubs for a nominal fee.

He told David he had no interest in that at the moment and would just happily develop with the club.

Richard got a list of the twenty-two players that made up the new under 23 team from Tom:

Goalkeeper:
Josh Taylor, Arben Gashi, Jack Simpson

Defender:
Lewis Adams, Thomas Bond, Les Hailey, Lee Baek-min, Francis Maphosa, Layne Moore, Thorsten Strømme, Ivan Terzic

Midfielder:
Richard Lucas, Tom Nelson, Max Roberts, Ashley Shaw, Danny Westwood

Attacker:
Rob Daniels, Owen Fairclough, Mitchell Farrows, Peter Knight, Paul Newman, Charlie Ranger

David said the club would be looking for some new players before the start of the season to complete the squad.

Richard and his friends gathered at the club's lounge the following Saturday to watch the first team's last game of the season, which was away to a team in Lancashire. They were in the relegation zone and desperately needed a win as well as hoping their rivals from South Yorkshire to drop points in their game at home against the team from Berkshire.

The club's first ever season in the Championship was a serious struggle, as players and coaches found their feet in one of the most competitive leagues in the world. The defence was relatively solid but the team didn't score enough goals, with last season's top scorer Kalifa finding the net only seven times before the last game of the season.

The first team played in the same 4-3-3 formation as the under 18's and Richard could see a lot of similarities in

123

the way they played. There was far less time available and the game was much more physical – Richard didn't think he was ready to take some of the challenges he saw.

With the home team in the safety of a mid-table position, the Black Dragons were able to score a couple of goals in the first half – one from Keith the big Irish centre back and the other from Luciano, the team's main wide attacker from Argentina. The bad news was that the team from South Yorkshire were also leading by a goal to nil at half time.

The visitors added a third goal at around the hour mark from Kalifa's penalty and looked secured for their victory. However, the team from South Yorkshire were hanging onto their one goal lead.

"I guess we will move back to League One then," Charlie said with a sigh when the matches reached the ninetieth minute.

"It hasn't finished yet! And even if we go down, we'll bounce back up in no time!" said the other local boy Tom.

"Look! Luciano has scored the fourth goal!" Layne shouted.

While Richard and the others turned their attention to the screen showing the Black Dragons' goal, Tom screamed wildly while watching the other one.

"Berkshire has equalised!"

They had indeed. South Yorkshire's goalkeeper fumbled a cross and gifted the striker a free goal at the ninety-third minute!

The referees soon blew their final whistles. The youngsters and the staff were absolutely over the moon – the team had survived at the very last moment of the season, against all odds!

Charlie and Tom started jumping up and down and chanted, "We are staying up say we are staying up! We are staying up say we are staying up!"

The rest of the team followed and they celebrated as if the team had won a trophy – for a small club like theirs, being able to survive at this level certainly felt like winning!

The youngsters continued their celebrations outside a pub near the stadium where there were plenty of fans. Most of them supported the club from its amateur years and it was quite something for them to hold on to another season in the Championship. Richard could feel the passion they had for the club and was proud to be a part of it.

Even though the football season had ended, Richard and Layne were staying at the Stevenson's until the end of their school term to continue their studies. They were given some training routines by the club to work on during the holidays, which they could either do at the club's training centre or locations they preferred. Richard spent most of his evenings at the centre with Danny who, like him, had to stay for his school work.

Layne was due to take his GCSE exams and Richard had been helping him with his revisions. He gave the youngster his notes from the year before and also his tried-and-trusted schedule for study leave: a solid nine-to-five block of hard work every day followed by as much exercise and/or entertainment as he pleased outside, before an early night. He patiently answered any questions Layne had and made sure he wrote them down on his notes, as he found doing so physically increased the chance of them being memorised.

He had cut down the amount of time he spent with Sarah outside of classes. He claimed he was too busy with studies, training and recently his driving lessons. She seemed to understand but one day she sent Richard a message after school.

"Balaclava Park at five? I think we need to talk."

Richard turned up on time to find Sarah sitting on a bench. He went over and sat next to her.

He had a bad feeling about this.

"Hey," he said softly.

"Hey," she turned over, "how are things?"

They didn't greet each other with a hug or a kiss.

"Busy," Richard continued his story. "School, football and driving lessons."

"I get that," she acknowledged. "I just think it'll be good to talk things through before we go into the summer break."

"About?"

"Us, of course. Where do you think we're heading to?" Sarah asked that in such a peaceful tone, Richard would have expected someone in this situation to be far more emotional.

"I don't really know, I thought we're doing alright?"

"I don't know either," she sighed. "Don't you think we're a bit early to be as settled as an old couple?"

"What… do you mean?" Richard tried to play dump.

"I think there's a lack of, what should I say, passion? Or affection? We shouldn't be acting like this only a few months in."

Richard chose not to say anything and let her continue, as he didn't really know what to say.

"What happened the night after the theatre? Don't you want to do THAT with me? Every time I felt we were close you backed off."

"Err… I just didn't think we were ready, or I was ready…" Richard muttered.

"I just don't think your heart is here."

Richard guessed she already knew where it was going, given how intelligent she was.

"I think you need to listen to what your heart really wants, and not what your head thinks is the right thing to do."

She knew how Richard was feeling. That last sentence hit him right on the head.

"I think you know me better than I do," Richard gave in. "Thank you, and I'm sorry."

"Don't be sorry. It's good to be clear. We'll always be friends, right?" Sarah gave Richard a kiss on his cheek and walked away.

Richard remained on the bench to have a think about it all. He felt bad for the way his relationship with Sarah ended. He thought it could work but maybe she was right, he just didn't have the affection and it wouldn't be fair to her if he pretended. The other part of him was relieved, his heart really was somewhere else and his head was losing its ability to overrule it.

Four weeks flew by and Layne had completed all his exams. He felt confident and all he needed now was to wait for the results. Richard planned the evening of his last exam to be the grand finale of their first season in the football management game. They were playing in the Champions League final and seemed to be well on the way having scored two goals early in the second half. However, they conceded twice in quick succession and were hanging on by the skin of their teeth.

"We made it!" the two screamed as their team won after a tense penalty shootout, with the last spot kick scored by the rookie striker that Layne insisted on bringing on as a substitute.

"Great call to have him on!" Richard praised the decision.

Layne got up and grabbed Richard to celebrate their "achievement". The two were singing "We Are the Champions" until Layne tripped over some cables and fell over, dragging Richard down to the floor with him. The strangled pair laughed at each other until Layne stopped and looked away with a blushed cheek. Richard felt a very strong urge to move closer but his head kept thinking that it would be the wrong action.

His internal struggle continued.

"Sorry," he said awkwardly before standing up.

"It's... okay, Richie."

"Well, we'd better call it a night then. I have my driving test tomorrow."

"Have a good night," Layne responded with a rather disappointed smile. "Thanks for your help on the exams."

Richard couldn't sleep that night. That look of Layne remained in his mind and he couldn't, and didn't want to, shrug it off.

We can't stay like this forever. I should either tell Layne how I feel, or completely move away. But what if it means giving up football... or him?

He managed to pass his driving test with minimum fuss the next day despite his lack of energy, partly due to his strategy of having it mid-morning when the roads were clear. That won him a bet against Charlie, who only passed at his second attempt a couple of weeks earlier.

Both of them bought a car straight away: Richard picked up a used MINI Cooper in white with black roof and bonnet stripes from the local dealership using his savings while Charlie put a new black Audi A3 on finance, with a guarantee from his dad.

They also planned a week-long holiday in Bournemouth with their teammates. Richard was supposed to take Thomas, Ollie and Rob in his car while Charlie had Tom, Danny and Paul, but Thomas pulled out at the last minute and they needed to find a replacement quickly.

"Why don't you ask Layne?" Charlie suggested.

Richard wasn't sure that was the best thing to do. Part of him loved the idea, but he was also worried that he might lose control of himself and make the wrong move. After all, while he knew how he felt about Layne, he wasn't certain if it was mutual. However, having been declined by all other possible options for the trip, he ended up asking his housemate.

"Hey Layne, are you free to join us for a week in Bournemouth?"

"I'm going to Madeira with mum the week after, so I guess I can? Who else is going?"

"It's Charlie and the normal crew. We'll be sharing rooms."

"Oh! Only if I'm sharing with you? I don't know the others too well."

"Yes... I think we can do that."

The group were staying at in a hotel by the main beach. Charlie moaned about not going for more luxury hotels but the down-to-earth organisers Richard and Danny insisted on not blowing their budgets. He also challenged Richard to a race there but was kindly declined by Mr Safety First.

The journey was painless for Richard, with the only problem being the tussle between the pop rock playlist of Richard and Layne and the hip hop one from Rob and Ollie. It was slightly different in Charlie's car. He tried to show his mates his racing lines and was involved in a couple of near misses. Danny vowed he would never get into his car again and demanded a seat in the Lucas mobile for the return trip.

The group had a great first day relaxing on the seven-mile long beach. They enjoyed a seafood dinner and at the end of it they split up into two groups for further entertainment: Paul, Charlie, Rob and Ollie stayed in town for drinks, while Richard, Tom, Layne and Danny headed to a bowling alley nearby, as they were not legally allowed to join the other group anyway and didn't want to sneak into places using a fake ID like Ollie.

Layne used to go bowling back in Bath and he tempted Richard to play with him regularly at the centre in Tolworth. They bought their own bowling balls and shoes as Richard hated the greasy house ones. They were only amateurs averaging about 150 points in a game but they beat Tom and Danny easily on the night, even without their usual gear. It was fun watching Tom getting frustrated – he might have all the power in the world, but he couldn't channel it properly and his balls nearly always ended up in the gutter. Danny found his rhythm late on and was delighted to have hit a few strikes. Everyone had a good time and they returned to the hotel after three games.

Richard was sitting on his bed, flicking through the rather limited selection of TV channels available, while Layne came out of the shower, wearing only a pair of red boxer shorts.

"The room is so hot even with the air con on!" he said.

"I think it's already set to its lowest temperature, you may just have to be patient," Richard responded. He tried hard not to look at Layne but couldn't help having a few little peeps.

"I guess you must be feeling it as well, your face looks boiling!"

"Err... yeah it's pretty hot..."

"What's available on tele?" Layne asked as he sat down.

"It's just the news channel, I'm not really watching."

Layne took over the remote control and randomly switched to a movie channel, which happened to be showing a romantic scene.

"Oh that's interesting!" he said as he focused on the actions.

Richard watched along but felt rather uncomfortable after a while as his mind automatically replaced the characters with him and Layne.

"Maybe... we shouldn't watch it?"

"Don't be such a saint Richie, I bet you have plenty of experience already!"

"What... what makes you think that?"

"Have you not slept with Sarah?"

"Err..."

"Come on Richie! I thought there's no secret between us? I'm just curious."

"You're right, there isn't..."

"So?"

"No, I haven't."

"Really? You've been together for a good few months?"

"I don't think we were ready for it..."

"Were?" Layne picked up on the past tense.

"Yes... we split up a few weeks ago."

"Oh why?"

"I'm not... passionate enough for her, apparently."

"That's a shame. Are you feeling okay? It's your first ever break up?"

"I'm fine. It's not like I don't have other things to focus on."

"So... you are still a virgin then? Are you back on the hunt? What type of girls do you actually like?"

Layne's questions troubled Richard and he became rather agitated.

130

"Stop asking stupid questions!" he said with a slightly raised voice.

"I'm... sorry, Richie," Layne was clearly shocked, as it was probably the first time he saw Richard being anything but calm and friendly outside matches.

"... no I'm sorry. I was being rude," Richard realised and apologised.

An awkward silence followed.

Richard looked at Layne helplessly as he struggled internally. There were moments when he opened his mouth but his mind stuttered and nothing came out.

Layne seemed to feel the tension and he asked, "Do... do you have something to say, Richie?"

"Err... I... we... well, no, I guess... you must be tired after a long day, let's go to sleep, we're meeting the boys for breakfast tomorrow."

He then buried himself in the duvet, even though he was sweating like hell. He didn't know how he stopped short on confessing his feelings for Layne. He wanted to, but he was far too nervous to gather his words together.

The team visited the popular Durdle Door after breakfast the next morning. The view from the top of the cliff was breath-taking and the water was some of the clearest, but there was a little scare as Layne slipped on the way down to the pebble beach and crashed into Richard. They managed to stay on their feet but Richard's heart stopped when he felt the youngster's warmth on his back.

"Thanks for saving me, Richie."

"It's... okay... just be careful, alright?"

The group returned to the main beach for dinner at a large fish and chips restaurant.

"What shall we do tonight?" Tom asked after Richard consumed the last chip.

"The club we went last night was really good, fancy it?" Charlie suggested.

"How about the under-age lads?"

"I'm sure they'll find something kiddy to do. There's an old playground the other side of the pier?"

"Cut the crap out, Charles," Danny cut in. "Don't you worry about us."

So the group split into the clubbing five and the younger Danny, Richard and Layne.

"Anything you two want to do?" Danny asked.

"I don't know... the cinema? I don't mind bowling again," Richard said.

"Actually... I quite like to head back to the hotel..." Layne suggested quietly.

"Are you not feeling well?"

"No, just a little tired."

"That's okay. You can take him back Rich, I'll have a walk to the football stadium," Danny concluded.

"Shall we take the long route back?" Layne asked after Danny disappeared from sight.

"I thought you're tired?"

"I just want to have a walk with you."

"Err... sure... where do you want to go?"

Layne didn't respond and simply led Richard towards the beach. It was finally dark after the long summer day and they walked past a few young couples before they reached the water front, far away from the crowd and the main attractions.

"The beach feels differently at this sort of time," Layne commented.

"Yes, it was vibrant during the day but very peaceful now."

"The waves sound so lovely," Layne said before he turned to face Richard. "I... I have something to ask you, Richie."

"Do you have feelings for me?"

"What... do you mean?"

"As in... a romantic... sort of... way?" Layne said as he shyly looked down to avoid eye contact.

Richard was stunned. The time had finally come for him to face the truth, one way or the other, and there was no point in dallying anymore. His throat gulped to release some of the pressure, before he set himself free.

"I... I... I mean... I do... yes, I do like you, Layne," Richard said as he grabbed Layne's hands. "Ever since day one."

Layne slowly looked up with a sweet little smile, before he asked softly, "Then why did you go out with Sarah?"

"I... I knew it was wrong but I forced myself to... so that I could stay away from how I really feel. But I was wrong. I wasn't happy at all.

"The one I fancy all this time is you, Layne. I know we're footballers and it's probably impossible but I... I just want to know how... how you feel?"

"I'm... glad that I get to hear your true feelings. Don't worry about what is to come because... because we can face them together. I like you too, Richie."

Layne finished with a beautiful smile, one that Richard would never forget. His dream had come true at that very moment. There may well be consequences in the future, but for the first time in a very long time, he felt genuinely happy. The weight had finally been lifted. He no longer needed to suppress his feelings.

He looked at the boy he wanted all along and slowly moved forward for a kiss. Layne closed his eyes in anticipation and was as adorable as the night of Richard's seventeenth birthday.

"May I kiss you?" Richard paused for a second and asked.

"You didn't ask the last time you tried!" Layne said softly.

The pair kissed. Richard finally got to be with Layne and this time there were no guilty feelings. He could take his time and enjoy every second of it – Layne's warm and soft lips, the lovely smell of him, and the odd moan in between kisses. He got what he had been dreaming for, for a long, long time.

It felt wonderful.

"You are so sweet, Layney boy," Richard said when they finally let go of each other for a breather.

"You nearly suffocated me... but it feels really good..."

Richard just couldn't stop smiling at Layne. And Layne couldn't stop giggling at him either. His joyful eyes were the most beautiful on earth.

They kissed again. And again. And again.

"I should have told you all this earlier. It'll save us all the waiting," Richard said when they finally had a break. "When did you realise how you feel about me?"

"I like you as a person the first time we met and I started falling for you when you comforted me. It would have been a dream come true when you got drunk and tried to kiss me that night... Then you treated me like a little brother and started going out with a girl! I wasn't sure how you feel ... until now."

"I couldn't control myself when I saw how cute you were but I didn't want to scare you away. The pessimistic me thought you only saw me as a bigger brother and I didn't want to ruin our friendship. There was a period of time when I hoped I could be 'normal' and work it out with Sarah, how silly was I?"

"It's okay now Richie, you can work it out with me."

"I couldn't be happier, Layney!"

"Hehe, Richie Richie!"

"Layney!"

"Richie!"

The two carried on calling each other's name childishly, leading to more giggles and further rounds of kisses.

"I've never imagined you to have a silly side. I thought you'll always be dead serious!"

"I am absolutely serious about us but I feel totally comfortable behaving like this. I guess this is reserved for you only!"

"I like it!"

"Mm... I guess we'd better head back. It's getting late."

"Sure! Let's walk back like those couples earlier!"

The pair held their hands during their return to the hotel. Richard felt very sweet and he loved every second of it. They resumed kissing once they were back in their room and it escalated quickly.

134

Richard's body was about to explode as the desire for intimacy intensified every time he felt the heat from Layne's breaths. Layne's hands were all over his body and it felt really good. It was something he never experienced before. And he wanted more.

He gently laid Layne onto the bed and took their t-shirts off. When his skin felt the warmth of Layne he could no longer control himself.

Layne went completely blushed as Richard started kissing and touching him. But when Richard looked at his pretty and innocent face again the remaining sensible part of him made a very last minute plead.

Layne was still only fifteen.

It felt like the ice bucket challenge hitting him three times in a row and he came back to his senses.

"We can't go any further," Richard whispered to Layne. "Not yet."

"Does it matter? I'm ready," Layne opened his eyes and said softly.

"We can't do it. That'll ruin our careers and possibly lives," Richard insisted as he lay down next to Layne to calm himself down.

"Do... you not want it?" Layne asked with a sweet and provocative tone.

"I definitely do... just look at the state I'm in. But in a month's time. Let's not cross the line now," Richard said as he kissed Layne on his forehead.

"I'm sure you cannot sleep like this..." Layne said while putting his hand on Richard's private part. "Do you need some help?"

"Isn't that the same as the real thing? We can't do that."

"Maybe you're right, Mr Sensible, but promise you'll wait for me," Layne gave in and just rested on Richard's chest.

"I promise, I've been dreaming about it since we met," Richard said as he gently stroked Layne's soft hair.

"You're such a pervert!" Layne giggled.

The two looked and smiled at each other again, still couldn't believe how things had finally developed.

"I never thought this could ever be true," Richard said.

"Me neither. There are so many things that I want to do with you. I want to take you to lots of places – my home town, holidays and all sorts."

"That would be so nice. I can't wait to spend all my time with you."

The pair carried on their little chat until they eventually fell asleep.

The group spent the rest of the beachside holiday exploring other local spots during the day and partying in the evenings. They visited both ends of the long beach – they tried their hands on windsurfing and jet skiing at Sandbanks, and went up the imposing clay and ironstone cliffs in Hengistbury Head.

The pair disappeared every now and then from the group to have their own time together – for a walk, a swim, some ice-creams, or whatever else they could think of. They also took plenty of lovely photos with the colourful beach huts.

The team gathered for dinner before calling it a day every day. Charlie and Paul loved the club so much that they went three nights in a row. Tom gave up after one trip and went to the cinema and arcade with the rest instead.

They had a poker tournament at Charlie and Paul's room on their fourth night there. Rob and Tom bought lots of drinks from a local supermarket and Layne helped himself to a few bottles. Richard had never seen him drunk before but wasn't surprised that he became even more cheerful and talkative. Luckily he wasn't showing too much affections towards him in front of the others, as he simply passed out on a cushion shortly after he blew all his chips. Richard paced himself to avoid a similar fate but started to feel the effects as the night went on. He carried Layne back to their room after he became the fourth player to bow out of the tournament, which was eventually won by Charlie.

He carefully placed Layne on the bed before crashing next to him. When he woke up it was already nice and bright in the morning. Layne was still soundly asleep and so he just gazed at how peaceful he was. There was a little smile on Layne's face and he looked absolutely gorgeous.

Richard couldn't help but give his boyfriend a little kiss on the cheek, and Layne gently woke up, carrying the same sweet smile on his face.

"Good morning Richie. Did you have a good night?"

"Yes it's really good... being next to you."

"That's how I felt the last few mornings!"

"You look lovely when you are asleep."

"Hehe, not when I'm awake?"

"You know I don't mean that," Richard cut the talking and gave Layne a kiss. The two continued for a while and ended up in another snuggle.

"I can't wait for your sixteenth birthday!"

"It'll be the best day ever!"

The beachside holiday continued and the pair enjoyed the remainder of their wonderful week away. On the return journey, Ollie got the shorter string so he had to get back in Charlie's car. To be fair he drove back carefully without any trouble.

The pair reluctantly headed home separately for the two remaining weeks of the summer break. Layne went to Madeira in Portugal with his mum but he was exchanging messages with Richard all the time, sending him pictures of almost everything – scenery, food and plenty of selfies.

9.

New Team

It was mid-July and the team were gathering for their first session of pre-season training as the new under 23 team. They learnt during the break that David had been appointed as the Team Manager, as Ron left the club to join another Championship club. The rest of the setup replicated the first team, with Nick as the Assistant Manager, Paolo as the Goalkeeping Coach, Tim as the Technical Coach and there were dedicated physiotherapists and kit management team for the younger side. Stuart headed up the newly rebranded Sports Science and Performance Analytics team that covered both squads.

Training would become full time, starting at half past nine and finishing at about one. There would be individual training programmes for each player which consist of both gym and pitch exercises.

Players like Richard who were doing, or looking to do, their A-Levels, would have their studies done through the partner school, if they fit in with the standard timetable, or private tuitions in the afternoons. Danny decided to call time on studying after GCSE's while Layne wanted to carry on.

The pair agreed to stay together at the Stevenson's at least until Richard turned eighteen, when he would legally be allowed to rent a property. They didn't tell anyone about their relationship and the plan was to continue sleeping in their own bedrooms... but Layne would often sneak into Richard's room at the middle of the night "for some warmth". Richard was comfortable with how their relationship had developed. He loved Layne to bits and was over the moon just to be able to see him happy every day.

David gathered all twenty-two players to make an announcement. He appointed Les, the towering centre back from the old under 21 team as the team captain and Max the slim centre midfielder with ginger hair as the vice-captain.

Then he introduced three new players that the club signed during off season.

The first one was a twenty-year-old right back called Viktor Svensson. He came from the Black Dragons' partner club in Sweden and had already played a few times for their first team. He certainly looked and sounded confident in his ability.

The second one was seventeen years old Kasper Boilesen. He came from the same club as Viktor and he played as a defensive midfielder. Upon hearing the Dane's playing position, Richard had a good look at him: he was about six foot two in height, had dark buzz cut hair and looked physically strong. He seemed friendly but Richard believed he would be a tough competition for his place in the team.

The third one was a striker called Alex Knight. He was sixteen and he came from the academy of a top club in Seville, Spain. He looked the opposite of Kasper – he was just under six feet but much, much leaner and had long bleached blonde hair tied up by a headband.

Richard noted his family name and looked across to Peter, who nodded and indicated that Alex was his half-brother. Layne was standing next to him and he gave Richard a funny face, which Richard pretended to ignore but couldn't resist a subtle smile.

He wasn't surprised by the new recruits today as he acknowledged that the team needed reinforcements in those positions, but with Kasper and the experienced Max in the team, he and Tom were far from guaranteed to be starters together. He actually thought that, out of all the under 18 players, only Danny's position was safe, and that was because Chris Williams the star midfielder of the old under 21 team was snapped up by a Premier League club in the summer. Charlie should get plenty of game time but he wasn't sure where Owen would be deployed, as he could play as a striker or on either wings.

David then gave the team a speech on his expectations of the season:

"As we said before the holidays, we set up this team to be the reserve to the first team and we want you guys to be capable of playing in the Championship and beyond.

"While there's no doubt that you are all talented players with huge potentials, you have to absolutely put in the efforts, in training and in matches, to become what you want to be. Remember, 'talent plus efforts equals success'.

"I want us to be the team that work the hardest in the division. I want you to put everything into every game: fight for every ball, jump for every header and run for every pass. We can be beaten on skills, but never, ever on efforts!

"But I'm not saying you should blindly chase after every ball and tire yourselves. We need to be intelligent with the way we use our energy. Be brave in attack and be responsible in defence. Never let your teammate face a challenge alone. We are one team!"

He then handed over to Stuart to talk about the pre-season training. He said that in order to make the players as fit as they could be, the training would be tough, but the loads and intensity would increase progressively to allow them to adapt and to reduce risk of injury. He also said that players would be individually tested and analysed to ensure the most appropriate programmes were designed. His team of coaches then gave every player a set of wearable devices that would gather their data during training and matches to monitor their conditions and progress.

"There's no hiding from now," he joked.

Richard had his tests and learnt that the results were categorised into five groups: body composition, lower body power, lower body strength, speed and fitness. He was told that his general fitness was good, he had extraordinary lower body power but needed work on his strengths and speed.

He had a look at Layne's report and it showed that his great muscle/fat ratio had enabled his blistering pace but like him he needed a lot of work on strengths, or he risked getting injured from the slightest of tackles.

Charlie and Tom were strong like an ox, Danny could run forever while Thomas had great springs.

Richard knew that the hard work was about to begin and he looked forward to it.

The intensive training commenced the next morning. The marathon-runner David led the team round the pitch three times as a warm-up, before Stuart put them through the drills: plenty of sprints combined with lunges, press-ups, squat jumps and planks.

"This is rather tough," Layne said while catching his breath after the first circuit.

"I guess that's the whole point of training, to get us fit," said Richard, who was in a similar state as his boyfriend.

"No pain, no gain," Danny coolly commented.

"This is easy! You guys just need to work harder!" Charlie bragged.

The second cycle was split by the players' positions. Centre backs would combine the sprints with jumps; full backs and midfielders were more of the same as the first round to build their stamina further; while attackers had spinning and shooting added.

Richard and Layne survived the full session but had to lie on the ground to recover. They could only look with admiration when the likes of Danny and Tom followed David for a few more laps round the pitch.

"Don't tell me we need to do these every day for four weeks!" Layne said with a sigh.

"Remember what Stuart said yesterday, young man – it will only get more intense as we move through the weeks," Les reminded the youngster.

"Is this the same as last year?" Richard asked.

"Pretty much. The coaches know how to push you to your limit!"

"Did you feel the difference during the season?"

"Yeah man. We could keep running at the death when other teams were all knackered. We scored plenty of late goals."

"That's good! We'll keep going!"

The coaches gathered the players soon after and asked them to plunge into some ice baths. Known as cold water immersion or cryotherapy, it is used to recover faster and reduce muscle pain and soreness after intense training sessions or competitions. Layne wasn't keen on it but had to follow the others. It was timed at precisely four minutes and the players were then allowed to have a more relaxing warm shower.

Plenty of healthy food was available for lunch but the pair were not too interested – they just wanted to go home and rest. They slept for the whole afternoon, until Mrs Stevenson woke them up for dinner.

The training repeated for a week before Stuart tuned up the intensity. It was surprisingly manageable and Richard and Layne continued to rely on having lots of rest to recharge their batteries.

Four weeks had passed and the players felt fully energised. David arranged a session for the team in the briefing room to talk about tactics. He told the team that the default formation would be 4-3-3, with a number ten behind three attackers. The wide attackers would run in field to create rooms for the full backs to overlap into, and the two centre midfielders would sit and protect the defence. He would prefer a short passing game with lots of triangles, but he was not against the odd long ball to stretch the opposition back line.

Overall, he wanted the team to be quick and precise in attack and to defend in numbers with a compact shape.

The key to those, he said, was transitional play. He defined a transition in football as the process of recognising and responding in the first few seconds after losing or regaining possession of the football. There were two important elements: the first was the decision making of the player who gained or lost possession of the ball –

how and where he could move the ball to commence the attack or what actions he should take to help the team defend immediately. The second focus was how the rest of the team reacted – what options they would offer in attack and which defensive positions they would cover. Speed and speed of thought were of the essence.

David used what the under 18 team did late last season as an example. They were using Charlie as the start of the attack. When the players won the ball, they looked for him and he would hold the ball up until the rest of the team were in shape: be it Layne on the outside, Danny at the edge of area or Rob at the far post. The players knew their roles in the attack and didn't need to think too much about it. The result was devastating.

However, David emphasised that it was only one type of transitional play and would be easily dealt with by an opposition who did their homework. He said that if the team wanted to be a successful side, they'd need to have multiple ways of playing these quick, synchronised attacks in their arsenal. And equally, the team would need to develop methods to defend multiple situations.

It would all come in the training, he said, and the first team would be doing similar things so that there would be minimal transition in between.

Richard was sitting next to Tom and what David said was like music to his ears – he was very excited to know that his ideas weren't too far from this concept that was so popular in modern coaching. Tom was amazed that Richard knew so much about these tactical stuffs already, without really studying them.

David then announced that there would be a practice match between the team the next day to push their understanding into the test. Richard's red team had Josh in goal, Viktor, Thomas, Ivan and Layne in defence, Danny, Tom and him in midfield, and Charlie, Alex and Rob in attack. The blacks had the six-foot-five Arben in goal, Baek-min, Les, Thorsten, Lewis in defence, Kasper, Max and Ashley in midfield and Owen, Paul and Peter up front. Poor Jack, Francis and Mitchell would be the substitutes to cover injuries or tiredness. David asked the teams to sit down separately and come up with a game plan. Nick would assist the reds while Tim would work with the blacks.

After four weeks of training, Richard knew that Alex was a great finisher. He didn't seem to like passing but he hoped he would do differently in a match.

The reds sat down in a different room to have their planning session. Nick was there with the white board that had a pitch drawn on it. He asked if anyone had an idea for the match.

Everyone looked at Richard, as they knew he would have some plans. But he just sat there and didn't say a word.

"Just tell us what you think Rich," Tom ran out of patience.

Richard sat up and started talking. He began with the characteristics of the blacks.

"They have the strongest centre back pairing in Les and Thorsten, we are unlikely to get anything out of high balls into the box.

"The wings will be hard to conquer as well: Baek-min is very strong defensively and has the stamina to recover from most situations and while Lewis may not have the raw pace to match Rob, his great positioning will make that route difficult too.

"So if we want to score, we'll need to go for quick movements and short passes through the middle. No offence to them but Kasper and Ashley are our best option.

"In terms of attacking threats, Owen crossing from the left to Peter will be lethal, as Peter is up against little Layne at the far post. We need to avoid that."

"That's all very good," said Viktor. "What's the plan?"

"I'm caught in two minds," Richard replied. "Shall we ignore all that and play to our strengths or shall we shuffle our starting line-up to match theirs? It depends on how confident we are to handle their threats while playing our game or being flexible enough to play in different positions."

"How would you shuffle your line-up?" Nick asked.

"I'm thinking about these: I'll play at right back to restrict Owen's influence; Viktor moves to left back to take care of Peter's aerial threat; Layne pushes up to left wing; Charlie and Tom in midfield to let Danny go one on one with Ashley. And when the chance comes, we overload on Thorsten on the ground."

"That sounds like a comprehensive plan," Nick said. "I can see it works for both attack and defence. The key is whether you guys can all carry out the tasks in unfamiliar positions, what do you think?"

"I think we would have to do something to mitigate their main threat from Owen and Peter anyway, so it's worth doing the whole plan," said Thomas.

"I agree. They knew about our usual moves as well and will surely put measures in place, let's confuse them," said Tom. "Shall we have a vote?"

The majority of players agreed to go with the plan, with the notable exception being Alex, who didn't vote at all.

"What do you think, Alex?" Tom asked.

"I don't mind either way," he said. "All you need to do is find me in the area and I'll do the rest."

"We'll take that as a yes then. Okay lads let's look at the individual movements and tasks in a bit more detail, we need to demonstrate that we can transit between attack and defence well," Tom concluded before getting everyone to look at the white board.

Richard found Alex's response a little bit odd, but he thought what he said was in a way in line with what the plan was all about, which was creating goal scoring chances, so didn't think too much into it.

It was practice match day. The weather was great, if anything it would have been too hot. The game was only going to be sixty minutes long so the players should be fine.

Richard had a look at the black's formation. They started as he expected, with Owen on the left wing and Peter in the other side. Kasper was playing as the anchor, with both Max and Ashley in front of him. They did look a little confused when they saw where the red players were standing.

The match started, and after warm up passes the ball was picked up by the black's star player Owen, who had Richard in close proximity. He shielded the ball from Richard and let it roll across him, before flicking it towards the corner flag. Richard chased after him while closing his path to the inside, but he stopped the ball sharply with the outside of his right foot, quickly pushed it right then left again and tipped it through Richard's legs.

To his surprise, Richard didn't turn around to chase the ball but ran forward towards the black's half instead. He soon realised that Ivan was right in front of him to pick up the ball and he passed it to Tom, who duly sent the ball to where Richard was running to.

Richard passed the ball in field to Danny, who dropped his shoulder and ghosted pass the approaching Ashley with ease. He then passed the ball to Charlie on his left and ran towards the area for the returning ball. Thorsten came out to close Danny down but he let the return ball go through both their legs. Alex was behind them and he placed it into the bottom left corner. 1-0.

Richard's plan seemed to have worked as Danny created the space against Ashley and his clever movement got Alex through. The transition from defence to attack was breath-taking.

The blacks continued to attack and reaped their reward minutes later. Lewis's cross towards Peter was cleared by Thomas, but it fell to Max the midfield general, who hit it on the half volley brilliantly pass the goal keeper to make it 1-1.

It was a stunning goal.

Richard thought there wasn't much the team could do against such outstanding quality and they just had to carry on with the plan to find another opportunity.

About ten minutes later, Tom managed to find Layne on the left wing. With the hard-working South Korean right back Baek-min (the team simply called him Bae) following him closely, Layne chose to run back towards his own goal with the ball, pulling him out of position. He then laid the ball off to Tom who immediately sent the ball through to the area behind them, where Charlie had drifted into. He found Alex in the area and ran for the return ball by the penalty spot, which was free. But Alex decided to turn and have a shot himself and it was blocked by Les for a corner. Charlie made a gesture to Alex saying he should have passed but he was ignored.

The half ended 1-1.

"I think we were doing okay," said Richard after he downed the remaining half of his energy drink as usual. "We just need to take our chances."

"Why didn't you pass there? I would have been clean through," Charlie quizzed Alex at half time.

"I didn't see you," Alex didn't look interested.

"Make sure you do next time then," Charlie decided not to follow it up for the sake of harmony and had a drink instead.

The second half began. The teams started to nullify each other as chances were hard to come by. After about fifteen minutes, Richard hit it long ball with heavy backspin towards Rob behind Lewis, and the winger made enough space for a low cross onto the path of Danny. But Alex was also there and he picked up the ball before it reached Danny. He then turned and hit the ball wide with his weaker right foot. The chance would have been better for Danny, who had been screaming for it. He didn't look impressed but he quickly moved back into position to defend.

With time running out, the teams were taking more chances and they weren't able to keep possession for long. Richard picked up a loose ball and hit a long diagonal ball towards Layne on the left wing immediately. He took on Baek-min but the defender forced him off the ball with his strength. He quickly passed the ball to Max, who hit a lovely first-time ball behind Richard for Owen. He controlled it beautifully as Richard turned and caught up with him. But before Richard could steady himself, Owen quickly executed a double touch to push the ball to his left, before hitting it powerfully with his left foot. The ball squeezed past the near post to give the blacks a 2-1 lead.

"Richie is beaten!" Layne looked horrified.

"Not so unbeatable now, are you?" Owen teased Richard who was on the floor.

"I never called myself that. Great play to open up that space and a good finish."

Owen was surprised by Richard's response, he looked slightly embarrassed to have made his earlier remark.

With minutes remaining and a goal behind, the reds carried out the next part of the plan – they reverted back to their normal positions for a final assault.

Charlie kicked off again and he passed the ball back to Richard, who was now back into the centre with Tom. They exchanged a few passes with the centre backs, while Charlie ran towards his usual position.

"There they come," said Les, who knew that was the sign before Richard hit a long ball.

But against a team familiar with their usual tactics, the reds made a small twist to their plan. Instead of Charlie being the outlet, it was Danny, and obviously Tom had changed his signal as well.

So Richard chipped the ball to Danny, who sneaked behind Kasper into the left channel. Layne was charging on the outside; Charlie had moved into the centre and Rob was running towards the far post. However, none of them was Danny's target, as he sent a perfectly weighted ball inside the area to Alex, who was in a great position to cut it back for Charlie to tap in. But again he ignored his teammates and chose to have a shot himself from the tight angle, and the ball hit the side netting instead.

That was the red's best and final chance, and the game ended 2-1 to the blacks.

Richard was very disappointed. He thought the plans worked, but it wasn't to be due to a lack of teamwork at the final step. He went over to give Layne a hug, and just when they started to talk, they saw something unpleasant happening in the far side near the black's goal.

Charlie had punched Alex!

They quickly ran over to the scene. The coaching staff were already there and Tom and Peter were separating the two. With everyone shouting in the background they couldn't hear what Charlie was saying – they could only see him swinging his legs trying to kick Alex.

"Enough!" shouted David. "This isn't some school playground!"

"We would have won the game had it not been this selfish prick!" Charlie complained.

"Who are you to say what I should and shouldn't do on the pitch?" Alex wasn't giving way.

"You fucking little shit!" Charlie approached Alex again but was held back by Tom.

"Just stop it!" David stood in the middle of the two. "Remember that you are professional footballers. Calm down and come to my office in thirty minutes."

"Listen to the boss," Tom told Charlie, "don't ruin it."

"Okay okay… I'm calm, I'm so gutted to lose the game like that," said Charlie after some deep breaths.

"We all are but violence is not the way," said Richard.

"Just go in and apologise to the boss," Danny said as he put his hands on both Charlie's shoulders, "but I'm with you on that."

"Cheers lads. I'll sort it out," said Charlie.

Richard felt sad about the situation – his friends had clearly teamed up against Alex, who was being selfish for sure, but how could the team play after that?

He learnt later from Charlie that he was given an official warning by David.

The first ever match for the new under 23 team was scheduled for the following weekend. It would be played at the training ground against a team from the US that were having a European tour.

David announced his team selection after Wednesday's training session. He wanted to have Josh in goal, Baek-min, Lewis, Les and Thorsten at the back, Tom, Max and Danny in midfield and Owen, Paul and Rob upfront.

Richard would be on the bench with the rest of the team, while Charlie would not be selected at all for his disciplinary issues.

Peter told Richard and his friends that Alex had a talking to from David but it seemed that the message hadn't really sunk in. He also said that he wasn't too close to his half-brother since their father left him and his mum for Spain when he wasn't even two years old.

"Are you feeling okay?" Layne asked Richard on their way home from training.

"I guess it makes sense to start with Tom and Max," Richard said. "I didn't play well enough in the practice game anyway."

"Still gutted that you were beaten by Owen?" Layne guessed that might be important to Richard.

"No I don't really care about that. I'm kind of glad that it did happen so no one says I'm unbeatable any more. I'm just thinking about how much competition there is in centre mid now. Tom and Max are good all-round players and Kasper has the strengths I can only dream of. What do I offer?"

"Don't be silly, your defending is much better than 'Boiler' and your passing has wider range and more accuracy than all three of them!" Layne was probably amazed that Richard could lack confidence. "I wish I can have those skills."

"Maybe I need to think less about tactics and focus on my actual game. Sometimes I think too much."

They had arrived back at the house.

"Yes you do that sometimes, but have a guess on what I'm thinking right now?" Layne asked as he opened the door.

"You?" Richard was finally smiling. "What else but a big cuddle?"

The pair laughed and walked in.

The under 23 team won their first ever game 4-1. Owen scored a hat trick to give the team a 3-1 lead in the first half and Max put away a penalty in the second. Tom and

150

Danny started the game as planned and Richard, Thomas and Layne came on the second half for their team debuts. Richard partnered Max in midfield for the first time and found him very different to Tom. He demanded the ball a lot more but he was also very happy to pass to Richard – he seemed to have faith in his skills, which was reassuring for Richard.

Layne replaced the fantastic Lewis late in the game and played reasonably well. He wasn't too adventurous in attack and made some good decisions, which was commended by David afterwards.

Alex also played in the second half but he was still more focused on his own game than linking up with others. He did win the penalty for Max though. Richard felt it was a shame as Alex was very good in getting into dangerous positions and could be extremely useful for the team.

Owen came over to Richard after the game to offer a handshake. He appreciated his performance during the second half, as Richard defended well and found him with his long passes a few times. He also took the chance to apologise for the tease in the practice match. Richard was delighted that he earned the respect of another one of the best players around. He looked forward to training every day and hoped he could break into the starting line-up very soon.

10.

Sixteen

It had been three weeks since the infamous practice match and the rift between Alex and Charlie showed no signs of improvement, even though they both had a lecture from David.

Alex was isolated by most of the team, apart from his half-brother Peter and the nicer characters such as Jack, Tom and Thomas. The older players tended not to care much about the rivalry of two junior players, and the younger ones didn't know what to do or which side to pick.

Richard and Layne had different views on this matter. Richard was the more inclusive one and thought the two must find a way to come together, while Layne was firmly in Charlie's camp.

One day Alex asked Richard if he could have some one-to-one training against him. He felt he needed more practice in taking on defenders and Tim suggested him to do it with Richard.

Richard accepted his request despite multiple nudges from Layne next to him to suggest otherwise. They agreed to meet up after normal training the next day.

"Why did you agree to help him?" Layne wasn't happy about it. "I thought we're friends with Charlie? He could easily do that with Bae?"

"We're all in the same team," Richard said calmly. "I want to find out if he's as bad as you guys think."

The next day, Richard and Alex spent an hour after training to practice take on's. Alex had a really good left foot for shots and his dribbling wasn't particularly bad, but he wasn't able to beat Richard once, no matter what he tried.

"You're really good at this, I couldn't beat you at all," he said when they had some drinks afterwards.

"It's nothing special, just years of practice," Richard was as humble as ever.

"It's not that. Your ability to attack the ball multiple times during a single movement is amazing. You must have really good balance. I've seen some great defenders in Spain, you're up there with them."

"What's it like playing against those two massive clubs?" Richard never thought he could ask someone with first-hand experience.

"It's different there. They are less physical but very skilful. They focus a lot on passing and movements. Kids from those two academies are from a different planet. They are better in almost everything and can walk into position effortlessly," Alex recalled.

"That sounds amazing. Why did you come back to England?" Richard would rather ask the question to Alex's face than guessing the answer.

"I didn't get a contract there. My agent knew Ron and he arranged it all in the summer," Alex was actually quite honest.

"You have an agent already?" Richard did think about it but he was just too happy to have signed for the Black Dragons.

"He's the one who got my schoolboy deal with Seville in the first place, he's well connected in Spain and England. Do you need his contact information?"

"No, not really. I don't see the point yet. How do you see the players here?"

"Honestly," said Alex before he had another sip of water. "There are some good players here but the overall standard isn't as high as in Spain."

"I get that. But I think we have a special bunch here. We are willing to fight for each other and make the sum bigger than its parts," Richard began his offensive into the topic.

"I see what you're trying to say here mate," he smiled. "I'm not against Charlie and the rest, but sometimes we make judgements on the ball in split seconds and we shouldn't lay into our teammates straight away and think they're the villains. And when I'm pushed, I'll fight back."

Richard thought Alex might have a point there. For Charlie and the rest, they had a plan developed over a few months and they saw Alex as the one who didn't follow it. But they didn't think from Alex's angle – he was new to the team and didn't know everyone's styles and movements.

"I see your point of view," Richard admitted. "I'll assure you that you'll find out the good things about the team over time. I admire your ability to beat offside traps and move behind defences at the right time – it could be the very key for this team to open others up."

"What makes you think that?" Alex was curious.

"Our front players, like Owen, Charlie and Danny, are very good at making late runs into the box. If you are there to hold it up in those advanced positions..."

"We can score a lot of goals!" Alex jumped in.

"Yes, that'll win us games and we'll all look good, right?" Richard concluded with a question.

"You're pretty good at these talks. I get your points, let's see how it goes," Alex stood up and got ready to go. "Same time tomorrow for more one-to-ones?"

Richard could see some hope.

The two players carried on with their extra training for another week. Alex's dribbling skills had definitely improved, but he still wasn't able to overcome "The Unbeatable". He had been more vocal during normal training as well. There were signs that the ice could be breaking, but it might still be some time away.

Richard went into the changing room after the last one of these extra sessions and was surprised to see Layne there. He had just finished his additional weights training and was having a drink before a shower.

Richard had a look inside to make sure no one else was there before sitting down next to him. The pair had been very careful on keeping a distance between them in training and matches since their relationship began a month ago. Although they had been seen by various teammates in town on their date nights, no one had raised any questions as they had always been close.

"Hey how are you doing?" Richard asked softly.

"I'm fine," Layne's reply was a little bit cold. "Are you done with your hottie?"

"You're not jealous, are you? It's just football training," Richard was a little bemused.

"I guess I'm allowed to be jealous – I'm not as tall as him, not as fit as him, I don't have blonde hair, and most of all, I'm not even old enough for you!" Layne complained.

Richard knew the last point had been the bugbear of their relationship since it started, as he politely declined Layne's advances a few times, including the time when he sneaked into his bed completely naked in the middle of the night. He followed the recent trial of the former England winger and was wary of the consequences of having underage sex with a minor, even though in their own case the age gap was less than two years and they were genuinely in love.

He actually found Layne's child-like angry expression highly adorable and he pulled him over to comfort him.

"Don't be silly baby. I'm not thinking about anyone else but you and I can't wait to give you everything in a couple of weeks' time."

Layne seemed to be settled by that. He broke out a little smile before he moved closer and demanded a kiss. Richard happily obliged.

He felt wonderful every time they kissed. He found Layne extremely cute when he closed his eyes in anticipation. And when they kissed, time seemed to have stopped. That warmth. That sweetness.

And they had forgotten where they were.

Someone opened the door and came into the dressing room!

The two boys separated quickly but Richard was certain whoever came in saw what they were doing. He looked over to greet the person with a sheepish smile.

155

Luckily, it was his friend Tom.

He seemed to be in shock for a second, before walking in calmly.

"Hey Rich and Layne, how's it going?" he tried hard to sound normal.

"We're alright, I suppose," Richard replied nervously and Layne was still completely blushed.

"It's okay, lads. I saw what was going on and I'm fine with it. Don't worry I'm not going to tell."

Richard and Layne looked at each other and shared a sigh of relief.

"Why don't you two come over to my new place for dinner tonight? We can talk more then."

Richard and Layne went to Tom's apartment that evening. It was in Surbiton by the river overlooking the marina. Richard was impressed.

"Hello lads," Tom welcomed the pair at the door. "Come in and make yourselves comfortable."

Richard had a look around and really liked the layout of the two-bedroom flat with a balcony facing the river.

"How did you find this flat? It's lovely!" he asked Tom.

"Do you like it? I'm a local boy, of course I know where the nice places are around here. You should have a word with Carla when you're looking, she has good connections with the estate agents. You can't stay at the digs forever, especially now that you two are…"

"Yeah we need to think about it, but we can't rent a property until I'm eighteen in December anyway," said Richard when looking at Layne.

"That's a good point. Layne is even younger. Oh, does it mean…" said Tom with a suggestive wink.

"No no no, we've been good!" Layne burst into a laughter as Richard vigorously denied any wrongdoing.

"Alright Rich I trust you are a law abiding citizen… Did you two start before, during or after Bournemouth? I sensed something when you two kept disappearing and how cheerful you became afterwards."

"During… I guess we didn't hide it well? Do the others know?"

"They may have guessed, but we haven't talked about it."

"Do you think they will be okay?"

"I'm sure they're fine too. It's quite normal these days and you two have always been close," said Tom before putting up a serious face. "You'll need to be careful with the rest of the team though, I don't know how they'd react. And the opposing teams and fans would be even worse. It's not an easy path in football."

"I know… I don't want to tell anyone yet, David included," said Richard with a sigh, before holding Layne's hand. "We're together no matter what."

To avoid further miserable thoughts, Tom changed his subject to the food of the night. He had made some Mexican style chicken and put them in the oven to go with tacos later. Mihara was working in the city and would join them later.

"It smells really nice! I didn't know you can cook!" Layne was impressed.

"I used to work in a restaurant! It's quite easy to do, you can't just rely on deliveries. Do you two know how to cook?"

"Not sure about this boy but I can follow some basic recipes. It's not rocket science," said Richard.

"I guess nothing is too difficult for your intelligence," Tom smiled.

Mihara was back just when the food was ready and they started their dinner gathering. Richard and Layne didn't stay too late given that they had training the next day.

On the short journey back, they talked about their future plan. Richard was keen to move to somewhere like Tom's, but he was worried that he might not be able to afford it on his own. Layne's schoolboy contract didn't pay him much but he was certain that he could get support from The Bank of Mummy.

157

David named his team for the second friendly game against the under 23 team of another Championship side. He wanted Arben in goal, Viktor, Les, Thomas, Lewis in defence, Richard, Tom and Max in midfield, and Owen, Alex and Danny up front. Charlie was named on the bench. With the experienced defenders behind the midfield duo and Max playing slightly deeper than Danny normally would, the defence was solid and the two were very effective with their covering and distributions.

Owen and Danny linked up with the supporting full backs and Max well on the wings and created plenty of chances for Alex, who didn't disappoint and put two of them away in the first half.

To continue his test on the strengths of his whole squad, David made five changes at half time and brought on Charlie, Layne, Baek-min, Thorsten and Jack for Owen, Lewis, Viktor, Les and Arben.

Alex stopped Richard, Charlie and Danny before they left the dressing room. He wanted to talk.

He said he had been observing the movements of Charlie and Danny and he wanted to confirm a few details. He then gave examples of his findings – to the surprise of Richard and the other two, they were very accurate.

"To be able to pass to you, I needed time to study your moves," Alex concluded.

"I'm good with that," Danny shook Alex's hand with his usual ice-cool face on. He then left with Richard, who gave both Alex and Charlie a pat on the shoulder.

"They can sort themselves out," Danny said to Richard on their way out. Richard couldn't hear what Alex and Charlie were talking about but knew that they were at least talking.

The other team kicked off just when Alex and Charlie stepped back onto the pitch.

Having served his sentence for disciplinary problems, Charlie was keen to play again. He closed down the defence quickly and eventually forced them to clear the ball, which was picked up by Tom in his own half. With the team two goals behind, the opposing players pushed out to hunt the ball back. Tom exchanged the ball well with Richard before finding a gap to pass it forward to Max near the centre circle. He spread the ball left for Layne and he played a quick one-two with Charlie to attack down the left flank. Alex made a good run to the channel but Layne hesitated and the path was closed down. He had to pass back to Richard to start another attack.

A few minutes later, the young Black Dragons attacked down their right with Baek-min bringing the ball out from defence. He hit it long towards Danny down the right, who trapped the ball nicely before hitting a low cross towards to right of the box. Alex was there to pick it up and after a couple of feints he chipped the ball back towards the penalty spot without even looking.

Charlie was completely free and he slotted the ball effortlessly into the bottom right corner to extend the lead to three. He then ran over to Alex and Danny to celebrate.

Layne looked confused towards Richard, who gestured to say "they had kissed and made up". The two laughed as they joined the team celebration.

With the new found harmony, the team were even more fluid in their attack and soon Alex opened up a space for Max to score the fourth. He then completed the drubbing and his first hat trick for the team with a tap-in set up by Charlie. The team crowded Alex to celebrate his goals.

"Thanks for helping me find the fun of playing football again," said Alex as he gave Richard a hug at the end of the match.

"That was lovely to see. Great play," Richard was glad.

Before the team disbanded for the day, Alex invited Richard and his friends to dinner that night. He heard that there was a good tapas restaurant in Richmond and was keen to try. Of course Richard wouldn't say no, and Charlie, Danny and Tom signed up too.

Richard and Layne picked Danny, Tom and Mihara up on route to the restaurant. Charlie was already there with his new girlfriend Heidi and the Knight brothers arrived shortly after.

"Thanks for coming, and a belated hola to you all!"
said Alex as he raised a glass of sangria.

"Salud!"

"Cheers!"

"To our new team!"

"Up the Black Dragons!"

Richard found the fruity drink easy to have, but soon he
knew he couldn't carry on – he was the driver after all.
Layne had a couple of cheeky ones and was even more
cheerful than he normally was.

The group ordered plenty of tapas on top of a couple of
paella's, to the point that the Spanish waiter thought it was
too much – but the team refused to cut down. He clearly
didn't know what a hungry Charlie and Richard could do.

The tapas came first: there were calamares, gambas, red
snappers, chorizo, jamon Serrano, Spanish omelette etc.,
and the team cleared each dish as soon as they arrived.
Then the two large paellas turned up and were gone in a
similar fashion.

Alex and Peter, who offered to pick up the bill, were
amazed by their teammates' appetite. The waiter was
equally in awe when he came back to see the empty dishes,
and was shocked even further when Richard asked him for
the dessert menu.

The group was fully satisfied after the last churros was
consumed by Richard, and the rift between the players was
finally gone for good.

"It's so good that the team are all friends again,"
Richard said to Layne when they got back to the
Stevenson's after dropping his passengers off.

"How did you play the mediator role so well?"

"I guess we all have the same goal – to play good
football and win games."

"It's good to hear that Alex is into girls."

"I never doubted that, it's only you getting jealous."

"Do you think he looks good though? Is he your type?"

"No he isn't. You are."

"I know that… When did you find out about what you
like?"

160

"Oh... I became so interested in other boys when I was about eleven or twelve but I thought it was just me having issues and I would grow out of it."

"Did you talk to anybody about it?"

"No way! I know my parents will go mad! How about you?"

"When I moved to high school, so about the same age as you?"

"Did you mum know about it?"

"Yes, she figured out quite quickly. She asked me one night and I just told her. She was very supportive – she said I don't need to worry about how the others see me and should just follow my feelings."

"She's so good, you're lucky, baby."

"I really am. Now I've got you too!"

"Ahh... I think I have to kiss you now!"

"By all means, Richie!"

It was late August and Layne had a day off training to pick up his exam results from school with Danny, Ollie, Harry, Andrew and Finley. The pair planned to meet up afterwards for lunch and they had a little side bet – Richard would buy if Layne had at least one A.

"Hey baby how did it go?" Richard asked when he met Layne back at the Stevenson's.

"Mm... I've got B's for Maths, English Literature and Geography, C's for Science and French, and... A's for English Language, History and PE!" Layne said with delight.

"That's very well done! Congratulations!" Richard said as he gave Layne a big cuddle. "I guess I'll be buying the lunch of your choice then!"

"You sure are! Do you know who I met at school today?"

"Danny and the others?"

"Of course I saw them – I'll tell you their grades later. But it was your Sarah! I didn't know Betty is her sister!"

"Oh, did you talk to her?"

"She asked me how we are doing! Are you aware that she knows about us?"

"I guess she does... She knew my heart was with you... when I was with her."

"She said that both of you saw me crying back at the cafe in Soho, why didn't you tell me earlier? How embarrassing!"

"You broke my heart that day... I didn't know she saw you too."

"You're such a bad boyfriend. Going out with her and thinking about me. It's good that you responded to your true feelings though!"

"That was the best decision I've ever made! Well, where are we going for lunch then?" Richard switched his attention back to his empty stomach.

"How about that Persian restaurant in Hammersmith?"

"That's an awesome call – I love their minced lamb... and their portions!"

Richard learnt the other players' results from Layne during their drive. Andrew did really well with all ten subjects in A* to Cs; Danny, Harry and Finley had a handful of passes while Ollie's results were "better left than said" – well he wasn't really surprised by that.

It was Layne's sixteenth birthday a few days later. The pair went to the famous Borough Market near London Bridge the day before for a late lunch after training. They visited various stalls and tasted plenty of delicious food. They sat down at a busy cafe for some iced coffee afterwards.

"Which one did you like most, Layney boy?" Richard asked.

"I love the oysters, they went down so well with some Tabasco," the young one said. "How about you?"

"It has to be the hog roast. It's so much better having it cooked right in front of us!"

"Where are we going next?"

"Mm... I'm going to take you up the Shard!"

"Huh?" Layne went completed blushed before he whispered, "It's not something you can say in public like this, Richie…"

"Why not? I thought it'll be a good treat for your birthday. Don't you want it?"

"I… I very much do, just didn't expect to be talking about it like this…"

Seeing how embarrassed Layne was, Richard thought for a second and realised what he was on about. He laughed and said, "I mean we are going up the very tall building a few minutes' walk from here! What were you thinking?"

"Err… Nothing…" Layne said while covering up his face.

"Let's get going then! I've pre-booked our tickets."

The pair went to the viewing platform at the Shard and admired the sight of London from the 72nd floor. They saw all the landmarks nearby and also managed to spot those further afield: they looked for Wembley Stadium and the other large sports grounds in the capital first, then they found Battersea Power Station, Hampton Court Palace near where they lived and finally Surrey Hills from far away. Layne took hundreds of photos, including plenty of selfies with Richard.

They then had a lovely early evening walk by the River Thames to see the Tower of London and Tower Bridge before returning to the new skyscraper for dinner. Having recently learned that Layne's mum was half-Chinese, Richard booked a table with an awesome panoramic view at one of the best Chinese restaurants in the capital. They had their signature dinner tasting menu and the food was fantastic – Richard was particular impressed with the Iron Goddess tea, with the way its aroma refreshed his taste buds in between dishes.

"How does this compare with the restaurants you used to go?" Richard asked Layne the expert.

"It's very good, but I'll ask mum to take us somewhere more dedicated to Cantonese dishes. They're different from northern cuisines like this."

"That'll be fantastic!"

"Are we heading back to the Stevenson's now?"

"What do you think? Is there somewhere you want to go? There's no training tomorrow so we don't have to hurry."

"I'll go wherever you want to... I'm sure you have a plan already?" Layne turned into the shy and adorable boy again.

"Follow me then," Richard said with a smile.

Richard took Layne back towards Waterloo Station. As they walked past a modern business hotel, he grabbed Layne's hand and pulled him in. He walked straight into a lift and activated it using a key card.

"Where did you get that from?" Layne asked. "Are we staying here?"

"I guess it's not right to stay at the Stevenson's for your big sixteenth?"

"But I... I haven't packed anything!" Layne's face turned bright red again.

"Don't worry, I've got everything you need."

The lift stopped at the third floor and Richard led Layne to room 316.

"Here we go, Layney boy!" he said after he unlocked the door using the key card.

The double room was neat and clean, which was typical for a business hotel, but it wasn't important – the boys had other ideas in their heads.

"How about... spending our night together here?" Richard asked as he felt the heat growing in his face and ears.

Layne, still wearing the beautiful blushing, kept his head down and said softly, "Yes, Richie."

Richard put his hands on Layne's burning cheeks and brought his head up gently. He looked into his eyes and couldn't hide his affection for his young boyfriend.

The pair started kissing. They might have done it hundreds of times already but it was wonderful – greater than ever before. Richard felt a hot stream going through his veins and his heartbeat accelerating rapidly. His body was about to explode.

"Shall… shall we have a shower first?" Layne suddenly asked.

"I guess… we should," Richard said before pointing at the wardrobe. "Your change of clothes should be there."

"Why… why don't you go first?"

Richard obliged but his head was full of Layne throughout the shower: the way he looked at him, his mix of shyness and desire, the warmth and softness of his lips, and the potential of being even closer with him later on…

The time was approaching midnight and Richard delivered his next surprise when Layne came out of the bathroom in the dressing gown provided by the hotel – he brought a small cake out from the mini fridge and started singing.

Happy Birthday to You
Happy Birthday to You
Happy Birthday to My Baby
Happy Birthday to You!

"Thank you so much Richie! I love you!" Layne said after he blew the candle. "Won't it be nice if we have some champagne?"

"Hehe, as you wish," Richard said after taking a small bottle out from a bucket of ice that he had been hiding.

"You've planned every single thing!"

"Hold on, you haven't had your present yet!" said Richard as he gave Layne a nicely wrapped box.

It was a beautiful cashmere scarf with blue and grey check. Layne loved it and happily tried it on to show Richard.

The two gazed at each other after they had the cake and champagne and said simultaneously, "What shall we do next?"

They shared a smile and got into another cuddle.

"Well, some time between you and me perhaps?" Richard whispered.

"Hehe, yes…" Layne's cheeks caught fire again. "What… do we actually do?"

"I can do anything that makes you feel good, baby."

"Same here... I want to be close to you, as in, very very close to you, Richie."

Layne sat on Richard as they kissed passionately on the small sofa. A moment later Richard lifted Layne up and gently put him on the bed. He carefully untied the knots of his dressing gown and started kissing and touching his smooth and firm body.

"Can... can you turn the lights off please?" Layne asked. "I'm... not quite ready for that."

"Sure, aren't you adorable?"

Richard was extremely excited – he fancied Layne from the moment they met and as they grew closer and closer he couldn't wait to get intimate with the person he loved, however hard he tried to hold on until it became legal. Layne seemed to be enjoying his every single touch, which only served to drive up his desire.

The pair had a wonderful time. Richard was bursting with joy – the physical pleasure was immense, and the feeling that they were now completely in love with each other was hugely satisfying.

"That was beautiful... I love you so much, my baby."

"I'm a hundred percent yours now..."

"So am I. There's absolutely nothing between us."

"I've never seen you this happy before. I love it!"

"That's because we've done something wonderful!"

"Did you... like it?"

"It's way better than what I imagine. I love the way you call my name!"

"Hehe... I'm glad you enjoyed your first time!"

"I'm so happy that I shared it with you. Did you feel good too? Did it hurt?"

"I didn't know what to expect, but you made it good... I like it. I like to be this close to you, I like to feel your warmth, I like that we are... connected. Thanks for being gentle with me."

"All the researches paid off!"

"You... you studied this too?"

"Of course! You are the best thing that has ever happened to me and I have to handle you with care!"

Layne giggled before he asked, "Why wouldn't you let me kiss you down there? I'm sure I can make you feel even better?"

"Kissing your lips is the sweetest thing on earth, I'd love to keep it that way."

"I've never imagined you to be such a romantic!"

"There's a lot more for you to find out!"

The pair carried on kissing and snuggling until they fell asleep – they just couldn't let go of each other.

Richard came out of his sleep early the next morning from an ache to his left arm, having let Layne sleep on it throughout the night. He tried to sneak it out but he woke Layne up in the process.

"How are you Richie?" Layne said softly.

"I'm good baby, did I wake you up?" Richard said before kissing Layne on his forehead.

"Why are you up so early?"

"My arm hurts a little bit..."

"Oh, you should have asked me to move."

"It's fine, I love holding you to sleep."

"You look different since last night!"

"In which way?"

"I don't know how to describe it... you look... relaxed?"

"Maybe I'm just too happy!"

"Hehe, now that we're up, shall we... have another go?"

"I'll be able to see everything this time!"

"Go on then, I'm all yours now!"

The young lovers giggled away and shared more fun time together. They had a joint shower before finally going downstairs for breakfast, when Richard revealed how he managed to book a hotel room and smuggled the champagne into it at the age of seventeen.

"Good morning sirs, can I have your room number and last name please?" the hostess asked.

"Morning, room 316 and the name is Nelson," said Richard.

He gave Layne a wink as the hostess led them to a table by the windows.

"I knew there was an accomplice!"

"Who else would it be? He gets staff rates!"

The couple had a buffet breakfast. There was a good selection of pastries, fruits, cold cuts and of course Richard's favourites – all the components of the traditional full English.

They then walked along the river to see the London Eye and County Hall.

"Oh I didn't know the Dungeons are here! Shall we go in?" Layne asked.

"I thought you're a little uncomfortable after this morning, maybe we should head home?"

"I'll be fine. Let's give it a visit, I know you like this kind of historic attractions."

"Thanks baby, you know me well!"

Richard enjoyed the visit as it demonstrated lots of historic events of London, including the Great Fire, Jack the Ripper and Guy Fawkes's plot to blow up the parliament. One of the demonstrations was held in a completely dark room and the pair got caught having a cheeky kiss when the host switched the lights on. It was embarrassing but the other tourists gave them a cheer and they were off the hook – luckily no one knew who they were.

The pair eventually boarded the train home after having some street food.

"Did you enjoy our trip up the Shard?" Richard whispered on the train.

"In a lot of ways, yes!" Layne giggled.

Richard found Layne a little different since their trip to central London. He would turn into a sweet and adorable boyfriend whenever they were in private, demanding plenty of physical affection, be it a kiss, a cuddle or more. Richard loved that and enjoyed spending every minute of their days together.

11.

Training

The under 23 team began their season in the Professional Development League 2 with a win, a draw and a defeat each, as David altered his starting line-up to find his perfect team. To his delight, the squad had plenty of depths at this level. He had a settled defence with Viktor, Lewis, Les and Thorsten. Baek-min, Ivan and Francis were ready to step in when needed, while Thomas and Layne could be introduced gradually. In midfield, he seemed to favour Tom and Max as two of the three, and would choose between Richard and Danny depending on whether he needed more in defence or attack. Danny could be pushed into the front three if Richard was required, and David could choose between him, Charlie, Alex and Rob to support Owen in attack.

The team repeated their pattern in October with another four points out of nine. Owen, Charlie and Alex opened their accounts while Danny and Tom registered their first assists. Richard played a part in all six league games but had no goals or assists to his name so far.

It was November and some of the under 23 players were invited to train with the first team for a week to give them some experience. They could also be useful if there were injuries and fatigue from the forthcoming festive schedules. Richard was one of the selected, together with Viktor, Les, Lewis, Tom, Max, Danny, Charlie and Owen.

Bob Warner was the manager of the first team and Richard found his approach to training very similar to that of David's. He thought that was probably what the club wanted to do in order to align the playing style, culture and development of both teams and prepared the players for a simpler transition.

Bob stressed the one thing he wanted his players to do when they lost the ball – to win it back quickly.

"There is no rocket science in that," he said.

He used the Spanish national team as his example and said the players could recover and have their breather when they passed the ball around for the other team to chase.

"Even tiki-taka can be used for defensive reasons."

He also played videos of defending by top European teams ahead of games, as he believed the players should learn from the best if they wanted to be the best.

Richard loved what he was seeing and hearing. However, he found the physical demand very challenging. He had a decent engine especially after pre-season but he wasn't used to the high intensity he was seeing with the first team – the challenges were so strong that even his great balance wasn't enough to counter.

"There's a lot to learn," he told Layne one night. "I don't know how Charlie and Tom can cope so well."

"Don't worry," Layne tried to comfort him. "It'll come with time. Just keep training."

He then examined Richard's body in detail, which made him quite uncomfortable.

"What are you trying to do, baby? I don't think it's time for that," he asked.

"Checking you out, obviously," the young one giggled. "Seriously, I think your muscles have grown a lot in the last few months. Have you not noticed?"

Richard had hardly realised until Layne mentioned it. He had a quick look at the mirror and he had to agree – he had indeed grown quite a bit.

Whilst it was a good sign, Richard thought there was so much more he needed to do.

"Let me see how much you've grown," said Richard before he grabbed Layne from the back.

Layne tried to escape and eventually they ended up laughing into another snuggle.

170

Bob named Lewis in the first team squad for their next home game. Lots of the young players showed up to support him from the stands.

Richard watched the play closely to study the formation and style of play. It was similar to how they played in the under 23's but he could see how much sharper the first team were with their transitional play, especially when they lost the ball, how they reacted quickly to close down the player with the ball and also cover paths to the key channels. He learnt a lot just by doing that.

Layne sat next to him and was watching the game like a normal fan. He had no idea why Richard looked so tense when some of the play was rather boring, and why he concentrated on writing when the team nearly conceded. He just stayed in his studious mode throughout the whole match.

"You're such a boring 'friend'," the youngster moaned.

"I'm here to learn," Richard replied. "We can go bowling or to the cinema later if you fancy some entertainment."

"I'm interested in something more physical today," Layne said. "How about some go-karting by the racecourse?"

"That's a good call, let's invite Tom and the others too."

"I'll do that while you carry on studying then…"

"Thanks. Look, Lewis has been summoned by Bob, is he about to come on?"

The team were leading 1-0 and Bob decided it was time to give Lewis his first team debut. He played well during his twenty minutes as the team held out for their victory.

"Look at Lewis lads, we can be next! First team isn't that far away!" claimed an excited Tom.

Having seen the game, Richard was convinced some more under 23 team players would make the switch, and he certainly hoped that he would be one of them.

Go-karting was a bit of embarrassment for Richard. Being one of the few players who had a driving licence, he was expected to do well but he finished second from bottom, only ahead of Ollie who crashed and did not finish.

His safety first approach remained the joke of the team throughout the evening. Layne missed out on the podium in fourth as Charlie, Rob and Tom finished ahead of him.

Richard had been viewing local apartments for the past few weeks with Carla, the Head of Football Operations. Layne wasn't involved as they wanted to keep their relationship as a secret and he said he'd trust whatever Richard chose. Although he did demand to have a balcony overlooking the river which restricted the selection by some degree.

Richard saw properties near where Tom and Mihara lived and he eventually set his sights on one that was two blocks away. Richard knew the area quite well and thought it would be nice for him and Layne to jog or cycle along the river in the evenings.

Carla did ask Richard why he was so keen on a two-bedroom apartment instead of a one-bed or a studio. It was quite a stretch for his earnings especially if he wanted one with river views. Richard told her that his plan was to flat share with Layne now that he was sixteen. He was relieved that Carla didn't seem to think too much about his cover story.

The young Black Dragons' next game was at home against a team from the West Midlands. Richard and Layne both started the match as they scored three goals within the first twenty minutes. Alex opened the scoring with a lovely volley from Danny's cross and Owen added two to his tally when he converted good plays from Charlie and Max. The game ended with no further goals but Richard was seriously tested when the away side launched a fightback late on. He stopped the attacking midfielder going through on goal as he pretended to focus on the runner but then dived in to tackle the ball back. The gamble paid off.

The team won their next match at Suffolk 2-0 thanked to goals from Danny and the substitute Rob. Richard held onto his starting position alongside Tom and Max but

Layne gave way to Lewis who returned from his first team duty.

Richard was called into David's office one day after training.

"Hi David, are you looking for me?" it's been a while since they had a one-to-one.

"Hi Richard, thanks for coming. We haven't spoken for a little while, how are you finding life in the under 23 team?"

"I really like it. I love playing with good players. There are some healthy competitions for places and the best of all, we are winning games."

"That's good to know. I'm sure you're one of those who understand what we are doing with the new structure. You're growing well. A lot have changed since I watched that unbeatable boy in Windlesham."

"Indeed. Thank you so much for bringing me on the journey. Last year or so has been life changing."

"Just keep up the good work in training and matches, there's a lot more in you. I have two things to discuss with you today. The first one is that we would like a number of you to be mentored by members of the first team. It should help you guys develop and be ready for the switch in the future."

"That would be great. May I know who my mentor would be?"

"We believe Michael would be good for you. Have you met him? How do you feel about the arrangement?"

"Michael the first team captain?" Richard was a bit shocked.

"Yes, he's seen you play and handpicked you to be his apprentice."

"That's unbelievable! He's a player I admire a lot – thank you for matching us together."

"That's good then, I'll leave it to you two to arrange," David paused before introducing his second purpose of the day. "The second thing I want to discuss is about your private life. We wouldn't ask players this normally… but are you and Layne together, as in a romantic relationship?"

Richard was stunned. He thought they had been hiding it from the others well – the only person who knew was Tom and there was no way he would inform David.

"Yes we are. May I know how you found out?" Richard thought there was no point denying it. In truth, he wouldn't want to deny it even if there was a valid reason.

"It wasn't hard for the host family to notice," explained David. "It really doesn't matter to us – remember one of our mottos is to be the most inclusive club in the country. I just want you to know that we are here to support. You two may need some help if you are to come out into the public world, as and when you play for the first team."

Richard couldn't believe what David was saying. He knew the club was good but he didn't know it could be this supportive.

"Thank you for that David. It means a lot to have your understanding and support," said Richard as he fought back his tears. "I know the road ahead would be very difficult but we're keen to go through it together."

"That's a good spirit. Just let us know how you would like us to cooperate."

"I would like to stay as low profile as possible. Layne is only young and I don't want him to face the cruel world. We won't be coming out in public any time soon," Richard said.

"It's okay. We'll support you that way. Just remember we're here if you need anything – come to me or Carla."

Richard told Layne about his conversation with David that evening. He was surprised that they were found out but he was of the view that they would have to be public one day and he was not afraid as long as they were together. Richard was far less optimistic – he had read about players before them and their stories were not particularly comforting. But he was keen to overcome whatever adversity to come their ways too, as he was not prepared to give Layne or football up easily.

Richard received a new intensive training programme from the Sports Science team the next morning. The aim

174

was to build up his upper body strength further while maintaining his balance and agility. There would be extra sessions in the afternoons.

Richard was glad that what he thought was lacking was also picked up by the coaches and he was keen to make it work. He mentioned it to Charlie and learnt that he also had additional gym work arranged for the afternoons so they would be doing them together.

The training was tough, but with the guidance of the coaches Richard felt that they were manageable.

One day after training, Charlie asked Richard if he would join him for a coffee. Richard accepted the invitation as he seemed to have something to say.

They went down to a local cafe. After some warm up conversations and the annual mocking of Richard's effort for Movember, Charlie started moaning about how his relationships had all panned out in the wrong direction. He had had plenty of fun but girls he met all seemed to be there because of his future as a professional footballer and not him as a person, and it felt so hollow. Richard agreed that it was not healthy – he couldn't really figure a way out so he suggested that maybe Charlie needed to hide his fame when he went out.

Charlie then asked Richard how he'd been doing with girls. He knew he had split up with Sarah but didn't know if he had met another one. Richard just told him he hadn't been with another girl since and was focusing on his studies and training. He didn't want to tell more people about Layne in case the news got out. He wasn't ready to face it all. He also felt very lucky that his relationship with Layne was pure and simple, he wouldn't want to deal with a partner who might have other reasons to be with him. What's the fun in calculating your every move even when you were at home?

On his way back, Richard walked to the apartment that he had agreed to rent and stood outside to imagine his life with Layne there. His head was full of hope – he couldn't wait for his next step in life to begin.

175

He wasn't picked by David for the next game away to Birmingham, which was hosted at their main stadium. It was on the advice of Stuart, who said that the additional strengths training had taken its toll in Richard's body and he needed some rest to adjust at this early stage. He travelled with the team anyway as Layne was in the starting eleven.

Several key players were not available due to international call-ups and injuries. Tom was captaining the under 23 team for the first time, in front of hundreds of supporters.

The game started reasonably well for the team as they created a few goal scoring chances. Mitchell and Layne combined well on the left for a cross to Paul who headed just wide, and Danny put a long-range effort over. The defending was solid with Kasper sitting deep to protect to back four.

However, the game changed after twenty minutes as the hosts took the lead through a rather soft goal. Their keeper's long kick somehow managed to bounce over Ivan and through to their striker who scored. Soon bad became worse as Rob's square pass to Tom was cut out by the opponent and the ball was quickly sent to the same striker to make it two.

The second half didn't start as David would have hoped for as the home team extended their lead from a free kick just outside the area. He tried to change things round with bringing three substitutes on with half an hour to go but the Black Dragons conceded two more goals to complete their miserable trip to the midlands. The fourth goal was from a good team move and the last one was a mix up between Layne and Thomas.

The young team were really downbeat in the dressing room.

"The result is disappointing, but it showed us the areas that we need to work on," David said in the dressing room. "We'll talk more about the specifics when we're back in training. Just get some rest now."

"Where did it go wrong?" Layne asked Richard on the coach journey back. He had, naturally, replaced Thomas as Richard's travel buddy.

"The other team were much more experienced than us. They figured out how we played and exposed our weaknesses. The lack of regular starters didn't help," Richard tried to reply without hurting Layne's feelings.

"But I thought we could just step up to the plate when they're away," Layne was rather sad to hear the truth that they might not be good enough just yet.

"You did alright, but maybe we can't lose so many starters at the same time yet. At the end of the day we literally had an under 18 team playing against their under 23's, it wasn't meant to be easy. But let's not dwell on it for too long. Have you packed everything yet?"

The couple were moving to their new apartment the week after. They had been living with the host family for over a year so they had built up quite a lot of belongings.

"I'm nearly there, but if we miss anything I can always go back afterwards," Layne was quite relaxed about it. "Don't you over plan again – it's not like a million miles away."

That was Layne's favourite phrase recently, he got a little impatient with Richard's meticulous planning on literally everything. The other current favourite was "get a life".

A few days later it was Richard's eighteenth birthday. He had made it a tradition for him and his friends to have a Brazilian barbecue to celebrate. The team returned to the restaurant in Kingston riverside and he had Layne, Charlie, Tom, Danny, Owen, Ollie, Rob, Baek-min, Alex and Peter as guests. Thomas was invited but he had to stay home at the last minute to look after Elle who wasn't well.

Richard and Owen had become friends since the beginning of the league campaign. Owen saw Richard's training with Alex and asked if they could do something similar. It was very challenging as the team's best dribbler took on the best defender and they both learnt a lot from it – Richard was able to win about half the duels.

He had also spent plenty of time with Baek-min, who was the other expert on defending one on one. They shared ideas on those as well as food – the London-born South Korean was a keen advocate of his country's cuisine and urged Richard to experience some at the nearby New Malden, which was known as the base of Koreans in London, if not the UK.

During the meal the group talked about how things had changed in a year, most of them were now professional footballers while they were just on their scholarship contracts with no certainty of a career in their favourite sport back then.

The quality of food was as good as the year before and the team once again enjoyed their unlimited meat selections.

Charlie said he was going to throw a party for him with some strippers "now that he's an adult" but Tom stopped him citing Richard was "such a serious person he'd hate a party like that". Richard thanked Tom saying that would indeed be awkward. He did have a couple of shots plus a few beers though – Charlie wasn't going to let him off those. He had his usual "nap" afterwards but woke up feeling fine a little while later. He amazed his friends as he returned to eating mode and had a few more steaks from the staff.

The night had gone quickly – Layne had a few naughty drinks as well and Richard had to carry him back to the Stevenson's.

"Open the door!" he shouted as they arrived.

"How could you get so drunk, baby?"

"Hehe, I'm so happy to be with you, Richie!"

"Me too silly, come on in."

As soon as they entered the house Layne started kissing Richard. He pushed and dragged him upstairs into Richard's bedroom and onto the bed.

"We have training tomorrow," said Richard as he put up a weak resistance.

"Oh come on don't worry about it. You're supposed to get a stripper so here I am!" said the young one before he started to undress.

Richard had all his disciplines in his head, but he also had the love of his life here kissing him passionately. His heart was beating at an unsustainable level and he felt like having non-stop electric shocks – all in a good way.

He gave in and answered the young one's request, "Go on then, to your heart's desire."

Training was a disaster the next morning.

Naturally, Richard had little energy after just a few hours' sleep. The worst was that he also pulled his groin muscle half an hour into it and had to go off.

"Oh no, not Richard 'The Saint'!" Charlie laughed. "Did you call the strippers in after dinner?"

Everyone came around to ask Layne, "Did you hear anything last night?"

"I have nothing to say," said Layne with a "I know but I won't tell" impression.

Tom didn't say anything, he just looked at Layne with an evil smile.

Rachel, the physio in her mid-twenties who started working with the team that day, took Richard to the side and did some checks on him. She said quietly, "It's okay, just a bit of tiredness. It happens a lot with you youngsters... I suppose you had a lot of fun last night?"

Richard went completely blushed and couldn't squeeze out a response. He lay down covering his face and wished the ground could just swallow him up.

"I know that's very difficult for you guys to not do it all the time, just don't overdo it, okay?"

Richard sheepishly nodded, he was far too embarrassed to make any eye contact.

Layne didn't fare much better. He wasn't able to run at full speed and was off colour the whole time – but at least he didn't catch the team's attention like Richard.

The pair had their goodbye dinner at the Stevenson's that evening. As their relationship was known by the host couple they didn't need to hide. Mr and Mrs Stevenson knew both of them well and were happy for them. Richard got to taste Mrs Stevenson's lovely fish pie again – possibly for the last time but the boys promised they would visit in the future.

"Do you know what Andrew asked me at school today?" Layne asked as they went back to Richard's room.

"What can he ask you? Isn't he better than you in studies?"

"No... he asked if I'm no longer a virgin!"

"How did he know? You didn't walk around telling everybody about us, right?"

"I didn't! I asked him why, and he said I looked different – in training and in school."

"It's true you haven't trained well this morning, you ran differently..."

"That's your fault! At least I didn't pull my muscle... Did you see Tom's face when you went down?"

"Oh no – I guess he might have figured out about it?"

"He just looked at me with a dodgy smile. I denied all knowledge."

"I guess that's the way to deal with it... did you tell Andrew then?"

"No I didn't, but he didn't seem convinced."

"Maybe he sussed it out from experience? Does he know you're not into girls?"

"He does... I told him a little while ago."

"I guess he knows about me and you then, as we will be living together?"

"Well it's a matter of time. Hey have you recovered yet? Shall we continue where we left off?" Layne asked a cheeky question.

"You never had enough baby! I'd love to, but we have training again tomorrow!"

"I wouldn't want it if it wasn't you... how about me taking the lead and make you feel good?"

"Oh you are so sweet! I'll enjoy the treat then," Richard smiled.

And they giggled away into another fun night.

Richard picked up the keys to the new apartment after training the next day. He didn't have lessons that day and he managed to get Tom to help him move a car full of boxes and bags. The apartment was fully furnished so it was ready to live in. It had two double bedrooms with one en-suite, an open plan kitchen and living area with a balcony overlooking River Thames and Ravens Ait Island.

"This is a great place, Rich. David must be paying you well if you can afford all of these on your own!" Tom was impressed.

"Don't be silly – I don't think my contract is any better than yours. Layne's mum is helping out with his share," Richard was desperate to explain.

"Oh yeah he's a rich boy, isn't he? Lucky you!" Tom teased.

"He's good, I won't deny that," Richard replied with a little smile. He chose not to rub it in by mentioning that Mrs Moore actually offered to buy an apartment for them to live in.

He then told Tom about the conversation he had with David. While Tom was keen to point out that he didn't tell anyone, he was glad that the club had stuck to its motto of being inclusive.

"Have you told your parents about it? How did they react?" Tom brought it up.

"I haven't yet. I think I know how they would react."

"By your impression I guess they won't approve? That would be tricky. How do you want to go about it?"

"I think I'll just keep quiet until I have to tell them – officially Layne and I are just housemates here."

"That can't be easy, good luck with that mate."

Tom left shortly afterwards and Richard was alone in the apartment. Layne wouldn't be back from tuitions for a few hours. He put some of Layne's items, including the giant polar bear, into "his bedroom" and started unpacking

181

others to where he thought was appropriate – he knew Layne would change them all later but he just wanted to see how different their preferences could be.

Richard picked Layne up from school hours later and drove straight back to the apartment.

"Welcome to our new home!" he said as he walked in holding Layne's hand.

"It's beautiful – thanks for sorting it out, Richie," said Layne before he gave Richard a kiss.

The pair unpacked the rest of their belongings for a little while before going for a walk along the river, all the way to Kingston Bridge and back down the other side of the river. Layne really liked the scenery there and he took lots of pictures of themselves with the lights from Hampton Court Palace as their background.

"Will you give me a kiss here in this beautiful place, Richie?" he asked softly.

"Of course," said Richard after checking if there was anyone around.

Richard felt wonderful – he really loved the boy in front and was so grateful that they could be together. The pair held their hands on the walk back – not one passer-by noticed in the dark, or maybe no one really cared.

They spent the rest of the evening finishing off any loose ends and as Richard expected, Layne changed the location of almost every item in the apartment. He framed up lots of photographs and there would be one in every corner.

Richard received a call from Tom when he was on his house duties one late afternoon.

"Hey Rich, are you and Layne free tonight? My mate's 7-a-side team are a few players short."

"When? Layne's having a nap but I guess he won't say no to more football."

"Kick off is at seven so you have plenty of time. I'll ask Danny too."

"Okay count us in… wait, are we allowed to play by the club?"

"Probably not but I'm sure we'll be fine, just be careful and don't get injured."

The pair got to the astro turf centre near Wimbledon and met Tom, Danny and their team for the night. Team captain Addy was having a nightmare with the number of absentees and he begged his school friend Tom to help. His team were bottom of the league and couldn't afford a forfeit, especially against another team fighting against relegation.

The other two players Sean and Manual were Addy's work colleagues and played in goal and upfront respectively. Richard played in defence alongside the captain with Layne, Tom and Danny in midfield.

The other team also had a couple of ringers – they were twin brothers Jesse and Samuel. Tom recognised them from previous encounters.

"The blonde twins over there are from Hounslow, Jesse is in midfield and Sam is a left footed attacker," he told Richard. "Don't underestimate them, they are really good."

The team from Hounslow were a local rival to the Black Dragons in both League One and the Championship and the youngsters were part of their newly established B team that replaced their academy at the beginning of the season. The club decided to pull out of the Professional Development League and arranged their own friendly matches instead, as they believed that to be a better way to keep and develop their young talents.

The hour-long match started and Richard was up against Sam soon after. Richard placed more emphasis on his opponent's stronger left foot to prevent him from taking a shot, but he skilfully dragged the ball in field using the inside of his foot before flipping it back to his left to create an opening. Richard lost his footing by that lightning quick move but managed to stick out a foot to divert the shot wide when he was on the ground.

That was some skill – his feet are extremely quick, he thought.

The two had another duel minutes later. Sam ran towards Richard at speed and attempted a Marseille turn, or a double drag-back. Luckily, it was one of Owen's favourite tricks and Richard was able to see that coming. He went down to block the ball from moving forward and sent Sam tumbling onto the turf. He then drove a low ball forward to Danny on the left, who opened the scoring with a sweet left foot volley.

"You're pretty decent," Sam said as he walked back to his half for the kick off.

The match resumed and Sam was on the attack again. But this time he opted for a quick pass and move with his brother instead. His pace took him ahead of Richard for the perfectly angled return pass and he sent the ball past Sean first time to equalise. It looked rather easy but that was the nature of the smaller-sized game – the key was the movements in both attack and defence, and goals were inevitable.

The two teams had a fairly even game and it was 6-6 after forty five minutes. Danny scored a hat trick and the rest came from Tom, Layne and Manual. The twins were responsible for four of the goals.

The game was played on the large court and its high quality attracted a sizeable crown. The spectators were cheering on both sides and the players wowed them with their skills, movements and finishes.

Richard was in the middle of defence when one of the amateur players approached him with multiple step overs. He instinctively slid in to tackle, sending the player flying in the process. He then saw the space in front of him and put his right foot through it for a powerful shot from the halfway line. The ball rocketed straight into the back of the net and the crown went wild – they were mesmerised by what they were watching!

"Bloody hell Rich, you're doing this for real!" Tom said.

"It's all or nothing, as always," Richard said with his serious face on.

The teams traded two more goals each afterwards and the game ended 9-8 to Richard's side. The players celebrated passionately and the crowd applauded their performance.

"What a game! I've never enjoyed it so much!" said Manual, who scored both of the last goals to complete his own hat trick.

"You guys brought the very best out of us," said Addy.

"It wasn't fair. You have four professionals and we only had two!" the captain of the other team joked.

"That was great fun, Dragons. I hope we'll play you in a full game one day," said Sam as he shook hands with Richard. "You must be 'The Unbeatable'?"

"Please don't call me that. I'm sure we'll meet again."

The overjoyed Addy gathered the players and offered everyone a drink from the bar. He knew he invited professional players to help but he didn't think it would improve his own level by that much.

"You guys pushed us to the limits. You never stopped running and telling us where to move. I'm completely knackered!" he said.

"It's good that you enjoyed it, I did too," said Tom.

"Can we take these snoods off now? It's boiling hot!" Layne had been complaining about the disguise the whole night.

"I guess so, now that we're not playing," Richard said.

"I hope the club doesn't find out about tonight," Danny said.

"I'm sure we'll be fine," Tom said confidently.

"Oh wait, the venue has posted a video of Richie's screamer online already!" said Layne. "No names were mentioned though."

"Sorry if I got you guys into trouble," Addy apologised, "but you did save my life – can I get you some drinks?"

"I'll have a pint but I'm sure these guys are on water only," Tom said.

"I would love a beer if possible?" Layne asked.

"I'm sorry mate, you looked far too young. The centre will have issues with that," said Addy.

"Oh well, water then…"

"Shall we go for some food instead? I'm starving," asked Danny. "Layne can also have his drink with the meal."

"What a plan Danny!" Layne agreed.

"Sounds good! How about the cheeky chicken place in New Malden?" Sean suggested.

"Great idea! Let's go!" Addy concluded.

At the popular chain restaurant, Richard went for his usual of four boneless chicken thighs with two portions of spicy rice. He put everything neatly into one plate, with plenty of hot sauce on top.

"You made it look like a chicken katsu curry again," Layne was impressed.

"I like it this way. How's your half chicken with salad?"

"Good! It goes down so well with the Portuguese lager!"

The team had a good time with their post-match discussion. They were impressed by the twins and wondered how they would develop under their club's new B team structure.

David and the club did actually notice the players' involvement in the 7-a-side game but they decided to give them a verbal warning only. He reminded them that they were not allowed to take part in sports that may cause them injuries. The players accepted the warning and apologised.

"If you don't want us to find out then don't score worldies in front of cameras!" David jokingly said at the end.

"It's all your fault, Rich," Tom agreed.

"I can't help it…" Richard shrugged his shoulders.

12.

Winter

The under 23 team's next game was at home against the club from the Welsh capital. David was able to pick a strong team with the majority of players back in contention, except Max who was still out injured.

Following the last defeat, additional training had been put in place on pressing as a team. There were gaps in that 5-0 drubbing and they needed to be closed. The coaching team also looked at how the team could control the pace of the game better so that they could maintain their stamina for the whole ninety minutes.

The players put their training into practice and with a far more settled side, they dictated the game and won convincingly 4-1. Owen scored another hat trick and Alex settled it at the end with the fourth, set up by Richard's first assist for the team. The other team preferred playing out from the back, which made the high press by the Black Dragons even more effective, often gaining possession deep in the final third.

The team had another game the week after, which was a trip to Nottinghamshire. The substitute Paul rescued a draw late on from a delightful pass from Tom for a 1-1 draw. They fell behind from a corner kick at the half hour mark but while they had opportunities throughout the game from gaining possession high up the pitch, they couldn't convert them until Paul struck the equaliser.

Richard had his first one to one session with his mentor, the 34-year-old midfielder general and club captain Michael Carter. The model professional and local hero joined the club from the age of eight and made his senior debut when he was only sixteen. He succeeded Charlie's father Miles as captain when he retired and played a massive part in the club's run of promotions with over 500 appearances.

Richard had a really meaningful time with him. When he asked him for his secret in being so calm on the ball in midfield, he said the key was being aware of the space around him and to have confidence in his own skills. He pointed out after watching Richard's games that one thing he could work on was his close controls to get out of tricky situations – maybe a turn, a dribble or a faint. The ability to create space and time for a pass. Richard took his advice on board and arranged additional training with Tim the Technical Coach.

The last match of the calendar year was a massive friendly against the under 23 side of a top Premier League team from north London. Given the profile of the visiting side the club had arranged the game to be played at The Dragons Stadium, which would be a first for many of the youngsters.

"Did you hear that the game next week will be played at The Dragons?" Tom said to Richard, Charlie, Danny and Thomas during lunch after training.

"Is the refurbishment completed? Will there be supporters?" Richard asked.

"Yes they are selling tickets, there should be hundreds if not more. Has anyone played in front of a proper crowd before?"

"The biggest crowd I faced was against the west London club in the FA Youth Cup last year, but I don't remember much of it apart from Steve's injury," Thomas recalled.

"I did with the England under 19's. It's great if you're playing well," Charlie said.

"I guess the home fans will just support us, right? They can't be too critical?" Richard was being hopeful.

"Isn't the team from north London the one you supported as a child? No pressure Richard!" said Danny.

"Thanks Danny – I used to idolise their midfield maestro, shame he moved on to play for the west London side afterwards."

"It'll be a great chance for us to make ourselves known to the supporters. With the stadium work done, we'll have another five league games hosted there as part of the PDL's rules. Maybe they'll start buying our shirts!" Tom said.

"Who wants to put number 48 Nelson on their back?" Thomas joked.

"Says Mr 45 Bond!" Tom returned some friendly fire.

The group laughed. They were all given official squad numbers in the forties, except Charlie who got number 38 and Layne who had 57. But when they played for the under 23 team they just shared the team shirts with one to twenty on the back.

Soon it was match day. Richard had visited the first team dressing room during his introduction but he was now there using it. His locker of the day had a shirt with his favourite number sixteen hanging on it. It felt so real – and the team were playing the mighty Reds.

David had named nearly the same team from the previous match, with the only change being Thomas replacing Thorsten. Max was back in the squad but wasn't quite ready to start.

In his pre-match team talk, David stressed again the importance of the high press. The team did it well in the last two games and he wanted them to do it again, this time against a team much better in retaining the ball and pressing high themselves.

"You have to be on top of your game today, Rich and Tom. Your ability to keep possession under pressure will be the key to victory. Everybody else, keep moving and make yourselves available for those two. Let's go and make yourselves a name out there!"

"Fly, you Black Dragons!!"

The team walked onto the pitch to warm welcome from the fans. Richard had a good look around the stands – it was quiet during warm up but there must have been over a thousand fans now. They were seated in the lower sections of all but the Family Stand, which was kept empty, and they sang the famous club anthem. The match day

189

announcer read out the names of the youngsters and the fans responded with a cheer after each and every one.

"So this is how it feels!" Tom said to Richard. "My blood is boiling!"

"Yes, let's win it for them," Richard wasn't a boyhood fan of the Black Dragons like Tom and Charlie but he loved the club and would do anything for them.

The match began. With the boost in spirit the team started the brighter side, putting enormous pressure on the ball and pushing forward when they got it.

They took the lead after fifteen minutes. Lewis's brilliant run on the left set Danny up for a shot but it was deflected wide. Richard's corner was flicked on by Les at the near post and Thomas was able to calmly swept it in from close range. He celebrated his first goal for the under 23's in front of overjoyed fans in the West Stand.

The young Black Dragons created another chance quickly afterwards as their high pressing brought success again. Alex cut out a pass from the goal keeper, played a quick one-two with Danny and sent Charlie through, who hit a measured left foot shot first time into the top corner for 2-0.

Richard joined the action with a dipping shot from far out but it was tipped over by the keeper at full stretch. The away team's only chance came late in the half, as Tom's mistake in midfield led to a shot but it was well saved by Josh.

The Reds started the second half strongly and they forced the Black Dragons into the back foot, having to pass around more without creating any chances. Richard's specific training on space awareness and tight control paid dividends as he was able to find enough time to plan and measure his moves even though he and Tom were made to work really hard in the middle. The team also did their part as they moved around tirelessly to offer them options.

The Black Dragons finally settled the match twenty minutes later with a third goal. Richard sent Owen through on the right with a high ball, and his cross was converted expertly on the volley by Alex. The home crowd went wild – the score line was way beyond their expectations!

With the team three goals up and twenty-five minutes remaining, David made some changes and brought Kasper and Max on to replace the tiring Richard and Charlie. The move seemed to have slowed the team's momentum and they conceded five minutes later. The tall left-footed centre midfielder Toby cut inside and sent the striker through to score.

The goal sent the Black Dragons into a bit of disarray and soon they conceded a second one – their hesitations in defence gifted possession to the visitors and the impressive Toby fired it into the bottom corner from outside the area.

David sent Layne on to replace Alex to make it five at the back. He wanted to an option out wide while keeping enough defenders at the back. The team regained their composure and managed to close the game out without further scares.

The crowd appreciated the young side's efforts and the team celebrated as they sang the winning tune. David was pleased with how they pressed as a unit and also their ability to finish their chances.

That was that for the calendar year. The team got two weeks off for Christmas, apart from Lewis and Les, who had been called into the first team squad as covers for the festive fixtures.

Richard and Layne went home separately for Christmas. Layne really wanted Richard to join him at his family home in Bath but he insisted that he should stay with his parents. He would visit Layne during the week between Christmas and New Year instead.

Since he was living the dreams of playing professional football and being with Layne, Richard had become more positive and cheerful. He smiled more often and spoke in a more friendly way, instead of his old, robot like, monotone. His parents especially his mum picked up on that and were happy for him, which eased a bit of the tension from switching away from full time education to the hybrid model. Richard was fearful of telling them about Layne and just kept it under wraps. The family of three had a joyful Christmas, one that Richard didn't have for ages.

Two days after Christmas, Richard drove to Bath to visit Layne and his mum. Mrs Moore had taken the time off and Richard was meeting her for the first time. He learnt from Layne a while ago that she knew about their relationship and was happy for him. He could only wish his parents were the same.

Richard arrived at Layne's family home just after midday. It was a lovely Georgian house backing into a large field. Richard drove past a private school nearby and imagined that must be the one Layne went to. An excited Layne was there waiting at the door, with a lovely smile on his face.

"Hey, Merry Christmas!" Richard got off the car and gave Layne a big cuddle.

"It's strange not seeing you for a week. Did you miss me?"

The two continued to have their little chat before Richard noticed that Mrs Moore had also come to the door to meet him.

"Hello Mrs Moore. Nice to meet you," Richard gently shrugged off Layne to formally meet his mum.

"Hi Richard, you can call me Jane, it's easier that way," she said with a welcoming smile before giving Richard a hug. "Come on in!"

Richard went inside the house and noticed straight away that the interior was heavily influenced by the Chinese culture – there were paintings, writings, furniture and other decorative items such as vases and teapots. He knew that Layne's maternal grandfather was originally from Hong Kong but wasn't expecting his home to be a mini museum.

"These are very nice. Were they from Hong Kong?" he was impressed by models of some old-fashioned fishing boats.

"Yes they were from my granddad ages ago," Layne said.

"What do the characters say here? Are these traditional or simplified?" Richard asked, as he hadn't noticed any signs that Layne knew the language before.

"I haven't got a clue! They're so complicated. Mum knows."

Richard sensed that Layne was behaving even more like a child when he was home.

After a tour of the exhibitions, Richard joined Layne and his mum for lunch. Looking at the variety of food on the table, Richard was certain that Mrs Moore knew about his eating habit as well as ability. There were multiple roasted meats and vegetables, with a perfectly blended gravy.

Richard and Layne had a walk after lunch. Layne took him up the hill to see where he used to play football and the various fields owned by the school. They then strolled towards the city centre for the Christmas market. Similar to the year before at the Winter Wonderland, Layne had a good time on the ice rink and Richard had his with the food stalls – sausages, hog roast and some Dutch pancakes.

They had some homemade mulled wine with Mrs Moore before they said good night. She asked if Richard would be staying in the guest room but Layne reacted quickly with a big "no way". The look on her face made Richard rather embarrassed – she wasn't angry, she just looked as if she was asking Richard "how dare you?".

"I thought your mum was going to punch me there," Richard whispered to Layne when they tiptoed into his room.

"For making me a grown up?" Layne giggled. "There's no way I won't have you here, I miss having you around at night."

"Same here, it's so strange to be sleeping alone."

"Let's cuddle up in bed then!" said Layne as he started kissing Richard like he normally did at their flat.

"Are you sure it's a good idea? Do we need to keep our noise down?"

"Hehe, maybe you can tune it down a little bit," Layne whispered. "I've been waiting for this moment since I was young."

"As in doing it right here on your bed?"

"Yes!"

The pair quitted their little chat and enjoyed their moment.

Richard and Layne went for a run in the hills the next morning. When they returned, Mrs Moore had already cooked up a full English breakfast, which was exactly what Richard wanted after the exercise.

"There's a reason why you are not as fit as Danny," Layne gave him an accusatory stare.

"I only eat as much as Tom and Charlie," Richard tried to defend his habit.

"But they work so much harder in the gym!"

"Alright, I'll have one less sausage then…"

"You two actually sound like an old couple," Mrs Moore was smiling at them. "Just help yourself Richard, I'm sure you'll be fine."

After breakfast, Mrs Moore asked Layne to make way so that she could have some time with Richard.

"Time with the barrister!" said Layne as he walked away.

Richard knew Layne's mum would want to talk to him, just like any other mum would. He was prepared, but it was still a bit frightening to be quizzed by a former barrister, especially when she seemed to be serious and got her little notebook out.

"So, when did you and Layne become together?" she started with a simple question.

"Since July, when we went to Bournemouth."

"What do you like about him?"

"He's so cheerful and… comfortable to be with? We share many interests and hobbies. He brings me lots of fun and a peacefulness that no one else does. He is uncomplicated and he allows me to be myself without all the calculations. Does it make sense?" Richard had never put his feelings together this way.

"I can understand that, that boy is still very simple minded. How do you see yourselves in the future? With football and without?"

"I wish we can progress in football, that's my, and I think our, aim at the moment. But if not, I would go to University to read Maths. I'm taking my A-level exams next year."

"That's good," she seemed a little impressed. "My worry is that you two will find it difficult in the cruel and macho world of football, as you would only be the one percent of all footballers."

"I am well aware of that. We haven't experienced anything nasty so far but my intention is to stay as low profile as possible for as long as possible so that Layne doesn't get exposed to that side of things. But if it does become difficult I'm sure we'll support each other to overcome it."

"Very well. It's good that Layne has managed to meet someone like you. My boy may be sixteen but deep down he's just a child living in fantasy. Do look after him, he's probably not the easiest to live with, for a mathematician."

"I will," Richard with a firm answer, but couldn't help smiling at the last comment.

Mrs Moore went on to ask if Richard's parents knew about them and felt sorry for him when he said they didn't and were unlikely to approve. She said she knew about Layne's sexuality since he entered adolescence and would always support him. She was worried that he'd get hurt in the real world but she was relieved after meeting and speaking with Richard.

Richard found Layne in the drawing room where he was playing some Christmas songs on the grand piano.

"I know you can play the piano but never imagine you to be this good!" he praised when Layne completed his latest song.

"I used to play a lot before I joined the Black Dragons. It's so nice to get my hands on this again."

"Did you take any exams for it?"

"I passed grade 8 before my fifteenth birthday. I don't think I would go for performance grade."

"I'm impressed! We should get a piano at our place then!"

"Maybe not, we can only fit an electric one in and that's no substitute for a proper one."

"But isn't it a shame that you cannot continue playing?"

"It's okay, I'll focus on football for now. Hey how did it go with mum? Is she happy with you?"

"I guess I've passed the test!"

"I knew you would, now come over here," said Layne as he pulled Richard over for a kiss. "Have a seat, I'll play you some of my favourite pieces."

He started with a couple of classicals; before playing "Call Your Name" by Hiroyuki Sawano, one of the theme songs of their favourite anime Attack on Titan; and finally surprised Richard when he played and sang one of his favourite songs, "Talking to the Moon", a powerful ballad about a failed relationship by Bruno Mars.

Richard was really touched by the performance as it reminded him the period when he was unable to tell Layne how he felt about him. He held onto his young partner tightly at the end of the song and said, "This is beautiful. I used to hope that you were the one talking to me from the other side of the moon."

"When I was merely on the other side of the wall," Layne chuckled.

"It's so good that it works out at the end."

"It is," said Layne as he gave Richard another kiss. "Shall we head out now?"

Layne planned to take Richard out for a tour of Bath. Richard had only visited the city once before and that was ages ago. He couldn't remember visiting the city centre or the various tourist attractions.

They started by walking to Lansdown Crescent nearby, before heading to the famous Royal Crescent. Layne said it had always been his dream to be walking the green there with his future boyfriend, and he grabbed Richard's hand when they arrived there. Richard felt a little uneasy to start but he didn't want to let go.

"Would you give me a kiss here, Richie?" Layne whispered.

"Here? In public?" Richard was a bit nervous.

"We did it back in Bournemouth and Hampton, didn't we?"

"But they were in the dark!"

"We're holding hands under broad daylight anyway, we may as well? I'll take the lead!" he said before moving in to kiss Richard on the lips.

Richard was worried about being seen by others but once Layne was there he couldn't resist – the pair kissed for a good minute or two.

"Thanks for making my dream come true!" said Layne with a lovely smile.

They moved on to the city centre to see the Roman Baths, Bath Abbey and the Parade Gardens. They stopped by the famous bakery that Layne bought a bun for Richard the year before for a light lunch.

They walked along the river before returning to the city centre for dinner. Layne had a table booked at an award-winning Italian restaurant and they had a lovely meal, even though the portion wasn't exactly to Richard's liking.

The pair had a few more relaxing days in Bath before heading back to south west London for the resumption of the season.

A week after the winter break, Richard's parents visited his apartment after training. They arranged with Richard a couple of days beforehand so he had time to prepare – he needed to put Layne's items back to "his room" as well as hide all their pictures.

His parents arrived in the middle of the afternoon, which was perfect as Layne was having tuitions. They had a little tour and were impressed.

Richard was keen to minimise their time there so he suggested to have afternoon tea at a popular cafe in nearby Ham. His mum was looking forward to it as she read about their dishes with edible flowers and the plant-filled glasshouse.

Just before they left, Mr Lucas senior went looking for the bathroom and accidentally opened the door to Layne's room. He spotted the pictures of the pair on the wall and he was not happy with his discovery.

"Who is this pretty boy that you're house sharing with?" he confronted Richard while holding one of the pictures. "What exactly is your relationship with him?"

Richard thought for a little while before he decided to go all out – he believed he had nothing to hide.

"His name is Layne, and he is my boyfriend."

"How dare you? How can you let us down again like that? I thought you've changed after what happened in Munich three years ago! You were dating a girl earlier this year! Why can't you just carry on, get married, have a few kids and be a normal person?" his father shouted while he forcefully threw the picture away. "Oh God forgive us!"

Richard picked up the broken picture and explained, "I tried and it didn't work. I can't lock up my feelings and pretend to have a so-called normal life just to be a son for you to be proud of. I'll be living with regrets forever!"

"How are we going to tell our friends and families of this shame?"

"Just tell them the truth. For once I want to do something for myself. It is my life after all!"

"Why can't you just listen to your dad? You don't have to carry on like this," his mum asked, with tears on her eyes.

"No way! I love Layne more than anyone and there's no way I would give him up!"

"What do you like about him? He's a boy, for goodness' sake!" his father challenged, with his hands on Richard's shoulders.

"Everything!" Richard raised his voice while pushing his hands away. "He understands me and allows me to be true to myself! I don't need to live with a mask on."

"But you can't love a boy, it's forbidden!"

198

"Says who? We're not doing anything wrong. We aren't harming anyone. Why can't we genuinely love each other in our own little world?" Richard asked, in despair.

"Whatever you say, we're not going to accept it – I hope you'll think it through and do the right thing," concluded his father before turning to his mum. "We're leaving."

"You just don't understand…" Richard was talking to himself as his parents left the apartment. His mum did turn around and gave him a sad and helpless look.

His worst fear had been realised. The day he dreaded all along. The conflict between his parents' believes and his true feelings. He had to choose between his parents and Layne. He made the choice, but half of him was now lost.

Why can't all parents be as open minded as Layne's mum?

Why can't they just accept what their children were and love them regardless?

Why was all that happening to him?

He was close to breaking point. Every moment of his life was flashing back into his head, good times and bad times, like a whirlwind into his mind. He didn't know what to do next. He lay on the sofa with a head full of anger, but it soon turned into sorrow. He may not have the best relationships with his dad, but he did value him being there and cutting ties broke his heart into pieces. He eventually passed out after exhausting himself emotionally.

"Hey Richie, are you okay? Why are you sleeping on the sofa? What happened? Did you cry? Oh dear…" Layne asked nervously when he found a distraught Richard.

"My parents found out about us…"

"I… I guess they didn't like it? But don't worry, you've got me here," Layne said as he helped Richard up and gave him a hug.

Layne's comment touched Richard's heartstrings and he broke down on his shoulder, "I don't want to lose them!"

"Don't say that. They… they'll understand eventually."

"Will they?"

"Yes! They are your parents after all, they would come around, trust me!"

"You're all I've got now!"

"It's okay Richie, don't worry," Layne kept comforting him by stroking his hair.

Richard didn't say anything else, he just held on to Layne as tightly as he could. He needed his warmth. He needed his support. He needed him.

"You'll be fine, Richie. I'm here, don't worry," Layne said gently.

13.

The Brawl

The under 23 team played two matches since the winter break: a comfortable 2-0 win at home and a goalless draw on the road. Goals by Max and Danny settled the home game against a club from north west London, while a solid defence wasn't enough for a win in West Yorkshire. Richard didn't play the first game as David noticed that he wasn't there mentally and he only played the last half hour in the second match.

Richard had reverted back into his quiet and emotionless way since his argument with his parents. He would break into a better mood when Layne was around but he would retreat into his shell otherwise. His friends noticed it and they sent Tom to check him out.

He grabbed Richard for a coffee after training one day and asked how he was doing. He thought there might be an argument between him and Layne but they seemed closer than ever. Richard told Tom the story and that he didn't need to be worried – he was getting over it. He never thought his parents would accept his relationship anyway so it was just a realisation of something he expected. But since the argument he felt that there was a hole in his heart and it made him rather sad.

The next fixture was an away trip across the capital to a club in south east London. Richard learnt from Tom that James Barton their former teammate in midfield joined them recently. Richard was not expecting a warm welcome as James accused him of stealing his place when he was released by the Black Dragons.

It was match day Saturday and the team had travelled to the training ground of this south east London club.

James was waiting outside the away dressing room to meet his old teammates. He shook hands with the likes of Tom, Owen and Paul but he purposefully looked away when Richard and Layne came close. Richard could feel the hostility – it wouldn't be an easy game.

David chose to start with Jack in goal, Viktor, Lewis, Thomas and Les in defence, Richard, Tom and Max in midfield and Charlie, Owen and Danny upfront. He wanted the team to continue their high pressing game with quick transitional plays.

Richard reassured David during the week that he was ready to play and his efforts in training also justified that. He believed that by concentrating on football completely he could forget the outside world for a while.

The match started. Richard could see that the home team was playing in a traditional 4-4-2 formation, with James as one of the two central midfielders.

He soon came up against Richard in midfield and he said, "I'll show you who the better player is today."

"I won't go easy, that's for sure," Richard replied.

James attempted to take on Richard with a couple of shimmies but the steady defensive shape of Richard made it too risky him to push through and he passed the ball backwards. The same pattern happened continuously through the half – James simply knew that he couldn't beat Richard.

The teams didn't have many goal scoring opportunities and the half ended in a stalemate.

"You're as annoying as you've ever been," James grumbled to Richard as they walked off the pitch.

"Just doing my job," said Richard, who had been emotionless since the start.

"Football is about scoring goals; it doesn't care about those man-marking other players."

"I wasn't even marking you. Maybe you think too much of yourself."

"And it is this attitude that makes me hate you the most! Don't you think you're superior just because the coaches liked your sucking up!"

"I didn't get to decide who stayed at the club, but I trust the coaches' decision."

"I'll sort you out right here!" James got angry and he gave Richard a hefty shove. Richard nearly lost his footing but he found his balance and stood firm.

"Back off!" Layne jumped in between the two. "What are you trying to do?"

"We'll settle on the pitch," James walked off with a gesture to suggest he had his eyes on Layne too.

"What is it between you and James?" Tom asked Richard back in the dressing room.

"I don't know. He seems to think that it's me who got him released by the club, and it's my fault that he couldn't get through the middle today," Richard shrugged his shoulders.

"Just be careful when you're out there. He has a pretty short fuse," Tom warned.

The second half kicked off and Richard noticed James had moved deeper in midfield as his team switched to a 4-5-1 formation. It suited him fine as he could focus on the forward who was now playing as an attacking midfielder.

However, he spotted a pattern soon that the centre backs always passed to James to spread the play. Max seemed to have noticed it too and he moved in to close him down. Richard saw a chance to double up on him and quietly sneaked up the other side of Max.

He predicted James's turn away from Max and picked his pocket. James dived into a sliding tackle straight away but Richard lifted the ball up and jumped over his challenge.

With James out of the way, Richard passed the ball to Owen on the right and ran into the space in front. Owen chipped it first time into that area behind the centre backs and Richard was clean through on goal. He calmly measured his side-footed shot into the bottom left corner to score his first goal for the under 23's. He ran over to the bench to celebrate with David and Layne.

"Great goal Rich!" Layne could be heard screaming from the side lines. "That'll show him!"

That comment seemed to have put even more hatred into James. He left his foot in for a couple of challenges on Richard but luckily he evaded both unscathed.

Twenty minutes into the second half and David sent Layne on to replace Lewis, who had a slight knock.

Just as he normally would, he ran into space on the left and received the ball from Thomas. He played a one-two with Max and continue his run into the final third.

Richard noticed James making a rapid run towards that area and he had a really bad feeling. As if it was in slow motion, he saw James launching himself into where Layne was running to with both feet off the ground.

"Layne, jump!!" he shouted anxiously.

But it was too late. James had made contact with Layne and sent him flying.

"That'll show you, little prick," he said to Layne, who was rolling on the ground, clearly in a lot of pain.

Seeing Layne suffer, Richard felt a flame lit inside his body. Together with all the negative thoughts he had been having recently the rage got the better of him. He lost his temper. He charged into James at full speed and sent him tumbling to the ground.

"What have you done to him?" Richard shouted.

James stood back up and tried to fight back. Richard dodged his punch and pushed him over again. The other players came over quickly and held Richard back. James got back on his feet again but he was shoved away by Tom when he ran towards Richard.

Players from both sides joined in and it was becoming a brawl with lots of pushing and shoving.

Richard was being pulled back by Thomas and Danny and when he wiggled his way out to challenge James again Owen came over and said, "Calm down, Richard. You don't need to beat him up."

"I won't let anyone hurt MY LAYNE!" he said loudly.

Players from both teams went completely quiet, clearly shocked by what they heard.

After a period of silence, James pointed at Richard and laughed, "I knew it! I knew from that day that you two are fucking gay! You're not the angel that everyone loves, you are just a child fiddler!"

Richard was stunned. But before he could react to James's vile comment, Charlie punched him in the face and knocked him down.

"Don't you dare talking to my friends like that!" he stared at James.

"Standing up for your queer boys now Charlie, well done!" James said with a few sarcastic claps.

The referee wasn't far from the incident and rushed over to stop Charlie going for more. He showed him a straight red card and ordered him to leave the pitch immediately. He then gave Richard his marching order for his part in the melee. He finished off with issuing James a yellow card for his initial challenge on Layne and then others for their involvement in the brawl. Richard stayed by Layne until the physios put him on a stretcher and took him off the pitch. He seemed to feel better after all the spray the physios managed to get onto him.

"Cheerio for the gay hero!" James mocked as Richard walked off. Some of his teammates laughed and added some wolf whistles.

Richard felt deeply ashamed. He felt lonely. Another fear of him had been realised. He walked straight pass the bench for the dressing room – David was saying something but he didn't hear any of it. He didn't want to face anyone. He just wanted to shut down. How could the world be so cruel?

Tom and Les complained to the referee about the homophobic remarks that James and the others made. The referee and his assistants said they didn't hear them and asked the teams to restart instead, and the incident could be reported to the FA later. Tom went to the bench and after a lengthy discussion with David he told the referee that the team would not continue with the game – they would walk off to protest the lack of actions. The referee said it would go down as a forfeit by the Black Dragons.

The team returned to their dressing room and found a shattered Richard, who curled up in the corner. Layne was in a separate room with the medical team. Charlie, Owen, Tom and Thomas all tried to talk to Richard but he just sat there motionlessly.

Richard could hear James shouting more abuses from outside the dressing room, which only ended when David went out to challenge him.

The good news was that the initial examination on Layne's right ankle was positive, it didn't seem to be broken but further scans would be needed. The medical team didn't think he needed to go to A&E so he would go back to south west London with the rest of the team. He remembered jumping when he heard Richard's shout, which had probably eased the impact but it was still extremely painful.

But the psychological damage to the pair was the bigger problem. After the confrontation with his parents, it was the last thing Richard needed. James's comment really got to him. He liked Layne ever since he met him but was he preying on him? He was indeed a year and a half older but he considered themselves to be of a similar age and not in an adult and kid relationship, even though he was more mature than his age and Layne the opposite. Was that how the others see them? Did it matter? He was so confused, completely tied up in knots.

He didn't even take a shower or talk to Layne on the coach, he was completely shut down. He did accompany Layne to his scan afterwards and they came home with Layne in a temporary leg brace and crutches. They wouldn't have the final results until the next day.

The pair eventually talked about what happened in the match and what was said by James. Layne assured Richard that he wasn't taking advantage of his age and he genuinely loved him, but Richard was still troubled by that comment. He was also worried about how the team felt and what else could happen if there were fans in the stadium – it was bad enough with one person making that sort of remarks.

"Don't think about it too much," Layne urged Richard to take a break and have some rest.

The story that a youth football team walked off the pitch to protest against homophobic remarks quickly reached national news outlets.

David asked all players not to engage anyone on social media and the club's media relations team had so far declined to comment on the identity of the players involved. The club had also asked the FA and the other club to withhold the release of the match report, which they agreed. There were lots of rumours online but with the lack of official communications they were just rumours.

Richard and Layne didn't read any of the news that evening. Layne gave some sleeping pills to Richard to help him settle and he was still in bed when Tom visited first thing in the morning.

"How's your ankle, Layne?" Tom asked at the door. "And how's Rich?"

"I'm not too bad," Layne said as he let Tom in. "Richie is still sleeping; I gave him some pills last night."

"Was he that bad? At least he can have some rest then. I guess you haven't seen the news?"

Layne quickly checked his phone and saw that the match was trending on social media. There were plenty of support from the main stream media and reasonable fans but there were also some witch hunt going on.

His account was full of nasty messages and a few of them threatened to kill both him and his boyfriend if they continued to "stain their beautiful game".

Layne had a look at Richard's phone and it seemed that the keyboard warriors hadn't identified him yet. It would be a matter of time anyway as it was easy to find out that they lived together.

"What should we do?" he asked Tom.

"I think Richard has spoken to David before and asked the club to keep it as low profile as possible. He doesn't want to go public. How do you feel about it? Do you need to refer to the police?"

"These threats don't mean much to me. It's probably just kids trying to look tough in front of their mates. I

207

don't mind coming out. I have nothing to hide and it's not something I can change. Sometimes I think he worries too much," Layne said.

"I don't want you to be on the receiving end of these abuses," said Richard as he came out from the bedroom. "Is it that bad? Tom mentioned the police just then?"

He tried to grab Layne's phone to have a look, but Tom beat him to it and took both phones away.

"Give it to me, I need to know," he asked Tom.

"You just need to ignore them. They always find something to attack players, whoever they are. Do you remember the racist abuses I got last month when I posted a picture of me and Mihara on holiday in Sri Lanka?"

"I understand that it's hard to avoid, but I need to know how bad it is and if it warrants any further actions," Richard sighed.

Tom passed Layne's phone to him and he read those death threats. He agreed with Layne that they were probably from some teenagers but they should still be reported. However, he didn't want their relationship to be exposed and he didn't want to come out in public.

"Should I get mum onto the case? She knows plenty of lawyers," Layne asked.

"I don't know what to do, maybe we'll just leave them for now," Richard said.

"I think those should at least be reported to the club, but in general you should just ignore comments from people you don't even know," said Tom.

"How about those on the pitch? What if we play someone like James again? How about the fans? We can't keep walking off..." Richard was really worried.

"We'll walk off again if it's that bad and they'll get punished for it, but you're right we can't avoid all of them," Tom agreed.

"We may just have to live with some," Layne added.

"It's easier said than done. You're not the one being accused of being a paedophile preying on young boys..."

"Don't be stupid. People say what they want. I'm not a kid," Layne looked serious when he said it. "And being a footballer means we will be in the public domain eventually, we just have to get used to ignoring them."

"I get that, but I only want us to be judged by our football skills and not our backgrounds, or because we are different. I don't want others' pity. All I worried about is you, but you seem more relaxed than I am."

"How do the team feel about all this?" he turned to ask Tom.

"Judging from yesterday, I think the majority, if not all, are fine with it, but I think you'll need to talk to them properly," Tom said.

"I suppose so. We shouldn't hide it from the team. I'll say something tomorrow before training," Richard agreed.

"It's good that you're back to your sensible self. You got me worried yesterday," Tom said.

"Thanks mate, I'm better now. I just need to grow up quickly," Richard smiled. "Fancy breakfast while you're here? We have some nice croissants and a new coffee machine."

"Oh go on then," Tom loved any food with butter.

That evening, Richard and Layne gathered with their best friends for dinner – something they did every other week on their day off. The group went to their usual Italian restaurant in Kingston that night for their good food and atmosphere.

At the beginning of the evening, the pair admitted their relationship for the first time and thanked their friends for standing up for them, especially Charlie who was due to receive another disciplinary warning from the club, on top of a suspension with Richard for their red cards.

"Congratulations. Didn't I say he'll lighten you up a bit, Rich? I just didn't know that you'll take it THIS far!" said a giddy Thomas.

"You could have told us much earlier, we kind of guessed anyway. You two looked different since Bournemouth," Danny said.

"I heard that you sounded like a Spartan with that 'THIS IS MY LAYNE' announcement, bro!" Ollie joked.

"Don't you worry about that James – he's just a loser. I'll fix him if he dares showing up again," Charlie said.

"You beat me to it Charlie, I wouldn't mind punching that piece of crap in the face," Owen joined in.

"Take care of this boy for us Layne, he worries too much," Tom said to Layne while pointing at Richard.

"He's the vulnerable one," Layne smiled.

"I'm happy for you guys, but how am I supposed to react to all the posts on my social media accounts?" said Alex, who had been receiving abuses as the witch hunt brigade thought he was "the other one", possibly due to his long blonde hair and fashion sense.

"Just ignore them or post some photos of you and your girlfriend... if you manage to find one!" Tom suggested.

"Or go and get caught clubbing with me and Paul?" Charlie came up with another suggestion. He was warned by the club earlier that month for an incident in Soho.

"Maybe I'll just keep posting pictures with different players to keep them guessing... it sounds fun!" Alex had his answer. "Do you want a photo with me for that, Layne?"

"Behave, he's MY boyfriend!" Richard finally joined in with the fun.

He was relieved that his teammates took their relationship well.

The group had also learnt that night that Elle, Thomas's girlfriend, was pregnant and would be due in the summer.

The gossips online naturally died down afterwards – they were only under 23 players after all and luckily they didn't have a lot of market value.

Richard and Layne were at the training ground next morning. David had gathered the team for them to make their announcement.

"Morning all," Richard cleared his throat to settle his nerves and began talking. "First of all let me thank you for giving me the time today and the support you gave us on Sunday. I'm sorry to have caused the team trouble with my conduct on the pitch. I should never have resorted into violence. But as you're probably aware since Sunday,

Layne and I are dating each other and I felt the need to stand up against someone who intentionally hurt him.

"I don't really know what to say next, but I sincerely hope that our relationship would be accepted by you, my teammates, and we can continue to play our beloved game and win as many as we can together."

"You don't need to ask, Richard. We're one team and you know it," said Les the team captain before turning to the rest. "What do you say, boys?"

"No issues with me," said another senior player Max.

"Same here, we don't need to worry about private matters," Lewis said.

"It's fine with me too," said Josh the first choice goalkeeper.

"You know how we feel. We're behind you all the way," Tom added.

"Thanks guys. That means a lot, it's wonderful to have you as teammates," Richard was touched, he felt well supported.

"Excuse me and I hope you don't mind me saying this. I have nothing against homosexual relationships, but how is it going to work in the dressing room? I suppose we can't be sharing the same shower, for example?" asked Francis.

"I don't really see that as a problem. Just cover up if you don't want to be seen?" Charlie said.

"We are one big family. It doesn't matter if our brothers bat for the other side, they're our brothers anyway," Owen added.

"That's very good, I like the team spirit," David took over. "We can talk about this offline if you are really concerned, Francis. Otherwise leave the PR side with me and the club. We said we will be the most inclusive club and we meant it.

"But I must say one thing: you are professional players and under no circumstances you should be fighting with other players. There are rules and conducts to follow, at all times."

"I'm sorry boss," said both Richard and Charlie.

"It's okay. Let's talk about it after training today. Now let's get on the pitch with Nick and Tim."

Richard looked over to Layne and they exchanged a smile of relief.

Richard felt some of the heavy weight on his shoulders had gone now that he had come out to his friends and teammates. He was grateful that his relationship with Layne was accepted and he realised that the world might not be as grim as he thought it was.

A week had passed since the game in south east London. Layne's scan returned a positive verdict – he should be back to full training in two weeks' time. Richard and Charlie received a three-match ban from the FA for their straight red cards, which they accepted.

Meanwhile, James received a two-match ban. The FA interviewed players from both teams and was convinced that he did make the comment – the official statement said that "Regardless of whether or not there were LGBT+ players present, the comment was abusive and deserved a suspension." That was requested by the Black Dragons, who did not want to confirm the identity of Richard and Layne. The match, however, would still be recorded as a forfeit by the young Dragons as the FA did not have a rule that allowed clubs to postpone games unilaterally.

Bob Warner, Thames Ditton's first team manager, said in a pre-match press conference for the first team that the issue had been dealt with and no further comments would be made. He would not confirm if any of their players were homosexual, he just urged the press and the public to support and respect players regardless of their personal characteristics.

A sports website analysed the under 23 team squad and narrowed down "the suspects" to a handful of players including Richard and Layne, but their article didn't get a lot of traction online so the story cooled down naturally.

The team won two and lost one of their next three games. Rob made the most of Charlie's absence and scored three goals. Owen and Alex also increased their tallies during the victory over the team from Shepherd's Bush at the main stadium and the trip to Warwickshire. The team then lost 2-1 away in Lancashire, Les's headed goal wasn't enough to claw back a two-goal deficit from the first half, in an exciting match hosted in the home side's main stadium.

The next game was against a side from South Yorkshire at The Dragons Stadium. There was a clear gap in abilities between the two teams and the Black Dragons came out 7-0 winners.

Layne made a full recovery from his injury and played in the second half. A match-hungry Charlie scored a hat trick in the first half and Alex, Tom and Viktor scored in the second. Richard completed the score line with a penalty late on to record his first official goal for the under 23 team, as his goal in the abandoned match against south east London didn't count.

The players returned in time for the team's tour of Germany and Austria.

14.

The Tour

The club arranged a five-day tour to southern Germany and Austria for the under 23 team. They would play friendly matches against the under 19 sides of Munich and Salzburg.

All twenty-five players were fit and they joined David, Nick and the rest of the coaching team for the journey. They would train at the world class facilities in central Munich the afternoon after their arrivals before a match with the local side on the second day. They would follow the same pattern and travel to Salzburg by coach on the third day, with the practice match scheduled for the day after.

Richard was very excited. He used to live in Munich when he was young and it would be the first foreign trip he had with Layne and all his friends.

The flight arrived at the Munich airport at about eleven in the morning. The training ground was about an hour away in the south of the city and the team had lunch provided by the host. The training complex, which was for both the first and reserve teams, had five grass pitches and plenty more facilities. The team were given a quick tour and were astonished at what was available for the sides there. They heard that a new state-of-the-art youth complex near their new stadium was due to open later that year, and they wondered how much better it could be.

As Richard spoke fluent German, his teammates relied him to act as a translator between them and the host team, which he was only too happy to do.

The team had a light training session in the afternoon where some of the Munich coaches were present to exchange ideas with David and the coaching team. Richard shocked the team when he made his way over to greet one of the coaches at the end of the session.

"Hi Tobias, it's so good to see you again," he said to one of the coaches.

"Hey Richard, I was very happy when I learned that you are part of this team," said a delighted Tobias who gave Richard a big hug.

"How do you know each other?" David was interested.

"He used to be one of us... did he not tell you?"

"No wonder why he has such good foundations! You've trained him really well!"

"It was a shame when his family decided to move back to England, we would have offered him a contract, you know," Tobias told David before asking Richard. "Are you happy now, Richard?"

"Yes I am. We have a great team here and I'm developing well," Richard responded, before he asked, in a more discreet manner, "... Will 'he' be playing tomorrow?"

"Yes, 'he' is in the squad."

"That's very well then. I'll see you in the match."

The team were amazed to hear that it was where Richard spent some of his early football years.

"Why don't you tell us anything about your past?" Tom moaned. "What else are you hiding from us? You were actually from Mars or something?"

"I've never said I didn't play football when I was living in Munich," Richard put up a defence. "I just don't want to brag about it, I prefer to be judged by my ability."

"Do you know about it, Layne?" Tom asked.

"He told me yesterday," Layne said with an unimpressed look.

"That's the privilege of being his boyfriend, I suppose," Charlie teased.

"I'm always honest with him. He just needs to ask the right questions," Richard said.

"I'll sort you out when we are back in the hotel, Richie," said Layne as he walked away.

"Now you're in trouble Rich, never mess with the other half," said Thomas.

"I guess I'm learning it the hard way," Richard smiled.

A Bavarian style team dinner was arranged for that evening. Richard's all-time favourite, the schweinshaxe, or whole pork knuckle, on a bed of sauerkraut was on the menu but Layne preferred the healthier schweinsbraten (roast pork) instead. For Charlie's disappointment beer was limited to half a stein (one pint) each due to the practice match the next day, but he managed to have nearly two steins as he took over the ones for Richard and Danny. The legal age for drinking in Germany was sixteen so Layne had his share too.

The players were asked to share hotel rooms and naturally Richard and Layne were assigned the same one. The coaches jokingly gave them a little reminder that players should refrain from sexual activities before matches, which they embarrassingly acknowledged. Layne didn't bring his annoyance from the afternoon up, but he did notice that Richard was somewhat anxious with the following day's match. He raised it at bed time but Richard wasn't going to tell.

The practice match was scheduled for eleven the next morning. It was played at the stadium within the training complex, which could probably hold three thousand spectators. There weren't many for the practice match, but there were some scouts from other clubs, who gathered on the press section in one of the stands.

David decided to go for his strongest team, with Josh in goal, Viktor, Lewis, Thomas and Les at the back, Richard, Tom and Max in midfield, and Charlie, Owen and Danny up front.

The home team started in a 4-1-4-1 formation, with a deep midfielder playing behind two box to box ones. When defending they would become a solid 4-5-1, while in attack they could change into a 3-4-3 with the deep midfielder dropping back further to enable the full backs and wide attackers to push forward.

Some of the home players remembered Richard and waved him over to meet them just before kick off. They were happy to see him again and were excited to play against his new team.

But Richard also saw "him".

"Hi… Ian, how… are you doing?" he asked.

"I'm okay. You?"

"Not bad, I suppose."

"Have you found… what you wanted?"

"Yes, he is on the bench today."

"That's good for you… I'm sorry for what I did back then. I should have handled it better."

"We can't change the past, but I appreciate it. I shouldn't do what I did too. Have a good match, I'll see you afterwards."

Richard was glad that Ian apologised. He was the reason why Richard's family moved back to England from Germany, when he brutally exposed Richard's crush on him and rejected him in front of everyone during in a family event for British expats at the company Richard's father worked for.

The friendly match started. Even though it was only their under 19 side, Munich's players were quicker on and off the ball. They passed around effortlessly, making the young Black Dragons work really hard in defence and in the off chance of gaining the ball, they lost it back quickly as they didn't have any time to think and any energy to run with it.

While Munich were completely dominating the game, the Black Dragons were solid in defence in the goalless first half. Richard and Tom formed their usual wall in the middle, with Richard amazingly winning all his six defensive duels and making five interceptions. His intensive strengths training during suspension was paying great dividends as he sustained the strong challenges by his German counterparts.

Both teams made some changes at half time. David replaced Viktor and Thomas with Baek-min and Thorsten as he always planned to share the game time between players of similar ability. He also withdrew Max and put Alex on. He wanted more pressure on the deep sitting orchestrator and he thought Danny would be better for the job.

He asked the team to slow the play down by keeping possession when they got the ball, and not to rush into an attack until they had their breather. It had been a recurring theme for the team when they were under pressure and David was keen to iron it out of the system.

He mentioned the "Fifteen Pass Rule" established by one of the most successful managers in the world, who used to manage their opponent's first team: "If there isn't a sequence of fifteen passes first, it's impossible to carry out the transition between defence and attack."

He stressed that he wasn't looking for fifteen needless passes between defence and attack, he mentioned it just to illustrate the important point of being patient in order to steady themselves. He said, "The player who wins possession back has to make the right decision: the team should have a breather if they have spent a considerable time to regain the ball, while they should go for a fast attack if their energy level is high."

The second half resumed and Munich were taking the initiative again. The Black Dragons resisted and when they got the ball they tried to pass around at the back to buy themselves some time. They were doing it well but the home team were very good at their pressing too. Soon the forward hunted the ball off Baek-min and squared it for the advancing midfielder, only for a last-ditch tackle from Richard to divert it out for a corner.

David was going to put Rob, Layne and Kasper on but decided to hold out after the corner, in order not to affect the defensive shape. However, it didn't matter as the corner was headed in by the towering centre back at the near post. His superior height had been giving Tom plenty of issues throughout the game and he finally prevailed.

The three substitutes replaced Charlie, Lewis and Tom. David wanted to keep Richard on to see if he could complete ninety minutes at this intensity following his additional training.

The team now needed to attack but Munich operated a very tight squeeze and it was very difficult to play against. The match looked destined for a 1-0 win for the home side. Owen had been playing on the left since Charlie was withdrawn. He gave a signal to Richard for their move when he won the ball in midfield. Richard passed it to him while Layne and the rest of the team went for their positions. The home side was tracking so well that Owen had to improvise – instead of just holding up the play he went directly for the middle himself. He dribbled past a couple of defenders brilliantly but was tackled by the third. The loose ball went out to Richard, who took up Tom's normal position in the move behind the play. He instinctively chipped the ball into the small space in front of Danny. The ball rolled backwards when it landed due to the heavy backspin and it gave Danny the split second he needed to hit it on his stride from twenty yards out. The ball flew straight into the top left corner and gave the goal keeper no chance.

Danny celebrated with Richard and the players were ecstatic – they somehow pulled level with their only shot on target!

The game ended soon afterwards and the coaching teams agreed to name Richard as the man of the match. Some of the coaches and scouts actually came over to congratulate his performance.

"It seems the additional training has worked, look how tough you were getting in there," Tom said.

"Yeah I felt good," Richard replied. "It was quite strange really that everything was instinctive – I didn't have to think but seemed to know what was the best to do straight away."

"That's what some called being 'in the zone'," Danny said. "When you are full of adrenaline and completely focused. Elite players can get into it before every game, that's what we should be aiming for."

"Is that what it is? You must have experienced it before too?" Richard asked.

"A few times. It felt like you were unplayable."

"Oh I can probably figure out which games those were. You looked to be on a mission!" Tom recalled.

"Think about how you got there today and memorise it – with your level of concentration normally it shouldn't be too hard," Owen added.

"Mm… I think I know what you mean. I'll try it next time."

Ian was waiting for Richard after the group handshakes and photos. Richard gestured Layne to head inside first and stayed for a chat.

"Well played Richard, that was some pass for the goal."

"Thanks. It's great to share a pitch with you again."

"It is. I'm glad that you're able to free yourself from the closet. You look far more confident this way."

"It is good. I have a strong support team behind me, and of course I have Layne."

"He seems a good match for you. I wish you two all the best!"

The two shook hands again and that was that, the long old chapter was finally closed for good.

Back in the dressing room, David was happy with the team's efforts. He was also keen to point out that they would have lost on most days, but they were also playing one of the best teams in the world.

It was free time for the players after the match and Richard had reserved a table at a specialist schweinshaxe restaurant in the city centre for him and his friends in the evening. He spent some time sightseeing with Layne prior to that. They had a quick tour of the BMW Museum near Olympiapark before seeing the gothic architecture around the old town centre. Richard specifically brought Layne to the English Gardens as his parents used to take him there every weekend.

"You can return the favour, baby. I used to imagine taking my future partner here for a walk," he said.

"Really? This feels so special!" Layne was excited and he duly gave Richard a few kisses, to the point that he felt quite embarrassed.

"Mm… that's enough, sweetie."

"Who's the blonde English midfielder waiting for you at the end? He looks really good! I have a funny feeling that he is your type, am I right?"

"… Yes he is. His name is Ian. THAT Ian."

"Oh God, is that him? Did you speak to him? No wonder why you were so fired up today!"

"We did have a few words. He doesn't mean much to me now. We've both grown up – we realised we shouldn't do what we did, we apologised to each other, and we moved on."

"What exactly did you do?"

"I used to follow him around a lot. He felt annoyed and rejected me publicly, in front of both our parents amongst others. That's why my dad transferred back to the UK office immediately and hated me. I must have affected his career progression."

"I get it now. Come here, Richie baby. I'll never let you feel like that again."

The pair had a hug – Richard felt warm, he was so glad to have Layne, who was probably the real reason why he was able to move away from the past.

They joined their teammates for dinner afterwards. Charlie challenged the team to have a pork knuckle each and the losers had to down a stein of beer. The task was easy for Richard and most others but Layne couldn't finish his. As it was legal for him to drink, he took the forfeit himself. He downed his stein like a true Bavarian and was fine afterwards. Everyone looked at Richard and couldn't help laughing at his inferior drinking ability comparing to his boyfriend. Charlie gave him a chance to redeem himself, but it was stopped by Tom, who reminded everyone that they had training the next day.

The drunk Layne was going for more drinks afterwards but he was dragged into a taxi back to the team hotel by Richard. Luckily, they returned early enough to sneak into their room without alerting the coaching team. It was a different story for Paul and Rob, as they came back at midnight and got caught red-handed by Nick. Charlie somehow escaped as he needed the bathroom and rushed to the one next to the hotel reception while his two mates were stopped.

The team left Munich for Salzburg the next morning. It was a two-hour coach journey through the beautiful mountains and they arrived at the host team's stadium before lunch time. After a light lunch and a tour of the stadium, the team had their session at the training centre nearby.

The training facilities were modern but much smaller than those in Munich. The training itself was focused on recovery and was quite light. The club had arranged a low-key dinner at the hotel restaurant. Richard had a traditional Wiener schnitzel with some pasta and decided to have an early night.

The practice match with Salzburg was again scheduled for eleven the next morning. David made lots of changes and started with Jack in goal, Baek-min, Layne, Thorsten and Ivan in defence, Kasper, Max and Ashley in midfield, with Mitchell, Peter and Alex upfront. Paul and Rob were scheduled to be starters but they were benched instead for their actions the night before.

Salzburg played with a flat 4-4-2 formation and so David believed the two key areas would be whether the Black Dragons' extra man in midfield could dictate the play and if the wingers were able to track their opposing full backs.

The game started and soon Richard noticed the home team nullified the Black Dragons' numerical advantage in midfield by pushing one of their central midfielders into Kasper and getting their wide midfielders in field to fill the space.

"The path in the middle is blocked. The only way out is the full backs," he discussed with David.

"Yes they need to demand the ball more," David agreed, before giving the instruction to Layne, who was nearest to him.

As instructed, Layne called for the ball more often, but he found all his paths forward blocked as the home side dropped their strikers into midfield when he got the ball, ensuring the defence's numerical advantage was intact. They shifted their midfield four towards their right and made the centre backs the only realistic passing option available for Layne. He could switch sides and go long to Baek-min, but the midfielders would have shifted to their left by the time he got the ball, so it ended up in the same pattern.

When the home side got the ball, they attacked through doubling up on the wings for crosses into the hard-working strikers, but with the Black Dragons' wingers tracking back, they couldn't create many chances. They only attacked on one side at the time and would revert back into their defensive shape very quickly so the away side couldn't gain much from counters either.

The half ended in a stalemate.

"What do you think, Richard? How can we break this disciplined team down?" David asked, probably trying to test Richard's understanding.

"We need the ability to win individual battles and break the defensive balance. I'll bring Charlie and Owen on," he said.

"Sounds good. I'll go further by bringing you on to replace Kasper, we need a bit more pace in passing the ball around," David then discussed his plan in more detail.

"Be mindful though, they will try to win the game by switching into attacking play at some point," he concluded with a warning.

The second half kicked off with Charlie, Owen and Richard on. Richard was on the pitch early and had a few deep breaths to focus his mind, as he tried to get "in the zone".

The home team defended in a similar way and the game followed the same pattern, with the Black Dragons having plenty of possession in their own half between their back four. Richard tried to stretch the play with a few long balls towards the flanks but still couldn't break through the resilient home team and the ball ended up back to his centre backs. Charlie and Owen did manage to dribble past their opponents on a few occasions but the compact shape of the home team limited their impacts to half chances only.

Twenty minutes into the second half, David brought Danny on for Ashley and Richard knew that it was time for the next part of the plan. He gave the signal to his teammates and sent the ball to Owen on the right. He worked it towards the corner flag under the watch of the opposing left back, and the rest of the home team continued their shift towards their left. Owen held the ball well and exchanged it with the supporting Baek-min, Alex and Danny. Having drawn the home team into a period of play on this side, Danny laid the ball off to Richard back in centre midfield and he hit a powerful low pass diagonally towards the advanced left back position, which was completely free by design of the home team's tactics.

But this time, Charlie was there.

He controlled the difficult ball by Richard expertly and brought the ball inside before the right midfielder got close to him. Layne was running outside him to occupy the right back, so it became a one on one between Charlie and the right-side centre back. Charlie pushed on to the corner of the six-yard box and cut it back to the penalty spot. Alex arrived in front of his marker and swept it in to finally open the scoring. Having been frustrated for chances the whole game, he celebrated wildly by jumping into Charlie, who lifted him up in the air for a good few seconds.

That was David's plan. He needed the close control and passing skills of Owen and Danny to keep the ball on the right to draw the attention of the defence there, before using Richard's passing ability to find Charlie quickly, utilising his ability to control such a pass and run at the defence before the home team's shift was completed. It was executed beautifully.

The home team had to attack and David brought Viktor, Francis and Tom on to replace Baek-min, Ivan and Max to refresh his defence. They stuck to their well-practiced low block and managed to deal with the threats.

But David's plan wasn't for the team to just survive the onslaught. With five minutes remaining, Tom picked up a loose ball from defence and he found Alex, who had dropped back into his own half with both centre backs behind him. Richard quickly ran up to offer him a return pass and chipped it up field first time. Alex, who immediately turned for the pass, was completely alone in the other half and was onside – the offside rules didn't apply if all defenders were in the attacking half of the pitch. He picked up the back-spinning ball and dinked the ball over the keeper beautifully to score.

That was game, set and match. The home team lost their spirit and didn't cause any further concerns for the remaining minutes and the practice match ended 2-0 to the Black Dragons.

"I didn't expect it to be such a tactical game, I had a lot of fun. But well done for reacting so well, you should be proud of your efforts," David said in the debriefing in the dressing room.

"That was hard work," said Layne who had been running non-stop for seventy minutes until Lewis came on. "It was good that Richard wanted an early night yesterday."

"Ahem... as opposed to what exactly? I thought you two have a twin room just like us?" Rob just couldn't help it.

Richard burst out laughing. He put his hands up as a gesture to say "that has nothing to do with me".

"Richard set a good example there. You are professional players and have to manage your health. Early nights, nutritious food and plenty of water," David ignored the jokes and brought the topic back to something proper.

"He's only good on one of those things though. Just look at the amount he eats! He doesn't drink anywhere near enough water too!" Layne pointed out.

"Okay, I'll keep an eye on those," said Richard after David gave him a stare.

The team got another free afternoon to explore the city. Kasper "The Boiler" had been to Salzburg before and volunteered to be a tour guide for the group. Layne made up his nickname after learning how to pronounce his family name Boilesen.

Kasper planned a cultural tour with visits to the various attractions associated with Mozart, one of the composers of all times, complimented by an Austrian meal at the end. To his surprise, Richard and Layne declined the latter as they had tickets for a concert in the evening. Charlie, Owen and others weren't interested in classical music and joined a river cruise instead.

The pair spent most of the time in Mozart's residence. The historian Richard studied every piece of the composer's items and the pianist Layne listened to all the exhibitions. They eventually joined the rest for a quick tour of the Mirabell Palace before going for some bratwursts from the food stalls near the theatre. They then enjoyed a ninety-minute concert performance of Mozart's masterpiece of The Magic Flute.

"That was truly amazing! The soprano from the Queen of the Night was just mesmerising!" Richard was delighted at the end of the concert.

"I don't know how she can go to such a high pitch for that long, it's awesome," Layne was very impressed too. "Mr Mozart certainly tested her limits!"

They returned to the hotel after getting some fast food in the city centre.

"This was such a lovely trip – the football, the food and now this," Richard said when they were back in their room.

"I enjoy every minute of it," Layne agreed. "Did you manage to get in the zone today?"

"Not quite. I think I was dipping in and out of it. It'll probably take some time before I can be in control."

"At least you know what it feels like and what to do."

"Yes, but let's switch off from football for now. I'm so glad that I was able to experience so much with you, my little Ping," Richard said while putting his arms round Layne's waist from behind.

Ping was Layne's middle name, which Richard loved calling him with in private since learning it from his mum over Christmas. It means "peace" in Cantonese.

"What are you thinking, Richie? Some romantic actions in Austria?" Layne turned around and asked softly.

"Won't that be a fitting end to our lovely trip?" said Richard as he started kissing Layne.

It was Charlie's nineteenth birthday the week after and he invited the team to an American restaurant well known for their barbeque ribs and lobsters in Chelsea for dinner. Fresh from another warning by the club after the events in Germany, he decided not to go too extravagant this time. Richard and Layne were there with plenty of others and their partners. Charlie generously paid for unlimited ribs, fajitas and drinks and it was a great night for everyone. He was there with his latest girlfriend (Richard couldn't remember her name, there had been too many) and he, Rob and Paul were absolutely hammered again.

"That sort of drinking really can't be healthy," Richard said on his taxi back home with Layne, Danny, Tom and Mihara.

"Yes, I've spoken to Charlie before but he wasn't listening," Tom said.

"Well he's still performing in the games so what's the problem?" Layne didn't understand.

"We're not at the top of our games yet. I'm sure we need to do a lot more to become professionals in the Championship and beyond," Danny said.

"Very true. Look at the under 19 teams we played against in Germany and Austria, how good were they? And how good will they become when they are a few years older?" Richard said.

"I'll try to tell him that again the next time I have a chance," Tom concluded.

15.

A Different Path

A few days after the tour of Germany and Austria, Richard received a phone call from his agent Jon. He was a friend of Layne's mum and Richard and Layne appointed him as their agent at the beginning of the year on her recommendation, when Layne got his first pre-agreement contract from the club.

Jon told Richard that he had been approached by a handful of German Bundesliga clubs after his performance against Munich and Salzburg. Some were willing to buy him outright from the Black Dragons for their first teams. They wanted to know if he was interested before officially submitting a bid for a transfer.

Richard was a bit shocked by the news and needed some time to think about it. It was of course a great recognition and the chance to play in the Bundesliga tempted him, especially that he was fluent in the language. However, he loved the Black Dragons for what they had done for him and most importantly, he didn't want to leave Layne behind.

He discussed with Layne that evening.

"Jon called me this afternoon and said some teams in the Bundesliga are interested in signing me," he said when he and Layne were in bed. "What do you think?"

"Wow! Is that on the back of your performance over there? I saw some scouts at Munich's stadium," Layne was excited.

"I guess so. I spoke to some of them after the match and they seemed impressed. That's one good thing about learning German when I was young."

"Do you want to go?"

"It'll be exciting playing in the top flight, but I can't be sure if they'll have me in their first team. What if it's just their youth teams? Then I'll have a better chance of breaking into the Championship with the under 23 team here."

"But it's a league well known for their youth development, you'll become a better player there, right?" Layne seemed positive about the move. "Will they offer better money?"

"I don't know yet but I don't think so. It's not too important at this stage anyway."

"I think you should consider going, Richie," Layne sat up and said. "I think you'll develop better there, it'll give you a chance to play at the top flight and I think... you could do with staying away from the limelight over here – I don't want you to get all those horrible messages on social media like me."

"They stopped bothering me a while ago. But I don't really want to leave the Dragons. David and the club have been so nice to me from the start and they supported us through that period too. What about you? I can't just leave you here."

"Maybe you can ask if they would sign me as well?"

"Won't that be a little awkward?"

"Honestly, I don't want to be the one holding you back. I'm sure we'll manage."

"I don't know if I can do that, living without you next to me... Let me think about it."

"Why don't you talk to David about it?" Layne knew Richard would say the last sentence every time he couldn't make a decision so he suggested him to ask for help.

"Would that make the interested clubs feel bad? It may look like they've approached us in the wrong way?" Richard wasn't sure about the protocol.

"Then maybe you can get Jon to ask the clubs to contact the Black Dragons first?"

"I guess we'll do that."

Richard called Jon the next morning to say that he would prefer the interested clubs to speak to the Black

Dragons first. Jon got that and would relay the message appropriately.

The Black Dragons played three games after the trip to Germany with some mixed results. They won the first one against the club from Suffolk 3-0; drew 2-2 at north west London and finally lost to the other team from Sheffield 2-1. Alex scored three of the seven goals and overtook Owen as the team's top scorer. Richard continued to experiment on how managing his mindfulness could get him into the optimum state of mind and felt a breakthrough was near – he believed he had found "the switch".

Their next match was the return match against one of their local rivals, the one from Shepherd's Bush. It was where Richard got his head injury the year before.

The home team included a handful of first team players in the starting line-up – some were recovering from injuries and some were fringe players of the squad. Leon the midfielder who injured Richard last season was also there. He came over to offer Richard a handshake and was pleased to see him making a full recovery.

Given the quality of the opposition, David went for his strongest team possible, with Josh in goal, Viktor, Lewis, Thomas and Les in defence, Richard, Tom and Max in midfield and Charlie, Alex and Danny upfront. Owen had a slight knock and started on the bench.

"Be careful out there, Rich," a concerned Layne told him before the team went onto the pitch.

"I'll be fine, don't worry."

Similar to the game last year, this was no friendly match. It was physical and competitive - even more so than the previous occasion because first team players were taking part. Some of these players had experience playing for the biggest clubs in the Premier League and their class was evident. Their touches, turns and passes were just that bit sharper and they seemed to walk into positions while the Black Dragons were chasing all the time.

It didn't take long for the home side to score. Their first team left back found the star midfielder at the edge of the penalty box and he tricked his way through both Les and Thomas to score a sensational goal.

Richard looked at Tom and they were both amazed. The two centre backs were not easy to beat and their player just whizzed past both of them in one go – was that the difference between first teams and reserves?

The away team gathered themselves and launched attacks of their own. They realised they needed to do everything a little quicker and make sure they kept their composure. The efforts bore fruits as Tom hit the bar with a long range shot and Charlie forced a brilliant save out of the keeper from the corner of the area. However, the home side had the last laugh of the half with a well worked set piece routine giving them a second goal. The striker was left unmarked at the far post to head in from a deep cross.

"Good efforts out there, that should show you guys the level needed to be playing for the first team," David addressed the team at half time. "You were playing in the right way though, just keep doing what you did and focus on winning the second half."

David made some changes to rotate his squad and inject some more pace into the team. Layne and Rob came on for Lewis and Max. He asked the team to utilise the added pace by playing more direct passes to the wings. Danny drifted to the left to overload with Charlie and Layne, and together they created a chance for Layne to hit a low cross towards Rob, whose shot was blocked by the opposition left back. The resulting corner was taken by Richard and Tom jumped the highest to claw one back for the Black Dragons. 2-1.

The Black Dragons pressed for the equaliser with both Layne and Viktor supporting the attack. But the home team exploited the space behind them in a counter, the skilful attacking midfielder picked up a pass at the edge of the final third and he dribbled past Tom soon after. Richard moved across to hold him up and it became a one-on-one.

The midfielder tried to flip to the ball to Richard's left before he settled but the agile Richard was able to shift his balance and keep tracking. The midfielder then amazingly drifted the ball back and forth repeatedly behind him using only the tip of his right foot. Richard attacked the ball multiple times and forced the midfielder to take the ball away to his right. After a couple of yards he tried to cut it back to his left into space but Richard read that, pretended to make a tackle and forced him to over hit the ball.

He knew his job was done – Les was there behind him.

The giant defender won the ball with a solid tackle and sent it up field to Alex. He controlled it on his chest before guiding it to the left for Charlie, who sent Layne through on the outside. Layne returned the ball to him at the edge of the penalty area and Charlie crossed it to Danny for a first time finish. 2-2.

"Brilliant goal lads – see, we can do it!" Tom shouted as he joined the group celebration.

But the quality players in the home team were far from finished. Minutes later the talented left back found some room to put it a beautiful cross for his target man to put the home side back in front again. They timed it to perfection again and little could be done about it.

The Black Dragons had to chase the game again. With ten minutes remaining, they threw caution to the wind and went all out. Les stayed forward to play as an extra striker while the rest worked the ball to the wings for crosses. There were chances but headers by Les and Charlie were saved.

And the home team hit the Black Dragons at the break again. The keeper found the attacking midfielder near the centre circle, whose brilliantly flick sent the advancing right back into the final third, with attackers outnumbered the defence by four players to three. Richard couldn't stop the cross and the ball eventually reached the striker for 4-2.

The game soon ended and the Black Dragons had lost the derby.

"Well played in the second half. You've put up a good fight against some top opponents. I'm proud of you guys," David said at the dressing room.

"How did you find it out there?" Nick asked the team. "Did you see a lot of difference between you and their first team players?"

"They were sharper than us – everything was that second quicker. But I think we weren't far behind. We could give them a match," Tom replied.

"That midfielder was so good. There's a reason why he was once highly rated by the best manager ever," Thomas said.

"Sadly he's ruined by his off-field issues," said Danny, with his eyes locked on Charlie.

"Hey he still couldn't beat our 'unbeatable' boy!" Charlie tried to divert the topic.

"He did on the face of it," Richard smiled before turning around to Les, "Thanks for having my back, Les."

"It was a good lesson. I think we know what to do next time we play them," Les concluded. "On to the next game, lads!"

That evening was Layne's turn to cook. He was making some meat-ball spaghetti and Richard was by his side to have a chat.

"How hungry are you, Richie?" he asked knowing the portion would end up being large or extra-large.

"Very, after that match," Richard said. "I know I've cleared the biscuit tin but I'm still starving."

"That's alright, you're in for a treat!" Layne said with a smile. "Do you remember the same game last year? You got me worried then."

"Yeah at least I made it out unharmed this time. Still a tough game but a different type of tough," said Richard as he wrapped his arms around Layne's waist from the back. "You got me mixed up after that game. I wasn't going to go for another boy but I couldn't stop thinking about you since."

"Hiding in a closet is not good for health. You would have gone mental," Layne said.

233

"I'm glad I've made the right choice," Richard replied as he rested his head on Layne's shoulder. "Let me see your cooking."

"I probably can't do it now you're in the way," Layne giggled and half-heartedly tried to wiggle himself out.

Richard just tightened his grip on him, "I don't think I can ever leave you behind. I love the way it is."

"You know I wouldn't say no to that," Layne turned around and gave him a kiss. "I guess you have an offer from the German clubs then."

"Not yet, but I won't go even if there is one," Richard replied.

"Let's see what happens first. Maybe I'll just follow you there if you get a big contract."

"That'll be interesting."

The food was nearly ready and the pair enjoyed the rest of their evening.

Richard was called into David's office after the next training session.

He told Richard that the club had received two bids from Bundesliga clubs for him. The offers were respectable in terms of market value, the club and David in particular didn't want Richard to leave but would understand if he wanted to develop over there.

"What do you think, Richard? I think you'll be worth a lot more in a few years but we won't stand in your way if you fancy it there," David said.

"I'm flattered to be recognised by the clubs there. Berlin and Hamburg aren't small clubs and I'm sure I can develop well, knowing the language and all that. But I don't want to leave the Black Dragons at the moment. The team are going strong and I owe you and the coaching team a lot."

"That's well and good, I very much appreciate your thinking but you need to be aware that we won't be able to guarantee you a place in the first team just because you turn them down to stay. I think you have a good chance, but it depends on how you train and play in the coming months and years."

"I suppose it's the same wherever I go. But I want to do it here, I want to grow with this team."

"I like that," David smiled, "but go and have a word with your agent before confirming it with me. We don't have to answer straight away, he could start the contract negotiation if you prefer."

"Thanks David," said Richard before he left the room.

He spoke with Jon after that and he recommended getting an idea of the contract being offered before making a firm decision. He believed he could use that to get a better deal from the Black Dragons. Richard wasn't keen to negotiate with the club but he'd let Jon do his job.

Richard and Layne were meeting his friends that evening for dinner, as one of their regular get togethers. This time Tom suggested they met at a pub restaurant near Thames Ditton station, as there was a lovely garden for them to enjoy the nice spring weather.

In addition to the pair and Tom, Charlie, Ollie, Danny, Thomas, Alex, Owen, Baek-min, Viktor and Kasper also joined.

"This is a nice place! I've never been to this part of town before," Viktor looked impressed by the beer garden.

"It's lovely around here," said Alex, who lived nearby.

"Where about do you live Viktor?" asked Owen.

"I'm in Molesey near the swimming pool."

"That's quite far away. Don't you cycle to training every day?" Layne asked. "I'll be exhausted before I kick a ball!"

"Really? You need more workouts," said Owen. "I'll join you for a ride in the morning Vic, I'm not far from where you are."

"Sounds good to me!"

"How's Elle doing? She must be due soon?" Richard asked Thomas.

"Three more months. I can't wait," Thomas said with a sweet smile on his face. "I've been talking to him every night."

"So it's a him then?" Ollie picked up the hint.

"Yes and we've been decorating his room," Thomas continued to behave like an expecting dad.

"That's lovely. Do you have names already?" Tom was curious. "I guess he won't be another Tom?"

"No he won't be another Tom. We're not sure yet, we have a shortlist but we have to see him to decide."

"You won't have time for football training soon. Sleep well when you can," said Danny, who instinctively linked everything to football.

"Taking about football, do you know what happened to Mr Lucas today?" Layne was excited, and Richard reacted by covering up his face.

"He received two transfer offers from Germany!" Layne proudly announced.

"What? Where? How much?" Ollie was full of questions as always.

"They're from Berlin and Hamburg," Layne said. "How much again, Richie?"

"Don't make such a big deal out of it... It's about two million pounds."

"Wowsers! That's amazing! What do you think about them?" Tom asked.

"I'm not sure. I've only just started here and I want to play for the first team," Richard said.

"I think you should seriously consider it. Not everyone gets a chance to play over there and you already know the language," Danny said.

"I know, but I want to play with you guys and win things together. I think I owe David for his support too."

"That's true, loyalty is important. Are they giving you good money for it?" Thomas asked.

"I don't know yet, Jon is dealing with it."

"What do you think, Charlie? You've been very quiet today?" Tom noticed Charlie wasn't drinking as quickly as he did normally. "Did you drive here?"

"I'm trying to give up drinking," he said.

Everyone burst into a massive laugh.

"Are you sure?" Ollie was completely shocked. "You giving up drinking is like Danny giving up his tracksuits!"

"Stop laughing!" Charlie looked serious. "I've been thinking after the derby game. I need to raise my level further. I can't let things like booze and women stand in the way."

"Yeah I felt that too. There is a lot more we need to do to get to that level," Thomas agreed.

"As for Richard, I think he should stay. We are building something great here, I strongly believe that. But that's ultimately your call," Charlie said.

"I agree. I love it here," said Richard as he naturally turned to look at Layne.

"Oh I think I know why you're staying," Ollie said. "You know what… that's important too. I can't imagine moving abroad without my Misha."

"Hey I think it's time for us to have some food!" Richard thought it was time to change topic, as the food arrived.

Jon reported back to Richard later that week with the contract offers from the two German clubs. They were willing to nearly double his wages – but given the low starting position he was in, it didn't make much of a material difference and was still a very long way from those astronomical salaries that footballers were known to earn.

Richard remained keen to stay with the Black Dragons, so Jon suggested to initiate a contract negotiation with them instead. Richard wouldn't mind getting a pay rise but insisted to Jon that he wanted to maintain his good relationship with the club.

Jon was told by the club that they were already preparing contract extensions for some of the under 23 team players and Richard was one of them. He would hear more when they were ready.

Training for that week was focused on playing in tight spaces. There were plenty of drills on close controls, movements, awareness and 5-a-side matches. Richard found that while he was good in these situations defensively, there was a lot to learn on his attacking side, as pointed out previously by his mentor Michael. Danny was great on both fronts as he had the engine to go non-stop for a long period of time.

Then came two breaking news. David announced that Lewis the capable left back had been officially promoted to the first team, to the excitement of all, but he also said that Paul had been suspended by the team on disciplinary grounds after he was caught drink driving after a night out with friends outside the club.

The young Dragons' next game was against the side from Bristol. Layne took full advantage of Lewis's move and played the whole ninety minutes. His cross halfway into the second half was flicked on at the near post by Charlie and Alex applied the finish at the far post to settle the tight contest.

They then travelled across south London to the main stadium of the Premier League club. The intense battle in front of one and a half thousand supporters ended goalless thanked to man of the match Les, who commanded the area with authority and made some important last ditch tackles.

The next game week took the young team back to The Dragons Stadium for their encounter with one of the Sheffield sides. Charlie's renewed focus on his life choices paid dividend as he scored both goals to complete the turnaround in a 2-1 victory. The home side fell behind early on to a tight offside call but the two thousand fans had the last laugh as the energised Charlie converted passes from Danny and Alex expertly late on.

The match marked the end of Richard's involvement that season, as he planned to go on study leave to focus on his A-Level exams. But before he left, the club's media team asked if they could interview him and Tom to talk about their teammates as part of a review of the under 23 team's first ever season. He was a little reluctant but Layne persuaded him to take part.

"The more you go in front of the camera, the better you become," he said.

The host would ask the midfield partners a series of questions about the team. It was in the format of a popular football show so they knew it well.

Host: We'll start with something easy. Which player trains the hardest?
Richard: Danny, without a doubt.
Tom: Danny is "The Machine", but Lewis worked really hard, too.

Host: Who is the most skilful?
Richard: It's either Owen or Charlie.
Tom: I'll say Owen is slightly better.

Host: Who's the hardest to beat?
Richard: ... Les?
Tom: (pointing at Richard) "The Unbeatable"!

Host: Who's the biggest moaner?
Richard: Max, he's a perfectionist.
Tom: Charlie, nothing is right for him.

Host: Who's the brainiest?
Richard: ... (blushed)
Tom: (pointing at Richard) Mr Lucas – he's going to get four straight A's this summer!

Host: Who's the quickest?
Richard: We actually had a race the other day, Layne came out on top. Rob was a close second.
Tom: Owen is pretty quick too, but yes it was Layne.

Host: Best and worst dress sense?
Richard: The best is probably Alex, he goes to all these fashion shows. The worst... Danny?

Tom: I'll say Owen is pretty cool, he looks like a model. The worst is either Danny or Boiler, I'm sure they wear their tracksuits to weddings.

Host: Who is the worst DJ?
Richard: Rob, I'm just not a fan of having hip hop non-stop.
Tom: Thomas and his old country collections.

Host: Who's the joker?
Richard: Well Ollie was in the under 18, but in the 23's I'll probably say Jack?
Tom: Ollie once hid inside my locker and scared the shit out of me… excuse me for the language.

Host: Who's the best dancer?
Richard: Baek-min? He loves his K-pop.
Tom: Rob and his break dance.

Host: One secret fact of the other?
Richard: Tom is a very good chef.
Tom: Rich is our Tetris champion.

Host: Final question. Who spends the longest in the shower?
Richard: … (face palm).
Tom: (pointing at Richard) HIM.

Richard and Tom watched the playback and it was actually quite funny. The media team did another clip with "cross bar challenge" as well, Richard missed and hit the post while it was won by Jack, Danny and Nick the Assistant Manager.

16.

New Coach

The Thames Ditton under 23 team completed their season with one win out of their three last matches. They won 2-1 away in Wales with goals from Les and Owen then lost their next game 4-3 against the second best team from the northern section, despite equalising three times, with the last one being Layne's first ever goal for the team. Finally, the top team from the south comprehensively beat them 3-1 at The Dragons Stadium, with three goals in the first half.

It wasn't highlighted by David or any of the coaching team but Layne believed Richard's absence had a big part to play for the eight goals conceded, as the top teams were able to find gaps against the less disciplined midfield pairing of Tom and Max. Richard brushed it off as nonsense and claimed that the other teams were just that much better, as their league positions suggested.

Disappointingly, the Black Dragons ended up third in the southern section of the Professional Development League 2, just a single point behind the south east London club, who qualified for the knock out stage against the top two sides from the northern section. The forfeited game against their rivals turned out to be crucial – had that been at least a draw the Black Dragons would have finished second. David still believed it was the right action to take and urged the team to have a good summer break and come back stronger the next season, but there were jibes from Ivan who suggested supporting the boys was the wrong idea.

A massive news followed when the players gathered for their end of season team meeting. David had been promoted to become Assistant Manager to Bob Warner in the first team, who completed their second season in the

Championship in sixteenth place, having secured their safety with five games to spare. He would be replaced by Martin Frisk, who used to work for the Black Dragons' partner club in Sweden and coached the likes of Viktor and Kasper.

Richard was happy for David but felt a bit lost with the uncertainty.

Alex and Charlie ended the season as the team's top scorer and assist provider respectively. Richard, having played a good amount of games, was offered an improved contract by the club alongside Tom, Danny, Charlie, Les, Max, Owen and Alex. He also learnt that Paul's contract had been terminated after his multiple disciplinary problems. He considered that a fair outcome but felt for Paul as his dream to become a professional footballer might have reached the end.

Following Lewis's footsteps, Les and Josh the goalkeeper had been transferred to the first team. Failing to negotiate a similar promotion, Max declined the new contract offered and joined a club from Sussex in League One instead. The club had also agreed the transfers of Ivan, Francis, Mitchell and Peter to League Two sides. Finally, the popular Baek-min had accepted the invitation to play for a top division club in Seoul, the South Korean capital.

The remaining fifteen players would stay with the under 23 team for the next season. They were joined by Andrew, Billy, Caden, Finley, Harry, Mason and Ollie from the under 18's and the club would be recruiting throughout the off season for new players. As part of their strategy to compete with clubs with bigger budgets in the division, they would apply their data-led approach to look for suitable young players either released by others English clubs or from other leagues.

Apparently, there were offers for Danny, Charlie and Owen from other Championship clubs but the Black Dragons turned them down. Charlie's father Miles, the Director of Football who was in charge of transfer activities, didn't think the prices were right for their potential. The players didn't want to leave either so it was an easy decision at the end.

Richard and his teammates gathered to have some farewell drinks with their friends Peter and Baek-min, who were leaving the Black Dragons.

Peter arranged it at a newly renovated pub restaurant by the sailing clubs, which was a stone throw's away from Richard and Layne's apartment. The two arrived early and found Peter, Alex and his new Spanish girlfriend Isa there.

"Hey Rich and Layne, you're early!" Peter welcomed the two.

"Well we only live up there," said Richard as he pointed at his apartment. "It'll be rude not to be early, especially on a lovely day like this."

"Now we are in off season, you have no excuse not to drink then?" Layne asked Richard.

"I guess you only asked because you want a sip?" Richard knew his young partner well. "We're not in Germany so you're a kid again."

"Oh come on! The local ale is so good!"

Richard gave him a smile and ordered a pint from the bar with Peter. He couldn't really resist Layne's demands.

By the time they came back, Baek-min, Charlie, Tom, Danny and Owen had arrived. The team chatted about the decision for the two players to leave, the prospect of playing first team football and their holiday destinations.

Peter told the team that he had a frank conversation with David near the end of the season, and he told him that his chance to play for the Black Dragons' first team was slim and it might be better for him to gain experience at a lower level. So he asked his agent to invite some bids and he ended up moving to Bedfordshire. He said that even though his new club was currently in League Two, they were very ambitious and the plan was to return to the higher levels in the coming seasons. He also said that his new manager wanted to play him as a centre forward again, so even though he was sad to leave the Black Dragons, he was looking forward to the move.

The case was slightly different for Baek-min. The Black Dragons were happy with his development but his father, who was also his agent, set up the transfer to the K-League using his network. The right back was tempted by the chance to live in his parents' home country as well as playing for a top division club.

Thomas, Rob and Ollie arrived and the former teammates toasted farewell for the duo. They were happy that Peter and Baek-min found their ways forward in the cruel world of football. There was no guarantee for those remaining that they would feature for the first team but they all treasured the time they had together and wished them the very best.

The group then moved on to discuss their plans for the summer break. Richard couldn't go anywhere for the first week because he would be taking his final A-level exams – he was fairly confident on getting good grades for his first two subjects and had prepared well for the last ones.

Alex was planning to go to Isa's home town near Barcelona for a month and asked if his teammates would join him in the city for a week near the end of it. Layne thought that would be a great idea and as Richard had never been there, he would be happy to join for both the city and its food. So were Danny, Owen, Ollie, Rob and Charlie, but the latter two wanted to go there earlier for a longer stay. Tom needed to check with Mihara and Thomas would be staying with Elle as their baby was due soon.

"It'll be a repeat of Bournemouth last year, only miles better!!" Charlie was excited. "Think about all the girls and, err, boys, on the Barceloneta beach!"

"I'd love to see the famous stadium," Danny said. "Shame there will be no games when we go."

"Jamón ibérico, fresh seafood and paella…" Richard could only think about the tasty Spanish cuisine.

"Yes! We're in. Mihara said yes!" Tom announced after checking her latest message.

Charlie volunteered to take charge of the accommodation, as he still couldn't let go of the "budget holiday" arranged by Richard and Danny the year before.

"Don't go over the top, not everyone is on your contract!" the sensible Thomas warned.

"It's five stars or nothing with the Ranger Tour!" Charlie claimed.

The traditional pub food arrived and the team had a good time by the river. Layne got a bit merry after a few drinks and Richard had to get him home early.

"I shouldn't really let you get drunk like this," Richard told him as he piggybacked him to the apartment.

"It's just a few drinks…"

"Here you go!" said Richard as he threw Layne into bed and began walking away.

"You're not going anywhere," Layne said as he pulled him back into bed.

"Okay, it's off season, you'll get what you deserve," Richard responded with a smile.

A week had passed quickly and Richard had completed all his exams. He had done all he could so it was just a matter of waiting for the results.

The pair had a discussion a while ago on where to spend their first ever holiday together between the exams and their annual trip with their teammates. Richard was keen to go to Italy for the historic architecture (and food), but Layne went there a few years ago with his school and didn't fancy going again so soon. He suggested the likes of Majorca and Mykonos but Richard didn't want a party style holiday with Layne not being allowed to drink. Somehow, they settled on Cornwall, because Layne had fond memories of the area due to it being one of the few places that he remembered visiting with both his parents when he was young. Richard was happy to go as he would like to do some driving.

So they spent a few days back at Layne's family home in Bath before continuing their journey to the seaside town of St Ives. Richard did ask his mum if they could visit on their way but his dad turned them down.

The two had a fantastic time away. Layne was keen to re-visit all the spots that he had pictures with his dad from back then and they followed the photo album to the various landmarks. They tried to maintain some distance when they were in crowded areas but would find a quiet corner on the beach for some private time together – holding their hands or a couple of kisses below the sunset.

They had a few days back at their Surrey home before they joined their friends for the team holiday, in sunny Barcelona.

Charlie had, predictably, booked THE landmark hotel on the Barceloneta beach. Layne was very happy – its own private beach and roof top swimming pool were pure luxury. Charlie arranged a king sky room with a far-reaching sea view for the pair.

"Imagine having sex while looking at this view!" Layne said giddily.

Richard and Layne had a walk along the beach after lunch at the beach club with the team. They were holding hands just like any other couples.

"Things can't get much better than this," Richard said as he kissed Layne on the cheek while they enjoyed the sea breeze.

"Glad I'm sharing them with you!" Layne was also loving the moment.

They continued along the beach until a five-a-side football game caught their attention. There was a little crowd watching it, seemingly excited by what they saw. They then noticed that Tom, Danny and Owen were playing barefooted for the "skins" team amongst the local beach goers and they were the ones wowing the crowds with their skills.

Soon the game finished and Danny's side were a couple of players short. He spotted Richard and Layne in the crowd and waved them to join in. They weren't so sure about it first but the people next to them urged them on, and when the pair took their shirts off, they gave them a big cheer and plenty of whistles.

"We'd better not let the team down then," he said when he gave Danny a high five.

Richard took a few seconds to steady himself into the mindset of playing. It was his technique to get "in the zone" and he did that every time he got on the pitch for real. He wouldn't play if he wasn't being serious.

That, obviously, became a nightmare for the youngsters in the other side. They couldn't manage to get past this new monster they were facing and Richard's side must have won the twenty-minute match by more than fifteen goals to nil. Tom the keeper had hardly anything to do.

"Maybe you were a bit too serious there, Rich," even Danny joked when they shook hands after the game.

"Was I?" Richard came back to normal from his match mode.

"You were flying in to tackle the poor lad – fair enough it wasn't a foul but it's a little OTT for a beach game?" Tom laughed.

"I'll say fair play mate – every game is a cup final," said Owen.

"You turning into beast mode reminded me of my first training match with the Black Dragons," Layne said as he gave Richard a hug. "Good that you're consistent."

The crowd gave them a huge round of applause and players of the other team joined in as well.

"You guys are so good! And you are a monster, my friend. Do you play for a team?" they asked Richard.

"We're from the Black Dragons," Richard pointed at Danny, who was wearing the team shorts.

"You guys are pros?" the youngsters realised what they were up against.

The players said their goodbyes and headed back to the hotel to get ready for dinner at the main restaurant with the rest of the group.

The restaurant was famous for its grill. Richard had one glance at the menu and knew his choice straight away – he wanted the massive tomahawk steak.

"Are you sure?" Layne shouldn't be shocked but he was. "It's over two kilograms!"

"You'll share with me, right?"

"Of course I will, but I'm not sure we can finish it, especially if you order side dishes as well?"

"Don't you worry about me and food."

"But I want to try the lobster…"

"Oh that's a curve ball… do you have to?"

"Err… sorry to interrupt your rather public private conversation… I can help with the steak if you don't mind?" Ollie came to the rescue.

After the group placed their orders, the sommelier came over and offered to match everyone's dish to a specific wine. When it was Richard's turn, he recommended a glass of Shiraz to go with his tomahawk steak with Chimichurri sauce. Layne then jumped in to ask what matched his grilled lobster and the sommelier responded, to the amusement of everyone, "Sir, the best one for you is a glass of limonada."

The food arrived and the waiter cut the tomahawk steak into multiple pieces. They looked absolutely delicious – cooked to perfection with a charred crust on the outside while the inside stayed juicy and colourful. Ollie took slightly more than a third and left Richard with the lion's share. He was truly satisfied.

The meat and wine went down really well and Charlie suggested a visit the nightclub near the top of the hotel afterwards. It was strictly over eighteens only so Richard, Layne and the other young ones went to the beach instead. There were plenty of parties along the beach clubs so they had a lot of fun too.

Richard and Layne turned up for breakfast the next morning after an early swim in the pool and met everyone apart from Charlie and Rob, who apparently were partying until the early hours. The former did say he would drink less, but the real effort remained to be seen.

They finally turned up at the end of the breakfast session and the plan for the day was for the players to visit both football stadiums in the city, and for the girlfriends to go shopping. He arranged a minibus for the nine of them and the first stop was the smaller RCDE Stadium in the west of the city. They saw the press room, the changing rooms, the dugout and the club's museum. It was the first stadium tour for many of the players and Danny was particularly excited. He read into every article, photo and finally the trophies. It was handy to have the Spanish speaking Alex next to him for the odd piece that didn't come in English.

Then came the big one, Camp Nou – the world-famous stadium for one of the biggest football clubs on earth. Charlie booked a tour that showcased the players' experience, including exclusive access to the changing room and a walk along the famous pitch. Danny was living his dreams.

"I've never seen you smile so much," Tom teased.

"I'll play here one day," Danny said.

It was late afternoon when they finished the tour and the minibus took them to the most extraordinary landmark of the city – La Sagrada Família, the unfinished church by Antoni Gaudi. Richard was amazed by the sheer size of the Basillica but he wasn't comfortable with the amount of tourists there when he went through the long queue just to buy a book on its history.

The group went their separate ways after an upmarket seafood dinner in Las Ramblas and the pair had a quiet walk around the Gothic Quarter then along the beach on route to the hotel.

"Have you ever thought about doing THAT on the beach?" Layne with a cheeky question.

"What?" Richard was shocked, "No, no and no!"

"Won't it be fun? How about one in the water?"

"No, no and no!" Richard wasn't interested.

"How about swimming naked?" Layne never ran out of idea.

"No, no and no!" Richard was getting agitated.

"Okay okay, let's just stick to 'sex with a sea view', granddad," Layne gave up, "… how about a bubble bath together?"

"I guess I can manage that."

The pair returned to find their room romantically decorated with rose petals and balloons. Layne was pleasantly surprised.

"Happy dating anniversary, baby!" Richard said while he presented Layne a little present.

It was a pair of silver necklaces with the date of that night in Bournemouth and its geographic co-ordinates engraved upon the pendants in the shape of a rectangular cuboid.

"Oh these are lovely Richie! Thank you so much!" Layne said before he wrapped his arms round Richard's neck and kissed him.

"Fancy a bubble bath together?" Richard asked, having pre-arranged it with the hotel.

Layne giggled at the idea and they found a beautifully scented hot bath with petals all over it already prepared for them. They enjoyed a lovely time together.

"What's so funny Richie?" Layne asked when Richard stopped midway through sex and burst into a laughter.

"I suddenly remember your earlier comment when I look up at the sea view! It's lovely even when it's dark!"

"Hehe, shouldn't you just look at me when we're at it?"

"Okay baby, eyes on you only!"

After spending the next day relaxing by the beach, Richard and Layne were ready to do some more sightseeing. Charlie, Rob, Ollie and Owen invited Richard to a super car driving experience near the hotel but he would rather go for a hunt of Gaudi's architecture with the others instead.

The first stop for the group of seven was Parc Güell in the north of the city. It was a park with plenty of colourful buildings and sculptures covered in mosaics. They spent a few hours there before visits to Casa Vicens, Casa Milà and Casa Batlló. They finally settled in a seafood kiosk inside the famous Mercat de la Boqueria in Las Ramblas.

The group arrived there early to beat the usual crowd and they sat on the high chairs at the counter surrounding the chef. The food was cooked right in front of them and it was fresh and delicious.

"Food tastes best when they are served hot," Richard claimed.

The rest of the holidays followed a similar pattern for the pair – a run or swim in the morning, a breakfast buffet, relaxing by the beach or pool and finished by a trip to some local restaurant. They spent most days with the more disciplined Danny and Tom, while the others enjoyed their more extravagant ways.

The week-long holiday went in the blink of an eye and the group returned home to the news that Elle had successfully given birth to a baby boy, whom the couple named Archie. Richard and Layne went to visit them a few days later and were glad to see them doing well.

17.

The Break

Richard's third season with Thames Ditton Football Club started with a speech by the new under 23 team manager, Martin Frisk.

"Welcome back from your holidays. I'm glad to see that you're all fit and raring to go. I have a few words to say before we begin our campaign.

"As you know, my name is Martin and I'm your new manager in the under 23 team. Nick and Tim have followed David into the first team so here we have Magnus your new Assistant Manager and Mads your new Technical Coach. We are from the partner club in Sweden and have been heading the youth department for over five years.

"Our philosophy is simple. We are here to prepare young players for the first team, both physically and mentally. We would follow the same shape and playing style of the first team so you'll have a smooth transition if and when you are called up. Train well, play well and I think you can all be there.

"During the last few weeks we have been studying your statistics as we learn about you. They are useful but for me, everyone starts with a blank piece of paper, if you train well, you play the next game. Reputation is not the telling factor. Are we all clear? Let's go for a successful season!"

With Les moved to the first team, Tom had been named as the under 23 team's captain, with Thomas as the vice-captain. The club had signed two players during off season, both of them were eighteen years old: left back Marcus Wolston from a local team and midfielder Stefan Wahlberg from Sweden.

Richard obtained the new twenty-three-man squad:

Goalkeeper:
Caden Cox, Arben Gashi, Jack Simpson

Defender:
Thomas Bond, Mason Brown, Layne Moore, Thorsten Strømme, Viktor Svensson, Ollie Wallace, Marcus Wolston

Midfielder:
Kasper Boilesen, Richard Lucas, Billy McCarthy, Tom Nelson, Harry Smith, Stefan Wahlberg, Danny Westwood

Attacker:
Rob Daniels, Owen Fairclough, Andrew Harding, Alex Knight, Finley Long, Charlie Ranger

Richard and his friends were given new squad numbers. Most of them were now in the thirties, except Alex who wanted to stay with 47. He started branding himself as AK47, and changed his goal celebration to resemble the firing of a machine gun. Richard had number 36 while Layne had his request accepted for 37. He just wanted to be next to Richard's.

Pre-season training was as tough as it ever was but Richard felt it was much more manageable this year, after his specific training the season before.

At the end of the fourth week the team set off to a pre-season tour in Portugal. They would play against under 23 teams from Guimaraes, Braga and Porto. They all played in the Portuguese top division and would certainly be tough opponents for the young Dragons.

The team followed the same routine from previous tours and played the first two teams in their first team stadiums built for the European Championships back in 2004. The latter was well known for their unusual architecture, with one of the ends carved straight from a cliff.

The first game saw the Black Dragons pegged back twice in an entertaining 2-2 draw against a team full of talented South American players. They fared better in the second game with a 2-1 win. Danny the second half substitute amazingly scored directly from a corner to settle the tight match.

The team then travelled back to Porto to their hotel, which was next to the main stadium in the north eastern part of the city.

The officials welcomed the team and gave them a tour of the stadium straight away. The 50,000-seated stadium was also one of those built specially for the Euro 2004 and was visible from miles away due to its elevated position. The youngsters were particularly obsessed by the vast collection of trophies on show, including all the major European ones.

However, they were a little bit disappointed that their friendly match with the home team would not be played there – it would be at the training complex in the south of the city instead.

"We'll play here in a competitive game one day Rich," Danny said.

The coaches had arranged a team dinner by the riverside that evening but the players had some free time beforehand, so Richard and Layne went to the city centre for a quick tour.

Their first stop was the main train station which was renowned by its elevated azulejo tile work. Richard spent a good thirty minutes to study the murals showing historic battles and daily life activities of people from back then. Layne ran out of patience and went to get a couple of milkshakes from the popular chain restaurant which was located in a historic café nearby.

They then visited the city's cathedral before venturing through some hidden paths between local residence to reach the river front by the iconic metal bridge, Ponte Luis I.

They spotted Charlie, Owen and Rob straight away, as they were enjoying coffee al fresco by the river.

"Hey Rich, do you fancy a visit to one of those wineries the other side of the river after training tomorrow?" Charlie asked, "I want to get some Ports for my old man."

"That'll be great – I'd love to see how they are done," Richard liked the idea.

The group caught up with the others at the restaurant for the team dinner. It was a modern steak house with a wine bar.

"Tomahawk ribeye is on the menu!" Ollie shouted across the table to Richard and Layne, "Are you having that?"

"Maybe not again so soon," Richard laughed.

He opted for a T-bone this time, as it was not a normal cut back home.

The meal was delicious and the team had a good get together. Richard didn't know the serious looking Martin had a funny side – he was having beer after beer and became rather rowdy soon. In contrast, the re-born Charlie was only having one for the night, saying he needed to be ready for training the next day. Richard had a glass of red wine to go with the steak but no further drinks. Layne asked for a mojito but the waitress gave him a nojito, or a virgin mojito, instead. However much he tried to look over eighteen, no one was fooled by his boyish looks.

Light training the next day ended at about one and it was free time for the team again. Richard and Layne went to the south bank of the Douro River for a winery tour with Charlie and others. A total of fifteen players signed up and so they literally occupied the whole tour. It was quite a scene as they were all in their team gears.

They visited the wine cellar of one of the oldest port producers in the Douro Valley. There were antique casks, vintage wines and plenty of pictures and videos from the past. There was a wine tasting session at the end and the players got to sample a typical ruby and also a tawny – a style of port that had a nutty flavour due to them "being aged in wooden barrels exposing them to gradual oxidation and evaporation". Layne, Andrew and Finley somehow managed to be seen as over eighteens and got their drinks too – to be fair, the staff was probably right to assume all members of an under 23 football team to be old enough. The tawny was quite strong and Layne got a little tipsy – it was easy to tell as his cheek turned red every time he had a tiny bit of alcohol.

After the tour the team were, naturally, led to the store for some souvenirs. Charlie bought a few of the expensive bottles for his father and Layne wanted to get a nice one for his mum.

"Do you want some for your parents?" he asked Richard.

"My dad is still mad at me. Do you think it'll help?" Richard said as Layne touched on a sore subject.

"A little gift won't hurt. Let's get this one for them," he said as he picked up a nice bottle of vintage wine.

The pair then went on a hunt for all the blue tiled buildings in the city. They saw the Capela das Almas, Igreja dos Carmelitas Descalços and Igreja dos Clérigos amongst others. Richard surprised Layne by taking him to the lavishly designed historic bookstore which was said to have inspired a scene in his favourite fantasy novel. To their annoyance, it was full of tourists and they had to give up on having a picture taken together.

They then re-joined their friends for dinner. They went to a traditional snack bar known for its unique hot dogs (cachorrinhos) and sandwiches (francesinha). Richard was particularly fond with the latter, which was made with bread, wet-cured ham, linguiça, steak, covered with an egg and melted cheese and a hot and thick spiced tomato and beer sauce. They noticed on the wall of fame that plenty of famous Portuguese footballers and coaches had visited there before and Layne asked the waiter if he would have one taken with "The Mighty Black Dragons", and he happily obliged.

Martin picked his strongest team to start the next day, with Jack in goal, Viktor, Layne, Thomas and Thorsten in defence, Richard, Tom and Danny in midfield, with Charlie, Alex and Owen upfront.

Being the under 23 team of a European giant, the home side was not an easy opponent. The players were quick, skilful and composed. They quickly took the lead when the pacy left winger made some space against Viktor and delivered a perfect curling cross into the head of the diving centre forward.

But the Black Dragons were not an easy team to play against either. They restored parity five minutes later with Alex, who held off the centre back's challenge to tip Danny's through ball into the back of the net. It was the result of some brilliant build-up play, where the team had a string of thirty passes together before the killer ball.

The home team went forward again and Richard broke down the attack just outside the penalty box with another great tackle. He heard a familiar shout of "Richie" from his left and immediately hit a long curling ball towards the left channel. Layne was there to bring the ball into the massive space ahead before cutting it back at the very last moment for the unmarked Danny, and he smashed the ball in to complete the comeback.

The exciting first half ended 2-1.

The second half kicked off in a similar fashion as the first, with plenty of attacks from both sides. The home side's left winger continued to be a nuisance and he soon created another chance. His cross was punched out by the substitute goal keeper Arben and the loose ball bounced towards their centre midfielder. He steadied himself and hit the ball first time.

Richard was about five yards in front of him and he blocked the ball with his right arm, which was in its natural position next to his hip. The referee didn't see that as a foul but Richard felt an extreme pain coming from his wrist. He knelt down on the ground holding it – he tried hard not to scream but his face couldn't hide the distress.

He had a look at his right wrist and it had a swelling lump the size of a squash ball already. He tried to generate some force from it and the extreme pain resurfaced again. He didn't know what to do.

"It looks like a Colles fracture, it's not good," Magnus the Assistant Manager said. "We need to take you to the hospital straight away."

"What does it mean?" a worried Layne asked.

"It's basically a broken wrist. His radius by the looks of it, I just hope the ulna is okay," Magnus said.

One of the home team's coaches drove Magnus and Richard to a hospital in the north of the city. He had an X-ray and the consultant confirmed that he had a distal radius fracture, which meant the radius was broken near the wrist. The broken end of the radius connected to the wrist tilted to the other side of his ulna, which was the reason behind the severe pain. The consultant also said he had to be operated on within the next twenty-four hours to prevent any lasting damage. His arm would be put in a cast for at least six weeks and he would be out of action for about three months.

By the time he moved to his ward, Layne had arrived. The match ended in a 2-2 draw, the home side equalised with ten minutes remaining, but that clearly wasn't his concern at the time.

"How are you feeling?" he asked.

"Better now with the pain killer," Richard said. "It was a bit tough before."

He told Layne the diagnosis and the next steps, that he would go through a general anaesthetic and would have to stay in Portugal for a few more days. The team was scheduled to fly back to London that evening but Layne obtained permission to stay with Richard until he could travel. Magnus would also be there for the whole duration.

The operation took place the next morning and it was successful. It was a massive relief for Richard as the night before was probably the hardest he had ever endured. The pain resurfaced every time he went asleep and he was staying in a completely unfamiliar place. Even though he was well informed, there were moments when he feared for his career, when memories of Steve's injury creeped up on him.

He was so sleepy after a general anaesthetic. When he woke up the first time, he could only see a blurred Layne by his side, and he muttered something like "don't worry" and "I love you" before falling asleep again.

The next time he woke up he realised he was in a private ward. His left hand was connected to some tube which led to a bag of drips hung on a metal frame on wheels. Layne was asleep on a chair not far from him and he was woken up by the noise of Richard's movement. He looked tired but wasn't as worried as before and was delighted to see Richard.

"How are you feeling? You've been sleeping for a long time," he asked.

"I feel better now. The arm still hurts, it's like something's stabbing me whenever I move."

"That's because they put two metal pins in your arm to stabilise the bones."

"That'll explain it. How long am I going to be in this for?" Richard asked while trying to hold his cast up.

"They said four weeks before they change you into in lighter one for another two."

"That's not good. I'll be out of the team for months!" Richard sighed.

"Bad things happen sometimes. You just have to go through it," Layne said before he gave Richard a kiss on his cheek. "I'll take care of you, don't worry."

"Thank you, Ping. Look, I can't even give you a hug now," Richard looked at both his hands and squeezed out a smile. "Can you help me with one thing first?"

"Sure, what do you need?"

"I need to go to the bathroom," Richard said embarrassingly.

"It's alright, it's not as if I haven't played with 'little Richie' before," Layne giggled and helped Richard up.

Richard was discharged from hospital the next afternoon and the pair flew back to London the morning after.

259

The team started the season in brilliant form, winning all of their first four games. Kasper played in Richard's position and he was impressive with his strengths and ability to break up play. The range of his passing was nowhere near Richard's level but he kept it simple and let Tom and Danny dictate the play. Alex was also in great form, scoring in all four matches.

Richard spent the whole of August with his right arm in a heavy cast. He needed Layne's help in almost all his daily activities, including a shower before he purchased a waterproof plastic cast protector. Tom gave him and Layne a lift to training in his new Lexus hybrid SUV every morning and he worked with the physios on cardio and some light exercises that didn't involve his arm.

The pair went to the school on A-Level results day in mid-August. Layne came along as he thought Richard might need his help with his arm still in the cast.

They were met with a familiar face when they entered the school.

It was Sarah. She noticed their arrival and came across. She was holding an opened envelope so she must have her results already.

"Hey Sarah, how are you doing?" Richard greeted her with a hug and kiss on her cheek.

"What happened to your arm? Football incident again?"

"Yes I broke my wrist when I blocked a shot in a friendly game."

"That must be very painful," she said before looking over at Layne, "but I suppose you're well looked after?"

"That's true – I couldn't ask for a better carer," said Richard with a satisfactory smile. "How did your results go?"

"Two A's and two B's, it's okay," she replied. "History is one of the A's."

"That's great, did you meet the offer from your university?" Richard asked. "And which one is that?"

"Yes I did. I'm off to Edinburgh," she looked delighted.

"It's beautiful up there, congratulations!" he gave her another hug. "Do you want to know my results? Just stay here for a second if you do."

"Well, I can't wait to see a letter with just A's on it!"

Richard and Layne picked up the results letter from the school office and came back to where Sarah was.

"Shall we open this?"

Richard promptly broke the seal and took the sheet of paper containing the results out. He had a look, folded it up neatly and put it back in the envelop. He did the whole thing in his usual emotionless look, without a change of impression.

"What are they like?" asked a concerned Layne.

"I'm afraid… you're buying the next four dinners, boy!" he said, finally breaking into a smile. The pair had a side bet, as always.

"You got four A's? Really? How did you do it?" Layne raised his voice in excitement.

Richard nodded, with an even bigger grin this time and opened up his left arm, inviting Layne to give him a hug.

"You can't be too surprised by that – he has an IQ of 147, which puts him amongst the top one percent of the human population," said Sarah.

"Top one percent? And you chose to be a footballer?" Layne was even more surprised now.

"There are professional players with a higher IQ, so don't be silly," Richard explained.

"Congratulations anyway. You had to manage all these together with your football," said Sarah.

"Thanks," Richard looked to Sarah while still having Layne in his arms. "It does feel great."

"Hey Sarah, are you done yet?" another student came over and asked. "Oh, hello Richard, how are you doing?"

"I'm fine, Terry. How are you?" said Richard as he reached out with his left hand for a handshake.

"Yeah I'm okay," Terry said while he put his arm on Sarah's shoulder. "Are we good to go?"

"Yes we are," Sarah said. "Well, all the best to you two, it's goodbye for now!"

"All the best to you too, enjoy university!" said Richard as he opted to wave her goodbye.

"Is that her boyfriend?" Layne asked after Terry and Sarah went.

"I suppose so."

"I sense that you're not best friends with Terry?"

"It's not that bad. Let's not drill into it."

Richard received a message from his mum that said, "Well done and please thank Layne for the wine", but she also mentioned that his father was still mad at him and criticised his decision to become a full time footballer instead of going for higher education.

The teammates branded Richard as "The Scholar" upon learning his results, some went as far as calling him "Professor Lucas". Richard was just relieved that chapter was over and he could fully focus on his football from now on.

Layne was called into Martin's office one day after training. He was told that Youssef and Lewis, the first team's regular left backs, were injured and they wanted him to deputise in the next few games.

"Your chance has arrived!" Richard was very excited, "I can't believe you'll play for the first team at the age of sixteen!"

Layne joined the first team squad for training the following few days and started their next game at home against a team from Lancashire. He informed the team of his relationship with Richard before the first training session and the players were supportive.

Richard watched the game from the Ditton End with Charlie, Tom and Danny. They saw Layne running onto the pitch, giving the mascot dragon a big high five and lining up with the rest of the first team. It was a proud moment for Richard when the announcer said "Number 37, Layne Moore". The home crowd gave him a big roar as encouragement but the away fans jeered and chanted a song asking who he was.

"I wish Layne can blank them out," said a concerned Richard.

"He'll be fine, he isn't as easily distracted as you," Tom said calmly.

The match started and Layne was playing conservatively, without too many forward runs and keeping things simple.

"That's the right way for a debut," Danny commented.

The Championship was known as a tough league for a reason. The intensity was really high and there was no holding back in the physical challenges. The opponents were clearly instructed to target Layne early on and the right winger was given plenty of the ball by his teammates. He tried to take on the youngster but was held at bay by some solid positioning. The right back overlapped on the outside but was tightly followed by the industrious Andrés, the Black Dragons' left winger. The rest of the first team players carried out their defensive duties and as a team they repelled the initial waves of attacks.

The away side altered their approach after their fruitless start and launched a few long balls behind Layne, but the youngster handled them extremely well, wowing the home crowd with his extraordinary pace in those situations. The settled Black Dragons began to take ascendancy as the half went on but they couldn't create a clean cut opportunity, as shots by Kalifa and Ross were not enough to trouble the goalkeeper.

The second half started with a bang, as George the striker who was playing on the right beat the offside trap and found Andrés for a simple finish.

The away team brought another striker on to push for the equaliser and they dominated the rest of the game. Layne was put under immense pressure as he was seen as the more probable option, but Bob replaced Kalifa with Les to play with three centre backs and pulled Andrés back to support the young debutant. The solidified team defended the remainder of match well and George managed to score the killer goal late on from a breakaway to seal the crucial victory.

"That was a great debut. He surprised me with how composed he was," Charlie said.

"That boy doesn't know fear," Richard was relieved.

"He's also grown up to be a really good looking man too!" Tom teased.

"Err... I... wouldn't disagree with that," Richard stuttered with a flushed face.

David invited him into the dressing room after spotting him waiting for Layne after the match. He went in and congratulated the youngster for making his first team debut.

"How did I look from the stands?" Layne asked.

"You were hot, as always," Richard with a cheeky response.

"Hehe, I know that, but I mean the football."

"You were nice and simple today, less adventurous but did the main job well. I guess you can be more effective with more forward runs, but it'll come slowly."

"I can do that. The match went so well – I'd love to see the day when we play together here."

"That day will come."

A 16-year-old making his debut for a Championship club made the news on a number of sports websites. Richard read most of the articles and was glad that all of them were positive and none mentioned their relationship. Some comments on social media mentioned Layne's involvement in that infamous game against the south east London club and highlighted their suspicion on his sexuality, which attracted a number of attacks online. But Richard finally realised what Layne and the others had been saying – if he wasn't specifically looking for these offensive comments, he wouldn't even notice them.

The next game was away to a team in Berkshire. Layne was in the starting line-up again as Youssef was still injured and Lewis was not match fit, having just returned to training. Richard went to the game with Tom, who drove there after their training session.

"I came here a few times when I was young," Richard told Tom.

"I've only been here once. It was a legends game between England and Germany about ten years ago."

"Really? I was here for that game too!" Richard was surprised.

"So we must have met when we were little!" Tom laughed. "Do you remember the rugby tackle by that politician?"

"Yeah, he's a clown on and off the field."

The match started. Richard didn't know if Layne was instructed by Bob but he was more attack-minded that day. He looked more natural with his movements and he connected with the team well. He put in a few dangerous crosses and, having pushed the home team backwards with the positive intend, he wasn't really tested in defence.

"Layne playing like this reminded me of his performance during the latter part of his first season. He was awesome back then with his aggressive movements and solo runs," Tom commented at half time.

"Oh that period," Richard didn't say much, as that was when Layne was mad at him for going out with Sarah.

"What made him that angry back then?" Tom didn't pick up the signal and kept asking.

"Err... I'm sure he was just going through puberty..."

"Oh I got it! You were with Sarah at the time... were you 'connected' with him already?"

"Let's say it was complicated... shall we get a burger?" Richard tried to change the subject.

"Ha-ha yeah let's do that," Tom finally picked up the message.

The second half started after some refreshments. Layne continued to balance his attacking and defensive duties well.

"His energy level is really good with all those running," Tom noticed.

"I worked him hard!" Richard joked.

"Mm... I don't need the details, Rich."

As they were talking, Layne was sent through on the left wing again and he put in a lovely cross to the near post, which was headed in by George!

Richard and Tom were screaming and jumping like mad with the other away fans as the players ran over to celebrate.

"My boy is amazing!" Richard was thrilled.

The Black Dragons held out for the remaining twenty minutes for their 1-0 win. There was a scare late on when the home striker ran through on goal but Layne's supreme pace got him back in time for a crucial block.

Layne was named as the man of the match and he became the main headline in the Championship news section.

"He's getting famous now," Richard said during the car journey back.

"Are you feeling the pressure?" Tom asked jokingly.

"Of course there's a bit. But I'm very happy for him."

Richard got home shortly afterwards and he couldn't stop thinking about Tom's casual comment. It had been five weeks since he broke his wrist and he switched into a lighter cast a few days before. He followed the rehabilitation schedule given to him to the letter and he felt good about his fitness level, but he wasn't allowed to kick a ball until his cast was taken off. Kasper had been playing really well in his absence and it seemed the team had got used to his more defensive style and made up their attacking play in other areas. Part of him felt rather insecure – would the team welcome him back? Would he be able to follow Layne's footsteps and play for the first team? He didn't know, he couldn't figure out an answer.

Layne returned home soon after.

"Welcome home, Mr Man of the Match!" Richard gave him with a big hug.

"It's good to be playing with my natural style, thanks for pointing it out after last week," said Layne as he happily showed Richard his little trophy.

"You really caught the eye today, even some home fans appreciated your performance."

"That was good. How are you feeling with the new cast today? Still painful?"

"Still that stabbing pain. I guess it won't stop as long as the pins are there. Let's not talk about that, what should we have for dinner to celebrate? Shall we head out?"

"Mm... steak house in Richmond, Korean in New Malden or Japanese in Chiswick?" Layne had plenty of ideas.

"I can't drive yet, so maybe Richmond, we can take the bus?"

"We can always take a taxi, don't be so tight."

"Actually, I can't use knife and fork yet... so sushi maybe good."

"Let's do that then! We can share the Tonkatsu like last time if you want?"

"Sure, but please don't try to spoon-feed me in public again!"

Layne's next game was at home against a club from East Anglia, on the day before his seventeenth birthday. He started alongside his former teammate Les in defence. Richard watched in the stands on his own as the under 23 team had an away match in north east London that morning, which they lost 2-1.

The first team had a tough match. Layne continued his good form with some solid defending and wing play, but the team couldn't find a breakthrough.

The game's only goal came in the second half and it was from the away side. They were awarded a free kick thirty yards out and their young midfielder Ben put it straight into the top corner. The Black Dragons pushed for an equaliser but they couldn't make the chances count and their good run of form ended.

Layne's run in the first team had also ended as both the regular left backs were back in full training. Bob and Martin decided it was better for Layne to continue his development in the under 23 team, as he was guaranteed a starting position there. Bob thanked Layne for his contribution in the three matches and vowed to call him up whenever the opportunity arose again.

The pair went out with Harry, Andrew, Finley and Dillon after the match to celebrate Layne's birthday. They had two games of ten-pin bowling in Tolworth before an all-you-can-eat Korean barbeque in New Malden. Richard wasn't able to play but he enjoyed the dinner very much – the sizzling king prawns, squids and beef short ribs were simply delicious. He kept going for more, to the amazement of his younger teammates.

The two went to the club office with Layne's mum the next morning to sign Layne's first professional contract. His agent Jon used his breakthrough performances to negotiate improved terms and succeeded in bringing his salary in line with the likes of Richard and Tom. They were pleasantly surprised by a rare appearance of the club's founder and chairman, the legendary entrepreneur Dr Phillip Edwards. He attended the contract signing and had pictures taken with the players. He seemed impressed when Richard asked him about his encryption algorithms – he probably wasn't expecting his players to be interested in those. He patiently answered Richard's questions in detail and suggested him to attend some lectures at the university where he developed his work to further his understanding. He went as far as saying he could fund Richard's study if he was seriously interested, but Richard said he would focus on his rehabilitation and the season ahead first. He would consider reading a part-time degree in mathematics the next year.

The birthday celebrations continued as Mrs Moore took the pair to a dim sum lunch in Bayswater. Richard had various dumplings with shrimps and pork, some with a rich and burning hot broth inside, rice noodle rolls filled with shrimps, steamed tofu skin rolls filled with minced pork, sweet cream buns and pan-fried turnip cakes. He was mesmerised but the variety of taste and texture and his appetite was truly satisfied when he finished the last portion of braised vermicelli with shredded roast duck.

"I never knew there are so many different ways of cooking!" he said afterwards.

"You've only just touched the surface Richard, there are plenty more for you to explore if you are interested," said Mrs Moore.

"We can come here more often but you'll need to work harder in the gym!" Layne laughed.

The pair said their goodbye to Mrs Moore and went to the large shopping mall nearby for the latest superhero movie. They went clothes shopping afterwards and completed the day with a visit to a popular restaurant for burgers and milkshakes. They didn't have a lot of opportunities to behave like a normal young couple and they had a great time.

18.

The Trialist

Since the start of the season, the under 23 team had seen plenty of trialists trying to get into the team. Most of them didn't make it – not that they were bad football players, they just couldn't improve an already strong team and squad space was limited.

It had been six weeks since his injury and Richard's cast was finally taken off for good. The doctor took the two metal pins out by force, which was a rather unpleasant process, and Richard could finally see his right arm again. It smelled of dead fish and was extraordinarily skinny. It would take weeks of training to get it back in shape, but the good news was that he was allowed to take part in training with the ball.

He was applauded by the team as he ran back onto the training ground. Stuart and the Sports Science team designed a special four-week programme for him to regain his strengths and touches. He would wear a protective gear made from fabric during training and matches for the next few months.

On the same day of Richard's return, the team had another five trialists joining them for the week. Richard had a glance of them as they walked past but had to look again at one of them. He turned his attention away but seconds later came back to have a third look.

He found the young-looking player incredibly attractive.

Oh that's a class A boy!

Being an analytical person, he split all boys (and girls) into five categories with A being the best. For him, Layne was an obvious A. Generally he would be interested in someone if they were classified as an A or a B. The best a girl could do was a B, which meant he would be willing to try if pursued.

It wasn't the first time he met others in such categories, so as normal he just turned away and focused on what he was doing – he had the lovely Layne after all.

There was a practice match at the end of training but Richard wasn't involved – his condition was not ready for physical contacts yet. He watched on from the side as he jogged along and he saw that young trialist again.

This time he had a good look. He was just shorter than him, with a small frame of lean build, his deep seated brown eyes sharply fit on his slightly pale face and his dark brown hair was in a curtain style with an undercut, like one of those young Korean pop stars. He may be young but he was quietly confident with his skills. He was predominantly right footed but he had a more than decent left. He played on the right wing and was equally comfortable cutting inside or hugging the touch line.

The trialist was on the same side as Layne and Danny, and Richard heard Layne calling him Ryan. He got the ball on the right and he dribbled infield along the edge of the box. He couldn't find a way through to goal so he kept going left. Layne was running into the space calling for the ball but Ryan flicked the ball back towards the right side of the area with the outside of his right foot instead. Danny was running in completely unmarked and put away an easy goal. That wasn't an ordinary pass.

He continued to impress with his tricks and movements. Richard noticed that he seemed to have a very strong change of pace and direction. He would use his first touch to push the ball into the area he wanted to go and had the explosive acceleration to get there ahead of his opponent afterwards. He looked more than a decent player.

The practice match ended with the trialist Ryan netting one goal and providing two assists. Martin looked satisfied but Richard wouldn't know for sure if he had done enough.

The trialists stayed with the team for another few days and Ryan kept up his good form – he worked hard in training, scored plenty of goals and created lots of chances.

Richard and Layne had lunch with him and his friend Kyle, another attacker, after training one day and found them pleasant and affable. They were surprised to hear that Ryan was a black belt in Taekwondo and had represented Great Britain at youth levels. At the end of their trial Richard wished them the best of luck – he genuinely hoped that they would be successful.

To his delight, Ryan came back to the Black Dragons' training ground a week later – he was offered a contract alongside another trialist called Zach, who was a centre back, but there was no space for Kyle. Martin introduced them to the team before the day's training.

"Hello everybody, please join me in welcoming two new players today, Ryan King and Zach Morrison. Ryan is a forward who can play across the front and Zach is a central defender who can also operate on the left. You might have seen them during their trials – I believe they are brilliant additions to our team, so please give them your support. Thank you."

"Hi everyone, I'm Ryan. I was born in Ireland but I've been living in Farnham since I was young. Nice to meet you all!"

"Hi I'm Zach from Croydon, pleased to meet you."

The two new joiners trained with Richard that day as they were put through some light training. Ryan was very agile – although he couldn't beat Richard in a take on but he certainly made him work hard to win the ball. Richard learnt that he only just turned sixteen years old, while Zach was eighteen.

Ryan was assigned some gym training and he did them at the same time as Richard's rehabilitation. They got to know each other quite well. Ryan took training seriously but he was happy to have a chat every now and then. He asked Richard about the club, the team members and what happened to his right wrist. Richard learnt that he was playing for the youth team of his local club in the National League before the Black Dragons invited him for a trial. He also learnt that Ryan was doing his A-levels during the afternoons and was a keen mathematician as well.

Richard was clear in his mind when he interacted with Ryan – he was only being friends and teammates, nothing more. He loved Layne to bits and wouldn't do anything to hurt him.

The pair took advantage of the lovely Autumn weather on their next day off and went on a boat trip along the River Thames. They had always wanted one since they moved into their flat having looked at the sailing clubs from their balcony but they never found the time, especially with Richard's injury.

They hired a small boat with an electric motor and the self-appointed skipper-of-the-day Layne "sailed" all the way to the Molesey Lock by the magnificent Hampton Court Palace before turning back towards the other end of the route, the Teddington Lock. They stopped by a mooring along the Home Park and had a small picnic.

"Do you remember our walk here when we moved in?" Layne asked, as the pair sat on the mooring with their feet in the river.

"Of course baby, that was so lovely!"

"Let's have a few more selfies!"

"As you please, silly."

The pair had a great time before they set off again. Richard took over the driving and steered the boat all the way, passing through both bridges at Kingston and the small islands.

"This is so good! We need to do this more often!" Layne said while he enjoyed the breeze.

Richard stared at Layne's childish impressions and smiled – he felt awesome being in a relationship with him and wouldn't swap him for anything.

The under 23 team played another four games when Richard was having his rehabilitation. They won the first one 2-0 against the team from Bristol, drew 1-1 away in Sheffield, 2-2 in a tightly fought out derby at Shepherd's Bush and then were soundly beaten 1-4 at home by the league leaders from east London.

After a total of twelve weeks away, Richard finally returned to the match day squad for the next game away at the blue side of Birmingham.

Martin started the game with Jack, Viktor, Layne, Thomas, Mason, Kasper, Tom, Danny, Charlie, Alex and Owen. Richard was on the bench sitting next to Ryan. It had been raining non-stop but the training centre was of top condition and the teams were able to play their normal passing game.

Richard was talking through the game as usual, pointing out the pattern he was seeing and where the potential space and risks were. Ryan seemed impressed by how much Richard knew as the home side picked up on that yard of space between Kasper and Mason he spotted and scored.

The Black Dragons replied quickly through Charlie as he played a neat one two with Alex and slotted the ball in before the keeper came out. But the parity didn't last long as the home side scored another goal from a free kick soon after.

The second half followed a similar pattern with both sides trying to outsmart the other on the break. Martin asked Richard to warm up since the restart and sent him on to replace Kasper at the hour mark. He had been away with the Danish under 19's and was visually tired.

"Welcome back, buddy," Tom gave Richard a high five as he came on.

"Martin wanted us to push further up to drive their midfield back," Richard whispered to Tom and Danny.

With the hunger from not playing for so long, Richard was into the action straight away and he hunted down every ball in front of him. That caused the home team's midfielders a few panics and disrupted their rhythm. The pressure paid off as Richard forced a midfielder to lose the ball to Danny, who sent Owen through to equalise.

The away side continued with their pressure and forced a number of corner kicks. Richard whipped them across with his typical accuracy and they nearly scored with a couple of them. Mason's header hit the bar and Charlie narrowly missed the target with his.

The high press since Richard's introduction turned the game on its head and the Black Dragons had the last laugh as Richard found Charlie on the left and his lay off sent Layne through on goal and he put the winner away. He ran over to Richard to celebrate and the rest of the team joined in for a big pile up on them. Richard ducked out of the group in time to protect his fragile wrist. The game soon ended 3-2 to the Black Dragons.

"What a turnaround! Well done boys!" Martin congratulated the team.

"Your command to press higher worked a treat," Richard responded.

Martin pointed his fingers on his eyes and winked, "Good to see your hard work paid off too!"

"Those long through balls you played were amazing!" Ryan told Richard, his eyes full of admiration.

"Thanks buddy," Richard said.

The under 23 team's next match was away to Suffolk. Martin decided to start with Richard in midfield ahead of Kasper and went back to playing with two deep sitting midfielders. His full team was Jack in goal, Ollie, Layne, Thomas and Thorsten in defence, Richard, Tom and Danny in midfield and Charlie, Alex and Rob upfront. Owen had been summoned to the first team as they needed more options in attack.

The match started with the Black Dragons on the front foot. A good combination between Charlie, Danny and Layne set up Rob for a shot but it was well saved by the keeper. Thomas then missed a great chance when his header went narrowly over the bar from Richard's out-swinging corner.

The young Dragons finally took the lead after twenty-five minutes. Alex was fouled in the box when he tried to meet a cross from Ollie and a penalty was given. Richard stepped up and sent the ball powerfully into the bottom left corner, despite the keeper diving the right way.

The away side made it two five minutes later when Danny chipped Alex's laid off into the area for Charlie to volley it home. The home team went close from a free kick late on but the effort was pushed out for a corner by Jack. The first half ended comfortably to the Black Dragons.

The home side staged an unlikely comeback in the second half, with two goals in quick succession ten minutes in. Both came from set pieces: the first one from a corner and the second one from a free kick not far from it. Martin wasn't happy with the lack of organisation at the back and swapped Ollie and Thorsten with Viktor and Mason. Ryan also came on for Rob.

Knowing Richard's ability to hit accurate long passes, Ryan kept making runs down the channel to push the home defence back. Richard tried to find him on the right and Layne and Charlie on the left at every opportunity but his intentions were read by the defence and a number of his passes were intercepted. He eventually created a chance with five minutes remaining when his through ball caused the central defender to clatter into Danny for a free kick some twenty-five yards away from goal.

Danny put the ball down and gave Richard the gesture to have a go. Richard steadied himself and focused on what he wanted to do – to curl his shot over the wall and into the top left corner. He put the ball down, took five equal steps backward, with his eyes on the target only. He ran up, hit it and the goal keeper had no chance. The game finally swung back to the Black Dragons' way. Richard lifted both his arms in the air and waited for Layne and others to crash into him to celebrate.

The home side launched a few desperate long balls into the box in their final assaults but the Black Dragons held out for another 3-2 victory.

"Great free kick at the end there Richard," Martin said as they shook hands after the match, "but you'd better watch your long passes going forward – they were a little bit off near the end today."

"Really? I thought we did okay," Richard was a little dismissive as he walked towards the dressing room.

"You're amazing again today, two goal hero!" Ryan told Richard as he was going for a shower.

"Thanks," Richard replied quickly but decided to take his time before going into the old school communal shower with him.

"Don't you want a shower?" Layne asked as he was also ready.

"Err… yeah, let's go," Richard followed him.

Some of the players met up for dinner that evening as they got a free day next. They met at the Italian restaurant in Kingston again and with the number of players and other halves this time they got the whole function room to themselves.

The pair turned up when about half of the party were there. After getting some drinks Danny showed up with his new girlfriend Grace, who was herself a professional football player playing for the big west London club. She was well known for being a tough tackler in midfield.

"I thought you'll always be a single machine," Charlie teased as he welcomed the pair.

"Who said two machines can't be together?" Grace replied with a joke of her own.

"She'll jump in two footed if you keep teasing her," a smiling Danny gave Charlie a friendly warning.

"How did you two meet? You never go out!" Tom asked.

Danny exchanged a smile with Grace before answering, "I was practicing in the park one day and this woman came over and challenged me to a duel. That's how it started."

"How romantic! That's the way for footballers!" Alex joined in.

"Who won the duel though?" Harry asked.

"I think we'll keep that as a little secret," Grace said with a smile.

"No comments from me," Danny added.

"Did you hear that Owen scored two goals on his first team debut earlier?" Tom said.

"Well that was never in doubt – he's that good," Andrew replied.

"I'll join his celebration party in town later tonight, Rob and Ollie are already there," Charlie said.

Young Ryan was the only player there without a partner. He moved to sit next to Richard and Layne. "Do you mind if I sit next to you guys? It looks like we're the only single ones here."

Richard and Layne smiled at each other and raised their intertwined hands up to show Ryan.

"I'm sorry mate, you may be the only one here," Richard said.

"Oh! Sorry I wasn't aware..." he was rather embarrassed. "So the rumours online are true then?"

"What did you hear? I'd love to know," Richard asked.

"Apparently a massive brawl broke out in our game against another club because a player made some homophobic remarks after injuring another," Ryan tried to recall what he read online. "Some said it was a love triangle and some said it was just tackles being overly aggressive."

"Love triangle with James? Oh God..." Layne was bemused and shocked at what he heard.

"That's funny. Did they figure out who were involved?" Richard asked.

"Layne's name popped up a lot as I think he was the one injured in the game, Danny, Alex, Charlie and you were also mentioned."

"I can see why they were picked out... Alright, let me tell you the truth," Richard took his time to tell Ryan what actually happened and the fact that the two of them were living together. He finished by asking Ryan not to tell anyone outside the club.

"It's okay I won't tell, it's good to know the club is so supportive, I-"

Before Ryan was able to complete his sentence, the food had arrived.

Richard and Layne ordered their usual, which was a margarita pizza, a spaghetti Bolognese and linguine alle vongole to share. Ryan had a fillet steak with Italian blue cheese.

"Oh that looks really good!" Richard was a bit food envy.

"Do you want a bite?" Ryan might have felt that he had to offer.

"Don't tempt him – give him a bite and he'll finish your plate!" Layne said.

"Is that how you ended up with him?" Andrew jumped in from the other end of the table.

"How are they even connected?" Richard felt a little hard done by his laughing teammates. "Alright I'll stick to my own food... I only said it looks good..."

The dinner went quickly and the pair went home after Richard had his big slice of tiramisu.

"What do you think about Ryan?" Layne asked Richard when they were in bed.

"In which way? He seems a good player."

"You know what I mean," Layne didn't sound impressed with Richard's answer. "Is he your type? Where is he in your class A to E system?"

"Oh dear why are you asking? It doesn't matter, right?"

"I saw you had a triple take on him when he was on trial. It's okay I'm not doubting you, just interested in your views," Layne explained gently.

"He's an A, if you have to know. But I've maintained a distance from the start," Richard hated lying to Layne so he didn't.

"That's the first one since me then. Was Ian an A, too?"

"Yes, but you're the best."

"Did you fall for anyone else in the team?"

"Err... most of them are quite macho so no, but I used to think Fin was attractive."

"Really? Did you make a move?"

"No way! It was clear from the start that he's one for the ladies."

"True. He's even more of a womaniser than Charlie and Rob!"

"How about you? You never told me about the boys you liked?"

"Well I've… maybe the odd celebrity…"

"Interesting! Which one?"

"Newt in the Maze Runner movies?" Layne said quietly with a blushed cheek.

"He's pretty good actually, have you seen his music video about domestic violence? He was lovely in that. You must have fancied a real person though, come on baby share with me!"

"Mm… there was one…"

"And?"

"I… I don't want to talk about it… But since I met you I don't want anyone else, Richie."

"Ahh… aren't you cute? How can I not love you to bits?" Richard stopped the conversation and snuggled up with Layne instead.

19.

Possession

"There's no 'but' Richard, I'm taking you off. You need to think about your actions on the pitch and the examples you're setting for the younger players!" Martin concluded before he stomped off to the dressing room.

It was half time between the Black Dragons' next match, at home against a strong team from South Yorkshire. Before it started Martin stressed to Richard that he wanted him to keep possession of the ball and be careful with his long passes. The away team was known for being well organised at the back and had a midfield of players with first team experience.

The Black Dragons' first eleven were Jack in goal, Viktor, Layne, Mason and Zach in the back, Richard, Tom and Harry in midfield, Charlie, Alex and Rob upfront.

The away team was set up with three centre defenders so there was space behind the wing backs. Richard tried to find the pacy Charlie and Rob in those areas as he would normally do. However, his passes were all cut out by the centre backs moving across. The away team then kept possession of the ball for long periods and forced the Black Dragons to be chasing all the time.

"Keep it easy!" Martin shouted from the bench as Richard got the ball again.

But Richard saw a gap ahead of Charlie and hit another long ball towards him. It was intercepted by a centre back again. It took another five minutes before the Black Dragons got the ball back and the pattern continued until half time.

"Why don't you follow the game plan? At this rate you'll all be knackered by the hour mark. We don't have to force the game like this!" Martin took Richard aside at half time.

"I could see space behind the wing backs-" Richard tried to explain why he did it.

"It was a false impression. By the time the ball travelled through the air their big centre backs would have moved out to deal with them. We'll be much better playing on the floor."

"But..." Richard was looking for things to say but he was shut down by an angry Martin.

Martin sent Kasper out to warm up and told the team of the change. He reminded everyone that the aim was to keep possession and to build their play from there.

Richard wasn't happy with the humiliation and it showed on his face. Layne tried to talk to him but found him too angry to respond. The team left for the second half soon after.

Mads the Tactical Coach stayed behind to have a chat with Richard. He explained to him that while his passing abilities and vision were very much key to the team, he would need to adapt different approaches against different opponents. At this level and beyond, other teams would study his play and plan accordingly, which was evident in this game. He urged Richard to visit the new Performance Analytics team and review his own statistics. He then pulled Richard out to join the rest of the team on the bench.

"Don't be disrespectful."

Richard heard what Mads said and on reflection he actually agreed with most of it. He took a few deep breaths, calmed himself down and joined the team on the bench. Martin looked at him and Richard gave him a nod. Martin smiled and nodded back.

The team implemented the game plan much better in the second half. The passes were shorter and more assured and they used their abilities on the ground to their advantage. Charlie and Rob were able to get the ball on their feet to drive at the less mobile centre backs. They managed to get a few free kicks and one of them led to the opening goal. Danny, who came on for Harry late in the game, scored with a direct free kick.

The team continued to keep possession well and the away team at bay. The threats were only from set pieces and the team managed those well, following the specific training they had since the last game.

The game ended 1-0 to the home side.

Richard felt good for his friends and was on pitch side welcoming the team back alongside the coaches.

"Are you better now?" Layne asked as he gave Richard a hug.

"Yes, I was being stupid," he said as the two walked towards the dressing room.

"It was strange for you to behave like that on the pitch, you were a bit… overly eager on those Hollywood balls?"

"I don't know, there was an urge to take more risks for some reason."

"Trying to impress someone?" Layne asked while looking at Ryan's direction.

Richard paused for a second to think about it. Maybe it was true. Ryan had been singing his praise for the ambitious passes and he felt inclined to carry on impressing him.

"Hey Richie, I'm talking to you," Layne got a little annoyed.

"Maybe you are right, maybe I was trying to please my young fan," Richard admitted. "I'll be more conscious in the future."

As suggested by Mads during the last game, Richard arranged a visit to the Performance Analytics team after training one day. He was pleasantly surprised to be welcomed by a familiar face.

It was Steve Fraser, his teammate who was forced to retire from competitive football during his first season with the club.

Richard knew that Steve didn't give up on his footballing journey and started studying a degree on performance analysis the year before. What he didn't know was that Steve asked the club if they could let him analyse the under 23 team's data as part of his project, and he ended up working part time in the new Performance Analytics team.

Richard explained the purpose of his visit and the frustration he was having from the last match. Steve brought up his data and showed him the statistics for games since the start of the previous season, when the data collection started. Richard could see for himself that his passing accuracy had significantly reduced this season, especially over long distances. Steve then compared his statistics to those of Tom, Kasper and the first team's centre midfielders Michael, Kalim and Mark. While Richard was the strongest in terms of interceptions and defensive take on's, he was miles behind in his passing. He was then showed the team's statistics in games with and without him playing, and the pattern was clear – the team kept the ball much better without him and their stamina was also better managed. The number of victories may be similar, but the nature of the games was very different. Matches with Richard in were more won through individual brilliance instead of good build up play.

It was like a moment of wakening for Richard. He realised how much his actions affected the team and what he needed to do going forward. He thanked Steve and arranged to re-visit him in three months' time to see if he could make any improvements.

One day after training Richard got a phone call from Tom.

"Hey Rich, Martin just told me that I'm in the first team squad for the next game!" said an excited Tom.

"Wow that's great news! Did someone get injured in the first team?"

"No, he said Bob and David wanted to give me a try, they said I may be able to offer something different."

"That's brilliant! Such a shame we couldn't come and cheer you on with our game away."

"It's alright, I'll make the team proud."

With Tom away with the first team, Martin kept Richard in the starting line-up in the next game, which was away in south London. Ryan was also given a chance to start after his impressive form in training.

The home side was known to be hard working and operated a high press. Martin reminded the team that there would be limited time on the ball and they had to help each other out with plenty of movements. The key was to pass through the press and attack the space behind.

The game started with the Black Dragons having most of the possession, as if the home team preferred hunting the ball up field instead of building up from their own half. Richard knew Martin had his eyes on him and he made sure he kept his passes short and safe. He would play the odd one two with Kasper and Danny to get out of difficult situations but he would then lay it off to either Layne or Viktor in the full back positions. Keeping it simple was his aim. Ryan had been making forward runs anticipating a long pass from Richard but it didn't come. His movement did stretch the home side a bit and the team did create some half chances but they were thwarted by some excellent defending by the home team. The half ended goalless.

"I don't get the gaffer's game plan. We need to play more forward passes," Danny said to Richard at half time. "We can't have both you and Boiler passing sideways all the time."

"It was about preserving our energy I think," Richard said. "I guess we can be more adventurous in the second half when they're tired. It's a reverse to the match last week."

"I think you're probably right!" said a smiling Martin after he overheard what they were saying, before he whispered to the two players, "We move when Rob comes on."

The second half followed the same pattern as the first. The Black Dragons were safe in their ball control but they couldn't create any clear-cut chances.

They were wearing the home team down slowly but time was running out. Martin had already brought Andrew and Marcus on for Charlie and Layne, and he was getting Rob ready with fifteen minutes left. But the plan didn't materialise as Viktor pulled up just before Rob came on for Ryan and Martin had to use the last substitution to bring Ollie on.

Richard and Danny exchanged a glance and agreed that they had to force the issue anyway. Kasper stopped a counter attack by the home side and gave Richard the ball. After a few short passes with players nearby Richard hit a trademark long ball to the right channel. Danny had slowly drifted to that side and was on the run for it already. He controlled the ball, flicked the ball past the centre back who was rushing out and drilled it low across goal.

Ryan was there to tap in his first goal for the Black Dragons. He went ecstatic and he ran over to Richard to celebrate.

"I knew you'd hit a killer ball sooner or later!" he said as he jumped into Richard before the rest of the team joined in.

The home team had to attack for the remaining ten minutes but they were visually tired after hunting the ball for most of the game. In contrast the Black Dragons still had plenty in the tank and they nearly took advantage of the gaps left behind of the home side, but Andrew's curling effort narrowly went out. The game finished 1-0.

"You've learnt well, Richard," Martin looked happy when he welcomed Richard back. "You were in control of the game. Did you see the difference?"

"Yes I did. Thanks for giving me the chance to prove it."

"You're welcome. We know you have good quality; we just need to make sure you understand more of the tactical side, you're as close to our brain on the field as we get. Well done!" Martin explained.

The team coach had the first team's game on the radio on the way back from south London. Tom started the game on the bench and the under 23 team cheered as he became the latest youth team player to make the transition when he came on with half an hour to go in the second half. The first team were winning 2-0 at that point with another two goals from Owen and the fans gave the local boy Tom a massive cheer. His job was to stabilise the midfield and he successfully protected the result in solid fashion.

The young players gathered for dinner that evening to celebrate Tom's debut. The regulars such as Charlie, Danny, Alex, Ollie, Richard and Layne were there, Thomas managed to get a night off from parental duties and Ryan heard about the dinner and invited himself. They went to a steak house in Richmond where there was plenty of room for large groups.

Layne passed his motorcycle riding test the week before and rode his new Italian scooter there with Richard as his passenger. He always wanted to have one and the inconvenience caused by Richard's injury made up his mind to go for it. Richard was a bit scared with the idea to begin with but he became more comfortable after seeing how mature and confident Layne was on the bike. They bought a pair of low profile helmets with matching details and Richard enjoyed holding Layne from the back when no one was around.

The players toasted for Tom's achievement and they talked about who was going to be next, with the festive fixtures coming up. Tom was told by Bob that he and Owen would be staying with the first team for the foreseeable future, making them the fourth and fifth former under 23 players to complete the switch. There were rumours that some regular starters in the first team were being targeted by bigger clubs, which meant there could be opportunities for the other youngsters too.

The group also congratulated Ryan for his first goal. He was overjoyed and couldn't stop saying how good the build-up was from Richard and Danny. Richard said it was Martin's plan all along and they just executed it. He was starting to understand the benefits of the club's statistics-based approach and he recommended everyone to pay Steve and his team a visit.

For the first time ever, the players were recognised by the other diners. Tom was popular with fans as he only made his first team debut that day, but Layne was also picked out by a few who remembered his performance earlier in the season. The group had a few photos being taken and they were glad that the fans were happy.

With Tom's promotion to the first team, Thomas had been named as the under 23 team's new captain, with Danny and Richard as his deputies.

Their next game was at home against the club from south east London. It was tightly fought out given the recent rivalry between the teams and the Black Dragons came out on top with a 2-1 victory. Alex scored early in the first half with a fine finish from Layne's cross but the away side equalised at the hour mark from a mistake by Thorsten, who was caught in possession at the back. The contest was settled by a sensational goal from Rob, who ran all the way from the half way line to curl his left foot shot into the far corner from outside the area. Richard was credited with the assist as it was his simple pass to Rob to begin with. James was not included in the matchday squad of the away side – the manager told Martin that it was due to injuries and no one really wanted to find out more about it.

Tom played another twenty minutes for the first team in the next game. The team was chasing a victory at 1-1 but the opponent held firm to deny them. Tom was neat in possession and had a chance from twenty yards out but his shot was saved by the goal keeper. Owen had another impressive game as he played the full game and created the chance for the goal.

The under 23 team lost their next game 2-0 away to the top team in Sheffield. They held the host at bay for most of the game but conceded two late goals to lose the match. Tom was an unused substitute in the next first team game.

It was early December and the club had their annual Christmas party at a local hotel in Surbiton, the one Tom used to work for. It was the first joint party for the senior side and under 23 team.

Knowing the date of the party in advance, Richard decided to celebrate his birthday with Layne in private this year and leave the big celebrations with the team to the party. They went out for a romantic dinner in a glamorous Grand Art Deco restaurant near Green Park and had a very good time. They shared half a dozen of oysters and a Soufflé Suissesse for starters and Richard had an entrecôte steak with béarnaise sauce while Layne had a steamed whole lobster with garlic and lemon butter sauce.

The pair went for a professional haircut together at a Japanese salon in Ealing before the party and Layne had a new style – he dyed the top to an orange-reddish colour and had his long bangs curled professionally to create more volume. He looked fantastic but Richard was worried about the attention he would get with that. They agreed that they would go to the party separately to avoid being pictured as a couple by the local paper. Layne didn't think it would have been a problem but Richard thought otherwise – he just didn't want their relationship to be in the spotlights unnecessarily.

Most players were there with their partners and the club had arranged for some stand-up comedians to perform during the traditional dinner with roast turkey and Brussels sprouts. They also had a live vote on goal and skill of the season so far. Rob won the best goal with his solo goal recently and the skill award went to Owen for a double nutmeg before a delightful through pass with the outside of his boot when he played for the first team.

After desserts there were other entertainments, Richard was keen to try his theory on the roulette table with fake money but he blew all his chips on his first spin as his plan with an 85% probability to succeed failed to materialize. Charlie and Layne laughed their hearts out at his embarrassment.

There was also a dance floor with a professional DJ. Richard was reluctant to join in to begin with but Layne somehow forced him to. He was a fan of the popular TV show on ballroom dancing and he invited Richard to dance with him after arranging some romantic ballads with the DJ. Richard was completely blushed to do something like that in public but his teammates urged him on. So he ended up on the dance floor with Layne and did a bit of waltz, just like what they did back at their apartment. He looked into Layne's joyful eyes and couldn't help himself from kissing him on his forehead.

"Thanks for everything you've done," Layne whispered. "The last two years were the happiest in my life."

"Words can't describe how much I love you, baby," said Richard as he kissed Layne again.

There were applauses for the couple from the club staff and players at the end of the song. Richard felt fairly embarrassed but he smiled and thanked the team for their support.

The DJ moved on to play some traditional Christmas party songs and Richard made his escape to the bar. Layne stayed on the dance floor to have some fun with the other young players.

Bob, David and Martin were there having a chat next to the bar. They saw Richard coming and invited him to join in.

"That was sweet out there, Richard," Martin said with a wink.

"Err… thanks boss," Richard's face turned red again.

"Things have moved on a lot since the day we met, Rich," David said. "You're no longer that arrogant little kid who ignores everyone and stops them playing."

"Yes, I've grown up a bit, I guess. Thank you for having confidence in me," Richard was genuinely thankful for how David changed his life.

The four of them went on to talk about the latest trends in football tactics. Richard was amazed at how much the three coaches knew and the plans they had in place to take the teams forward. He was keen to try some of his latest learnings in his football manager game.

The event ended at midnight and the pair walked back to their apartment. Layne was overjoyed at being able to dance with Richard and talked about it non-stop, saying it was the best Christmas party ever.

But Richard was shocked the next morning when he was sent a link to an online story by Jon his agent.

It was on a minor sports website with the headline "Young footballers came out at Christmas party" and there were a couple of blurry photos of him and Layne dancing and looking intimate. The story described the party and how the team celebrated the two's actions. It also made references to the match last season where the under 23 team walked out.

There was clearly a leak to the media by one of the team or the hotel staff. Jon asked how Richard would like to respond. Richard didn't really know. Most of the story was indeed true – but it didn't need to be public. It made Richard uncomfortable and he was worried by the public's reactions to it.

He discussed this with Layne when he woke up. Layne was far less concerned – what was reported was true and he was quite happy and proud to tell the world about his relationship with Richard. The article somewhat painted a positive picture for the club being inclusive as well. He understood why Richard didn't want it to be public but as it was already out there he didn't think they should, and could, do anything about it, just let it run its course and people would forget or get used to it.

Richard saw his points but just felt grumpy about it, he said it wouldn't have happened had Layne not forced him to go on the dance floor. Layne didn't like the way the blame was laid and they ended up having an argument over it. They didn't get anywhere and soon they calmed down to agree that the best action was no action. They also agreed that they wouldn't say anything if they were asked by the press. All their social media accounts were already set to private so they wouldn't be able to receive any of the nasty comments or threats anyway.

20.

Debut

Similar to the season before, the first team called up a number of young players to train with them ahead of the festive fixtures and Richard was selected along Viktor, Charlie, Danny and Layne. They had a mini injury crisis with a number of regulars out and they wanted the youngsters to be ready physically and mentally to step up during the busy festive schedule.

Charlie was an unused substitute in the next game, which was an away game to the north east but Owen and Tom made another appearance in the second half. The home team took all three points in a 2-0 victory.

Owen and Tom started the next game at home against a team from Yorkshire. Both Charlie and Danny were on the bench and both came on halfway through the second half to make their first team debuts. Charlie went close with a header from a corner and Danny made some good runs to the box in a narrow 1-0 win.

The next game was away to the south east London team where the under 23 team infamously walked out a year ago. Tom, Charlie, Danny and Layne were all in the squad as substitutes while Owen started again. Richard travelled to the game to support them.

It was a tough match and the home side took advantage of some sloppy defending to take an early lead. The Black Dragons were chasing the game from then on but they couldn't create any good chances.

Tom and Danny were brought on early in the second half to bring some fresh ideas. They combined well to create a chance for Owen but his shot was deflected wide by a defender. Layne came on to replace Youssef with ten minutes to go and was met by a very hostile home crowd –

they clearly remembered the match against the under 23 team the year before. The jeers were deafening and homophobic chants could clearly be heard from a section of the stands.

The fourth official overseeing the substitution raised the issue with the referee and representatives of the home team. A tannoy announcement was made immediately saying the club would not tolerate any such chanting and offenders would be ejected from the stadium and potentially banned for life.

The jeers continued from the home fans, be it without the specific homophobic remarks. The away fans tried their best to counter them but the sheer difference in numbers drowned their efforts.

Richard was really upset. He felt bad for Layne. Some of the away fans sitting next to him recognised who he was and gave him encouragement. Richard was grateful but he started to fear that he might have been pulling Layne's progression in football backwards.

Layne's situation was very unpleasant. The home fans sitting next to the touchline were giving him grief every time he was near – they whistled, gestured, made funny noises and some threw coins and other objects at him. But he looked determined to ignore them and play the game.

Minutes later he chased the ball down the left flank and crossed it in. It was too high for George the centre forward but Danny flew in at the back post and met the ball with a diving header. The ball squeezed in between the keeper and the post and the Black Dragons had finally equalised!

Danny ran towards Layne near the touchline and celebrated his first professional goal in front of the home fans with a shush gesture. The crowd reacted angrily but the other Black Dragons players joined in – they were eager to show their support to Layne.

The referee showed Danny a yellow card for provoking the crowd.

The away fans went wild – Richard was amongst them jumping up and down on the stand, chanting repeatedly for their new hero.

The Black Dragons pushed on for the winner from the re-start but it just wouldn't come. The game ended 1-1. Layne and the other players went to applaud the away fans and were well received.

There were some ugly scenes when Richard and the away fans left the stadium. Hundreds of home fans gathered outside and they blocked the path to the train station. Richard felt intimidated – he was trapped inside a dimly lit tunnel with the others for nearly an hour and all he heard was the crowd shouting how they would "kill the gay boy".

He had never been in such situations and he started to fear for his safety. He was also deeply worried – football fans in the real world seemed nastier that he imagined.

"Don't worry Richard, we won't let them hurt you," Geoff the regular supporter spotted the disoriented youngster and pulled him over to stand with his group.

Richard was relieved and managed to calm down. He learnt from Geoff that it happened there all the time and the police would eventually move in to help. He also said that the drunk fans would always find something to pitch their anger towards and asked him not to take it personally.

He was right – a large amount of police arrived and they formed a human chain with their shields to escort the away supporters to the station. Some objects were thrown at them but they managed to escape unscathed.

"Thank God you're picking up! Where are you Richie?" Layne said when Richard finally answered his call.

"Sorry baby, I've just got on the train. We were trapped in a tunnel where there was no signal."

"What happened? It's been one and a half hour since full time? I'm already home!"

Richard told Layne what he experienced, without mentioning the specific homophonic chants. He simply didn't want to add any more negativity to Layne's day. He soon returned home and ever though he had calmed down from the events, all he wanted to have was a deep hug with his beloved boyfriend.

"Oh Richie… are you okay?"

Richard didn't answer. He just held on to Layne tightly, to escape into that world of their own.

It took him a good few minutes to settle.

"Thanks dear, I'm better now."

"Was it that bad? You seem terrified!"

"It was a little frightening. I didn't know what was going to happen, but luckily Geoff and his friends were there. What was it like on the pitch? It looked pretty bad from the stand."

"It wasn't great – they were mocking me all along, they kept giving me wolf whistles, some girly chants, asked me where my boyfriend was, if he knew I was there and some of them threw things at me – coins, bottles, pizzas. I just blanked them out and focused on the match – I wanted to show you how keen I am to make this work. And we did it – Danny put them back in their place."

Richard looked at the determination on his young partner's face and couldn't help from giving him another hug.

"Sorry I put you through all these, baby."

"Don't be ridiculous. I chose to be with you, I'll never regret that."

The boys held onto each other for a good few minutes, before an alarm sounded – it was from Richard's stomach. He hadn't eaten the whole day.

"Poor Richie. Let me make you something to eat… Korean ramyun?"

"Double the portion but half the chilli, please!"

"Hehe, I think I know your taste by now!"

Layne was in the provisional squad for the Boxing Day game against a top team from Birmingham so the pair had a quiet Christmas Day. They visited Layne's mum in Richmond after light training in the morning and she roasted a goose for the three of them – her gravy was as good as what Richard recalled, but the boys needed to control their portions and have plenty of vegetables and water to maintain their physical condition. They had a great time together. Richard did message his best wishes to his mum but didn't think their relationship was good enough for him to visit yet. When he did eventually visit, he would want to do it as a pair and not just on his own.

Layne was on the bench with Tom on match day while Charlie, Danny and Les started. Josh the ex-under 23 team goalkeeper finally got to make his debut, having transferred to the first team at the beginning of the season.

The away team, who were relegated from the Premier League the season before, had a strong team and a good young attacking midfielder called Ted, but they were in the middle of a poor run. They also started with Darren, who they signed from the Black Dragons' academy two seasons ago.

A home game on Boxing Day was most footballers' dream as they didn't need to be stuck in a team hotel on the evening of Christmas Day. The home stadium would also be similar to a carnival with plenty of families in the stand.

The Black Dragons started strongly with the lively Charlie, who tested the keeper early on with a curling effort from the left. The hard-working Danny then forced the ball off the defensive midfielder to Luciano the prolific right winger, and he took the ball round the keeper to score. But the away team equalised before half time, when Darren headed Ted's brilliant cross in from six yards.

The hosts picked up the pace again in the second half and it took a last-ditch challenge from the centre back to stop Charlie opening his account for the first team. He was denied again minutes later as the keeper tipped his powerful shot wide of the post.

Bob brought both Layne and Tom on after the hour mark and the latter made an instant impact. He won the ball in midfield and after a quick exchange with Danny he sent the ball through to George, who controlled his volley expertly to retake the lead. Charlie should have scored the third goal late on but his shot hit the bar. The Black Dragons extended their good run and won the game 2-1.

The media were impressed by the Black Dragons' graduates and the official Football League website did a special report on them. It featured the established squad members such as George, Andrés, Lewis and Les, the rising stars like Owen, Tom, Charlie, Danny and Layne and the up-and-coming Josh, Richard, Thomas and Alex. The article described how the club invested in their youth facilities and gave the players game time to develop. It concluded with an interview with David.

The team were in action again four days later and were at home against the blue team from Sheffield. Richard was named on the bench for the first time alongside Charlie and Danny. Owen, Tom and Les were in the planned starting eleven while Layne gave way to Lewis, who returned to the bench following his injury.

Similar to Layne's call up before, Richard joined the team in the morning for a light training session followed by the final briefing on tactics and a healthy team lunch. He was then assigned one of the twenty five players' rooms at the training facility to rest – they were designed to be as relaxing as possible, with minimum lighting, soundproof walls and some peaceful background music. Richard managed to have a 2-hour nap and felt fully recharged for the actions.

The match day squad then entered the stadium through the VIP lounge, where they were welcomed by around a hundred supporters. They had some quick interactions before being led to their dressing room.

Players' shirts, footwear and the rest of their team kits were neatly placed at their allocated space. Richard was given a shirt with his name on the back for the very first time – he had finally caught up with Layne and his friends.

Bob, David and the rest of the coaching team came into the room once the team had changed into their warm up gears and the manager gave the team his pre-match team talk.

"Today we welcome Richard from the under 23's. He'll be our cover for defensive midfield and please offer him your strong support as usual."

The team gave him a round of applause and Bob continued with the rest of his speech on tactics, completed with the motivating cry, "Fly, you Black Dragons!"

The starting eleven for the match were goalkeeper Gordon, full backs Jonas and Youssef, centre backs Alain and Les, captain Michael supported by Tom in the centre behind attacking midfielder Ross, and finally Owen, Luciano and George upfront. The long-serving keeper Matt, defender Matias and striker Kalifa were on the bench with graduates Lewis, Charlie, Danny and Richard.

Richard followed the team out for the warm up. While he had seen it as a spectator plenty of times, it was his first time as a player in front of a decent crowd. He spotted Layne and the other youngsters in the Ditton End straight away, and he gave them a wave before focusing on his tasks.

The routine for a substitute was not as rigid as the starters. He followed Tim's instructions for some quick runs and turns then was free to have some ball exchanges with Charlie and Danny. The team returned to their dressing room to change into their match outfits, including the all-black presentation track top. They marched onto the pitch at the end of the fans' singing of Queen's "I Want It All" and Richard followed the other substitutes to the bench, which was installed with a heating system in order to keep them warm.

The match started after the formalities and the Black Dragons, who were comfortable at mid-table, went for a fast start and took the lead after fifteen minutes. The skilful Owen continued to amaze with his pace and technique as he opened up some space on the left for a cross that George headed in brilliantly. They kept pushing for the decisive second goal but the away team defended well and kept them at bay.

The second half became very tense as the away side put on the pressure, with their deep lying playmaker dictating the play. Richard watched on the sideline during his warm up as Gordon the assertive Scottish goalkeeper made some fantastic saves to deny them, but it looked as though it was a matter of time before they levelled the score line. Bob summoned Richard back and asked him to ready himself. He wanted him to replace Ross and played as the advanced destroyer – it was also known as a suffoco in Europe and its role was to suffocate the deep lying playmaker.

Richard stepped onto the pitch, wearing his protective gear on his right wrist, completed the checks by the assistant referee and stood by waiting for a break in play, while the chant of "Black Army" were echoing around the stadium. This was the moment he had been dreaming for – to play for the senior team.

"Are you nervous, Richard?" David asked him before he went on.

"I'm well prepared, David," said Richard with his match face on.

"Go and show the world what you are capable of."

The home crowd cheered as another home-grown talent made his debut – Richard's travels to the away games also gave them a good impression. The visiting supporters took their opportunity to boo and send him insults but he had learnt from Layne to ignore them.

"Remember what we talked about Richard – you're good enough to be here and just play your game," said Michael his mentor, who was now one of his midfield partners.

"Welcome to the party, buddy," Tom said as he had a fist bump with Richard. "Make us proud."

The match had twenty minutes remaining. Richard moved towards his target, the deep lying playmaker, to carry out his task of man-marking him. His very presence made the other players less inclined to pass to the playmaker, but the player being marked was not giving up easily. He moved about to shake Richard off and connected with his players with some quick, one touch passes, but his influence was vastly reduced as Richard was in position to tackle if he held on to the ball any longer. He tried to evade Richard but he found his young and energetic opponent very difficult to beat and retreated.

Danny and Lewis were sent on to replace Luciano and Youssef with about ten minutes left. Richard continued to restrict the impact of the playmaker, who became frustrated and decided to take on Richard one more time.

He shuffled his footwork to con Richard but the youngster held his ground on the left, trying to shepherd the playmaker to the other side, knowing that Danny would have quietly closed in there to help.

The playmaker noticed he was surrounded but it was already too late. Just as he flipped the ball back away from Danny, Richard made his move – the black boot with gold sprinkles struck for the first time in the Championship.

The loose ball rolled towards the left of the area and Richard had a decision to make: Did he have the pace the burst through the gap between the centre backs? Or should he play safe and retain possession?

He opted for neither.

He surprised everyone and hit the ball first time with his left foot from 35-yards out – he noticed the keeper was out of position and he chipped him!

The world went into slow motion. The ball flew over the desperately jumping keeper and down into the back of the net. The referee whistled in acknowledgement, and the score board switched to show 2-0 to the Black Dragons. The home fans behind the goal were electrified, they all jumped up at the same time, their arms, their crisps, their pizzas, even some of their Bovril were up in the air, and everyone was screaming at the top of their voices.

Richard had scored. In front of the West Stand. Minutes into his first team debut.

He couldn't describe how he was feeling. He stood at the same spot with his fists clenched, roaring towards the sky. All the hard work, all the setbacks and all the sacrifices – they were all worth it.

His teammates went wild for what happened. Richard indulged in the passionate celebrations and felt immensely proud – he did something truly unbelievable.

As he made his back to his position, Richard pointed to the stand where Layne was sitting and kissed his left ring finger. The crowd gave them a massive cheer, with some good humoured whistling in between. The deflated visitors had nothing more to fight for after that killer goal and the match finished 2-0.

"You've done more than we expected, Richard!" David congratulated Richard for his excellent debut.

"I didn't think I would score, just thought I'll give it a try," said a delighted Richard. It was probably the first time David saw Richard smiling as genuinely as that.

The teammates took in turns to send him their congratulations.

"I can't believe you scored for the first team before me mate. Well done!" said Charlie as he shook hands with Richard.

"You were a brave man to hit it from there," Danny joined in and gave Richard a pat on his shoulder.

"He'll be in the run-in for goal of the season with that," said Owen as he put his arms round both Richard and Danny.

Richard felt great – he was fulfilling his childhood dream. He remembered that he should really thank the fans and he ran back to the West Stand to show his appreciations of their support. The fans reacted with a new chant for him:

We've got Richard Lucas!
We've got Richard Lucas!
We've got Richard Lucas!

A young fan asked if he could have Richard's shirt as a souvenir but his dad stopped him in time to save Richard's dilemma – it was his first senior game and he wouldn't really want to give his shirt to anyone.

Tom was named as the man of the match and the reporter invited Richard along for the post-match interview.

Host: Thanks for joining us Tom and Richard. So it's another win for the Black Dragons. How do you feel about that Tom?

Tom: It's great to be winning games. Today was particularly tough as we were put under a lot of pressure in the second half, well, until this boy came in to settle it all.

Host: Was it a tactical move by the manager to man mark the deep lying playmaker?

Tom: It was. He was dictating the game from behind and we were made to do a lot of chasing. We needed to cut the supply to him and luckily, we did that.

Host: That's very true. Richard, congratulations for making your senior debut today. Can you talk us through your goal please?

Richard: Thank you very much. Well the manager asked me to suffocate the playmaker and with the help of Danny we got the ball off him. I had a glimpse of the keeper's position so I thought I'd have a go. I didn't think it would go in but it did – it was just amazing. I still couldn't believe it.

Host: Can you tell us a bit about your celebration? Was that a gesture to someone in the stand?

Richard: Err... I'm not sure if I should talk about that...

Tom: He just made his debut today so let's not embarrass him too much. It's something between the team – we know what he meant.

Host: Well I hope we get to see more appearances and goals from you two. Richard, can you present the prize for Tom please? He's the man of the match today.

Richard: Sure – well done Tom, great play.

Tom: Cheers buddy.

The two went back into the dressing room and Layne had made his way in to give Richard a massive hug.

"That was quite an impact, Richie!" he said.

"Yes, I love every second of it!" Richard was still over the moon.

Richard and his teammates went back onto the pitch later for some warm down exercise. He noticed that a spectator was still in the stand and was waving at him. To Richard's delight, it was Simon his coach from the youth team back in Windlesham. Richard ran over and caught up with him, thanking him for his recommendation to David that started everything. He heard that the youth team was doing well as the Black Dragons had paid them a decent sum for his transfer. David came out to meet Simon later as they had plans for dinner afterwards.

The win moved the Black Dragons into eighth in the league, three points behind the team in sixth. In the Championship, the top two teams were promoted to the Premier League, the top level in English football, automatically. Teams finished in third to sixth would qualify for a mini knockout tournament called the playoffs, with the winner claiming the third and final promotion spot.

The next game during the brutal festive period was only three days later and it was away at the runaway league leaders from the West Midlands. Bob gave most of the younger players a miss as the first team regulars were back in contention, with only Les and Charlie travelling with the squad.

The league leaders were top of the league for a reason. They dominated the game from the beginning to end with the Black Dragons barely surviving and seriously struggling to create any chances of note. The home team won the game comfortably 2-0 with a goal in each half. Charlie came on at 2-0 but he didn't have much impact against such strong opposition.

The transfer window had opened and there were rumours of incoming offers for a number of Black Dragons' players. Charlie mentioned during their regular dinner gathering that the club had a reasonable offer for him from another Championship team. Mr Ranger senior told him that he and the club were not keen to sell him but they might accept offers for one of the first team wingers, who also had a few interested parties.

Four days after their defeat in the midlands it was the FA Cup third round tie at home against the Premier League's leaders from Manchester. Bob continued to play the regular starters and of the former youth team players only Owen started, with Les, Tom, Charlie and Danny all on the bench.

The game started brilliantly for the Black Dragons and they led 1-0 after the first half. Owen's good work on the left created a chance for George, whose shot was parried by the keeper and Luciano was on hand to score from the rebound. However, the goal only seemed to have awakened the visitors. They might have rested a few of their top players but they still had a team full of internationals and their quality shone through, as they put four goals past the Black Dragons in the second half. Tom and Charlie did come on as late substitutes, but they could only watch first-hand the gulf between them and one of the best teams in the world.

Bob was naturally disappointed with the result but he was encouraged by the team's efforts and he urged the team to move on and focus on the league, where they were definitely in the mix for a place in the playoffs.

The Black Dragons' next league game was at home against a team from Teesside, who were one of the teams fighting for a playoff place. Richard and Layne were on the bench with Tom, while Les, Owen, Charlie and Danny were in the starting line-up. The unfortunate Lewis was injured again and would miss another four weeks of actions.

The Black Dragons played some excellent football with the home support and they scored two goals in the first half. Charlie finally opened his account for the first team when he controlled George's lay off with his left foot and slotted it instantly to the far corner with his right. He celebrated wildly with multiple fist pumps with the last one towards the sky.

The second goal was scored by George after a great run by Owen. He picked up the ball on the right and forced his way past three defenders before cutting back for the striker to tap in. His transition to the first team had been nothing but spectacular.

Tom, Richard and Layne were brought on to much fanfare after seventy minutes. Their task was to protect the two-goal lead. Richard and Tom replaced the tired Michael and Kalim and they formed their usual defensive wall in the middle. With Les and the powerful first-choice centre back Keith behind them, they comfortably held the away team at bay. Richard made four interceptions and won two take on's in his twenty minutes of solid performance.

"It's so nice to have you playing next to me," Tom told Richard after the match.

"We've been playing together for more than two years, I think I know the way you move by now," said a smiling Richard as he shook hands with Tom.

The Black Dragons' next game was away at Wearside. Owen, Charlie and Tom remained in the starting eleven while Richard, Layne and Danny were named on the bench. Les missed out through injury.

Richard was never great for long coach journeys and a five-hour commute was like torture for him. Luckily the first team travelled to away games the day before so it shouldn't affect his match performance. By the time the coach arrived the hotel in the early evening Richard was already half dead, with a massive headache that wouldn't go away, even though he took his usual travel sickness tablets. He only had a tiny portion of food at the team dinner, which spoke volume given his normal appetite. The club's rule for the first team was for each player to have their own room but Layne hung around Richard's to make sure he was okay before returning to his.

Richard felt much better the next morning. The game was at the standard kick off time at three in the afternoon so the team had plenty of time to prepare. An injury to the regular attacking midfielder Ross during warm up meant Danny started the game instead.

With a capacity of 49,000, it was the biggest stadium Richard visited as a player. It was almost full at kick off and the roar from the home fans was deafening.

The home team played a direct game and Bob pointed out the key to victory would be the ability to attack on the break. His game plan worked well as the Black Dragons scored two goals from counter attacks in the first half.

305

The first one was scored after twenty minutes by Owen after some quick interchanges between him, Danny and Charlie. The second goal was a screamer from Danny, who hit a clean dipping shot unchallenged from thirty yards out. It was the first time he scored with his well-practiced technique and he pointed at Richard on the bench as he performed his usual celebration with a double clap.

Similar to his previous appearances, Richard was called upon around the seventy-minute mark to close the game off. There were boos and questions asking who he was but they weren't too aggressive – the score line helped. Due to the direct, long ball style of play by the home side, Bob asked Tom to sit in between midfield and defence to utilise his strength in the air, with Richard and the captain Michael either side in front of him to direct the play.

The Black Dragons held on to their lead and won the game 2-0, the same score line for all of Richard's three league appearances.

"You seem to be our lucky mascot in the league!" Michael said to Richard as they walked off the pitch.

"Thanks cap, glad I could help," Richard said with a happy face.

Layne was an unused substitute. He was his usual cheerful self and was delighted to see Richard perform well.

The team left Wearside straight after the match and eventually got back to south west London before midnight. Richard doubled his intake of antihistamine to cope with his travel sickness and slept through the trip. Layne got him a sandwich from the motorway services for dinner but he opted for a delivery from his favourite burger place nearby – the one he went with Danny when he first joined the club.

Richard received a call from his agent Jon the next morning, who told him that he had secured a sponsorship deal with the major US sports company that he always bought his boots from. There were no fixed sums of money but Richard would be effectively given the boots he wanted from the available range and he would receive an annual allowance for clothes and other gears. There would be bonuses if Richard was selected for the England youth teams. Richard was absolutely delighted to be recognised by such a global brand.

Layne was next to Richard on the phone and he jumped in to ask Jon if he could negotiate the same from the German brand whose gears he played with. Jon said he was already on the case and given that Layne had more appearances for the senior team it should be an easy sell.

The pair met up with their teammates for their dinner gathering that evening in a seafood restaurant in South Kensington. The usual suspects were there plus the young Harry, Andrew and Ryan. Harry and Andrew were good friends of Layne and Ryan would join any event that Richard took part in.

It was near the end of the month and the team asked Charlie if there were any developments on his future. He said there was an improved bid but the club still turned it down. Personally he was fine with it as he didn't want to leave anyway. He felt the team could get promoted in the next few years and would like to achieve it with his friends.

The shock for the team was that the club had accepted an offer from a Premier League club for Owen. After his impressive performance since moving into the first team, there were lots of interest and the club decided an 8-figure sum was enough to tempt them into selling. Personal terms were being discussed and it was likely to be the reason why the club didn't want to entertain selling Charlie as well.

Layne then raised the topic on sponsorship deals. Apparently, Charlie had one a while ago as he played for England under 17's and 19's. Danny and Tom had theirs recently and it was quite similar to Richard's. Layne was rather frustrated that he didn't get his when he was the first player in this group to play for the first team. He sent a few more messages to Jon as a result.

Soon it was the end of January and the transfer window. As expected, Owen joined the Premier League club from

East Sussex on deadline day for fifteen million pounds plus add-ons. He had a call with Richard on the day to say goodbye – he was sad to leave the Black Dragons but he couldn't turn down the chance to play in the Premier League as well as a much improved package.

Layne got his youth player sponsorship deal he wanted – all he received was a pair of new boots and some allowance, similar to what the others did, but it was enough to make him happy for a few days. He opted for a pair of pink and black boots – having dyed his hair back to his natural colour, he wanted something catchy to wear. Richard declined to try them on despite the pair sharing the same shoe size.

With the festive season over and the Black Dragons out of all cup competitions, Bob and David had informed Richard, Layne and Danny that they would return to the under 23 team for the rest of the season. There might be the odd call-up to the senior team in emergency but it was better for them to get more match practice with the junior side. Richard was glad to have tasted first team football and was eager to be selected again.

21.

Triangles

The under 23 team went on a tour of Poland in early February. They would play the under 23 sides of two top division clubs during their three days in Gdańsk, the northern port city on the Baltic coast. The winter break of the Polish season was to end in mid-February and clubs were keen to play friendly matches to build up their players' fitness level.

The team arrived in the evening and stayed in the seaside resort town called Sopot, which was known for its long wooden pier that extended well into the Baltic Sea.

With Charlie and Tom moved to the senior side and Owen left, opportunities were there for the likes of Andrew, Rob, Ryan and Kasper to stake their claims to the starting eleven. Having had their fair share of first team actions recently, Martin decided to give Richard, Layne and Danny some rest. He started the lunchtime match against Gdynia with Jack in goal, Viktor, Marcus, Thomas and Thorsten in defence, Kasper, Stefan and Harry in midfield and Andrew, Alex and Rob upfront.

The home team were very good technically and they played a fast passing game in a 4-3-3 formation. But the younger players in the under 23 team had grown a lot and they were much more ready physically. The regular defence was solid, and although it was done without the elegance and intrigue passing from Richard and Tom, the midfield duo of Kasper and Stefan were effective in possession. Harry linked up well with the front three and set up runs for Rob and cut in opportunities for Andrew. The only thing lacking was a goal, as the tall keeper managed to save all the five shots on target.

Ryan spent the whole of first half sitting next to Richard to hear his views of the game. He was full of admiration of Richard's knowledge and he kept asking sensible questions. Layne wrapped himself up with a few blankets as he found the Baltic weather in February a little bit too cold. It was not until Martin asked him to warm up during half time that he got out of his layers. He was still well covered though – wearing a turtle neck under shirt, leg warmers and gloves throughout.

Richard, Layne and Danny were introduced at half time in place of Kasper, Marcus and Stefan. Martin kept the impressive Harry on and play both him and Danny as attacking midfielders, leaving Richard as the single pivot.

The range of passing and movements offered by Richard and Danny respectively made a big impact on the match, as the away side opened up the space between the home team's midfield and defence. Andrew was sent through on the left by Harry and Alex finished his low cross coolly on the turn to make it 1-0. Minutes later a long left foot drive from Harry was parried by the keeper only onto the path of Alex and he put it into the empty net on the half volley. The home team had a consolation goal late on and the game ended 2-1 to the visitors.

The players had their afternoon off and Richard visited the wooden pier with Layne. It was the longest wooden pier in Europe built in 1827 and the pair took their time to enjoy the views. Richard noticed a popular restaurant on the way there and decided to pay it a visit when they returned.

"What's so special about this place? It's just selling fish and chips," Layne was a little disappointed when looked at the menu.

"You wait, baby. I'm sure there's something good here – look at the number of customers," Richard was confident he had unearthed a gem.

He ordered two fish soups from the counter and brought them to Layne, who just about managed to find a table for two in the packed restaurant. They had a sip of the hot soup and they were amazed – it was full of flavour and there was a good amount of fish in it. They enjoyed every single bit of it.

"How did you know their fish soup is good? Did you check on the internet?" Layne asked.

"No I didn't. Just look around here, all the local diners are having one, so it must be decent," Richard revealed his secret.

"You're crazy with your observations, but thanks for the delicious treat," Layne gave Richard the credit he deserved.

The team dinner at the hotel was reasonable but there was nothing really to write home about. Ryan was again sticking around Richard with his questions about football and other topics and Layne was a little annoyed.

The team had a light training session at Gdańsk's training complex the next day, which was next to their historic stadium.

After training the team were free to visit the city of Gdańsk. Together with Gdynia and Sopot, these three cities formed the so-called Tricity. The historian Richard was keen to see the various landmarks, especially the medieval Żuraw, or the crane, which was unique in Europe with its two fortified towers facing the beautiful Motława River.

After hearing their plans, Ryan invited himself to the sightseeing trip along Richard, Layne, Danny, Thomas, Alex, Harry and Andrew. They visited the crane before returning to the Neptune's Fountain for a traditional Polish dinner. Throughout the trip, Ryan was very interested to hear all the historical stories that Richard knew of the area and was talking to him non-stop, again to the dismay of Layne, who made it known that night.

"What's going on with Ryan? Does he not know that you have a boyfriend?" Layne moaned when the pair were back at their hotel room.

"Maybe he's just bored? He doesn't seem to have a lot of friends in the team," Richard tried to find an answer.

311

"Maybe you're not just a magnet to the ball? He's a class A boy deserving a triple take after all!"

"Don't even go there. I know my place and I love it."

"He may not be so clear about it."

"As long as I know the line, it's going to be fine. I don't want to cause the team any more troubles," said Richard as he got into the bathroom for a shower.

"Maybe you're right... Oh wait!" Layne went after him into the shower.

"Okay, no more talking of Ryan then, it's just you and me," said Richard as he gave Layne a kiss.

The match against Gdańsk was played in their new stadium which was purposefully built for the European Championships in 2012. It could host over 42,000 spectators and was, perhaps surprisingly, nearly half full for the under 23 friendly game. It was on a Saturday and the match was part of a double header, with the first team coming on for their friendly with another team afterwards.

Martin started with Arben in goal, Ollie, Layne, Mason and Zach in defence, Richard, Kasper and Danny in midfield, and Andrew, Ryan and Rob upfront. Richard was named as the captain for the first time.

It was Ryan's first game in front of thousands of spectators. Richard noticed and went over to offer him some support.

"Just think about the training and all the games you've played. This is no different, just go out there and enjoy your game. We'll back you up," he told the youngster, who turned seventeen the month before.

"Thanks Richard, I'll do what I can," Ryan replied with a smile.

The home team played in a 4-5-1 formation and looked keen to utilise the wide areas. With Rob's tendency of not tracking back, Richard asked Kasper to cover the left half of midfield while he went to the right to offer Ollie some support.

But that might be unnecessary as Ollie won his first challenge against the left footed left winger. He sent the ball over the head of the advancing left back to his cousin and Rob had a free run at the centre half. He got to the byline and crossed it low towards the edge of the six-yard box. Ryan was there sliding in but he didn't time it well and the ball went harmlessly wide.

"Don't worry about it, there's always another chance," Danny told Ryan as he still seemed a little nervous.

Minutes later Kasper intercepted a through ball and passed it right to Richard. He swung it left first time to the space in front of Layne, who played his typical one two with Andrew then repeated what Rob did earlier and crossed it low towards Ryan. But instead of hitting it first time he hesitated and tried to control the ball. The delay led to a challenge by a defender and it ended up being a corner to the Black Dragons.

"Just listen to your instincts," Richard said to Ryan before picking the ball up for the corner.

Minutes later the goal keeper gifted the ball straight to Andrew on the left wing. He brought the ball towards the centre, played a one two with Ryan at the "D" and continued his move to the right. He pretended to pull the trigger but cut the ball back to his left at the last moment, and Ryan was completely free. He tried to side foot it to the bottom left corner, but the ball hit the post and out.

Ryan was beating the ground in anger, having missed three good chances. Richard picked him up and said, "Take it easy, the more frustrated you are the less likely you'll score."

The Black Dragons created another chance just before the first half ended. Danny got the ball from Rob just inside the final third, evaded his marker with a swift drop of his shoulder, before chipping the ball to Ryan inside the area. The young striker tried to hit it towards goal on the volley but the ball hit his standing foot instead. The bounce inadvertently sent Danny through on goal and he blasted it into the net to finally open the scoring.

"Thanks for the assist, Ryan," said Danny as he patted him on his head.

"You're welcome…" said the embarrassed Ryan.

The first half ended and Richard spoke to Martin during the break.

"I'm not sure if you would, but please don't take Ryan off at half time."

"You're worried about his confidence?" Martin hit the nail in the head straight away.

"Yes I think he just needs a bit of luck to find himself again."

"Okay I'll have a think Richard."

But changes were needed as Martin wanted to give all players some play time on tour. So off went Kasper, Rob and Andrew and on came Stefan, Harry and Marcus. Danny moved to the right, Layne moved forward to left wing and Ryan stayed as centre forward.

"The boss hasn't taken me off!" Ryan whispered to Richard who sat next to him.

"He's giving you more chances to prove yourself. Relax and make the most of it."

The second half began with more possession from the home team. Plenty of supporters had arrived and they cheered their young side on. The Black Dragons were put to the test at the back but Ollie and the more defensive assured Marcus were handling the threats from wide well with the help from wingers Layne and Danny. Richard made plenty of interceptions in the middle but he found it hard to pass it forward as the team were pushed back by the home team. They were hanging on – and he signalled Layne to stay up field to offer a way out.

The home team's left winger was forced in field by the strength of Ollie and he tried to take on Richard who was covering that area. He thought he put the ball through Richard's leg but it was cut out by his trailing foot. He passed it to Harry on the left, who sent it forward to Ryan at the edge of the area. Feeling that the centre back was too close to him, Ryan flicked the ball to the left with the outside of his right foot and ran after it. The centre back couldn't react quick enough and an opportunity opened up for Ryan to shoot with his left foot.

Just put everything through it! Richard shouted in his head.

Ryan put every ounce of power into it indeed – and the ball rocketed straight into the top left corner before the keeper could react!

"I did it!" Ryan screamed with joy as he ran towards the bench to celebrate his goal.

That was his typical move. He did it in training frequently and his ability to change direction like that was really special.

Martin completed the change of guards with Thomas, Viktor and Alex on to replace Zach, Ollie and Layne. Ryan moved to left wing to accommodate Alex's arrival.

With the home team deflated by the second goal, the Black Dragons pushed for a third to finish the game off. Thomas stopped an attack and passed the ball wide to Viktor, who centred it to Richard. He was unopposed so he brought the ball forward to the right and eventually crossed it towards Ryan. Knowing the striker's outstanding athletic ability, he intentionally hit it further for him to volley it home from the angle for 3-0.

Ryan threw himself into Richard to celebrate his second goal of the game. He couldn't believe how accurate the cross was – he didn't need to move much to guide the ball into the net.

The home team found a consolation goal late on and the friendly match ended 3-1. The 30,000 home fans appreciated the football on show and they gave the teams a standing ovation.

Ryan was very excited after the game and he was talking to Richard non-stop. Martin gave him a pat on his shoulder, as his persistence to give Ryan more time worked out well.

The under 23 team returned to action a week after their victorious tour of Poland. It was late February and they played the team from north west London. With the loss of Charlie, Tom and Owen the team played a number of under 18 players and gave Richard, Layne, Danny and

Alex the Saturday off to recharge their batteries. They drew the home game 1-1, with Dillon scoring the goal on his under 23 debut.

Alex took the opportunity to go to the London Fashion Week Festival at the Strand. Richard was going to read the papers on encryption from Dr Edwards so Layne joined him for a trip to central London. He returned home for dinner in the early evening.

"Look what I've bought for this season!" he showed his souvenirs to Richard.

Richard recognised some of the brands but was not really interested in all the mix and matches that Layne loved. He watched Layne tried all the outfits on as he prepared some pasta for dinner. Layne also modelled the clothes he bought for Richard – he knew exactly the type to get – elegant, comfortable and low profile, in black, grey or navy, all from his favourite Italian brand. Richard liked them and would probably be wearing them for years.

Layne's own fashion show ended just when the meal was ready.

"Oh do you know who I met today at the show?" Layne asked during dinner.

"Who? A famous designer?" Richard had no answer for such an open question.

"No it was Leo, someone I used to go to school with back in Bath. He's an online influencer these days with tens of thousands of followers."

"At your age? That's quite an achievement!"

"He's a year older. He's always into fashion and said he could interview me in one of his clips."

"What does he want to interview you for? Football, fashion or old school days?".

"Not sure yet, we'll arrange later."

"That sounds like something you'd like to do, just don't count me in – 'the teammates' was the best I can offer," Richard still remembered the embarrassment he had the season before.

316

There was some severe weather between the end of February and early March, with heavy snow falls across the country.

The under 23 team's game at home against a team from Wales had to be abandoned shortly after the second half started. The team were leading the chaotic match 4-2 with goals from Thorsten, Alex, Danny and Ryan.

The club's training ground was covered by inches of snow the next day. The first team were given priority to the only artificial pitch for their on-field training and the under 23's were restricted to the gym – extra sessions on strengths building and plenty of cardio instead.

With the odd occasion of a heavy snow in the capital, Richard and Layne went to Primrose Hill after training, having seen reports of it being turned into a skiing paradise.

The reports were true – people were skiing and snowboarding there as if they were in the Alps. Both Richard and Layne knew how to ski: Richard used to go to Austria with his parents and Layne had his annual school skiing trips. As professional players they were not allowed to take part in dangerous sports during the season so they picked a nice spot and watched the skiers do their twists and turns.

"It's funny how you know how to ski but not how to skate."

"I need the pull of gravity!" Richard replied with a rare joke.

"We need to have a skiing holiday one day. I miss my time on the mountains."

"I guess we have to wait until we retire from football. We can't even get Christmas Day off."

"Do you think we'll still be together when we grow old?"

"Of course we will, baby. Nothing is going to separate us," Richard said as he gave Layne a hug before kissing him on his cheek.

Layne blushed a little and gave Richard one of his sweetest smiles. Richard felt blessed, and he pulled the hood of Layne's big coat up so that they could enjoy a moment of intimacy.

"This is wonderful," he said after a long round of kisses.

"I love how you keep me warm in the cold Richie..."

"I look forward to doing that for many, many more winters with you."

The snow only lasted a few days and the under 23 team were back to their usual outdoor training schedule. Richard received a call after he and Layne returned home one day. **It was from the Football Association.**

The official on the line told Richard that he had been selected for the England under 21 squad for their next two games. Richard couldn't believe what he heard and checked a few times just to make sure it wasn't a hoax. He knew it was definitely true minutes later when he picked up congratulations from Martin and David. Charlie, Tom and Danny were also called up for the first time. The England under 20 team won a major tournament recently but a number of the regular players were not available so the coaching team decided to bring in some new blood.

The games were a few weeks away and the players would get together to train at the FA's headquarters in St. George's Park.

"That's so exciting!" Layne congratulated Richard.

"I never thought that would be possible. And it's going to be with the boys too," said a happy Richard.

The young Black Dragons played two away matches since and they were both draws. The first one was against the team from Bristol, where Alex and Ryan rescued the game with goals in the second half, while the second was a heartbreak in Lancashire – a late penalty cancelled out Danny's brilliant opener.

Richard played the full ninety minutes in both games and felt good with his fitness level, ahead of joining the England setup the week after.

Richard and his friends arrived at St. George's Park in Staffordshire to join the England under 21 squad. Richard gave Danny a lift there as he still hadn't taken his driving lessons – Charlie offered but Danny was still scarred by the journey to Bournemouth. Tom kept him company instead.

Charlie was a regular in the under 19 team but this was his first call up to the under 21 side. He knew most of the players and he introduced them to his teammates. Most of the players were from Premier League clubs and the young Dragons made up half of those from the level below. Richard played against a number of them before and knew the standard was really high. He also caught up with his old teammate Owen, who was settling in well at his new Premier League club.

The youngsters would train together for three days before a home friendly against Romania on Saturday and an U21 European Championship qualifier against Ukraine three days later.

The training wasn't particularly tough comparing to what Richard did with the Black Dragons. The players were all talented and supremely fit physically and they just needed to learn and practice the shape and style of the national team together. The pitch condition was of the highest standard and was perfect for the passing game. The coaches commended on Richard's defensive capabilities and his calmness on the ball – something he learnt from Martin and Michael this season.

The evenings could be quite boring for the young players as they stayed in the training complex. Tom, Danny and Owen hung around Charlie's room as he had his Xbox with him. Richard brought a few books with him to read and he called Layne every night before he went to bed. Layne told him that he would spend Friday evening with Leo for an interview – he spoke to the club's PR department and they were comfortable for him to do it, but they also gave him the relevant policy to read, on things that he should and should not be saying.

Richard also exchanged a lot of text messages with Ryan. It started after the trip to Poland and they talked about all sorts of topics – from the obvious football to views on current affairs and philosophy of life. Richard found Ryan's values close to his own and they could talk non-stop if he had the time.

On the third night of staying at St. George's Park, Ryan asked a few questions about relationships and he touched on Richard's with Layne.

"It's so nice that you and Layne can be together – it's not easy to find a partner that you really love," he wrote.

"It's true, I'm the lucky one. But you're young and will have plenty of chances," Richard responded with an encouragement.

"No I won't be able to. It's too late."

"Why? You're only seventeen?"

"No… he's already taken. I have no chance," he replied after a few minutes' silence.

"If that's what you know then you should consider moving on, there's no point drilling on it if it's impossible?" Richard noticed the "he" in the reply but acted as if it was a normal crush anyway.

"But I keep thinking of him though… Do you think I should tell him?"

"My head says no, especially if you know there's no chance, but I understand why the heart would want to tell. It may probably be a good way to close the chapter?" Richard didn't know what the right answer was. He'd been through it before with Layne and he would probably regret holding it in for life if he didn't break the silence that summer in Dorset.

"Thanks for the advice, Rich," Ryan replied before following up with a second message shortly after.

"Richard, I know it's impossible, but I just want you to know that I like you. I dream of having someone as nice and caring as you with me all the time. I'm happy to see you doing well with Layne but it also hurts me like hell. You don't need to do anything. Like you said I just want to let you know my feelings, I'm not expecting anything."

Oh dear. What have I done? Richard asked himself. Like his admission to Layne before, he was physically attracted by Ryan, but he never considered making any moves as he was very happy with Layne. He also thought that it would be unlikely for another footballer to be like him and Layne. Ryan's confession wouldn't have changed anything but Richard now had a problem at hand – what should he say?

"You don't have to answer. I know. Maybe it was better left than said. But I honestly love you," Ryan sent another message after a few minutes, resembling the lyrics of one of Richard's favourite old songs.

Richard could sense the sadness from Ryan's message – he didn't want to hurt him but he couldn't accept him either. He needed to say something.

"I'm sorry, Ryan. You are a nice boy and I like your company. But I am with Layne and that will never change. We've been through so much together and it's well beyond an ordinary relationship. He's also my best friend, my soul mate, my everything. I'm sure you can move on and find your true love in the future," Richard typed his response, amended it a few times and eventually sent it off.

"I get it. Thanks for being honest with me. You'd better have some rest before training tomorrow. Good night," Ryan replied a few minutes later.

Richard wished that would be the end of it. He wasn't sure if he should tell Layne given he was rather hostile to Ryan recently. He decided to leave it until he went home.

He didn't sleep well that night. He was never good with strange beds but he couldn't stop thinking about the situation with Ryan. He was concerned for his wellbeing but also worried about any fallouts in the team. It would be such an embarrassing situation to have a love triangle in the team and wouldn't fare well if it became public.

He went training the next morning with his head full of thoughts. He struggled to get in the zone and he wasn't concentrating when he was on the ball during a practice match. He suddenly realised he was tracked down by another player and when he rushed to get out of trouble by clearing it in a sliding motion, he twisted his left ankle in the process.

It hurt.

The swelling developed quickly and he couldn't walk. The physio helped him to the bench and said he would need at least couple of weeks off, so there was no way he could take part in the two upcoming matches.

It was heart-breaking for Richard. He knew it was the once in a lifetime opportunity for him to fulfil his dream and play for England – the regular players would be back in contention at the next call up and he may never be selected again.

He might be a calm person, but as the thought went through his head he couldn't hold his tears back. He was sad, angry and disappointed. His dream was so close but yet so far. The physio told him that while it was good that he cared, he needed to pick himself up and be professional.

"Your time will come. Don't worry about it."

As he was no longer able to train and had no chance of appearing in the two games, Richard was allowed to leave the England camp and go home. But he opted to go along to the match in the Midlands first to support his friends, all of whom were on the bench.

The match started brilliantly for England as they scored a goal early on and became in control since. They eventually scored a second with twenty minutes to go before Romania pulled one back late on. Richard was very happy to see Charlie, Danny, Tom and Owen played a part in the second half.

Just before Richard started driving home, he received a link to a video from Ryan, with the message "Your everything may not see you as his everything".

Richard played the clip. It was only a few seconds long and it was from someone named Leo Harrison. It had the caption "good to have you back" and a few hearts, and he was in the video having drinks and fun with… his very own Layne!

And the background was Richard's flat!

"What is going on?" Richard asked himself after watching the clip repeatedly. The feeling of rage built up inside his head. He called Layne multiple times but there was no answer.

He drove home straight away – he wasn't holding back on speed at all, but it still felt like the longest two-hour journey ever, and in those two hours plenty of negative thoughts had manifested.

He angrily opened the door of the apartment and Layne was there, casually sitting on the sofa reading a magazine and listening to some music.

"Hey Richie, how's your ankle?"

"Why didn't you pick up the phone?"

"I must have left it in my bag. Did you call?"

"Forget about that. What did you do last night?"

"Last night? Leo came over for dinner and we recorded the interview. I told you that on the phone yesterday, what's the matter?"

"Is this what you called an interview?" Richard showed Layne the clip he got from Ryan.

"Oh when did he take that? Did he put it online?" Layne was a little shocked but remained calm.

"Tell me what happened!"

"We had some drinks and laughs, alright? What's the problem with you?"

"What else did you do? What does he mean by 'good to have you back'? What did you do behind my back?"

"Nothing happened between us! I got drunk and went to bed, I was never unconscious."

"Were you two together before me then? Was he the crush you never wanted to tell me about?" Richard wasn't having it and he inadvertently raised his voice.

"No we were never together and I never liked him in that sort of way!" Layne got annoyed and started losing his temper as well.

"But he clearly does! Why is the bedroom in such a mess?" Richard went mad after seeing the state of their bedroom.

"Nothing happened!"

"How can I trust you when he's bragging it online!"

"Is that what you've said? You can't trust me?" Layne's face went pale.

"Tell me, did you cheat on me?"

"That's fine. Don't bother asking. I'm not trustworthy anyway," said Layne before he walked into the spare bedroom and slammed the door shut.

"So you are admitting it then! How dare you do that to me?" shouted Richard.

"I'm not your toy, Richard William Lucas!" Layne shouted before he stopped talking on the other side of the locked door.

Richard stormed out of the flat. He was going to have a walk by the river but with his injury he sat down on a bench instead. He downed a bottle of beer he bought from the convenient store. Having two heartbreaks in a row wasn't easy for him to take.

By the time he finished his third bottle, he got a text from Layne.

"Believe it or not, I did not cheat on you. You are my one and only."

Richard didn't know what to do. He was confused. On the face of it, Leo was clearly interested in Layne and they had a fun night in. But to what extent? Layne had never lied to him before, and he didn't look like he was lying earlier. He may not be the most intelligent but he would have tried to hide the evidence or make up some cover story, instead of casually telling him what happened.

Richard asked himself a series of questions:

Did he make the wrong assumptions about the whole story?

Did he incorrectly accuse Layne of cheating?

What if Layne did cheat on him?

What would he do?

Deep down, Richard loved Layne to bits, and would have forgiven him if it was a mistake, maybe he was too drunk and got taken advantage of? But the absolute denial made Richard suspect if he was lying, which would become intolerable.

He made a call to Thomas – he needed some help. He told him what happened and asked what he should do. Thomas said that, with the evidence available, he couldn't conclude if Layne had cheated on him and so he might have overreacted – it was understandable given he just had his disappointment from his injury, but he should behave in a mature manner. They needed to move on from being childhood sweethearts if they wanted to be in a long-term relationship.

"It's about trust, Rich. You should think about his side of the story rather than just what you imagine. He's your partner after all. It hurts him to be considered by you as not trustworthy. Just calm down and talk through it with him peacefully. You love him, right?

"I'm not sure if I should tell you this, but I heard from my agent that Layne turned down a number of Premier League clubs to sign for us. It is well known by the circle of agents that he is the one with the most potential and market value out of us lot. Why would he do that if it wasn't for you?"

Richard was shocked by what Thomas said at the end. Cold sweats broke out as he realised that he wasn't the only one having to sacrifice for their relationship and he may well be the one pulling Layne's progress backwards. He tried to calm himself down before heading back to the apartment.

But Layne was not there.

Richard did some forensic work – their bed smelled just like normal, it was messy but actually not much more so than how Layne would leave it normally, and he found a new and half-opened duvet cover set in the wardrobe, which had a Saint George's Cross on it.

Richard started to think that maybe Layne was telling the truth, he slept alone after the drinks, he was just messy and he was halfway through trying to change the bedding but gave up? The latter was quite possible as Richard did most of the housework normally. And clearly, he bought that duvet set to celebrate his call up by England.

Richard had a look at the second bedroom. He opened the drawer where Layne put all his documents and found what looked like an official letter from the big west London club.

Thank you for the interest you showed on your response. However, we regret to inform you that we do not have intentions to sign Mr Lucas at this moment. We admire his qualities greatly but we already have a number of players of his calibre at our disposals. Our offer to you remains unchanged and we would be grateful for your acceptance.

So not only did Layne reject an offer from one of the biggest clubs in the world, he went back and asked the "awkward question" if they would sign Richard as well.

He suddenly remembered all the time he spent with Layne – from the early days at the Stevenson's to the training, matches, tours, all the wonderful moments they shared. He realised he couldn't live without his young partner. The despair of losing him and hence everything went through his mind.

I need to find him, where is he?

As he turned around, he saw a picture on the wall – the selfie they took at the field backing into Hampton Court Palace, the day before Layne's sixteenth birthday. Layne looked extraordinary cute and sweet holding onto him.

Richard rushed out of the apartment. He ran along the river and crossed the bridge – he thought he knew where Layne would be. His ankle really hurt, but he didn't care.

He got to the field and there was Layne, sitting on a bench in his running outfit.

"There you are," he said while catching his breath. "I've been looking for you."

"Isn't it beautiful here? Do you remember our first visit?"

"I do. It was one of our greatest moments."

"Did you run all the way here with your bad ankle?"

"Yes, because I really want to see you. Shall we talk?"

"Will you listen to me?"

"Yes I will, I promise."

"What do you want to talk about?"

"I... I...," Richard stuttered. "I don't care what happened. I only wanted to tell you that I can't live without you. I'm so sorry for lashing out earlier. Will you forgive me, Layne?"

Layne looked at Richard for a moment before throwing himself into Richard's arms. His eyes were full of tears.

"I'm sorry for what happened, but I really didn't cheat on you, Richie. We had a takeaway and some drinks after we recorded the interview. I felt tipsy so I called it a night. I offered him the guess bedroom but he decided to leave. I didn't know he has feelings on me and he posted that video online. I see him as an old friend and nothing more. I've told him to delete the interview and I'll never see him again," Layne said slowly.

Richard was holding him tightly and he believed what he said. "I'm so sorry, baby. I should have trusted you."

"I would never cheat on you."

"I believe you. I'll never doubt again. I'm so sorry."

He realised how important Layne was to him and he never wanted to let him go again. He didn't want to bring up the offer from the big club but he treasured what Layne did to be with him.

Leo's video caught the attention of the tabloids and stories of an affair between a popular online influencer and a footballer emerged.

Martin summoned both Richard and Layne to his office after the next training session on Monday. He told the pair that while the club would not get involved with players' private matters, Layne was seen drinking while he was still under the legal age to do so and that was against the club's policies. Layne admitted his wrong doing and accepted the official warning from the club, but he also made it clear that the stories were not true. Martin was fine with that.

With Leo's removal of the video and the lack of follow up material, the story died down quickly. The pair's relationship was slowly becoming an open secret – they never admitted it or came out officially, but it was presumed to be the case by the media and the fans. They got used to be at the receiving end of boos and abuses from a minority of the crowd every time they played but luckily, they had not faced anything more sinister since the game against south east London in December.

The pair watched the next England under 21 game against Ukraine with their teammates and some fans at the local pub close to The Dragons Stadium. They cheered when Owen and Charlie came on in the second half as the team snatched a 2-1 win late on.

Richard returned to training two weeks later. He told Layne about the messages he received from Ryan but he urged him not to take offence and continue to be teammates. Layne was okay with it as long as Ryan didn't follow up on the matter.

22.

Run

The Black Dragons' first team only picked up five points out of fifteen in March and were winless in the last four. Their momentum for a playoff place faded as they had to win nearly all remaining games to stand a chance. However, it was already some achievement as they had effectively secured their safety from relegation with ten games to go.

One day, Charlie asked Richard and Danny if they could stay behind after regular training to help him work on his first touches. He wanted to be able control the ball with minimal delay and be ready to either run at speed with it or take a shot straight away. Richard and Danny's role was to hit powerful low passes to him from a short distance. He had plenty of work done with the ball launcher robot already and he wanted the randomness from real passes. They started with some easy balls and slowly increased the difficulty to some really awkward ones as he improved.

Charlie tried to control a number of the passes with his back foot – in order to bounce the ball forward into his path for a run or a shot. He kept practicing it until he felt comfortable to execute it for moves into all directions, and without noticing the trio spent over two hours before stopping to have some drinks.

"I think it'll be good to have you two in the first team, I miss Rich's long balls and the space your runs create, Danny," Charlie said.

"It was great to get a run during Christmas, but it's unlikely that they'll promote two youngsters in centre midfield," Richard highlighted the problem he was facing.

"I'm confident in my abilities but Ross and Mark are good players. Competition for places is tough," Danny said.

The three of them weren't aware that Bob the first team manager was nearby.

"Doing extra work, boys?" he asked as he walked towards them with a smile.

The players turned around and greeted him. They had a chat about the teams' recent performances and how they were developing individually, in particular their call up by England under 21's. Bob closed by saying that he would take Richard and Danny into the first team "really soon".

"Did he mean it, that last sentence?" Richard asked Charlie afterwards.

"He's a man of his words," Charlie coolly responded. "Keep training well and you'll be there."

The under 23 team's next game was a friendly against the under 19 team from Seville at the main stadium. Martin chose to start with Jack in goal, Ollie, Layne, Thomas and Zach in defence, Richard, Kasper and Danny in midfield and Andrew, Alex and Rob up front.

The game meant a lot to Alex, who was released by the Spanish side a couple of seasons ago. Martin let him give the team talk in the dressing room before kick off.

"I'm sure you guys know my history with today's opponent. I won't hide the fact that I'm desperate to win this game – not just to show them how good I am, but to show them how great my new team is. Please don't try too hard to set me up to score today. Just pass to the player in the best position – the team wins, I win. Fly high you Black Dragons!"

"Well said. Up the Dragons!" Thomas the captain concluded the pre-match ritual.

From Alex's information his former team tended to play in a similar 4-3-3 system to theirs and they were very good at pressing up front. Their lone striker Ruben was known to be lethal in front of goals and he broke into their B team in the second division earlier that season. He was only travelling with the under 19's because he was recovering from an injury.

"We have to be quick today, Boiler. Play safe if you have to. The rest of you, keep moving for us... Hey baby are you listening?" Richard was reminding his teammates of the key points before kick off and noticed that Layne wasn't paying attention.

"Err... baby?" Andrew picked up the rather amusing part.

"I mean Layne, of course," even the ever-serious Richard chuckled at what he just said.

"I think we know!" Ollie with a cheeky answer.

"Let's get back to business lads," Thomas joined in to re-focus the team, before he said to Layne. "Be ready to run down the channel for us, baby."

"Oh God..." Layne turned away from the team.

"Come on guys we're playing!" Alex shouted as he was about to kick off.

The unintended lapse in concentration put the Black Dragons on the back foot. The away team gained possession quickly and launched their attack. They created a chance from their crisp passing but was denied by good goal keeping from Jack.

But the away side succeeded with their second opportunity as Ruben the lone striker read Ollie's intentions and tackled him. Jack forced him into a narrow angle but he curled the ball into the empty net brilliantly to take the lead.

"Don't worry about it. Keep talking to each other and we'll pass our way out," Richard said to the team.

The visitors continued to press from the re-start. They did their homework and didn't allow any time for Richard to pick his passes. He was being suffocated like what he did to his opponents in the past. He gave Danny a gesture and decided to make a move. While Richard dragged his marker to the left, Danny dropped deep to receive the ball near the centre circle. He turned and ran into the space ahead of him on the left and dribbled past one of the midfielders, before passing the ball forward to Andrew on the left. He quickly sent the ball back into the space created by Danny's run in the centre, along the edge of the area.

Richard had moved there to pick up the pass, having left his confused marker behind and formed a two against two situation against the centre backs with Alex. While everyone expected him to pass to Alex on his left, he surprised them all to pull out a trick of his own. He feinted the pass and flicked the ball to his right at the last moment to dribble past the centre back. He went through on goal, spotted a tiny gap in the far post and hit the ball with the outside of his right boot.

It bent round the keeper, hit the post and in!

"Where did that movement and dribbling come from?" Layne was completely surprised.

"I've been watching Danny and Charlie all this time and it just came into my head," Richard said with a smile.

"We're going to win from here!" Alex encouraged his teammates.

The away side's high press ceased as the players tired towards the end of first half and Richard started spraying his passes freely across the pitch. He sent Layne through on the left, and with some fantastic movement by Andrew, he was able to run all the way to the byline. His cross was met by Danny in the six-yard box and he made it 2-1 for half time.

"Lovely cross, baby!" Danny continued with the theme of the day as he performed his usual celebration with a double clap.

"Thanks, Richie. Look what you've done..."

The Black Dragons scored another goal quickly after the re-start. Danny won the ball in the opponent's half, sent it to Alex, who held on to it long enough to lay it off to Andrew for a shot. The keeper saved it but the loose ball fell back to Danny for a tap in. 3-1.

With the gap widened the young away side found it hard to restart their momentum. Kasper and Richard were winning most balls in midfield and they slowed the play down with some safe passes.

Martin sent Ryan, Finley and a trialist on at the hour mark in place of Rob, Andrew and Kasper. The tall midfielder on trial named Cheikh was about seventeen and looked rather nervous.

"Just keep it simple, Cheikh. You can do it," Richard told him as he settled into his position. He gave him some easy passes to build his confidence when he had the chance.

The Black Dragons had another chance near the end of the match. Cheikh found Ryan on the right wing and his cross was controlled by Alex at the near post. He turned quickly and sent a hard ball across goal. Layne arrived at the far post and poked it in with his right foot to make it 4-1.

"Great finish, baby!" Alex and the others gathered around Layne to celebrate his goal. Richard couldn't stop laughing while he gave him a hug.

"Thanks to you, dear."

"You're welcome, baby."

The match ended soon after. The couple of thousand home fans, with the majority being youngsters, were delighted to see their team dominated an established club from Europe and showed their appreciation at the full-time whistle. They heard how the players called Layne throughout the game and came up with a chant for him in the tune of the nursery rhyme "Baby Shark", with the word shark replaced by his surname Moore. They sang it repeatedly since his goal near the end and had a lot of fun.

Alex caught up with some of his old teammates and was ecstatic when he returned to the dressing room.

"We did it! Cheers lads!"

"How did your old mates find it?" Rob asked.

"They were amazed at how good we are. They name dropped Danny, Rich and 'The Baby Boy'."

"Oh, stop it! Even the fans were singing baby shark out there," Layne complained.

The team picked up on that and started singing it as a result. Of course they did. Layne pretended to cry in

Richard's arms, who just laughed and embraced the harmony of the team.

Martin asked Richard, Danny and Layne to see him at his office afterwards.

"Well done today all three of you," he welcomed them in. "It's been a pleasure to have you in my team, and it was fitting that you all played so well in your final game."

"Final game?" Layne was a bit shocked.

"Yes this is the last game in the under 23 team for you three – we're transferring you to the first team tomorrow!" Martin proudly announced.

He went on to say that the club saw them as a core part of their future together with Les, Charlie and Tom.

"That's brilliant, thanks Martin," Danny calmly said.

"Thanks for your help along the way, Martin, I appreciate all your support and advice," Richard gave Martin a firm handshake.

"You've learnt well – I'll become a supporter from now on," he said with a warm smile.

The first team were about to enter a run with six games in twenty-one days, the last two of those being local derbies against the teams from Putney and Shepherd's Bush. Seven of the twenty-three first team players were out injured at the time and so there should be plenty of game time for the youngsters.

The three young players were given their first team gears and lockers the next day.

"This feels so real now," Layne said.

They were then welcomed by the club captain Michael before training started.

"Well done for graduating into the first team, you're one of us from now on. I expect to see you on the pitch very soon," he said.

"You're now officially part of the team, my fortune-telling boy," said Matt the veteran goalkeeper.

"Welcome to the big stage," said Les the former under 23 captain.

"Now we can have more fun in one to one's," said Luciano, who had a few duels with Richard when he trained with the first team previously.

Richard managed to get a list of the latest first team squad:

Goalkeeper:
Gordon, Matt and Josh

Defender:
Jonas, Jan, Youssef, Lewis, Layne, Keith, Alain, Les, Matias

Midfielder:
Michael, Ed, Kalim, Tom, Richard, Ross, Mark, Danny

Forward:
George, Luciano, Charlie, Dennis, Andrés, Kalifa

The first team's next game was away at Bristol, the team Layne supported when he was young. Bob started with Gordon in goal, Jonas, Youssef, Keith and Les in defence, Michael, Tom and Ross in midfield and Charlie, George and Luciano up front. Richard and Danny were on the bench with Josh, Lewis, Alain, Dennis and Andrés. Layne travelled with the squad but was not named in the final eighteen.

The game kicked off at Saturday lunch time and was shown live on national television – a first for Richard if he was to play.

The opponents were in a similar situation as the Black Dragons – they were as far from the bottom of the league as the top, but it was by no means an easy game. The teams cancelled each other out in a tightly contested first half. Charlie created two chances for the team but they were both defended well.

The second half continued in a similar fashion and Bob decided to bring Danny on for Ross to change the pattern of attack. Richard also came in to replace Michael, who picked up a knock. Bob wanted Danny to play close to the striker and Richard and Tom to hold the line as a midfield two.

The arrival of Danny restored some much-needed urgency into the play and more chances were created as a result. But the team still failed to put them away.

The Black Dragons had a throw in on the left near the half way line with about fifteen minutes left. Youssef threw it to Richard and looked for a return pass. Richard sent the ball into space for him first time but the left back was clattered into by the home team's right midfielder. The collision was bad and he had to be replaced by Lewis.

Richard stood over the ball for the free kick. Charlie gave him a glance and he duly hit a high curling ball towards the left of the penalty area. The winger had a running jump on the centre back and he headed the ball down across. Danny knew exactly where the ball was going and met it with a left-footed volley – he actually sliced it but it went in off the post to finally break the deadlock!

The home team tried to force an equaliser and inevitably, the Black Dragons retreated to protect the lead as full time approached. Richard defended heroically as he made five successful tackles in a row to foil an attack through the middle. He then dived in to block the follow up shot with his head just outside the area. It was on target and the keeper Gordon might not be in place to save it.

The referee blew the full-time whistle when Les won the header from the resulting corner and cleared it down field. The Black Dragons won the surprisingly hard-fought battle 1-0.

Danny was named as the man of the match and the presenter dragged Richard into the live interview as he walked past.

Presenter: Thank you for joining us live. How are you two feeling as you are now permanent members of the first team?

Richard: It's great to become part of the squad, it's a dream come true.

Danny: Yeah I'm very happy to make the switch and a big thank you to Bob, David, Martin and the coaching team. I hope they like what they saw on the pitch.

Presenter: That was a tough battle, how are you finding it out there, comparing to matches for the under 23's?

Danny: Not that games for the under 23 team were easy but this is another level. Everything is that bit quicker but I think we're adapting well. The experience we gained during the festive period really helped.

Richard: I think the club made it easier for us to make the transition as the teams play in a similar style and we train next to each other every day. The senior players were great and of course having other old under 23 teammates in the team helps too.

Presenter: Can you tell us a bit about your goal please, Danny? You seem to know exactly where the ball was going before anyone else?

Danny: Charlie and I worked together a lot on the training ground and it becomes instinctive – I'm glad it ended at the back of the net.

Presenter: Richard, tell us about your amazing defending near the end there. What were you thinking diving in head first?

Richard: I didn't know much about it to be honest. I was on the floor after I think the fourth tackle and I saw him pulling the trigger, so I pushed myself up to block it. Luckily it hit my face and went out. It'll be sore for a few days, I guess. It's probably not the best day to be in front of the camera!

Presenter: That's wonderful stuff. Well thank you both for your time and congratulations again for the win. Danny, you've been nominated by the studio as the man of the match and Richard, do you mind presenting the trophy for us?

Richard: Sure, here you go mate.

Danny: Cheers Rich.

David told the youngsters afterwards that Bob was very happy with their performance and urged them to keep up their hard work.

Layne arranged to visit his old school friend Grayson back in Bath after the game. The pair caught up with him and his partner Jeremy at a pub not far from Layne's family home. It was the first time for Richard to meet another gay couple and he found it quite relaxing as he could honestly talk about his feelings towards how he and Layne were received in the football world and the challenges they were facing. They got plenty of encouragement and felt positive for their future.

The pair went to meet Layne's mum at their family home for dinner afterwards.

"Hello Mrs Moore~ How are you doing?" Layne was very happy to see his mum after a few drinks at the pub and was acting like a child again.

"What's going on with my little Ping here? Have you been drinking, naughty boy?"

"Just a few, it's all good-"

"Ahem, I thought I asked you to take care of him, Mr Lucas."

"Well, you know what he's like. I can't stop him all the time," Richard shrugged his shoulders and smiled.

Mrs Moore had just returned from a business trip to Japan and she bought quite a lot of souvenirs for Richard and Layne. Richard had the miniatures of Tokyo Tower and Kaminarimon (aka The Thunder Gate) to add to his collection of landmarks and Layne got plenty of anime merchandise and hair styling products. She also bought them a genuine replica shirt of characters from Captain Tsubasa each.

"Thank you – Danny will be so jealous!" Richard was very happy.

"I have a bit of news for you too – I've quit the job, so I'm done with all the travelling!"

"Really? That's the greatest news ever!" Layne was absolutely delighted.

"It's been a good experience exchanging ideas with all the international colleagues but five years was about enough. I'll be having a break before my next move."

"We can see each other much more often then!"

"We sure can, you need to get me tickets to all your home matches from now on. No pressure!"

"That's easy, we've never used all our allocations."

"There's my good boy!"

Mrs Moore was cooking a traditional Cantonese meal for the pair. There was a steamed sea bass, a roasted duck, some stir fried bean sprouts and green vegetables and finally a dish that Richard thought he recognised.

"Is this sweet and sour pork?" he asked pointing at the dish with small chunks of meat wrapped in a rich red sauce.

"No, it is eel with roasted honey sauce, have you tried an eel before, Richard?"

"Oh no, is it really edible? Isn't it like a snake?"

"You'd love it – the roasted honey sauce is wonderful, and mum does it boneless," Layne helped out with the convincing.

"Okay, let's see what it's like," Richard tried to look brave.

The meal was really good. The chopped eel was soaked in the honey sauce before being fried. Its texture was a bit like fish but there was a layer of fat between the meat and the skin – Richard could understand if people didn't like it but he found it delicious.

Richard enjoyed the family dinner very much. He was glad to have some normal life, considering his relationship with his parents. He touched on that with Layne when they travelled back to London the next day. Layne suggested to pay them a visit one day.

"Maybe they'll kick me out… or maybe they won't?"

Richard had a lot to think about.

The Black Dragons' next game was at home against a team from Lancashire five days later. It was another team in the middle of the table and Bob went for the same team with the exception of Lewis replacing the injured left back

Youssef. Layne was named on the bench as a result, alongside Richard and Danny.

The home team were on the attack from the start with both wingers causing troubles, but again the finishing was a little lacking. The visitors tried to hit them on the break but the defence did their job well.

After a goalless first half Bob brought Danny on. Similar to the last game, he instructed him to push forward as a support striker and made himself a nuisance to the away team. He did exactly that and his efforts paid dividend after seventy minutes. He picked the pocket of a defender and set Luciano up for an easy finish.

Bob brought Richard on for Tom to restore energy to the midfield and protect the lead. He continued where he left off at Bristol and helped the team to another victory. Layne was an unused substitute and he went on the pitch to congratulate Richard.

"Have you noticed that the team haven't conceded a goal with you on the pitch yet, Mr Unbeatable?" he said.

"Oh don't say that, you'll jinx it," Richard joked as he embraced Layne for a hug.

With the tight match schedule, the team had a recovery training session the next morning instead of a day off. For players who played the majority of the game, it involved plenty of foam rolling, yoga and time in the hydrotherapy pool; while for those with less minutes, it was similar to a full session. The video analysis and tactical planning came in the afternoon and the team set off for their next match away in Nottinghamshire after putting the plan into practice the next morning.

On match day, Bob decided to start with both Richard and Layne, as Michael needed some rest and the unfortunate Lewis suffered another injury during training. He was likely to miss the rest of the season.

It was Richard's first start for the senior team. He looked around the 110-year-old stadium to soak up the atmosphere as he stood in the starting line-up between Layne and Tom. He wasn't nervous, as he never was, but he did get a sense of immense proud – he had achieved another milestone.

The home team had been going through a goal drought but they started the game strongly, with the striker hitting the bar with a pot shot from twenty yards out after a good link up play with the centre midfielder.

Charlie was playing in his father's home city for the first time and he was particularly keen to impress in front of his grandparents. He received the ball from Richard on the left and drove directly into the centre, evading three players on his way. He took a shot from outside the area but it whizzed past the post in the far side.

Richard had another busy game in midfield but he lived up to the expectations with plenty of successful tackles and interceptions. He consciously kept his distribution short and safe, with ninety five percent of his passes reaching their targets. He created a chance for Danny with a measured pass, but his first time shot went into the side netting.

The second half continued with the same pattern until the home team brought a young right winger named Rory on twenty minutes in. Richard played against him in the PDL and knew that he was very good on the ball, so he dropped a little deeper in case he needed to support Layne.

Soon after his introduction Rory got the ball on the half way line and he dribbled past Layne relatively easily. Richard was right there in front of him ready to pounce and so he chose to pass it backwards. But he didn't know the young Black Dragons' habit of hunting in a group – Danny was waiting for that. He picked up the ball and laid it back to Tom on his right, who then rolled it back to Richard.

Layne was sprinting towards the penalty area at full speed so Richard delayed on the ball a little before hitting it powerfully to Charlie who was further ahead. The winger cushioned the ball nicely onto Layne's path with his head and the left back charged towards it, touched it slightly to push it through the legs of the on-coming centre half and then dinked it over the keeper with the outside of his left foot.

It was a stunning piece of counter attack and the Black Dragons took a one goal lead!

Layne ran all the way back to the away fans and celebrated his first senior goal with a knee slide. When he got up, he turned around and made a heart with his hands towards Richard, who felt fairly embarrassed but he went on to hug him anyway.

"You're not hiding it anymore, are you?" he whispered.

"I'll give you a kiss next time!" joked the young one.

The home team had twenty minutes to find an equaliser. They were not yet safe from relegation and they needed to fight. High balls were launched into the Black Dragons' box and they were looking dangerous. Bob brought Les on to replace Andrés and asked Danny to drop deeper to form a 5-3-2 with Charlie moving up front with George. The arrival of the giant centre back settled the defence, but the Black Dragons were down to ten men with five minutes remaining when George pulled his hamstring and went off, after all substitutions were made.

Charlie offered to come back to help the team defend but was pushed away by Richard.

"Stay up there and occupy their centre backs, we'll find you," he told him.

After Les won another header, Richard hit the loose ball high into the right wing with added backspin. It looked like a lost cause but Charlie knew exactly what it would do and went after it. The left sided centre back was a split second late to react and Charlie took the ball past him. Danny's supporting run distracted the other centre back and gave Charlie a chance to go direct. He completed the job emphatically, with a powerful left foot shot straight to the top corner. He took his top off and threw it away as he ran passionately to the stand where his family were to celebrate. He was duly booked afterwards for that.

The Black Dragons won the game by two goals to nil – a third victory in a row since promoting the three young players from the under 23 team, and they still hadn't conceded a goal since having Richard in the team.

A selection of first team players were summoned to model club merchandise for the next season. The new match day jerseys were presented by the established stars such as Gordon, Michael and George, while the younger players were asked to showcase the other product lines. The muscular Charlie and Tom were selected for beach wear, Danny was, naturally, picked for tracksuits and Richard was assigned the shirts and jumpers for his studious look. Layne was reserved for the new cycling series and he modelled the figure-hugging Lycra outfit. The tight cutting revealed his slim but firm body and Richard was dazzled by what he saw, even though he had literally seen everything Layne could offer.

"Don't stare at me like some kind of pervert!"

"You look really good in these…"

"Should I keep them?"

"Well… maybe… yeah…"

"Hey Rich, everyone in the studio can see what you're thinking! Get a room!" Tom laughed.

Richard wasn't aware that they were watched and was really embarrassed. He dashed to the canteen to calm himself down away from the scene.

The pair and Danny were invited by the media team for an interview afterwards. It will be published in the next matchday programme, for the derby game against the team from Shepherd's Bush in ten days' time.

The host started by asking the youngsters to introduce themselves – Richard talked about his time abroad and in Windlesham, Layne mentioned his private school days in Bath and Danny gave a bit of information on his time in the children's home in Slough.

They then talked about coming through the Black Dragons' academy and the under 23 team. They described the structural change, how the training intensified, how the matches became more competitive, and finally how they started playing and performing for the senior side.

The interviewer then asked who the players' inspiration had been. Richard said it was David for him – he discovered him from the youth team, took him under his wings through the junior teams and now into the first team. Layne had a little blush before claiming Richard was his inspiration – the way he helped him settle into the team from day one and led by example on how to behave on and off the field. Danny told the host that Nick and David had a great impact on his development and he couldn't help but thank them.

The next question was who their favourite teammates were. Richard named Tom as their understanding meant they knew exactly how to complement each other in the middle of the park. Layne said he loved playing with Thomas behind him for his clear communication when he ventured up to support the attack. Danny found it difficult to pin down to a single player, as he really enjoyed playing with his under 23 team teammates but he also found the first team very welcoming too. He did miss the chemistry he had with Owen and wish he could line up with him again in the future.

The last question was on what the youngsters called each other during their youth team days. Layne gave away all the nicknames they had in the team but Danny slipped out a comment saying the audience probably didn't want to know what Richard and Layne called each other. Richard tried to recover the situation by saying he called Layne "The Baby", just like everyone else. Of course he didn't mention why everyone was calling him that to begin with. The boys had a good laugh and closed off the interview.

23.

Double Header

Four days after their trip to Nottinghamshire, the Black Dragons made the twelve-mile journey to one of their local rivals, the team from Putney. As the club progressed through the Football Leagues into the Championship, the rivalry with teams in the local area naturally grew. The supporters seemed to have taken a significant disliking of the team from Shepherd's Bush, while being on slightly more friendly terms with those from Putney and Hounslow.

The home team were one of the front runners that season and were challenging for automatic promotion. A win would move them back to second, while anything else would confirm the promotion of the league leader, the team from West Midlands. The Black Dragons, on the other hand, had moved back up to eighth following their three wins in a row and were four points behind the team in sixth.

George was still out injured so Bob moved Luciano to the middle and called Alex up from the under 23 team to be one of the backups. Richard got a feeling from the first team players that they didn't have a great impression of Alex, seeing him as a prima-donna type of player with his long blonde hair and rather extravagant fashion style. But he surprised everyone in training the next morning when he came in with a short and neat haircut. It was still blonde, but already way more like a sportsman than before.

He also showed everyone why he deserved to be called up with some brilliant skills in training – his movements, first touches and finishing were all impressive.

Bob started the local derby with Gordon in goal and Jonas, the fit-again Youssef, Les and Keith in defence. To counter the attacking threats from the hosts' midfield, he opted for three centre midfielders with Michael, Tom and Kalim, who returned to the starting line-up after a few months out. Charlie, Luciano and Danny completed the line-up. Richard, Layne and Alex were on the bench.

The away team dressing room was one of the smallest in the league. Even though some clubs intentionally made them tight and poorly-equipped to gain some psychological advantage, it was genuinely due to a lack of space in the old stadium. It posed a challenge for the supporting staff as they needed to squeeze all the kits, drinks and equipment into the very limited space. The players had to take turns to put their footwear on using the old-fashioned benches to avoid suffering from accidental muscle problems.

The Black Dragons played well in the first half with some impressive passing and movements. The solid midfield gave Charlie and Danny the licence to roam in the final third, and Danny went close with a solo run. They also combined to set up Luciano but his goal-bound shot was deflected wide by a brilliant piece of defending from one of the centre backs. The entertaining first half ended goalless.

The break was a blessing for the home side and they came out strongly in the second half. Their passing was more positive and they opened up the Black Dragons' defence a number of times. They scored with one of those ten minutes into the half when their star striker smashed the ball in from the edge of the box after some brilliant one-touch passes in the build-up.

Alex was introduced at the hour mark to make his first team debut. He came on alongside the right winger Andrés to replace Luciano and Tom. Danny moved back in field into the number ten position.

The Dragons launched their bid to rescue the game and their season. With just three games to go and the team in sixth place drawing, a defeat would all but end their unlikely push for the playoffs. But the home team were holding firm with their three centre midfielders all sitting back and wingers tracking Jonas and Youssef, effectively putting ten men behind the ball.

Bob brought Layne on with five minutes to go and he asked him to focus on running down the wing at every opportunity. He did exactly that during stoppage time and his pace drew Charlie's marker away for a split second. He went infield and controlled a hard driven pass from Danny with his back foot just outside the box. With the speed of the move he took the ball past the centre back in front of him first time and, just before the other one dived in to tackle him, he flicked the ball towards the middle of the six-yard box. Alex slid in at pace and tipped it past the keeper!

The Black Dragons equalised five minutes into stoppage time in an important derby!

The away fans, the coaching staff and substitutes all went absolutely mad for it – they screamed, cheered and jumped on their old wooden seats – Richard thought the sound of which was quite terrifying.

Alex ran behind the goal to the stand that hosted the away and neutral fans and threw himself into the crowd. They had all forgotten who and where they were – just celebrating wildly.

The referee blew the whistle seconds after the re-start and the game ended 1-1. The team in sixth nearly snatched a victory late on, but their missed penalty meant the Black Dragons were still only four points behind them with three games to go – still an unlikely chase, but the dream lived on another day.

The team had the luxury of a full week to prepare for their next match against the team from Shepherd's Bush and the players got the next day off to recharge their batteries. It was a beautiful Sunday and Layne arranged a round of footgolf at a centre in Greenford with his teammates. The under 23 team were on tour in Ireland so only Charlie, Danny, Tom and Alex took part. Alex's brother Peter, who played for a League Two team in Bedfordshire, also joined.

Footgolf is a new sport that combined the concept of football and golf, where players kick their balls into the holes instead of using golf clubs. The team competed against each other at the 18-hole course full of testing slopes and tricky decisions. It was the first time for all of them and it took them a little while to get used to the game. Richard was really good with his distance but he was held back by his putting. He still won the day with two shots under par but it was only decided after a final playoff against the ultra-competitive Danny. Layne came last after slicing his ball into the woods at hole eleven. Everyone had fun and it was a thoroughly enjoyable experience.

"Let's take a photo, team vibes!" Charlie requested with his latest large-size smart phone.

"Be careful with posting pictures of me and Layne... You'll get some mad responses!" Richard reminded him.

"I'll only have it as a story, don't worry. Do you want me to tag you as 'baby Moore'?"

"Whatever, Mr Figo..." said the baby.

The team had some lunch at the clubhouse after the game.

"Congratulations to Alex our latest graduate to the first team, thanks for the goal that keeps our hopes alive and well done to Rich our footgolf champion! Come on you mighty Dragons!" Tom took the lead and raised his pint.

"Cheers everyone!"

Peter had become a regular starter for his team and they were on the brink of automatic promotion to League One – they were ten points ahead of the team below with just four games to play. He was involved in eleven goals, scoring five and assisted the others.

"I told you lots it's an ambitious club. We'll be playing against you soon, hopefully in the Prem!" he said.

Charlie told the team that he heard some rumours from his friend Darren, who was playing for one of the Championship clubs in Birmingham.

"Apparently they've shortlisted Bob to replace their manager in the summer," he said.

"That's big news! He's a boyhood fan of that club, isn't he?" Layne asked.

"Not quite, he's indeed from that area and all his family were fans of that club," Tom corrected him.

"Does it mean he'll go?" Danny asked.

"Quite likely if they approach him. It's a much bigger club with a much bigger budget – they are still receiving parachute payments from the Premier League," Richard came with his analysis.

"I wonder what it means to us? Will the new manager be as good as Bob to young players?" Layne sounded worried.

"A new manager shouldn't deviate from the club policy, right?" Tom asked.

"We just need to keep working hard and play well, that's what we can control," Alex said.

The group had a quick meal and decided to reconvene at a riverside pub back in Thames Ditton later that afternoon. Richard and Layne went to their local supermarket to pick up some essentials first and were stopped by a television crew on their way out. The national news channel was running a special on the forthcoming derby and would like to interview residents for their thoughts.

"Good afternoon lads, do you support Thames Ditton Football Club?" the reporter asked after using his microphone to intercept the pair, who were in their hoodies and wearing their glasses.

"Err… we… are players…" Richard was bemused and rather embarrassed.

The reporter didn't seem to register what Richard said and carried on with his script, "How do you feel about the derby match against the team from Shepherd's Bush this weekend?"

"I hope we get a result against them, it's important for the fans and can really define our season."

"Will you be cheering the team at The Dragons Stadium?"

"Err… sure, we'll do our best."

"Thanks lads, have a good rest of the day!"

The reporter moved onto other residents and the pair took their shopping back to the car.

"That was weird, did he realise who we are? I literally played in the last game!" Layne asked.

"I don't think he did. I guess we need to work harder on our reputations!"

They told their friends about their encounter later at the pub and Tom easily found the clip of the live interview online, as it was trending on social media after being shared by fans as a joke. The residents interviewed after the pair actually pointed out their identity to the reporter but it was too late for him to rescue the situation. The club's social media team added fuel to the post by replying to thank the two "young supporters" and the story made it into several footballing sites.

The team returned to training the next day. When Richard and Layne arrived, they saw Alex having a chat with the regular right winger Andrés and they joined in.

They learnt that Andrés came to England from his native Spain when he was sixteen and he spent three years at the famous academy in Barcelona before. He was only two years older than Richard but he had already played over fifty matches for the Black Dragons.

His advice to the youngsters was to be more proactive in showing themselves to the team and be more vocal in team discussions before and after the games.

"You've earned your rights to be here and you should start behaving like one of us. I'm not saying you should act like super stars but you don't have to be little kids either. You're professionals and you can express yourselves. The guys respect your opinions."

Richard had thought that as he came from the youth team, he was always going to be seen as a youngster. But Andrés was right when he asked them to consider themselves as players purchased from another club – the management team brought them in for a reason, because they had something to offer and were good enough. He felt much better after thinking it through. He also observed how Les, Lewis, Charlie and Tom behaved and noticed how naturally integrated they already were.

Five days later it was the second west London derby in a row, with the Black Dragons at home against the team from Shepherd's Bush. Richard played against their academy and under 23 teams and was finally there to meet their first team.

Bob started with Gordon, Jonas, Youssef, Les, Keith, Michael, Ross, Danny, Charlie, Andrés and George, who was back from his injury.

He decided to swap Charlie and Andrés because he believed the latter's trickery could be an advantage against the visitors' right back and Charlie could dominate their left back in the air on the other side. Richard was named on the bench with Layne, Tom and Alex, who retained his place on the bench following his scoring debut the week before. Luciano was rested.

Contrary to the team from Putney, the one from Shepherd's Bush were in a relegation battle and they needed a result to stay up. They had been on a bad run so they started the game cautiously. The Black Dragons played to their game plan and frequently gave the ball to Andrés to attack the opposition right back. He created two chances within the first five minutes. George headed his cross into the keeper and Michael sent his cut back narrowly over the bar.

The Blacks continued to attack down their left and finally succeeded after twenty minutes. A great link up play between Andrés and Youssef ended with the former slotting in the latter's low cross outside the six-yard box.

The home team kept dominating the game but the away side scored late in the half against the run of play. Their left back, who played for the under 23 team that beat Richard's side the season before, delivered a beautiful cross from a free kick and the striker headed it in.

The half ended 1-1.

Richard, Layne, Tom and Alex were out warming up during the break and when the first team returned Bob asked Alex to strip off to replace George, whose injury had resurfaced and was taken off as a precaution. He also asked Charlie and Andrés to continue playing in their less familiar side as it was working well.

The second half started with a similar pattern to the first – the Black Dragons' attacking down the left and the away side relying on counter attacking and set pieces. Charlie was getting to the end of Andrés's crosses but he didn't have a clear chance to score with. He headed a cross back for Alex but he first time shot went over the bar. The match dragged on and Bob decided to send Richard on for Ross after an hour to completely released Danny from defensive duties.

He made his mark straight away. Michael laid the ball off to him on the left of midfield and he hit a long diagonal ball behind the left back with his right foot. He had been practicing a new technique that kept the ball going straight without any bends, be it inwards or outwards. Charlie his training partner knew exactly where it was going and was there ahead of his marker. He side-footed it on the volley and the ball flew straight into the back of the net.

"What a beautiful ball!" said a thrilled Charlie to Richard as they gathered to celebrate.

"Your finishing made it look easy!" Richard was equally delighted.

The visitors had to fight for their survival and they piled on the pressure. Richard covered the ground in well in his usual fashion, making plenty of tackles and interceptions. On one occasion the opposing midfielder cut out a square pass from Youssef and ran past Richard while he was off balance. Richard remembered what Bob and Michael said about transitional play and decided to bring the player down before he moved closer to the area. It was a professional foul and he was given his first ever yellow card in the senior game.

The resulting free kick was tipped over the bar by Gordon and Bob brought Tom on to replace Danny after the resulting corner was cleared to solidify the midfield.

The home team survived the remaining ten minutes and took all three points from the derby. The team in sixth suffered a surprise defeat and so the Black Dragons moved within only one point behind them, although they were still sitting in eighth. Their two remaining games were a trip to South Yorkshire against a team deep in the relegation battle and a home game against the other Birmingham team who were already safe. The unlikely pursuit had become real.

"What a pass, Richie," Layne congratulated as they walked to the dressing room. "Nice professional foul too!"

"I thought I had to do it, how did it look from the bench?"

"I think you're fine – Bob was shouting 'Bring him down' at the time!"

"They won't fine me for getting booked then!"

Back in the dressing room, Bob was happy with the team's efforts and he singled out Charlie for some special praise – he was attacking the far post non-stop and got his reward at the end. He commended Richard's passing and decision making as well, saying sometimes the players needed to assess the situation and take the necessary actions.

With the trip to South Yorkshire another week away and the team having a rest day, Richard and Layne went to watch the latest superhero movie at a cinema near Waterloo. They had seen all the previous ones and were very excited to have secured their tickets for the first weekend of its release. They were a bit sad about its ending but couldn't wait for the finale the year after.

After the movie, the pair went to Chelsea to have dinner with Charlie, Tom, Danny and their other halves. Grace heard from her Japanese teammates about a teppanyaki restaurant and wanted to try it out.

Richard had always wanted to taste Wagyu beef but was a little put off by its price. The dilemma was settled when Danny, the ever so stingy Danny, said both he and

Grace would have the Wagyu set. The team looked at him with surprise, but he calmly responded with the reason.

"Grace wants to try it."

The whole table burst out laughing.

"Well done, Grace. Only you can get him to spend. We all tried!" Charlie said while clapping his hands slowly.

"I know they don't pay much in the women's game, but I'm financially independent," the tough-tackling Grace was keen to point that out.

"That settles it then, Wagyu and sake set it is!" Tom concluded and waved to get the attention of the waitress.

The drinks arrived shortly. The sake was served warm and with its high alcohol content it was lethal for Richard – he had a small cup's worth and he felt dizzy already. Layne was having cups after cups with the others and was very happy. He seemed to have forgotten that there was training the next morning.

After some prawn appetiser and an onion soup, the chefs started cooking the Wagyu in front of the party. They cut the meat into identical cubes with their extremely sharp knives, and then grilled the steak to everyone's preference after few minutes of immaculate performance on the iron griddle.

Richard found the Wagyu steak's texture very different to normal steaks. They didn't need much chewing and seemed to have melted inside his month, releasing the aroma of the meat. They were very tasty – he wished he was able to have more and he wondered what the even more valuable Kobe beef tastes like.

"Say 'arigato' to your teammates for the tasty treat, Grace," Richard said.

"I will – it's such a great call."

"I want more sake!" Layne was clearly in the mood.

"We'd better stop now, we all have training tomorrow," said Danny the professional.

"Get your boyfriend under control please, Mr Lucas," Charlie with another banter.

The pair were back home soon after. Layne was still fairly tipsy and he was holding onto Richard as they entered the flat.

"It was such a good night, Richie!"

"I enjoyed that, the Wagyu is so good!"

"The meat made me rather horny... Is it too late for a bit of that?"

"I'm afraid so. We have training tomorrow."

"Just a quick one, please-"

"You're such a naughty boy," Richard smiled.

Layne had a massive hangover the next morning. He managed to complete the training session and went for a massage straight away. Richard was keen to practice more set pieces and stayed behind. He did an hour of extra training and went to the dressing room for a shower.

He was aware that someone was having a shower when he walked in, but he minded his own business as usual. Right after he took his boots and socks off, the player came out from his shower, completely naked.

And it was Ryan.

Richard saw him and kept his head down immediately to avoid eye contact, but Ryan started a conversation as he put a towel on.

"Hello Richard, how are you doing?" Ryan noticed he was there and asked.

"Err... yeah I'm okay, you?"

"Why are you looking down?"

"I just... don't want to see you... mm... naked," Richard explained, rather awkwardly, with a red face.

"You are funny... oh wait," Ryan was slowly realising the truth. "You like me as well, don't you?"

"But I can't. I am with Layne," Richard said with his head staying down.

"You don't have to be like that."

Richard suddenly felt Ryan getting closer. He looked up and at that very moment, Ryan kissed him on the lips.

He was shocked but he didn't push back. He felt very bad but at the same time he felt really good. He knew he shouldn't be doing it but he found the boy in front irresistible.

The two kissed for about half a minute but when Richard felt Ryan's hands on his body he woke up.

"We can't do this," he said as he pushed Ryan away gently.

"Why not? We like each other, it's only natural."

"No, I'm taken, it's wrong!" Richard said firmly.

Ryan wasn't giving up and he closed in for another kiss.

This time Richard pushed him away forcefully, causing him to lose his footing and fell onto the floor.

At the same time, someone closed the dressing room door.

Richard broke out in a cold sweat and ran for the door. He saw two shadows moving away quickly at the other end of the corridor and he definitely recognised one of them.

It was Layne.

How long was he there for?

How much did he see?

How is he going to react?

Why didn't I push Ryan away earlier?

Plenty of questions went through Richard's head as he kept chasing after Layne. He couldn't afford to lose him.

He went onto the training grounds and finally found Layne at the other side of the pitch. He spotted him too and waited there while he ran across.

"Why are you running barefooted?" Layne asked with a smile on his face.

"I... I... I..." Richard was catching his breath. "I wanted to see you, badly."

"Why's that?"

"Were you... there in the dressing room?"

"Yes I was."

"What did you... see?"

"I saw my boyfriend kissing another boy," Layne answered in an emotionless tone, which was frightening.

"It's not what it seems-"

"What is it then?"

356

"I didn't want to do it…"

"He can't really force you into it, right? You're an adult."

"I know… I'm sorry… I was lost for a moment… I didn't mean to…" Richard tried hard to explain.

"Look," Layne put his hands on Richard cheeks and said. "I saw it all the way through, including the last bit where you turned him away. It's okay, I'm just toying with you."

Richard came out from his despair and looked at the boy in front of him. Layne was smiling at him, before wrapping his arms around his neck and kissed him.

Richard was relieved. The pair were going to have further kisses but thought better of it as there could still be others around.

"Does it mean I've kissed Ryan now?" Layne joked afterwards.

"Please don't go there, baby. I don't want to think about it."

The pair walked back to the dressing room amid questions from everyone on Richard's bare feet. They just laughed it off and ignored them. Ryan left, of course.

"Who was here with you at the time?" Richard suddenly remembered that there was another witness.

"It was Harry," Layne said. "It goes without saying that he was horrified. I'll text him later to clear it up."

"Thanks baby, now I know how easy it is to cross the line."

"Temptation is everywhere, but I trust you."

The pair received a written note from Ryan in their lockers the next morning. He apologised for his actions and vowed not to do it again. They agreed to reply with a short one saying, "Apology accepted, Fly you Black Dragons". They hoped that was the end of the matter.

357

24.

The Late Challenge

The Black Dragons entered the final two games of the season in eighth place, one point behind the teams in sixth and seventh with an inferior goal difference of eight and two. They had to win their last two matches and hope the other two slip up to break into the playoff places. Their penultimate game was a trip to South Yorkshire, to a club that was in the relegation zone and in desperate need for points.

Bob started with Gordon in goal, the usual back four of Jonas, Youssef, Les and Keith, captain Michael, Tom and Ross in midfield and Charlie, Andrés and George upfront. Richard was on the bench with Matt, Layne, Alain, Danny, Luciano and Alex.

The manager believed the home team would come out all gun blazing from the start in their 4-4-2 formation and the team needed to stay compact at the back and play on the break. The plan worked as the Black Dragons created several half chances from counter attacks within the first twenty minutes. Charlie's shot went wide and George's header was deflected out by a defender.

But the home team scored against the run of play after twenty-five minutes. The right back hit a cross from deep from the winger's back pass and it took a massive deflection off Charlie's back. Gordon was completely wrong footed as the ball flew over his head and in.

The Dragons were clearly frustrated and tried to force an equaliser for the rest of first half. But the lack of composure didn't help their cause and the half ended 1-0 to the home side. Michael pulled up at the final moments of the period and had to be replaced by Richard at half time.

"This body can't take much more battering. The future is for you young ones, help us get to the promise land, Richard," the captain told him.

"Stay calm and play to our game plan. The goal will come," said Bob in his half time team talk.

The home team continued to attack in a bid to score that decisive second goal to kill the game. They were wary of the Black Dragons' fire power and decided attack was the best form of defence.

The waves of attacks kept Richard and Tom very busy but when they had the ball, they needed to make good use of it in order to win the game – they needed the three points too.

Robbie the centre midfielder that Richard was up against had been talking to him ever since the beginning of the half. It wasn't particularly unusual to face a chatty opponent and it didn't normally bother Richard, but Robbie seemed to have some cruel intentions.

"Hey, you must be the 'special' youngster that everyone talks about?" he asked when he met Richard for the first time.

"What do you mean?" Richard responded with his usual game face on.

"Nothing, just heard that you're a little 'abnormal'."

"We'd better focus on the game," Richard decided it was better to ignore him but he kept coming back to it every time they encountered each other again.

Is your partner on the pitch?

Are your teammates okay with what you do?

What's it like doing it with a man?

Are you the giver, taker or both?

Richard tried not to listen to him but his remarks did make him a little frustrated. They were said quietly so there was no point complaining to the referee and he just had to concentrate on his game. He did inadvertently become more aggressive in his tackles and committed a couple of fouls – he received a warning from the referee to control his temper.

Bob brought Danny and Luciano on for Andrés and Ross at the hour mark. The team needed two goals and had to throw everything at it.

The game opened up and in an attack by the home team their right back launched a long ball into the big centre forward, he headed it down and after a few ricochets the loose ball favourably came to the space on the left, where the left winger was free and he looked odds-on to score.

"There's no way I'll let you in!" Richard thought as he launched himself into a last-ditch block.

He managed to do just that at the expense of a corner. The winger was caught in the aftermath and he exaggerated the impact with some rolling around on the floor.

"Great block," said Tom as he offered a hand to pick Richard up.

But there was a big roar from the crowd and Richard turned around to see what happened.

The referee had given the home team a penalty!

The Black Dragons' players challenged the decision as they were adamant that Richard had got to the ball first. But the referee wasn't having it and followed up with another surprise.

He showed Richard the red card!

"What did I do wrong? I won the ball and you sent me off!"

"I've told to calm down but you didn't listen. You were the last man and you denied a clear goal scoring opportunity. Now go, young man."

Richard was stunned and he stood there, motionless.

"It shouldn't be like this," he talked to himself.

"Off the pitch please," the referee said again.

"Be professional, man, we'll take it from here," said Les as he tried to wake Richard up.

"Time to go back and cry to your boyfriend then?" Robbie said.

Charlie confronted him but was taken away by the other players.

The home crowd booed as Richard walked off. There were plenty of jeers, whistles and gestures, but Richard wasn't thinking about them.

I've lost the game for the team. Their season ended because of me. I'm useless. I'm the weakest link. I'm not good enough, after all.

His confidence was collapsing like a house of cards.

David was there on the touchline. He gave Richard a pat on the back and walked to the dressing room with him.

"Before you say anything, let me tell you that it was a good tackle," he said.

"But why did the ref give a penalty and send me off?"

"Maybe he didn't see it. We'll appeal."

"How about this game? How about the season?" Richard was getting emotional and tears were dropping.

"Bad things happen. In football and in life generally. Don't worry about it. We have a young team and time is on our side."

They heard another roar from the crowd as they got to the dressing room. They looked at the screen and found that Gordon had parried the weak penalty away for a corner!

"See? The boys are still going strong!" David said.

"You should go and help Bob; I'll be fine here."

"Are you sure about that? Good, I'll see you afterwards."

Richard watched the game from the dressing room. The numerical advantage made it extremely difficult for the Black Dragons to fight back, but his teammates were desperately trying. Bob moved Charlie into a midfield three with Tom and Danny, and they were running tirelessly to close down every ball, to find a pass, to attack. The defenders were stretched, there were plenty of last-ditch challenges and blocks, but they never gave up.

Richard was really touched by their spirits, he realised that he was with a team of warriors.

But spirits and efforts were not enough to conquer the mountain in front of them, and the game ended 1-0 to the home side. The three points took them out of the relegation zone and their fans were ecstatic.

"We are staying up say we are staying up!" they chanted.

Richard's teammates slowly returned to the dressing room. He was there at the door to greet everyone as they walked in, to apologise for his sending off, but none of the players put the blame on him.

Layne was the last player back. The pair had a hug before sitting down together. Bob came in and he gave the team his post-game summary.

"Great efforts today boys. We were up against it and it just wasn't meant to be.

"We had a tremendous run towards the end of season that you should be proud. We just need to make sure we do that for the whole year. We have some exciting young talents in and the future is bright.

"As for the red card and penalty, Richard, I don't agree with it and we will contest it with an appeal. Don't beat yourself up with it, you've done well since coming into the team."

"The team still haven't conceded with you playing," Layne whispered.

"It doesn't matter if we're not winning... I appreciate your positivity though," said Richard with a polite smile and a pat on Layne's head.

The Black Dragons' late challenge for a playoff place ended as the team in sixth won their game and extended the gap to four points with one game to go. They also dropped to ninth on the table but it didn't matter much. The season was over.

The team were very quiet on the coach journey back – much quieter than usual. Most players were on their headphones, some were sleeping, some were just staring at the window.

Richard and Layne were listening to a football phone-in on the radio and one of the callers was a Black Dragons fan. He complained about the penalty and said how unfair it was for the referee to give that as well as a red card to the "poor lad, who looked absolutely distraught". The hosts agreed with him and said that it was harsh, and they discussed the danger of diving in for a challenge in this sort of situations. The guest said that Richard had to go for the ball or the Black Dragons would have conceded that vital second goal that would have killed the game and their season. The host believed that he did get to the ball first, but he risked the consequence of what happened today. They were of the opinion that the forthcoming plan on video assisted referee should help in these situations. The caller also praised the club for bringing up a number of youngsters, which the hosts also agreed.

"See, we're not alone to think that was a good challenge," Layne said.

"The most important person thought otherwise though. Oh well, whatever happened happened. We have a game next week and let's win that one, if I get to play."

Training resumed on Monday. Bob made it clear to the team that he would use the last match of the season to give the young players some game time. He also called Thomas up to the senior squad, to the delight of Richard and the rest of former youth team players.

The players were quite relaxed in training as there wasn't anything left for the team to fight for. But Bob was very keen to get a victory, saying it was the last home game of the season and the team ought to put the efforts in for the fans, as an appreciation for their support.

Tom was one of the players that were completely on board with the idea and continued to work very hard in training. It was his debut season in the first team and he was keen to put on a show for the home fans, many of whom his friends and families.

Charlie was also eager to perform well in the last game. He had scored three goals for the first team so far and was levelled with Danny. He wanted to win that personal battle.

Richard had his red card rescinded by the FA on Wednesday after an appeal. Even though the damage was done, he was glad to have cleared his name. Supporters on social media started calling him "The Unbeatable" as they discovered the statistics that the Black Dragons had not conceded a single goal with him on the pitch.

One evening Layne was on the phone with his mum, who told him that she would also come to the match on Sunday, having been in the stands for the last two home games. Then he took the conversation out to the balcony for about five minutes and came back with a giddy smile. Richard asked him about it but he just wouldn't tell.

The under 23 team were playing their last game of the season at the main stadium on Friday in a friendly against the blue team from Manchester, who beat them 4-3 the week before at their ground. Richard and Layne went to watch it after training with Charlie, Tom, Alex, Thomas and Danny.

Martin started the game with Jack in goal, Marcus, Viktor, Mason and Thorsten at the back, Kasper, Stefan and Harry in midfield and Andrew, Rob and Ryan up front.

The teams were warming up when Richard and the others arrived, and the first under 23 team player they met was none other than Ryan. It was the first time the pair saw him since the event in the dressing room and Richard was rather nervous. Fortunately, Layne stepped up to offer Ryan a handshake and the awkward moment Richard dreaded did not materialise.

Seven first team players wearing their team outfits sitting amongst the one thousand fans attending the game soon became part of the spectacle and they were surrounded by supporters seeking autographs and photographs. It wasn't until kick off that Richard got a chance to have a bite of the double cheese burger he bought from the food kiosk behind the stand.

The match itself was a treat.

The home team scored within the first ten minutes. Rob broke through on the right and his cross found Andrew on the far side, who cut the ball back onto his right foot and smashed it in.

"That move is so familiar. Andrew is like a better-looking version of Charlie," Tom commented.

"Have you seen his girlfriend Emily? She's very attractive too!" Alex added.

"No one beats me and my Julia," Charlie coolly responded.

"You've been with Julia since the trip to Barcelona, that must be a record?" Thomas asked.

"Yeah it's a year soon, we've been good."

"It's great that you're settling down," Richard joined in. "I can't imagine changing partners all the time."

"Of course you'll say that in front of Layne," Tom pointed out the obvious.

"Oh look! Ryan's on the ball. Come on Ryan!" Layne cheered.

Richard looked over to Layne and he gave him a wink. They had a bit of giggling between themselves, to the confusion of others.

Ryan's shot was saved by the keeper and the away side launched a quick counter attack. The keeper's long throw was picked up by the left winger, who played a first-time pass to the centre midfielder and ran down the side. The midfielder found him and his cross was headed in by the centre forward with minimum fuss.

"That break was lightning quick," Danny said.

"Yes they hit us a couple of times in the last game up there. They're a tough team to play against with all their movements and skills. That young kid in midfield called Wayne is a real handful. One minute he's there, the other he's completely gone. And he's really good on the ball," Thomas added.

The away team completed the comeback ten minutes afterwards when the seventeen-year-old Wayne found a gap in the Black Dragons' defence and passed the ball into the net from the edge of the area.

"Like you said Tommy, he's special," Danny said.

"He'll be in their first team one day, playing at the highest level," Thomas nodded.

The first half ended with the home team trailing 2-1.

"The boys need to do something about that Wayne. They should send Richard the monster on to teach him a lesson," Tom suggested.

"He's good at bullying kids," Charlie joked.

"He's probably too quick for me," Richard commented as he was munching the foot-long hot dog he just bought from the kiosk, having signed another batch of autographs on the way.

"Yes if you keep eating like that," Layne teased.

"You can't beat the Bratwurst from behind section D, it's the best!" Richard said. "You'll go for a run with me this evening, right?"

"I may join you guys later," said Thomas, who had just moved to the part of Surbiton where Richard, Layne and Tom lived.

"Oh we can visit little Archie afterwards then," Layne loved playing with the little boy, who would be two years old soon.

The second half started positively for the under 23 team, as Martin decided to man mark Wayne with the Swedish midfielder Stefan. He limited his influence while the other players handled the threats from the rest.

The away side withdrew their young midfielder at the hour mark and the Black Dragons took control of the game. A nice passage of play between Stefan, Harry and Andrew created a chance for Ryan in the area, and he slotted the ball home to level the game.

They re-took the lead late in the game when Ryan's brilliant play on the right set up Finley, one of the substitutes, for a simple tap in.

The game finished 3-2 to the home team. They ended their league season in third again, having won 13 of their 29 games.

Richard and his friends joined the under 23 team's celebrations in the dressing room. Ollie bought a few bottles of champagne and was splashing it around the room. The graduates were not immune and ended up completely soaked together with Martin and the coaching team. The atmosphere was wonderful and Richard loved it, even though he needed another shower.

The Black Dragons' final game of the Championship season was at home against a team from Birmingham.

As Bob announced earlier in the week, he started with plenty of young players. He had Josh in goal, Layne, Thomas, Les and Jonas in defence, Richard, Tom and Danny in midfield, and Charlie, Alex and Andrés up front. The reliable German right back Jonas was named as captain for the first time, Thomas was making his first team debut and Alex had his first start. The average age of the starting line-up was just over twenty. It was a sell-out game and the home crowd cheered their young players on.

It was Richard's first start at the home stadium and he stood between Layne and Tom as he always did before in under 23 matches. The crowd cheered every name read out by the public announcer and Richard felt rather emotional when it was his turn. He raised his hands and clapped as a response to the supporters. He made sure he waved at the stand where Layne's mum and her guest were as well.

The away side also fielded a number of youngsters as they were already safe from relegation. Richard recognised some of them.

"Today is about showing yourselves to the fans and winning them over. Remember your teammates as well – we don't need super heroes!" Bob said before the team got going.

"Let's show them what we've been training for!" Tom with the rallying call.

Alex kicked off the game with one of the under 23 team's usual moves. He started by passing it back to Richard, who sent it left into space for Layne. He steadied himself and hit it up field into the left channel for Charlie, who beat the right back to the ball and knocked it back down to Danny in the centre. He did his part of the move and squared the ball onto Tom's path, just outside the box. Tom played a one two with Alex inside the area and had a shot – the keeper pushed his powerful ball out at the expense of a corner kick.

The home fans had barely settled into the match and were excited by the breath-taking move from the youngsters. Richard jogged over to take the corner and the home fans were singing his name. He gave them a nod but maintained his focus.

He could see that Charlie, Thomas and Les were all in position for their well-practiced move and he hit his typical dipping corner towards the target zone. It was Les's turn to attack it – the giant defender rose the highest and expertly guided the ball into the far corner. That was 1-0 to the Black Dragons.

The fans went absolutely over the moon as they watched Les and the rest of the team gathered around Richard at the corner flag to celebrate. It was the perfect start.

The away side restarted the game but came under serious pressure straight away. Danny, Alex and Charlie were hunting them down like hungry lions released into a drove of sheep and they didn't give their young visitors a second to breathe. They forced the ball back to the keeper and his clearance was picked up by Jonas at right back.

He passed it back to Les, who kept possession at the back with Thomas, Richard, Tom and Layne. The away team were drawn towards the Black Dragons' half but they couldn't get near the ball. Richard picked up a sideways pass from Tom, who also gave him the signal. He hit a long forward pass towards Charlie first time and the Black Dragons were going again.

Charlie controlled the ball with minimum fuss and drew the attention of two defenders. Just before he got tackled, he flipped the ball to his left, where there were acres of space for Layne. The young left back whipped a lovely ball to the far side to Andrés, and his cut back fell perfectly into Danny's path. He feinted a shot before rolling it across goal and Alex was there to smash it past the keeper with his right foot. The young Black Dragons had scored again – all within the first ten minutes!

Soon two became three. While the away team were still wondering what hit them, the Black Dragons put them to the sword again. Richard picked up a stray pass in midfield and immediately drove a powerful low ball forward to Charlie. He threaded the ball through into space for Alex on the left of the goal and Alex's return ball was perfectly weighted for him to run on to. The rest was easy as he slotted it into the far corner to make it three goals in twenty minutes. It was truly like "hot knife through butter", one of the most frequently used (and rather annoying) catch phrases in a popular football video game.

To avoid the score line becoming more embarrassing, the away team sat back and defend for the rest of the half. They did achieve their new target as there were no further goals in the first half.

"There were some scintillating stuffs out there – well done boys. Keep control of the game and the victory is ours," said Bob in his half time team talk.

The second half started with the Black Dragons in control. Richard and Tom were dictating the play with their passing and the team kept possession of the ball without being too advantageous. Bob brought the top goal scorer George on for Andrés at the hour mark and he created a chance straight away. He dribbled past a couple of players on the right but his low cross was cleared by the centre back for a corner.

With twenty minutes remaining, Bob brought Michael and Youssef on to replace Richard and Layne. The fans were impressed by the youngsters and gave them a standing ovation. They clapped to appreciate their support and hugged each other when they were back to the bench.

"Well done you two. Good job controlling the game today, Rich. Great running up and down the wing, Layne," said Bob to the pair.

"Thanks boss!"

There was enough time for the Black Dragons to score another goal. Danny picked up a loose ball on the left after his corner kick was headed out, and he hit it hard across goal again. It bounced off the shin of a defender and went in to make it 4-0.

"I'm claiming that one and we're back on level terms for our mini competition," he told Charlie with a smile.

"I'll write to the dubious goal committee to argue it the other way!" Charlie laughed.

Josh was made to work for his clean sheet late on when he dived at full stretch to push a long shot wide. There was no time for the resulting corner kick and the season had ended.

Richard, Layne, the other substitutes and all the coaching staffs joined the team on the pitch to celebrate. They had an end of season lap of appreciation to show the fans their gratitude.

Bob addressed the fans with a speech. He apologised for the poor form early in the season, the disappointing cup exits and thanked them for their unwavering support in turning the season around. He also mentioned the emergence of the club's youngsters and urged the fans to aid their development with patience. The fans chanted his name and the club's anthems in response.

The Black Dragons finished the season in ninth place with seventy-one points. George was the top goal scorer with thirteen.

Back in the dressing room, Bob gave the team his end of season speech.

"Thank you for your efforts this season. We've been through some ups and downs this year, played some great football and suffered some heartbreaks along the way.

"We played our games, we stuck to our style and we were never beaten on efforts. You should be proud of your achievements, especially the youngsters who moved up a few levels to become part of this team. You've earned your place here.

"I'm going to make an announcement today before you go off to your well-earned holidays. I am leaving the team to take over at the other club in Birmingham next season. As you know my family live there and I'll be making my old man proud.

"It has certainly been enjoyable to work with you, to see you develop over the years and we shall be seeing each other again. Well, at least twice next season. The club will make their announcement on my successor in due course, and I wish you all a wonderful career ahead. This club will live forever in my heart.

"Fly, the Black Dragons!"

Even though he had heard the rumours before, Richard was still shocked to learn that Bob was actually moving away from the club. He knew that managers come and go in modern day football, and with the club's long term vision in place, there shouldn't be wholesale changes with a new manager, but it felt unreal and he was really grateful for what Bob had done for him and Layne.

The pair came out to meet Layne's mum and her guest after their showers. Richard didn't know who Mrs Moore's guest really was until now.

It was his own mum!

He hadn't seen her for over a year and he was genuinely surprised and touched to see her at the stadium. He went over to give her a massive hug.

"I didn't know Mrs Moore's guest is actually you, mum. Did you enjoy the game?" he asked.

"Jane was keen for me to come. I'm glad that I did. You've grown so much stronger since I last saw you," his mum said with tears in her eyes.

"I've lived well. Training was hard every day but it's worth it – look at me on the pitch, I can play at this level, if not higher."

"I'm so glad that you are happy," she said before turning to Layne. "You must be Layne? Thank you for all your messages and the invitation today."

"Do you know each other?" Richard asked curiously.

"Yes Richie. Layne has been sending me messages and photos of you, and I met him at the hospital when you bumped your head, remember?" she said. "... You've made a good choice."

"Does... does it mean you approve of our relationship?" Richard couldn't believe what he heard.

"I'm not sure about your dad, but I only have one child and I'm happy as long as he is," she said with the kindness that Richard had been missing for ages.

"Mum, thank you! It means a lot to me," said Richard while holding her hands. His tears were coming down slowly.

"Well, shall we head off for some dinner? It's half six so you'll be hungry really soon," Layne said as he wiped Richard's tears off.

"Do you still eat as much as you used to?" Mrs Lucas asked.

"If not more! Look how much muscle I've got now?" said Richard as he childishly showed off his biceps.

"Alright alright, let's go and talk about it later," Layne concluded.

The four of them went to Eton for dinner – Richard wanted to drive his mum home afterwards and Layne found a nice Italian restaurant near the Eton Walkway. They had a great time – Richard told his mum all the little things that happened to him and Layne during the last year and all their plans for the future. He carried on talking so much that he didn't even have time for the massive plate of spaghetti al Frutti di mare – a first for Layne to see.

Richard eventually took his mum back to the family home in Windlesham. His dad was out on a business trip so they didn't have a chance to meet – it was good as Richard wasn't sure if he was ready for it.

His mum invited them into the house and Layne had a look at Richard's old room.

"So this is where you used to live? It's so tidy – exactly what I would expect," Layne said. "Look at all these boots, how many pairs of black boots with gold details do you have?"

"Look at these," Richard picked up a smaller pair of boots and said. "These were my favourites, I used to play in them when I was in Germany."

"I was meant to ask you this before. Why didn't you join a bigger club when you came back? You must be able to, as you played for Munich?"

"I was a bit lost after what happened there. I wasn't sure if I wanted to be surrounded by others. It took me six months to finally join the village team, after the PE teacher alerted Simon of my abilities."

"Well I guess if things didn't happen this way we would never have met, so it's all good at the end!"

"Yes I wouldn't want it to go any other way," Richard agreed before he gave Layne a kiss.

The pair eventually left the room to re-join Mrs Moore for the trip home. She was having a chat over some mint tea with Richard's mum anyway so there was no hurry. Richard promised to visit again.

"Was this what all your secret conversations the other night were about?" Richard asked Layne on the way back.

"Yes, mum wanted to see if she can help you make up with your mum, so I gave her the contact details and she did the rest."

"Thank you so much, Mrs Moore."

"My pleasure – I'm glad it worked out fine between you two. Every mum loves their children. Layne's messages helped too!"

The pair went back home after dropping Mrs Moore off at Richmond.

"What a day, baby. We started for the first team together at home for the first time, won it 4-0, mum was there to see me and she is happy for us to be together. Thank you so much for arranging it," said Richard as he gave Layne a kiss.

"Don't worry – you know I'll do anything for you."

"You're the best baby in the world."

"Oh stop this baby thing…"

"Now the season has ended, shall we?"

"We most certainly shall…"

Richard picked Layne up and heard him giggling their way into the bedroom.

The players got six weeks off before pre-season and Richard and Layne had it all planned out. Layne completed his A-Levels exams during the first two weeks

373

of the break before the pair headed off to southern Italy for a couple of weeks. They enjoyed the sun and food in Sorrento and the surrounding islands – but Richard's seasickness prevented them from visiting the famous Blue Grotto on the coast of the beautiful island of Capri. They also visited the famous stadium in Naples but Layne hated the city after he nearly got mugged close to the train station. The shady pickpockets unzipped the front pocket of his backpack and took some loose changes. They would have gone away with his more expensive gadgets inside the main compartment had Richard not been alerted and intervened in time.

During their time away they learnt that the club had appointed David as their new first team manager. It was probably the best news for the former youth team players.

For the third year in a row, the pair joined their friends for a week-long holiday together. It was Tom's turn to arrange and he picked a 5-star resort in Malta.

The hotel had its own private beaches, swimming pools and three restaurants. Tom opted for the all-inclusive deal so everything was catered for.

All the usual suspects signed up to the trip, including Charlie, Danny, Alex, his brother Peter, Rob, Ollie, Owen, Andrew, Harry, their other halves, and finally Thomas, Elle and young Archie.

The hotel was like a palace overlooking the Mediterranean Sea and Richard and Layne enjoyed their stay very much. For Layne the best part about Malta (and Tom said it was his intention all along) was that their legal age for drinking was seventeen. Charlie, Rob, Ollie and Owen spent most their nights in the casino adjacent to the hotel. Richard and Layne went there once to have a look and thought that was enough for them – Richard still remembered how his well calculated plan failed spectacularly at the Christmas party.

The holiday went like a blink of an eye and pre-season training resumed in early July.

The former youth team players were given their new squad numbers after being asked for their preferences.

They didn't get to choose numbers that were already taken by other first team players but the club was fine for them to get any vacant ones.

As a result, Les was given number 6, Tom got 8, Josh had 12, Danny his dream number 14, Richard his favourite 16, Layne 17, Charlie 18 and finally Lewis, Thomas and Alex stayed with 30, 35 and 47.

David gave a speech on his preferred playing style and expectations of the players. Being true to form, he believed for the team to stand out in the division, they needed to be working the hardest, running the furthest as well as being the sharpest in their decision making. It was a continuation of the club's long term vision.

All Richard remembered was the last part.

"This is your season to shine. Work hard and make it happen – we will create our own history!"

25.

New Era

Richard's first full season with the Black Dragons first team started with four weeks of pre-season training. It was similar to previous years but much more intensive. Stuart the Head of Sports Science told him that their schedules were similar to those given to Premier League players so they were probably the hardest they could be. It included the dreaded 1,000 metre run test, where the players were asked to run as fast as they could over a 100 metre distance ten times. Jonas came out the fastest, followed by Danny and George. Richard and Layne were somewhere in the last quartile. Richard was glad that he was able to sustain that level of requirement and he felt fitter than ever. He also noticed how much stronger Layne had become, he was now a proper athlete instead of just a skinny teenager.

The club sold a few players to help fund the extension of their stadium. The most notable ones were first choice centre back Keith and defensive midfielder Kalim, who made big money moves to two Championship teams. There were also moves for Alain, Youssef and Kalifa to other Football League clubs. The former caught the club by surprise when he handed in his transfer request after Keith was sold, which left the club short in the centre back area. Matt the veteran goal keeper, who was part of the team that clinched promotion to the Championship, had retired.

A few young players from up and down the English Leagues had been signed as their replacements. The intention seemed to be giving the team's younger players more game time but also making sure there will be some fierce competitions too.

They were Mazibo, Kieran, Samuel and Toby. Mazibo, or simply Maz, a 22-year-old right back, and Kieran, a 20-year-old centre back, were regular starters for clubs in the lower leagues; Samuel or simply Sam, the 21-year-old winger whom Richard and his friends played against in a local 7-a-side match, joined from the team in Hounslow and finally the 20-year-old Toby came from the youth setup at one of the biggest clubs in north London. The tall left-footed centre midfielder played against Richard and the young Black Dragons at the main stadium during Richard's second season at the club. Richard was really happy with Sam's arrival but he was a little concerned by Toby – he was well aware of his ability and believed he would be in a direct competition against him for a place in the team, behind the ageing but still highly capable Michael.

David had also promoted Jack the goalkeeper and Thorsten the centre back to the first team. The former was registered as the third-choice keeper but would likely be spending most of his time playing for the under 23 team. The same was probably true for the big Norwegian and the likes of Thomas and Alex, but at least they were seen by the club as part of the first team.

Richard obtained a list of the new twenty-five-man squad:

Goalkeeper:
1 Gordon Blackford, 12 Josh Taylor, 33 Jack Simpson

Defender:
2 Jonas Schulz, 4 Kieran Rowe, 6 Les Hailey, 17 Layne Moore, 22 Mazibo Ndinga, 28 Thorsten Strømme, 30 Lewis Adams, 35 Thomas Bond

Midfielder:
5 Michael Carter, 8 Tom Nelson, 10 Mark Whitby, 14 Danny Westwood, 15 Ross Davies, 16 Richard Lucas, 23 Toby Archer

Forward:

7 Andrés Iglesias, 9 George Walton, 11 Luciano Romero, 18 Charlie Ranger, 24 Samuel Hughes, 27 Dennis Potter, 47 Alex Knight

He was asked to be Sam's buddy and he showed him around the club and the surrounding area. It was the young winger's first move away from home and Richard helped him organise the daily essentials to make sure he got off to a smooth transition. He also invited him to the younger players' regular gatherings and they became personal friends.

The team played five pre-season friendlies and David altered the starting line-up to test his players and formations.

To Richard's surprise, David had been experimenting with 4-1-2-3 and 3-4-3 instead of his usual 4-2-1-3. He seemed to have settled on the former with an anchor backing up two box-to-box midfielders.

The defence was rather settled with Gordon, Jonas, Lewis, Les and Kieran. The latter was pacy and decisive and David seemed to favour him over the other two young centre backs Thomas and Thorsten. Layne would be competing for a place on the bench with the other reserve full back, the new signing Maz.

The three former under 23 team midfielders Tom, Danny and Richard found themselves in rather tough competition. While Richard would have the opportunity to play as the anchor in the early fixtures, Michael the club captain would be the sure starter when he returned from the injury he sustained at the end of last season. Ross the newly-appointed vice-captain had been redeployed as a box-to-box midfielder to make the most of his strengths and energy and he would start ahead of Tom and Toby. He could also be used in the attacking role in place of Danny and Mark. The three youngsters' position in the match day squad, let alone the starting eleven, was nowhere near certain.

George and Luciano were the two definite starters upfront as they could both play as a centre forward or out wide. Sam the very skilful winger would be fighting for the last spot against Andrés and Charlie, with Alex and Dennis as backup. The overall squad depth was very good. Richard played in all five warm up matches, starting three of them and coming off the bench in the others. Layne appeared in four, starting the two games which David played with wing backs in a 3-4-3 system. It was a more natural position for him given his tendency to attack from deep.

The Black Dragons began their new season at home against a newly promoted side. David, who began wearing a black suit over a black t-shirt instead of the team tracksuit since he became manager, started with a 4-1-2-3 with Gordon in goal, Jonas, Lewis, Les and Kieran in defence, Richard behind Ross and Danny in midfield and George, Luciano and Charlie upfront. Tom was on the bench alongside Josh, Maz, Thomas, Mark, Andrés and Sam.

The home side started brilliantly with Danny playing on the left-hand side of centre midfield. He received the ball from Richard, played a quick one two with Charlie and then cut it back for Luciano to emphatically open the scoring from inside the box.

The lively George then created a chance on his own when he dribbled past two players only the see his left foot shot hitting the far post and out.

The Black Dragons kept up the high tempo and were rewarded with a second goal after twenty minutes. Danny sent a delicious reverse pass between the full back and centre back for Charlie to cut in and send the ball into the far corner.

Minutes later Danny claimed another assist as his in-swinging corner found the unmarked Charlie for a free header into the roof of the net to make it 3-0.

David was very happy with the fast start and asked the team to manage the second half without taking unnecessary risk, by controlling the tempo of the game.

The team did exactly that for the first ten minutes of the second half, as Richard, Ross and Danny dictated the flow of the game, spreading it around beautifully away from the visitors.

Richard found Ross a very good partner in midfield as his movements and strengths gave him lots of passing options. His communication on the pitch was clear and precise as well.

The young Dragons conceded a goal five minutes later as they were punished from a moment of over-playing. Lewis's pass to Danny was intercepted in midfield and after a string of good passes the ball fell to the away team's striker, who put his shot out of reach for Gordon.

An exciting thirty minutes followed as the teams fought for the next goal. David brought Mark on for Danny to improve the defensive capability of the team while Sam was introduced for his debut, in place of Charlie. George moved to the left to cater for the new left-footed right winger.

Richard's job was to protect the back four and he managed to block the path through the middle with his good positioning. However, when the visitors tried to force through, he was often outnumbered and had to resort to some last-ditch tackles – he won the majority of them but was booked for the one that he mis-timed.

The game was eventually settled with ten minutes to go as the tricky Sam won a free kick just outside the area. Mark placed the ball on the spot and gestured Richard to have a go. He did his measurement and duly curled the ball into the top right corner to open his account for the season. He celebrated in front of the Ditton End where Layne and both their mothers were.

The game finished 4-1 and the supporters were very pleased. David was happy with the high tempo and the composed finishing by the attackers. He was delighted by Richard's free kick as well.

The match day reporter spoke to Charlie and Richard after the game to discuss the goals and their expectations of the season. Charlie was keen to state his ambition to score more than ten goals that season and to win promotion to the Premier League, while Richard simply wanted to establish himself in the team as a regular and make the supporters happy. He was then asked if he felt sad to have finally conceded a goal while playing for the Black Dragons and he just laughed and said the key was for the team to win – having a clean sheet was great but nowhere near as important as the three points. Charlie was named as the man of the match and Richard presented him the small trophy.

He then met Layne and their mothers after the game. Mrs Lucas had become good friends with Mrs Moore and they agreed to come to more home games together going forward. The pair took them to a Chinese restaurant renowned for their natural ingredients and high quality tea in Surbiton for dinner. It was Mrs Moore's first visit there and the expert was impressed.

At the end of the evening, Richard's dad came to pick his mum up and the pair went out to meet him.

"Hi Dad," Richard tried to start a conversation.

"Hey Richard, I heard you played well today," said his dad in his typical serious tone.

"Yes we won 4-1 and I scored the last goal."

"I guess you're enjoying this life of yours?"

"It couldn't be much better. How are you keeping?"

"I'm fine."

"Let me introduce, this is Layne, my other half."

"Hello Mr Lucas."

"Don't you think I'm okay with what you two are doing just because your mum came to see you, I don't agree with it. And to you, young man, I will never like you for turning Richard into this."

"Don't say that, dad. We are genuinely together."

"It's not right and you know I'll never accept it. We're going," his dad said before driving away. Richard looked at the leaving car and he felt sad. He had hoped that it could become the beginning of their reconciliation but that still seemed very far away.

"Don't worry about it, Richie. At least he didn't punch me!" Layne tried to make him smile.

"Maybe you're right," he sighed.

The Black Dragons' second game was away at the club in Berkshire. David rewarded the good performance by Richard, Danny and Charlie in the first game with another start. Layne was also in the first eleven as David believed his pace could be useful against the home team's makeshift right back – they had an injury crisis and started with a centre back there. Poor Tom and Alex travelled with the team but didn't make the final eighteen.

David's plan to overload on the left was successful, as the Black Dragons scored two goals in the first half. Layne's pace gave the right back a torrid time and his cut back set up Charlie for his third goal in two games after fifteen minutes. The home team doubled up on him afterwards but that left Danny with plenty of time to pick his through pass to George on the right to register his first goal for the season with a fine finish.

Richard thwarted the home team's second half fight back almost single-handedly. He was everywhere in midfield and the home side's momentum finally ended after the Black Dragons hit them on the counter and scored the third goal. Jonas's lovely cross from the right was met by Mark the substitute in the area with a perfect side foot volley.

Richard was named as the man of the match for the first time in his senior career. He put his little trophy next to the one Layne won the season before, which was against the same opponents.

The first mid-week game of the season saw the Black Dragons visiting a League One club in north Kent for the first round of the League Cup. David wanted to give some of the players a rest while staying competitive, and he opted for Josh in goal, Jonas, Lewis, Thomas and Les in defence, Toby, Ross and Mark in midfield and Andrés,

Alex and George upfront. Richard and Layne were on the bench with Jack, Thorsten, Tom, Dennis and Sam.

The home side, fielding their strongest possible team, started the game brightly and attacked the Black Dragons with intent. They survived the first half with Josh having to make a number of important saves. David urged the team to push the play back up field as they had been retreating to their final third, which attracted even more pressure onto them.

The team responded in the second half and started to show their superior ability. George and Andrés were fed a few good balls and they created several half chances. David sent Sam and Layne on at the hour mark to improve the attack further but the home team were holding firm.

With fifteen minutes to go, Jonas had a knock and had to come off. Richard came on to replace him at right back.

"Let's give that a go, Rich," Alex came over and whispered as Richard ran onto the field.

Richard soon got the ball on the right at the halfway line. He saw where Alex was heading and hit a massive cross towards the box. It looked over-hit as it sailed past every player in the area, but Alex was on the chase and he acrobatically hit the ball back from the edge of the area with an overhead kick. George was diving in and he diverted the ball into the net.

The deadlock was finally broken in sensational style!

The players couldn't believe what Alex did and celebrated wildly. They knew that it was a move that he and Richard had been training for, to make the most of Richard's long pass and Alex's movement and technique, but to see them succeed in a real match was something special.

The home side pushed forward for the equaliser but they were punished again late on. George beat the offside trap and ran all the way to score the decisive second. The game soon ended and the Black Dragons progressed to the second round of the cup, which was two weeks away.

383

Layne went back to school with Alex, Andrew and Emily to pick up their A-Level results the next morning. He received some respectable grades, including an A for English Language, B's for Business Studies and History, and a C for French. He achieved the conditions offered by a University for a degree in Law but he would defer it to focus on his football career.

The other three did well too – Alex had three C's, Andrew got one A and three B's and finally Emily had two A's and two B's. The group celebrated by going to a nicely decorated Mediterranean restaurant in Surbiton for lunch. Richard joined in after training and enjoyed his Turkish steak and chips.

The weekend after saw the Black Dragons back in the Championship, hosting a club from Greater Manchester. The visitors were in a financial crisis and had a much trimmed down squad. David restored Richard, Danny and Charlie to the starting line-up but Layne remained on the bench with Thomas and Tom. Maz made his debut at right back, replacing the injured Jonas.

Despite fielding an inexperienced team, the away side managed to repel the Black Dragons' attack throughout the first half. Their compact defensive shape limited the time on the ball for Ross and Danny and crosses from Luciano and Charlie were well handled. Richard went close when he hit the corner of the goal frame from a free kick thirty yards away.

Tom made his first appearance of the season when he replaced Richard at the hour mark. Andrés also came on to replace Charlie and he made his presence felt straight away with a shot from the edge of the area after finding his way past two defenders. It was saved at full stretch by the keeper for a corner.

Danny's wicked delivery found the towering Les at the front post and the resistance had finally crumbled!

The young away side staged a fight back and nearly caught the Black Dragons on the break. Tom made the sensible decision and brought the player down to halt the play. The referee duly showed him a yellow card.

But his afternoon took the wrong turn minutes later as he slipped during a tackle and caught the opponent instead. The referee gave him a second yellow and the red card – the team had to play the final ten minutes with just ten men.

Tom was devastated but he accepted his punishment and walked off. Richard met him on the side line but he just shook his head and went straight to the dressing room. Richard felt for his friend as his hard-earned opportunity to play had ended badly. He decided to follow him into the dressing room.

"Hey Tom, are you alright?"

"I can't really be alright after getting sent off, mate."

"Sometimes it can't be helped, don't worry about it."

"Don't worry about it? That was my chance to impress David and look how I fucked it up!"

"I'm sure he knew you were going for the ball, you'll get another chance."

"Who knows? It's easier to say that in your position, Mr Golden Boy."

"Don't say that, you know that's not what I meant."

"… I'm sorry Richard, just let me stay here for a little while."

"It's fine, but is everything really okay? You look a little jaded."

"I don't know, mate. Mihara is going to New York next week and she said we are over."

"What? I'm sorry, Tom."

"Don't be silly. Her company is sending her to work over there and she thought long distance just wouldn't work. I understand that but I… I couldn't bring myself to face it. What should I do?"

Richard didn't know the answer. He was nowhere near an expert on relationships and what Mihara wanted was indeed the logically outcome. Deep down, he did give up the chance to play in Germany for Layne but what if he went, would they be able to continue on a long-distance basis?

385

He didn't answer Tom's question. He just gave him a pat on his shoulder. Tom appreciated his support and they watched the remainder of the game together from the dressing room.

Thomas was brought on to replace Luciano to play as a defensive midfielder. He looked a little nervous as he hadn't played in that position for a while and it was only his third senior game after all. Ross and Danny dropped deeper to offer him support and together they survived to maintain the Black Dragons' hundred percent record.

David had a word with Tom after the game to remind him to be careful in those situations – although he was unlucky to have slipped, it might not be the best idea to dive into a tackle while carrying a yellow card.

The Black Dragons' fourth league match was a Tuesday evening away at a club in Staffordshire. It was a fixture well known in the football world to be a tough physical challenge. David was wary of that and he pondered if he should match up to that physicality. He spoke to Richard during training to see if he was up for it.

"How do you feel about Tuesday's game, Richard?" he asked.

"It will be combative for sure, but we can cause them troubles with our fast passing," Richard said.

"Are you confident?"

"I'm ready – let me show you, David."

"Good, I'll think about it."

On match day, David decided to stick with Gordon in goal, Jonas, Layne, Les, Kieran in defence, Richard, Ross and Danny in midfield, and Charlie, George and Luciano upfront. Josh, Thomas, Lewis, Mark, Andrés and Sam were on the bench together with the recovered Michael. With four wins on the trot he was keen to maintain the momentum and play to their strengths rather than adjusting for the opponents.

The home team's reputation as a tough side was there for a reason, but they were not just a physical side. They operated an aggressive high press in a 3-4-3 formation that

Richard hadn't faced before. They had spent good money during the summer to improve their squad further, with the former Black Dragon midfielder Kalim being one of them, even though he was injured for his previous clubmates' visit.

David told the team that if carried out effectively, this high press could force the play into the compact central area and the ball would be lost there. Long balls would not be useful as they had three experienced and dominant centre backs. The key was for the three midfielders to find the full backs quickly, bypassing their first line of pressure, and for the full backs to either switch play with a cross field ball or send the ball down the line for the wingers. He opted to start with Layne for that very reason, but he asked the young full back to be mindful of overly aggressive play at the beginning of the match.

"They'll see that you're young and try to destabilise you with some rough treatment, be mindful of that, protect yourself and stay professional," he told Layne.

The match began. As in David's briefing, the home team pressed high up the pitch straight away. With seven players in the first and second lines, it was a very tight squeeze. The Black Dragons were not allowed any time on the ball. They repeatedly ended up passing it back to the keeper for a clearance and lost it to one of the three big centre backs.

Fortunately, the Black Dragons' own defensive shape restricted the home team's attack from those deep starting positions to long balls into the channels and they were dealt with competently. So the game was becoming a stalemate.

The home team's right winger did give Layne his best "welcome" possible, as he left his foot in and caught Layne on the ankle for their first get together. Layne saw that coming and exaggerated the impact with a painful scream and some time on the floor in order to get the attention of the referee. He duly gave the offender a verbal warning.

"Don't be such a pussy, pretty boy!" he shouted afterwards.

He continued his rough treatment on Layne and he dived in dangerously when the ball from Richard was rather weak. Layne got to the ball first before jumping over the tackle. He did get clattered but he wasn't hurt. The referee showed the offender a yellow card this time.

The first half ended 0-0.

"That was a hospital pass, Richie," Layne said as they walked to the dressing room.

"I'm sorry. I was surrounded by four players and that was the best I could do," Richard apologised. "That press was so hard to beat!"

"That was better than I anticipated," David said during his team talk. "Not once you were caught out in possession in the central area, well done. But we need to work on the way out through the wide area, let's focus on the left now that Layne's marker has been booked. Use our ability to pass to each other and move. Two touches max. Don't assume they'll get tired later on, these players are really fit and would probably be pressing the whole game."

The second half started with the home side pressing high again. As planned, Danny and Charlie moved closer to Layne to create the triangles for short passes. Richard had also drifted slightly to the left to support. He received the ball from Kieran through the first line of press and quickly lay it to Layne. He played a one two with Danny ahead of him and broke through the second line of press with his pace. He then passed the ball to Luciano in the centre and he sent a delicate through ball to Charlie behind the defence. He raced clear of the centre backs and dinked the ball over the oncoming keeper with his left foot to score his fourth goal of the season.

With the deadlock broken, the home side moved up a gear in their attacking play and started to take more risk. That left a gap in the back and the Black Dragons exploited it. Instead of passing through the compact middle as in the first goal, Kieran hit a long ball towards the left where Charlie was heading and his lay-off found

Layne on the inside. He tried to run straight through the gap between two of the centre backs using his pace, but he was forcefully tackled by one of them. There was no escaping this time and he was badly hurt – Gary the physio suspected there was some damage to his left knee and advised David to take him off. Lewis came on in his place.

Richard was worried but he had a job to do – the team had a free kick in a good position. He took a few deep breaths to settle his mind and hit a curling shot over the wall towards the top left corner.

But it went past the post by a whisker.

Richard held his head in disbelief, as he did the hard part right and it looked certain to go in.

"Don't worry about it. It happens," Ross the captain said as they moved back into positions.

As Jonas and Lewis did not possess the same raw pace as Layne, the Black Dragons' options to break the high block was restricted to long balls down the side to Luciano and Charlie. Their ability to hold up play became vital for the remainder of the match.

David decided to withdraw Richard and Danny at the hour mark with the Michael and Mark. Layne had some ice packs tied to his elevated knee but he looked relatively comfortable, which was a relief for Richard.

The Black Dragons defended well for the next thirty minutes and the game ended a goal to nil for the visitors, making it twelve points out of twelve for them.

Layne would be out of action for two to four weeks with his knee injury. Luckily it was just a minor sprain and there would be no lasting damage. David did commend him for his brave display and urge him not to rush back into training.

With the next game against the club from Bristol at home only four days away, David decided to give some of the players a rest. He was wary of potential burnouts for the younger players as they were not used to the intensity and frequency of a season in the brutal Championship.

389

Richard was one of those players rested along with Danny, Charlie and Kieran.

Richard and Layne were in the stands with their mums. It was the first time he watched a football game with his mum and he spent the whole time explaining the rules, the work behind the scenes and the ins and outs of various tactics. Mrs Lucas probably didn't understand what he was talking about but she looked very happy to see his son's passion. She also told Layne not to worry about what Richard's dad said a couple of weeks ago.

The game was a comfortable victory to the Black Dragons. The fast start favoured by David produced another goal for Luciano as he put away Andrés's cross and they combined to set up Ross for a drive from outside the box near the end of the first half to make it 2-0. Tom played the last twenty minutes when he came on with Toby and Alex in the second half.

With five wins out of five, the Black Dragons were top of the league together with the team from East Anglia, who were also their next opponent, but there was the small matter of a League Cup second round game in mid-week before that.

The Black Dragons played against a League Two club from West Sussex in the League Cup on Tuesday night. David played a weakened side with Richard on the bench, but they still won the game relatively easily with a 4-0 score line. Sam scored his first goal for the club after twenty minutes from a cut in from the right, Alex also opened his account shortly afterwards with a penalty before Kieran diverted Tom's header in from a corner at the end of the first half. They controlled the play in the second half professionally and Andrés added a fourth at the hour mark with a neat finish. Richard and Charlie remained on the bench throughout.

It was Layne's eighteenth birthday two days after the cup game and he had it all planned out. Richard joined him and Mrs Moore for a late lunch in her Richmond flat after training before they met their friends and teammates at a

Bavarian restaurant by Kingston riverside later that evening.

They had a re-run of the pork knuckle challenge from their trip to Munich a couple of seasons ago. Richard guessed it was probably intentional that Layne, who had a few drinks already, gave up on the meat halfway through and volunteered for the penalty, which was a boot-shape glass filled with litres of Bavarian wheat beer. He downed the drink in one go, to the cheer of his guests, and had to rest on Richard's shoulder for the next thirty minutes.

"This little alcoholic is finally eighteen! No one can stop him from having one now!" Ollie said.

"That can't be good for his football. His pace would suffer if he carries too much weight," Danny commented.

"The odd one won't hurt," said Harry, who was trying to defend his friend.

"Don't be hard on him Danny, he's allowed to be smashed on his eighteenth. We've definitely done worse!" Charlie the old alcoholic said.

"The only one who's hard on him is over there!" Andrew said while pointing at Richard. He was always reliable for an embarrassing comment.

"I love it when he's hard," Layne suddenly woke up and made it even more awkward.

Richard covered up his face as the whole team laughed uncontrollably, "Who's idea is it to get this little man drunk?"

"He's your boyfriend Rich, you sort him out," Thomas said while he was still chuckling.

Just when the team were laughing their hearts out, the waiting staff brought the birthday cake out and started to sing. The team joined in and Layne made a demand after he blew the candles.

"Can you give me a kiss for my birthday Richie?"

The team went wild and some chanted "Kiss him, Richie" repeatedly.

Richard looked around the table with an embarrassed smile before fulfilling his partner's wish and kissed him on the lips. The whole team cheered and whistled:

He's got Richard Lucas!
He's got Richard Lucas!
He's got Richard Lucas!

Layne was over the moon and celebrated as if he scored in a cup final. Richard loved the atmosphere, he liked seeing Layne happy and felt wonderful to be surrounded by his friends.

The group had plenty of drinks at the restaurant and eventually moved on to the next venue, the popular nightclub complex in a converted 1930s cinema in Kingston.

Danny, Alex and Thomas decided to call time on the night after the meal and they left with Tom, who wasn't really in the mood the whole evening, and Ryan, who wasn't eighteen yet. That left Charlie, Rob, Ollie, Harry, Andrew, Finley, Sam, Layne's old school friend Grayson and his boyfriend Jeremy on the guest list.

Richard reserved a VIP room in one of the two clubbing spaces and the group entered through the special entrance. Layne was half-carried in but he came into life once he heard the rather loud music. He jumped straight into the dance floor with Harry, Andrew and others and had a good time. His knee seemed to be holding up well as he tried out all his different moves.

Richard remained in the nicely decorated booth to have a chat with Charlie, who used to be a regular at the club. He paced himself on drinks carefully throughout the night and managed to avoid getting in a mess – unlike Layne, he did have training the next morning.

After about half an hour, Finley suddenly ran up to them and said "Hey Richard come with me!"

"What's going on?"

"Just come!"

Judging by the sheer panic, Richard had a bad feeling and rushed off with him, towards where the washrooms were.

There he saw Harry and Grayson on their knees looking after a motionless Layne while Andrew and Sam were having a fist fight with three unknown men!

The massive bouncers quickly moved in and separated the youngsters.

"What happened? How's Layne doing?" Richard asked nervously.

"That guy in the black shirt was trying to rape Layne in the loo!" Grayson said.

"What?"

The perpetrator had already disappeared when Richard turned round. His two friends denied any knowledge and claimed that they were just trying to stop the assault from Andrew and Sam.

Richard and his friends took Layne back to their room and woke him up with a cold towel. He couldn't remember anything and was shocked to hear that someone tried to take advantage of him when he was unconscious. He then started crying badly in Richard's arms.

"It's fine now, Layne. You're safe," Richard tried to comfort his distraught boyfriend.

"But... but... what if he really did it?"

"But he didn't, don't worry."

"That would have ruined everything! What if you don't want me anymore?"

"I won't do that, silly."

"Are you sure, Richie?"

"Of course I am. Get up and have this glass of water. You'll feel better."

Layne had his water and slowly calmed down. He stayed nestled in Richard's arms, as if he needed his protection.

Richard expressed his gratitude to Grayson, Andrew and Sam for their intervention, especially the latter who suffered a cut to his face. He then took Layne home on a taxi after leaving the matter with the staff.

"Are you feeling better now baby?" Richard asked as they entered their flat.

"Mm. I still don't remember what happened, but how horrible it must be... Grayson said that man had already taken my pants down..."

"That taught us a lesson. You're a very good looking young man nowadays, please don't ever get that drunk again."

"I know that now. It would have been so bad – what would you do if I was really raped?"

"I don't want to think about that... it would be so painful, but I'm with you no matter what."

"Thanks Richie. I won't put us in that situation again."

"That's okay baby. Now let's go to bed and have some rest."

"Can you hold me tight for the whole night?"

"Of course I will, baby."

26.

The Midfield

The first real test of the season came when the club from East Anglia visited The Dragons Stadium. The two teams were levelled on points with their hundred percent starts but the Black Dragons were one goal ahead on goal difference.

The game was televised at Sunday lunchtime so the teams had one extra day of preparation since their midweek games in the cup.

Having analysed the strengths and weaknesses of both teams, David opted for a more experienced side. He started with Gordon in goal, the settled back four of Jonas, Lewis, Les and Kieran, a midfield three of Michael, Ross and Mark, and the attacking trio of George, Luciano and Andrés.

The bench was fully occupied by former under 23 players Josh, Thomas, Richard, Tom, Danny, Charlie and Alex. Layne was still out with his knee injury.

The away side was the bookies favourites to win the Championship that season and had a good mix of youth and experience in their starting eleven.

David's plan was to operate a high press to guide the opposition build-up into the central area for the solid midfield three to regain possession. The wingers would defend high up the pitch, blocking the pass to wide areas with their cover-shadows, while the striker George would press the central defenders. This would leave the passing lane towards the centre midfielders as the only viable option. Once the Dragons won the ball there, they could hit the opponents on the break deep in their half.

The match started with the home crowd urging the team on. The front three carried out the game plan well, closing the defenders down and forcing the play into centre midfield. However, the visitors' two young wingers came in field to provide options for the midfielders and, with Jonas and Lewis unwilling to be dragged inside, the Black Dragons were not able to win the ball back in that area. But with the middle of the pitch completely packed the away team couldn't create any good chances anyway.

Because they couldn't regain possession high up the pitch, the Black Dragons had to build up from deep when they had the ball and it was easily defended as the wide players lacked the necessary pace to break through.

The first half ended goalless.

"Well done with the pressing. You've kept one of the most prolific teams in the division quiet," David said in his team talk. "We need to figure out how to score ourselves. Their young full backs are surprisingly quick, we may be better to force some set pieces and try to score from those."

The second half resumed and David sent Danny, Charlie and Alex out to warm up.

"I guess we won't play a part today?" Tom whispered to Richard on the bench.

"Michael and Ross are playing really well, there isn't much we can do," Richard said.

"At least you've played in five of the seven matches this season, I've only played twice, and one was cut short by the red card."

"It's never meant to be straight forward mate. This time last year I was still in a cast with my broken wrist and you were playing in the under 23's. We've moved up so quickly and it won't do us any harm to settle slowly."

"I'm worried about losing our momentum, once we're out of the picture it's so hard to get back in!"

"That's true, but we can only carry on working hard in training and give David a headache."

"I guess we have to."

"How's the home situation?"

"She's leaving tomorrow, and that would be that."

"That's so sad. Are you okay with it?"

"I have no choice. I just have to move on."

"Yeah, we're still young!"

"We shall see. I may have to join Rob and the others on the lookout again. What do you know about those dating apps?"

"I have no idea. Layne will literally kill me if I download them! But I'm more in favour of knowing the person before sleeping with them."

"But I have friends who met their other halves that way."

"It may work for some, but I'm not so sure."

The game remained goalless after an hour. The Black Dragons did get some corner kicks but nothing of note came from them. David sent Danny and Charlie on to replace Mark and Andrés.

Charlie played against the away team's young right back the season before and he knew he was a difficult player to play against. But he had a distinct advantage – he was much stronger. He asked Danny for a ball to his feet to instigate a foot race and before the right back caught up with him, he cut across his path and forced him off balance, creating an opening for him to pick a cross.

He sent it to Luciano and his downward header bounced off the ground to go in!

"Yes! That's a goal created by the lads!" said Tom.

"Charlie used his strengths so well!" Richard echoed.

With twenty-five minutes to go, the Black Dragons looked good for their sixth win out of six. David asked Richard and Tom to warm up as he considered his options to manage the rest of the game.

However, the away team equalised before he made his move. The skilful left winger ran directly into the heart of the Black Dragons' defence with the ball and was taken down by Jonas just inside the area. A penalty was given and the striker calmly slotted it in.

With the game back to square one, David decided to take the risk and send Alex on to replace the tired George – he wanted to win.

Alex had a chance to score late on, but his curling effort from the edge of the area was pushed onto the post and out by the fingertips of the keeper.

The Black Dragons were caught in a lightning fast counter attack from the resulting corner. The skilful left winger picked up the loose ball, dribbled past Lewis brilliantly and set the striker free to take it past Gordon, making it 2-1 with hardly any time left.

The referee blew the whistle soon after and the Black Dragons' perfect start to the season ended.

David was disappointed but he praised the efforts of the team, who were, naturally, a bit deflated in the dressing room.

"We put up a very good fight, the win could easily be ours. There are a couple of things that we need to work on – we'll do those during the international break," he said.

A small Championship club like Thames Ditton did not have a large number of international players. Therefore it was a good time for the players to have a couple of days off to recharge their batteries and for the coaches to arrange some specific training. Only three players were away on international duties: Thorsten, Charlie and Kieran for the Norway and England under 21 teams, with the latter selected for the first time. As expected, Richard had not been picked since his last call up – the regulars were back and he was overlooked, together with Tom and Danny.

"Good luck for tomorrow mate," Richard said to Tom before he left to meet Layne and their mums for a late lunch.

"Why don't you guys come around for dinner tomorrow?"

"Yeah I can do that after some studies, but Layne is out with the under 23 boys."

"That's cool, I'll ask Danny too."

The players had their Monday off so Richard spent some time working on the follow up material on cyber security from the chairman. He studied the first set of papers and raised a few questions to Dr Edwards, who was only too happy to supply him with more details. He also read a report produced by Steve from Performance Analytics.

Meanwhile, Layne went to a theme park nearby in Surrey with other young players. They were out for the whole day and so Richard joined Tom and Danny for dinner.

"Hey Rich and Danny, I didn't think you'll arrive together," Tom said as he welcomed the two.

"We just saw each other downstairs," Danny said.

"How's your day?" Richard asked.

"Well, she left. Off to chase her dreams, leaving the country and me behind."

"Poor you. Be strong, buddy," said Danny.

"I'm sure you'll get over it soon. Let's change the subject, what's on the menu?" Richard asked.

"You and your food, Rich. I'm baking some penne with chicken, broccoli and mozzarella, should be good in half an hour. Fancy some drinks?"

"Water will be just fine," said Danny.

"Coke Zero for me please," said Richard.

"Oh come on guys, I'm expecting my friends to at least share my sorrows with some drinks!"

"Alright then, I'll have a beer," said Danny as he picked up a bottle from the fridge and then threw one to Richard.

"Oh, okay," Richard said as he just about caught it.

The three had a chat about the season so far and the games ahead. Tom moaned about his lack of game time and Richard shared his worries now that Michael was back to full fitness and reclaimed his place in the starting eleven. Danny thought they need not worry as there would be plenty more chances as the season went on. He predicted that, bar any unfortunate injuries, all three of them would end the season with at least thirty appearances.

Richard brought up the report he read from Steve and highlighted the importance for Tom to offer something different in midfield. He drew a few radar charts and asked Tom and Danny for their inputs.

"Midfielders can be measured by nine different strengths: Non-penalty expected goals and assists, shot on target percentage, progressive pass distance, key passes, shot-creating actions, tackles won, successful pressures, blocks and progressive carrying distance. Let's come up with our own radar charts and see how we compare."

While the charts of Richard and Danny clearly reflected their superior defensive and attacking strengths respectively, Tom's showed his all-round abilities – he was reasonable in nearly all fields, but there was no special talent.

"Oh my words, what should I do to get better in these?" he asked.

"It's good to be an all-rounder anyway, but I think there are little changes you can make," Richard explained. "For example, you can definitely improve on shot-creating actions by breaking the lines more. At this level we can't both sit deep all the time, you have to be that link between defence and attack. Shall we plot the graph for Ross and see the difference he makes?"

"Oh I get that, but will I leave too much space behind for the counter?"

"That'll be down to your decision making – a good centre midfielder has to evaluate the situation and gamble at the right time," said Danny.

"Interesting stuff! I'll definitely speak to David and Steve about this and pick up their advice, thanks guys!"

"Glad to help. It'll be great if we are the midfield three," Richard said.

They then moved on to talk about their respective relationships. Tom's break up with Mihara was well documented and he asked if the other two were doing okay with theirs other halves. Richard said that Layne started becoming more independent with his own circles of friends, which he thought was good for their settled relationship. They had complete trust between them and would always inform each other of their whereabouts. In Layne's case, it meant lots of pictures.

Danny and Grace had a more distant relationship as they were busy with their respective careers. Their games always seemed to be at different times and locations, and they ended up not being together much. But they were both highly independent and extremely serious about their football so they complimented each other well.

The chicken pasta bake was delicious and the three had a good time watching the live Monday night game from the Premier League. Richard hoped that would help Tom through this tough period, as even though he was laughing and chatting most of the time, there was more than a piece of sadness on his face every now and then.

Layne came home a little tipsy that night and he couldn't stop telling Richard about all the rides he went on, the dinner they had and all funny things he learnt from the new under 23 players. Of course he also showed Richard the hundreds of photos he took that day. Richard enjoyed learning what Layne went through and was delighted to see him happy.

After two weeks of international break, the Black Dragons' next game was away at Sheffield, another front runner in the league. Danny and Charlie started in place of Mark and Andrés and Richard was on the bench again. David told him that he would be the cover for defensive midfield as well as both full back positions.

The home side was known to be strong defensively with a 5-3-2 formation, with one of the centre backs being Keith, whom they signed from the Black Dragons for good money during the summer. He welcomed his former teammates when they lined up prior to kick off.

The match started with the Black Dragons taking a surprise lead after twelve minutes. Charlie was surrounded on the left wing but his deflected cross somehow found its way to Luciano, who smashed it into the back of the net with little hesitation.

The home team reorganised quickly and mounted a serious assault on the Thames Ditton defence. Kieran followed his England under 21 call up with another excellent performance as he stopped numerous chances and won all his aerial duels. The Black Dragons retained their lead going into half time.

David commended Charlie's determination and the defence's performance. He urged them to stay focus and used the space behind the home side for counter attacks.

However, the Black Dragons' solid defence was breached early in the second half, as a clever chip from the central midfielder after a period of short passes found the striker behind the line and he slotted home the equaliser.

The home team stepped up a gear after the goal and with the waves of attack coming at them, David decided to bring Richard and Tom on at the hour mark to replace Michael and George.

Richard's defensive statistics since transferring into the first team had been nothing but immaculate, and other teams started actively avoiding the areas he covered. The hosts were one of them and they switched their attacks to the wide areas. They sent crosses after crosses into the Black Dragons' box and they eventually succeeded – the left wing back's attempt found the towering midfielder at the far post, who beat Richard in the air and headed the ball into the top right corner. There wasn't much Richard could do, as it was such a mismatch of heights.

The Black Dragons launched a late fight back but the home team's young goal keeper Brandon denied them brilliantly with some extraordinary saves.

The match ended soon after and the Black Dragons had lost after taking the lead for the second match in a row. David didn't look impressed as the team were inviting those crosses, which eventually proved to be their undoing.

"I'm sorry boss, I couldn't beat him to the header," Richard confessed in the dressing room.

"It wasn't your fault, Richard. It shouldn't be you tracking him. I'm a little disappointed that he wasn't picked up by Tom. We should also do more to stop those crosses coming in."

Richard looked over at Tom as he was shocked by David's direct comment.

"That's a bit unfair, boss. I was on their number eight," Tom protested.

"But he's only five foot eight, Tom. You should have focused on the player your size and not left the tall one to your midfield partner."

"It's only natural to mark the closest player."

"That's exactly the wrong way of thinking. You'd fall straight into the other team's tactics; they planned a mismatch all along. You should know better – have a think about it and we can talk it through after training on Monday."

While what David said made sense, Richard was worried about how Tom would react to such a public humiliation.

The Black Dragons were off to another away game at Teesside the Wednesday after and they repeated their latest pattern, when they surrendered another early lead to lose the match 2-1. There seemed to be the same issue of the team losing their energy and more importantly their concentration near the end of the game. Danny and Charlie did come off the bench in the second half to rescue the match but Richard was an unused substitute throughout. Tom didn't even make the travelling squad.

The team's bad run of form halted the next Saturday when they beat a club from East Yorkshire 2-0 at home. Richard started in midfield with Ross and Danny and they dominated the game. George controlled Ross's through ball beautifully to open the scoring in the first half and Luciano converted a penalty in the second, when Danny was fouled in the area. Charlie also started but Tom was yet again overlooked for the matchday eighteen.

He was instead sent to play in the under 23 team's game the next day, which was a friendly at the main stadium against the white team from north London. Layne had returned to full training following his knee injury and he also started the game alongside Thomas and Alex. Richard and Danny were in the stands with hundreds of supporters.

Tom wasn't very happy at what he described as a demotion but Thomas talked him round – he needed the minutes to show David and the coaching team what he was capable of. An excellent performance for the under 23 team would do him a lot of good.

And he put in a virtuoso display in front of them all, as he demonstrated his all-round abilities from tackling, passing to winning headers and taking set pieces. He set up Alex for the opening goal with a free kick from the right and then Ryan from a through ball. He communicated well with Kasper and Harry around him and inspired a great spirit from the team as captain. The on-form Finley completed the scoring when he tapped in Andrew's low cross. Layne added an hour to his recuperation and felt good with his left knee.

"Tom is clearly a class above the under 23 team's level," said Danny. "The trouble is how he is going to get into the first team."

"There will be injuries and fatigue, he just needs to be patient," Richard said. "I hope he is. I'd love partnering him in the middle."

The next game for the senior side was an away tie in the League Cup third round against a Premier League team from East Midlands. The home side rested a number of key players but was still full of internationals and had plenty from their title winning squad a few years before.

David started the game with Gordon in goal, Jonas, Lewis, Les and Kieran in defence, Michael, Ross and Danny in midfield and Andrés, George and Luciano up front. Richard returned to the bench with Josh, Thorsten, Toby, Mark, Charlie and Sam. Tom was not included again but David told him explicitly that he would take part in the next league game when they travelled fifteen miles across the river to Hounslow on Saturday.

With a stronger team and home advantage, the Premier League side quickly stamped their authority on the game. They opened the Black Dragons' defence at will and put two past them in the first half: a close-range header by the striker and a neat finish from their England under 21 winger Damian. It could have been more had their finishing been sharper. A change for the Black Dragons beckoned.

David decided to replace Andrés and Luciano by Richard and Mark. He wanted Danny to support George upfront with four midfielders behind them, with Richard and Michael deeper than Ross and Mark, in order to break the home team's dominance there.

The change worked as the midfield four were able to force the play away from coming in field and avoid those killer passes. The two-goal lead held by the home team probably played a part in that as they eased their foot off the pedal. Maintaining possession seemed to sit higher than scoring the third goal on their list of priorities.

That effectively stopped the Black Dragons' fight back as they couldn't get hold of the ball. George, Danny and the rest were chasing around but the home team were simply too good – players were composed on the ball and they were fluid in switching positions to support their teammates.

The contest ended when the home team scored their third goal late in the game. Their star midfielder Ben, who scored a free kick against the Black Dragons when he played for a Championship club, repeated the trick with another brilliant shot from twenty yards out.

The game finished 3-0 to the Premier League side.

"That was embarrassing," Danny sighed as he walked off the pitch with Charlie and Richard.

"We have to learn from that – there is a gap at the moment but one that we can close in time," Richard was optimistic.

"We'll create our own story," Charlie claimed.

David was pleased with the efforts in the second half but told the team that to be able to compete against such top oppositions, they needed to attack and defend together as a team and not just through individual brilliance.

The brutal fixtures of the Championship campaign resumed a few days later as the Black Dragons travelled to Hounslow for their tenth game of the season and the first west London derby. With eighteen points out of twenty-seven, the team were fourth in the table but they desperately needed to rediscover their form after only one win in four.

David started with Gordon in goal and the same back four, the youthful Richard, Tom and Danny in midfield, with Charlie, George and Luciano up top. He wanted to give some rest to Michael and Ross, who just came back from a long-term injury and had a knock respectively. Jonas was named as the captain.

"Let's show David that this is his best midfield," Tom said to Richard and Danny.

"Yes, we'll fight together," Richard echoed.

"Just win," said a determined Danny.

The game began and the home team pressed ahead in their 4-3-3 formation. They were in mid-table and with the home support they were out fighting for their three points. Sam's twin brother Jesse, who was promoted to the first team this season, started on the bench.

They attacked through the middle and their number ten tried to take it pass Richard, who patiently waited for an opportunity to poke the ball away. Tom swiftly passed it right for Luciano, who sent it towards the far post after a couple of step-overs. Charlie jumped the highest to meet the cross and his powerful header went through the keeper's hands and in. The Black Dragons' favoured fast start struck again as they took another early lead.

The challenge, as in previous games, was to hold on to it. The home side continued to attack through the middle and they were stopped brilliantly by Richard and Tom: the former won his tackles and the latter his headers, and they swept up the second balls for each other. Tom was dangerous with his well-timed forward runs, which created several chances for the second goal but they didn't go in for one reason or another. The half ended a goal to nil.

Hounslow swapped one of their centre midfielders for another forward to make it a 4-4-2. Their intention was clear, they wanted to capitalise on the Black Dragons' fragile second half form.

"They'll attack out wide now," Richard said to Tom.

"Okay, I'll track the taller number six and you can take number twelve. Let's keep talking to each other," Tom said.

With the two strikers in the middle, the home team indeed switched their play to the wings as their full backs pushed up to support the attack. Learning from their previous defeats, Charlie and Luciano tracked back to prevent them from having free crosses, and when they did manage to cross, it was well dealt with by Les, Kieran and Tom, who took care of the taller midfielder running from deep.

By sheer grit and courage, the Black Dragons succeeded in defending their one goal lead. David was impressed by the determination and maturity from Richard and Tom.

"Well done you two. I always know your capabilities but you showed us today that you can do it together at this level," he said.

"Cheers, partner," Richard said as he reached out to Tom for a fist pump.

"That was good, buddy," Tom responded.

As if David needed any further proofs that Richard, Tom and Danny were his best option in midfield, he got it from the next game in midweek, when the Black Dragons surprisingly lost at home to a team from Yorkshire with Michael, Toby and Mark at the helm.

They started brilliantly again and scored early on with Luciano, but their soft underbelly resurfaced again in the second half as the away side put not just one or two, but three goals past them. A rare mistake by Gordon started the onslaught and the left winger outpaced Jonas twice to score goals two and three.

"David must be very annoyed by that," Richard said to Layne as they watched from the stands. "We shouldn't be losing to teams like this."

"I think it's time he starts playing you guys in the middle more."

"We need to keep up the good work in training and show him that in matches."

David restored the young midfield trio to the starting line-up for the weekend game away in Suffolk, but he asked Danny to play as a right winger in place of Luciano, who was due a rest having started the last seven games. Ross was back in midfield following his injury and Layne was back on the bench after missing the last nine matches.

The change proved to be a master stroke as the Black Dragons won the game comfortably 3-0. George headed in Danny's beautiful cross early on before Charlie adding a second from Richard's corner near the end of the first half. Tom then drove a long-range effort home at the hour mark to register his first senior goal and complete the excellent display. Layne came on during the second half to add more minutes to his recovery.

After twelve rounds, the Black Dragons had twenty-four points with eight wins and four defeats. That put them in fourth – not a bad position to be in by all means, but it could have been much better after that brilliant start to the season.

27.

The Chant

During the two-week international break after the Black Dragons' game at Suffolk, David and the coaching team had been training the team with their new formation – a return to their previous 4-2-1-3 but with the front three much closer to each other. The width would be provided by the wing backs while the two defensive midfielders would cover the space they left behind together with the two centre backs.

There were two reasons for the switch: David wanted to add more widths to the attack while ensuring that the team's compact defensive shape remain intact, and the devastating news that their captain Michael had suffered another serious injury, which made it very hard to operate with just one defensive midfielder.

Based on their statistical analyses of the players, the coaching team believed Layne, Richard and Danny would be essential for this tactic to be carried out effectively.

Layne would provide the pace for the transition on the left while the more disciplined Jonas could tuck in to form a three-men defence if necessary.

Richard's defensive capabilities and range of passing would become the foundation at the bottom of midfield with either Ross or Tom next to him, with the tireless Danny in front of them in a number ten role against weaker teams or a deeper role against tougher ones. David's view was that while Richard was growing in confidence, his contribution to the attacking play would increase significantly if he was paired up with a box-to-box midfielder.

Danny could also be utilised as one of the front three if David fancied having Ross in the advanced role. They would interchange regularly while staying close to each other for those quick passes through defence.

The team's main attacking threat would be from the left with Layne pushing up and the rest shifting over to form an overload. The right would be less adventurous but Danny could also operate there occasionally to make use of the space.

Their first test was against the other team from Sheffield at home, the exact fixture where Richard made his senior debut and scored the season before. David opted for the planned setup, with Tom partnering Richard in midfield and George, Danny and Luciano up front. Charlie was a little tired after playing in both England under 21 games and so he started on the bench. David also believed that Charlie could be extremely dangerous with his superior strengths and dribbling skills if he was introduced later in games.

The away team started with the same orchestrator from last season between defence and midfield but this time he was up against the powerful Ross, who restricted his influence with his tracking and physical challenges.

The Black Dragons instigated their attacking moves down the left at will, with Layne travelling up and down the line for crosses and small triangles with the overloads. They scored two goals in the first half. Luciano slid one in at the near post from Layne's low cross and George headed in the second from Richard's cross from the left. The game was under complete control.

The second half followed a similar pattern, even though the away team moved their orchestrator further up the pitch to play as a number ten. Richard took over the marking and he stopped him getting any service, by either cutting out the pass or forcing the ball off him.

There was no goal from Richard this time, however, as he sent his only opportunity, a free kick from twenty-five yards out, harmlessly over the bar.

The Black Dragons did score a third and decisive goal after seventy minutes, as David's plan to unleash the power of Charlie late on paid an immediate return. He ran directly on goal from the left through two tired defenders and blasted the ball into the back of the net. Danny was credited with the assist.

The home supporters enjoyed their team's second successive three nil victory and pundits were singing their praises as they went back to third in the league, only five points behind the leader, the team from East Anglia.

They continued their good form into the next four games, all squeezed into the two weeks before the next set of international fixtures. They recorded two comfortable wins at home and two draws away. Six goals were scored with only one against. Luciano was the hero with three of those goals, while George, Charlie and Andrés got one each. The defence was solid, with the only goal conceded coming from a penalty.

Richard, Layne and Danny started every single one of those games and established themselves as the first names on the team sheet. Tom also played a part in all four games, starting three of them. He was glad that his contribution to both attack and defence was valued by the coaching team and fans, with specific praise from David on his decision making.

Layne's raw pace and crossing ability offered the team a unique weapon and when utilised properly it became a major threat to other teams. He was involved in five of the six goals scored by the Black Dragons during these four matches, with three of them directly credited to him as assists.

He also received his first ever call up by the England under 19 team and played in both friendly games at home against European oppositions. Richard and Mrs Moore travelled to both games together to cheer him on.

Sadly, with his increasing fame the amount of abuses he attracted went up as well. He switched his social media account back to public to post a message thanking the fans' support after the last home win for the Black Dragons, but within minutes he got disgusting memes, nasty comments and even death threats. Football fans online may not be ready for him to come out officially, however much he wanted to. To Richard's surprise, he didn't revert his account back to private. He just reported the threats to the police and vowed to ignore the rest.

The Black Dragons' next league game after the international break was away to Nottinghamshire. With an eye on the west London derby against the team from Shepherd's Bush in midweek, David decided to give Layne a rest following his exploits with England under 19 and started with Lewis. Maz also got a rare start at right back as Jonas failed a late fitness test. The rest was unchanged, with Richard, Tom and Ross the midfield three and Danny, Luciano and George upfront.

David's game plan was to play with the same tactic but switch everything to the right, as Maz was the more attack-minded defender. It worked at the early stages of the match as the Black Dragons created a number of chances from the right, but they couldn't make them count with the tall goalkeeper in fine form.

The home team's young right midfielder Rory, who had his pocket picked by Richard and Danny for the defeat in the same fixture last season, started the game and had his revenge, as he curled a shot past Gordon after thirty five minutes.

The first half ended 1-0 and the Black Dragons had a lot to do in the second.

The match resumed with largely the same pattern as the first half, as the Black Dragons focused their attack on the right but without returns. Richard and Danny were replaced by Toby and Charlie at the hour mark but they didn't fare much better against the home side's spirited defence. There were some more half chances but they just couldn't find the equaliser, and their six-match unbeaten run ended.

David was disappointed with the defeat but he urged the team to bounce back for the next match, one of the biggest on the calendar – the local derby against the team from Shepherd's Bush.

412

Three days after the disappointment in the Midlands the Black Dragons travelled to Shepherd's Bush for the second west London derby of the season. The match was a sell-out as always and the home fans were all fired up for the game.

David started with Gordon in goal as usual, with Jonas and Layne restored to the defence but Kieran was out with a knock. He was replaced by Thomas, who resumed his old partnership with Les. Richard, Ross and Danny were in midfield, with Charlie, George and Luciano upfront. Tom was on the bench with Alex and the others.

The home supporters were trying to gain an advantage for their team by disrupting the Black Dragons players. They seemed to have picked on Layne and Richard and were throwing all sorts of abuse at them.

Shortly after kick off, they started singing the infamous "Rent Boys" chant, which was usually reserved for the big west London club and had more than a sense of homophobic intentions. Every time the pair received the ball loud booing could be heard, with a minority of fans chanting "Does your boyfriend know you're here" or "Do you take it up the arse" at them. The former was obviously quite pointless but the latter was downright offensive.

Ross the Black Dragons' captain brought this up with the referee during a break in play. He halted the match and asked the club officials to send a warning to those responsible through the public announcement system. The two offensive chants calmed down since but the "Rent Boys" and booing remained throughout the first half, which ended goalless. Chances were at a premium during the feisty contest which saw two players from both sides on the book already.

"How are you doing, Ping? We've never had it this bad before," Richard asked as they walked towards the dressing room amid aggressive jeers from the home supporters.

"It's like south east London all over again with all these people screaming 'bum boy' or 'twink' at me everywhere I go, but what can we do about it? At least my boyfriend knows I'm here!"

"I think mine knows where I am too. I got to hear all sorts when I took those corner kicks, apparently I'm a 'sausage jockey' as well as a 'shirt lifter' now!"

"Hey lads, joking aside, are you guys really alright?" asked Ross when they were back in the dressing room.

"We are fine, but I'm sorry to drag you guys into it," Richard said.

"I complained to the referee just now," said David as he walked in, much later than everyone else, "but he said the 'Rent Boys' chant was not classified as offensive in their world."

"We can live with that, don't worry about it," said Layne. "I'd rather silence them with the ball."

"I like that spirit! We will certainly bring it up with the FA after the match. With regard to the play, I think we can do with a bit more risk taking now that we're attacking our end. Let's try the 'other plan' on them."

The second half resumed. For the first ten minutes or so the Black Dragons continued to attack down their left and were well contained by the hosts.

Then Richard saw the signal from Ross and switched to the new game plan. For the first time in the match, he hit a long ball from deep towards the right, where Danny had quietly drifted to. Jonas made a lung busting run on the outside and all three forwards moved to their designated positions: George to the corner flag, Luciano into the area towards the near post and Charlie on the edge of the area. The defenders were busy going after their runners and they left a gap for Danny to drive into. He brought it all the way to the edge of the box, played a little give and go with Charlie and then rolled the ball across to the far side, where Layne was arriving completely unmarked, having left the right winger for dead.

But before he connected with the ball for a simple tap in, he was tripped by the desperate right back. He had a little scream as he fell to make sure the referee knew about it. He did not hesitate and duly pointed to the spot.

The home players were not impressed with the way Layne exaggerated the impact and they challenged him as he got up. One of the defenders named Stan was particularly angry.

"That was a fucking dive, you prick!" he shouted.

"He did make contact, should I just tumble and give you the ball?" Layne responded calmly.

"It's a men's sport, it's not for little poofs like you!"

"What did you say?"

"I said, there's no place in football for fucking queer boys like you and your boyfriend! Just go home to suck each other's dicks and stay away from the football pitch!"

"What the hell… are you talking about?" Layne said, with a quavering voice.

"That's completely out of order!" Richard moved in between them to protect his young partner.

"Don't you dare joining in, you little shit!" Stan shouted and forcefully shoved him away.

Richard wasn't expecting that. He lost his footing and banged the side of his head against the goal post heavily. He tried to get back on his feet straight away but felt disoriented and had to sit down. The right side of his head really hurt.

"Are you okay Richie?" a worried Layne asked. "Oh God you're bleeding!"

The referee saw his injury and signalled the physios to come up quickly. He also reached his pocket and showed Stan a straight red card.

The already hostile home crowd went completely mad – the booing was deafening and they were shouting all sorts of insults towards the pair and the officials. Players were shoving each other and both managers had to come onto the pitch to separate them. Charlie, Gordon the goalkeeper and another home player were cautioned for their involvements.

Once the dust settled, Luciano kept his cool in front of the highly aggressive crowd and put his penalty away to open the scoring for the Black Dragons.

Gary the physio managed to stop Richard's bleeding and wrapped layers of bandage around his head. He felt okay to carry on playing.

With the game being a local derby, the home team continued to attack despite having a man less. That fell perfectly into the Black Dragons' quick transitions as they exploited the space behind expertly. Thomas found Danny with a clearance and he quickly sent the ball through to Charlie on the left. He cut inside the stranded centre back with his sharp control and put the ball into the far corner.

With the buffer established, David decided to withdraw both Layne and Richard. The crowd gave them the loudest jeer they could manage and a significant number of them were shouting homophobic slurs at the pair. Layne used his fingers to tell them the score line and that caused them to become even more aggressive.

"That's enough, baby. Let's not provoke them further," Richard whispered.

"Okay, I was going to tell them my boyfriend is here," Layne giggled.

"Well done you two, that was tough," Tom said as he stood on the touchline, ready to replace Richard.

"I guess they won't ask you those questions," Richard joked as they shook hands.

"They'll boo me all the same, they're football fans after all."

He was partially right. The crowd continued their hostility as he and Lewis entered the fray, but they didn't ask those specific, homophobic questions.

The home team carried on with their gung-ho approach in search for a way back in the game. Tom was busy in the defensive role, holding the line together with Ross. He also played a part for the Black Dragons' third goal near the end of the match, as his flick on from Danny's corner fell to Jonas for a simple finish.

The first derby of the season against the team from Shepherd's Bush ended in a convincing victory for the Black Dragons. The broadcaster invited Layne and

Richard for the post-match interview but it was declined by the pair, with the support of the coaching team.

The ugly scene in the second half prompted the FA to charge both clubs for failing to control their players. The Black Dragons filed a complaint for the homophobic chanting and Stan's remarks towards Layne, but disappointingly the FA's response was the typical "The matter of homophobia is taken seriously and will be investigated thoroughly." It was more lip service than any concrete actions. Stan received a mere three-match ban for his violent conduct and there was nothing for his vile comments to Layne.

The incident sparked a sizeable debate on social media, as fans and charities came up en masse to support Layne and condemn the chanting and the FA's lack of actions. That was despite him not coming forward to confirm or deny his position, on the request of Richard. He would prefer them staying away from the limelight – he just wanted to stay as two youngsters playing the sport they loved.

Sadly, they were up against the bigoted and old-fashioned brigade who believed football should be a masculine sport "only for the real men".

While the aftermath of the ill-tempered derby was ongoing, the Black Dragons had another match to play at the weekend, a home game against a strong team from West Yorkshire. It happened to be on Richard's twentieth birthday, and he was given another start by David as his head injury was only minor. Layne, Danny and Charlie also retained their places, but the return of Kieran pushed Thomas back to the bench.

The away team were only a point behind the Black Dragons at fourth, and they had been on a good run of form with four wins from five. Their 4-1-4-1 system was very strong defensively, and highly effective when coupled with their energetic high press.

The Black Dragons struggled throughout the match to break them apart and were nearly punished when they lost

417

the ball in the back, but they snatched the win late on with their prowess in set pieces. The giant Les headed them ahead halfway into the second half from Richard's corner, who then capped his birthday with a fantastic free kick in stoppage time. His shot from the edge of the area had just enough curl to beat the keeper at full stretch. He celebrated with his now standard way of kissing his left ring finger, even though he wasn't wearing a ring, as it was a symbolic gesture for Layne.

He was named as the man of the match by the sports channel showing the match and did a quick interview with the presenter. He drew a line under the incident during midweek by saying it was in the hands of the FA and he would appreciate it if fans and media could respect his personal life. He did, however, let it slip at the end when he told the presenter he would be celebrating his birthday with Layne and their parents later that evening. The host picked up on that but decided to let the youngster off the hook on air. He did have a laugh with Richard afterwards and wished him a happy birthday.

The pair and their mums went to a restaurant well known for lobsters in Knightsbridge for dinner. Layne informed the restaurant that it was a birthday celebration and reserved a massive lobster for Richard. He opted for it to be grilled with clarified butter and he was well satisfied. His dad came to pick his mum up afterwards and had a short conversation with him, although he completely blanked Layne again.

The Black Dragons' next game was away to the south east London club. With the backlash of the last derby still lingering on, the management team decided it was better to keep Richard and Layne away from a ground that was extremely hostile even on the best of days.

The pair did insist to David that they expected no special treatment from the club and were willing to play, but David decided not to risk it and there were plenty of players available for selection anyway.

But the plan backfired as the Black Dragons lost the match 2-1. They conceded two goals early on and could only score one through Danny in the much better second half.

The home fans were singing the "Rent Boys" chant throughout the match and kept asking where the pair were, in some derogatory ways.

They returned to the starting line-up the next weekend at home against a team from Derbyshire. George and Ross were injured so Tom and Andrés came in.

The away side had a number of exciting young players on loan from Premier League clubs including Adam Jenkinson, the former academy player at Thames Ditton. They played a part in the pulsating match, where the Black Dragons hit back twice to draw 2-2.

The young Dutch winger Koen scored a lovely free kick fifteen minutes into the first half but it was cancelled out by Luciano, who turned brilliantly from Danny's forward pass to score. Then the two England under 21 stars combined to score for the away team halfway through the second half. The pacy centre back Oscar set Adam up for an easy finish with a cushioned header inside the area. The Black Dragons levelled again five minutes later when Charlie's cut back found Tom for a smashing finish. The timing of his forward runs was getting better all the time and there were now goals and assists to show. There was another chance late on but Alex's acrobatic effort was deflected wide by the equally impressive Oscar.

With nearly half of the season gone, the Black Dragons were fourth on the table with forty-two points, having won thirteen games, drawn three and lost six. The team achieved its first target of the season, which was to secure their survival in the division, much earlier than anticipated and were ready to set sight on the next – promotion to the Premier League.

28.

Friends and Enemies

The Black Dragons' last game of the first cycle of fixtures was away to the Birmingham club that Bob, their previous manager, joined during the summer. They were two points ahead in second place.

The festive schedule wasn't the most kind for the Black Dragons this season. The match against Birmingham was the first of four consecutive away games within ten days. The coaching team would have to manage the players' physical and mental conditions carefully. Similar to previous seasons, they had called up some under 23 players to train with the first team.

On match day, David decided to start with Gordon in goal, Jonas, Layne, Kieran and Les in defence, Richard, Ross and Danny in midfield and Charlie, Luciano and George upfront. He wanted to win the toughest game in this sequence, and to do that he needed his strongest team.

With Bob's knowledge of the Black Dragons' players and systems, David thought they'd need to make some adjustments to create an element of surprise. So instead of the normal fast start that he deployed, he would like the two wingers to sit deeper for the first twenty minutes and play on the counter using the ball holding ability of the interchanging George and Luciano with support from a more advanced Danny, effectively playing a 4-4-1-1 system.

The match started well for the travelling side as the home team were confused by their steady approach. As the half went on, the home fans were frustrated by the lack of actions and they urged their side to come out from their deep positions to win the ball. That led to the opportunity that David had been planning for – a small window where a gap in the home defence appeared.

Richard noticed the change in mentality and hit a low driven pass towards Luciano upfront. He was surrounded by both centre backs but he managed to lay the ball off to Danny, who held on to it for a few seconds while all four wide players sprinted up field. The obvious option was to pass it to Charlie on the left, who had Layne on the outside. However, as Bob was fully aware of the threat posed by the young left back, he instructed the hardworking right winger to track him all the way, closing off that path. With his options restricted Danny passed the ball back to Ross on the right of midfield, and he released Jonas on the outside. His cross from deep found Luciano at the near post and he expertly guided the ball over the keeper into the back of the net.

The first half ended one goal to nil for the visitors. David told the team to continue with their plan to counterattack but there would be a lot of pressure from the home side and possession would be at a premium.

Bob switched his formation from 4-2-1-3 to 4-4-2 with a diamond midfield at half time, by replacing a midfielder with the ex-Thames Ditton forward Darren. He was a good friend of Les and it would become a great battle. Their number ten and talisman Ted also moved from left wing into the tip of the diamond.

The change gave the home side an advantage in midfield and they started to dominate possession of the ball. Ted moved between Richard and Ross all the time to link up his midfield and forwards, to the point where Ross asked Richard to man mark him and pulled Danny back to help. That changed the Black Dragons' shape and their mentality to focus on defending. Bob seemed to realise that and instructed his full backs to push forward at all possible opportunities.

The Black Dragons' defence was finally breached at the hour mark, when a cross by the left back was flicked on by Darren and smashed in by the other striker. The goal was coming and the Black Dragons needed to make some changes.

"Stay calm on the ball and use the width," Layne passed on David's instruction from the technical area to Ross and Richard.

The Black Dragons regained their composure and started countering the home side's attack by utilising the width, with Charlie and George occupying the home team's full backs. They created a few half chances but couldn't get past the solid defence.

With the clock ticking, Ted demanded the ball to initiate an attack from the left and tried to take on Richard. From his homework Richard knew he had to stay on his feet and watch the ball closely. His opponent was very good with his feints and controls – once the defender made a wrong move, he would drift the ball away and run past.

Richard managed to restricted Ted's advance, but he couldn't prevent him from creating the space for a pass and he sent the ball between Kieran and Layne towards the striker on the right. Layne was caught on the wrong side and lost his balance in the resulting physical challenge. The striker struck the ball across the area and Darren was there to complete the home team's come back, to the heartbreak of the Black Dragons. They did have a chance to level the game again but Danny's long-range effort went off the post. The match ended 2-1.

"Great defending mate, I couldn't find a gap to get past you," Ted said to Richard as they shook hands.

"Still not enough to win the game," Richard responded with a polite smile.

David wasn't too happy with the way the team retreated in the second half and also the marking for the decisive goal, but he was encouraged by the efforts shown and urged the team to move on to the next game.

Both Richard and Layne were selected for the Boxing Day match, which was away in Bristol. The players were meant to stay the night before in a hotel but the pair were given permission to drive there themselves. So they went to Layne's family home in Bath after training to spend some of the Christmas Day with Mrs Moore, before meeting the team at the hotel for a festive but healthy dinner – lean turkey, pasta and plenty of vegetables.

The match turned out to be another disappointment as David made a number of changes to rotate his squad. The team conceded early when a corner kick was somehow scrambled in. Layne made amends for his mistake in the last game with a brilliant cross for Alex to pull level late in the first half with a right foot volley.

The Black Dragons went on the offensive in the second half but they couldn't take their chances, with the substitute Andrés missing a glorious opportunity at the hour mark. Richard carried on what he left off last season as he blocked a number of shots late on. Luckily, he didn't have to do it with his face this time.

The game ended 1-1 and the Black Dragons dropped to fifth in the league.

The pair took Danny and Tom for a trip to Bath after the game. They visited the various tourist attractions and had dinner in a small Vietnamese restaurant before heading back to London. They didn't plan it but Richard couldn't resist the smell of the beef broth and led everyone in. Pho noodles with beef brisket was his go-to comfort food and the one there was one of the best he ever had.

David rested both Richard and Layne for their next trip to Greater Manchester. The Black Dragons won 2-0 against the struggling side with Charlie and Les scoring the goals. Viktor marked his first team debut at right back with a solid performance.

The team returned to Greater Manchester only two days later for the New Year Day match against another team deep in the relegation zone. The pair started the game as the Black Dragons put three goals past the hosts in the second half. David saw a gap in the home side's defence on their left and brutally exploited it by sending both Danny and Charlie there. Luciano benefited with two goals and the third came from George.

David was happy with seven points out of twelve from the difficult festive fixtures and the Black Dragons returned to fourth, before a FA Cup third round tie at home and the beginning of the transfer window.

The team had three days to prepare for their FA Cup third round tie at home against a team from Bedfordshire, the leaders of League One. It would see the return of Peter Knight, the stepbrother of Alex, who used to play for the under 23 team with Richard and his friends. He had been in prolific form up front, having scored eleven times and created six for his teammates.

David continued to shuffle the team following the festive period and started the match with Josh in goal, the taller Viktor, Lewis, Thomas and Les in defence, Toby, Tom and Ross in midfield and Charlie, Luciano and Andrés upfront. Richard and Layne were on the bench with Jack, Kieran, Danny, Sam and Alex.

The plan was to nullify Peter's aerial presence with a bigger team and use the pace and trickery of the front three to attack.

The first half was lively, with the away team attacking from wide with plenty of crosses and the Black Dragons trying to catch them on the counter. Both teams went close on several occasions but no goals were scored.

The second half started favourably for the away side, as Peter headed in a perfectly delivered corner into the net five minutes in. David waited another five minutes before making his move – he brought Danny and Alex on for Ross and Andrés.

With the great understanding between Charlie and the two substitutes the home team equalised quickly. Alex drifted to the left for a through pass and his low cross found Danny in the area after a brilliant dummy by Charlie.

Richard came on for Toby with about twenty minutes to go as the Black Dragons sought the win that would not only see them progress to the next round but also avoid another match in the already congested fixture list. He played a quick one two with Tom before sending the ball into the space on the right for Viktor. His cross into the area was a little high but it wasn't a problem for Alex – he performed an audacious overhead kick and the ball flew straight into the back of the net!

The fans went ecstatic for the amazing winner. Alex ran towards the bench and jumped into David to celebrate. The tie had been turned on its head.

With just fifteen minutes left, the away side had to throw everything into finding the equaliser. They hit high balls after high balls into the Black Dragons' final third but these straight balls were easy to defend against. Tom dropped deeper as usual in such situations and Richard was in front of him sweeping up the second balls. He found Danny in front of him and he set Luciano free on the right. He ran all the way towards goal and rolled it across the box at the final moment. Alex arrived to finish it off – it was game, set and match.

The tie ended 3-1 to the Black Dragons. Richard caught up with Peter at the final whistle to wish him the best of luck for their promotion push, only to be told that he would be joining the young Black Dragons' gathering that night.

"That was an exciting half! Did you enjoy playing against good old Peter?" Layne asked.

"It was great to see him out there. I still can't beat him in the air but luckily I didn't need to!"

"It's funny, isn't it? We're friends off the pitch but enemies on it."

"We're just competing against each other, not really enemies, don't think like that, baby."

"You may be right; Peter isn't James after all! Did you hear that he's been promoted to their senior side?"

"Good on him, I guess?"

"Don't you hate him for what he did?"

"I did for a while but can't be bothered now, especially that he didn't cause you any damage."

"You're such a nice guy, Richie."

"I'd rather not remember all the bad things, it's not good for health!"

The pair met their friends for dinner at a sushi restaurant in Wimbledon. It was their first gathering for a while and plenty of players turned up. Tom, Danny, Les, Kieran, Thomas, Harry, Andrew and Ryan were already there when Richard and Layne arrived, before Rob, Ollie, Finley, Viktor, the Rangers and the Knights showed up.

Peter the giant congratulated the Black Dragons for the victory on the day.

"I thought for a second we could nick it, but then you brought Danny, Alex and Richard on! That was so unfair!" he joked.

"At least you're only beaten by a worldie from your own brother!" Charlie said.

"What were you thinking having an overhead kick from there?" Ollie asked.

"I just thought I'd had a go; it was too high for a header!" Alex explained.

"You have to credit the cross!" said Viktor who, obviously, supplied it.

"You're right there Vic, drinks on me tonight!" Alex said.

"We all hear it! Can we have some sake over here please?" Harry picked it up quickly.

"Cheers Alex, the two-goal hero!" Layne completed the stitch up.

"It wasn't meant to be for everyone, but go on then, put them all on me!" Alex was in celebration mode.

The team ordered a few bottles of Junmai Daiginjo, the premium Japanese sake. The team went for it – they had the next day off and for the first time in months the next match was a full week away.

The pair took a taxi there so they both joined in. That, of course, meant a little sleep for Richard before the food arrived and a very cheerful Layne. Richard couldn't remember much about the sushi, only that he had a lot of them. There were plenty of yakitori skewers too – he was particularly fond of the one with Emmental cheese wrapped in bacon.

Richard noticed during the night that there was something different about Rob. He couldn't really tell exactly but he was quieter than usual.

After four tough away games in a row, the team's next two league matches were both at home. First one up was a team from Teesside, who beat the Black Dragons 2-1 in their last encounter. They were sixth in the table and definitely a rival competing for the promotion places.

David selected his strongest team having rested a number of players in the cup tie. Richard, Layne and Danny were back in the starting line-up with Tom moving to the bench, but the surprise was that the regular centre back Les was omitted from the match day squad altogether. Thomas started in his place.

The away side was known to be physical and they played in an unpredictable 3-4-2-1 formation with a target man upfront. He scored halfway through the first half from a cross by the wing back, who combined with the inside forward to overload on Layne. The Black Dragons found it tough to play, their opponents seemed to be switching formations at ease and were everywhere.

David pulled Richard aside during the break and he asked him to move a little forward in the second half, to the space between the attack and midfield. He wanted him to exploit the gaps between the lines. He then called others over to tell them to attack the space between the wing backs and the defence, particularly behind the adventurous right wing back.

Finally, he said that the plan was a gamble and the absolute key was for Richard not to lose the ball in the middle.

"No pressure, Richie!" Layne joked.

David's plan worked well as Richard found plenty of passing options when he was in that zone between the away team's attackers and midfielders. Luckily for him the attackers were not the best in tracking back.

Ten minutes into the half Richard found George in the inside right with a delicate chip and he drove straight into the heart of the opponent's defence. Luciano and Charlie drew the other defenders away and George passed the ball back to his right, where there were acres of space for Danny to run into, and he drilled his shot into the far corner expertly to level the match.

The experienced manager of the other side made a change immediately. He brought an additional centre midfielder on in place of one of the inside forwards. He felt the need to match up the numbers in midfield.

The move closed the space for Richard to explore and the Black Dragons switched back to attacking the wide areas with their full backs. They had some rewards with a number of crosses but they were dominated in the penalty area by the three big centre backs. Meanwhile the "little and large" strike partnership in the other end were dangerous. The intelligent movement of the little inside forward meant Richard was going backwards more often and that in turn dragged Danny back into central midfield.

The match ended 1-1. The Black Dragons remained at fourth place while the away team dropped into seventh.

The team returned to training on Monday to a shock announcement by David. Les Hailey, the towering centre back who progressed through the youth teams to be one of the first team regulars, had followed Bob to sign for the club from Birmingham for an eight-figure transfer fee. He had been a solid performer for the Black Dragons that season and would be sorely missed. With just three recognised centre backs in the squad, David called Mason up from the under 23 team and indicated that he might get another from the transfer market. Tom also received some training for the position in case there was an emergency.

Richard also learnt that his friend Rob had moved to a League One club in east London permanently in search of first team football. That explained his rather mixed mood the other night. Richard texted him his best wishes.

Training did not go well that day. It was the first day back to full training for Michael the captain and he was badly injured halfway through. He seemed to have twisted his left knee when he changed direction to evade a rather routine challenge from Richard, who heard a couple of terrifying cracks before his mentor fell to the ground. He was clearly in a lot of pain as he lay there motionlessly.

It was later diagnosed as a grade 3 anterior cruciate ligament (ACL) tear, which meant it was torn completely in half and was no longer providing any stability to the knee joint. The 35-year-old would need to have surgery and face another lengthy recovery. He reluctantly decided that it was time to end his long professional playing career.

Richard felt guilty for his mentor's injury and kept apologising, only to be told that it had nothing to do with him. The captain urged him to play with no regrets and keep performing for the team he loved. He wanted to see Richard achieve the maximum of his potential and he would be cheering him on. Richard vowed to do his very best and thanked Michael for all his support.

The Black Dragons' next game was at home against the club in Berkshire, a mid-table team whom they beat by three goals to nil back at the start of the season. The starting eleven remained unchanged apart from Alex replacing the injured Luciano, with George switching to the wing.

The home side had a frustrating time as they couldn't break down their resolute opponent. Only some half chances were created and they couldn't put them away. Richard and Tom, who came on at half time to replace the injured Ross, defended the midfield well in the stalemate.

Richard and Layne had Andrew, Harry and Ryan over for dinner that night. The latter, who came out to the team at the beginning of the season, had become a good friend of the pair as Layne was keen to look after a teammate who shared the same sexuality. The changing room incident was long forgiven and forgotten.

The attacker scored a "perfect" hat trick for the under 23's in their 4-0 victory earlier that day – he registered with his left foot, right foot as well as his head. That took his tally to fifteen for the season, which was quite a feat as it was only January.

"You must be looking for your chance in the first team, Ryan?" asked Layne as they waited for the main course from Richard.

"That'll be awesome but I'm not in a hurry – there are some great forwards in the first team," Ryan was more realistic about his chances.

"Will you go out on loan? I've heard that you have an offer," Andrew asked.

"It's from a League Two club and David thought it won't help me develop as they play long balls all the time."

"That's quite right, it isn't really our game," said Harry, who were as tall as Ryan at five foot seven.

"You'll be staying to break the under 23 goal record then," Richard said as he put the massive tray of pasta on the table.

"Yes I'm sure George won't mind that," Ryan said before he changed his subject. "Oh Layne do you know what's on the latest magazine?"

"What's on it? I haven't bought it yet," said Layne.

"They've done a poll on the most shipped celebrities. Guess what? You two came ninth, only behind some proper movie stars!"

"What does it mean by shipped?" Richard had no idea.

"You need to keep up with the urban language Rich, after your 'taking Layne up the Shard' comment last time!" Harry laughed.

"Oh you didn't tell everybody about that, did you Mr Moore?"

"Only my best buddies, Mr Richie," said Layne with a cheeky smile.

"It's from the word relationship," Andrew explained slowly. "To say, 'I ship that couple,' is a short way for someone to say that they believe in a couple, that they're rooting for them to succeed in a romantic relationship."

"Really? So everyone knows about us then?" Richard was concerned.

"Not quite," Ryan said. "The fact that you two didn't confirm it either way makes people more curious though."

430

"Let me check them out when I get it, they'd better have some nice pictures! Why don't they ask us for an interview?" Layne sounded excited.

"Just some official photos, don't get too pumped up for them," Ryan said.

Richard wasn't too comfortable with the added publicity but he would just leave it – there wasn't much he could do.

To cap the period in which the Black Dragons played against a number of their old colleagues, the FA Cup fourth tie was an away trip to East Sussex, none other than the club that one of their former star youngsters Owen Fairclough played for. He had established himself as a first team regular at the Premier League side that were battling against relegation, with five goals under his name so far. He went into the away dressing room to greet the Thames Ditton players before the match and he had a joke with Richard that he would challenge him for a duel during the game.

David picked a youthful side, with Josh in goal, Jonas, Layne, Kieran and Thomas at the back, Richard, Tom and Danny in midfield and Charlie, George and Andrés upfront.

"You will be up against Owen on your side. Remember what I taught you about defending. I'll back you up," Richard said to Layne before the match started.

"I'll show him how much I've grown," Layne said. "Oh look at those over there, no wonder this is known as the unofficial capital!"

Richard turned to where Layne was pointing and saw a few rainbow coloured banners, with one specifically saying "Welcome home, little Dragons". He felt touched but also a little embarrassed.

"I guess we won't be booed today."

"Until we score against them!"

The home supporters gave the pair a special cheer when their names were announced, as if they were one of the home players.

"Don't even think about leaving us to join this club, Rich!" Tom joked.

"Seriously? I may have to consider it one day, mate," Richard replied.

The match began and the home team started in their standard 4-3-3 formation with two combative players and a great passer in midfield.

Owen was on the right wing as expected. He soon received the ball to have his first run at Layne. He took it to the outside and initiated a foot race against the young left back, who had the raw pace to match him. He then performed a double step over to cut inside. To his surprise, Layne reacted quickly and stuck out his right foot to poke the ball away.

"You have improved your defending, matey," Owen said to Layne.

"I have some decent mentors," he smiled.

The star player of the old youth team was much more than a one-trick pony. The next time he came up against Layne he duly executed a flip flap to change direction, leaving Layne behind with ease. But his advance came to a stop as another ex-teammate slid in and took the ball from him – it was Richard "The Unbeatable". The loose ball was collected by Tom and he passed it back to Josh in goal for a re-start.

The double up by the pair on Owen worked as he couldn't dribble past both of them, but that left the centre midfielder free and Owen found him with a lovely back heel after pulling the pair towards him again. The midfielder had time to measure an inch-perfect pass behind the Black Dragons' defence and the left winger arrived first to open the scoring ten minutes into the half.

"We can't be marking Owen with two players all the time, Rich. What shall we do now that we need to chase the game?" Tom asked.

"Yeah maybe I was too fixated on not letting him go free. Let's focus on stopping the ball getting to him in the first place and put some attack together."

Richard let Layne know the plan and asked him to track Owen closely without going into a tackle, effectively holding him up for others to come and support.

The match resumed and the Black Dragons started to attack. Charlie was up against a very tall right back named Adrian who was a centre back by trade, so he demanded the ball to his feet. Danny found him and he managed to run past his marker relatively easily. He continued to dribble towards goal until he was tackled by one of the centre backs for a corner.

Danny took the corner kick but with the three big defenders in the area he hit it towards the edge of the box instead. The skilful Andrés was there and he hit it on the full volley. The whole stadium gasped as the ball bounced off the post and out.

Minutes later Tom decided it was a good time to gamble and he gave the signal to the team before sending the ball towards Charlie. For the first time in the game Layne left Owen behind to support the attack. Owen was a bit late in tracking him and he was free to hit a low cross from the byline. Danny met it first time near the penalty spot and guided the ball into the bottom corner to make it 1-1.

The away side completed their comeback minutes later, as a forward pass by Tom found George at the edge of the area, who combined with Andrés to create an opening for a simple finish.

Owen had a few more one on ones against Layne but he was held up long enough for other Black Dragons players to close in. The away side also managed to hunt down the ball further up field to stop the supply to the front three. The first half ended 2-1.

"Good efforts out there, boys. It wasn't the easiest with the high press but you've made it difficult for them. Good recovery from the early goal too," David said in his team talk. "Keep that going for another fifteen minutes or so and try to score a third. We'll have to switch to a more compact shape after that as you won't be able to keep chasing for that long."

The Black Dragons started the second half as planned, as they went after the ball high up the pitch. The home team were forced into clearing the ball up field and they were won comfortably by Kieran and Thomas. Layne was on the attack again as he collected Charlie's pass from the touch line, played a quick give and go with Danny and crossed it low towards George, was met it ahead of the keeper to make it three.

With a two-goal advantage, the Black Dragons moved into the next phase of their game plan and sat deeper in a compact shape. They would maintain possession for a patient build-up with less risk taking.

On the other hand, the home side had to throw everything at it. They swapped into a 3-4-3 formation with Adrian moving into the centre, and a right wing back brought in to support Owen on the right.

The ball soon found its way to Owen and he took it forward with the wing back running outside him. Charlie did his part of the defending by tracking him but Owen kept dribbling, eventually winning a corner kick off Layne. He then hit a perfect ball towards Adrian who jumped the highest to head it in.

With ten minutes to go, the giant defender stayed up field to play as an emergency target man. David reacted by bringing the fierce Thorsten on for Andrés. But instead of just launching high balls to the target man from deep like the team from Bedfordshire did in the previous round, the home side sent the ball in from wide to create a tougher angle to defend against. One of Adrian's knock downs found the left winger, whose low shot was blocked by Josh, but Owen reacted quickest to the rebound and equalised with a diving header!

The last five minutes of the match became completely open, as both sides threw cautions, and tactics, to the wind. It resembled a basketball game as the teams took turns to attack. Charlie was sent through on goal by Richard's long low pass but he was tackled, desperately at the last minute, by the combative midfielder. Then Owen dribbled past three players only to suffer the same fate as Richard dived in to block his goal-bound effort.

With seconds remaining before a replay was needed, the home team launched another ball towards Adrian, who again won his aerial battle. However good Tom was, he couldn't make up the seven inch difference in height all the time. The knock down found Owen, who had switched sides to the left. He evaded tackles from Viktor and Thomas on route to the middle, but his shot was again blocked by Richard. The ball ricocheted off his knee but it inadvertently fell through to the striker, who put it away first time. The stadium erupted as the home team finally secured the tie. Fans and players celebrated wildly but it was heart-breaking for the Black Dragons.

The referee blew the final whistle seconds after the restart and that was that – the exciting cup tie ended 4-3 to the home team. The Black Dragons were in disbelief, as they sat on the ground wondering what went wrong. Richard had to console Layne who was in tears.

"What went wrong? We were two goals ahead!" he asked.

"We did what we could – it just wasn't our day," Richard said.

Owen came to the pair and said, "You guys have done really well today. You've made it such a tough game and we were lucky to win it at the end."

"Well played mate. You brought the best out of us – there's nothing left in the tank," Richard said as the two shook hands.

"You've grown a lot, Layne. Your defending was first class."

"Thanks, but…" the young one's voice was still quavering and inaudible.

"Leave him with me mate, he'll be fine," Richard said as he put his arm round Layne's shoulder.

"Be nice to your other half, looks like he's suffering from some domestic abuse!" Owen left with a joke.

It took Layne a little while to settle down but he was okay when they returned to the dressing room. David was disappointed but he wasn't critical of the way the team performed. He said it was a game that they could easily have won but it just wasn't to be. But being able to compete with a Premier League side like that was an achievement on its own.

The high scoring match was selected as the main feature for the highlights programme that evening. They showed Layne's tears at the end to emphasise the importance and appeal of the cup competition, very much to his annoyance. His friends and teammates sent him more than enough reminders through various memes to make it worse too.

"That'll teach you not to cry in public, baby," said Richard.

"You guys are cruel!" Layne said in a childish tone.

"It's okay, you can use my shoulder again if you need it."

Layne pretended to be angry and pushed Richard away, but then giggled and came back for a cuddle.

"I could do with some other parts of your body," he said in a seductive tone this time.

"Oh dear, I guess… I can make you happy that way," Richard responded with a smile as he started kissing his lovely boyfriend.

With the team out of both domestic cup competitions, there was only one focus left – to maximise their points intake in the league to either win it, gain automatic promotion, or secure a place in the playoffs.

29.

The Heartbreak

The Black Dragons' January transfer window closed with two further pieces of business. Mark the midfielder demanded a move to another Championship club in search of guaranteed first team football while Ethan, an experienced left footed centre back, joined from the Belgian first division on a short term contract. As a result, Mason moved back to the under 23 team while Andrew stayed to train with the first team as a backup.

After twenty-eight games, the Black Dragons were fourth in the table with fifty-one points, seven behind the top team from East Anglia, four off Bob's Birmingham club and just two lower than a club in Sheffield. They were on course for a playoff place but their eyes were really on securing one of the two automatic promotion spots.

Their next game after the exhausting cup match was away to South Yorkshire. The home team had been in the relegation zone for a long time and it was their new manager's first game in charge.

Richard and Layne didn't make the trip as David rested a number of players. Ethan got his full debut partnering Thorsten and Tom started in midfield with Toby and Ross. Luciano returned from injury to resume the normal front three with Charlie and George.

The pair watched the game from the players' lounge at the training centre with Danny, who was also rested. The team struggled to break down the spirited defending by the home side.

"That low block is so tight and compact, we need to either pull them out or break in from wide," Richard commented at half time.

"I had a bad feeling about this, the lads have been trying all sorts but still not getting anywhere. We needed to score when we are on top. The home team will have at least one chance, I hope we can deal with that when it comes," said Danny.

His fear materialised at around the hour mark. After another period of consistent pressure the home team broke out in numbers and won a penalty after Charlie tripped their right back in the area, having tracked him all the way from the front. Gordon dived the wrong way and the team fell behind.

"Can't really blame Charlie there, he ran all the way back to help and tackling wasn't in his repertoire," Danny said with a sigh.

The home team resumed their compact defensive shape, even pulling the striker back. The Black Dragons couldn't go through the ten men behind the ball, despite David's introduction of Andrés, Alex and Maz. The match ended 1-0 and the struggling team completed a surprise double over the high-flying Black Dragons.

With the match schedule back to a manageable level, David played a consistent team for the rest of February. Thomas seemed to have secured his place in defence as the replacement of Les and partner of Kieran. Ethan looked more than a decent player in training but he needed time to settle.

The team won their next three games, which were all played at home. A free kick from Richard was enough to see off the aggressive club from Staffordshire, despite the return of their former midfielder Kalim; Charlie scored his first hat trick in professional football in the 3-0 victory over the one from Suffolk; and finally a brace from both George and Danny won the exciting derby match against the team from Hounslow 4-2.

Richard's reputation as a solid defensive midfielder was growing by the day. As part of the club's community project he was invited by the school he attended while a youth player at the Black Dragons' academy to share his story, alongside another alumni Tom. They gave a speech to the year ten and eleven students on where they started, how they moved up the levels to become first team players and what professional training was like every day. It all went well until the host opened up the floor for some questions.

The first question by the crowd was already straight to the point – a girl asked if Richard was dating Layne as rumoured. Richard admitted they had been house mates for four years but that was all he would share. The second question was equally awkward, when a boy asked Richard if gay players should come out in public. Richard said it was really up to the player, as privacy should be respected and sexuality should not be a telling factor for football players, or anybody for that matter. The last question for Richard was whether he felt unfair to be targeted by a section of fans because of stories about his private life. He just said he already got used to it and he couldn't control how others behaved.

"That was hard work," Richard said to Tom as they drove away from the school. "Kids these days sure know what to ask!"

"I think you handled it well, all those PR training was worth it!"

"Thank God for that – imagine not knowing what to say in front of hundreds of teenagers. Plenty must be live streaming that in secret!"

"Honestly have you thought about coming out? It's like an open secret anyway."

"I really don't know. Layne always wants to but I just don't feel the need. You wouldn't go in front of the camera to tell everybody that you're now dating Immy, who happens to be a girl, would you?"

"I see your point. People say what they want to say anyway so yeah maybe doing what you regard as normal is the best way."

Richard had a chat with Layne that evening, after he came back from his part of the community project, which was to support Danny as a PE teacher for a day at a local primary school. Layne's view on the subject was that although he was comfortable on coming out, he would happily respect Richard's preference. He also liked Richard's way of describing things – they would do what was deemed normal for ordinary couples, not being particularly high profile nor hiding away from others. Richard was glad that they shared the same understanding.

After a weekend off due to the team not being in the FA Cup fifth round, the Black Dragons' next game was away to Humberside. David stuck to the same team that beat the team from Hounslow ten days ago, and the team dominated the first half in terms of both possession and chances. However, they couldn't break the deadlock.

The second half started badly for the Black Dragons as they conceded from a set piece ten minutes into it. The skilful left winger sent in a lovely cross for the big centre back to head in at the far post. David replaced Luciano and George with Alex and Sam at the hour mark for some fresh ideas and they made an instant impact. Sam tricked his way into the box and his low cross found Alex for a tap in. They had another chance late on but Charlie's shot was well saved by the keeper and the match ended 1-1.

The Black Dragons began their March fixtures with a return to Yorkshire. David rewarded Alex's goal with a start, in place of Luciano who was injured in the last game. He repaid his faith by setting up both goals in a 2-0 victory. His layoff found Ross in the first half and he sent the substitute Toby on goal with a pinpoint through pass in the second half. Richard was at his usual best, stopping plenty of attacks in midfield, but he also picked up his fifth yellow card of the season when he committed a professional foul when the team were only a goal up. Luckily it was after the halfway point of the fixtures and he won't get an automatic suspension.

The team picked up another four points from their next two matches as they beat another team from Lancashire 3-1 at home and drew 2-2 away with one from Birmingham. The goals were scored by George, Danny, Tom, Alex and

Kieran. Richard claimed another assist with the corner that the latter scored from.

The Black Dragons' thirty seventh and last game before the March international break was a visit from the other club in Birmingham. It would be the first visit for both Bob their former manager and Les their previous regular centre back.

With five wins and two draws from their last eight games, the Black Dragons had moved up to second place, three points behind the league leader from East Anglia and a point ahead of their visitor. But they had to face all the other five top teams in their next six games. It was make or break time.

Les went straight into the heart of his new club's defence and continued his excellent form. Bob named him in the starting line-up in a 4-1-4-1 formation against the Black Dragons, but their star attacking midfielder Ted was injured so there would be no repeat of his battles against Richard.

The home supporters gave both Bob and Les a warm welcome as they remembered their achievements with the club well.

David was able to pick his strongest eleven as Luciano returned having missed four games due to injury, as Alex moved back to the bench alongside Tom, Andrés and the others.

The two teams cancelled each other out during the exciting first half, as the players matched up for their respective battles and winning their fair shares. Richard was busy dealing with the two attacking midfielders with Ross and Layne had an excellent half against their right winger.

The second half continued with a similar theme until Bob introduced Darren as a replacement for his regular striker. He ran behind Thomas for a through ball but his shot was deflected wide by Richard's last-ditch block. Les won the aerial battle from the resulting corner but his header hit the top of the bar and went over.

441

David brought Alex on to replace George and asked Danny to move to the right to play a 4-2-4 formation for the last twenty minutes of the match. He wanted to use the front two's movement to find a way through the solid defence, and he gambled on Richard and Ross being able to hold the fort in the middle.

He reaped his reward as Charlie's clever reverse pass created a chance for Luciano, who scored expertly from a tight angle.

There was no time for the visitors to come back and the Black Dragons won the six-pointer 1-0 to open up a two-point lead over the club from Sheffield, the new team in third.

Bob congratulated David for his tactical victory but vowed to keep fighting for promotion until the end of the season.

Richard was over the moon after the game as he received a call from the Football Association to inform him that he had been selected by the England under 21 head coach for their next two friendly games, at home against Belgium and away in the Netherlands. He was joined by his teammates Kieran, Danny and Charlie. Layne was also called up by the under 19's alongside Ryan to face Scotland away and Portugal at home.

The pair had dinner with Mrs Moore at her Richmond apartment afterwards. She was going to cook but they ended up calling for deliveries as she felt a bit unwell. She told the pair that she had lost some weight with her new diet routine and that she would travel to Glasgow and then St. George's Park for Layne's under 19 matches.

Richard and Layne joined up with the England setup at St. George's Park on Tuesday together with Danny. The various age groups would be staying in separate camps before travelling to their respective matches in due course.

Having made over thirty appearances for the Black Dragons first team, Richard had faced plenty of his new teammates: the brilliant goal keeper Brandon from Sheffield, Oscar from the club in Derbyshire, Rory from

Nottinghamshire, Ben and Damian from the Premier League side that beat the Black Dragons in the League Cup, the young centre midfielder Wayne who played for one of the big Manchester clubs against the under 23 team last season and finally Owen and Adam who used to be his teammates. They all recognised Richard and welcomed his arrival – he was pleasantly surprised by the warmth from Adam, as he thought he might be a hostile figure given the clash he had with his close friend James.

The training was as intensive as before, in the same professional yet friendly manner. The coaches commended on Richard's improved strengths, his positioning and how he managed to create the time and space to execute his excellent passes. The dead ball specialists had a little competition amongst themselves and Richard came second only to Ben who was already well known in the Premier League.

Richard felt a lot more comfortable to socialise with the other players during this call up, which was probably due to him having established himself as a regular first team player. He commanded respect from the other players and plenty of them tried to talk up their (parent) clubs as potential destinations for Richard and his young teammates in the future. Charlie often went on the defensive when such topic arose and told everyone that there was no plan for anyone of them to leave the Black Dragons, and that they would be playing in the Premier League in their own rights really soon. Richard agreed with what he said but found it funny that he was so desperate to say that out loud.

Despite them being in the same campus for the first couple of nights, the pair agreed not to see each other and to act as independent players. But Richard broke the pact and came around to see Layne off as the younger team set off to Scotland for their first match, he just didn't go as far as a goodbye kiss.

Richard was on the bench alongside all his club mates for the under 21's first of two friendly matches, at home against Belgium on Friday evening. He was given his favourite number sixteen and he made his debut at the hour mark, when England were leading 1-0 by a goal from Owen. He had Wayne and Danny, who came on with him, for company in midfield. Kieran was also introduced to replace one of the centre backs.

Richard played a string of neat and short passes with his teammates around him as England sought to control the rest of the match. He found Owen on the run once with a long ball and Charlie a few times when he came on after seventy-five minutes. The away team didn't pose too many threats as England maintained their possession well and Richard's defensive skills were not really tested.

The game ended 1-0.

The head coach was happy with Richard's solid performance and Richard hoped he would get more playing time when the team travelled to the Netherlands a few days later. He heard from Layne that he played the full ninety minutes in the under 19 team's 2-0 triumph against Scotland. Ryan made his debuts as a substitute.

The England under 21 team travelled to Amsterdam on Sunday for their friendly game on Tuesday night.

"Have you been to the Dam before?" Charlie asked Richard on the coach.

"Only when I was really young, my parents took me to see the windmills and tulips. Have you?"

"Ahem, yes, I visited with Rob and Paul a few years ago."

"Oh… judging by your companions I guess I don't want to know the details!"

"That was a wonderful trip," Charlie said with a rather filthy smile.

"Don't you share that story to our Richard here, it'll be too much for him to take," Danny, who sat behind them, climbed up and said.

"Oh I'd love to hear it, where did you go?" said the eighteen-year-old Wayne, who sat next to Danny.

"Charlie, why don't you swap seats with Danny so that you can share all your adventures back there?" Richard suggested.

444

Charlie did exactly that and he started to talk about his experience of the city, "Well, promise me you won't tell Julia this…"

Richard put his headphones on in time to avoid listening to the rest of the story. He heard the odd laughter from behind him and shook his head with Danny, who by the looks of it must have been told those plenty of times before.

The team had some light training at the world-renowned stadium in the city on Monday. They were given some free time in the afternoon before a team dinner together at the hotel. Richard went to the Van Gogh Museum with Danny and Kieran before buying some souvenirs for Layne, Mrs Moore and his parents.

Richard was given his first start for England under 21 the next day. He sat at the bottom of the three-man midfield with Wayne and Ben. Charlie also started on the left wing, but Owen was on the bench with Danny and the others.

A three-man midfield with a single defensive midfielder was quite different to the one with two that Richard was used to with the Black Dragons. He did play it at the beginning of the season when David was trialling it and he knew what he needed to do – sniffing out danger before it happened, covering the gaps left by the advancing full backs and always providing the keeper an option for a pass. He received some specific training from the England coaches on those as well.

The Dutch team played in their traditional 4-3-3 formation and they had two really good wingers, both preferring to cut inside to have shots with their stronger foot. They also had a classic number ten pulling the strings in midfield, so he would likely to be Richard's main opponent.

The match was played under the closed retractable roof as it was raining heavily outside. Richard felt immensely proud when "God Save The Queen", the English national anthem, was played. He hummed along quietly and was amazed at how Charlie belted it out wholeheartedly. The

445

stadium was only half full – respectable for an under 21 match on a rainy Tuesday night. But the roar from the 25,000 fans after the Dutch national anthem was still deafening due to the echo inside the arena.

It's a shame Layne couldn't see this moment here, we'll have to watch the recording later, he thought.

The Dutch number ten, who was playing on his home turf, was lively from the kick off. He wasn't a dribbler trying to go past Richard all the time, but he consistently ran behind him for little passes or give-and-go's, causing him a lot of headaches. He dropped deeper to restrict that space available but then the number ten would move back for a ball to his feet. It became a bit of a cat-and-mouse game between the two. Obviously, when Richard got the ball, the number ten closed him down quickly too.

Contrary to the Black Dragons' cautious approach of having one full back attacking at a time, the England setup was for both to be flying up field at all time. This meant the midfield three would have to be alert, communicate with each other and press well. It wasn't as far as overwhelming for Richard, but he was at least kept on his toes throughout the first half, which was goalless.

"You had a tough one out there, Rich!" Danny said at half time.

"Yes I had to be at 100% all the time, it's so much faster at this level."

"That's great experience for you."

Richard played another fifteen minutes in the second half as the teams continued to nullify each other, before he was replaced by the regular defensive midfielder. Danny and Owen also came on.

"Well done Richard! It's impressive how you adapted to this level so well. It was against a top side too!" the coach was full of praise.

"Thank you for giving me the opportunity. I've learnt a lot just from the hour out there."

"That's good! We expect a lot from you."

The teams exchanged a goal near the end of the game. The pacy left winger exploited the gap behind England's right back and curled a lovely ball to the top corner at the eightieth minute, only to be pegged back by Danny, who scored his first goal for England with a sweet half volley from the edge of the area.

The team travelled back to St. George's Park the next day. Layne was waiting for Richard there as the under 19 had their game at home the day before, which was a 3-1 victory against Portugal. He was named as the man of the match so he had another little trophy to take home.

The Black Dragons' first game after the international break was an away trip to the league leaders in East Anglia. They were still five points behind and ideally needed a victory if they were to catch them. But as demonstrated in their 2-1 home defeat early in the season, their opponents were not easy to handle, especially when they had the home advantage.

David selected a slightly more defensive-minded team, with Gordon in goal, Jonas, Layne, Kieran and Thomas in defence, Richard, Tom and Ross in midfield, and Danny, Luciano and George upfront. He wanted to use the extraordinary energy and work rate of the two inside forwards to operate a high press.

The plan seemed to work as they disrupted the rhythm of the home team and won the ball higher up the pitch. Richard was like a magnet as he intercepted numerous loose passes in the middle. But the Black Dragons couldn't take advantage of the counter attacks in the first half, as they found the home goalkeeper in fine form.

The second half started with a bang for the home side, as their tricky left winger cut in from wide having danced through both Jonas and Tom. Richard ran over to hold his progress but he sent the ball through his legs towards the centre forward, who played a blinding first time back heel to put the right winger behind him through on goal. He chipped it over Gordon and established the one nil lead for the league leaders.

The Black Dragons responded with an excellent piece of play themselves. They pulled the home defence out with a string of passes before Danny put Layne through on the left. His low cross found Luciano in the area and his lay off set Tom up for a thumping finish.

The away side followed up with another great display but Danny's screamer was tipped over by the keeper at full stretch.

David brought Charlie and Andrés on to push for a winner. They had some half chances but the Black Dragons were nearly caught out at the back instead. The left winger went behind the defence and was tackled at the very last minute by Tom – any mistake in that and he would have been sent off. The match finished 1-1, which meant the league leaders maintained their five-point lead with eight games to go but the Black Dragons were now levelled on points with the team from Sheffield, ahead only on goal difference of just one. Bob's team also won their game and came back to just two points behind. The race for the all-important second automatic promotion place was truly on.

The Black Dragons' next match was only three days later and it was the home game against the south east London club, who were seventh in the league, pushing for a place in the playoffs.

With the recent history between the teams, there was a lively build up to the game, with fierce debates on social media between fans and the topic of homophobia in football being the focal point for the pundits and writers.

Richard was sitting next to Layne one evening when he received a rare call from his mum regarding these – they did chat regularly but it was the first time she mentioned them specifically. She was concerned by the nasty and vile attacks online and worried about their impact on Layne. He reassured her that he always ignored them and together with Richard there was nothing to be fearful of. She then asked, to Layne's embarrassment as he thought Richard was listening in, that if he had any future plans with Richard such as getting married or registering as civil partners.

"Mum I'm only eighteen! We're great together but that's surely too early!"

She said she was just saying it as she considered Richard to be a good partner to have, someone who could look after him, but she would leave it with the pair. She also said she had an appointment on Tuesday and couldn't go to the match. Layne moaned about her promise to go to every home match and got her to agree to going to the away game in Derbyshire on Saturday as a compromise.

"What did your mum say that made you that excited?" Richard asked afterwards.

"She asked... if we have plans to get married," Layne said quietly.

"Wow I haven't thought too much about that, do you want to?"

"You're not proposing now, are you?"

"No no no, don't get the wrong idea baby. I love you to bits but like you said you're only eighteen and I'm merely twenty. I'd love to spend the rest of my life with you but I think it's too early to consider all that?"

"To be honest, I'm quite happy to be with you forever too but yeah let's not think about getting married yet!"

"Talking about it, I do want to kiss you now though, baby."

"You never need permission for that!"

It was match day for the televised game against the south east London club. The police's presence was heavier than normal but there were no serious troubles before kick off.

The Black Dragons remained unchanged apart from Charlie coming in to replace Ross, who took a heavy knock during the last game. Jonas was named as the captain.

The match started in the Black Dragons' favour as Danny opened the scoring after twenty minutes. Richard intentionally rolled the ball forward with heavy top spin for him to hit on the run, and the perfectly executed dipping shot went into the back of the net beautifully. Just as he did the year before, he celebrated in front of the travelling fans before exchanging double claps with Richard.

The incensed away fans took their anger out on poor Richard later, when he went in front of them to take a corner kick. All sorts of abuses could be heard but the stewards moved in to stop any items being hurled at him. They reserved the same treatment for Layne as well, every time he attacked the byline there would be massive outpouring of wolf whistles and insulting chants.

The pair had the last laugh of the half as Richard curled in a free kick from twenty-five yards out. They repeated Danny's trick and celebrated in front of the away stand.

The second half took an interesting turn as Jonas the captain was sent off for a professional foul after he wrestled the inside forward to the ground after he went clean through. David replaced Luciano with Toby and moved Richard to play at right back.

The resulting free kick was saved by Gordon but the away side pulled one back at the hour mark. Richard was beaten in the air by the big centre half from a corner kick and his header deflected in off Layne, who was guarding the post. This set up a frantic last thirty minutes as the ten men fought to protect their slender lead.

David brought the experienced Ethan on for Charlie to restore some calm at the back and he did just that, as the Black Dragons held out for a valuable home win. All other top five teams won so there were no changes at the top of the table.

The Black Dragons travelled to Derbyshire for their next league game four days later. The home team were sixth in the table and they were a tough side to beat, as proven by their 2-2 draw at The Dragons Stadium earlier in the season. Their three loanees from Premier League clubs continued to perform really well.

Ross returned from his injury and pushed Tom back to the bench. Maz came in to replace the suspended Jonas.

Mrs Moore kept her promise and drove to the match, to the delight of Layne, who was playing his fortieth game for the Black Dragons – quite an achievement for an eighteen-year-old.

The match started with the home team on the front foot, with the Dutch winger Koen coming close with his free kicks. Layne was up against him and was booked early on for a late tackle.

There was a break in play fifteen minutes into the game and the Black Dragons' bench signalled a substitution – Lewis was coming on for Layne. Richard could see the shock on Layne's face but his frustration quickly turned into a sense of panic as he rushed off into the tunnel with Nick, the Assistant Manager. Richard had no idea what was happening and had to focus on the game.

The match was still goalless when the Black Dragons made another surprise first half substitution after forty minutes – this time they were taking Richard off!

Something isn't right, he thought as he sprinted to the bench.

"What's going on?" he asked David.

"It's about Layne. I think he desperately needs your help, go straight to the hospital, we'll handle it here," David said.

Richard put his tracksuit and trainers on and followed a club official out of the stadium, where a taxi was already waiting for him.

The twenty-minute journey felt like years:

What's happening?

Is Layne okay?

Why is everyone panicking?

He got to the Accident and Emergency department, where a nurse led him to a ward and he saw Layne sitting by a bed, with Nick next to him.

He noticed Richard's arrival and looked up, his eyes were completely red and swollen, he seemed lost and frightened.

"What happened, dear?"

"My mum… my… mum… has… died…"

"What? H… how?"

451

Layne pointed at the bed and burst into tears, his body was shaking and he was mumbling something inaudible.

Richard felt cold sweat at the back of his head as he looked at the bed – Mrs Moore was indeed lying there, but she was motionless and extremely pale, so pale that he felt frightened. The machine next to her, which Richard assumed was there to measure her pulse, was completely silent. So it was true – she was no longer with them. But why? She seemed fine last time he saw her, what happened?

Before he could ask those questions, he went over to sit next to Layne and do what he really needed to do – take care of his loved one.

He put his arm round Layne's shoulder and he immediately collapsed into his arms, sobbing painfully. The normally calm and impassive Richard felt really bad for Layne, and his tears were in free fall – it hurt him to see the person he loved so much suffered, and of course he knew Mrs Moore well too.

Layne settled after a while. He wiped his tears, took a few deep breaths and said, "I need to be strong, there's a lot to do from here."

And he was right. Jon their agent who was also a friend of Mrs Moore had arrived by this point and he was helping out with the formalities. But there were still plenty for Layne, the only relative, to handle.

He gave his mum a final kiss on her cheek before the hospital staff moved her away. He broke down again and again in between the processes but he soldiered through.

The pair eventually returned home at midnight. They didn't talk much throughout the day but Richard gathered that Mrs Moore collapsed at the stadium and her passing was confirmed at the hospital. The pair found out from her medical record that she had terminal cancer and was in her final days.

"That's why she gave up work, that's why she lost so much weight, that's why she's been feeling unwell. Why didn't I notice any of these, and only whinged and demanded her to go to the match today?" Layne questioned himself when he was in bed.

452

"Don't be hard on yourself. We just wouldn't know if she's keen to hide it away."

"Why did she do that? She could have told me about it! I'm her son!"

"I can only guess but I think she didn't want you to worry, she didn't want to affect your playing, especially that your career had just started."

"But I could have done something about it! I could have made it memorable... Why did everyone leave me without saying goodbye?"

"She was only doing it to protect you."

"I'm not a child! I'm old enough to handle it, I don't need protection... Don't ever leave me like that Richie! Please!"

"I won't do that, I'll share everything with you, I promise."

"You're all I have now-"

"It's okay baby, let it out. I'm here for you."

Layne had another breakdown in Richard's arms before finally falling asleep with exhaustion.

Richard couldn't sleep – with the chain of events happening his brain had gone into overflow. He checked his phone to find out that the match had finished 1-1. Adam scored a late equaliser for the home side.

There were also a whole host of messages from his teammates asking if they were okay. And there was an email from... Mrs Moore, sent only an hour ago!

Richard was a little bit scared but he opened the mail anyway:

Dear Richard,

If you are reading this email, it means I'm already gone. I've asked my best friend Sue to take care of things and this is a part of it.

As you probably know by now, I was diagnosed of stage four liver cancer before I returned to London and only have months to live. I'm glad that I was able to spend so much of it with my dearest Layne, when he was having the time of his life, with you and his football. I have no regrets.

I know you are a good person, Richard. I know you love my little baby as much as I do. I know he's in good hands, whether you are together or not. Please don't take this as me pressurising you to stay with him forever, I just want you to be the someone whom he can always fall back on when he's in trouble.

Regardless, it was a pleasure to meet an aspiring and courteous young person like you, and I'm sure you would achieve what you set out to be, whether it is football or studies. I hope you would guide my little Ping along the way too. For that I thank you sincerely.

Sue is also the executrix of my will and will be in touch in due course. Please stay with Layne during this period – he's driven by emotions and I'm worried about his reactions.

It's time for me to say farewell. Don't be sad – I've lived well and I'm happy with how my baby has grown. I'm finally united with his daddy and we'll be watching you two play from above.

With lots of love,

Jane

Richard read the email time and time again and couldn't stop crying. Why on Earth must such a loving mother be taken away so soon? She was all Layne had, how was he going to cope?

He looked at the tired out Layne next to him and swore to himself that he would look after him forever.

Richard woke up quite early the next morning. He didn't sleep well at all. He went to the living room to avoid waking Layne up and he decided to read up about liver cancer – he wanted to know this horrible killer disease.

"Richie? Where are you?" Layne got up and called for him hours later.

Richard sensed the panic in his voice and rushed into the bedroom to give him a hug, "Baby I'm here, it's okay."

"Can you tell me it was all a dream, a really really bad dream, please?"

"I'm sorry Layne. You know it's true, we just have to face it, together."

Layne's lips started quavering and he cried in Richard's arms.

"How did the game go yesterday?" he asked when he eventually calmed down.

"It was 1-1, Thomas scored first but we were pegged back late on."

"That was a shame. I guess we are third now?"

"Yes, Sheffield won their game and are now two points ahead of us."

"Have you spoken to David or Nick?"

"I did talk to Nick when we were in hospital. He said you can take as many days off as you need."

"How about you?"

"They said I don't have to report for the midweek game against the West Midlands team but they want me back for the trip to West Yorkshire."

"That's fair enough."

"I'll make sure someone is with you when I'm away. It'll mainly be Jon but Ryan, Harry and Andrew have all offered."

"Don't worry too much, I'll be okay."

455

"Just let us keep you company for a while."

The doorbell rang when Layne was getting ready. Richard opened the door and there was a lady that he never met before.

It was Sue, Mrs Moore's close friend from Law School and the executrix of her will.

"You must be Richard. I know it's probably not a good time to visit. I'm only delivering Jane's note to Layne today. How is he doing?"

"He's just about managing. I've read Mrs Moore's email last night, thanks for sending it."

"That's okay. I'll be working with Jon on her funeral and other things as well. I'll leave the note with you then. I'll be in contact."

Layne came out just after Sue left, "Who was that at the door?"

"That was Sue, your mum's friend. She wanted to give you this," Richard said as he handed the note over.

"Is this… from mum?" Layne saw the handwriting on it and started feeling anxious.

Richard nodded and said, "Do you need some time on your own?"

"Stay with me please, Richie."

The pair sat down on the sofa as Layne opened the envelope and took the handwritten letter out. Richard let him read it without interfering and was there when Layne inevitably broke down in tears again.

He stopped crying after a while and he carefully put the letter back in the envelope and took them to the drawer where he kept all his documents.

"I guess I just have to be strong from now on. I'm no longer a child," he said when he came back to the living room.

"I'm always here if you need me, we can grow up together," Richard said.

"Thanks dear, I don't know what I'll do without you."

"Shall we get something to eat? You haven't had a meal since yesterday lunchtime."

"I don't really feel like it. Shall we just grab a coffee and have a walk?"

"Sure, maybe some fresh air will help."

30.

The Kiss

"Are you sure you are ready for this, Layne?"
"Yes, that's what mum would have wanted me to do."

It was the last match day of the Championship season, a month after Layne lost his mum during that away game in Derbyshire.

The Black Dragons played five games during the period and unfortunately lost four of them: a shock 2-1 defeat at home by the West Midlands club, a 2-0 loss at another promotion-chasing team in West Yorkshire, a painful 3-1 setback at home against second-placed Sheffield and finally went down 2-1 at South Wales. The only victory was the local derby at home against the team from Shepherd's Bush, one that they won 2-0.

Their hope of securing automatic promotion vanished with those defeats but their fifth place finish secured their involvement in the playoffs. The first leg of the semi-finals would be played in a weeks' time, with the second leg three days after.

While Richard had been involved in four of those five games, it was Layne's first game back from his time off for bereavement. He returned to training a week after his mum's passing but was in no shape to compete mentally. The club arranged counselling sessions for him and he gradually recovered.

The pair arrived at the training centre the morning ahead of the game against the team from Nottinghamshire and met up with their teammates.

"Hey, you two are early today. Are you ready for the game, Layne?" Tom asked.

"It's all sorted after yesterday, I'm here to complete our mission."

"Good that. I'm sure the gaffer is keen to have you back, we missed your threats on the left."

David saw them and walked across to meet them.

"Boys you're early. Can I have a word with you please, Layne?" he said.

"Sure boss," said Layne as he followed David into his office.

Richard and Tom went to the dressing room. The rest of the team started to arrive one by one and soon everyone was ready apart from Layne.

He eventually entered the room with David, Nick and the coaching team.

"Right boys," David started his team talk. "As you found out from our defeat up there, today's opponents are a tough side to beat. But today we're not only going to win, we are going to win big. We will build our momentum for the playoffs and go to Yorkshire with the wind on our backs.

"Don't give them a second to think, we'll hit them with all we have from the very start. The fans deserve it for the last home game of the season."

The light training reflected the game plan and the players had their usual lunch together followed by a power nap in their rooms.

"Did you have a good rest?" Richard asked when he met Layne again.

"It was okay, I did fall asleep."

"What did David say in the morning?"

"Just checking on my readiness, nothing special."

"Good, let's go!"

After the usual player-fan interaction at the stadium lounge, where the supporters gave Layne plenty of encouragement, the team received their final instructions from David in the dressing room.

"Here's the starting line-up: Gordon in goal, Jonas right back, Kieran and Ethan centre backs, Layne returns to left back, Richard and Ross centre midfield, Danny number ten, Charlie left wing, Luciano right and George up top. Josh, Thomas, Lewis, Toby, Tom, Andrés and Alex on the bench.

"They would have done their homework on us so we need to be flexible on how we attack. Make them play at our pace and overload when you see the opportunities. Rich and Ross, be crisp and sharp as always, we need you at your very best today."

The team went onto the pitch for their warm ups. The stadium were half occupied and the away team were already there. Richard saw Layne staring at the empty seats in the stand and moved over to comfort him.

"She'll be watching from the sky, don't worry," he said.

"I'm sure she will. Maybe she'll bring dad along?" Layne wondered in an innocent tone with added sadness, but he promised he won't be crying again.

The team returned to the dressing room after their warm up and Tom gave everyone a black armband in memory of Mrs Moore. Layne looked at all his teammate and was genuinely touched.

It was time for kick off. The team returned to the pitch to the thunderous welcome from the home fans in the now full stadium. They were singing the club anthem and chanting "We are going up". The match day announcer read out the team sheet and fans gave the loudest cheer when he said "Welcome back to our number 17, Layne Moore" – they knew what he went through recently.

The Black Dragons had a team huddle before kick off.

"Last home game of the season, whatever happens we win this for the fans. We'll hit them at a hundred miles per hour. Remember what the gaffer said, focus and composure!" Ross the captain gave the rallying cry.

"Fly, you Black Dragons!" the team roared.

The away team won the toss and decided to kick off first. They were also aiming for a fast start and they swiftly launched the ball forward. Ethan won the first aerial battle and the ball dropped to Richard.

"Man on!" he heard a shout from Ross and he passed it first time to Layne who was in space on the left. The away

460

team put him under pressure straight away and he sent a low and hard pass towards Charlie in front of him.

Charlie, who had grown a full ginger beard, controlled the driven ball effortlessly and sent it forward to George, who was stationed on the edge of the area. He received the ball with his back to goal, feinted a pass back to Charlie with his left foot and laid it off towards the "D" instead with his right, without even looking in that direction.

Danny was charging towards that space and he hit the ball first time. The ball went straight into the bottom right corner under the goal keeper's dive and it was a goal to nil within five minutes. It was Danny's eleventh goal of the season and his fourth from outside the area. He was slowly becoming a fans' favourite with his endless running as well as end products.

The Black Dragons scored a second goal at the half hour mark. Charlie was involved again as he controlled Danny's pass on his stride and took it pass his marker at the same time with a smart turn. He reached the byline and cut the ball back to the corner of the six-yard box.

Layne arrived at speed and slotted the ball into the far corner with his left foot.

He sprinted towards the stand where his mum used to sit and emotionally knelt down, pointing his fingers to the sky. He also took his shirt off to reveal an undershirt with "I miss you, mummy" written on it. Richard and the rest of the team joined in to pay their tributes.

The referee had to follow the rules and showed Layne a yellow card for taking his shirt off, but he sent his condolences verbally at the same time to make sure Layne knew why he did it.

The half ended 2-0. David was happy with the team's performance but he demanded more. He wanted the team to be even more ruthless and scored a few more goals. Although their fifth place was already confirmed, he was keen to put on a show to make their opponents in the playoffs worried. He asked if Layne was able to carry on after his emotional display but the left back was keen to continue. They agreed to review the situation at the hour mark.

The first fifteen minutes of the second half went quickly as the teams fought for possession in midfield. The reorganised visitors held the Black Dragons at bay with their compact formation while their counter attacks were thwarted the home team's mean defence, with Richard making a number of crucial interceptions.

David decided to withdraw the visibly drained Layne at the hour. Richard ran over to give him a hug before he went off, and the home fans gave him a standing ovation for his performance over the season, which he contributed with two goals and seven assists.

Thomas also came on for Kieran and he completed the splendid afternoon for the hosts with the third goal. Danny's in-swinging corner was cleared only as far as Richard on the left, and his cross found Thomas onside and unmarked for a simple header. He celebrated his second goal of the season with a "rocking baby" gesture to mark the birth of his second child, Sebastian, a few days before the game.

The match ended 3-0 to the Black Dragons. The players had the traditional end of season lap of appreciation for the fans, even though they had an extra home game the week after – the first leg of the playoff semi-final against the team from West Yorkshire. The other half of the playoffs would see Bob's team from Birmingham against the club from Derbyshire, who sealed their sixth place finish on the last day.

Richard and Layne were at the office of the executrix of the will the next morning. Sue the executrix listed the properties owned by Layne's parents and all the other investments. There were five properties in total, all were either fully paid before her passing or covered by her insurances: three in Bath, one in Wiltshire and the flat in Richmond. The estate came to a total just short of five million pounds and Layne was the sole beneficiary.

462

Layne had no idea how much his parents had and was rather shocked – he knew they had a few properties but he wasn't aware of how they were funded.

The value of the estate didn't mean much to him anyway as the pair were financially comfortable and he would definitely swap all that to have his mum with him a little longer. He tried hard not to cry but he broke down again after hearing Sue's memory of her childhood friend – Mrs Moore was intelligent, kind and passionate, and she always had her only child in her mind, even when she went through the very harsh medical treatments. She left a message saying Layne was her biggest accomplishment and she was very proud of him.

Richard and Layne returned to their flat soon after.

"How are you feeling, Ping?" Richard asked gently.

"I'm okay. I just don't know what to do with all those properties."

"They're all rented out apart from the family home in Bath and the flat in Richmond, right? You just need to think about what you'd do with those two. Maybe you want keep them as they are?"

"You're right, I think I'll leave those for now, I can't deal with making them different to what they are."

Layne's lips started to quiver so Richard stopped talking and got him a glass of warm water.

"It's okay. Let it out if you need to, I'm here," he told him softly while putting his arm around his shoulder.

Layne didn't have another full breakdown, only a few tears in Richard's arms and he was better. "What shall we do for lunch? We're meeting the lads tonight so just an easy one now?" he asked.

"Yeah let me see what we've got in the fridge. Why don't you go and wait in the balcony?"

He quickly made some chicken breast and lettuce sandwiches and brought them to the balcony, only to find Layne snoozing on the lounger. He put a blanket over him and covered the food for later.

Layne woke up after about ten minutes and found Richard sitting next to him reading a book on number theory.

"Sorry I fell asleep, Richie. You shouldn't wait for me."

"It's alright, baby. You must be tired after everything. Come and have a drink, I've made you a nice cup of hot white chocolate."

"Thanks," Layne said after having a sip of the not-so-hot chocolate. "I haven't been out here for so long – look at those flowers in full bloom over there in the island!"

"I'm not surprised, you've been so pre-occupied recently."

"It's been difficult but I think it's time to move on. Sorry I haven't talked to you much during this time."

"Don't be silly. We're supposed to support each other."

"It couldn't be easy for you with me crying all the time, but honestly I wouldn't survive without you. I'll treat you well from now on."

"You're always good to me anyway… but if you can take the dishes out of the dishwasher later you'll be even better!"

The pair had their light lunch and a long overdue relaxing afternoon. They had a run by the river and felt energised for their team gathering in the evening, which was in a top Italian restaurant in a riverside location near Hammersmith.

Richard took delivery of their new white BMW M4 convertible from their local dealership earlier that week. They went there a few months ago to have their eight-year-old MINI serviced and were talked into buying a new car by the Sales Manager, who was a Thames Ditton supporter and immediately recognised the two first team players (and the sales opportunity) when they walked in. Layne was sold by the looks of the car almost right away and he helped persuade the prudent Richard to agree to buying it, after he examined the financial offer in detail and determined that the monthly payment was sustainable for what they were earning.

The pair had the retractable roof off on their way to the restaurant and they really enjoyed the drive – the engine had an awesome soundtrack. They got there at the same time as Charlie and Julia, who were in the yellow Porsche Cayman that he bought at the beginning of the season.

"Is this your new motor Rich? Looks flashy in that metallic white! Fancy a sprint later?" Charlie asked.

"No thanks, but I can take you out for a ride if you want?"

"Wowsers Lucas! Is it new car day?" Tom asked as he parked up his Lexus 4x4 with his new girlfriend Immy.

"Excuse me? Why does everyone think it is his car? I have a license too!" Layne moaned.

"Why don't you drive us home later? I can have a few drinks!" Richard teased.

"No way! You're my driver!"

Richard smiled and agreed – he was glad to see Layne behaving like he used to.

Just when the six of them were ready to enter the restaurant, Danny also arrived with Grace... in a taxi. He still didn't want to learn how to drive, claiming cars would all be autonomous soon anyway.

Charlie was the organiser and he booked the restaurant's private dining room for the team. Alex, Andrés, Luciano, Kieran, Sam and their other halves were already there.

The restaurant was famous for being inventive with their seafood and Richard was well satisfied. The group was relieved that Layne was back to normal, as he got completely drunk having indulged himself with all the lovely wines recommended by the Italian-speaking Luciano.

Richard gave Danny and Grace a lift home afterwards. Layne was screaming all the way demanding for the roof to be taken down while it was raining cats and dogs outside.

"How embarrassing, sorry guys," Richard said when Layne finally fell asleep.

465

"That's fine Rich, I'd rather see him like this. He had a hard time."

"True. He's still only eighteen to be fair, bless him."

The pair went to see the final instalment of the long standing superhero movies in Esher after training the next day. They sat at the back of the small luxury cinema and enjoyed the thrilling actions until one of the main characters sacrificed herself for the sake of her friends and the mission. The scene touched Layne's feelings and he began sobbing in Richard's arms. He continued on and off throughout the movie but recovered well enough for the exciting final battle.

A group of teenagers walked over after the ending credits to see who the "annoying crying man" was and recognised the pair. Fortunately they were supporters of the Black Dragons and they knew what Layne went through.

"So you two really are dating then?" asked one of the boys.

"We are very good friends," Richard responded with a polite smile.

"I saw your new motor on the paper today, it looks awesome!" said another boy on his way out.

"Paper?" Richard and Layne swapped glances and shared a thought that something not very nice might have happened.

They went home to find out that one of the tabloids had "Young footballer splashed out on sports car the day he collected his inheritance" as their main headline. They had some blurry pictures of the pair with the car at the team dinner, and rough details of Mrs Moore's estate.

Layne wasn't normally bothered by stories about him but he was absolutely livid this time. He asked Jon to put out a statement to say that they bought the car on finance themselves months ago and it had nothing to do with his inheritance, but Jon warned that it could be twisted as a confirmation that he and Richard were together as a couple. Layne discussed with Richard at length and they agreed to go ahead with it, as it was more important for them to show the respect they had for his mum.

As expected, the tabloid responded with "First gay English footballers confirmed – young Championship stars live together and share car finance" as their headline the next day. The pair decided not to comment any further. Other newspapers reported on the dispute but didn't highlight the connection between their statement and them coming out. David was questioned about it during his pre-match press conference but he laughed it off by saying it wasn't impossible for young players to be housemates or even share a car. He urged the papers to focus on the football and not players' private lives.

Thames Ditton's under 23 team completed their season with twelve wins out of twenty-nine league games. Ryan was the top scorer with twenty six goals followed by Finley in second with fifteen. The former broke George's goal scoring record for the junior side on the last day and was earmarked for a promotion next season, while the latter and the likes of Harry, Andrew and Dillon were not far behind but could be up for a loan elsewhere. Kasper, the tough tackling defensive midfielder from Denmark, had agreed a return to his former club on loan for the next season and said his goodbye to Richard and others before Tuesday's training.

The Black Dragons were up against the club from West Yorkshire in their playoff semi-final. It wasn't going to be a straight forward tie as the two teams won their respective home match by two goals to nil during the season. As the away goals rule did not apply in playoffs, they just needed to focus on winning the first game with a big enough margin.

David decided to play mostly with the team's strengths instead of being too wary of their opposition. He did make one change though, as he started with the more defensively disciplined Danny on the left wing in place of Charlie. The first eleven were Gordon in goal, Jonas, Layne, Kieran and Thomas in defence, Richard, Tom and Ross in midfield, and Danny, George and Luciano upfront. The West Yorkshire club came in their usual 4-1-4-1 formation and they had one of the meanest defence in the division.

The Black Dragons began the game in their usual fashion, a fast and high tempo start aiming to score before their opponents settled. But the away team planned for it and repelled with a compact low block. They actually looked the more dangerous side as they counter attacked on the break, with both full backs energetically sprinting up field in support.

The home team had to switch to their next plan after twenty minutes. They slowed the play down and focused on building it up from more assured passes and movements. It mitigated some of the risk from the counter attacks but they couldn't generate enough chances themselves too. The highly tactical first half ended goalless.

David was satisfied with the performance and he said during his team talk, "Everything's going according to plan so far. We knew they would be hard to beat and we contained their counters well. Keep passing it around to wear them down, we'll hit them later on."

The match resumed in pretty much the same way as the first period, with the Black Dragons controlling possession and keeping the away side on the back foot. They visitors seemed content to take a draw home for the second leg.

David made his changes twenty minutes into the second half. He brought Charlie on for Tom and Alex on for George.

"It's Ranger time," Richard whispered to Danny.

It was indeed. Charlie wasted no time to show his worth, as he dribbled past two players to hit a shot at goal, which brought out a great save from the keeper.

It marked the beginning of the Black Dragons' onslaught. Charlie, Danny and Layne linked up nicely on the left and they created an opportunity for Charlie to cross low from the byline. Luciano controlled the ball inside the six-yard box with his back to goal. His lay off found Alex coming in from the right and he smashed it into the bottom corner – it's one nil to the Black Dragons!

They had a go at getting the second goal but Ross's late effort was pushed away by the keeper and Richard put his free kick narrowly wide.

"It wasn't the biggest advantage to take up there but it was a good performance – well done boys!" David said after the match.

The players had another lap of honour for the home fans, who gave them a great sending off to the second leg, with chants of "We Are Going Up" echoing round the stadium.

The pair visited the cemetery where Mrs Moore was laid to rest after the recovery training session the next day. They tidied up the area and decorated it with some fresh flowers.

Layne was sitting quietly next to his mother's grave so Richard stood aside for a moment. He wasn't crying, but Richard could feel his sadness.

Who wouldn't miss their parents, especially ones taken so young?

Richard remembered the burial there a couple of weeks ago – it was so painful for him to see the devastated look on Layne's face. But he was strong and his determination took him through it all. Plenty of teammates and coaching staff were there with friends and colleagues of Mrs Moore's and the handful of relatives. It was as good as it could be. Richard was particularly touched when his parents showed up to pay their respects, even though his father claimed that he was only there to accompany his wife.

Layne stood up after a while. He gave Richard a hug and told him he was ready to go. They had a light lunch and decided to have a drive around the local area. They cruised along the huge Richmond Park with the roof down and they met a large group of deer.

"Slow down Richie, look at how many deer we have here?"

"Wow, there must be at least thirty! How did we not notice them before?"

"We need to come here more often, look at those lovely antlers!"

"Yes, maybe we'll join Danny and Viktor for their bike rides?"

"No thanks, I'll drive behind you three!"

"Cheering us along? Nice thoughts…"

"Goodbye deer! Have a nice day!" Layne said as he waved at the mammals.

"That's a bit silly, baby."

"Oh Richie, I've been thinking about this. Shall I sell one or two of the rental properties to buy one around here? We can't carry on renting forever."

"Houses here are expensive, I'm not earning enough to pay my share yet…"

"No, I meant I'll pay for all of it. I want to share what I have with you. I'm sure mum would agree."

"You don't have to do that…"

"I insist – you're the one I want to be with forever, Richie."

"Me too baby. I'll happily accept your offer then – let's plan after the playoffs."

The Black Dragons went up to West Yorkshire for the second leg of the playoff semi-final three days after the first game in London. They were dealt not one but two huge blows as regular starters George and Ross failed their fitness tests. Andrés and Charlie came in their places and David altered his plans to cater for the different style of players.

The home crowd was very hostile towards the visitors, as they tried to help their team overturn the one goal deficit from the first leg. They weren't shy to give Richard, Layne and the other players all sorts of abuses – they sang various offensive chants including the infamous "Rent Boys" and gave the pair plenty of nasty gestures. Their recent dispute with the tabloid only gave them more ammunitions.

The home team's veteran manager stuck to his usual 4-1-4-1 formation but with a very different intent. They scaled up the tempo and didn't give the Black Dragons a second to breath. They kept attacking from wide and one of their centre midfielders, who was great in making late runs into the box, opened the scoring from one such runs early on.

The Black Dragons tried to settle their nerves by keeping possession but they nearly conceded a second goal straight away. To the delight of the crowd, Layne was muscled off the ball by the right winger and his cross nearly found the centre midfielder again. Richard was there to make the crucial block and he flicked the ball clear when he was on the floor.

But the away team restored their overall lead against the run of play in the dying seconds of the first half. Despite the deafening jeers, Layne remarkably ran through two challenges and found Andrés in the far post for a simple finish. The half somehow finished 1-1.

The Black Dragons started the second half in comfortable fashion as they slowed the tempo down and maintained good possession of the ball. They created a few half chances but the shots from Charlie and Luciano didn't trouble the keeper.

Minutes later they opened up the home defence again with some great passing and movements to send Andrés through. He was hacked down by the goalkeeper and the referee pointed straight to the penalty spot. The Black Dragons argued for the keeper to be sent off but the official only gave him a booking.

Richard stepped up to take the penalty after the lengthy debates. The keeper stood right in front of him in order to look bigger and one of the players behind him said loudly, "We know all about you, kid."

A piece of hesitation got into Richard's mind. He was going for the same spot he always hit with precision – the bottom right hand corner, but the comment led him to believe that the keeper might have done his homework and knew his intentions. So he ended up sending it the other way.

The keeper dived the wrong way but the ball hit against the bar and flew over!

The crowd reacted with all sorts of abuses – from the usual whistles and jeers to the more specific "go home, homo" and "this is a men's game". Richard was too occupied to pay them any attention; he stood there in disbelief – it could have been all over but he somehow missed it!

To make matters worse, the home side took the lead again with a lightning quick attack at the seventy fifth minute. The Black Dragons' substitute Alex was tackled in the seemingly harmless right-wing area but the home side launched a counter and a few passes later the ball was with their left winger, with the Black Dragons' defence in disarray. He hit a high cross towards the far post and the centre forward beat Layne to the ball and headed it in.

The Black Dragons needed to find another goal within the next fifteen minutes plus stoppage time or the tie would go into extra time. Layne was devastated by the goal and some home fans added further insults by chanting "Where's your mummy now?" repeatedly. It was absolutely disgusting. He was next to the technical area and David asked if he would prefer to be substituted. Layne declined as he was keen to stay on and win the game.

With minutes left to go, Richard managed to find Danny in the middle with a forward pass. He performed a quick Flip Flap to create room to pull the trigger but was clattered and the referee blew for a direct free kick.

Richard put the ball down amid massive jeering from the thirty-five thousand home fans. The keeper set up the wall to block the right of the goal while he covered the left. The only way to score was to bend it up over the wall and down into the top right corner. With the ball so close to the box it wasn't straight forward.

Richard took his five steps back, had a deep breath and sprinted towards the ball… but he ran over it. While everyone in the stadium was surprised a left footer came up and sent it straight into the top right corner.

It was Layne the speedy left back!

He had been training his free kicks with Richard but it was the first time he hit one in a real match – and what an important match it was to launch his secret weapon!

The pair celebrated passionately in front of the home crowd, who were shouting all sorts of homophobic remarks at them. Having suffered these for the whole game and heard the chant directed at Layne's mum, Richard exploded and did something that he would never dream of doing.

He kissed Layne in front of the stands!

The world stood still at that very second. Layne was as shocked as anyone and he broke down in tears soon after. The home fans went absolutely mental but the pair didn't care – they were congratulated by the rest of the team and together they moved back into position to see out the remaining minutes of the game.

The home team launched everything upfront but the Black Dragons held firm. Kieran won a high ball and the referee blew the final whistle as Richard hoofed the loose ball up in the air. The Black Dragons had made it to the playoff final with a 2-2 draw in the second leg and a 3-2 win overall.

Layne was named by the broadcaster as the man of the match and Richard accompanied him on camera.

Presenter: Hi Layne and Richard, that was a tough game. Can you tell us how the team prepared beforehand?

Layne: The boss's plan is to contain the home team and play on the counter. We were doing that until they scored their two goals, so we had to dig deep and find our own reserves to equalise, luckily we did.

Presenter: There were some controversies throughout the game, did you think there was a push on you for the home side's first goal?

Layne: Well it was a bit physical but I thought it was a fair challenge, he was just stronger at that moment.

Presenter: That's very sporting of you. Richard, do you think it was a penalty, and what went through your mind when you hit it against the bar?

Richard: It wasn't too clear from my angle but I thought there was enough contact to bring Andrés down. As for the kick I just hit it too hard, maybe I was a little nervous.

Presenter: Now tell us about the winning goal. Was it planned for Layne to take the free kick?

Richard: It surely was. The position was better for a left footer and we've been training it for a while. It was beautifully executed.

Presenter: It was indeed. How about the celebration? Were you trying to tell us something there?

Richard: I just thought I needed to stand up against the abuses we were getting from the stands. I understand that the game is full of passion and so on, but there has to be a limit on what people can and can't say. Layne is an eighteen-year-old boy who just lost his mother. How dare were they mocking him on that? How low do you go to affect the opposition team? How about all those homophobic chants? Is somebody going to do anything about it? It doesn't just hurt me or other players what you said, but all those fellow supporters who are also from the LGBT community. You are insulting fans of your own club! And for those who kept asking if my boyfriend knows I'm wherever, I'm going to make it clear here – Layne and I are indeed in a relationship, or in other words, yes we are gay! Nothing is going to stop us playing football, and we'll continue to do whatever we can to win our games!

Presenter: That... was some statement, Richard. Please accept my congratulations for your bravery, for standing up for Layne here and the wider community. I'm sure our audience at home heard you well, and I wish somebody somewhere will indeed do something about it.

Richard: I'm sorry if it came across as an outburst, I was getting a bit emotional. But even if we are just one percent of all footballers, or indeed the only two in

England, we will still be who we are. Judge us by our performance on the pitch and not who we spend our private time with.

Presenter: Don't worry about that, you've put your message across well. In a lighter note, the studio has named Layne as the man of the match and here's your little reward.

Both: Thank you.

Once they were off air, Layne crashed into Richard and they cried in each other's arms. He was touched by what Richard had said and done, the fact that he overcame his own fear of coming out to support him in front of the whole world. The television crew gave them a round of applause and wished them well for the future.

David took them aside in the dressing room after learning what Richard said in the live interview. He was supportive of the idea of the pair coming out, but as there was no doubt that there would be some kickbacks from the cruel world of football fans he was asking if they needed any further help. Richard appreciated his offer and told him that he would report any abuses to the police and leave them with his legal team. David said the club would issue a statement to support them and to condemn the vile attacks.

The Black Dragons teammates were surprised by Richard's on-air announcement but were fully supportive of the pair. They said they would join the club's actions.

Two English professional footballers coming out on live television made massive waves in the media. The pair's kiss was on the front pages of every major newspaper but the reception was generally positive. The papers denounced the crowds' chanting and the FA's lack of actions to protect the players. The latter responded with a statement saying that they were appalled by the ugly scenes and were considering the banning of homophobic chants in stadiums.

31.

The Last Kick

The club standing between the Black Dragons and the Premier League was the one from Derbyshire. They made it to the final after beating Bob's team from Birmingham against all odds, having lost the first leg 2-1 at home. They won on penalties after edging the wild and dramatic second leg 3-2.

The two teams drew both their matches during the season, with the last one being the one that Mrs Moore passed away in, so the final meant even more than a final to Layne and Richard.

Since their public announcement after the semi-final, the pair had received plenty of encouragement from clubs, players past and present, pundits and fans across the world. Many applauded their bravery in coming forward and netizens came up with a campaign with #EveryonesGame to support them. They decried any form of discrimination against any kind of personal characteristics, be it ethnicity, religion, sexuality and so on. It attracted the attention of some top players and they joined in to help spread the word. Several clubs followed the lead by Thames Ditton in announcing new "zero-tolerance" policies and vowed to identify and eject anyone who spread hatred towards players and other fans.

Inevitably, there were abusive messages sent to Layne's social media accounts but as Richard planned they were all referred to the pair's legal team and reported to the police. Richard's own accounts were still set to private so they were immune. However, some posts made their way to the pair's home address, including death threats with bullets and small blades. The authorities took these seriously and advised the pair to be vigilant when they were in public space. The pair restricted their movements to between their home and the Black Dragons' training ground as a precaution.

The Championship playoff final was widely regarded as the most valuable one-off football match in the world, as it unlocked the door to the lucrative Premier League television revenue and parachute payments. It was scheduled to be ten days after the semi-finals and it would be played at the Wembley Stadium – the home of English football.

Richard and plenty of his teammates had never played there before and were obviously very excited. The Black Dragons were allocated a third of the 90,000 tickets, which was over three times the capacity of their own stadium. The players were given ten tickets each for their friends and families – Richard invited Simon, Mark and others from his youth team and other childhood friends. He did ask his parents first but his father flat out refused to come. Layne told him he gave all his share to friends such as Grayson and Jeremy back home.

The Black Dragons' game plan focused on maintaining a compact defensive shape to avoid being exploited by the clever movements from their opponents' key player, England under 21's Adam and quick transitions to catch them off guard at the back, as they had a tendency to over commit in attacks. They also needed to be mindful of not giving free kicks away, as the young Dutch winger Koen was a major threat in those.

Richard was given the key role of tracking Adam and he would be partnered by Tom as Ross was still out injured. George was back in full training but was only rated fifty-fifty by the medical team.

While Richard was really good at positioning and tackling, man-marking wasn't one of his specialities. So he spent a couple of sessions literally playing cat-and-mouse with Alex – the best in business for the Black Dragons. He felt confident he could accomplish his mission – hours studying Adam's movements helped too.

477

The Black Dragons chose to stay at a hotel in Richmond the night before the final despite Wembley was only twenty miles away, in order to ensure the safety and conditions of the players. On the other hand the team from Derbyshire were staying in a hotel out in St Albans.

On match day, the Black Dragons arrived Wembley a couple of hours ahead of kick off and the players were able to have a walk on the pitch to soak up the atmosphere. The weather was lovely – a sunny and warm spring day with a soft breeze, the perfect weather for a game of football.

"We're finally playing here," said Danny on fulfilling one of his football dreams.

"I would prefer winning promotion outright but this would do," Charlie added.

"I can't believe nine of us under 23 lads have made it to Wembley in such a short period of time," Tom said.

"We just have to keep going, it's the Premiership next!" Thomas vowed.

"Why are you so quiet, Richie?" Layne asked.

"I don't know. There's a strange feeling that I'm having," Richard said.

"You're not nervous now all of a sudden, are you?"

"Maybe I am. I feel a little anxious about how the 90,000 spectators would do to us."

"So what? We're used to getting booed at every away game!"

"Isn't that a bit sad? We're expecting to be jeered in our national stadium."

"I feel fine, and you should too!"

"Sorry for bringing you all these troubles, baby."

"Instead of not being together or not being able to play the game here at Wembley? Let them scream – we'll silence them, just like the semis."

Looking at Layne's young but determined impression, Richard's fighting spirits were reignited, "Yes, together we'll break through it all!"

The stadium started being filled up with spectators as the Black Dragons came back for their warm ups. Richard jogged over to the side of the pitch to retrieve a loose ball and was surprised to receive some nice encouragement by opposition fans.

The other team turned up a little bit late for the match – they underestimated the north London traffic and had to rush their warm ups. Richard could see that all three young players Koen, Adam and Oscar were going to start. He had a word with Adam after the warm ups, as they became friends since the England matches. Adam was impressed by Richard's recent actions and they exchanged their best wishes for the game.

David gave his pre-match speech before the team headed out for the big kick off.

"They said we'd never make it to the Football League. They said we'd never last. They said it's impossible for such a small club to survive in the Championship.

"We had no chance. We were odds on to go down. We'd suffer second season syndrome and come back down in no time.

"Where are we now? History is in front of us, our family, friends, supporters, all out there, singing our song, with one voice. They want it all, and they want it now!

"What do we want to show them? Where will our names go in the record books? How do you want us to be remembered?

"We will compete. We will fight. We. Will. Win.

"Fly, You Black Dragons!"

The team reacted with a massive roar – David rarely showed his passions but that was some inspiration!

The two teams walked onto the pitch to a thunderous welcome by the full Wembley Stadium. The stands were split into two, black for the Dragons on one side and white on the other. The teams were introduced to the match officials and various dignitaries on the pitch, and they had their pre-match handshakes.

Layne pointed Richard towards where his guests were and he saw two familiar figures waving at him – his parents were there in the stands! He turned around to Layne looking confused and he just smiled and said, "Enjoy your big day, Richie!"

The Black Dragons started with their fiery keeper Gordon in goal, the calm vice-captain Jonas at right back, the lightning fast Layne on the left, the agile Kieran and composed Thomas in the centre, the unbeatable Richard, energetic Tom and lethal Danny in midfield, and the powerful Charlie, the fit-again and clinical George and skilful Luciano in attack. The bench was made up of Josh the young keeper, the experienced Ethan and the exciting Lewis, Toby, Andrés, Sam and Alex. Other first team players and youth teams were all in the stands to support.

The club from Derbyshire were in their usual 4-1-2-3 formation, with Oscar playing in central defence alongside their experienced captain, Adam as the attacking midfielder slightly left to the middle and Koen on the right wing.

The Black Dragons kicked off the match with their supporters behind them. They tried to dictate the tempo and went for a fast start. Layne launched the ball down the line towards Charlie and his flick on found George inside the area on the left. He hit it with his left foot and forced a save from the keeper, and the Black Dragons had a corner within twenty seconds of play.

Danny sent the ball into the area towards Thomas, but he was beaten in the air by Oscar. His header went as far as Tom at the edge of the box and he volleyed it back towards goal, only to be tipped over by the keeper for another corner kick. Richard jogged towards the corner flag to take the kick. There were the usual jeers from the opposition fans but to his surprise he didn't hear any nasty chanting or comments apart from some wolf whistling, which he considered to be light-hearted – maybe the online campaign had eased the situation a little.

His corner kick was cleared again by Oscar and the ball went out for a throw.

The sixth-place team tried to settle into the game with some slow build ups at the back. The Black Dragons were hunting them down high up the pitch but they managed to keep them away from the ball.

With fifteen minutes gone without scoring the Black Dragons switched to their next plan, which was to engage only after the halfway line. They wanted to draw their opponents out and hit them with quick transitions.

Richard had been marking Adam throughout the opening minutes and was able to restrict him to just a few quick touches. With his room limited his team focused their attacking on their right with Koen. He was up against Layne out wide and given his tendency to cut in, he was a real handful for the young left-footed left back. For the few occasions where Koen ran at him, he focused on showing him wide, which worked as the Dutchman's right foot wasn't particularly impressive.

The Black Dragons did have a chance late into the half as Charlie managed to go behind the defence from Danny's through ball but his shot from a tight angle was saved by the keeper. The first half ended with a scare for the Black Dragons, as the opposition's target man drew a foul from Thomas at the edge of the area but Koen fired it narrowly over the bar.

David was satisfied with the first half performance but he wanted to team to be more decisive when they attacked. There were times when the player on the ball hesitated for a split second and the opportunity was gone.

"Just listen to your instincts, believe in yourself and your teammates," he said.

With the players' energy restored, David wanted to go for another period of fast attacks. The team pressed high up the pitch again with both full backs joining in. The opposition players were forced into clearing the ball up field, which invited the Black Dragons to formulate more attacks. Tom sent the ball to George on the right and his run drew a couple of defenders to him. His cut back to Danny was perfect, but before he could take his shot he was tackled by the hardworking Adam.

The midfielder steadied himself before hitting a fantastic cross field ball to Koen on the right. He controlled it expertly and managed to cut in field, with Layne tracking him closely. The rest of his team supported in numbers and the counter was on. Koen played a clever reverse pass behind Layne to the target man who, having dragged Kieran out of position, flicked the ball back into the path of the box-to-box midfielder. Tom was behind him and he made the decision to take him down professionally before he ran into the box. He was only given a booking as Thomas was, fortunately, the last man.

The free kick was in the perfect position for a left footer like Koen. Gordon set up a five-man wall to cover his left and he stood in the middle of the goal. But Koen's shot was exquisite – he curled it round the wall, hit the inside of the post on Gordon's right and went in! The Black Dragons went a goal behind after fifty-five minutes.

With the significance of the match weighing on them, the young Dragons were a bit disoriented and lost their momentum for the next five minutes. They were fortunate not to concede another goal as the target man's header from a corner was saved on the line by Layne.

David made a change at the hour mark and brought Alex on for George, who just returned from injury and hadn't been effective.

The Black Dragons gathered themselves to re-establish their rhythm. Richard had to leave Adam alone some of the time in order to support the attack – he had to gamble. His involvement improved the variety of attacks and his long ball set Alex up for a volley from the left. He hit it brilliantly but it was deflected wide by a brave Oscar.

The opposition started retreating to their final third. They were defending desperately as the Black Dragons created chances after chances. Charlie, Danny, Alex and Luciano all had opportunities to shoot but they either missed the target or put it straight at the keeper.

With time ticking David brought Andrés on for Kieran. He had to throw everything at it. Richard and Tom dropped a little deeper to allow the wingers and full backs to focus on attacking only.

The nimble Andrés made an immediate impact. He picked up the ball on the right and dribbled past the left back with some brilliant close control. He cut it back for

Luciano just before it went out but the experienced centre back brought the Argentinian attacker down before he could connect with the ball.

Everyone turned to the referee. He thought for a long second and pointed to the spot – the Black Dragons had received a lifeline at the ninetieth minute!

Richard had been the designated penalty taker for the second half of the season but he missed the one in the semi-final last week. He had extra training since and David re-appointed him as the kicker again during his pre-match team talk.

He stepped up and put the ball down once all the appeals were over. Opposition players tried to distract him but Tom stood there and pushed them away. He made up his mind on where he was going for – the bottom left corner. He had his five equal steps back and began his run up. The whole world went quiet as he hit the ball with his right foot.

The keeper dived the right way but the shot was too good for him – it went straight into the bottom left corner!

Richard felt the adrenaline and raced towards the bench to celebrate with David and others.

"Nerves really are for the unprepared Richard, it's not for you!" David shouted passionately.

"Yes Richie yes!" Layne jumped on the back of him and pushed him to the ground before the rest piled on top.

The Black Dragons supporters were ecstatic and they chanted his name repeatedly.

We've got Richard Lucas!

We've got Richard Lucas!

We've got Richard Lucas!

It was quite a feeling when over thirty thousand people were screaming his name. He just loved this club and its fans.

The match went into extra time as the referee blew the final whistle soon after the re-start. It consisted of two 15-minute halves and teams would change ends immediately in between.

The teams had a five-minute break on the pitch. The physios were busy giving players quick massages and assessing their conditions. David decided to replace Charlie by Toby and restore the team's usual shape with Tom moving into central defence. He urged the team to stay focus, maintain their composure and take their chances when they occurred.

"It depends on who wants it more now," he said.

The first period of extra time started with the Black Dragons attacking the end where the opposition fans were, just like the first half of normal time. With both teams low on stamina, the game inevitably slowed down and gaps started to appear. Adam was still making his runs and he kept Richard on his toes all the time. After some good passing in triangles, Danny set Layne free on the left and his cross found the head of Luciano at the far post, but he couldn't keep it on target under pressure from Oscar. Koen had another free kick later on, this time on the right, but his shot hit the outside of the post and out.

The first period of extra time went quickly and the game remained at 1-1.

After some quick drinks, the second period of extra time began. The club from Derbyshire had replaced their target man by a more mobile centre forward and he was making runs deep into the Black Dragons' territory. Balls were launched from the full back areas and one of those resulted in a corner kick on the right.

Koen sent an in-swinging ball towards the near post and Oscar was there first. His header hit the underside of the bar and the loose ball fell to the feet of Adam at the far post, who completed the simplest of tasks to put his team ahead again!

With just five minutes remaining, the Black Dragons had to throw cautions away and went for it. Thomas was playing as an emergency striker with Alex. Jonas and Layne were sending balls into the area but the defence was holding firm. Adam picked up a loose ball and he immediately released Koen in front of him near the centre circle. He was onside as all Black Dragons players were in

484

the other half but Layne managed to catch up with him with the very last drop of his energy and slowed his momentum with a tackle. Richard was back in time and he took the ball off the exhausted winger.

He drove a low ball towards Luciano on the right and his desperate cross deflected high into the area off the left back's head. The keeper came out to collect the seemingly harmless ball but he was beaten to it by a determined Danny diving in – he managed to flick it over the keeper and into the empty net!

The Black Dragons had equalised, again, in the dying minutes of the final!

The stadium erupted as the Black Dragons' supporters celebrated like mad. Danny the goal scorer, however, paid a heavy price as he was completely taken out by the keeper in the process and lay unconsciously on the ground. The medics rushed onto the scene and, to everyone's relief, revived him, but there was no way he could continue with the remaining of the game.

The match resumed after the delay with about two minutes left. Tom intercepted a tired pass out from the centre back and gave the ball to Richard in front of him. With seconds remaining, Richard launched the ball towards Andrés on the left, who controlled it beautifully and took it past the oncoming right back. He eventually forced a corner kick off Oscar.

With time ticking away Andrés took the corner kick quickly but it was headed clear. The ball bounced towards Richard in the centre, and he only had one thing in mind.

He ran towards it for a shot.

It's now or never! Come on Rich! he told himself as he connected with the ball from thirty five yards out.

As if it was in slow motion, he could see every player's impression as the low shot travelled through the crowd – shocked, nervous, hopeful, worried. Nobody was able to react, and the goal keeper haplessly looked on as the ball flew past him and smashed into the top right corner.

The stadium went silent at that split second – Richard could hear clearly the sound of the ball rattling the Wembley net, before the volume completely exploded.

It was a sensational goal!

The Thames Ditton supporters behind the goal went into an absolute frenzy and it brought Richard back from his momentary absence from the world.

He subconsciously ran to the section of the stand where his parents were to celebrate. They were there waving at him, with big smiles on their faces.

The jubilant fans changed the way they chanted his name to reflect his goal.

We've got Rocket Lucas!

We've got Rocket Lucas!

We've got Rocket Lucas!

Richard lifted his arms in the air and soaked up the admiration. It felt wonderful.

Layne caught up with him and jumped onto his back. The rest of the team, including those on the bench, crowded in, euphoric with what just happened.

He was finally convinced that it wasn't a dream when he heard the announcement from the PR system and another roar from the crowd. He had really scored with the last kick of the game to turn the match around. He had really sent the Black Dragons into the Premier League for the first time ever. He had really accomplished his mission.

The match eventually resumed but before the opposition team had a chance to do anything the referee blew the full-time whistle – the Black Dragons had done it, they had won the Championship playoff and with it promotion to the Premier League!

"We've done it!" Tom cried with his fists clenched.

"Yeeeeees!" Charlie could be heard screaming from the bench.

"Fair play, Richard. That was a great goal," Adam offered a handshake. "I'll see you in the Premier League next season."

Richard ran across to join his teammates' celebrations near the technical area. Danny was barely standing a moment ago but he was there jumping up and down like everybody else.

"How dare you taking a shot from there? I brought you to the team for your defensive skills and you gave us two goals in the playoff final!" an excited David said. "You really are my golden boy!"

The Black Dragons supporters were chanting "We are going up" at their stands and the players went over to join them. The stadium began playing the song "We Are The Champions" and Richard jumped on top of the advertising board to lead the singing. Multiple cameras were focussing on him but there wasn't a care about them, he was completely in the spirit.

We are the Dragons, my friends
And we'll keep on fighting to the end
We are the Dragons
We are the Dragons
No time for losers
'Cause we are the Dragons, from Ditton!

The supporters repeated the chorus for a few extra rounds after the music ended before they switched back to chanting Richard's name.

The foreign players managed to put their national flags on – Richard could see those from Argentina, Belgium, Congo, Germany, Norway, Spain plus the other Home Countries. Layne was handed a rainbow flag by a supporter and he duly tied it round his waist before giving Richard a massive hug.

"You're the greatest boyfriend in the world!"

"I'm glad you like it!"

The television crew cut in to invite the man of the match Richard to a pitch side interview. They were looking for Danny the other goal scorer but given his condition they pulled Tom in instead. The two players talked about the goals, the game in general and how they looked forward to playing in the Premier League next season, until Charlie interrupted by spraying champagne onto the party. The completely soaked hostess decided it was best to call time at that point and let the players have their celebrations.

The organisers invited the teams to the middle of the north stand for the trophy presentation at the prestigious Royal Box. The Black Dragons, led by David their manager, followed the team from Derbyshire and climbed the famous 107 steps. The troubled Danny went up with the support of Thomas and Tom either side of him. They received their winners medals in turn and waited at the presentation area for the big moment. Ross the injured club captain, who changed into a full kit with a Welsh flag round his neck, and the retired Michael, who had just started walking unaided following his knee reconstruction surgery and was scheduled to take over the under 18 team the following season, came up last.

The two captains shouted the famous club slogan before lifting the silver trophy.

"Fly, You Black Dragons!"

They held it aloft for the players and fans to celebrate their triumph. Thousands of confetti exploded and fireworks were set off. The exuberant players were jumping for joy, taking turns to kiss and lift the trophy in front of tens of cameras. Richard and Layne had one taken with just the two of them.

The players stayed on the pitch for another good ten minutes before the celebrations moved indoors. Charlie found more champagnes to spray around the dressing room and the team formed a circle to dance to Andrés's emotional singing of "Campeones, Campeones, Olé Olé Olé" – the Spanish song dedicated to winners.

"I've never experienced anything like this," Richard said to the overjoyed Layne, who was downing a bottle of champagne as they sat down on a bench.

"It's all thanks to you and your rocket!" Layne gave him multiple kisses.

For a second, Richard thought he should really stop Layne but he was feeling so good that he didn't want it to end. The pair ended up kissing for a little while.

"Get a room, boys!"

That was from David the manager.

The pair were suitably embarrassed and pulled apart immediately. David gave them a wave and asked them to join him and the others. They giggled with each other and did exactly that.

Pictures and videos of the celebrations were posted to social media and were soon trending. There were the odd insults saying that there was no place for gay players in the Premier League but the pair simply ignored them.

He got a message from his dad saying "Congratulations son, come and visit with Layne one day". He couldn't believe it – he knew Layne must have done something but he just smiled and wouldn't tell.

On top of all of these, Richard received a call from the FA to say he'd been selected by England for the forthcoming European Under 21 Championship, together with Danny, Charlie and Kieran. Layne was also called up by England under 19 for their tournament.

The Black Dragons had a celebration party that night back at the hotel near Richmond Park. The players were given a special shirt with "Premier League" printed on the back by the staff. There was a stage in the centre and when the pair arrived Charlie was there singing "A Little Less Conversation" by Elvis Presley. He was clearly drunk by the sound of it – Thomas was right about his singing, it really was one you couldn't "un-hear".

Having downed a bottle of champagne earlier, Layne wasn't in the best shape himself. But he resumed his drinking straight away with the welcome cocktails.

"Know your limit, baby," Richard tried to slow him down.

"It's the night to let everything go," he said playfully and jumped into the dance floor with the other young players.

Richard wandered around the venue and found Thomas chatting with David, Martin the under 23 team coach, Stuart the Head of Sports Science and Steve their old teammate and now one of the Performance Analysts.

"Here comes the boy with the rocket!" Steve said.

"Thanks for the two goals earlier. Are you ready for the Prem?" David asked.

"Don't worry – he has it all prepared!" Martin said.

"Double session every day for pre-season, right?" Richard with a one-liner to Stuart.

"Well, with the intensity of the Premier League, you're not far off there," Stuart responded with a smile. "I've spoken to my friends at Premier League clubs, their training isn't that much different to ours."

"You trained us hard, in other words," Thomas said.

"There's some truth in that – statistically you guys ran the most distance in the division, with Danny being the top of the league," Steve came up with the stats.

"Did I get the highest pass completion rate by any chance?" Richard asked.

"You're close at 85%, but Michael was the best with 89% followed by Kieran's 88% and Tom's 86%."

"Too many Hollywood balls, you see," Martin said with a pat on Richard's shoulder.

"And shots from way out!" David added while patting Richard's other shoulder.

"You did win the most defensive duels and have the most interceptions amongst midfielders in the league," Steve tried to restore some pride for Richard.

"I guess I didn't disappoint then, gaffer?" Richard with a tactful question.

"Not enough goals, surely," David joked. "I expect at least ten free kick goals a season and you gave me just four!"

"No pressure, Rich!" Thomas joined in.

The group moved on the other topics and had plenty of laughter. Richard excused himself from the discussion later in search for some food. The venue offered plenty of finger foods and he walked around to taste them all. He found a merry Layne dancing with Harry, Andrew and Ryan by the stage. He saw him and gave him a big hug.

"Oh I missed you, Richie!" he said.

David walked onto the centre stage and the team slowly gathered around it.

"Are you having a good night, Black Dragons?" he asked to a loud cheer by the team.

"As you know, we are going to play in the Premier League next season. It's the first time ever for the club and it will surely be tough for all of us. But I have every faith in you, your ability and your spirit. We will give it our best shot and give the supporters a season to remember!"

The crowd gave him another round of applause, while the waiters brought a few pints onto the stage.

"Well, as it's the end of season we have some awards to give out. While we are here, the prize is simple – just come up and down your pint if you hear your name!"

"Oh dear you'd better not win anything!" Layne said to Richard.

"I'll read them out one by one. We'll do the easy ones first: most appearances, Kieran!"

"Most goals with sixteen, Luciano!"

"Most assists with eighteen, Danny!"

All three players went up on stage while the others chanted their names. Kieran and Luciano downed their pints with ease but Danny wasn't allowed to drink after his concussion during the match.

"Next up, goal of the season. We had lots of contenders but who would argue with the rocket today? It's you, Richard!"

"I'd love to see you downing this one, Richie!" the rowdy Charlie couldn't stop laughing, while the team gave Richard a big round of applause and urged him on to the stage.

We've got Richard Lucas!

We've got Richard Lucas!

We've got Richard Lucas!

"Come on Richie! The stage is yours!" Layne shouted.

Richard slowly walked up to the stage, shook David's hand and picked up his pint. He downed it in one go, to the cheers from everybody.

He had a few drinks already that evening and downing a pint was a really bad idea.

He managed to get back to where he was standing with Layne, but seconds after that the dizziness struck him and he passed out once he reached the nearest sofa. He heard lots of laughter when he was down; someone was talking to him but he couldn't hear a word; he felt someone kissed him on the cheek – he hoped that was Layne but he couldn't tell.

He didn't know how long it was but he gradually woke up a while later. The party was still going strong and he could see Layne sitting next to him, looking at him with his lovely big round eyes.

"You're such a lightweight," he said softly. "Get up and have some water."

"Were you here with me all the time?"

"Of course, I need to take care of you too."

"Have I missed anything? Did everyone laugh at me?"

"We had a group photo taken with you passed out in the background, it should be trending on social media now."

"Oh really? How amusing…"

Richard stuck to water for the rest of the night and felt better. He learnt that Danny was named as the players' player of the year, and David downed the pint for him, to the delight of everyone.

The party ended at midnight. Richard had to carry the completed wasted Layne to their room and helped him to bed.

"It was such a wonderful day, Richie. Thanks for making it happen!" Layne said.

"I still can't believe it went in, but thank God it did," he said as he lay down next to Layne.

"You are God's gift to me," Layne rolled over and rested his head on Richard's chest.

"I've been thinking about our journey here. You were everything for me in the last four years, be it football or life. I couldn't have done it all without you. Thank you, baby."

"Back at the Stevenson's, have you ever imagined that we'll be together and playing in the Premier League one day?"

"Yes but I thought the chance was very slim."

"How slim? What is it in probability?"

"Maybe one percent?"

"Mum used to say something like that too, but with you it became possible."

"That's because you're there to motivate me."

"No, everything started with you, Richie!"

"What do you mean? You must be drunk."

"I'm going to tell you this. I was having a trial at the Bristol academy when they played against the Dragons four years ago…"

"When I made my under-18 debut?"

"Yes. I saw you in action and… all I could think about since then was you."

"Which means…?"

"You are my crush, my one and only one, Richie!"

"So you fancied me before we even met?"

"Hehe, I wouldn't go that far. I just wanted to see you again and get to know you. It turns out to be the best decision of my life!"

"You… are such a silly boy, but I like how it went!"

"Our story will go on forever, right?"

"I'm a hundred percent sure on that!"

32.

Top Tier

"We are Premier League!"

"A bit more conviction please, Richard."

"We are Premier League!!"

"Mm… Remember the emotion when you won the playoff, the moment you scored that goal, then say it out load."

"… WE. ARE. PREMIER. LEAGUE!!"

"That's it, good take!" said the director. "Thanks and good luck for the season Richard, we're done here."

Richard was at the west London studio of one of the major media companies, recording their promotion clips for the new Premier League season. Like the previous year, he did the individual videos used to introduce the line-up before every live game with his teammates but this year he was one of those chosen to perform some extras. Charlie was shouting "We're here to win" before him and Danny was simply asked to perform his double clap and shush celebration.

The players were wearing the new home kit for the season, which was the traditional black shirt with a stylish dragon scale pattern and a golden yellow collar, completed with plain black shorts and golden yellow socks. They also had new colour combos for their travels: a red shirt with layers of diagonal patterns in black, matched by a pair of black shorts and red socks; and a white shirt decorated by multiple shades of grey, navy shorts and white socks. The goal keepers had a choice of golden yellow or pink outfit, both subtly decorated with tree branch patterns.

The club had also released their new logo following a competition over the summer. The traditional shield had been replaced by a two-dimensional circular design, which had a rising dragon in front of a black backdrop in the middle, surrounded by a golden ring with the letters TDFC printed over it, at ninety degrees apart. It was easy on the eyes and much more digital-friendly – it looked beautiful as the face of the club's mobile phone app and its black-and-white version was used for the away shirts.

Richard walked over to the studio next door to see if Layne had completed his part. He was there, with his left foot stepping on a block about two feet high, tying his rainbow-coloured shoelaces, while whispering "It's everyone's game" to the camera. Being the only two openly gay football players in the top division as well as the country, there were plenty of attentions from the media and Layne wanted to make good use of them to promote a more inclusive environment. Richard supported his ideal but he politely declined to take part – he didn't want to be seen as a celebrity couple.

The director was happy with the take and Layne came over to meet Richard.

"Am I the last one to finish?" he asked with a smile.

"Probably. We'd better hurry back to the coach, we're heading over to the other studio in Stratford next."

After another few hours of recording, where Layne performed a rainbow flick for the inclusivity campaign, the pair returned to their riverside apartment in Surbiton.

"It's been such a long day! Media day is more draining than a training session!" Richard said.

"I think it's fine. It'll be fun to see the clips on air during the season!"

"I'll be cringing to see my goal celebration clip, I was like a robot… shall we have a cup of tea before unpacking the rest of the stuff from Greece?"

"Oh Richie, can't you help me with mine?"

"Only if you make me one of your nice brew."

"I can certainly do that!"

While Layne prepared the beverages, Richard opened one of their two suitcases and unloaded its content: plenty of clothes, a deflated football and lots of souvenirs.

The pair had a two-week holiday in Greece during off season after their exploits with the junior national teams, where Layne played a major part in winning the under 19's European Championship while Richard's under 21's lost to Germany on penalties in the semi-final. They only returned to London the day before the photo shoot. The annual team holiday was cancelled for the first time, as everyone's commitment was too much for the organiser Sam to shoehorn into.

Richard and Layne started their break with two nights in Athens, where Richard enjoyed visits to the historic spots: they spent a day up at the Parthenon, then went to the Panathenaic stadium, where they had a race on the same track as the first ever Olympics, before heading to the Pireas district for a stadium tour of the biggest football club in the country.

They then flew to the island of Santorini for a week, staying at a hotel with multiple whitewashed cave houses on the cliff top near the town of Oia. The view from the hotel was ridiculously scenic – sitting at the north of the reversed moon-shaped island, it overlooked the underwater caldera at the centre and the small islands (and cruise ships) in the west. The pair visited other towns and attractions on the island during the day riding their rented scooter but insisted on returning to the hotel in the afternoon for the magnificent sunset from their private swimming pool every day.

"I'm happy to stay here forever," Layne said after their last sunset there.

"We can always visit again. Remember it's your dream destination next," Richard pointed out.

"Oh I can't wait! Have you decided if we're going to THAT beach or not?"

"Why are you so keen on going to a nudist beach?"

"I just want to explore, you can stay textile if you're scared!"

"I'm not scared, just not really into it."

"It's such a shame that the full moon party is not until next month."

"Maybe it's a blessing in disguise, I can't imagine drinking nonstop for so long!"

The pair's final stop in Greece was the island of Mykonos. They stayed at a romantic boutique hotel near the Super Paradise Beach, which was once considered the most famous homosexual beach of Greece, if not the world. Layne had long wanted to visit but Richard kept him waiting until he was over the legal age for drinking.

They were a little disappointed when they found that the beach had become more tourists oriented and attracted plenty of straight sun seekers. So on their second day on the island, they went to the nearby Elia beach which, according to the locals, had taken over from Super Paradise as the gay beach on the island. They weren't disappointed this time, "like-minded" visitors were everywhere and the pair felt completely at home.

Layne originally heard that Elia was the beach for the nudists but with it being crowded he didn't see plenty there. One reveller recommended him to go over the rocks for Agrari, which would be quieter. He also annoyed Richard when he gave Layne a creepy "360 degree scan".

But the pair followed the advice and found the much more peaceful Agrari beach, which did indeed look like a paradise.

Layne was going to go natural right away but Richard stopped him. He wasn't comfortable with showing his naked boyfriend to other people.

"I just want to keep you to myself," he said.

"That's very sweet Richie, but I want to have a full body tan…"

"Mm… maybe only if we can find a quiet corner?"

The pair did exactly that and found a secluded spot at the very end of the beach for Layne to enjoy his sunbathing. Richard was glad to have fulfilled his partner's desire but couldn't help to be on the lookout for any people passing by – there were some, but they were minding their own businesses and couldn't care less, which made Richard's rush to cover Layne up with a beach towel rather embarrassing.

They spent the rest of their holidays in Elia and Agrari before flying back to London via Athens.

Layne wasn't impressed by Richard's choice of flying budget airline after they left on a very early ferry only to learn that the connecting flight was severely delayed.

"We're literally millionaires, why can't we do better than this?" he moaned.

"I get that now. I'll loosen up the strings in the future," Richard admitted his misjudgement as he suffered from a massive headache from his travel sickness. "I thought we'd better control our spending after committing to buy the house but sometimes it's worth paying the extra."

The pair had agreed to buy a property together in east Esher, a detached house a few streets from the school they went to and about ten minutes' drive from the training ground and stadium complex. Layne sold Mrs Moore's flat in Richmond to fund it and completion was due in August. But they won't be moving in until October as they had work planned to refresh the interior to their liking.

The Thames Ditton first team reported for pre-season training the day after the photo shoot. David and the coaching team welcomed the players back and Dr Edwards the chairman made an appearance to announce his expectations for the club's first ever season in English football's top tier, the Premier League.

"Welcome back from your summer break, Dragons!" he said, to the applause of the players. "Here we are in our maiden season at the Premier League, well done again for winning the playoff final but the challenge is now on – we will face unprecedented difficulties, we will play against the very best teams, and we will inevitably lose plenty of matches. But our mission is to learn from these and evolve to become one of those very best teams. I fully believe our principles, our spirits, and our efforts will get us there – I believe in all of you! It's time to fly, The Black Dragons!"

The players roared in response – Richard felt his adrenaline rising, he couldn't wait to start playing at the highest level with his friends and teammates.

Once the team's energetic response settled, David came into the fore and announced, "We had a very good look at the squad and we decided that we would make minimal changes to it. You won us the place at the top table and it's only fair for you to have the chance to show your worth. As you already know, there were some changes but the core of the team remains. Work hard in training as you always do and we'll show the world who we are!"

In addition to Michael's retirement, the club decided not to renew the contracts of Ethan and Dennis and they reluctantly sold Jonas the first choice right back as he wanted to have a go at his native Bundesliga. To install some top level know how into the team, Miles the Director of Football signed former Welsh international centre back Graham from the Premier League side in east London. While he might be on the wrong side of thirty, his vast experience would be immensely welcomed in the dressing room. Four under 23 players were also promoted to complete the squad: Viktor the composed right back from Sweden, Harry the tiny and tricky attacking midfielder, Andrew the speedy winger and Ryan the deadly centre forward / second striker.

Several players took advantage of the vacant squad numbers, with the ambitious Charlie securing the prestigious number ten. Richard obtained a list of the new twenty-five-man squad:

Goalkeeper:
1 Gordon Blackford, 12 Josh Taylor, 33 Jack Simpson

Defender:
2 Mazibo Ndinga, 3 Lewis Adams, 4 Kieran Rowe, 5 Thomas Bond, 6 Graham Pugh, 17 Layne Moore, 22 Viktor Svensson, 28 Thorsten Strømme

Midfielder:
8 Tom Nelson, 14 Danny Westwood, 15 Ross Davies, 16 Richard Lucas, 23 Toby Archer, 30 Harry Smith

Forward:
7 Andrés Iglesias, 9 George Walton, 10 Charlie Ranger, 11 Luciano Romero, 19 Ryan King, 24 Samuel Hughes, 31 Andrew Harding, 47 Alex Knight

During the summer break, Richard and Layne were offered a contract extension by the club that included an entry-level Premier League salary, with an option to scale it back if the team got relegated. Jon their agent requested the addition of a release clause – an amount in transfer fee that other clubs could pay to trigger the acceptance from the Black Dragons to sell the player. The club was quite happy to set Richard's at £25 million but Jon had to negotiate hard to get Layne's to £35 million. Both of them accepted the offers and signed their new five-year contracts, but they heard that not every player had done the same.

Similar to previous seasons, the team had four weeks of pre-season training followed by two weeks of friendly matches. With just twenty teams in the Premier League comparing to twenty four in the Championship, the team had eight less league matches to play and so the plan was to maximise the players' fitness level for each game while putting less attention on the ability to recover quickly. David said that with the highly energetic style the team played with, injuries would be inevitable and so there would be playing opportunities for every player. He urged them to be ready to step in when called upon.

"All of us may only have one shot at the highest level, let's make the most of it in every single match," he said.

At the end of the first session that invoked lots of testing and some general fitness training, the pair were invited to a discussion with David and Carly. It was about their standing as the only two openly gay footballers in the country. They had an uneventful summer in terms of abuses but the club expected them to pick up again when the season started.

"Sadly, fans of the Premier League are not an upgrade from the Championship," said Carla.

The club had reaffirmed its commitment to inclusivity in its communications and would continue to operate a zero tolerance policy for any discriminations, but David asked the pair to expect atmosphere at away games to be hostile.

"There will also be moments when your sexuality is to blame for your performance, even from our own fans," he added. "We had them on racial and religious grounds in the past, and this will be no different."

"We understand that. We will ignore them," Richard said.

"I would suggest you not to provoke the crowd by kissing Layne in front of them," Carla made reference to the infamous playoff semi-final where Richard broke the silence and came out.

"Why not? Players have all sorts of weird and wonderful celebrations anyway!" Layne said, cheekily.

"It's only our recommendation, you don't have to follow, but I'll say don't give them ammunition," Carla responded with a smile, which looked a little suspicious.

"It's fine, we won't do it," Richard said.

"Do let us know if things get out of hands though, whether it's in the stadium, on the streets or online, okay?" David closed off the conversation.

"That was rather awkward," said Layne when the pair were driving home.

"I guess they foresee the issues and are trying to give us a heads-up. It won't be easy."

"We're always prepared for that. I'm a little worried about Ryan. Do you think he will come out publicly too? Those nasty fans may be too much for him."

"True. He's easily distracted by the crowd as it is. We need to give him some advice if that's his intention."

"Did you hear that he has broken up with his boyfriend?"

"Oh the great-looking Swedish boy? That's a shame, they looked very sweet together. Do you know why?"

"Not the exact details, but I think he wanted Ryan to spend more time with him but he couldn't."

"That's going to hurt. He adores that boy."

"Yes, it's not easy for him."

Richard got a text from Tom when they got home, which said "Hey Rich I didn't know you're a nudist?" with an eyes emoji.

"What about it?" he replied.

"Just check you two's favourite paper today."

"Oh dear," Richard thought as he clicked into the tabloid's website.

There they were on the front page, with the headline "Gay footballers went all out in Greek paradise". Richard clicked into the article and, after scrolling through numerous ads, saw a picture of him and Layne sunbathing in Agrari, with their bottoms blurred by mosaics.

"We were done by the paparazzies, baby."

"Let me see," Layne grabbed Richard's phone to have a look. "Did you take your trunks off too?"

"I didn't and that's the worst bit! They made it look like I did with those mosaics!"

"Mm... what can we do about this?"

"Probably not much, again," Richard said with a sigh, "but I told you not to do it, you never listen!"

"How is it my fault that some creepy paparazzies took photos of us when we're on a private holiday? I need to live!"

"But we're their target, we should have been more careful."

"Now that they've done it, we can only learn our lesson and go somewhere more secluded next time."

"Oh that's what Carla's smile was about, she must have seen it before the meeting! How embarrassing! Everyone can see them too!"

"Well, your body isn't something to be ashamed of, Richie!"

"That's not the point! I don't need to show everybody!"

The pair continued to argue over the photo, until Richard decided it was pointless and took a timeout in the spare bedroom. He soon fell into an afternoon nap.

He woke up to the smell of cooking and when he came to the kitchen he saw Layne battling with the pots and pans – it seemed like he was trying to fry a couple of steaks in one pan and some eggs in another, with a pot of overflowing penne pasta next to them.

"Stop laughing and help me!"

"I thought you don't need me," Richard referred to one of the lines Layne said during their argument.

"I do, I always do!"

"Fine. Just move over and watch."

Richard took over the cooking and served up the dishes soon after. Layne was happily waiting at the other side of the kitchen island, which also served as their casual dining area.

"They look delicious! How did you turn a mess into a meal so quickly?"

"Shame there isn't time to make a fresh pizzaiola sauce, but this will do."

"Are you not mad at me now?"

"I'm not over it yet. Still don't know how I'd react to the boys in training tomorrow."

After a rather quiet dinner, Richard went back to the spare bedroom for some reading. Layne came in when it was nearly bedtime.

"Stop being mad at me," he asked softly as he climbed on top of Richard.

"What do you want now?" Richard didn't look impressed. He had calmed down from the photo incident already but he played along to see what Layne was up to.

"You know what," Layne said while moving Richard's hands to his bottom. "Maybe everyone can see these online, but only you can touch them... and more."

Richard didn't say anything, he just enjoyed the treat at hand.

"Remember your promise when we first got together. You said we'll resolve all our differences before we go to bed every night? Forgive me Richie, pretty please~"

Richard smiled and gave Layne a good squeeze.

"Hehe," Layne giggled. "I take that as a yes then!"

He then started kissing Richard and they soon snuggled up as normal.

As expected, the pair endured numerous teasing and taunting from their teammates during training the next day. The usual suspects such as Charlie and Andrew made fun of them at every opportunity, but it was peak when Rachel the physio commented on how nicely tanned Layne's bottom was in front of everyone in the massage room.

"How come yours is not as tanned?" asked Alex, who was on the massage bench next to Richard.

"Because I didn't go naked on the beach!"

"You can't deny it now, we have photographic evidence!" said Jack, who was on the other side.

"They're trying to mislead you..."

"I can't believe you've changed so much Rich, from falling asleep watching porno to swinging it on a nudist beach!" Tom said from the far side of the room, followed by another round of laughter from the rest.

"You showed him the wrong porno!" Charlie jumped in.

"Let him off lads," said Howard the physio massaging Richard. "His cheek is hot enough to fry some eggs now!"

"Layne!!" Richard shouted while wrapping his completely blushed face with a towel.

"Sorry Richie," Layne replied with a cheeky tone. "I'll let you cover up next time we go."

"I didn't do it!"

"Yeah right 'Richie', we trust you on that," Danny said as he walked past Richard for the exit.

The team had a session on tactics a couple of weeks into pre-season training.

David opened it by introducing the "pass network" chart – one that is used to demonstrate a team's most common passes and the number of passes in each position made throughout a number of games. Using data from the previous season, the midfield three were clearly the busiest and the most frequently used route was the one from centre midfield to the left full back. While it was a useful tactic, it quickly consumed the stamina of those involved and then the play slowed down. At the same time some players were isolated and they ended up breaking out of the team formation in order to get a touch.

He then talked through the charts for all other Premier League teams and highlighted the difference in style. What he wanted the team to achieve was to involve all players in a narrow and tight patch of the pitch to share the workload and carve out openings for crosses or through balls. To do that every single player would need to be fully concentrated at all times and be able run nonstop for long period of the game.

He went on to describe a new tactic: he wanted the front three to drop deeper together to create quick passing triangles with the midfielders to squeeze the play into the middle third, while both full backs sprinted into the space behind. Once the ball was in a crossing position, all three forwards plus two of the midfielders would attack the box. The key elements were the timing of through balls and the quality of crosses. It was a big gamble as the defence would be almost completely open if they lost the ball, but it was one that David believed to be worthwhile, especially when the team were desperate for a goal.

"Are we not open to through balls behind us if we push too far up? We're not the fastest," Thomas asked.

"Good question," David said. "That's why when we lose the ball, all front players need to carry on running and press immediately. We cannot allow the other team a second to settle and pick their through passes."

"That sounds suicidal when we're up against Premier League teams. Shouldn't we focus on not conceding in our first season in the division?" Ross commented.

"It's reasonable to play safe but I believe we'll end up losing more games that way. Plenty of promoted team did that before – the bigger teams have developed ways to break them down. And once you go a goal behind against them there's normally no way back. I'd rather we take the initiative and have a go," David explained.

"I think the main difference at the highest level is the ability to take chances, if we can create some good ones early on and score first we can really change the dynamics of the game," Richard added. "It's also easier to defend when we're a goal up."

"That's right. If we let the other team dictate the tempo, we will just be tiring ourselves chasing the ball with nothing to show our supporters," David agreed.

"I still think it is too risky," Ross wasn't convinced.

"We'll probably have to agree to disagree," David said, "but rest assured, we won't be going gung-ho all the time. It'll be for particular periods of the games and we need to adapt to the flow."

After four weeks of tough pre-season training, the Black Dragons first team headed off to the Czech Republic for a training camp. They stayed at a large hotel in the south of Prague for ten days and played against three top division sides from the area.

They beat the reigning champions of the Czech First League from the capital 3-1, with two goals coming from their new tactic in the second half. But first choice goal keeper Gordon suffered a hip injury near the end of the game and faced being off for up to six months.

A makeshift team then overcame the side from Plzen 2-0, before the strongest XI defeated another team from Prague by the same score line.

The club arranged a meet-and-greet buffet at their hotel the evening before their return for the several hundred supporters who followed them all the way to the Czech Republic. Richard and Layne met plenty of fans throughout the event, signing autographs and having their pictures taken. Geoff, one of the most loyal supporters that Richard met a few times when he travelled to away matches during his time at the youth teams, was there as well.

"Hey Panenka boy," he said when he approached the pair.

"Great to see you Geoff, you keeping well?" Richard said as they shook hands.

"All good! You've been one of our outstanding players last season, it was the happiest moment of my life when that shot went in!"

"It was probably mine too," Richard said while instinctively looked into Layne's direction.

"How're you two lads doing? Did you have a hard time from other supporters?"

"We nearly always get booed anyway, but we haven't played enough games since coming out to feel any difference."

"It's a shame, isn't it? You're probably better examples for youngsters than those multi-millionaire playboys!"

"Maybe we'll get there one day."

Geoff moved on to talk about the friendly matches and, just like what he did in the past, kept rumbling on and on. Layne excused himself when some young fans asked him for autographs, and poor Richard stayed in the conversation for another half an hour or so, until Geoff was taken away by his son.

"I saw you were Geoffed again?" Tom said when Richard joined him and Charlie for some water.

"You guys could have come and rescued me!"

"It's great for players to talk to fans… especially if you are doing it for us!" Charlie laughed.

The team flew back to London the next morning. They had four days to prepare for their last friendly match against a top division team from Belgium at The Dragons Stadium.

Richard and Layne picked up the keys for their new home after training one day. It would need plenty of renovation work to become the modern home the pair dreamt of, but they could start visualising their future there.

"I want to put the grand piano by the bay window in the front room," Layne suggested.

"That'll be good, we can have some comfy chairs there for me and the audience!" Richard agreed.

"Shall we turn one of the bedrooms upstairs into a home gym?"

"Sure. We can also put all the shirts we swapped with other players on the walls?"

"Do we need a cabinet for the trophies and medals?"

"Baby we don't have that many yet..."

"We need to be ready for the future!"

The pair spent the rest of their day discussing their plan for the house and Richard was really looking forward to their time there.

The Black Dragons eased past their opponents in their last friendly before the Premier League season started. Goals from Danny, Charlie and George early in the second half were enough to secure their 3-1 victory in their first outing at the expanded stadium hosting 11,000 supporters. Both Richard and Layne played the majority of the match and felt good physically and mentally for the challenges ahead.

With the season opener at home scheduled at Sunday lunch time, Richard visited his parents with Layne after training on Friday. His dad never formally accepted their relationship but became open to see them since the end of last season. Mrs Moore's passing seemed to have an impact on him and he invited the pair to dinner during the summer break. It was awkward to begin with but the cheerfulness of Layne soon broke the ice and the family was reformed. Mr Lucas senior offered his help when he learnt that the couple were buying their first house and negotiated a good price for them.

Mrs Lucas roasted some Bavarian schweinshaxe with beer gravy and mashed potatoes for an early Al fresco dinner in the garden. It was a dish she learnt and had plenty of practice in while living in Munich and was the one that Richard missed the most. It was thoroughly enjoyable and he felt that the distance and the barrier between him and his father were disappearing slowly, which made him very happy.

After one last training session on Saturday, it was finally happening – the first ever game in the Premier League for Richard, Layne, their friends and Thames Ditton Football Club.

Their first opponent was one of the longest serving clubs in the top flight, the blue team from Merseyside. David had the full team available apart from the injured Gordon and he opted for the more experienced eleven of Josh, Maz, Lewis, Kieran, Graham, Richard, Ross, Danny, Luciano, Charlie and George. Layne was on the bench with Jack, Thomas, Tom, Sam, Andrés and Alex. Only Graham and Luciano had experience at the top flight and twelve of the match day squad were from the Black Dragons' academy.

"You'll be the first openly gay player in the Premier League ever then, Richie," Layne said upon hearing the final line-up.

"It makes no difference to me. I'm just another footballer having his top tier debut."

"That's true. Let's win the game regardless!"

The players had their warm up and Richard spotted a few new banners being hung up in the stands. Some of them were player specific and one illustrated his best known celebration, the kiss in the playoff semi-final, with the words "Football knows no boundaries". He felt fairly embarrassed but was warmed by the support.

"So," David started his pre-match talk when the players were back in the changing room. "Here we are. The Premier League. Our destination. What we've been working for. I don't need to tell you how proud we all are – the club, the coaching team and the fans. We have created our own history and this is our next chapter. Go out there and show them that we are not here for fun, we are here to win every single game and be the team that everyone fears!

"Fly, you Black Dragons!"

The home team kicked off with their supporters behind them as usual. After a few short passes, Luciano found some space on the right but the goal keeper beat George to his cross and collected the ball. He sent a long drop kick up field towards his centre forward Carl, who headed it down for the number ten and he, without any hesitation, chipped the ball over the defence towards his right. The supremely quick right winger was on the chase ahead of Lewis and he poked it in against the hapless Josh. The Black Dragons had conceded their first goal in the top division within two minutes of play!

"That was lightning quick," Richard thought. "Is that the difference at the top level? The utilisation of their natural strengths and timing, we can't do much against that."

"Welcome to the Prem," said Carl as he ran past Richard. He was part of the England under-21 team and Richard knew him well.

"Don't worry about that," said Graham the experienced centre back. "Settle down with some possession, track your players and don't panic."

The Dragons restarted the match with some assured passes and slowly got back into the game. Graham pulled the back line deeper to counter the pace of the winger and it gave the visitors more space in midfield to explore, which forced Richard and Ross to sit behind more. They succeeded in keeping the attack at bay but it also limited the options upfront, with the wingers tracking back all the time and George completely isolated. The half ended 1-0 to the visitors.

"It wasn't too bad," said David. "We had a lapse of concentration at the beginning but recovered well. Stick to the same approach and wear them down, we'll decide the match late on."

The second half played out as David planned: the Dragons continued to play safe and frustrated the away side. He brought Layne, Sam and Alex on for Lewis, Luciano and George at the seventy fifth minute and that was the signal for the onslaught. The team moved into their shape and started putting quick passes together in the opposition half, with attackers and midfielders exchanging balls and positions regularly, and the full backs getting ready to pounce.

After a series of passes in the right half of the pitch, Richard found Charlie on the edge of the area on the left and he dribbled towards the centre, taking the right back with him. He created some room for a shot and just before he pulled the trigger, he chipped the ball towards the left, where there were acres of space. Layne ran in at full speed and he smashed the ball into the back of the net to level the match!

The stadium erupted as Layne celebrated with a knee slide towards the West Stand.

"We want Moore! We want Moore! We want Moore!" fans were screaming his name repeatedly.

The visitors were deflated at not getting their three points and the Black Dragons took full advantage. Following another string of quick passes, Richard sent the ball left to Layne, who feinted a cross as he controlled it, brought it inside the area and drove a low cross towards the penalty spot. Sam was there to lay it off for Danny to put the left footed winner away, in emphatic fashion!

The response from the stands was deafening. Everyone was on their feet with their arms in the air. Even the usually calm Danny lost his cool and jumped into the crowd to celebrate. It was simply amazing to have scored at the last minute to complete the turn around and pick up their first ever victory at the top level!

The match ended after another five minutes of continuous chanting by the home supporters, as the away team struggled to overcome the turn of momentum.

David, the coaching team, and the substitutes all ran onto the pitch at the final whistle to celebrate. Fans were singing the winning tune non-stop and Richard and his teammates soaked up the fantastic atmosphere.

"I can get used to this," Charlie said.

"What a feeling!" Danny added.

"Well done lads! What a turnaround!" Tom joined in from the bench.

"The new plan works so well! Great finish, Layney boy!" Richard said as the pair hugged.

"I've captained myself in my fantasy team!" Layne whispered.

"You did well there, but I have captain Westwood!"

511

"Oh my, you'll be ahead of me then, he got man of the match!"

"Mind the gap, baby!"

The players did a lap of honour for the supporters before going back to the dressing room. Richard, Layne and Danny were stopped by the match day reporter for a live interview. After the usual questions on the game, the hostess at the studio asked how Richard and Layne felt to be the first openly gay players in the top flight.

"I honestly don't really want to talk about this," Richard said. "We're just two boys playing the game we love. Sexuality doesn't come into it."

The hostess was rather embarrassed by that response and she apologised for posing the question in the first place. The reporter then quickly rounded off the interview by asking Danny about the season ahead and presented him the man of the match trophy.

"That was a bit blunt Richie?" asked Layne afterwards.

"I just don't want us to stand out and become the target of those vicious abuses," Richard replied.

"I think that's fair enough mate," Danny said. "We should all be judged by our performance on the pitch and nothing else."

"Couldn't agree more!" Richard nodded.

David was very happy with the players' efforts and of course the result.

"It's a very tough league but we showed that we are capable of competing here," he said. "Great start, and onto the next game!"

33.

Mentality

"Look at you Rich! You must have worked really hard on these, they're solid!" said Tom as he patted Richard's biceps after his latest reps. The players were having an additional gym session after regular training.

"It's all part of Stuart's program for my upper body strengths," Richard explained. "He said I need to be stronger to play my role well in the Prem."

"Yes those players you came up against on Sunday were as fit as a fiddle! They're not even known to be a tough side!"

"How did you feel on Sunday Charlie?" Richard asked as Charlie joined the conversation. "You are stronger than the veteran right back?"

"He was no match on strengths but he managed to stay tight on me the whole game. I guess that's what experience gives you."

"We did create two goals down that end, did we not?" Tom asked.

"That's purely because the right winger was tired and didn't track back," Richard said. "The boss played a blinder by introducing Layne late on."

"How will we approach the next game? Do you think we'll go with the same tactics?" Charlie asked.

"They are very compact and hard to beat at their home ground, we'll need to tempt them out and go for a quick break," Richard said.

"Plenty of running then!"

"I don't mind that. I just want to play!" said Tom.

The Black Dragons travelled to the south coast on Saturday to play against the team from Hampshire. The host drew their opening match against the team from Tyneside and were keen to register their first win of the season.

David recognised the opposition's highly effective 4-5-1 formation but he identified their right hand side to be the one to exploit, as their tricky winger Imad wasn't keen on defending and the attacking right back Miguel had a tendency to over-commit. They did have their industrious captain Jay in right centre midfield to cover that gap but David believed it was still worth focusing on it.

"The key is the understanding between you two on our left," he told Charlie and Layne during his team talk the day before. "We are likely to win this match if you two can attack and defend as a unit more than your opponents."

The starting eleven was unchanged apart from Layne replacing Lewis. Tom was again on the bench while Harry could make his senior debut if called upon.

David's plan was in jeopardy when the team news came out, as the home team went for a 4-4-2 and started their captain Jay on the right!

"They've clearly done their homework and saw Layne as a threat. We'll have to carry on overloading our left and improvise," said David.

The match started and the hosts launched their offensive, backed by the strong vocal support from the stands. They were keen to go from their right hand side, with Jay and Miguel sending crosses into the box for the front two – a traditional centre forward and a hardworking runner. Josh, Graham and Kieran just about managed to defend the crosses and Richard and Ross were there to sweep up the loose balls. They tried to initiate a fight back but struggled to find a route out under the home team's aggressive high press. There was no time to think and their rushed forward passes failed to find their targets.

After another five minutes of intense pressure, the Black Dragons finally got a breather when they won a goal kick.

"We need to settle down," Graham said to Richard and Ross.

"They are not giving us any time to do that," said the captain.

"You need to bypass us," said Richard. "Let's be brave and take the game to them."

"Good call, get Charlie and George to hold it up for us," Graham agreed.

"Sounds like a plan, I'll let them know," Ross confirmed.

The Black Dragons started utilising the wide areas bypassing the press and got back into the game. Players provided support behind the ball for those on it and together they managed to exploit the space out wide. Layne received a few through balls and his crosses caused havoc in the area, with both George and Luciano close to opening the score.

The hosts reacted by having both Jay and Miguel back to guard that area, but Danny had other ideas. He received the ball from Richard on the edge of the penalty box after another string of fast exchanges, rolled the ball to the left to feint a pass to Charlie but flipped it back to his right for a quick side-footed shot with minimal backlift. The keeper was flat footed and could only watch on as the ball curled into the top right corner. The double clap celebration followed.

"Captain Westwood strikes again," Richard referred to his fantasy team selection when he walked back to the dressing room with Layne at half time.

"I guess you claim the assist then? Well done for opening your account!"

"Good reaction from their high press and great skill for the shot, Danny," David said at his team talk. "Keep that going for another twenty minutes and switch to protection mode, okay?"

The hosts made one substitution at half time: one of the defensive midfielders was replaced by their usual right winger Imad, and the captain Jay moved back into his normal position. They planned to attack and their target was clear – they would test the defensive capabilities of Layne.

515

The tricky Imad received the ball soon after the restart and brought it up against the young left back. He went to the outside after a few step overs, with Layne following him closely. Then he shifted his body weight discreetly and moved the ball to his left with the outside of his left foot in a very smooth motion. Layne wasn't expecting that and lost his balance completely. Imad got a free ride into the centre but he was swiftly taken down by Kieran. The referee blew his whistle and gave the home team a free kick, some 35-yards away from goal. He also showed Kieran a yellow card.

Jay was a well-known set piece specialist and he took the direct free kick. It flew over the wall towards the top right corner beautifully but luckily for the Black Dragons, it bounced off the post and went out.

"We need to do something about that," Richard discussed with Ross. "I drop deeper to block his route to the middle."

The change nullified the immediate threat from Imad and the team traded half chances for the next period of play. It involved plenty of movements at both ends and Richard had to be on high alert throughout. Layne managed to win a few duels against Imad but he was also booked for a mis-timed challenge.

David made three changes after seventy minutes and replaced Layne, Kieran and Luciano with Lewis, Thomas and Tom. He wanted to refresh the team in order to protect the one goal lead without taking any unnecessary risk.

With time running out, the hosts intensified their attack and tried to force the issue with direct passes to the two strikers, who seemed to have endless energy and kept stretching the Black Dragons' defence with their clever runs.

The away team successfully repelled the waves of attacks, but were simply hanging on, waiting for the final whistle. A minute into added time, Imad picked up a headed clearance from Thomas and dribbled past Lewis with a double feint. He dropped his left shoulder as Richard approached him and drove towards the area at pace. Richard might be tough to go past in an one-to-one but he was nowhere near unbeatable in a race. He had no choice but to bring Imad down before he entered the box. The referee blew for a free kick, and didn't hesitate to add Richard's name to his little black book.

The free kick was on the edge of the area, perfect for the expert Jay. The whole stadium grasped as he approached the ball and hit another curler – this time it went straight into the back of the net!

Richard stood there in disbelief. Two valuable points had just slipped away and he was responsible for the free kick that led to it.

"Don't be harsh on yourself," Thomas tried to comfort him. "You did the right thing. If you didn't take him down, I'd have to!"

"I get it, just gutted that it had to happen this way," he replied.

The tense match ended 1-1. Supporters from both sides appreciated the quality and efforts on show and applauded the teams. Richard and his teammates went over to the away end to thank the travelling fans as usual and he saw a child waving a piece of cardboard asked for his shirt, which was a first.

"You're getting popular!" said Tom after Richard obliged and gave the youngster what he wanted.

"I wish I was giving them three points," Richard said. "If only I didn't commit the foul."

"Can't believe you've costed me my clean sheet bonus – in real life and the fantasy league!" Layne came over and said.

David said it was disappointing to drop the points having been so close but he was happy with the way the team battled. He asked Richard not to worry about the foul.

The team had a week to prepare for their next game, which was at home against a club from Lancashire. The visitors were known to be a physical long ball team with plenty of height across the pitch. Training was therefore focused on being quick and agile in attack, pressing high up the field and covering each other in defence. It had been raining all week and the weather forecast suggested the match will be played in treacherous conditions.

The Black Dragons had a mini match during the last training session on Friday to finalise their work on their game plan. Richard was with Josh, Thomas, Ross and Luciano while Layne's team had Jack, Kieran, Danny and George. It was going fine despite the heavy rain until the very end when the pair injured each other following a collision. Layne was hunting the ball from Richard but he lost his footing and caught Richard's left ankle instead. He also pulled his calf muscle in the process. The physio team examined the two of them and advised that both would be out for about two weeks. David wasn't pleased with the news but he asked the pair to have plenty of rest and leave the game to their teammates.

Lewis and Tom came into the otherwise unchanged side on match day. Richard and Layne watched from the stands with Ollie, Harry and Ryan as the game played out in torrential rain. Even though the pitch was well equipped for most conditions due to its modern hybrid grass system composed of natural grass combined with artificial fibres, it was difficult to play the team's usual passing game, as the flow was constantly broken down by misplaced passes and poor controls.

The visitors took the lead after twenty minutes with a well worked corner routine. The in-swinger found one of the centre backs at the front post and his flick on was converted at the far post by the other one. They then turned into defensive mode and shut down any attacks from the Black Dragons for the rest of the half.

"It's tough for the boys out there," Ollie said during the half time break.

"Hopefully we'll improve in the second half now that the rain has calmed," Harry responded.

"How do we break down this solid defence? It's two very disciplined banks of four," asked Ryan.

"We need to draw those deep lying defenders out then create wide overloads," Richard said. "I'd move Tom into a three-man defence and set the full backs free."

"Shame I'm not playing! I'd love to play as a wing back," said Layne.

"Lewis may not be as quick as you, he can do well in that role too. Let's see if David thinks the same."

David did make a change. He gave Viktor his senior debut, replacing Maz who had a knock, but kept the same shape for the restart. The downpour might have eased but the Black Dragons continued to struggle to impose themselves. The away side sat back and the hosts were frustrated at their lack of progress, especially in the final third.

The coach finally made the switch after seventy five minutes – he surprised Richard by pulling Lewis into a back three and bringing Andrés on for Luciano to play as a left wing back, with Danny moving behind George on the right.

"We're going for the squeeze," claimed Richard.

Andrés's ability out wide was evident straight away as he evaded his marker to release Charlie for a cross. It was headed behind for a corner but the sign was there – the Black Dragons were going for the width. They played their well-trained tactic with multiple short passes in the middle third before sending the wing backs through, looking dangerous on a few occasions.

They finally found their equaliser into stoppage time. Andrés broke in behind the defence again and his cross from the left eventually found its way to Danny, who smashed the ball into the net. It was his third goal in three matches and the fans were absolutely delighted!

Charlie picked the ball up and brought it to the halfway line in order to get the match restarted quickly. He wanted all three points but it wasn't to be – the match ended as the visitors kept possession for the final minutes. It looked rather comfortable with the Dragons offering little organised pressure, only individual ones from the likes of

Charlie and Danny. There was a lengthy discussion between Ross and Charlie afterwards.

"Charlie doesn't look happy there," said Layne.

"I would be pissed off too! We could have gone for it but somehow didn't!" said Ollie.

"Maybe Ross thought it's better to secure the point than risk losing it?" asked Ryan.

"The players may be too tired to keep chasing," Richard suggested. "I'll check with Charlie later."

Richard and Layne were meeting their friends for dinner at a steak restaurant by Richmond riverside that evening. Charlie didn't give them a second to settle down before lodging his complaint.

"Do you know what Ross said at full time today?" he asked.

"What did he say?" Layne went along.

"I asked him why he slowed the play down and he said we should be glad to pick up a point! We were at home against a mid-table team for goodness sake!"

"Is that what he said?" Richard asked. "A point isn't bad in the circumstances but I agree we should have gone for it. We seemed to have all the momentum at that point."

"That's just the wrong mindset, we're in this division to win, not just for survival. That's two points dropped in my eyes!" Charlie rumbled on.

"Mentality is a hard thing to change. The club and players are used to be happy just being good enough, but I think we need to aim higher now," Danny added.

"But come on boys, five points out of nine isn't that bad for a newly promoted side!" Thomas the peacemaker tried to cheer the team up.

"Oh don't get me wrong. It's good but we could have been much better! I'm just gutted that we didn't do everything we could," Charlie said.

"Hey let's draw an end to this and enjoy our dinner, it's been a while!" Tom closed the topic and waved for the waiting staff. "I'll get the champagne!"

The group sat at the waterside terrace for an al fresco dinner. Richard ordered some seared diver scallops for starters and a tira de ancho steak to share with Layne.

"I can't wait for our next game in the League Cup against the team from southeast London," said Charlie.

"Is Rob going to start?" Tom asked.

"He's been in great form lately so probably yes," said Ollie.

"It'll be so good to play him again," said Thomas.

"When are you guys back?" Danny asked Richard and Layne.

"I should be okay for the next league game, but Layne may sit that one out," Richard said.

"You're out for the England games as well then," Danny added.

"You two should stop injuring each other," Charlie joked.

"Well it wasn't me diving into a challenge in wet training," Richard pointed out.

"Oh I'm sorry Richie, but it was slippery," Layne said before leaning onto Richard.

The food and wine were awesome and the team had a great evening. Since the season started Layne had cut his alcohol consumption right down in order to stay fit. He only had a glass of red wine after the champagne but it was enough to make him cheerful for the whole night.

The first midweek match of the season saw the Black Dragons visit southeast London for their League Cup second round tie. Richard and Layne sat with the travelling fans at the away end – in the same section he was in five seasons ago, when he cheered the first team with Charlie and Tom. They were easily recognised and were treated like royalties by the supporters.

David gave some squad players a chance to impress and started with Jack in goal, Viktor, Lewis, Thomas and Thorsten in defence, Toby, Tom and Ross in midfield and Sam, Andrés and George up front. Danny and Charlie were on the bench alongside Alex and the others in case

521

they were needed. Rob Daniels, the flying winger who left Thames Ditton for the hosts the season before, played as the right winger.

The Black Dragons started the match strongly, with Sam sending some lovely through balls from the left to the other forwards, who were denied by the home goal keeper in tremendous form. Rob had a few runs at Lewis but the defender was able to keep him at bay. He looked as fast as ever, with added strengths and discipline on the ball.

Andrés and Sam swapped sides in the last quarter of the half and it created the opening goal for the visitors. Sam cut in from the right and his deep cross found George at the far post, whose header back across goal was scrambled in by Tom. The away side went for a second but George missed a glorious opportunity when he hit his shot at the keeper, having been put through by a clever reverse pass from Ross. The half ended a goal to nil for the visitors.

The hosts made a change at half time, bringing in another winger and moving Rob into centre forward.

"I never knew Rob can play in the middle?" Layne asked.

"With his pace and added strengths, he has the raw talents to make it there. He just needs to time his runs better – it used to be his weakness," said Richard.

The home side was certainly trying to play to his strengths, as Thomas and Thorsten were no match for his pace. But they were indeed let down by Rob's timing as he was caught offside for the first few through balls. However, for the one opportunity that he was onside for, he opened his body up and bent the ball beautifully into the bottom right corner to make it one all. He did not celebrate his goal out of respect for his old club, just a few claps towards the home stand.

The Black Dragons countered his threat by having their midfielders and forwards pressing higher up the pitch to stop the through balls and Jack acting more as a sweeper keeper. There were scares, but no further goals.

With twenty five minutes left, David replaced Toby, Andrés and George with Danny, Charlie and Alex to add creativity and restore energy to the side. Danny wasted no time to show the stadium that he was probably the best player on the pitch by playing multiple smooth give-and-go's with his teammates before unleashing a dipping shot from twenty-five yards out. The keeper miraculously got his fingertips to the ball and diverted it over the bar.

The movement of the three substitutes gave the hosts plenty of problems but the Black Dragons could not get pass the inspired keeper. The match went into extra time and both teams had chances to win it. Charlie was put through on goal by Alex but his dink over the keeper was cleared off the line, while Rob raced cleared from the defence late on only to be denied by a well-timed sliding tackle by Jack outside the area. Harry made his senior debut with ten minutes to go as the additional substitute for extra time, but he had little impact on a match that was destined for penalties.

The teams had about five minutes to sort out their takers and Richard could see from the stands that some players were not keen. Being the team's first choice penalty taker he felt bad for not being able to help.

The Black Dragons won the toss and the kicks would be taken in front of the away end, where Richard and Layne were.

The home team's captain and centre midfielder was the first player up. He sent Jack the wrong way and put the ball into the bottom left corner.

Thames Ditton's first penalty taker was the ultra-confident Charlie. His eyes remained as intimidating as ever and he coolly slotted the ball home. He gave the crowd a solid fist pump to celebrate.

Jack wasn't strong enough to keep the second spot kick out despite diving the right way but Tom equalised with an equally powerful finish.

The hosts' third penalty went in off the post, while Lewis's placement was also too good for the keeper.

Jack became the hero when he blocked the fourth kick with his legs. Danny followed it up with a thunderous strike into the top right corner – it was probably the hardest spot to pick but he did it with enormous confidence. He gave the fans a double clap as always.

The fifth and last kicker for the home team was Rob and a miss here would mean the end for his team. He put the ball down, had about five side steps to the left, before running up to the ball. Jack dived to his right, but he went the wrong way – Rob scored to keep the game alive!

Alex stepped up for the decisive penalty. He was the team's third designated taker behind Richard and Luciano so had a good record in training. He pushed the ball towards the top left corner, but it was tipped over the bar by the keeper!

The home supporters had a collective sigh of relief followed by a massive roar. Richard might have been to bigger stadiums but not many could match the volume there.

The shootout went into the sudden death stage, where one player from each team took a kick until there was a winner.

The home team's experienced right back came up first. He had a decent game against Andrés and then Charlie, and he placed the ball into the bottom left corner out of Jack's reach.

Next up was Thomas. He took a deep breath, had a long run up and hit the ball powerfully.

But it went over the bar!

The stadium erupted with joy and the thrilled fans started running onto the pitch. The devastated Black Dragons had no time to react as they were escorted away by the stewards while the hosts celebrated with their supporters. Richard could see that Thomas was consoled by Danny and Viktor but Charlie was having another heated conversation with Ross, who evidently did not take a penalty despite being the senior player and the leader of the group.

The pair left the stadium with the away fans and by the time they arrived home Richard's phone rang. It was Charlie.

"Did you see the shootout?" he asked after the usual greetings.

"Of course I did. Is Bondi okay?"

"He'll be fine, just need some time to recover."

"Why was he taking the sixth anyway? He's not high up in the pecking order."

"That's where the problem was! Ross, our bloody captain, refused to take one! So Bondi stepped up for Harry!"

"Why didn't he take one? Was he injured?"

"No, he was just too scared."

"Are you sure about that?"

"He looked the other way throughout, that fucking coward!"

"That's not good. Is that why you challenged him after the game? What did he say?"

"He said it's none of my fucking business! What sort of leadership is that?"

"That's shocking. What did the boss say?"

"He didn't say much, just the usual 'let's discuss in training'."

"I guess we'll find out tomorrow."

The call ended. Layne was listening in on the speaker and he looked confused.

"Why wouldn't Ross take a penalty?" he asked.

"Maybe he had a bad experience before?"

"It still doesn't take the responsibility away, he's our captain!"

"I know. It doesn't feel right. Like Danny said the other day, it may be an issue on mentality here."

To the players' surprise, David didn't bring up the incident in the recovery training the next day. He wanted the team to focus on the first London derby at the weekend, against the white team from north London. Charlie tried to mention the penalties but was immediately shut down by Nick, who asked him to speak to David privately.

Both Richard and Layne were back in full training but both were deemed not ready to start. They were in the squad as backups.

It was Layne's nineteenth birthday the day before the match and the pair had a low key celebration. They visited Mrs Moore's rest place after training before heading to the world famous department store at Knightsbridge for coffee and some shopping. Richard bought Layne an expensive watch as a present and the couple also purchased a pair of matching bracelets. They went home for dinner in order to stick to the pre-match diet recommended by the Sports Science team.

The match was played at the hosts' new state-of-the-art stadium, which was only completed earlier that year and could house over 60,000 spectators. The Black Dragons started with Josh in goal, the fit-again Maz, Lewis, Kieran and Graham at the back, Tom, Ross and Danny in midfield and Charlie, Luciano and George up front. Richard was on the bench with Jack, Thomas, Viktor, Andrés, Sam and Alex, while Layne and Thorsten were the unused contingency players.

The home team fielded a star-studded side full of international players, with both their main attacking threats available: England's top striker and the friendly but lethal inside forward. Oscar Mayat-Fletcher, the young centre back who was on loan at the club from Derbyshire the previous season, was also in the starting line-up. It was by far the biggest challenge for the Black Dragons in their debut season at the top tier.

Richard watched the first half in horror as the home side completely tormented his teammates with four goals within the first half an hour. The star duo were in top form, scoring two goals each. The Dragons' defence could not cope with the movements and understanding between them, and their finishing was simply clinical. David asked Viktor, Sam and him to warm up during half time as he pondered his response to the humiliation.

He made his changes when the teams returned to the pitch: Richard and Sam came on for Charlie and George, with Danny moved to the inside left position.

"There was another argument between Charlie and Ross in the dressing room," Tom whispered to Richard when they were in position. "It wasn't pleasant."

"Oh no, this wasn't the time for that."

"Yeah, but let's focus on getting some pride back."

David's plan was to limit the damage with a solid midfield five and to counter when Luciano managed to get hold of the ball up field. He demanded at least a draw for the second half.

The referee signalled the beginning of the half and Luciano kicked off with a pass back to Richard. The home team came out pressing straight away and the England striker was quickly closing in. Richard pretended to pass the ball to the left but dragged it back to his right with the underside of his foot. He managed to lose the striker but the second wave arrived before he could measure up a pass. Fortunately he spotted Danny in front of him and chipped him the ball. Danny turned having controlled the ball on his chest and began driving forward. He changed direction swiftly for the centre as he was confronted by Oscar but was taken down by the retreating centre midfielder. The referee awarded a free kick twenty five yards from goal to the visitors.

"Are you ready for this buddy?" Danny asked as he placed the ball on the spot where the official marked with his disappearing spray.

"Trust me," Richard said confidently.

The home team's keeper set up a five-man wall to block the left of the goal while he steadied himself on the right. A sixth player was also deployed to lie down behind to allow the wall to jump without fears for a cheeky low shot.

"The only way is to go higher up than normal and down into the top corner," Richard measured up in his head.

He took his usual five equal step back, but moved slightly more towards the left. He took a deep breath and

527

began his run up. His eyes were fixed on his target – the top left hand corner.

He hit the ball from a lower angle with the top of his right foot, moving it towards the right just as he made contact to create the swerve. The ball flew towards the centre of the goal before bending aggressively to the left.

And it went in!

Richard celebrated with a quick gesture towards where Layne sat before rushing to pick up the ball from the goal for the restart. It might have been a great start to the half but the team were still three goals down!

With the clear gap between the sides, the hosts reverted into game management mode to put a curb on the Black Dragons' momentum. They used the full size of the pitch brilliantly and kept possession for the majority of the next twenty minutes, slowly wearing the visitors down.

"Let's forget about chasing the game and focus on keeping it like this," Ross said to Danny, Tom and Richard during a break in play. "Sit deeper and engage only in the final third."

"We can't do that. We can't give up," said Danny.

"It's not giving up. We need to avoid draining ourselves and letting them score more later."

"I disagree. I think we should carry on and show the fans that we care," Tom said.

"Don't be so immature. We have to settle for some defeats, this is the Premier League for God's sake!"

"I see the points from both sides, but let's go for another ten minutes then decide?" Richard suggested.

"Fine. Let's see who knows more at the end," Ross reluctantly agreed.

The Black Dragons regrouped and re-launched their offensive. Players supported the forwards in numbers and they found a second goal – Danny picked up a loose ball after Sam was tackled and smashed it into the back of the net!

So it was 4-2 with ten minutes left. The away team might have the momentum, but they had completely run out of gas. Danny the machine and the two substitutes were still running, but the rest had visually slowed down. Maz the right back, who recently returned from injury, pulled up badly during another forward run and had to be replaced by Viktor. Sensing the lack of energy from their opponents, the home side went for the kill again. They struck twice in the final minutes: a through ball for the inside forward to complete his hat-trick and a close finish from a low cross for the attacking midfielder.

It was all over for the Black Dragons and the match ended 6-2. Players were exhausted, physically and mentally.

"That was the biggest defeat we've ever had together," Tom said while he was catching his breath.

"Did we make the wrong call?" Richard asked.

"I don't know. We gave it our all," Danny said.

"What did you gain from that, boys? A full on humiliation. We could have walked away with 4-1 and Maz didn't need to be stretchered off!" Ross said.

"I wouldn't agree with that," Graham joined in to defend the younger players. "I think the fans preferred to see us giving our all, in a glorious defeat instead of a timid surrender."

While the players debated, the 3,000 supporters at the away end started chanting at full voice again. Lewis and others were there apologising to them but the crowd appreciated their efforts.

"We should join them," said Tom as he jogged towards the corner of the stadium where the fans were.

Richard, Danny and Graham followed him but Ross decided to go straight back to the dressing room instead.

The supporters welcomed the late arrivals with some heart-warming applause. Richard was not emotional normally but he was a little tearful seeing the fans' response.

"There's no shame in trying," said David as he gave Richard a pat on the back. "Like I said at the beginning of the season, we'll never lose on efforts! I'm convinced that we'll get enough results playing this way over the season."

The league had two weeks off for international matches. Richard and Layne were not selected due to their injuries and they took the opportunity to have extra training to re-build their fitness. The club arranged a closed door friendly with the team from Hounslow and they played the full ninety minutes together with Tom, Thomas, Alex and others. Goals from Sam and his brother Jesse cancelled each other out for a 1-1 draw.

The Black Dragons' next match was a home game against the red team from Manchester. Both Richard and Layne were back in the starting eleven but it was another game to forget. The visitors opened the scoring against the run of play with a swift counter attack after fifteen minutes, only to be pegged back five minutes later when George headed in Danny's in-swinging corner. The first half ended on level terms but the second took a turn for the worse as the away side demonstrated their superiority with three goals. The range of passing and speed of thought of their midfield general was the clear difference, as he set up all three goals with his inch-perfect through balls. He never attempted to take on Richard, as he only needed to create that yard of space to execute those killer balls.

Charlie was an unused substitute even though the match was crying out for his ball retention ability. David explained during his post-match press conference that he was tired following his exploits with the England under 21 team, but Charlie believed it was to do with his outburst against Ross during the previous league game. He made his feelings heard when the young players gathered at his house that evening. Danny shared his frustrations but urged him to keep working for the team. Richard agreed that it was not the time for the squad to have any divisions.

The players were going to have dinner out but with three bad results in a row they'd rather keep a lower profile. Charlie asked the private chef he regularly hired to cook up a brilliant meal at his performance kitchen for the party of ten. It was served with matching wine and the guests were well satisfied.

Charlie said that the private chef cooked his everyday meals there and left them in the fridge with heating and serving instructions. It saved him and Julia time on cooking but also gave him the balanced diet that was specific as well as pleasing to a sportsman. Richard picked up on that and planned to do the same when he and Layne moved into their new home, which was only about a hundred metres away from Charlie's.

The team travelled to Sheffield for their televised game the following Friday. The fellow promoted side was doing well, having picked up ten points from the fifteen available. Their flat 3-5-2 formation with a very compact midfield and centre backs responsible for both carrying the ball forward and over/underlapping their wing-backs proved to be very effective.

Having studied their two defeats last season in detail, David put specific training in place for the team on pressing, counter attacking and maintaining their defensive shape. The wingers had to block passing routes of the wide centre backs as well as occupy the wing backs, while the full backs had to control their forward runs and not be exposed.

Charlie was again omitted from the starting eleven as Andrés and Luciano were the preferred wingers either side of George. The rest of the team was unchanged, with Viktor keeping his place at right back despite having a terrible time against Manchester the week before, as Maz was still out injured.

The hosts began the match with a high tempo and they took the lead after eighteen minutes with a good piece of play. The target man cushioned a cross with his chest for his strike partner and he sent the ball to the top corner on the half volley. The half ended 1-0 with the Black Dragons struggling to create chances – the wingers were able to get the ball, but they couldn't hold on to it long enough for the rest of the team to arrive, with Andrés particularly ineffective against Keith the ex-Thames Ditton centre back.

531

Richard thought that a change was needed. The team could really do with Charlie's ability and fighting spirit but for some reason he wasn't used. He felt slightly disheartened by the situation but he could only carry on and fulfil his own duties. He didn't want to upset the team's harmony any further. Contrastingly, Layne had no such concerns as he duly pointed out the team's problems when prompted by David. He didn't have any opportunity to contribute to the attacking play as the ball was lost way before he could make a run.

"You should bring Charlie on," Ross surprised everyone when he followed up Layne's comment. "The team come first."

"That's what I am going to do," said the boss. "it's good that you see that too."

Charlie returned to the big stage and he made his impact ten minutes in. It had little to do with his wing play though, as he headed in Richard's corner at the near post. He celebrated with the away supporters behind the goal before bringing the ball back to the centre circle for a quick restart.

The home team were a little rattled and the Black Dragons dominated the next fifteen minutes of play. They utilised Charlie's physical presence on the wing and used him as the starting point for their offensives. Layne, Danny and George were there to pick up his passes to launch waves of attacks and they succeeded not once, but twice to settle the match. Layne went through on the outside and his cross was brilliantly volleyed onto the ground then into the roof of the net by Luciano; then Danny picked up Charlie's knock down before crossing it beautifully with his left foot into George's head in the far post.

The hosts launched a late fight back but were denied by the Black Dragons' defence. Richard and Tom, who came on to replace Luciano late on, were impressive with their tenacious display.

The match finished 3-1 to the visitors and they moved up to thirteenth in the league with their eight points.

Charlie and Ross shook hands at the final whistle and Richard hoped that they would put the past behind them.

34.

Rivalry

The Black Dragons' next game was at home against one of the surprise front runners of the season, the club from east London. They had a good mix of experienced and up-and-coming players, with Chris the former star of the Thames Ditton academy in the heart of their midfield.

Charlie returned to the starting eleven but it wasn't enough to overcome the in-form side. The extraordinary Chris held the upper hand against Richard and Ross throughout and he set up the game's only goal after seventy minutes, when he left the former on the floor with a quick Double Flip Flap and sent his striker through.

"I've never seen someone beat you so comprehensively before," Layne said after the match.

"I heard that he was amazing back at the academy but never expected him to be this good," Richard sighed, "I guess this is what top players are like."

The pair visited the big west London club with Danny the following Thursday to watch them play an Ukrainian side in the Europa League. They got tickets through Danny's girlfriend Grace and they witnessed the European debut of Adam, their teammate in the Black Dragons' academy, who was on loan at the Derbyshire club the season before. He returned to his parent club for the new season and had been playing well.

The match was a classic. The visitors scored two early goals through their exciting left-footed right winger Andrei and managed to hold on to their lead at half time despite the home side having the lion's share of possession. The fight back continued into the second half and the pressure finally paid off when Adam beat the offside trap cleverly and set up his striker for a simple finish with ten minutes remaining. Then one became two as Adam ran clean through again and put away the equaliser. The turnaround was completed in stoppage time when the centre back headed in Adam's corner.

"That's the kind of spirit I've been calling for," Danny said on their way out of the stadium.

"It's amazing how they always seem to believe in themselves," Richard added.

"Your friend Adam played really well," Layne jumped in.

"Yes, but so was that winger Andrei, he changes direction with minimal efforts. He'll be a nightmare for left backs."

"Lucky that I won't be facing him then."

"Who knows?" said Danny. "Maybe we'll be in Europe next season."

"You guys better focus on your game on Sunday, it's not easy up there," Grace said.

She was right. The Black Dragons' next match was away at Tyneside, a team struggling for points but very tough to beat at home.

The team flew to the northeast on Saturday for their lunch time game the day after. David had most players available and he started with Jack in goal, Maz, Layne, Thomas and Kieran at the back, Richard, Ross and Danny in midfield and Charlie, Andrés and George up front. Graham and Luciano were out injured and Josh was dropped after some unconvincing performance.

Having picked up just four points from seven games, the home team played in a defensive 4-5-1 formation, with a deep lying orchestrator behind two combative midfielders and two hard working wingers.

The visitors began the match on the front foot but they couldn't create any clean cut chances against the compact defending despite having the majority of possession. Richard's influence was severely restricted as he was constantly denied time on the ball by the young Scottish striker Connor, who wasn't shy in leaving his studs in. Richard complained to the referee after being on the receiving end of several late tackles but was simply told to play on. The half ended goalless.

The second period continued to be a frustrating affair as rain started to fall and the home team continued to sit deep in their half. David tried to alter the pattern by switching into three at the back after the hour, replacing Maz with Lewis and playing Andrés and Layne as wing backs, but things didn't improve and the game was heading to a dull draw.

Richard was on the ball near the centre circle with minutes remaining and he noticed that Charlie was offside just before he hit a long ball towards him. He hesitated for a moment and that proved to be fatal game changer.

He was dispossessed.

Connor approached him from behind and forced him off the ball with his superior strength. He immediately sent the left winger through and Richard's hope vanished when he dribbled past Jack and slotted the ball into the empty net.

He had made a costly error at the dying minutes of the match.

He covered his head with his shirt to hide away from his mistake. For the second match in a row his direct actions had led to a goal for the opponents. The home supporters mocked him and it sank right into his head.

"Come on Richie get your head up!" Layne offered him some encouragement.

"What have I done?" Richard was still in a state of shock.

"Get yourself together! We're kicking off!" Layne shouted as he ran back into position for the restart.

"Maybe you should listen to your boyfriend," teased Connor. "I'm sure he'll pamper you well tonight!"

Richard didn't react to the remark. He was trying desperately to get his head back into gear.

Having achieved their target, the hosts returned to their defensive tactic to use up the time. The Black Dragons launched their final attack: after a series of quick passes in the middle of the park Danny set Richard up for a pass to

536

Layne as some space appeared behind the right back, but he took an extra touch before releasing the ball and Layne was caught offside. The final whistle followed.

"Why didn't you hit it first time?" Layne asked.

"I thought my foot wasn't in the right place," Richard muttered.

"You can't take your time there! That ruined our final chance!"

"I know… I'm responsible for dropping all three points again, okay?"

Richard felt awful and he walked away from Layne and the others for the dressing room after a quick gesture to the travelling fans.

"That wasn't great but let's pick up the pieces during the international break," David said afterwards.

Richard didn't speak to Layne during the flight back home. He later overheard a call between Layne and the England under 21 coach confirming his first ever call up, but with no further calls in the next hour he knew that there was no place for him.

It was naturally very good news for Layne but Richard couldn't bring himself to celebrate with him. He felt depressed – his poor performances in recent games rocked his confidence.

"Are you feeling better now?" Layne asked gently when they were in bed that evening.

"Just leave me alone," Richard answered without even looking.

"I'm sorry for what I said after the match. The words just came out."

"You were only speaking your mind. I played badly, I got that."

"Oh don't act like that. We all know you're a very good player. It's just a bad day in the office."

"Two rubbish games in a row and no way back to the England team, and you said I should relax?" Richard turned around and asked.

"It's all well and good that you have high demands of yourself, but you can't let a few mistakes affect you."

"What's wrong with wanting to be the best of yourself?"

"Nothing wrong with that but you need to be able to learn from them and not keep drilling on it."

"... Just leave me alone."

"How about... me helping you relax and make you feel good?" Layne asked while putting his hand on Richard's body.

"No! I definitely don't need pampering by my boyfriend!" Richard flicked his hand away and turned back facing the other side.

"What's wrong with that?" Layne had absolutely no idea why Richard was triggered.

"Just go away and leave me alone," Richard repeated his plead and abruptly ended the conversation.

Layne went to central London for a piano performance alone the next day. He bought two good tickets in advance but Richard refused to go at the very last minute. He was still angry with himself and everyone else and he went for a very heavy session in the gym instead. He was in bed already when Layne returned, but he did give his partner a minimal send off when he left to join the England camp with Danny early next morning.

David had a lengthy discussion with Richard after training that day, as he nearly injured Sam with a way-over-the-top challenge. He said while he understood Richard's frustrations at his recent form, he needed to learn how to stay calm and concentrated in both training and matches. He also touched on the importance of mindfulness off the pitch and recommended him to visit the club's specialists to explore it further.

Upon reflection Richard understood what he did wrong and realised that his reactions the day before would have hurt Layne's feelings, especially when he broke their promise not to let disagreements go overnight. He sent him a message to apologise after failing to get through on the phone but the response was not the warmest. Layne did call back later that night but it was just a brief conversation, as he wanted to be fresh for training the day after.

The England under 21 team visited Lithuania for their European Championship qualifier on Thursday. Layne came on for his debut after an hour, when the team were already 3-1 up. Danny opened the scoring with a fine free kick and Wayne added two more brilliant finishes before the hosts pulled one back. The young left back linked up well with Damian ahead of him and his low hard cross found Noah the striker from north London sliding in at the near post for the fourth and last goal.

Richard called him shortly after to congratulate his first appearance but to no avail. He went to bed without making connections after a few more attempts. He got a message from Layne the next morning to say that the team returned to St. George's Park late last night and would be resting that day.

The next few days followed the same pattern: Richard tried to contact Layne but found him too occupied to have any meaningful conversation. He started to grow a little impatient: he knew full well that he was in the wrong to begin with and Layne was busy with England, but he felt that he had been the one making all the efforts to diffuse the situation while Layne had been playing him for fools. Being alone at home all this time only served to grow this ill feeling further.

Noting his foul mood, Tom invited Richard over for lunch on Sunday, but Richard declined his offer as he wasn't ready to talk to anyone about his latest rift with Layne.

The England under 21 team's next game was against Ukraine, played at the new 30,000 all-seated stadium in Milton Keynes on Tuesday. Richard went there alone and watched the game from the stands.

Layne's good performance against Lithuania was rewarded with a start. He lined up against Andrei the excellent right winger whom he watched with Richard and Danny not long ago, and it proved to be an exciting duel. The Ukrainian was lively from the start and he twice twisted and turned his way through to the middle to have a shot at goal. Both were saved by the newly selected goal keeper Roy but the warning signs were there. Layne started to show him the outside instead but that didn't stop the threat, even though his weaker right foot was indeed much weaker. He dribbled to the corner and surprised Layne and the others by crossing with his left foot using the difficult rabona technique, where the kicking leg was crossed behind the back of the standing leg. The brilliant cross was headed in by the giant striker Oleg, despite the challenge from Kieran.

Having been on defensive duties up until that point, Layne was able to unleash his attacking abilities after the restart. Wayne carried the ball up field, played a sublime one-two with Danny then sent it through to the left with the outside of his left foot. Layne was on the chase and, after tricking Andrei to create the room, his cross towards to edge of the penalty area found Noah for a cool side-footed finish.

Layne and Andrei continued to battle until both were substituted at around the hour mark. England won the game at the death with a penalty from the clinical Noah.

Richard was supposed to drive Layne and Danny home, but Layne invited his new friend Aaron, an 19-year-old midfielder from south London who made his debut that day, along. That would have posed little problems normally, but given Richard's recent bad feelings towards Layne and the fact that Aaron was selected ahead of him, it didn't give him any pleasure. He held a long face throughout the journey and only had the odd exchange with Danny. Layne wasn't happy with that and made himself heard when they were back home.

"Why were you so rude to Aaron?" he asked.

"Should I be nice?" Richard responded, in a stone cold manner.

"He's my new friend and a fellow footballer. You shouldn't give him a cold shoulder."

"Where does he play?"

"Centre mid… oh, you think he took your place in the team?"

"Is that not the fact?"

"So you're jealous. When did you become such a narrow person?"

"Yes I'm rubbish and not a high-flyer like you guys."

"This isn't going anywhere, Richie... I wish you'll be better over time."

Layne ended the conversation and went to bed. No cuddles. No kisses. Not even sharing the same blanket.

Richard didn't know how the conversation with Layne that he craved ended up making their relationship worse. He was no longer mad at Layne but it seemed whatever came out of his mouth had a negative impact. He didn't know how to handle the situation and decided to focus on training first – maybe an improvement there would help.

The Black Dragons played twice in the following two weeks: a 4-0 thrashing at the other Manchester club, winner of the Premier League last year and a 1-1 draw away against the one from East Anglia, winner of last season's Championship. Richard was left out of the squad completely for the first game, in which the young Wayne humiliated the midfield pairing of Ross and Toby; and played well for ninety minutes alongside Tom in the second. He felt well enough on the pitch, but he had to be ultra-careful with his every touch, which limited the creative part of his game.

While the "Cold War" between Richard and Layne carried on, the renovation of their new house was completed. They quietly moved into their new four-bedroom detached home after training on the Wednesday. Layne had his grand piano carefully transported from his family home in Bath and resumed practicing straight away. He would only see Richard outside of training at meal time, when they heated up the pre-cooked food from the private chef recommended by Charlie. They might have the odd conversation, but it felt rather distant.

Richard was saddened by the situation. He tried to bring it up with Layne but he didn't seem interested. He wanted both of them to focus on the next game, the home tie against the red team from north London, the one Richard supported as a child.

With just nine points out of a possible thirty, the Black Dragons were in need of a win. There were calls from fans and the media to alter his tactics but David stood firm to his ideas. He did keep the midfield trio of Richard and Tom behind club captain Ross but started with Danny as a false nine instead of the regular starter George.

A false nine is a centre-forward who repeatedly moves towards the ball from a high starting position, often dropping to receive centrally. The main intention is to get on the ball away from the opposition centre backs – and, in doing so, to draw players out of position and disrupt the defence.

The match started well for the Black Dragons as they had plenty of possession from effectively having an extra midfielder. Movements from the front three were good and they linked up with the supporting casts well. The only thing missing was a goal, with the finishing not as sharp as the build-up play.

The away side might be going through a transition and having a mix start to the season, but they did boost a world class striker in their ranks and it showed after fifteen minutes, as he expertly volleyed what seemed to be a half chance at best into the top corner. Jack, who was restored after Josh dropping another howler against East Anglia, stood there in awe as the ball rocketed into the back of the net.

Richard was closest to the striker when he scored and he started thinking it was his fault that led to the goal again. The self-doubt resurfaced and he became unsteady for the next passage of play.

"Get yourself together Rich," Tom told him during a break. "We need you."

"How? I'm just a liability to the team!" Richard asked.

"The goal had nothing to do with you. Remember, David put you in the team for a reason. He believes in you! You're our rocket boy!"

He believes in you!

The phrase repeated inside Richard's head, and brought memories of his footballing journey along. From the moment he started playing for David, to the goal at the playoff final. All the friends he played with, all the landmarks he achieved.

"Yes, I've earned my place here!" he said, with the sparks of his eyes reignited.

He became more assertive in his passing and began to pick out the defence splitting runs from his teammates. He sent Viktor through on the right with a delightful low ball, and his cross found Luciano for a tap in.

"That's more like it, Rich, welcome back!" Danny came over to give him a high five.

We've got Richard Lucas!

We've got Richard Lucas!

We've got Richard Lucas!

Richard heard the fans singing his name once more.

"They believed in you too," said Tom.

"Yes, loud and clear," he smiled, for probably the first time in a long time.

The half ended 1-1. There was a scare near the end when the striker broke clean through on goal, but Jack somehow tipped his shot wide of the post to keep the score levelled.

The home side regained their dominance in the second half and created chances after chances, but they lacked the necessary composure to score that decisive goal. Minutes were ticking away and the match was heading to a draw. In probably their last attack, Richard found Layne on the left and he sent it forward for Charlie near the corner flag. Spotting a gap at the near post, Richard made a run towards it hoping to draw a defender away. But no one followed him when Charlie sent the ball over, and he managed to flick it into the top corner!

He scored the winning goal in a crucial match!

The Dragons Stadium erupted with joy and his name was loudly echoed across the stands. Their hero was back again.

The players surrounded Richard to celebrate his winner.

"The rocket boy is BACK!" shouted Charlie the provider.

"This is what football is about, Richard. You lose some, you win some!" Graham said.

"Hopefully more of the latter!" Tom added.

Layne was there with the group, but he limited himself to just a pat on Richard's back.

The referee blew the full time whistle shortly after the kick off and the Black Dragons climbed out of the bottom six with their twelve points. Richard was named as the Man of the Match in the Premier League for the first time and he happily received his trophy from Ross after an interview. He was asked about his form and that of the team, and he duly responded that they would continue the hard work to maintain their standard.

Layne had another piano concert in London to attend the next day but this time he only bought one ticket. Richard apologised again for missing the last one and said that he would be willing to join the next time. Layne gave him a polite smile before telling him that he would also have dinner out and there was no need to wait for him.

Richard felt disheartened but he accepted that he was the one to blame. He urged himself to keep working on it to regain Layne's attention.

He was half asleep when Layne returned home late that night. He had a few drinks evidently and seemed to be in a very good mood. He gave Richard a kiss before undressing himself for bed and fell asleep almost instantly.

Looking at his blushed cheeks, Richard's heart began to race and he moved over to give him a kiss. Layne giggled and said, in his dreams, "Stop it, Niccolò!"

"Nic...co...lò...?"

Cold sweat broke out from the back of Richard's head, tears were pushing to break the floodgates, and his lips were shaking, chilled by what went through his quick thinking mind.

He had a scan at Layne's phone and found what he was looking for straight away. Someone named Niccolò de

Rossi had been sending Layne messages since about a month ago. It began with Layne congratulating Niccolò over something and it developed quickly – the two seemed to have attended the music event at 1901 Arts Club that day together followed by dinner at a fine Italian restaurant nearby.

A quick search on the internet showed that this Niccolò was the 25-year-old Italian pianist whose performance Layne went to see a month ago. He was, by Richard's standard, terribly good looking with his well-groomed dark curly hair and stubble, blue eyes that were a-fire with passion, and his flamboyant yet elegant dress sense over a slim but firm frame. The very worst part of his biography stated that he was openly gay.

Richard returned to bed to gather his thoughts, with Layne still sleeping like a baby next to him. He didn't think Layne had crossed the line but he clearly had a good time with Niccolò.

Should he confront him?

What if they were just friends?

Was he the reason why Layne became distant?

What could he do to stop it?

The pair might be having a bad period but he still absolutely loved Layne. No way he would want to lose him. He decided to bite his time and pretend he didn't know about it. He would wait for Layne to bring it up.

And that was exactly what he did the very first thing next morning.

"Do you know who I went out with yesterday?" he asked cheerfully.

"I have no idea, who was it?" Richard acted along.

"It was Niccolò de Rossi!"

"Who is that?"

"Don't you know him? He's the hottest young pianist in Europe!"

"Oh was he the one performing last night?"

"No his was a month ago, the one you didn't go? We went to see a different one yesterday."

"Was he good company?"

545

"Yes he knows so much about the pieces and gave me many tips on how to play them!"

"That's good, are you seeing him again?"

"He has another performance next weekend, do you want to come along?"

"Sure! I'd love to meet him too."

"Oh I forgot to say, he's 'one of us' as well."

"That's nice to hear. Does he have a boyfriend?"

"He's single, having split up recently."

"Does he know you have a boyfriend?"

"Of course he does, who doesn't know the only two gay footballers are together?"

"Mm... I'm not sure if that's such a good thing."

"Anyway, let me get the tickets before we go training."

Richard felt a lot more relaxed from that rather innocent conversation. Not only Layne was happily talking to him just like before, the relationship between him and Niccolò seemed normal as well. Maybe he really was just overthinking, but how could he explain Layne's sleep talk?

Training was tough but full of fun that week. Layne was back to his cheerful self and the team atmosphere was great from its latest victory, but, as always in the Premier League, another challenge was just round the corner.

The Black Dragons' next match was a lunch time fixture at East Midlands. It was where they suffered a comprehensive 3-0 defeat in the League Cup the season before.

David continued with Jack in goal, Maz, Layne, Kieran and Graham in defence, Richard, Tom and Danny in midfield then Charlie, Luciano and George upfront. Tom kept his place over Ross after his impressive performances in the last few games and in training.

"It's time for our revenge," said Danny before he went onto the pitch.

The home team, who were sixth in the league, came out strongly in the first half. Their midfield five were lively and together with the two forward-thinking full backs, they kept possession really well and created a number of chances. Ben the attacking midfielder curled a shot inches wide and Damian the young winger had a powerful left foot drive pushed over by Jack.

The Black Dragons scored against the run of play ten minutes before the end of the half. Layne earned a free kick thirty yards from goal with his direct run forward. Richard sent the ball towards the top right hand corner with a high ball and it somehow made it all the way after the keeper was distracted. He ran to the north east corner to celebrate his third goal of the season in front of the travelling fans.

The hosts stuck to their game plan and claimed their rewards in the second half. Ben the expert on set pieces wasted no time to equalise with a lovely free kick after five minutes; and he doubled his tally with another brilliant effort from open play ten minutes later to turn the game on its head.

David brought Alex, Sam and Viktor on to rescue the situation. The former won a free kick on the edge of the area near the corner flag on the right soon after. Richard whipped it across and Kieran jumped highest in the goal area to meet it – but somehow he headed it over!

The Black Dragons kept pushing with time ticking away and was awarded another free kick at a similar spot. Sam drove infield with the ball and when he looked to pull the trigger for a shot he passed to down the line for Viktor, who was duly taken down by the left back. Richard stood on the ball, giving his teammates the signal for another whipped cross, but he overheard the keeper's shout at the wall and changed his mind. He had his usual run up, but insisted of a high ball over the jumping wall he sent it underneath.

And Danny was there to tap it in!

The away fans behind Richard went wild for the dramatic late equaliser. He exchanged double claps with Danny before following the scorer to salute the supporters.

The exciting match ended 2-2.

"Well done mate," Ben said when he and Richard shook hands. "One free kick each today!"

"Yours was a proper one, I was just lucky," Richard said with a smile.

"A goal is a goal! Let's see who gets the most at the end of the season!"

Ben was referring to the friendly competition between the dead ball specialists. So far after twelve rounds, Richard had two from direct free kicks, one fewer than Ben but both were behind Jay, who had four.

Richard and Layne went to the Royal Festive Hall that evening for Niccolò's concert. It was within the Southbank Centre, minutes away from Waterloo Station in London.

"He must be decent if he can sell out a venue like this," Richard commented.

"Oh yes he's one of the brightest talents around!"

Niccolò came on stage at show time to the applause of the full audience, wearing a black floral jacquard two-piece suit, a white shirt and a black bow, completed with a very nice pair of black Oxfords made with a single piece of leather. He elegantly composed himself on the piano bench before performing his purposefully selected pieces.

The title of the performance was "il mio viaggio", which meant "My Journey" in English. The mixture of powerful and tender display soon led Richard to a trip down memory lane. It brought him back to the shock and excitement when he met Layne for the first time, the desire he developed on him, the despair from the uncertainties they faced, and finally the joy of becoming together. He looked at Layne lovingly halfway through the performance and the young one smiled before leaning on his shoulder. He felt wonderful.

"That was really nice," he said during the intermission.

"You looked totally engrossed, did you like it?" Layne asked.

"Very much so. It got me thinking about all the time we spent together."

"That's very sweet," Layne said before giving him a discreet kiss on the cheek.

Niccolò took his audience to a different kind of emotion in the second half of his performance. He drew them to how electrifying but fragile romance was, the pain in going through with it, the deep sadness from a break-up and the delight in rediscovering it again. Richard never imagined that music had such abilities but he thoroughly enjoyed the rollercoaster.

The pair met Niccolò at the back stage following the conclusion of the show. He seemed absolutely delighted to see Layne as he kissed him on both cheeks as a greeting. Layne giggled, in exactly the same way as in his sleep talk the other night.

"Did you enjoy the show, signor?" he asked as he had a formal and firm handshake with Richard.

"It was mesmerising. You seemed to be telling us a story and it resonated with me a lot. It's a wonderful experience," Richard said.

"I love this feedback, it gives me lots of satisfaction. How about you, Mr Moore?"

"I like your dynamics in S178. How can you memorise it all? It's nearly thirty minutes long!"

"Do you want to learn it? Come this way, I'll show you."

Niccolò led the two into another room where there was a spare grand piano, and he held Layne's hands and started showing him how to play. The two then entered a deep conversation on music theories that Richard had no idea about for another good fifteen to twenty minutes.

The pianist invited the pair to a cocktail bar nearby for some drinks afterwards. Layne needed the bathroom so he and Richard had a chat.

"Thanks for showing Layne the technique, he's very keen to pick it up again," said Richard.

"It's my pleasure. He has good potential," Niccolò said. "No wonder why he loves you so much, you're such a thoughtful and caring gentleman."

"I'm sure I'm the lucky one here," Richard said with a little smile.

"You are," Niccolò said, "and I'll say it now. I'm going to fight for him. He's exactly what I would love to have as a partner."

"I beg your pardon?" Richard could not believe what he just heard but he was able to give a firm response. "Layne's mine and I have absolutely no intention of giving him up."

"We'll just have to pull out all the tricks and let the man choose for himself."

"......," Richard was lost for words for a moment and Layne happened to return at that point.

Niccolò moved over to tell Layne that he was leaving, before giving him another round of kisses on the cheeks and walked away.

"What happened between you two?" The confused youngster asked. "Why is he suddenly leaving?"

"He has something important to do I guess," Richard said after taking a few seconds to recover from the shock. "Well, shall we have a drink before we head back?"

"Of course, this place is popular with its cocktails!"

Richard had a chat with Layne that night, as he contemplated if he should tell him about the challenge he received from Niccolò.

"How did you find Niccolò?" he asked when they were in bed.

"He's lovely! It's so kind of him to share his knowledge and agree to teach me how to perform!" Layne said happily.

"Oh is he going to give you lessons going forward?"

"Yes, I'll see him one evening a week until he goes back to Italy in spring."

"Where would they be?"

"His apartment in Westminster. I can ride my scooter there."

Every alarm bell inside Richard's head was ringing but he wasn't sure what to do – he had just managed to make up with Layne and blocking his lessons with Niccolò would more than likely jeopardise it all.

"Can I join in?"

"No way, you'll just be a distraction!"

"Are you sure it's going to be okay?"

"Of course! What could possibly happen?"

"… No, it's all fine, as long as you are careful with the commute etc."

However unwilling he was, Richard felt that he should not stop Layne. He had to trust him.

"Thanks dear," Layne gave him a kiss and rested his head on his chest. "Are you still mad at me for what I said after the Tyneside game?"

"No, it stopped ages ago. I was wrong."

"Why did you push me away when I tried to cheer you up?"

"That… that was because of something Connor said…"

"So you're saying you'd love me to make you feel good then?"

"Most certainly, baby!"

"In any way I want?"

"Mm… yes, whichever way you like."

"Hehe, sit back and enjoy it then!"

The couple had a long overdue fun night in. While Richard might have major concerns with Niccolò's intentions, he wouldn't dare bringing it up to upset Layne.

Richard got a call from the England camp the next morning. He was asked to join Layne and the under 21 team for their next two matches, at home against San Marino and away at Austria, due to a withdrawal caused by injury.

So instead of driving Layne and Danny to St. George's Park, Richard was joining in as well. There were plenty of personnel changes since his last call up, as the likes of Adam, Ben, Brandon and Oscar were no longer eligible while Wayne the young midfielder was fast-tracked into the senior squad. There still a good number of familiar faces though: his current teammates Charlie, Danny and Kieran, his old friend Owen, left winger Damian, right midfielder Rory, as well as Aaron the midfielder whom he met when he picked Layne up after his previous call up.

Richard was in the starting eleven alongside Charlie, Danny, Owen and Kieran in the first game, played at the stadium of a Premier League side in the midlands. As there was a sizeable gap in talents and experience, England came up easy winners with a 5-0 score line. Goals from Owen and Charlie brought the match under control in the first half, and Noah the young striker scored a hat trick in the second to take it beyond any doubts. Richard played seventy five minutes until he was replaced by Aaron, who came on at the same time as Layne.

The team then flew to Salzburg for their next game in the European Championship qualification round. The match was played at a stadium in Ried im Innkreis, a town approximately thirty-five miles north of the city.

Richard played the full ninety minutes together with Danny and Layne. The left back's pace and movement caused plenty of trouble for the home side and he set up the opener for Damian after twenty five minutes with a whipped cross. The hosts came back strongly in the second half, equalising at the hour mark with a well-timed run from the main striker. But England had the last laugh as the substitute Charlie curled one into the far corner five minutes from time.

The never-ending Premier League fixture resumed three days after the international games, and the latest visitors to The Dragons Stadium was Owen's team from East Sussex. Richard and Charlie were left on the bench after their England duty and Thomas got a rare start as Graham had a knock during training.

The prolific Owen wasted no time to establish a two-goal lead, and his second was a gem. He left Layne on the ground after some mesmerising footwork, lifted the ball over Tom's sliding tackle, did a Marseille turn to get away from both Ross and Thomas, then put the ball into the bottom left hand corner with the outside of his right boot. It was most certainly a contender for goal of the season.

"I should have played you from the start," David said after telling Richard to warm up.

He came on for George at half time. His role was to restrict Owen's influence and to explore the space behind him with his long passes. He found Andrés on the left ten minutes into the half and the winger set Danny up for an expert finish from a tight angle.

Charlie was introduced from the restart with the Black Dragons on the ascendancy. The crowd gave Andrés a standard ovation for his contribution but couldn't hide their excitement for their powerful winger's introduction.

And he didn't let them down, as he put away the equaliser late in the game, when he headed in Tom's cross at the near post. The match ended 2-2.

"It was never easy with you guys," Owen said to his former teammates at full time.

"What was that goal about? I'm going to appear in the Best Premier League Goals programme for the next fifty years now!" Thomas said.

"That's your claim to fame then!" Tom laughed.

"You're on it too!" Thomas reminded.

"It's always good to play against you mate," Charlie joined in and gave Owen a high five.

With fourteen points from thirteen games, the Black Dragons sat in the relatively safe position of twelfth, seven points ahead of the relegation zone. They were not quite title challenges as Charlie claimed, but were good value for a place in the league that nobody expected them to even be in.

The team travelled to northwest London for their next game. It was the first part of a double header on Sunday, followed by the north London derby.

It was also Richard's twenty-first birthday, and he had a memorable match as he created both goals in the comfortable 2-0 win. His out-swinging corner found George at "the spot" in the first period and they repeated the trick late in the second. He was named as the Man of the Match for his efforts.

Layne then took Richard to a grand Parisian Brasserie with an authentic Art Deco interior in the heart of Piccadilly for his birthday dinner. Richard was very impressed by the authentic setting and the vibrant atmosphere brought by the live band.

"How do you know this place? It's awesome!" he gave Layne his praise.

"It was recommended by Niccolò. He knows so much about good places in London!"

"Oh was it," Richard was a little disappointed to hear the name but tried not to let it get to him. "Let's see what's on the menu."

The pair ordered a dozen of escargots for starter, then a choucroute with garlic sausage and French style fish stew for main. Both dishes were Richard's old time favourites – one from his German days and the other from his time at the Stevenson's.

A surprise guest showed up right after they had their starters.

"Hey Layne and Richard, what's the luck of seeing you here?" It was Niccolò, the elegant Italian pianist and Richard's least favourite person.

"We're celebrating Richie's birthday. Are you here with friends?" Layne happily responded.

"I'm alone. My friend didn't show up. Non si è presentato!"

"Oh that's a shame. Would you like to join us?" Layne asked before Richard had a chance to say no.

"Are you sure? I hate to be a bother."

"No, just sit down. I'm sure Richie's fine!"

Niccolò quickly settled down and ordered himself a steak tartare. He and Layne then went into a long conversation on classical music, which left Richard completely sidelined.

Richard was not pleased by the situation but he politely had his main course on his own. He then gave the waiter a firm "no" when he presented him the dessert menu – he only wanted to leave the place as soon as possible.

554

"Why weren't you happy earlier? Was the food bad?" Layne asked on the taxi home.

"It was fine, but I was hoping to enjoy it with my other half."

"Oh are you referring to Niccolò? Don't you think it was bad to leave him on his own? I also wanted to ask him about the songs he gave me to practice."

"But it was my birthday…"

"Oh I'm sorry. I'll make it up to you when we get back!"

Layne did pull out all the stops later. He had Richard's favourite white sesame cheesecake and a bottle of English sparkling wine readied in the kitchen diner before he played, and sang, an extravagant version of the happy birthday song on the piano.

"Happy 21st my Richie!" he said with a beautiful smile.

"Thank you baby, that was lovely!"

"I'm glad you like it! Nico taught me that!"

"Can you just… not mention him for a while?"

"Sure sure, it's our time now."

Layne carefully cut up the wonderful looking cake and served Richard a big slice, which went down really well with the sparkling wine. Richard felt more pleasant after two glasses then Layne began his offensive, which was very satisfying.

Richard lay in bed cocooning a tired out Layne afterwards. He was happy but had plenty of thoughts in his mind. He was seriously worried by Niccolò's intentions and when he would make his move on his beloved boyfriend.

35.

Loyalty

The Dragons Stadium welcomed their biggest ever visitors on Wednesday night – the reigning European champions, the current league leaders, the red team from Merseyside. They were on a rich vein of form, unbeaten in their fourteen matches with only two points dropped. Their style of play could be summed up by the word "relentless" – they ferociously pressed high up the pitch, condensed the play massively and attacked every minute of every match. It would be by far the toughest challenge for the young Black Dragons.

David believed that the only way to counter such powerful opponents would be to attack the gaps behind their back line, but with their dominant centre backs, it would have to be done with precise through balls on the ground. The team would have to be on their toes at all times to stand a chance – be fully focused on their defensive duties but ready to transit into attacks swiftly, with absolutely no margin for errors, in timing or execution.

He made the controversial call to leave the on-form George on the bench and played Danny as a false nine. The rest of the starting eleven resembled the previous game: Jack seemed to have secured the temporary number one spot ahead of Josh, with Maz, Layne, Kieran and Thomas in defence, Richard and Tom behind Ross in midfield and finally Charlie and Luciano as the inside forwards. With the false nine, the team could play in their standard 4-2-1-3 or switch into a 4-4-2 with a diamond midfield. There were plenty of variations.

Knowing that the team would come under severe pressure, David asked them to follow a simple pattern: win the ball, give it to Tom or Ross, they set Richard up for a forward pass to Danny, who would either send it to behind the centre backs for the inside forwards or recycle possession with a back pass.

The match began. It did not take long for the visitors to launch their first attack. The prolific right winger received the ball into the final third and had a go at Layne. While the young full back's defensive skills had been brought up to standard, he was still no match for a world class opponent and he was left stranded after the winger tricked him into a tackle and shifted the other way.

The right winger continued to drive towards the centre and attracted the attention of both centre backs. He tipped the ball behind both of them at the very last second to set up his equally productive teammate on the other side. He coolly dinked the ball over Jack but the vigilant Richard spotted the danger and was there to clear the ball off the line.

The resulting corner kick was caught cleanly by the commanding Jack and the Black Dragons launched their counter. The keeper's long throw found Luciano on the left and he skilfully released Danny who only had the pacy left back in front of him. He carried the ball forward to the left of the area, dragged it back to his right foot and took his pick – Charlie and Ross were closer to him but he went for the far side, and Tom was there to put it away.

The stadium erupted with excitement by the shock lead. Tom ran all the way back to the West Stand and kissed the club badge on his shirt in front of the jubilant supporters.

The Reds were top of the table for a reason and they soon equalised. The right back hit a glorious cross field ball from deep and left-sided forward expertly guided his side-footed volley to the bottom corner. The perfect pass met by the perfect finish.

While the Black Dragons were still in awe of the amazing skills on show, the visitors added another goal. Tom was robbed of the ball near the half way line by the Reds' captain and he sent a long through ball to the left-sided forward again. He controlled it elegantly and his low

557

cross was converted emphatically by the right winger from the edge of the area to make it 2-1 after twenty five minutes.

Bad became worse at the end of the first half, as the same winger demonstrated yet again why he was considered one of the best players in the world when he danced through the whole Thames Ditton defence to score a magnificent solo goal. He took it past Layne on the outside, cut back in to evade Kieran's challenge, dragged back to his right then left to leave Thomas on the floor, delayed his shot to tempt Richard into a failed block, before calmly sent his curling shot out of Jack's reach to the top left corner. The crowd was absolutely stunned by the unbelievable actions unfolding before their eyes.

"That was, frankly, some breath-taking stuff," Tom said at half time.

"I just couldn't figure out where that winger is going, he keeps the ball so close to his feet and they are so quick!" Layne added.

"I'll appear on the Best Premier League Goals programme twice now," said Thomas with a bitter smile.

"At least we've earned our rights to play against them," Richard said. "They are one of the best sides in the world after all."

"Get your heads up. We'll fight back in the next half," Danny joined in with his style of encouragement.

And what a fight back he led. Ten minutes into the second half, he picked up a forward pass from Charlie and he took on the big centre back, who had a reputation of being one of the hardest defenders to dribble past. He executed a lightning quick Flip Flap to his right, before chopping the ball back to the left using his back foot. As he was about to run clear of the defender to have a left foot shot, he was taken down by the retreating defensive midfielder, about twenty five yards away from goal on the left.

Richard stood over the direct free kick with Layne and Danny. He measured up the angle to overcome the big wall in front of him but he was concerned by the

558

positioning of the keeper. He was standing right in the middle of the goal, which made a shot to the top left corner very difficult to go in. Then he saw Charlie on his right and had an idea. He whispered it to Danny for him to pass on the message.

He took his usual run up but before he took a shot, Layne moved the ball slightly to change the angle and he chipped it to the far side instead. Charlie was completely free and he headed it in!

The home crowd rediscovered their voice and rallied behind the Black Dragons. They were all over the visitors for the next ten minutes: passing incisively, creating chances, pressing vigorously and Richard performed his heroics to cut out a number of key passes. If they were going to get an equaliser, it had to be then.

And they did. In fantastic fashion.

Richard raced in front of one of the midfielders to intercept another pass in his own third and quickly sent the ball right for Maz, who followed the pattern set by David and gave it to Ross in front of him. The captain shielded the ball from pressure and rolled it back towards Richard. He threaded it through the gap in midfield to Danny, who found Layne on the left ahead of the opposition right back and he squared it for Charlie on the edge of the area. He swiftly turn inside and crossed the ball towards the six yard box.

Danny arrived and he made it 3-3 with a minimum of fuss!

The dramatic turn of events pushed The Dragons Stadium into a frenzy. The eight thousand home fans went absolutely over the moon and continuously sang one of their (and every football club's) favourite chants.

And it's Thames Ditton
Thames Ditton FC
We're by far the Greatest Team
The World has ever seen

With another twenty five minutes or so to go and the ferocious backing of their fans, the Black Dragons pushed for the winner. However, the experienced and flamboyant manager of the visitors had other ideas. He restored the energy in midfield with yet another two international players and brought on another striker.

The strengthened midfield regained control and resumed their domination of the game. Having covered plenty of grass in the match as well as playing the full ninety minutes on Saturday, Richard was close to running on empty and had to restrict his movements. His teammates were probably feeling the same and they started to sit deeper and deeper, playing into the hands of their superior visitors. David tried to bring George, Toby and Lewis on for Luciano, Richard and Layne, but before the substitutions were completed, Ross limped off after a collision and Richard had to stay on.

He continued to track his players, sniff out the danger and make his tackles, but his legs finally reached their limits with just the added time to go. He stretched out to intercept a pass and his right leg gave way. His calf muscles cramped up and he fell to the ground. It hurt.

It wasn't the first time he got in such situations but he couldn't pick a worse time. The game played on when he was on the ground and he had to witness, in pain both physically and mentally, his team's downfall. The prolific right winger collected the pass he failed to cut out, came inside Lewis with a brilliant two-footed feint, and found his partner-in-crime, the excellent left inside forward, yet again and he headed it home to surely win the pulsating football match.

Richard punched the ground in frustration. He was hapless to prevent what he knew was happening and he was angry with himself, for his lack of fitness. Tom helped him straighten up his leg to overcome the cramp but he was merely walking for the remaining minutes of the game, which had no further drama to offer.

"You should be proud of yourselves," said the Reds captain when he shook hands with Richard. "I can see you guys doing really well in a few years' time."

"Thanks. It was a very good lesson," he replied respectfully.

The home supporters had a dip in their enthusiasm when the winning goal went it, but they were back in full voice at the final whistle to applaud their team's efforts. David pulled everyone together to have a lap of appreciation to show their respect. He said the team might have lost the game, the way they competed against such a top side showed what they were capable of and they deserved to be proud.

The Black Dragons played another three matches over the next three weekends where they picked up seven valuable points. David continued to deploy Danny as a false nine to great effects, as he scored the winner in a 1-0 win in the West Midlands and contributed two more in the 3-1 home derby win against the team from south London to take his tally to nine. Charlie scored a late equaliser in a 1-1 draw against the Dorset side following a great run by Luciano. George was barely used in the games and he was far from impressed. Richard learnt that he had been having a contract dispute with the club and that might have played a part in his recent struggles.

Layne had his weekly piano lesson with Niccolò throughout the period and looked very happy with his improvements. He played a variety of classical and modern songs to Richard during the evenings and it was enjoyable. They spent their Christmas Eve with Richard's parents back at Windlesham before joining the team for their trip to Lancashire for their Boxing Day match. The team climbed up to ninth with their twenty four points from eighteen games, while their opponents sat just above the relegation zone at seventeenth.

It was a game to forget as the battling home defence repelled waves and waves of the Black Dragons' attack to secure a goalless draw. The only plus point for the visitors was the return of their first choice goal keeper Gordon, who was injured during pre-season.

The last fixture of the calendar year was a home game against the blue team of Manchester, the other title challenging side three points behind the one from Merseyside.

With the visitors' well-known possession-based game plan with fluid movements and little balls behind the back line that completed unpicked the Black Dragons in their first encounter, David picked a slightly more defensive line-up, with Gordon in goal, Viktor, Layne, Kieran and Graham at the back, Richard, Tom, Danny, Charlie and Andrés in a midfield five and Luciano up front on his own. Ross was still recovering from his injury while George was again put on reserve. Ryan, who had been in great form in training, was also on the bench for the very first time.

The away team rested both their world class midfield general and veteran striker but were still full of top class internationals, with Wayne the young England player in midfield. They asserted their dominance as soon as the match began as they calmly passed the ball across the pitch, patiently waiting for an opening in the defence. The Black Dragons were doing lots of running, but they remained compact as a group and were alerted to the danger when the visitors went for those clever through balls.

The goalless first half might feel flattering for the home side but it was deeply worrying for David and the coaching team. With the manic festive schedules, the first eleven were low on stamina and it was a matter of time before they succumbed to the pressure, be it a lack of concentration or an ever-so-slightly delay in their reaction. The youthful bench was full of energy and passion, but they did not possess the experience and tactical know-how to compete against such a well-drilled side.

So the coaching team reluctantly decided to carry on and hope the players could stay focused as well as being able to conjure up a chance for themselves.

Even though Richard was supremely fit and ran the most distance alongside Tom in most games, he was feeling the drain with keeping track of the movements of all the players and covering any gaps in the defensive shape. But most importantly, he soldiered on with his teammates and continued to hold the visitors at bay.

The resistance could only last so long and the persistent of the reigning champions finally claimed its reward at the sixty fifth minute. After another string of short and incisive passes, Wayne found the tireless winger behind the exhausted Layne and he applied the simplest of finish to open the scoring.

David made three changes straight after conceding, replacing Layne, Richard and Luciano with Lewis, Thomas and Ryan, with the latter making his debut in challenging circumstances.

And the little forward announced his arrival at the big stage with a bang.

The team worked an opening on the right for Viktor to cross towards Charlie the makeshift centre forward, and he managed to flick it left ahead of the centre back. Ryan sneaked behind the attack-minded right back and he went for the audacious – he hit a sensational left-foot volley from the corner of the penalty box!

The ball left a beautiful arc in the air and went into the top corner – the keeper had absolutely no chance, and the youngster had scored with his first touch in top flight football!

The overjoyed taekwondo master secured his cult hero status with the fans almost immediately with an equally amazing celebration – an acrobatic triple spinning kick accompanied by a powerful roar to send the supporters completely wild.

The experienced visitors made sure the positive atmosphere was short-lived though, as they re-established their authority with not one but two beautifully crafted goals. The hard-running winger turned provider as his mazy run drew both Kieran and Graham towards him which left the striker completely unmarked for a simple tap in. Minutes later Wayne played a fantastic give-and-go with the same striker before laying the ball on a plate for his fellow midfielder to secure the victory.

Richard and Layne watched from the bench how another heroic performance ended in defeat. While they were not under any immediate danger of getting relegated, which was a great place to be for a newly promoted side, he wanted to be able to challenge the very best sides and time and time again they fell short at the end – was it an issue with their fitness, their playing style or a lack of capable options from the bench?

The team had a recovery and tactical session the next morning. With it being New Year's Eve, Richard and Layne invited their friends over for a small gathering that evening, which doubled up as their house warming party. They had the athlete-friendly food prepared by their private chef in their large kitchen diner and Layne performed a few of his well-practiced songs on the grand piano afterwards. Their teammates never knew he could play and were amazed by his talents. The alcohol-free event finished early as the players had a full session the next day, before the coach journey to their next destination, the grand theatre in Manchester.

Considering the physical condition of the players, David had no choice but to rotate his team, with both Richard and Layne on the bench.

The stadium was the biggest one Richard visited for club football and when over 70,000 fans were screaming (or booing in his team's case) it was quite a scene. The home side, currently third in the table, made five changes to their line-up but still boasted a team full of international players.

Their midfield general also started and he continued where he left off in the last encounter as he quickly put his team ahead with a delightful free kick from the edge of the box at the twentieth minute. He brought the ball past Ross in the middle and Tom had no choice but to take him down before he set the pacy inside forward free on goal.

Having picked up a yellow card for that challenge, Tom had to be more cautious when he encountered the midfield general and that gave him the extra inch of space to create the next goal: he lifted the ball behind the back line beautifully for the forward coming from the right to put his first time shot through Gordon's legs for 2-0.

Richard and Layne were warming up at half time with the rest of the substitutes. There was also a penalty competition for some local youth teams and Richard spoke to one of the teenagers when he retrieved a loose ball.

"Can you pass me the ball please?" he asked from a distance.

"Sure!" the youngster was going to simply kick it but decided to run over with it as he realised he was talking to Richard.

"Here you are Mr Lucas," he said before turning his voice down. "Thanks for setting the example by coming out."

"Oh, we're just trying to stay true to ourselves. I hope it'll make lives easier for others in the future."

"I'm sure it will-"

"Stay away from my son, you filthy bastard!"

Richard looked over and saw a man aged about fifty shouting from the stand.

"You see it's not that east at home," the youngster said.

"You'll find out what's best for you when you're older. Contact me if you need any someone to talk to?"

The youngster nodded and told Richard his name was Callum.

David asked Richard to come on for Tom when the team returned from the dressing room. He said that while Tom performed admirably in the first half, the team couldn't afford to give the midfield general the space to dictate the game with him holding back because he was on a yellow card.

The first fifteen minutes of the second period were rather uneventful, as the home team slowed the play down having taken a two-goal lead. David then sent Charlie and Ryan on and it was time to have a go. The team moved into position to begin the squeeze – centre backs operating a higher line, full backs hugging the touch lines, and forwards dropping into the area between the hosts' defence and midfield. They played multiple quick passes between them and set Richard up for the switch.

However, the hosts were well-prepared and their defenders moved forward simultaneously to catch Maz and Lewis offside. Seeing the change in situation, Richard sent the ball to Ryan, who was onside some ten yards ahead of the centre circle.

The young striker decided to turn and run after the ball instead of controlling it – as the centre backs were rushing out for the offside trap they were completely caught out by the move. His explosive acceleration took him away and he went clean through on goal. He calmly dribbled past the experienced goal keeper and slotted the ball into the empty net with his left foot.

He scored with his first attack in two consecutive matches!

The outrageous triple kick celebration followed and the Black Dragons were back in the game with twenty-five minutes remaining. They continued with their tactic but with the home team's awareness of it the match became very intense, as everything was happening in the middle third of the pitch and both teams were living on the edge with every touch and move.

The skilful midfield general became the difference again. In a repeat of the first half, he collected the ball from his centre half and turned away from Ross with relative ease, creating a space for a through pass to the pacy left inside forward behind Maz. Richard noticed that and had to do exactly what Tom did in the first half – taking him down at the expense of a yellow card.

Fortunately the free kick came to nothing and the Black Dragons were able to launch a counter attack. The delivery was well defended by Lewis and his header found Charlie in front of him. The winger dribbled past a couple of defenders brilliantly to break through and his little through ball set Danny up for a clean left-footed finish.

They came from two goals down back to level terms with ten minutes to go!

The home side needed the three points to keep pace with the top two and with the large crowd encouraging them with their famous chant of "Attack, Attack, Attack Attack Attack" repeatedly, they upped the tempo and went for the kill. The left back found the the midfield general again, who looked to shoot from twenty-five yards out. Richard was in a good position for a block so the midfielder changed his mind and tried to evade Richard with a Marseille turn instead. He dragged the ball back with his right foot, spun his body to shield the ball then use his left foot to drag the ball away. However, his standing foot caught Richard, he fell over and the ball was poked away.

But the referee blew his whistle for a foul.

The Black Dragons protested against the decision but the official was having none of it. He then followed up with issuing Richard his second yellow card of the game, duly followed by a red!

He couldn't believe it. He was merely standing his ground and the midfield general stepped onto him. He didn't even tackle.

Charlie and others challenged the referee ferociously and he was also booked as a result.

Richard walked towards the dressing room located at the corner of the stadium amid the usual jeers and cheerios from the crowd. Callum's father managed to come to the side of the path and gave him some nasty gestures.

"Fuck off you bloody faggot!" he shouted.

Richard could see the genuine anger on the man's face, as if he was responsible for the murder of his entire family.

That level of hatred.

Considering the impact on poor Callum, Richard didn't want to take the matter any further. He had a quick scan of the other fans surrounding him: some looked rather shocked, some supplied even more vile abuses, but the majority were there, laughing at his misery.

Just like what he always knew, the world was a cruel place.

He continued his walk of shame into the tunnel and left the stands behind. He felt bitter by the decision, but ultimately he felt lonely. He knew that football was a masculine sport and some fans were bloodthirsty, but it was tough going through it, again and again. It was wearing him down.

As if his day couldn't be worse, the cheer from the stands told him that it could – the midfield general must have scored the winning goal with the resulting free kick. Disheartened, Richard fell to his knees and began crying on the dressing room floor. Then he felt a comforting and familiar warmth on his back – Layne had followed him in and was holding him from behind.

"Don't give up, Richie," he said with a soft and caring voice.

Richard turned round, looked at Layne's eyes and collapsed into his shoulder. The pair cried hugging each other.

Why were things so hard?

Why was it a crime that they loved each other?

Will the world ever change?

They couldn't figure out the answers, but they simply had to soldier on. At least they had the support of each other.

The match ended 3-2 to the home team. Another late defeat at the hands of a traditional top side. The consolation was that the matches and the score lines were much closer than those the first time round. The Black Dragons had definitely improved, but the gap between them and the top persisted.

The congested fixture list took the Black Dragons to a National League club based in north east London for their FA Cup third round tie three days later. Having seen how the team exhausted and collapsed in recent matches, David reluctantly played a weakened side against their high-flying opposition. He couldn't afford to have players suffering from burnout when the team entered the business end of the season, as it could easily derail their progress for the prime objective – to stay in the league.

So he started with the youthful eleven with Ryan and Alex upfront, with the blonde striker making his return from an ankle injury that had kept him out for the last five weeks.

Richard was given a one-match suspension across all competitions from his red card in the last game, but he travelled with the squad to support Layne, who was on the bench.

The hosts started the match brightly with their composed passing and coherent pressing. They were only denied the opening goal by some outstanding goal keeping from Jack.

The vocal crowd was finally silenced by a great piece of play from the visitors near the end of the first half. Alex beat the offside trap to collect Harry's lovely through ball and he sent it across for the unmarked Ryan to slot home his third goal from three appearances.

The home side tried to work up another head of steam in the second half but they suffered a hammer blow as the Black Dragons caught them in a break. The tricky Andrés dribbled past a couple of players before sending Viktor through to score his first senior goal.

The visitors added two further goals quickly afterwards as the hosts deflated. Alex and Ryan exchanged assists for each other after being sent through – instead of becoming rivals fighting for the same position, the two worked well together for the benefits of the team. Ryan rounded off the splendid afternoon with his third goal of the game as he chipped the keeper from the edge of the area following some good footwork by Andrew, who made his senior debut after replacing Alex for the last ten minutes.

The team had the rarity of a full week to prepare for their next match, which was the first west London derby of the Premier League season, to be played at The Dragons Stadium. The broadcaster tried to build the live game up in a similar fashion to the north London equivalent and aired a series of documentaries ahead of the tie. It showed the Black Dragons' journey from the lower divisions, including landmarks such as their crowning moments of the National League, achieving automatic promotions in League 1 and 2, and the playoff victory in the Championship. It also featured the kiss between Richard and Layne and how the exposure of their relationship had positively impacted the footballing world. There would always be die-hard homophobes but in general the environment had become more inclusive. A handful of players overseas had come out since, to the support of their teammates, clubs, fans and fellow professionals.

Callum's father had been identified and charged by the Manchester club and a five-year stadium ban beckoned. The youngster made connection with Richard via social media privately and received advices on how to handle his situation at home.

David had nearly all players available and he opted for a mix of youth and experienced with Gordon, Maz, Layne, Kieran, Graham, Richard, Tom, Danny, Charlie, Luciano and Ryan, with the veteran centre back Graham as the captain.

The visitors were fourth in the table and had their team of world class players available. The former Thames Ditton youngster Adam started on the left as an inside forward in an otherwise experienced line-up.

"I hope you can show them your very best today Richie," Layne said when they lined up in the tunnel.

"I always do baby, but thanks."

Richard thought that was a little odd, but he realised after a while – Layne was referring to the big west London club's refusal to sign both of them a couple of seasons before.

The Black Dragons started the match in their typical high tempo, with the supporters backing them in full voice. Layne charged down the line from the off, demanded the ball from Danny and forced a corner kick after instigating an exciting foot race against the experienced right back. He turned to Ditton End behind him and drummed up even more support from the crowd – fans were on their feet, chanting loudly the usual "Come on you Blacks" designated for set pieces.

Danny sent a hanging ball towards the far corner of the penalty box. Ryan was sprinting towards it and he duly hit it on the full volley!

The ball arrowed straight into the top right corner despite the efforts from the player guarding the post and the already vibrant stadium went up a few more decibels as they celebrated Ryan's amazing goal – his sixth in his first four games.

The Black Dragons continued their fast start and pushed for the second goal. They hunt the ball down as a team but the visitors were a top side for a reason. They calmly passed their way out of the press and created a chance of their own. Adam found some space on the left behind Maz and he drove in field looking for a shooting opportunity. He sped past Graham but as he pulled the trigger he was blocked by the determined Richard. The loose ball was picked up by Tom and he sent it down the line for Ryan near the halfway line. He flicked the ball through the legs of the left back and was fouled by the centre back outside the area on the right. It was a good position for either Richard or Layne to cross in.

The pair had a quiet discussion before Richard ran over the ball for Layne to take the kick – and he took a direct shot towards the near post!

The keeper fumbled across to block it, but he could only parry it back to the middle and Ryan was there to head in the rebound! The overjoyed youngster performed multiple somersaults in front of the home fans to confirm his status as their new favourite player!

The Black Dragons ceased their high press to conserve their energy towards half time but they somehow managed to score again. A seemingly harmless cross from Layne made it all the way to the area and Ryan was there again to capitalise from the confusion with a sweet left foot finish!

He completed a perfect hat trick against the club's new rivals in the first half!

The team returned to the dressing room to a standing ovation from the crowd – they were witnessing something special. David warned the team of their visitors' fighting spirit and urged them to stay focus and secure the three points.

The visitors made a tactical change. They switched into a 3-4-1-2 formation to solidify their defence while bringing a target man on to pair up with the young and mobile striker. Adam returned to his favourite number ten role and would no doubt be battling against Richard.

The new arrival wasted no time to demonstrate his tremendous ball holding ability. He chested down a clearance from deep under the attention of Kieran and he found Adam on his left, just over the halfway line. He tricked Tom into a tackle and took the ball forward into the final third, but before he engaged with Richard he sent it behind Maz for his left back, who put in a high cross towards the target man. He flicked it over Gordon but Layne came out of nowhere and headed it out for a corner! The stadium breathed a collective sigh of relief before they rallied behind the team for the corner kick. It was taken by Adam but cleared by Graham.

The next fifteen minutes were tensed. Richard dropped deeper to handle Adam's threat while Danny and Tom tracked the other runners from midfield. Layne and Maz concentrated on their defensive responsibilities and limited their counterparts' influence.

Richard had been fulfilling his duties under the radar the whole match. While he acknowledged what Layne said before the game, he had no ill feelings towards their opponents and didn't feel the need to be too expressive, especially with the team three goals to the good. However, he was called into serious action at the hour mark. The target man cushioned it down perfectly onto Adam's path and Richard had to make a decision: whether he should commit a professional foul before he entered the penalty area or be confident in his own pace. He chose the latter and pushed himself forward. Adam got to the ball first but Richard's position forced him to take a touch. He created

572

an opening for a left foot shot instead, but he still couldn't escape from the determined defender, who dived in to block his shot.

The visitors finally found a way back into the game at the seventieth minute. The target man found the left wing back with a flick on after, and the cross was met by the young striker who gambled at the near post ahead of Graham!

Given their recent poor record against bigger teams, the Black Dragons were clearly troubled by the potential come back and they sat deeper and deeper as a result. Players were nervous and they gave the ball away rather cheaply. Richard had to make tackles after tackles as he marshalled the area in front of the back line, but a breach looked imminent.

David replaced the hat trick hero Ryan with Thomas to have five defenders at the back for the last fifteen minutes, but that seemed to have played into the opposition's hands as they launched waves of attacks. They soon pulled another goal back as the target man, who won most, if not all, his aerial duels since coming on, jumped the highest again to divert a cross into the back of the net.

"We need to do something. We're waiting to be slaughtered here," Tom said to Richard.

"Yes we are inviting pressure at the moment. I think we need to keep them away from goal. Let's pull Bondi into midfield with us and push Danny up."

"Will we have the energy to do it?"

"I'd rather lose exhausted then dying a slow death."

The Black Dragons restarted the match with a different intention. They pressed higher up the pitch and denied the visitors any time on the ball. And if their opponents found their way out they stopped them with professional fouls. Soon there were yellow cards for Richard, Layne, Tom and Charlie, but most importantly, they were running the clock down.

The relentless visitors managed to create one last chance on the left. The wing back put in another great cross towards the target man but it was punched out by a brave Gordon. The ball only went as far as the edge of the area and Adam was there, steadying himself for a volley that would surely end up as the equaliser. Richard was too far to have any impact but he saw Layne in front of him and had an idea.

"Sorry baby," he apologised as he gave Layne a very heavy push.

Layne fell into the path of the shot and blocked it with his head. The ball went out of touch and that was it – the referee blew the final whistle and the Black Dragons won the gripping derby 3-2!

"What a block Layne! You're our saviour!" Tom shouted as he celebrated with the youngster, who was rubbing his forehead to ease the pain from the block.

"Did you-" he had a question for Richard.

"That was such a brave act, you took one for the team well!" Richard said as he picked Layne up with a giddy smile.

"I'll let you off, Richie," Layne whispered before the two giggled and hugged each other.

The supporters celebrated their first ever victory over their new local rivals with a prolonged version of their winning tune, "We Are The Dragons". It ran on and on and on and the players took turns to be the orchestrator in front of the West Stand.

Ryan was, naturally, named as the man of the match but David was full of praise for the determination and grit shown by the rest of the team.

The young attacker was invited by the broadcaster for the post-match interview for the first time and he grabbed Richard along for company. The studio congratulated him for his goals and his rich scoring form, but they also asked Richard about Layne's block at the end as they noticed that he gave his teammate and boyfriend a hefty push. Richard laughed and said that he was certain that Layne was about to dive in and he was only giving him some "guidance" on where the shot was going.

574

With the next match a full week away the coaching team gave the players the Monday off to recharge their batteries. Charlie took the opportunity to call for a team dinner out at a classy steak restaurant at Knightsbridge.

The food was fantastic, but the evening had an unpleasant twist as one diner approached the pair and shouted homophobic abuses at them. He was going to pour some red wine onto the players but a waiter selflessly shielded them before escorting the offender away. The incident took the celebratory mood away from Ryan, who wasn't quite ready to face the public and the attacks that entailed.

The players came back to training on Tuesday to two pieces of transfer news. The first was for last season's regular striker and academy graduate George, who joined the club down the south coast for eight million pounds. It was expected after he rejected the club's new contract offer and forced them to sell him instead of losing him on a free transfer.

The other move was more surprising, as club captain Ross signed for the team in Putney. They were relegated the season before and would offer Ross the guaranteed playing time he craved in familiar surroundings in the Championship.

David said that the club would be looking at the market for reinforcements, especially in midfield, where they would be a little light.

The team travelled to Merseyside on Friday for their game against the blue side there the next day. The struggling team's fans expressed their "welcome" with a firework display near the team hotel at the middle of the night, in order to disrupt the players' rest. Richard was one of those abruptly woken up by the loud noise, and he couldn't fall back to sleep until the equally suffering Layne sneaked in to snuggle up with him.

The team put on a tired performance as a result. Ryan opened the scoring with another excellent goal to take his tally to nine in five games but the former England under-21 striker Carl headed in a cross late on to salvage a point.

Richard played the whole game with a massive headache and had to sleep through the journey home.

Match day twenty four was only three days later, as The Dragons Stadium welcomed the team from the West Midlands. Charlie was the star as his thunderous left foot drive from outside the area rescued the team from a goal down for another 1-1 draw. Richard was an unused substitute as Toby and Tom played the full ninety minutes.

The team only had four days to prepare for their FA Cup fourth round tie away at the League One club in Bristol and David decided to rest a number of first team players. Layne was one of those and he rescheduled his usual piano lesson with Niccolò on Wednesday to Friday instead, so that they could have dinner at a hotel in Mayfair afterwards.

Richard wasn't exactly pleased with the arrangement but he had to go with it. He trust Layne and hoped that he only saw Niccolò as his tutor and friend, and nothing more.

He travelled with the match day squad on Friday afternoon and stayed at a hotel far away from town. The Logistics Manager said it was specifically arranged after the troubles with fireworks the week before. This, in theory, should give Richard a good night's sleep but he was completed restless after Layne texted him to say that he'd stay over at Niccolò's after having some wine during dinner. He seriously wanted to reply with a "no way" but he couldn't – he believed he had to respect his partner and have faith in his judgement.

"Take care, baby. I miss you."

He tried to sleep after sending his reply but the pessimism over losing Layne to Niccolò grew as the night went on. He couldn't stop imagining what the two were doing and his head was filled with rage and anxiety.

He reached breaking point soon after and resorted to taking some sleeping pills, but with his troubled state of mind he took more than the recommended doses, hoping for a quicker reaction. He eventually dosed off into a dream, away from the hell that was in his head.

He was in a park, walking alongside a crystal clear stream on a sunny autumn day. It looked like the English Garden in Munich, where he used to go every other weekend. Someone was talking to him in a deep but youthful voice, in a perfect royal accent. He recognised who it was straight away – it was Ian his first crush.

"I think it's scary," he said.

"What is?" Richard asked anxiously.

"The way you followed me everywhere. It's creepy."

"We... we just... happen to be in the same school and live near each other?"

"It's not that, is it? Why do you keep our picture in your wallet?"

"I... I just think it's a good photo..."

"It's scary."

"I... I..."

"Look, Richard. It won't work. Just leave me alone."

"But..."

"Richard, I'm not interested in men. Leave. Me. Alone."

Ian swiftly walked away, leaving the distraught Richard in the middle of the park. People gathered and laughed at him – some faces were familiar but he couldn't tell who they were. He had this deep sense of shame and he kept his head as low down as possible, eventually shutting his eyes to escape.

He didn't know how long it was before someone helped him up. He opened his eyes and saw a young and joyful Layne holding his face up to kiss him. It was warm and wonderful.

But it didn't last long. Someone forcefully pulled him and Layne apart – it was the Italian pianist Niccolò, wearing his elegant performance suit.

Richard's heart broke into pieces as Layne was pulled away and he couldn't do anything about it. The despair hit him, hard.

And he woke up at this point.

He found himself dripping in cold sweat in the small hours, still feeling the sorrow he experienced in his dreams. It was a mixture of actual events and his imaginations –

the unforgettable conversation between him and Ian was true to the letters and they did visit the English Garden together before, but the actual heartbreak happened during a gathering in a clubhouse. Then of course Layne kissed him that way plenty of times in real life, but he hoped the part with Niccolò wasn't true.

The in-fighting carried on in his head as he dipped in and out of his consciousness, until he decided enough was enough and got up for good at about six in the morning. He had a shower to freshen up and then some press-ups to focus his mind. He set off for breakfast at about half past seven, but someone was at the door when he opened it.

It was Layne!

"Good morning Richie! Why are you up so early?" he asked with a lovely smile on his face.

"What… what are you doing here?"

"I took the first train from Paddington!"

"Why?"

"Because I miss you too," Layne said before pushing Richard back in the room, until they fell into the bed.

"Weren't you staying over with Niccolò?"

"I did, but I can't stop thinking about you after seeing your text."

"Really? I thought you two would…"

"What were you thinking?"

"I think… he would… turn you away… from me…"

"How do you know he's interested in me?"

"He told me when we first met."

"Why didn't you tell me about it?"

"I didn't know how you would react, you seemed to like his company and you may think I'm bad-mouthing him out of jealous…"

"Oh Richie… is it why you've been so tense recently?"

"I guess so… I didn't really know what to do, and I couldn't stop imagining what would happen."

"You're being silly, as always."

"So did he…?"

"We had a few more drinks at his apartment and he told me that he wanted to bring me back to Italy with him. He's

578

even spoken to his friends over there to arrange a transfer to Serie A!"

"How... how did you respond?"

"I said no of course! I'm taken!"

The way Layne said the last sentence. The way he said it with zero hesitation. It made Richard feel extremely foolish for worrying over it the last few months.

"Yes you are baby, thank you."

"I meant it when I said I'm yours and will treat you well forever!"

Gazing into Layne's eyes, Richard felt completely in love. He felt liberated from all the anxieties that surrounded him in that split second; he wrapped his arms round Layne tightly to pull him closer, and closer, to the point that they were literally one.

"I want to tell you something too. I know I'm not the most romantic or entertaining partner in the world, but it is my life mission to treasure you, Layne."

"I know that Richie, and that's the one thing I love you the most!"

The world was wonderful again.

"Hey guys, would you mind closing the door when you do this kind of things please?"

The pair turned round to see a rather embarrassed Tom at the door, and quickly pulled him in before he said anything else.

"You're not even supposed to be here, Mr Moore! I don't think we welcome WAGs, or... HABs, into the team hotel!"

Richard was keen to point out that Layne had only just arrived and wasn't there overnight, but Tom gave them a suspicious look and laughed away.

"I'll leave it to you two to explain to the team later! See you downstairs!"

The pair did go for breakfast together after Layne put on Richard's team tracksuit. Richard told everyone that he'd forgotten his lucky shin pads and got Layne to deliver them first thing in the morning. Their teammates were surprised that even he could fail to prepare all his match day gear and praised Layne for his dedication.

"You dressed it up well, buddy," Tom said when the pair sat down with him.

"When push comes to shove, I can be a little less righteous," Richard said with a subtle smile.

"Now you'd better win the game with your lucky shin pads!" Layne laughed.

The match was a more straight forward affair. David played a youthful side and they secured their passage to the fifth round with a comfortable 3-1 victory. Alex partnered Ryan upfront in a 4-4-2 formation again and they were responsible for all the goals, with the former netting twice. Andrew made his full debut and provided one of the assists alongside Harry and Viktor.

"You played well in your sixty minutes or so on the pitch today, but you looked more than a little jaded?" Layne asked when the pair returned home.

"I didn't sleep well," Richard explained.

"You thought I may run away with Nico?"

"How can I not be worried? You're all I have!"

"Hehe, it's fine now. You'll have to put up with me for the rest of your life!"

"I'm only too happy to. How did Niccolò react when you told him no?"

"He was sensible about it, saying he's disappointed but respects my decision. He admitted that I belong to a lovely man already!"

"That's a surprise. Will you still have lessons with him?"

"No, yesterday was the last one. That's why I had the farewell dinner with him."

"Is he leaving?"

"Yes he goes back to Italy next week."

"Well that's the end of this chapter then."

"You may say that, but I did learn a lot for my piano though."

"That's very good, will you play me a song then?"

"Of course I can, but you'll go clothes shopping with me tomorrow, right?"

"Do you need me there? I thought you have an appointment with the personal stylist?"

"Yes, but I want him to dress you up too. We can visit the new restaurant there afterwards?"

"Okay, if you tempt me with something delicious!"

The couple enjoyed their evening as normality finally resumed.

As the end of the transfer window approached, rumours surfaced on some of Black Dragons' players. The strong performers such as Charlie, Kieran and Ryan attracted plenty of interests but the hottest gossips were on their prized asset, the goal-scoring midfielder Danny. Speculations had it that a number of top teams from the Premier League and beyond were tracking his progress and bids matching his release clause were imminent. The club had offered him another improved contract but he remained tight lipped on his future.

Charlie called for a mini gathering at his house the evening before the transfer deadline day and he didn't give Danny a second to settle before he popped the question.

"Hey Danny have you got offers?"

"Not yet," Danny answered coolly, as usual.

"Oh no, are you expecting one tomorrow?" Thomas asked.

"Quite possibly. My agent said one's being prepared, and the Dragons cannot reject."

"Are they going to meet your buyout? That's a lot of money!" Layne said.

"Which club are we talking about? Can you tell?" Richard followed up.

"Between these four walls, it's the white one from north London."

"Wowsers! Are you going to say yes?" Tom asked.

"I think it's likely-"

"No way! You are not leaving us!" Charlie cut in with a raised voice.

"Calm down Charlie. You know I love you guys but it's a much bigger club and they're playing in Europe. How can I refuse?"

"Are they going to give you much play time?" Richard tried to analyse the situation.

"They do have plenty of great players but I have to believe in my own abilities."

"They won't waste that much money to have you on the bench, right?" Layne added before the others gave him a stare.

"I really think you should stay for another year or two," Charlie said, having calmed himself down. "We can really achieve something here together, don't give it up just yet."

"And if we do, you'll get to play for even bigger clubs!" Tom did his part of the offensive.

"You guys really are giving me a headache. What do you think, Rich?"

"Without being selfish, I hope you would stay. Yes the other club is playing in Europe now, but I'm certain we'll get our chance in the not too distant future. We really can build our own history!"

"But these opportunities don't come along that often..."

"Like you said, you need to believe in yourself! Better chances will come, no doubt!" Tom said.

"Why don't you stay for the rest of this season at least and think about it if we don't qualify for Europe?" Richard continued his efforts.

"Let me think it through tonight... there's no guarantee that they'll bid anyway."

"I don't normally say this sort of things, but stay with us please, Danny! I really want to win trophies with you," Charlie concluded with a heartfelt plead.

"I know we won't be together forever, but let's make our first season in the Premier League as memorable as we can!" Tom added.

With the massive shadow hanging over them, the rest of the dinner was rather quiet. Everyone was occupied by what could have happened the next day, and the very different future after that.

Training next day was interrupted by the players' worst fear – Danny was given leave by the club to have his medical at the north London club halfway through the session, as a bid meeting his release clause of thirty million pounds had been received. The training ground was immediately filled with doom and gloom, as the star midfielder departed with his agent.

The young players gathered at Richard's that afternoon to watch the deadline day special together. They anxiously waited for news regarding Danny but nothing official had come from either clubs.

The Black Dragons did announce that they had recalled Kasper Boilesen the combative midfielder from his loan spell as the replacement for Ross. He gained plenty of first team experience in the Swedish top division and should be a useful addition to the squad. There were also rumours that the club was in talks with other clubs for an attacking option should Danny leave.

The players heard that their old under 23 teammate Max Roberts had joined the Premier League club in Tyneside after two successful seasons in League One, and Richard was surprised to hear that the same club had also signed his friend Hakim Benchekroun on loan from Munich.

"Who's this Hakim guy?" Layne asked after he saw Richard's reaction.

"He's a wonderful winger, one of those who can beat me regularly at one-on-ones."

"Does someone like that even exist?" asked the amazed Tom.

"Yes of course. We'd better be careful when we come up against him in the future."

The team suddenly heard the ringtone of a mobile phone and looked into its direction – it was Richard's, and it clearly showed the name Danny Westwood on the screen. Richard nervously gestured everyone to keep the noise down before he picked it up.

"Hi Danny."

"Hey Rich, are you with the boys?"

"Yes, you're on the speaker, how… is it going?"

"Good, that'll save me calling you all one by one then."

"What… are you trying to tell us?"

"Well… Open the bloody door first, Rich!"

"What?"

Richard ran to the front door and there he was. Danny was standing there, with a rare smile on his face, holding two bottles of champagnes.

"I thought you're in north London?"

"It's all finished. I reckon you guys will all be here and bring some drinks along."

"What do you mean by finished? Have you signed for them?"

"I'll tell you if you let me in!"

Richard led Danny into the kitchen where everyone was waiting.

"So…?" Tom ran out of patience and broke the silence.

"So what?" Danny just smiled.

"Stop acting up, are you still one of us?" Charlie asked.

"Of course. Who do you think I am, some sort of traitor?"

"Do you mean you've turned them down to stay with us?" Richard said slowly to confirm.

"Yes Rich. I waved goodbye to twenty grand a week just because some idiot begged me to win some trophies with him!" Danny said looking in Charlie's direction.

"You fucking bastard!" Charlie said jokingly. "I didn't go as far as begging!"

"This is the best news I've heard all day! Well played Danny!" Thomas said while giving Danny a high five.

"How did the other club react? It must have been quite late into the process when you told them?" Alex asked.

"Yeah I had my medical and everything before telling them that I want to stay at TDS for the rest of this season. I promised them I won't sign a contract extension before then, and they can come again if we don't make it into Europe."

"Is that the condition then? To make it into Europe?" Tom asked.

"That's a big ask! We're only ninth in the league!" Layne said.

"Well you guys better show me all you've got then!"

"We'll win them all!" Charlie said loudly, before leading the team into a group handshake.

"Fly, you Black Dragons!"

Richard quickly iced the champagnes and the team toasted to celebrate their long-standing friendship. They vowed to do all they could to bring success together.

36.

Scandal

Richard and Layne woke up to a shocking piece of news the next morning. The tabloid that they had a few run-ins with previously published a story outing Ryan's sexuality, backed up by details provided by one of his ex-boyfriends. They showed pictures of the two together, including some captured from a video of them in rather compromising positions.

"Have you seen this Richie? Oh my God it's horrifying!" Layne said when he discovered the story on social media, and with it plenty of comments linking it back to him, Richard and the club in a derogatory manner.

"Yes it's bad. I left Ryan a message but he hasn't come back yet."

"Let me give him a call," Layne said before trying, to no avail.

The pair joined the match day squad at the training ground as scheduled and the article was on everyone's lips. They were worried by the lack of response from Ryan until David confirmed that he had spoken to him directly and advised that he would not play a part that day. Sam was included in the match day eighteen against the club in south London instead.

Supporters of the home side were all fired up for the Black Dragons' visit, as they welcomed them chanting "Where's your King?" continuously. They reserved the loudest jeer available for the pair – they might not have said any homophobic words, but their intentions were clear.

David went for the same team from their last league game with Toby and Ryan replaced by Richard and Alex. The team were ten points away from reaching the magical forty expected for Premier League survival and he was

586

keen to achieve it as soon as possible to avoid being dragged into the gruesome relegation battle.

The Black Dragons tried to take the initiative from the start but were pushed back by some strong pressing, with Aaron the England under 21 midfielder particularly industrious. He didn't give Richard and Tom any time on the ball and forced them into playing safe passes.

Charlie was determined to gain an edge on the pitch following his vow to Danny. He was running into space nonstop and when he finally created an opening for a shot from outside the area, his piledriver was inadvertently blocked by Alex, who sprained his ankle in the process. It looked bad and he would probably be out of actions for another four to six weeks.

David remained calm in his half time team talk despite losing all his three recognised strikers within a short space of time. He asked Charlie to move into the centre to be flanked by Luciano and Sam in the second half.

The home team came out strongly in the second period. Their star left winger gave Maz a torrid time and he was sending crosses into the Black Dragons' box again and again. They were adequately defended and the visitors had a throw in on their left, which Layne was going to take.

Some fans in the stand took their opportunity to give him all sort of insults.

Did you take one up your arse last night?

Where's your queer striker today?

Why don't you leave the pitch to the proper lads?

Even though he was used to hearing these, Layne wasn't happy with them taking aim at Ryan. He talked back to one of the abusers but it prompted a ferocious response from the crowd and objects started to rain on him. One of them hit the corner of his right eye and left him bleeding quite badly. Richard rushed to the scene but Aaron was there before him, shielding the left back from more projectiles. Players from both teams joined forces to escort Layne away from the stands, as the medical team gave him some emergency stitching and patched him up.

The referee ordered the teams to gather around the centre circle while the stewards tried to control the crowd. A public announcement was also made to remind the supporters the club's zero tolerance policy towards homophobic slurs. The disturbance lasted for about ten minutes and the match resumed after the players had another warm up. Layne was replaced by Lewis as a precaution.

With the lengthy break in play, both teams had to rebuild their momentum and it wasn't until five minutes before the whistle for another shot at goal. The hosts' star winger cut inside Maz and his driven shot flat-footed Gordon and went in off the near post!

While the stadium was still celebrating, the Black Dragons put together a lightning quick move from the kick off to open the home defence. A through pass by Richard found Sam on the left and Danny laid his cross brilliantly for Charlie to level the match!

"We'll never go down without a fight!" cried the goal scorer Charlie.

The visitors went for the kill at the dying seconds with another beautiful build-up to send Luciano through. He took it round the keeper and applied the simple finish to surely put the match away! The players went wild and lifted the Argentinian in the air to celebrate, but it was short lived.

The linesman had his flag up for offside and the goal had to be checked by the video assistant referee!

It wasn't the first time for the team to go through this new process but it was certainly one with the most at stake. The decision took ages to arrive and it wasn't good – Luciano was fractionally offside. The match ended soon after and the teams had to settle for a draw. The Black Dragons dropped to eleventh in the league and the gap to top six was extended to fourteen points. Charlie apologised to Danny for not winning the game but was strongly rebuffed as Danny insisted it was his decision to turn the transfer down and the team did not owe him anything – as long as everyone pulled together as one he had no regrets.

Richard was invited to an interview along with Aaron and they jointly expressed their disgust at the homophobic chanting and the attack on Layne. Fortunately the injury was minor, but players needed better protection from rogue spectators in the stands. The clubs stated that they would cooperate with the police to identify the culprits and enforce appropriate punishments.

The pair decided to visit Ryan straight from their dismissal at the training ground. They were given the spare key to his apartment a while ago and they went in after getting no response from inside.

"Richie! Come here quick!!!" Layne screamed after he looked into the bathroom.

Richard rushed in and saw an unconscious Ryan in a bath of blood. He was absolutely horrified but remained calm enough to act. He raised Ryan's arm with the wound out of the water to reduce the bleeding and asked Layne to call for an ambulance. Ryan looked extremely pale and was barely breathing. He was in a really critical situation.

The wait for help felt like years. The pair kept encouraging Ryan to carry on the fight but when they looked at each other they were petrified at the thought of the unthinkable.

"Ryan's going to be alright, right?" Layne said, shakily.

"Yes! He'll be just fine!" Richard was probably comforting himself as well as Layne.

"Are you... sure?"

"Yes! He's a fighter, he'll make it!"

The paramedics arrived minutes later and began the rescue. They lifted Ryan out of the water, strapped up his wounds, fitted him with an oxygen mask and transferred him into the ambulance. Layne accompanied him to the hospital while Richard followed the ambulance and informed David of the situation on the way.

David and the pair waited in a cordoned off area for a couple of hours as the accident and emergency team battled to save Ryan's life. He got the distraught couple a change of clothes as their team tracksuits were soaked in blood. The youngster's parents and brother arrived later and they joined the worried party.

Ryan was immediately given a blood transfusion to counter the severe blood loss and his condition stabilised gradually. The medical team advised that he was no longer in a life threatening situation but would have to be monitored in intensive care for a few days. They claimed that the pair's early intervention was the absolute key in Ryan's revival.

Richard and Layne held each other upon hearing the news, weeping tears of relief that their friend was saved. They were genuinely scared that it might not be the case when they first encountered his lifeless face.

Ryan's parents thanked the medical staffs and the pair, and vowed to stay close to Ryan to oversee his recovery, both physically and mentally.

Rumours appeared online regarding the incident but they were firmly denied by the Black Dragons. They issued a statement saying the health and safety of the players were of paramount importance and they would not disclose any information. They also strongly condemned the actions from sections of the media in exposing players' private lives in an irresponsible and demeaning manner.

The players were shocked by the news and they shared the anger towards the tabloid. Charlie called for a boycott online and gathered support from players, pundits and supporters, but it also attracted the keyboard warriors and bots from around the world who came up with some horrendous comments. It became a battle of words between the two sides with politicians joining in to express their views and the matter occupied social media for a good few days.

The Black Dragons travelled to the league leaders in Merseyside the following weekend for match day twenty six. With the week dominated by negative press the team's preparations were far from ideal. They were seriously short on options upfront and David called Finley up from the under 23's to be Luciano's backup.

Richard and Layne were physically available for selection but David left them out of the match day squad as he noticed that the traumatic experience had effected their mental stability. Ryan came out of his induced coma on earlier that week but was still very fragile. He managed to have a brief conversation with his family but was not ready for anyone else.

The pair went bowling at their usual centre as a way to counter the stressful situation. They went in wearing their glasses and hoodies and specifically requested the lane at the far side to stay away from attention. After winning a tight game each, Layne offered to get some drinks from the bar. Richard took the opportunity to polish the balls but he soon heard an altercation from Layne's direction and headed over immediately. He saw three men in replica shirts of the Black Dragons' opponents that day taunting Layne with the match result, which was a straight forward 3-1 victory to the home side.

"You fucking rent boys aren't even good enough to lick our boots!" Richard heard one of the fans bragged.

"Or suck our dicks in your case," another one followed.

"You what?" Layne asked.

"You're just a team full of queers! Look at how your fucking striker enjoyed getting bumped!"

"Don't you talk about Ryan like that!"

"Oh I'm so scared! What the fuck are you going to do about it, you little wimp?"

The thug approached Layne with a "hit me" gesture before giving the youngster a hefty shove, sending him crashing to the floor. He got up quickly as the thug came forward again.

Richard intervened in time and stepped in between the two.

"Don't you dare touching him again."

"Of course the gay husband is here too, I'll shut your big mouth off right here!"

Richard dodged the thug's punch and charged into him with his shoulder to send him flying.

591

The thug wasn't expecting a fight back from the studious looking player but he duly drew out a pocket knife from his back amid laughter from his friends.

"You think you're hard yeah, come and get this!" he threatened as he waved his knife at Richard.

"Be careful Richie!" Layne sounded really scared.

Richard was well aware of the danger before him but he was desperate to protect Layne from harm. He was not a seasoned fighter like Tom and Charlie so he thought he must put every effort into ending the conflict in a single, powerful blow. He couldn't allow any mistakes or hold anything back.

He focused on the attacker's movement and stamped on his left quad muscles as hard as he could when he came into range. The full force of a professional football player was not something to be sniffed at and the thug fell heavily onto the ground, groaning painfully. The other two men seemed frightened by what they saw and fled.

Richard paused for a second to confirm that the threat was eliminated before turning round to check on Layne, only to find his boyfriend absolutely terrified.

"Are you okay, Richie? Does... your arm hurt?"

Richard looked at his left arm and realised its outside had been slashed open all the way up to his elbow. Blood was bursting out like a waterfall and there was a strange chilling feeling from his wound. He started to faint soon after and he slowly crashed down.

Layne stopped him from falling to the ground and pleaded with bystanders for help. A first-aider laid him down on the floor and wrapped his arm up, but the bleeding carried on and he was slowly losing his consciousness against an extraordinary strong urge to close his eyes.

"Don't sleep Richie! Don't sleep! Don't leave me here! Don't..."

He heard Layne's desperate call and tried hard to stay awake. He saw the panic in his eyes and attempted to say something, but he was too weak to make any sense.

I won't leave you, baby. I won't... We'll be together forever, remember...

He eventually ran out of energy and passed out.

His mind switched into a completely dark space and he wasn't able to think. He didn't know how long it was until he suddenly felt an injection of fresh air and regained some of his consciousness. He wasn't aware of where he was, but he could feel Layne's hands holding his, which gave him some comfort. He fell asleep again soon after.

The next time he woke up he was in Kingston Hospital, the very same place that they took Ryan to the week before. He knew because he was being treated by the same emergency medical team, who were asking him for his name and other questions. His blood loss was apparently minor in comparison and he started feeling better after the doctors stitched him up to stop his bleeding and gave him some drips.

His concerned parents were there with Layne when he was transferred to the private ward where he would be staying for the night. He tried to comfort them by claiming he was okay but they all knew that there were more to worry about than just his injury. The tide against a more inclusive environment in football seemed to have gathered pace and it felt impossible to rid those violent and bigoted views.

The incident was well-publicised with videos doing the rounds on social media and plenty of journalists stationed outside the hospital. They stopped David and Nick when they visited after returning from Merseyside and they got excited when they spotted Richard's parents leaving. They pushed and shoved each other to get the best pictures and ask questions. Richard's father gave up trying to find a way out and decided to issue an impromptu statement. He expressed his anger at the verbal and physical attacks aimed at his son's sexuality and strongly condemned some media for inciting the hatred with their coverage. He also highlighted the lack of actions by the Football Association and Premier League, accusing them of paying lip services without any real substance.

"The boys simply love each other. It makes no difference whether they are footballers or not."

Richard watched his dad's statement in tears as it was really some journey for him to change from being completely against his wishes to supporting him publicly. Layne was sitting next to him and he gave him a tight hug, with tears of his own.

"Can you promise me that you won't get into danger for me again, please?"

"I can't, baby. I will protect you no matter what."

"How am I supposed to live if something happens?"

"Don't be silly. That guy could have stabbed you if I didn't step in."

"You should just grab me and run!"

"If I knew he had a knife, yes, but at that moment I had to face up to him."

"But he could have stabbed you…"

"That's why I tried to kick him before he got closer, but he cut my arm in the process."

"That was quite a kick. You could have dislocated his knee if you hit lower."

"I've read that it's the best place to hit if you only want to immobilise someone."

"Where did you get this sort of random information from?"

"I think it read it from the UFC in passing."

"And you remember it when someone was wielding a knife at you?"

"It just came up. I was thinking about hitting his knee cap or his shin, but I thought they may cause permanent damage."

"He deserved it. I hope he gets a lengthy sentence."

"He can't escape, not with so many witnesses."

"I wish this is the end of these horrible things, but it just feels like the beginning."

Richard didn't know what to say, he could only hold onto Layne and hope for the best. They had no choice but to carry on and face it all.

The pair visited Ryan the next morning. The striker's physical condition might have improved, but he was in no mood for a conversation. He was grateful for their life-saving actions the week before, but he remained completely broken throughout the brief encounter.

"It's so sad to see Ryan like that," Layne said to Richard back in their room. "That spark he used to have has disappeared..."

"Yes. It's bad enough being outed against his wish, but nobody, regardless of their sexuality, wants their privacy to be exposed like that in public."

"Why did his first boyfriend do that to him? I know they didn't end well but this hurts so much!"

"I guess he's paid handsomely by the paper for that..."

"Do you think Ryan can sue them?"

"There probably is a case, but will that bring even more damage to Ryan? It's so tough."

"What can we do to help him recover?"

"I don't know. I'm no expert on psychology but I guess we need to keep showing him that there are people in this world who understand and care about him."

Richard was discharged from hospital in the evening. He considered various methods to escape from the reporters outside but chose to face them directly at the end. He wanted to follow his dad's example and send a message to Ryan that there was nothing to be fearful of. He gave some short answers to the press while Layne got the car ready, condemning the return of homophobia and the knife culture in London. He urged authorities to do more in both areas.

The Black Dragons were back in action the following weekend, when they entertained the white team from north London at home. It was the teams' first encounter since Danny turned down their approach on the last day of the transfer window. They scrambled to sign 22-year-old Dutch attacking midfielder Dex instead, which might indicate the end of their pursuit of the Black Dragons' ace.

David restored Layne to the match day squad but Richard was not allowed to play when his wound was still healing. He did attend the match and joined his teammates to present a banner with "No place for discrimination" on, to a big round of applause by both sets of supporters.

The Black Dragons did well to stay toe-to-toe with the fourth place side for the first half an hour but they were caught in a counter attack soon after. The awesome inside forward broke the offside trap and rounded Gordon to make it 1-0 to the visitors at half time.

The home team's hope for a comeback in the second half was dashed by the same forward, who turned provider with a brilliant back heel to set up the striker for a smashing finish. Danny pulled one back at the hour mark after some nice footwork by Charlie but Dex the substitute had the last laugh as he ghosted past Kasper and Graham to complete another great move by the north London side.

Richard watched the match from the stands and noted the team's lack of fluency with three key players missing. He felt sorry for Danny – they made all promises to persuade him to stay but for one reason or another they only picked up one point from the next nine available. With just thirty-one points they were down to thirteenth, a massive twenty points behind the team in sixth and were in fact much closer to the relegation zone with seven. European football next season seemed like a pipe dream.

With the League Cup final the following weekend, the team had a week off before their next league game the following Tuesday, at home against the team from East Midlands.

Richard was back in full training ten days after his injury and started alongside Layne in a freezing February night.

The Black Dragons made a good start as Kieran headed in Richard's corner after fifteen minutes. They held on to their lead for half time but rued their luck as Luciano's close range finish bounced off the bar near the end.

The regrouped visitors levelled the match five minutes into the second half, as their veteran striker latched on to

Damian's low angled cross from the left between two centre backs and expertly diverted the ball into the bottom corner.

The teams had an intense battle for the decisive goal in the next twenty minutes, as the Black Dragons took the gamble and squeezed the play. Charlie couldn't direct Layne's driven cross on target, while Ben sent a free kick inches over the bar. Damian had a chance to break through after flicking the ball past Maz, but Richard slid in from way out to block his progress. He captivated the crowd further with an amazing cross field pass to Layne on the opposite flank, who sent in an equally astonishing cross first time, and Charlie was at the far post to complete the breath-taking move with an outrageous flying scissor kick on the volley. He jumped on top of the advertising board and indulged himself with admiration from around the stadium.

The phenomenal goal seemed to have stunned the away side, as they struggled to keep their passing together to re-build any momentum. David gave Finley his Premier League debut five minutes from time, and his nonstop closing down helped the team secure their first win in six league games.

The Black Dragons were back in action quickly as they made the trip to Birmingham to face Bob's team in the FA Cup fifth round four days later. Their opponents had been flying in the Championship and automatic promotion was well within their grasp.

"I feel a little nostalgic coming back to this stadium!" Charlie joked when the Black Dragons' coach arrived.

"We only played here last year, you dumbass," Tom pointed out.

"But it felt like years ago!"

"They may be a division below us now, but they're not to be under-estimated," said Danny.

"We may well meet them again in the league next year judging by where they are now too," Thomas said.

"I was only joking! I know how tough they are and how important this match is, it's our route to European football next season!

"Fly you Black Dragons!

"Glory to Thames Ditton!

"To Europa and Beyond!"

Richard and the team roared to each of Charlie's battle cry. They knew the significance of the match as the cup was the only realistic way to qualify for Europe and keep the team together.

David opted for a slightly changed starting eleven with Jack in goal, Thomas and Kieran as centre backs, Viktor and Layne the offensive fullbacks, Kasper as the anchor man behind two box-to-box midfielders in Richard and Tom, then the interchangeable Charlie, Danny and Sam upfront. Tom was named as the captain for the young side, whose average age was only twenty-one years and seven months.

The home team had half an eye on their busy Championship run-in and fielded a slightly weakened side. Their new signing during the January transfer window, Rory the England under 21 right back from the Nottinghamshire club, started alongside the two former Thames Ditton players Les and Darren. Bob also gave his highly rated 16-year-old forward Phil his first start for the club, while Ted their captain and attacking midfielder was only on the bench alongside several other regular starters.

The hosts tried the take the initiative right from the word go as they wanted to avoid the tempo being dictated by the Black Dragons like previous encounters. They overcame the visitors' typical fast start with direct passing coupled with plenty of running, successfully pushing their opponents onto the back foot. Balls were hit into the channels where the two strikers drifted into and midfielders and fullbacks were making plenty of supportive runs.

They broke the deadlock after twenty minutes as Rory picked up Darren's knock down on the right flank and delivered a beautiful cross towards the back post, where the young Phil raced ahead of Viktor to poke home his first senior goal.

The strong home support kept pushing their side forward and they nearly scored a second goal minutes later. The centre midfielder collected a cut back from Phil and his shot went just wide of the post, with Jack completely beaten. It would have gone in had Richard not managed to deflect it away with the tip of his boot.

David decided to change the team's shape at half time. He asked Tom to drop into a back three and pulled Danny and Sam into wide midfield. He wanted to three defenders to cope with the two forwards and let the fullbacks concentrate on the wingers, to allow them to push the play higher up the pitch without worrying about being exposed.

"We will create chances and you need to put them away, you're the key of this," he said to the lone striker Charlie, who gave him a reassuring nod.

The Black Dragons contained the hosts well in the second half and slowly forced them backwards. They enjoyed a good spell of possession but couldn't find a way through the sold defence marshalled by their former graduate Les, who had the physique and strength to deal with Charlie.

Richard had been protecting the back three with Kasper throughout the match but as time went on he needed to do more for the attacking side. He waved Danny to move inside as he overloaded the left with Layne and Charlie. He had a tiny bit of space with the ball at the corner of the box, feinted a shot and dragged it onto his left foot for a cross. The low ball was too hard for Danny inside the six yard box but Sam was at the far post to slide it into the net!

With just fifteen minutes to go, both sides made changes to go for the winner. Bob brought Ted and the regular striker on while David replaced Kasper and Viktor by Lewis and Maz. The former moved into the back three, pushing Tom back into midfield with Richard and Danny.

Richard's new task was to manage the threat of Ted and was soon called into action. The attacker received the ball at his favourite left flank and brought it to the edge of the area. Richard was shepherding him all along, eventually gave away a corner kick. He refrained from committing to a tackle, as he knew Ted would either change direction at the very last moment or make contact with him for a free kick.

Rory took the set piece and found the giant Les at the back post, but his goal-bound header was bravely diverted over the bar by Layne, who was guarding the post. He roared towards the travelling fans behind him to celebrate his effort and received a massive cheer in return.

Jack came out to attack the next corner kick and managed to pluck the ball out of thin air. He threw it quickly to Danny on the left who controlled it beautifully and immediately ran forward with it. He drew one of the two defenders towards him before releasing the ball into the middle for Charlie, whose first touch took it behind the last defender and ran through on goal. He didn't wait for the keeper to make his move and smashed it directly into the back of the net to complete the breath-taking come back!

He celebrated by brushing Danny's right boot to highlight his amazing contribution, and Danny replied with thumping the club crest on his chest!

Bob brought another striker on to launch his final offensive for the last five minutes – it was "throwing the kitchen sink" time. David responded by sending Thorsten on for Sam. Layne moved to left midfield as a result.

The home team bombarded the Black Dragons' area but they couldn't get past the three centre backs as well as Tom and Charlie in front of them. Richard, Danny and the fullbacks were fighting for the second balls and together they defended resiliently.

With seconds to go, Richard picked up the loose ball in the left back area and he hit a very high ball towards the final third after a quick glance. The goal keeper rushed out to collect it but he was up against Layne, who sped past Rory the last defender and knew exactly where the back spinning ball was going to land. He hit it on the volley and lobbed it towards goal first time!

The hapless keeper was in no man's land and could only watch on as the ball bounced towards the empty net. Layne sprinted all the way back to the away end and jumped into Richard to celebrate with his ecstatic teammates and supporters, with his name being echoed in the stadium. It was truly amazing.

The exciting cup tie ended 3-1 to the Black Dragons. Pundits ran out of superlatives to praise the team's energy and counter attacks. They were amazed by Layne's wonder goal at the end and joked that if there was anyone in the world who could anticipate Richard's wicked ball it would have been him. The Black Dragons went through to the FA Cup quarter finals for the first time ever in their history and they would play at Merseyside in three weeks' time, against the blue team there.

37.

Resolve

"What do you mean we can qualify for Europe by finishing seventh?"

Richard and Layne were having breakfast at home the day after the cup game and Layne was shocked to hear Richard's latest analysis.

"Let me explain. Ordinarily, Premier League teams placed between first and fourth qualify for the group stage of the UEFA Champions League. The fifth-placed club and the winners of the FA Cup enter the UEFA Europa League group stage, while the team who lift the League Cup enter the UEFA Europa League at the second qualifying round.

"You already know that because the team currently in second place won the League Cup, their Europa League place goes to the team in sixth. Now looking at the teams in the FA Cup quarter finals, if any one of the four top six sides win it then the team finishing seventh in the league will get it."

"Wow! So instead of the massive twenty-point gap, we may only be six off!"

"That's a lot of 'what ifs' at the moment, but it's definitely possible. Of course the best way is to win the cup ourselves!"

The Black Dragons were twelfth in the league after twenty-eight rounds, having picked up thirty-four points from eight wins and ten draws. The top six places were occupied by the six traditional big clubs and they had opened up a fourteen-point difference from the seventh-place team, the one from the West Midlands. The Black Dragons' remaining fixtures were slightly more favourable, as they only needed to play two of the top clubs in their ten remaining matches.

Having said all that, Richard reminded Layne that they needed to focus on bringing their own form back on track first, as they only managed to win one of the last six.

The next fixture took the team to the east London club. David rewarded Jack's good performance with another stint in goal and he started behind the back four of Maz, Layne, Thomas and Graham, who was playing against his old club. Danny returned to midfield with Richard and Tom while Charlie, Andrés and Luciano were upfront.

The sides exchanged a goal early in the first half. A forward pass from Tom to Luciano was cut out in midfield and the right winger muscled past Layne to control the subsequent through ball before firing it into the bottom corner. Then Charlie chested down Richard's long pass at the edge of the area on the left, passed it in field for Danny before threading his return ball to Luciano inside the area. The Argentinian hit it first time with the outside of his right foot into the far corner to equalise.

The match then became a tight affair as the teams fought for supremacy in the middle of the pitch. Richard had a few battles with Chris and managed to push him backwards. The rest of the team were also winning their fair share of personal battles and the half ended levelled.

The pattern continued into the second half until David utilised his bench. He brought Viktor and Sam on to freshen up the right hand side and also replaced the tiring Tom by Kasper. He wanted to free Danny from his defensive duties.

The gamble nearly backfired straight away as the home team's defensive midfielder timed his run well to connect with a cross at the edge of the area, only to see his powerful shot tipped wide by Jack at full stretch.

The deadlock was finally broken five minutes from time. The liberated Danny drifted to the right to collect an over-hit cross from Layne and he passed the ball back to the supporting Viktor. The Swede with spiky hair cut inside the left back and crossed with his left foot towards

Charlie, who knocked it down for Sam to hit on the volley with his less favourite right foot. The rather miscued shot took a massive deflection off the centre defender and went it, having left the keeper completed flat-footed!

The hosts had to push forward for an equaliser. The ball was given to Chris and he brought out the audacious – he approached Richard slowly, had a single outward step over with his right foot before dragging the ball all the way back, round behind his standing left foot and tipped it through Richard's legs with the "rabona" technique. It was a fantastic piece of skill to watch, except for poor Richard on the receiving end.

Chris went on to finish the move with a delicate chip from twelve yards out, it went over Jack but a defender slid in in time to lift it over the crossbar!

Richard looked up to see the team's saviour – it was Thomas the gentle centre half. Charlie ran over to pull him up and Layne jumped straight into him to celebrate his goal-saving effort, but he just coolly said, "Get back in positions, we still have a corner to deal with."

And indeed they did as Chris sent over the out-swinging corner kick from the right. It was over Richard and when he turned all he could see was a towering attacker meeting it at the back post. The world stood still at that moment as the powerful header flew towards goal in slow motion.

But it hit the post and went out!

The Black Dragons survived the late scare and picked up their fourth away win of the season. They were only three points away from safety with nine games to go. It really couldn't go wrong from there.

David was delighted with the hard-earned victory and he praised everyone's efforts.

"We're nearly there for our number one objective, well done boys!"

"Yes but we want more than that! We want to play European football next season, be it from finishing seventh or winning the bloody cup!" Tom claimed, to the cheer of the players.

604

"That's the spirit! Every game is a cup final from now on!" Charlie added.

"Fly! You Black Dragons!"

David waited for the team to settle down before giving Thomas special credits for his goal line clearance, "That's the difference between one and three points today."

"Cheers boss! But can 'The Unbeatable' stop being beaten please?"

The whole dressing room laughed while Richard put his hands up and apologised.

"To be fair, I didn't think that piece of skill was even possible. He's some player that Chris," Danny came to Richard's defence.

"He was always that good with his feet, like a freestyler," Andrés said.

"Well, thanks for sorting my old club out chaps, onto the next one!" Graham the captain concluded.

Richard and Layne visited Ryan that evening. The youngster had returned to training a week ago while he continued to receive counselling. His conditions had stabilised significantly since his last boyfriend Nils learnt about his suffering and re-united with him.

"How's your fitness test yesterday? Did they say you're ready to play?" Layne asked after the four settled down with some drinks in the living room.

"It went well. They said I'm physically good enough."

"That's amazing! You'll be back in the squad in no time!"

"I'm not really… sure about going in front of others. What if people bring the video up again? I don't know if I can concentrate…"

"But you'd love to play again, right?"

"I do, but I don't know…"

Noting Ryan's shaky voice, Richard stopped Layne from going further and shared a story that he had never spoken about before, not even with Layne.

"I've quit football once before," he said, to the shock of his audience.

"When Ian outed me publicly in Munich and we moved back to England, I didn't want to play anymore. I didn't want to be in amongst a team of cruel boys again. I just... wanted to stick my head in the sand, to study, to go to university, to find a job, and to live 'normally' for the rest of my life.

"I still loved the game. I read about it whenever I had some free time and watched all the matches. I went to a summer fete in Windsor with my mum one weekend and I entered the 'Beat the Goalie' competition thinking no one I knew would be around. I won it with a near perfect score but then realised Mr Clarke my PE teacher was there helping out. He asked why I never showed that side of me to anyone at school and why I refused to play in his lessons. I told him my worries, that I wasn't comfortable to be surrounded by others.

"Then he told me something. He said that he used to play at a decent level in his youths, with a good chance of making it professionally. But he suffered two bad injuries in quick succession and had to give it all up. He was just seventeen at the time.

"He went on to ask me a very simple question: whether I like football. I nodded and then he told me to play when I was able to, because it just won't last forever.

"I still remember his impression at that moment. He tried to look relaxed, but that piece of sadness and that sign of regret were something I'd never forget. I had a trial at Simon's youth club the next Monday and never looked back. There were times when the going got tough, when the world was against us, and I thought about packing it all in. But his words would come up in my head and I would find the strengths again.

"So, I would ask you the same question, Ryan. Will the love of the game help you overcome your anxiety? Will you regret not giving it your best shot, when you are fit and capable, in later life?

"Do you like football?"

"I... I... I do. But..."

"The human brain is a strangely simple thing. When you're dedicated to one thing and focused on it alone, you won't be able to see or hear anything else. Just do what you love to do, and the rest will sort itself out."

Ryan nodded. With tears in his eyes.

"Wherever you go, I'll be there to support you," Nils said before he gave Ryan a hug.

"No wonder why you're always so serious, Richie," he said. "I can totally imagine you smashing the top corner every time in 'Beat the Goalie' too!"

"I became more and more so after witnessing the footballing journeys of so many: Steve's injury, Peter and Rob's departures, Paul's release, Michael's forced retirement, even when Matt hung up his gloves. He was so proud of his achievements but yet he was also sad to stop playing. We really need to treasure every opportunity we have, when we get to play the game we love, with the people we love to play with."

"In your case, with the person you love!" Layne couldn't help pointing it out.

"Yes Layne," Richard gave his boyfriend a little smile. "Do you get what I mean, Ryan?"

"Yes I do. You're right. I can't afford to waste more time. Plenty of other kids had their dreams smashed just for us to be here. I'll focus on being match fit again."

Richard was glad that Ryan was willing to resume playing. It wasn't so much that the team needed his potency upfront, he didn't want to see Ryan wasting his undoubted potential.

The Black Dragons' next match was against Sheffield at home. Having moved up to tenth with their last win, they were only one point behind their opponents, who were in rather patchy form.

The in-form Charlie, who scored three goals and assisted a further four during the last seven games, took advantage of the visitors' lack of confidence at the back to put his side in front after ten minutes. He demanded the ball from Danny when he started sprinting in field from the left, put it through the legs of a defender as he controlled the driven pass, then smashed it into the top left corner before the other defenders could tackle him. It was his eighth goal in the league and ninth in total – quite a productive first season in the top flight.

The away side launched a fight back but was caught by a lightning quick counter attack. A cross from the right was punched out by Jack and Tom cushioned it down for Richard, who hit a long, non-spinning ball first time towards Sam on the right. He chested it down nicely and eventually forced a corner off the left back. Richard's found Thomas at the near post and he diverted it to the top corner for his first goal of the season. He celebrated in front of Elle and the two boys in the Ditton Stand, where players' family members were seated.

With the team on course to achieve Premier League safety, the "We are staying up" chant was echoing around the stadium nonstop. The players switched to match management mode and kept their opponents at bay for the rest of the half.

The visitors improved after the break and threatened with their direct passing. The Black Dragons survived a scare midway through the half as a midfielder fired wide from close range after running through from deep, but they conceded five minutes later. The hardworking striker received the ball between Lewis and Thomas and his layoff found the supporting midfielder for a powerful finish from just inside the area.

The goal set up a frantic end to the game as the young Black Dragons panicked and lost their composure on the ball, which invited more pressure from their opponents. Having taken Richard and Layne off earlier in the half to manage their energy level, David sent the fit-again Alex to close down the defence. And the striker made the decisive difference in rather fortuitous fashion minutes later, as he deflected the keeper's clearance into the back of the net after the ball smashed him in the head.

The match ended 3-1 to the Black Dragons. With forty points secured, they had reached the traditional safety mark from relegation. The eighteenth-placed team might only be twelve points behind with another twenty-four available, but once all matches between the teams were taken into account, at least one of them would fare worse and so they were mathematically safe. Supporters were having a party in the stands as they danced to the tunes played by the stadium and players, including all those that didn't feature on the day, gathered in front of them to celebrate together.

The coaching team were in celebration mode as they lined up glasses of champagne to welcome the team back to the dressing room. Charlie took one of the unopened bottles to spray at everybody and the singing and dancing resumed.

David indulged in the celebrations before seeking everyone's attention for a speech.

"Hey gentlemen, we've done it! We've hit the magical forty points, and we get to play at the highest level for another season!

"Thank you for making this happen. I appreciate that the style we try to instil is extremely demanding and we had plenty of ups and downs, but I firmly believe that this gives us the best chance to succeed, and with the tremendous efforts from every single one of you, we've shown the world that we're here to stay, a full eight games ahead of schedule. Cheers everyone! But-"

"Oh don't you give us another 'Bob's moment' boss!" Tom jumped in.

"No no no, this is only the first part of our project and there're plenty more. What I was going to say is that, we have more business to finish this season! The west London derby next week, the club's first ever FA Cup quarter final the one after, and seven more top flight matches! I want you to win all of them! Are you with me?"

The team gave the gaffer a big roar.

"To Europa and beyond!" Charlie shouted his favourite slogan to another round of applause.

Richard was really happy with how the season turned out. He exchanged a satisfactory smile with Layne, held his hand for a quick second before going for their showers.

The players were given the next day off and Charlie called for a dinner together. He asked Layne for recommendations and the youngster suggested a seafood restaurant by Teddington riverside. The group enjoyed some sparkling cocktails and a sumptuous collection of fresh fish and shellfish in the company of a lively jazz band. The tipsy Layne later took over the grand piano and wowed the diners with a few of his favourites. The night reached its climax when he played and sang the Black Dragons' winning tune, "We Are The Dragons". Richard and the rest joined in and had a wonderful time.

A video of his performance soon trended on social media and it attracted a large amount of reactions. The Thames Ditton supporters naturally praised his talents, others criticised the players' extravagant celebration of the mere achievement of securing Premier League safety and some said he should just focus on his football. There were also the usual homophobic comments from the "No Place for Gay" brigade, which sparked fierce challenges from the inclusive fans. Richard read some of them but he had learnt to ignore and move on.

Thames Ditton's next game was a short journey to the west London club. The hosts sacked their manager after their 3-2 defeat by the Black Dragons and the players were keen for a revenge. They provided the in-form side a reality check as they won the match comfortably 2-0. The new tactically astute manager instructed his team to sit deep and counter quickly against the visitors' high tempo squeeze and they succeeded twice early in the first half through their precision in passing. Ryan made a cameo appearance near the end, with both sets of supporters giving him a warm welcome.

The Black Dragons' four-game winning run ended, but they remained ninth in the league, four points behind the team in seventh. They had a week to recharge their batteries and rediscover their form, before they travelled to Merseyside for their first ever FA Cup quarter final.

Richard and Layne received their call up from the England under 21 team as they resumed their European Championship qualification campaign away in Greece a week later. They were accompanied by the usual Kieran, Danny and Charlie, plus Tom who was recalled after missing out for over a year and Jack who was selected for the first time.

The club's logistics team had learnt from their previous visit to Merseyside and arranged to stay at a countryside hotel outside Manchester instead. As always they had to test the four key elements: temperature, lighting, noise and pillows to ensure the players get the rest they needed. The home supporters were still able to locate them but couldn't cause any disturbance as the hotel security team blocked their attempt to go near the premises to set off their fireworks.

They found another way to intimidate the Black Dragons on match day as they ambushed their team coach with eggs and stones when they arrived the stadium. Players were asked to move away from the window seats while the police cleared the way amid chants of "Bum Boys" from the crowd. It wasn't a pleasant experience.

David picked a strong eleven for the clash, with Gordon back in goal, Viktor, Layne, Thomas and Kieran in defence, the usual midfield of Richard, Tom and Danny and finally Charlie, Luciano and Ryan in attack. The talented young striker was selected after impressing in training.

However, he was clearly the home fans' target as they threw all sorts of abuses at him ever since he appeared for the warm up. Gestures, whistles and chants directly referring to the video intensified as kick off approached. The hosts sent warnings to the perpetrators, which seemed to have calmed the actions but loud jeers continued whenever Ryan, Layne and Richard were near the ball.

The Black Dragons tried to take the initiatives on the pitch with their high tempo attacks but they failed to convert the chances they created, with Ryan particularly hesitant. Typically in a football match, they were punished by their opponents' first meaningful move, as a counter attack found its way to Carl for a powerful headed finish.

Ryan continued to be ineffective and after he wasted two further opportunities the hosts scored another goal. Their veteran left back curled in a beautiful free kick from twenty-five yards after a handball by Layne.

"We can't let the game slip away like this," Tom said to his teammates prior to the restart.

"I'm really sorry guys, I'm not sure if I can handle this," Ryan said with his hands on his head.

"Don't be daft. It's just some stupid chants and you can't let them get into you," Danny said.

"Yes we'll carry on playing our game and you'll convert the next one!" Charlie joined in to encourage the youngster.

"We'll rely on you, as we always do," Richard added.

The Black Dragons created another chance at the half hour mark. Viktor found Danny at the edge of the penalty box and he slipped a little ball in to send Ryan through on goal. The whole world watched on as he dithered for a few tenths of a second and the chance was smothered by the keeper!

The crowd laughed at Ryan's miss and some started shouting "Bum Boy" repeatedly at him. It was soon echoed by half the stadium and it was too much for the youngster – he crumbled to the ground, covering his ears with his hands.

Richard and others rushed over to support him while David and Gordon complained to the officials. The referee decided to pause the game and sent the players back to the dressing rooms. The fans reacted angrily and started clashing with the stewards. It was a mess.

Richard looked around the stadium while he and other players escorted the distraught Ryan away and he felt incensed. He was not a hateful person but he absolutely loathed what he was seeing – people picking on Ryan's vulnerability and pressing him to breaking point. That feeling was shared amongst his teammates and they were fuming in the dressing room. Nick invited Nils into the dressing room to console Ryan while the players waited for further updates. David came in a few minutes later to relay the message that the match would resume once public order was restored and there would be no forfeit or postponement.

Ryan asked David if he could be substituted and the manager understandably accepted. Alex was his replacement and he vowed to win the game for Ryan.

"We'll sort it out on the pitch! Who's with me?" Tom asked.

All players raised to the call and showed tremendous spirit and togetherness. Ryan was touched and he tearfully thanked his teammates.

The match resumed after another ten minutes plus a short warm up. Amid the boos and jeers from the crowd, the Black Dragons pushed forward to turn the game around, but they might have been too eager – possession was lost up field and a break was on. The ball was cleared towards the right winger with Layne miles away and he sped past Thomas with an exceptional first touch. He brought it inside towards goal and was ready to pull the trigger. Richard tracked back in time but just before he launched himself for a block, he noticed the winger having a glance at him and he gambled on him cutting back to his left foot instead. He put the brakes on by jumping into the ground with his left foot and bounced back superbly to take the ball off the surprised winger. He tried to find Layne on the left but as the left back was retreating at pace he slipped and the ball went out of touch.

"Calm down lads! We're over-committing!" he shouted.

"He's right. We can't win this way," Danny shared his view and gestured his teammates to refocus on their shape.

With the Black Dragons tuning down their overzealous approach, the two teams played out the remaining ten minutes in a stalemate and the half ended 2-0 to the home side.

The young team were back on the pitch earlier than the time allowed for the second half, fully fired up for the battle. The home crowd did their best to discourage them with their singing of the song associated with playing at the national stadium but they were determined not to be distracted. They moved as a team and passed to each other with conviction, building up a steady steam of possession and chances started to arrive.

Luciano thumped his shot from the angle just wide of the right hand post after being put through, then Alex set Charlie up for a curling shot to the far corner that whizzed past the same post. Minutes later Richard found Charlie on the left and he put Layne through after pulling the experienced right back towards him. The youngster had time to whip in a high cross towards the far post and Tom timed his jump perfectly to head it down past the keeper! The goal scorer then beat everyone to the ball again to take it back to the centre circle for a swift restart.

The hosts solidified their defence with two substitutions and repelled the waves of attack from the Black Dragons for the next phase of play. David sent Sam and Andrés on for Luciano and Viktor with fifteen minutes to go as his final throw of the dice. His message to Richard and Tom was to push higher and hunt the ball up field – there was no time to waste.

The Black Dragons' final push forced a clearance from the keeper. It fell to Richard, who saw a small space in front of Danny and sent it there first time. He drove towards the right and with Alex's clever movement across the back line a gap appeared on his left. Danny rolled it into that area and Charlie arrived to drill a powerful shot into the top right corner!

The three thousand travelling supporters went absolutely wild at the late equaliser. Charlie and others celebrated in front of them briefly as they again took the ball back for a quick restart.

They were rewarded with another chance late on. Sam earned a free kick on the right after a mazy run. Richard sent a seemingly overhit lofted ball towards the left of the area, but Alex was there to volley it onto the ground and through the near post to complete the come back!

He took his shirt off and waved it in front of the most vocal home fans, those who targeted Ryan throughout the match.

"Have a bit of that, suckers!" he provoked.

The crowd was livid and a number of spectators ran onto the pitch to attack the goal scorer. The stewards moved in to block most of them but Charlie had to step in to throw the heavily drunk intruder to the ground before he managed to lay a hand on Alex. More officials arrived at the scene and the players returned to their half to celebrate.

The match eventually resumed but there wasn't much left. It was the Thames Ditton supporters' turn to sing the famous song for the national stadium as their team edged towards another trip to Wembley, after their victorious playoff final the season before.

Que Sera, Sera
Whatever Will Be, Will Be
We're Going to Wembley
Que Sera, Sera

The deflated hosts weren't able to create any chances and soon the referee blew the final whistle, which confirmed the Black Dragons' first ever advance to the FA Cup semi-final, having come from two goals down at half time!

The players were urged to return to their dressing room quickly to avoid further clashes with the crowd. Ryan was waiting for the team and he sincerely thanked them for their show of solidarity. Richard and Layne gave him a big hug and they celebrated their victory with the rest of the team.

The Football Association fined the Merseyside club for failing to control the crowd and ordered them to play their next two matches behind closed doors as punishment. Players from all over the country condemned the fans' behaviours and many contacted Ryan and the pair directly to offer their support. The young striker's mental state remained unstable and the club arranged further counselling for him.

The pair and their England under 21 teammates set off to Athens for their fifth qualifying match for the European Under 21 Championship. With four wins out of four, they were in a strong position but there was still a long road ahead with six more matches to go.

Richard and Layne started the game and the visitors had a dream start, as Danny's sweet half volley from Owen's cross went in through the keeper's hands after just three minutes. Layne then went on a great solo run from deep and his low cross found Noah unmarked for a simple finish. There was a scare late in the half when the striker was sent through after some good build up play, but his shot was brilliantly blocked by Kieran.

Richard and Charlie were withdrawn at half time and replaced by Tom and Damian respectively. The former was keen to stake his claim to further call-ups as he intercepted a loose pass and immediately drove into the space in front of him. He nearly went all the way but was fouled just outside the box. Danny lined up the free kick but he left it for Layne to curl it home for 3-0.

Jack was given his England under 21 debut but he wasn't able to celebrate it with a clean sheet, as the hosts had a consolation goal late on. The match ended 3-1 to England and the hundred percent record continued.

The team travelled back to London the next morning. The flight was perfectly normal until it was due to land. Richard and Layne watched the live footage from the camera underneath the plane in horror as they saw a coach full of passengers on the runway in front of them just before the plane touched down. The pilots had to take an emergency lift off on full power and shot the plane straight back into the sky. Layne was absolutely terrified and cried in Richard's arms.

"Don't worry baby we've stabilised. We just need to find another slot to land."

"I thought we were going to crash into that coach and explode!"

"We didn't. The pilots did a great job there. We're safe."

"But I can't stop thinking about it..."

"I'm here with you, silly. There's nothing to be afraid of."

"... That's true. We'll be together no matter what."

Richard couldn't help giving his boyfriend a little kiss after seeing his relieved smile. The pair went on for a while until they were brutally stopped by Tom sitting behind them.

"Hey you two, we can all hear and see what you're up to!"

Richard and Layne pulled apart quickly amid laughs from their teammates, but kept smiling at each other lovingly, knowing that their most important person was right there with them, which made the fear of the unthinkable much more bearable.

The plane landed successfully the second time round. Layne was holding Richard's hand tightly but he was no longer frightened. They joined other passengers in applauding the pilots and cabin crew.

Richard recalled the incident that evening in bed with Layne soundly asleep next to him. He looked at his cute face and wished the world would just stay like that forever. He believed it was time for them to tie the knot – he wanted to marry his young boyfriend. He may only be twenty-one years old but he felt ready to make such commitment. After all, they had experienced so much together in less than four years and he couldn't imagine himself to be with anyone else.

He searched for engagement rings online and he really liked one in platinum with an emerald-cut diamond. He called the store and asked if he could order one but there was a small issue to resolve – he didn't know Layne's size. The lady on the line offered him a practical and discreet method: he could measure it by tying a string on Layne's finger when he was asleep. Richard proceeded to placing the order first and faced another interesting twist. The customer service representative noticed that his address was already registered on the database. Richard imagined it was just one of the previous owners of the house but found that Layne was a recent customer. It didn't surprise him but his hope of finding his ring size from the database was quickly dashed. He had to find out himself.

Now holding a little secret from Layne, Richard couldn't help feeling giddy every time they spoke. He completed his secret mission that evening and confirmed Layne's size for the order the next day. It would take a few weeks for it to be ready.

The Black Dragons played at home four days later, against the team from Hampshire. It proved to be another tough match with plenty of running, but it was settled by two excellent finishes from Alex either side of half time. He guided his first time shot beautifully into the bottom corner from Charlie's chip into the area and then sent a lovely curler into the top left corner after a sharp turn. He could have had a hat trick but his late effort from a narrow angle was denied by the post.

Richard caught up with Jay the captain and dead ball specialist of the visitors at the end. He still only had two goals from direct kicks that season while Jay already had five, Ben had one less, followed by Rory and Aaron with three.

The club remained ninth and four points behind the team in seventh. It would likely to be enough for European qualification as two of the top six clubs were in the FA Cup semi-finals: the white side of north London would entertain the Black Dragons whilst the red team from Manchester were up against the one from Tyneside.

With their cup semi-final at Wembley set for the following Sunday, the Black Dragons' next league game was rescheduled into midweek. They had a tough evening away at north London against the Reds who were fifth in the league and in desperate need to fight for every point to get into the top four. They were in the middle of an injury crisis and had to field a side full of academy graduates, apart from their captain and star striker.

David decided to rest both Danny and Charlie, who had been involved in nearly every game since the beginning of the season. Harry and Andrés were their replacements.

It was Richard's first visit to his boyhood club as a player. He had been to the modern stadium several times during his youth and he looked forward to a good performance there.

The home team started nervously and frequently gifted possession to the Black Dragons. Their ill-disciplined centre back was far too eager with his challenges and committed a number of fouls. He was finally booked after fifteen minutes when he tackled Harry from behind twenty-five yards from goal.

Richard put the ball down, moved back by five equal steps, had a deep breath and hit it over the jumping wall. The ball swerved heavily towards the left, out of reach for the goal keeper and went in underneath the bar!

He ran all the way back to the corner where the travelling fans were and kissed his ring finger before celebrating with Layne and the others – the gesture had more meaning than ever.

The hosts equalised against the run of play shortly after. Their teenage right winger cut inside Layne and his left-footed cross found his captain deep inside the area for a simple headed finish.

The game-changing event happened after the half hour mark when the rash centre back was sent off for another challenge on Harry. The young attacking midfielder might not have Danny's amazing abilities to travel with the ball at speed or shooting accurately from distance, he was very difficult to dispossess with his low centre of gravity and bag full of tricks.

Richard repeated his trick and scored his second direct free kick of the game, as he placed the ball in exactly the same corner. The excited fans chanted his name repeatedly for the rest of the half, which the Black Dragons held on to their 2-1 lead.

The second half started badly for the visitors as the hosts equalised again despite having a player less. A seemingly harmless cross was unnecessarily headed out for a corner by Layne and the world class striker ran across to the near post to flicked the resulting corner kick past Gordon.The surprise turnaround was completed when Noah the England under 21 striker dribbled past Maz on the left and crossed for the star striker to complete his hat trick with a simple tap-in.

The frustrated David brought Andrew, Sam and Lewis on to replace Andrés, Luciano and Layne with ten minutes remaining, and the former created a chance late on, as his direct run inside from the left forced another free kick off the makeshift centre back twenty yards away from goal.

With seconds remaining, Richard placed the ball down and carried out his usual preparations. His mind was totally focused and he put his years of practice into play again.

He sent the ball into the top left corner for the third time in a single game!

He might have been very confident in his abilities but even he couldn't believe that he pulled it off – his first ever hat trick, a feat that he had never achieved even when in junior football!

There's only one Richard Lucas
One Richard Lucas
He scores all free kicks
He falls in love with his teammate
Walking into Layne Moore's wonderland

The Thames Ditton supporters to his left came up with a new song as he celebrated with them again. He and the other players couldn't stop laughing when they listened to the lyrics.

"That's amazing, Richie!" said Layne as he kissed Richard's cheek.

"Thanks baby. Shame it didn't bring a win!"

The final whistle went soon after the restart. While it was good to have rescued a point, the gap between the Black Dragons and seventh place had been extended to six.

With just five games left, they couldn't afford to drop more points. Their run-in included all four bottom clubs, which may well prove to be tough as they would be fighting desperately for their survival.

As per tradition, Richard picked up a match ball signed by all participated players as a souvenir for his hat trick. He was named as the man of the match and was interviewed together with the other triple goal scorer, the captain and world class striker of the home side, who commended him for his composure in set pieces and jokingly suggested that his boyhood club could do with his abilities. He also received a text message from Jay and the other dead ball specialists congratulating his achievement.

The first FA Cup semi-final was held the Saturday after and it was a shocker. The massive underdogs from Tyneside pulled off a surprise 2-1 win over the mighty reds from Manchester. Hakim the winger on-loan from Munich scored a wonderful early goal as he cut inside the left back and powered it through the near post. He had been a star for the team since his arrival, having been involved in eight goals in his first ten matches and winning the fans and pundits over with his no-nonsense display – he might be a very skilful player, but he didn't waste his efforts on showboating and often opted for a simple but highly effective faint or a shift of bodyweight. The tie was seemingly secured when Connor the fierce striker converted Max's through ball emphatically in the second half, until the reds scored a late goal to set up an exciting finale.

The result provided a major twist for the Black Dragons' quest for European qualification. Had the reds won, they only needed to focus on finishing seventh in the league. Now that route was only viable if the north London club beat them on Sunday and did them a favour by going all the way.

"We basically have to win the cup," Richard concluded with his teammates.

While the Black Dragons' record of two wins and a draw from twelve league matches against the top six teams was impressive for a newly promoted side, their two defeats against their semi-final opponents with an aggregate score of 9-3 said otherwise.

David altered his starting line-up for their latest showdown at Wembley. He restored the rested duo of Danny and Charlie to the side and opted for the more defensively sound Lewis ahead of Layne to counter the threat posed by the brilliant inside forward.

"Here we are again!" Charlie said when the players were having a walk on the Wembley turf before the game.

"That is where you scored your rocket goal, Richie!" Layne said. "It'll be great if you can give us another one of those today!"

"We managed to beat a team in white here last year, we can do it again!" Thomas tried to talk up some superstition.

Ryan, who was still the team's joint second top scorer with ten goals, travelled with the team but wasn't included in the match day squad. He watched from the stands surrounded by his teammates and the under 23 players.

The Black Dragons started with Gordon, Maz, Lewis, Thomas, Kieran, Richard, Tom, Danny, Charlie, Luciano and Alex. Jack, the fit-again Graham, Layne, Kasper, Toby, Andrés and Sam were on the bench. The team from north London also fielded their strongest eleven, with Oscar in defence and the new Dutch playmaker Dex on the right wing. The lethal inside forward started on the left, which placed the burden on Maz's shoulders instead.

The first phase of the match saw the Black Dragons playing conservatively with plenty of possession. They tried to create chances without exposing themselves to the lightning fast counter attacks that their opponents were famous for. The supporters, plenty of whom didn't have lots of opportunities to watch the team play, cheered them on patiently – they were well aware of the tough challenge facing their team.

The young attacker Dex was an isolated figure on the right. While he did his share of closing the Black Dragons' defence down, he didn't get to the ball once and his frustration grew. He went after a slightly loose pass from Kieran to Thomas and dived into a tackle, but the defender calmly flicked the ball over him before sending it forward to Lewis.

With the space ahead of him the left back brought the ball across the halfway line and squared it for Richard, who sent a typical first time ball low to Charlie on the left. He came in field with the ball as Alex went the opposite direction and he slipped a little through ball into the left of the six-yard box. Danny ran onto it and found the back of the net with a delightful left footed chip over the experienced keeper!

Wembley Stadium erupted with joy as forty thousand Thames Ditton supporters jumped as the goal went in. It was Danny's thirteenth goal of the season.

The goal served as a wake-up call for the top six side and they started stamping their authority on the game with some sharp passing and movements. They created an opening for their left back to cross from deep in the final third but the star striker headed agonisingly wide under strong pressure from Thomas.

They soon created another opportunity as a solo run by their world class inside forward went all the way into the Black Dragons' penalty area and he set Dex up for a left foot finish. But Thomas somehow managed to divert it wide with a last ditch tackle. He roared towards the sky like a warrior claiming his victory, while his teammates surrounded him to celebrate.

But another chance arrived immediately as Gordon's punch out from the resulting corner kick only went as far as Dex at the edge of the area. He looked odds on to score as he hit a first time shot but it was Richard's turn to perform heroics as he jumped in to head it wide.

The consecutive missed chances irritated Dex further and he finally lost it near the end of the first half. Thomas intercepted yet another loose pass from him and brought the ball out towards the halfway line. Dex chased after him at full speed and launched himself into a tackle with his studs up. He caught Thomas on his left ankle. Richard was near the incident and was horrified – Thomas's ankle was twisted in an unnatural position after he fell awkwardly and he was screaming in agony.

It was Steve all over again.

"What the fuck were you doing?" Charlie was seen pushing the offender Dex, who looked as shocked as anybody.

Other players stepped in as peacemakers while the medical staffs rushed onto the scene.

The referee pulled Dex and his captain to one side and showed him a straight red card. It was a dangerous tackle from behind and had caused a serious injury.

"Am I going to be like Steve?" Thomas asked in desperation while the medics eventually put him on a stretcher.

"You'll come back stronger Bondi! Take some rest, we'll win this for you!" Tom gave him the reassurance.

Graham came on to replace the unfortunate Thomas and the match resumed with five minutes left before half time. But instead of taking advantage from having an extra player, the Black Dragons conceded from a fast attack. The inside forward, having stayed closer to the main striker to work as a pair after the sending off, combined with his partner brilliantly to create an opening for a long range effort that rocketed straight into the top right corner. Richard and the rest just looked on in shock as the world class players demonstrated why they were considered world class.

The half ended 1-1. Richard and the team learnt from David that Thomas had been sent to a hospital straight away with a suspected fracture ankle. He also said that plenty of players had come back from similar injuries before but it will be a lengthy recovery process. The team were gutted and vowed to win the game for the gentle father-of-two.

The second half kicked off to a completely different tempo to the first, as the Black Dragons aimed to take the initiative against the Whites who were sitting back to play on the counter. They supplied the full backs with through balls but their crosses, be they low or high, were well defended, with Oscar the young centre back particularly impressive. The route through the middle for Danny was blocked by design with all three midfielders marshalling that area.

With the team eager to win the match for Thomas and their dream of European qualification, they subconsciously moved more and more forward in search for an opening and that fell right into the experienced opponents' hands. The keeper caught another cross from Maz and he threw it towards his star striker upfront, who won his aerial battle against Tom to flick it onto the path for the inside forward on the left. He evaded Kieran's challenge and sped past Graham almost immediately as he picked the ball up on his stride. Richard caught up with him but before he settled the forward took a big step towards the right again. Richard kept chasing and managed to force the forward wide, but the attacker was still able to send a high hanging ball into the penalty area.

And the England striker jumped the highest to complete the turnaround against the run of play!

It was a devastating blow to the Black Dragons, as it felt like the inevitable fall against the big teams was happening again. The opposition supporters celebrated wildly and started taunting the Black Dragons for being a tiny village club with no rights at the top table.

With just twenty minutes on the clock, David rolled the dice and sent Layne and Kasper on for Lewis and Luciano. There was nothing to lose and they simply had to gamble, but the manager had a plan.

"Push Maz back into a back three and play as a right back," he asked Kasper to relay the message to Richard. "Overcrowd the far post."

It was a tactic that the team had practice in training and it depended on Richard's ability to send accurate high balls from the right. Charlie, Alex, Layne and eventually one of the centre backs will attack that area and hope for a breakthrough.

A chance arose soon after, as Danny and Tom combined well to create some space for Richard. His high, swerving cross reached the desired destination, but Charlie's dangerous knock down was cleared over the bar by Oscar.

The Black Dragons continued to attack down their right and Richard's crosses were becoming more dangerous. The opponents reacted by replacing the inside forward with a more defensively minded midfielder. His task seemed to be all about stopping Richard and it worked – with less time and space available he couldn't deliver the right balls.

Time was ticking away and the Black Dragons needed some fresh ideas. Richard picked up another ball from Maz but his new marker closed him down quickly again. He couldn't create a big enough opening for a cross so ended up cutting in field and hitting a low ball towards Charlie using the outside of his foot instead. The rushed pass wasn't of his usual high standard and the right back looked favourite to cut it out. However, Charlie somehow found an extra gear to get to it first and took it pass him. He drove at the defensive midfielder and ran past him with a lightning quick two-footed feint – he was desperate to win, to fulfil his promise to Danny and the team.

He then pulled off multiple step overs against the centre back and charged down the left towards goal. The keeper came out to block him and the loose ball looped back towards the edge of the six-yard box, but before anyone arrived Layne dived in to put it into the net!

The ecstatic youngster sprinted back to the Black Dragons' corner and celebrated with an exaggerated knee slide. Fans responded with their usual "We want Moore" chant repeatedly and the game was back on!

The dramatic turnaround had dampened the Whites' spirits and the Black Dragons intended to take full advantage, as they created another chance before full time. Richard hit a measured first time ball towards the far post and a towering Charlie was there to meet it with a downward header!

It beat the stranded keeper but hit the foot of the post and went out!

The whole stadium went absolutely silent for a second before a collective groan / sigh of relief. The referee blew the full time whistle at that moment and extra time beckoned.

The north London side made their final substitution before the restart, bringing another defensive midfielder on to maintain the competitiveness in the middle of the park. Their intention was clear, they wanted to drag the semi-final into a penalty shootout.

David moved Richard back into a midfield three with Tom and Kasper. Maz returned to right back while Danny drifted to right wing.

Having been a man down for nearly an hour of play, the Whites were short on stamina and they retreated to their final third to hold out. Space was only available on the wings but crosses were not effective when the box was full of defenders. Fifteen minutes flew by and the first half of extra time finished goalless.

With players of both teams drained of energy, the final period was played at a very slow pace. There were half chances for both sides but nothing spectacular. The Whites' striker had a long range shot turned away by Gordon and Alex suffered the same fate for his effort from twenty yards out. Richard hit the resulting corner kick towards the usual spot but Oscar was there to head it out. The loose ball was picked up by Danny and he brilliantly tricked past the defenders rushing out to open up a chance for a final shot.

The ball hit a defender's outstretching arm on the edge of the area and the whole stadium looked at the referee, who blew his whistle and gave the Black Dragons a free kick!

It was just outside the area, slightly right of the "D". Richard put the ball down and measured up his options together with Danny and Layne. Layne whispered to ask Richard to take it, as the taller player in the middle of the wall was likely to block the trajectory of his shots. Richard acknowledged and readied himself for it. He took his usual five steps back and curled the ball over the wall towards the top right hand corner.

But it sailed inches over the top of the bar and that was that, as the game headed into penalties.

"Well done boys for pushing them this far, we just need to finish them off now!" David rallied the team as they gathered at the technical area for some final encouragement. "Who's keen to pull the trigger?"

"I'll do it," Danny came up coolly.

"Count me in," Charlie followed.

"I'm happy to," said Alex, despite missing one at the League Cup tie earlier in the season.

"Same here," Tom said with his hand up.

Everyone then turned to look at Richard, who was the team's designated taker.

"I'll have the fifth," he said confidently.

"Good! Just make your mind up and go for it!" David concluded.

"Fly! You Black Dragons!"

The toss came up reasonably well for Thames Ditton as the shootout will be held at the end where their supporters were, but the north London club will go first.

Gordon, the bearded Scottish keeper and captain of the day, prepared himself in goal against the first penalty taker, one of the centre midfielders. He jumped up and down waving his long arms like an octopus, in his golden yellow jersey, trying to get into the mind of the kicker. Richard used to laugh at his movements when they practiced in training, but he knew that it could be an effective weapon.

The referee blew the whistle and off they went. The player took his shot, aiming for the bottom left corner.

And it was pushed away by a flying Gordon!

Supporters behind the goal burst into a massive cheer as the keeper threw his fist in the air to celebrate. It took them a little while to calm down for the next spot kick, by the ultra-cool Danny.

He smashed the ball into the top left corner with zero hesitation!

The Whites' second penalty taker was their reliable left back. He calmly sent Gordon the wrong way and slotted the ball into the bottom left corner.

It was Tom's turn next. He had a fairly long run-up and he drove the ball towards the left of the goal.

But it was saved by the experienced keeper!

Tom covered his head with his shirt in disbelief, and the scores levelled again.

The third set of spot kicks began with the right midfielder of the north London club. He moved a few steps to his left and coolly sent the ball to the top right corner, giving Gordon no chance.

Charlie stepped up for the next ball. He had a slow motion run-up, trying to tempt his opponent into making a move first. The keeper did pick a side and dived to his right, but Charlie's placement to the other side hit the post and out! The Black Dragons were now a goal behind!

The left midfielder who came on to stifle Richard's efforts from right back was up next. The tie was likely to be over if he scored to put his team two goals up, as their fifth taker would have to be their lethal striker who had never missed a penalty kick in his career. Gordon continued with his octopus moves to distract the young kicker.

And he acrobatically tipped his shot over the bar!

A lifeline had been earned and it was up to Alex the next taker. He didn't look the most confident, as his miss in the previous shootout might be playing on his mind.

But he placed his shot perfectly into the bottom left corner to level up the match again!

The star striker of the north London club stepped up with the shootout tied at 2-2 after four rounds, and he made no mistakes in firing his shot accurately into the bottom right corner.

So, it had come down to the wire and Richard had to score to keep the semi-final, and his team's dream of playing in Europe next season, alive.

He began his walk towards the penalty spot, but was stopped partway by a familiar voice. Layne caught up to give him a hug.

"I love you no matter what," he whispered.

"Thanks baby."

He resumed his approach. He picked the ball up from the referee and placed in firmly on the penalty spot after rolling it backwards a couple of times.

His eyes were on the prize – the top left hand corner. He knew it was the hardest spot for this keeper to reach from his researches. He had plenty of practices but he needed to be precise. There was only one chance – the power and accuracy had to be a hundred percent spot on.

The whole stadium took a deep breath as he ran up to the ball. He hit it in exactly the same way he always did, and it arrowed towards its target.

The keeper dived the right way and got a fingertip to it, but it went in anyway!

It took Richard a good few seconds to realise what happened, but with the explosive cheer from the stands he knew he had done his part in keeping the game going!

The shootout moved into sudden death phase, where teams would have one shot each to decide the winner. The first round of those went quickly, with the last midfielder of the Whites and Graham cancelling each other. The seventh kick fell to the opposition right back. He wasn't the most confident but his shot went in despite Gordon diving the right way.

The next one up, was Layne.

Richard returned the encouragement with a deep hug and wished him all the best.

"Just focus on where you want to put it and go through with it."

Richard watched Layne put the ball down from the halfway line. He felt a lot more nervous doing so comparing to his own kick. He hoped, wished, and even prayed that he would successfully complete the task.

And Layne ran up, connected with the ball, and sent it to the top left corner!

He sprinted back to base and jumped straight into Richard's arms.

"Well done baby! That's a great shot!"

"I was so nervous... I'm glad it's over!"

Oscar the young centre back was the north London side's eighth taker. He had a lengthy run-up and hit the ball powerfully.

But it flew harmlessly over the bar!

Richard celebrated the miss with Layne and their teammates. Even though he felt a bit sorry for his friend Oscar, he couldn't help the excitement of having a chance to win the match for good.

Kasper the young combative midfielder was named as the next taker, but Gordon waived him away, claiming that he would "end this madness myself".

He duly put the ball down, began his run-up and hit it firmly.

And it went straight into the bottom right corner!

The stadium erupted once more, with half of it full of joy and the other half emptying quickly. Richard and the players ran towards the goal to celebrate with Gordon the hero. David and the coaching team followed suit quickly and together they lifted Gordon up in the air, to the cheers of tens of thousands of supporters.

Que Sera, Sera

Whatever Will Be, Will be

We're staying at Wembley

Que Sera, Sera

The fans sang the slightly edited song repeatedly and the players applauded their support. Richard had a quick word with the distraught Oscar before he joined the party as Layne led the crowd into their usual winning tune.

The team eventually returned to their dressing room and David played them a message from Thomas, who recorded it before he went into the operation theatre for his emergency ankle surgery.

"Great result boys! Wonderful resolve to level the game and then winning it! Big hands to the goalie but you're all my heroes! I'm sorry that I can't join you on the pitch for the final but I'll be back next season no doubt. Now pop those champagnes and have a good one!"

Richard was relieved to see Thomas in good spirit and wished the operation to be successful.With another league game scheduled for Wednesday, the team were not encouraged to have too much of a celebration and it was limited to a glass of sparkling wine in the dressing room. Richard and his friends did gather that evening at Tom's new house near the cricket green but it was all under control.

"You saved our cup run with the late goal today," Tom raised a glass to Layne when he served up the welcome drinks.

"It's Richie's pass that started it... but I didn't think Charlie would have got to that rather 'hospital ball'!"

"Yeah cheers for that Rich, it took every ounce of energy from me!"

"It was indeed a bit off," Richard said before a thought got into his head. "Oh wait, we could turn that into a new weapon for us."

"What do you mean, Rich?" Alex asked.

"We can play these 'hospital balls' intentionally to give defenders a false sense of security and Charlie and others the chance to burst past them."

"No everyone has that sudden change of acceleration, but it's worth practicing for sure!" Danny agreed.

"One for tomorrow then!" Tom said.

The host and his assistant Richard cooked up a delicious two-course meal for the party of seven, with freshly made tagliatelle with garlic and chilli oil for starter and roasted chicken breast in satay sauce with a roasted broccoli and quinoa salad for main.

"You're getting good with your cooking! The seasoning was perfect!" Richard praised.

"I'm just following some recipe online, nothing special, just plenty of practices!"

"Like how we train for football!" Danny added.

"To the Final!"

"To Thomas!"

"Fly, you Black Dragons!"

The players toasted for the latest achievement in their footballing journey.

38.

The End

Richard and his friends presented their new idea to David next morning and put it into practice the day after. Rather naturally, they discovered that only a handful of players, namely Charlie, Layne and Ryan, possessed that additional boost of acceleration, and they built that into their plans.

The pair visited Thomas after he was released from hospital. They were pleasantly surprised to see Dr Edwards the club owner there ahead of them and they had a quick catch-up. Thomas's operation was successful and the recovery process was expected to last at least nine months, but he was optimistic and more importantly, feeling much more comfortable.

David gave most of the regular starters a rest for the next league game at home against the team from East Anglia. It was a "do or die" match for the visitors, as anything less than a win will confirm their relegation back to the Championship. It was a big contrast in fortunes comparing to the previous season, when they secured promotion ahead of the Black Dragons, who now sat proudly at ninth.

Layne was in the starting eleven together with Ryan, who played for the first time since that infamous game at Merseyside. His counsellor recommended David to ease him back into actions in home matches only and the manager happily agreed.

The visitors made a dream start as they scored from their first attack. A misunderstanding in midfield between Toby and Kasper gifted the forward plenty of time to measure his through pass to the left winger, who finished the move confidently to give his team a fighting chance to stay up for another day.

First-time captain Kieran pulled the team together to steady themselves and they slowly got back into the game. Alex had plenty of the ball and his layoff set Sam up to equalise near the end of the half. It was his third goal of the season and he celebrated with his well-practiced series of hand gestures – Richard had no idea what they meant but he believed they were some kind of symbols between him and his girlfriend.

The team from East Anglia came out attacking in the second half, but having conceded at the worst possible time and the desperation for three points, the players were not in sync and their shape was carved wide open by the Black Dragons. Alex picked up his second and third assists of the day as he set Ryan up for two clinical finishes – a first time side-footed shot from the edge of the area and a glancing header at the near post. Then Andrew the substitute rounded up the day with his first senior goal from a breakaway late on.

Players of the visiting team were devastated at the final whistle, as they lay on the pitch exhausted, both physically and mentally, and faced the cruel reality of relegation. Richard didn't like what he saw, but he accepted that as part of being a professional sportsman. He was also glad that Ryan managed to play the whole ninety minutes and slowly moved out of the shadow, as his public celebrations with Nils showed.

The busy fixture list took Richard and the team to Dorset for an early kick off the following Saturday. The hosts were also in the fight against relegation, being three points adrift of safety in eighteenth place. A defeat would all but finish off their dreams of survival and hand safety to the side currently fourth from bottom, Owen's team from East Sussex. The former Thames Ditton forward did jokingly call his old teammates asking for a favour, and was rightly told that they would go for a win regardless. The Black Dragons were up to eighth following their midweek victory and only three points behind the team in seventh, who were soundly beaten by the table-topping side from Merseyside.

David reverted to the usual team and formation, apart from Luciano who was ill.

With a dream FA Cup final on the horizon, the Black Dragons were a little risk-averse subconsciously and didn't play their usual fluid passing game. Richard was "in the zone" as always as he broke up plenty of attacking play by the hosts but he had to be less adventurous with his ball distribution as movements from his teammates were lacking. The first half flew by with no goals from either side.

David was not happy with the shortage of efforts and demanded the players to show the coaching team why they deserved to be in the team for the cup final.

"Play with less than a hundred percent out there and you may not have a chance to prove yourselves again," he warned.

With the kick up the backside the team committed more to the play and created a few good chances to open the scoring, but they were up against Roy the England under 21 keeper in inspired form. He tipped a long range shot destined to the top corner by Danny over and miraculously blocked Charlie's close range header from Layne delicate cross. Sam seemed to have finally broken the resistance when he slotted a low shot home, but he was adjudged to be offside by the video assistant referee.

The hosts were rather lacklustre in attack despite their need for three points, but it only took a second to change. A cross from the left was routinely headed out by Kieran but the ball was met by the young right winger and his brilliant volley from outside the area shot straight past Gordon into the back of the net!

The home supporters rejoiced at the goal – with just five minutes left that was surely going to be the winner. The Black Dragons created a couple more chances in the time remaining but they continued to be denied by Roy, who was predictably named as the man of the match.

The defeat widened the gap between the Black Dragons and the seventh place team to four points while they dropped into ninth. The East Sussex club lost their match away at Manchester and was only outside of the relegation zone by their superior goal difference of two. The race for survival was really heating up.

"It won't be easy hearing this, but that first half performance was unacceptable. With the shaky start they were there for the taking but we ran with the brakes on. Second half was much better but luck stood on their side and we got a sucker punch at the end. That's the pattern we've been talking about – we need to score when we're on top, no holding back. Push yourselves to the limit every time you are on the pitch. Remember, when you're fully committed the chance of you getting injured is actually less," David gave the team a lecture in his usual calm and considerate manner.

"Can't believe our return to this special city ended with a defeat!" Layne whispered, in reference to their first summer trip together.

"It's disappointing, but I guess we needed a wake up call to remind us that every game at this level is competitive," Richard said.

"Shall we re-visit the city again this summer? We can even stay at the same hotel if you want to be nostalgic!"

"Won't that be nice? Let's plan at the end of the season."

The Black Dragons' next opponent was the team from north west London. They were barely holding on at second from bottom and a defeat would seal their relegation.

David continued to play Ryan at home and he started with Alex and Charlie upfront.

The hosts attacked the match straight from the kick off and got their reward after ten minutes. Alex's great run to the left channel was found by Charlie and his cross was headed in by Danny at the far post, as he extended his lead over Ryan to two at the top of the Thames Ditton scoring chart.

They soon had another chance as Ryan flipped the ball pass the centre back in his usual move, but before he caught up with the ball Charlie was there first to send it into the bottom corner.

"I'm on eleven now, I can still catch you two!" he said to Danny and Ryan.

The visitors were given a lifeline just before the end of the half, as a weak headed clearance by Maz was played back into the area and the right winger beat Layne in the air to claw one back.

With the teams from Dorset and East Sussex losing by a sizeable margin at half time, the north west London side threw everything into play in the second half. Thankfully Charlie and Ryan did their parts of the defending and together with team they succeeded in conceding chances and dampening the visitors' beliefs.

David decided to go for the killer goal at the seventieth minute, when he brought Andrew on for Alex. A square ball was cut out by Kasper and the break was on. Both full backs and Richard ran up at full speed to support the attack and they massively outnumbered their opponents. It was eventually converted by Charlie after a good run infield by Ryan.

"I'm on twelve now boys!"

It was game, set and match for the visitors. They may still have the courage to fight for their survival but the match was completely controlled by the Black Dragons, as they strung passes after passes using the full width of the pitch beautifully, to the sound of "Olé" by the home supporters.

Richard and Layne were withdrawn with ten minutes left and witnessed a second opponent being relegated from the bench. They joined their teammates in offering their sympathy to the players and wishing them a swift return to the top tier.

"I hope we won't be saying these to Owen when we play them in a couple of weeks' time," Layne said to Richard on their way back to the dressing room.

"We have to do our best to respect them in a sporting manner," Richard said. "but yes it'll hurt me to send them down."

After thirty-six matches, the Black Dragons had fifty points and were eighth, still three points behind the team in seventh, even though that had become meaningless for their quest for European qualification.

Their next league game was a rehearsal of the FA Cup final against the club from Tyneside at The Dragons Stadium. With it being the last home fixture of the season David decided to play his strongest team possible to secure a victory, instead of worrying about giving away tactical insight. He believed that it would actually be beneficial for his players to go into the final being more familiar with their opponents.

Richard received a phone call from Hakim the German born Moroccan winger on loan at the Tyneside club during the week. They exchanged their best wishes for the forthcoming league and cup encounters and caught up on the old days. The two players used to be close training partners at the Munich academy, but with the nature of Richard's abrupted departure they had not been in contact in the years since. He informed Richard that his crush Ian had moved to a 2. Bundesliga club during the January transfer window and recently made his debut in the German second division. Richard was glad to hear that Ian had found a way forward in his football career, as it was extremely difficult to break through the ranks at the giant club.

He also picked up the completed engagement ring after training one day. He hid the small black leather box in one of his drawers and started planning on when he should make the move. He couldn't wait to see Layne's reaction – he imagined that it would be one of their best moments in life.

With the league title secured by the Merseyside team the week before, the big match of game week thirty-seven was the life-and-death relegation battle between Dorset and East Sussex at lunch time on Saturday. Owen's side travelled to the south west ahead on a goal difference of one and absolutely had to avoid a defeat. They went two goals down in the first half and dramatically rescued the situation with two late goals. The Thames Ditton graduate scored the first one of those and had a hand in the second. They had to better their rival's result in their final game, which was at home against none other than the Black Dragons.

"It's going to be tricky next week," Tom said as the team warmed up for their three o'clock kick off.

"Owen wouldn't want us to let him win. It would have to be done the hard way," Danny said.

"Yes, and we are obliged to play our strongest side possible," Richard added.

"Why can we rest our players? We have a cup final to play the week after?" Layne asked.

"It is to maintain fairness to the other teams involved. I guess we can justify some rotations, but not a wholesale change," Richard explained.

"David has the final call, but I would love to play another competitive match before Wembley," Danny concluded.

For their game against the club from Tyneside, whose mid-table position was already confirmed, David had selected Gordon in goal, Viktor, Layne, Kieran and Graham in defence, Richard, Tom and Danny in midfield, and Charlie, Ryan and Luciano upfront. It was his strongest possible team except Maz, who picked up a slight injury during the last match. On the contrary, the visitors rested a number of usual starters but Max, Connor and Hakim were all in the first eleven.

The away side played in a 4-4-2 formation but their two centre forwards were instructed to sit much deeper, in order to disrupt the Black Dragons' foundation.

Richard came up against the fierce Connor soon after kick off. Having learnt from their previous encounter, he didn't take any chances with the ball and opted to either spread it wide to the full backs or send it home to Gordon. With the two solid banks of four in front of him, options were severely limited anyway.

The Black Dragons had to find inspiration from some exceptional play and got it from their tricky winger

Luciano. He picked up a pass from Tom, turned the left back with his quick feet but his cross was headed behind by a centre defender before Charlie could meet it.

Danny and Layne created a chance for the former to cross with a short corner routine. He found Ryan inside the six-yard box but his clever left foot flick went agonisingly wide. There was another chance before half time but Layne's free kick was tipped over by the goal keeper.

"Well done boys for creating those chances out there, it wasn't easy with such disciplined opponents," David said in his half time team talk. "But it's good that they are playing exactly how we thought they would. I have a few ideas on how to break them down, but I think we shouldn't show them too much ahead of the big day."

"We still want to win this game, right?" Danny asked.

"Of course, don't get me wrong Danny, but we just have to do it in a conventional way," David said before giving the team some specific instructions.

The second half started with the visitors remaining hard to beat and offering little going forward. Hakim and the left winger were restricted to safe passes, without taking on Layne and Viktor once.

It changed when the match approached the hour mark. David's plan was to overload on the less mobile centre back with short passes and movements, and the team succeeded in creating an opening for Charlie. He opened his body up and took a shot towards the far post, past the hapless goal keeper.

But it bounced back off the post!

Max picked up the rebound and hit a sweet left foot pass to Hakim near the halfway line. The left-footed Moroccan winger, for the first time in the match, made an attacking move as he flicked the ball over Layne effortlessly and drove down the touchline. Richard came across to halt his progress but before they engaged Hakim moved up a gear and accelerated down the side. Richard followed him closely but just when he thought he could make a tackle, Hakim put the brakes on, flicked the ball over Richard's foot with his left foot and when Richard made a rather super-human turn to re-engage, put the ball through his legs to enter the penalty area. Gordon and Graham approached him at the same time but he coolly chipped the ball into the empty net before running back to the East Stand to celebrate with his teammates and fans.

It was an amazing solo effort.

The home supporters were stunned as they witnessed a truly wonderful goal. Richard always knew his friend was highly capable but that was just mind blowing. He made eye contact with Hakim when he ran past and gave him a nod as a mark of respect for what he did, and the winger gave him a thankful smile.

As David was keen not to lose the last home game of the season, he sent Alex on for Luciano and asked him to pass on a message to Richard.

"Try that, but be subtle," he said.

Having established a one-goal lead, the team from Tyneside continued to sit back and defend in their rigid shape. The Black Dragons had the possession but found it very difficult to create anything meaningful.

Ten minutes later Tom received a pass from Viktor and he played it first time forward to Danny on the right side of midfield. He took the ball past his marker with a smart turn but before Max came across he passed it behind him on the left, where Richard had sneaked into. But he was followed by the hard-working Connor and ended up sending an under-hit ball forward towards where the slower centre back was guarding, without a teammate in sight.

Naturally, the centre back moved towards to ball to collect it, but before he realised, someone arrived at speed to tip the ball past him and was tripped over in the process!

That was Charlie picking up a "hospital pass" by Richard – their new idea had won the team a penalty!

"It couldn't be more of a hospital pass, Rich!" Charlie said when they exchanged high fives.

"We can't create the false sense of security otherwise. Great acceleration that, though."

After the usual debate over the penalty, Richard stepped up and scored his seventh goal of the season, putting the spot kick away into the bottom right corner! Both coaches made changes before the re-start to withdraw their key players. David replaced Layne and Danny by Lewis and Andrés, while the visitors took Hakim and Connor off. With both teams seemingly satisfied with not losing, the match inevitably slowed down and no further goals were scored.

The Thames Ditton players, coaches and staffs had the traditional lap of appreciation round the stadium, to the thunderous reception of the eight thousand home fans. They had exceeded all expectations and achieved wonders in their maiden Premier League season, where they could still finish seventh being just two points behind. And it didn't end there, they still had their first ever FA Cup final to look forward to.

Charlie arranged a team gathering at a pub in Esher that evening. He reserved the whole garden area for the players to enjoy some drinks.

"Hey here comes the goal scorer!" Charlie welcomed Richard and Layne as they walked into the patio.

"And Best Actor for this year's Oscars!" Tom made reference to his "accidental hospital pass".

"David said we needed to be subtle so I took advantage of the pressure," Richard explained.

"You did look like you lost the ball there, I'm impressed!" Sam praised.

"There were lots of swearing from the stands at the time!" Ollie added.

"That's good then! The other team may think we're just lucky!" Layne said.

"I hope so. I didn't think we would need to use that," Danny said.

"I guess we didn't expect to concede that goal!" Thomas, who was there in a wheelchair, said. "At least I won't appear in the reply!"

"That Hakim guy is crazy! I've never played anyone like him!" Layne said.

"I did say that he's very good. He is very simple but extremely effective," Richard commented.

"How did he get past you there? I thought you've recovered well!" Harry asked.

"He probably knew that I wouldn't give up that easily and planned for it."

"We have to be very careful when we play him again in the final," Alex concluded.

"Hey boys we're here to celebrate our successful league season. The first round is on me!" Charlie offered and brought the party to a start.

Richard and Layne spotted Ryan sitting by himself and joined him for a chat.

"Are you okay there?" Richard asked.

"I'm fine, just having some thoughts," Ryan replied.

"About whether you'll play in the final?"

"Nothing gets past you, Rich. Yes I'm quite worried about playing in front of 90,000 people."

"It could be the biggest game of our career. Are you prepared to swap that for some chants?"

"I really want to play a part, but... what if..."

"Ryan," Layne joined in. "We need to accept who we are first. Remember, there is no shame in being who we are. Once you understand that, whatever they say becomes irrelevant."

Ryan looked at Richard and Layne, had a thought, then broke out a relieved smile.

"I think I know what you mean. I am who I am, and everyone is the same on the pitch."

"Exactly," Richard agreed. "it doesn't hurt me if people shout to my face what I already know."

"It would only spur me on to play even better against them!" Layne added.

"Use that fire to keep yourself in the zone, you can do it," Richard encouraged.

"I get that. I'll tell David that I'm ready for East Sussex and Wembley!" Ryan made up his mind.

"East Sussex should be the most inclusive stadium anyway!" Layne laughed.

The players re-joined their teammates and enjoyed the rest of their celebrations. With a couple of games still to be played, they were well moderate and good-natured.

All Premier League matches on the last game week were scheduled to kick off at three o'clock on Sunday. This was to prevent any team gaining an unfair advantage from knowing other results. The timing had to be exact for games that were linked, such as title and relegation deciders. Thames Ditton's last game of the season was one of those, as they travelled to East Sussex, the team sitting in seventeenth place. The team from Dorset were due to play away at the big west London club, who were themselves desperate for the three points that would secure the fourth spot and their participation in next season's Champions League. Following their dramatic late draw the week before, Owen's team only needed to better the result of their rivals to achieve safety from relegation which, on paper, was the more than likely outcome.

With their historic FA Cup final scheduled for the following Saturday, there were debates online on whether the Black Dragons should play their reserves for this meaningless fixture. Naturally, supporters of the Dorset club claimed that anything less than the strongest possible side should be punished by the Football Association and the Premier League, but others understood why they wouldn't, as most of Thames Ditton's key players had featured in a large amount of games in what was a long and gruelling season.

Taking all factors into considerations, David came up with a strong starting eleven, as he believed the players' conditions were good and a competitive match against a team desperate for a result would be the best mental preparation for the players. He had Gordon in goal, Viktor, Lewis, Kieran and Thorsten in defence, Richard, Tom and Danny in midfield and finally Charlie, Alex and Andrés in attack. Ryan was on the bench alongside Jack, Graham, Layne, Kasper, Harry and Luciano. Owen started on the right wing in a 3-4-3 formation, with the tall centre back Adrian in defence.

Given the challenging opponents that the Dorset team were up against, the East Sussex side was not too adventurous at the early phases of the game. The Black Dragons had plenty of possessions, but with their own final in mind, the players were happy to play safe passes, without taking any unnecessary risks.

It all changed at the half hour mark, as the home fans suddenly got agitated and turned up their volume asking their team to attack – Dorset must have taken the lead against all odds. But a football match was not something that could be switched on immediately, even though the contrary was true. The East Sussex players started to press but as they were doing so in an uncoordinated manner the Black Dragons were able to pick them off. Tom took advantage of a gap in midfield and drove straight into the final third, before sending a delicately weighted ball behind Adrian for Charlie on the left. The winger hit a powerful cross towards the six-yard box and Alex was there to divert it inside the near post expertly, to make it 1-0 to the visitors.

The goal crushed the mood of the home supporters and the home side spent the rest of the first half in disarray. Passes were rushed and tackles were somewhat overzealous – the frustrated players were arriving late into challenges and were unnecessarily physical in doing so. Danny was the victim as he picked up a knock near the end of the half. It was a worry as he stayed on the ground for a lengthy treatment. He was withdrawn by David at half time as a precaution, with Ryan coming on to make it a 4-4-2. There were so boos at his arrival, but not much more than a usual away game.

The second half kick off was again synchronised between the two matches and the hosts were given a major boost ten minutes in. The big west London club had equalised through their target man and they only needed to pull one back to be safe again. They had been calmer with their possession and slowly building up some momentum, as the Black Dragons players inevitably turned their focus to not getting injured.

Owen had a frustrating match so far as he was well marshalled by the defensively sounded Lewis. Opportunities were scarce as both Richard and Tom sat deep in midfield and left any attacking imaginations to the four players in front of them. In order to change the dynamics, the manager switched him with the left winger to see if he could initiate attacks with the left wing back Cody, who was well known to be a good crosser, instead. The move succeeded some ten minutes later, as Owen's sudden change of pace caught Viktor off guard and brought him inside before sending the left back through, whose cross found the striker ahead of Thorsten in the near post to equalise.

The stadium exploded with joy and relief as the home team moved back into safety. The sound of "We Are Staying Up" echoed nonstop as both teams slowed the play down, seemingly settled for a draw. David replaced Charlie with Harry for the last fifteen minutes and reverted to the usual 4-2-1-3 with Ryan on the right. Kasper also came on for Tom.

With two minutes remaining, Ryan picked up a pass near the halfway line on the right and brought the ball in field away from Cody. He played a neat one-two with Harry to by-pass the centre midfielder and drove towards goal, facing one of the centre backs. He pulled off multiple step overs to squeeze the ball through the centre back's legs, but was taken down by the other centre back before he could go any further. The referee duly whistled to give the Black Dragons a direct free kick twenty-five yards away from goal and issued the offender a yellow card.

Richard picked the ball up and placed it on the spot sprayed by the referee. It was slightly to the right of goal and the goal keeper set up a five-man wall to cover the near side. The stadium went dead quiet and when he measured up his options he could see the concerned on the players' faces. His friend Owen was one of them and a thought crossed his mind.

"Will it be cruel if my shot ends up sending Owen down when we don't really need to win?" he thought. "But I am a sportsman, there's no way I would miss intentionally."

He made up his mind and had a go. The ball flew over the jumping wall towards the right of the post, before its usual bend came into effect.

It was another well-executed free kick!

The atmosphere completely collapsed. The players and supporters were in disbelief, and tears started to appear on younger (and some older) fans' faces. The match was in stoppage time and their team were going down.

Richard wasn't sure how to react – he had scored his sixth direct free kick goal in a season, which was itself a wonderful achievement, but he might have become public enemy number one in one of the few cities he loved in the process.

He didn't celebrate. He acknowledged the congratulations from his teammates and walked back into position. He did put his hand up to apologise to Owen and received a nod.

The East Sussex side launched the ball forward, looking to rescue the situation late on for the second match running. But it wasn't to be. Their last cross into the area was picked up by Gordon and that was that. The Black Dragons had ruined the party by winning the match 2-1 and condemned the third team to relegation.

It was heart-breaking for the players and fans alike. Richard and his teammates gathered to console their friend Owen.

"I'm sorry it ended like this," Richard said when they shook hands.

"It's not your fault mate. You only did what you needed to do," Owen gave him a hug. "It hurts, but we'll be back."

As other players joined in to send him their best wishes, a massive roar came up from the stands and fans were getting excited. It soon spread over the stadium and it was all jubilant again.

The big west London club had scored a late winner in their game!

The East Sussex players couldn't believe it. They checked with the coaching team and it was real – the other match had also ended 2-1 and they were staying up after all!

A large number of supporters ran onto the pitch to celebrate their last day survival. Stewards were quick onto the scene to escort the Thames Ditton players away but there was no danger – the fans were just happy and didn't cause any trouble.

"I guess we are still allowed to visit the city then," Layne joked.

"I hope they'll forget my goal quickly," Richard said.

The Black Dragons ended the thirty-eight game season with fifty-four points. They finished eighth in the Premier League, which was an astonishing achievement for a newly promoted side. David and Danny were nominated for the Best Manager and Best Young Player awards respectively but both lost out to their counterparts from the title winning team. The 20-year-old goal scoring midfielder did pick up his second consecutive Player of the Season award voted by the Thames Ditton supporters, ahead of Charlie and Richard.

The young players gathered for dinner that evening. For old times' sake they returned to the riverside pub restaurant opposite Richard and Layne's first apartment in Surbiton, reserving the whole of their first floor. Most of the matchday squad were there, while ex-players Owen, Peter and Rob also joined.

The three former Thames Ditton players had some mixed fortunes that season: while Owen survived relegation from that day's results, Peter's team from Bedfordshire won their second promotion in three seasons having clinched second place with three games remaining, but Rob's team from east London were relegated to League One the previous week, despite him finishing as one of the top scorers of the division.

"Shame about the drop Rob, we could have played in the same level!" said big Peter.

"Don't worry about that. My agent is working on a way back already," Rob said.

"That'll be great, you're too good for League One," Danny said.

"I can't wait to meet Bob and Les in the Premier League next season," Tom said, referring to the latest champions of the Championship.

"You guys still have another game to play, don't forget that!" Owen pointed out.

"Of course! That's the game of our lives! We'll win our first ever trophy and qualify for Europe!" Charlie claimed.

"Fly, you Black Dragons!"

The pair had a good night and left the party at about eleven. Layne suggested a walk along the riverside path that they used to run every evening and Richard was only too happy to oblige.

"I can't believe we've moved away six months ago, this place is still so familiar," Layne said.

"Yes, it feels just like yesterday."

"We need to have another boat hire one day, that was so much fun! Oh look! There's a wedding reception over there in the island!"

Just as Richard turned to the party's direction, the firework began and the pair stood by and admired the colourful display.

"This is so nice," Layne said as he leaned into Richard.

"Yes baby," Richard responded while putting his arm across.

Wouldn't it be nice if I can propose now? he thought, but he was there without the ring.

"What are you thinking Richie?"

"It's beautiful. The island is such a nice place for wedding receptions."

"Hehe, it's so true!"

One day, Layney boy, Richard continued in his imagination.

"Why are you smiling?"

650

"Nothing, I'm just happy to be with you here."

"You're being silly, as usual!"

The pair laughed and enjoyed the rest of their evening.

Training for the cup final was similar to normal, with the one additional focus on penalty taking. The coaching team provided plenty of information on opposition players but David asked the team not to spend too much time on it, claiming that over-analysing could lead to a lack of preparation to surprises. Maximising physical capabilities and maintaining a balanced mental state were the more important. He urged the players to have plenty of sleep as well.

Soon it was the big day. Similar to the Championship playoff final the year before, the Black Dragons stayed at a hotel in Richmond the night before to ensure the safety and conditions of the players. As the Wembley Stadium was only twenty miles away they had their usual routine for a home game – a short, light training session in the morning at the training complex followed by an early team lunch and a two-hour nap. They set off for Wembley two and a half hours prior to kick off time, at about half past two, to the cheers of all staff members who were staying behind.

Players were wearing their new charcoal slim fit suits and white shirts, sponsored by a large British retailer, together with the club's black and golden yellow striped ties. They had a casual walk on the Wembley turf to inspect the pitch and have some photographs taken.

"Third visit in a year, can you believe it?" Charlie said.

"This one will be the toughest," Richard commented.

"We're wearing red today, let's hope it's our lucky shirt!" Layne said.

"We did win more than we lose in that so maybe you're right," Ryan said.

"We'll be fine if we stick to the plan and keep our composure," Danny was full of confidence, as always.

The players changed into their special edition training kit and listened to David's announcement of the starting eleven.

"Goal keeper Gordon. Maz and Layne full backs. Kieran and Graham centre backs. Rich, Tom and Danny the midfield three. Charlie, Luci and Alex up top. I've no doubt that the rest of you will have a vital part to play. It's not an easy opponent and you could turn out to be the match winner. Follow Nick and Tim out and get yourselves ready!"

The stadium was nearly half full when the players had their warm up. Richard waved at his guests in the stand – his parents, his youth team coach Simon and former teammates, his PE teacher Mr Clarke, and his former hosts Mr and Mrs Stevenson. Layne gave his allocation to his private school friends and auctioned the rest for local charities. The club gave plenty of tickets to students from local schools as well and made it a very family friendly atmosphere.

The Black Dragons suffered a major blow during their warm up, as captain and centre back Graham pulled his thigh muscle and had to be replaced by Thorsten. Gordon picked up the captain's armband and Viktor was called up to the bench instead, together with Jack, Lewis, Kasper, Andrés, Sam and Ryan.

The players returned to the dressing room amid cheers from their supporters and David gave his final team talk.

"This is it. Our first ever cup final. I'm probably as nervous as you are, but let's remind ourselves why we are here.

"Six rounds. Two Premier League teams. That tough semi-final on penalties, against a so-called top six side. Through blood and tears, we made it here. In our own rights.

"Throughout the last few seasons, we've proved time and time again that we're a formidable group. A team of great abilities, a team of unbeatable efforts, a team of tremendous togetherness, a team of dragons! It is that time again, for us to rise and write another chapter in our history! In our first of many major finals! As victors! As champions!

"We are ready for the challenge! We are ready for the fight! We are ready to WIN!

"Fly! You Black Dragons!"

Players roared at the top of their voices and followed Gordon out into the tunnel full of spirit. There they met their opponents, the team from Tyneside. They might have been one of the traditional clubs with a big fan base, they had not picked up a major trophy for more than sixty years and it was their first final in over ten.

Richard shook hands with former teammates Hakim and Max before calming himself to switch into competition mode. It had become a natural part of his pre-match routine, having made over ninety professional appearances.

The team of officials arrived and after a quick chat with the captains they led the two teams onto the pitch, to the deafening cheers of ninety thousand spectators, with one side of the stadium in red, the Black Dragons' changed colour for the day, and the other in black and white.

Once the pre-match formalities with the Football Association dignitaries were over, the whole stadium raised for the national anthem, elegantly performed by an opera singer.

"This is it Rich. This is all I ever wanted. To compete for trophies with you guys. Let's do this!" said an excited Tom, who stood next to Richard as always.

"Let's put our names on the famous trophy!" Layne, who lined up on the other side, echoed.

"Yes. Only one thing matters now!" Richard agreed.

The team from Tyneside started with the same 4-4-2 formation that played well against the Black Dragons a fortnight ago. All their key players were back in the side, but Max, Hakim and Connor kept their places.

The experienced referee blew his whistle and the final began as Connor passed the ball back to his long-serving captain, Wilfred the centre back. The Black Dragons started with their fans behind them.

After a period of possession in the back, the ball was passed to Max just behind the centre circle. He feinted a long pass to the right to tempt his marker Danny into a block, switched back nicely with a Cruyff turn, and sent a delicate left footed chip into the area between Richard, Layne and Kieran. Hakim chested it down beautifully and flicked it behind the young left back for Connor, who was onside and he angled the return ball perfectly onto the winger's path between the two centre backs. Gordon rushed out to sweep it up but Hakim arrived first and he was clattered by the goal keeper!

The referee blew for a foul and showed Gordon a straight red card for denying a clear goal-scoring opportunity!

The whole stadium held their breath as the decision was checked by the video assistant referee, and after a long and anxious wait, the verdict was out.

It was deemed to be a foul and… the contact took place inches inside the penalty area!

Richard and his teammates couldn't believe it – their dream cup final had come to the absolutely worst possible start!

Half the stadium showed their disapproval of the decision but it was difficult to argue against it. Gordon angrily walked off after handing Tom the captain's armband while David reluctantly withdrew Alex to bring on the substitute goal keeper Jack. The striker was naturally heartbroken but he sportingly applauded the supporters and urged the team on as he walked off.

After the lengthy delay and amid massive jeers from the Thames Ditton fans behind the goal, Connor placed the ball on the penalty spot and steadied himself for the kick.

He sent his side footed shot to the right of goal but Jack was able to parry it! Hakim latched onto the loose ball but instead of a first time shot at goal he cleverly flipped it over the desperately sliding Layne and placed it into the bottom corner!

The Black Dragons went a goal and a man down after just five minutes of play!

"Relax lads! There's plenty of time for us to turn this round!" Tom did his job as captain to encourage his teammates.

David instructed Danny to move slightly forward to occupy the false nine position and asked the team to steady themselves for the next fifteen minutes to avoid conceding another goal.

Sensing the shock for their opponents, the team from Tyneside pushed for the decisive second goal. They were comfortable with the ball given the numerical advantage and explored the gaps in the Black Dragons defence. Their left winger was given time to pick his cross and Connor's layoff set Hakim up for a shot, but Richard was there diving in to block. Then Connor ran through on goal from another killer ball by Max but his lob was cleared off the line by the excellent Kieran.

The Black Dragons eventually settled back into the game with some possession but they found it hard to create any chances from open play. They forced a handful of set pieces but they failed to test the goal keeper. Richard disappointingly hit a free kick against the jumping wall from a good position and Thorsten's powerful header from Danny's in-swinging corner was agonisingly wide.

The first half ended 1-0 to the northern side.

"It wasn't the best start but well done for limiting it to one goal. We need to keep focussing on getting those set pieces and make them count. Gamble but refrain from using the squeeze straight away – they would have prepared to hit us on the break. I'm sure that there're goals in this team even with ten men. You know you can do it, go and show them hell!" David gave the players his half time team talk.

The second half began with the team from Tyneside trying to slow down the tempo. They spread the play using the whole width of the pitch and held back from taking unnecessary risks, but with the pace and skills of Hakim they were always only one good pass away from a breakaway, as they showed in the league encounter.

The Black Dragons maintained their defensive shape and focused on having meaningful counter attacks when they won the ball back. They had to consider their stamina level when they did – quick bursts ahead if they felt strong or had a breather if the tank was low. They were patient and not in danger of conceding again but at the same time the match was slowly ticking away.

The balance of the tense game was finally broken after seventy minutes. Richard cut out a slightly loose pass from Hakim to Max at full stretch and immediately released a "hospital ball" to the area in front of the two centre backs for Charlie. He got there ahead of the right sided centre back but was tackled legitimately by the covering Wilfred, who gave the ball to Max in the process. The midfielder sent a first time ball towards Hakim on the right, in exactly the same way as in the league game, but Layne had learnt his lesson and didn't commit to a challenge that could allow the winger room to run behind.

Hakim was still able to open up some space for a pass and he sent the left winger through with a magnificent diagonal ball. He attracted the attention of Thorsten and crossed the ball towards Connor, who was completely free.

But Tom returned in time to cut out the pass!

He deflected the driven ball out of the penalty area and Richard was there to collect it. With no time to waste, he hit it long towards Luciano, who was behind the left back. The Argentinian forward controlled the ball in mid-air brilliantly and sent it forward towards Charlie in the centre, who helped it onto the left with a first time scoop ahead of Max. Layne reached it with his electrifying pace and his first time cross was headed in by a diving Danny at the near post!

Thames Ditton had equalised with a breath-taking counter attack!

The Black Dragons supporters behind the goal were invigorated by the sensational turn of events and rediscovered their full voice when Danny performed his double clap celebration in front of them.

To take full benefit of the momentum, David staked his next bet and replaced Thorsten the centre back with Ryan the striker. Tom and Danny would play deeper roles to facilitate the change and it was, certainly, make or break time.

Knowing how dangerous the small forward could be and how fragile his mental state was, the opposing fans did all they could to distract him. But Ryan stood tall in front of them: he ignored the jeers and focused on his task – closing down the defence using his fresh energy and creating chances.

The team pressed high up the pitch straight from the re-start – they were going for the squeeze. The team from Tyneside had not fully recovered from the setback and were caught in possession straight away. They were forced into a clearance that was picked up by Tom and he initiated an attack from deep. He carried the ball into midfield and put a string of first time passes together with his teammates, which resulted in Layne running behind on the left again. He whipped a high cross towards the edge of the six yard box, and Charlie was there to meet it!

But the keeper miraculously pushed it onto the post with his fingertips and Wilfred was there to clear it up field!

The ball fortuitously fell to Hakim and he controlled it with his left heel and took it past Kieran first time to run clean through from the halfway line!

I can't let you do it! Richard thought as he pushed himself to the limit and sprinted back.

He managed to hold Hakim's progress from his right and forced him into a one-on-one situation. Sensing his inferior momentum, the attacker chopped the ball back to his right before a quick double step over to push it forward again to his left. Richard lost his balance reacting to that lightning quick movement but he crawled back up and caught Hakim up again as he pulled the trigger just outside the penalty area. He threw himself forward and managed to block the shot with his out-stretching right foot!

The ball was deflected over the oncoming Jack, but the keeper rushed back in time to scramble it out for a corner!

The usually calm and composed Hakim punched the ground in disbelief – he could have hit the winner and killed the Black Dragons off but was somehow denied by his old friend!

There was a lengthy delay for the resulting corner kick as Richard suffered badly from a cramp. It took the physio a little while to get him back to his feet – the challenge really took out the most of him.

David made his final change and replaced the tiring Maz with the versatile Andrés. He was going all out for the winning goal – he knew the team would not have the stamina to compete in extra time.

The corner was defended successfully while Richard waited off the field after his treatment. The team from Tyneside seemed to have figured out their potential advantage in having extra time and switched into game management mode. They were keen to run down the clock and drain out any remaining energy from the Black Dragons with numbers behind the ball. The match was frustratingly heading towards the ninetieth minute.

Andrés was relatively quiet since coming on but he had a chance with five minutes remaining. He dribbled past the tired left winger with a quick turn and played a nice give-and-go with Luciano to open up some space for a cross. It was punched clear by the keeper and the clearance was picked up by Layne on the left, ahead of the halfway line.

Instead of attacking the byline as he had done all game, the young left back brought the ball in field, tricked his way through Max and sent it towards Ryan in the middle, who had dropped into the space between defence and midfield.

He was closed down quickly by Wilfred but he magically flipped the ball past the approaching defender on the left using the tip of his right foot while turning the other way to meet it on the right using his explosive acceleration. He took a small touch to move the ball forward and he was in the clear – he had a chance to have a shot.

Just put everything through it! Richard screamed in his head.

But Ryan didn't.

He saw the goal keeper rushing out with a starfish style block and scooped it over him instead!

Richard witnessed, in slow motion, with his heart in his mouth, the ball flying over the keeper's hands, and into the back of the net!

He paused for a second to process what he saw, before releasing all his emotions into a massive cry.

"Yeeeeees!"

His team had scored the decisive goal with barely minutes to go!

He instinctively ran towards the goal scorer Ryan and jumped into his teammates there with absolute joy!

"You. Fucking. Beauty!" the excited Charlie was there having a big smooch on Ryan's cheek while everyone else jumped up and down round them.

Layne crashed into Richard and screamed passionately, "We've done it! We've done it! We've turned it around!"

The jubilant players kept celebrating until Tom shepherded them back into position – there were still a good few minutes plus added time to see out!

The team from Tyneside had to throw everything forward to rescue their cup final. Players ran into forward positions while balls were launched into the final third. The Black Dragons pulled everyone back to defend and heroically repelled waves after waves of aerial bombardment.

The fourth official held up his electronic board to indicate there would be a minimum of four minutes of added time.

"Four more minutes and the victory is ours!" Tom shouted to focus his team's concentration.

Another ball was launched into the Black Dragons' penalty box by the keeper and it was cleared as far as the right back. He crossed it dangerously towards the far post and Andrés had to deal with it at the expense of a corner kick. The keeper received the signal from the bench and sprinted up to join the attack. That was it – the final attack. Max sent the ball towards the keeper on the edge of the six yard box but Jack managed to get a hand to it and punched it out of the box!

The loose ball was collected by Danny on the left and he held off the right back's challenge before squaring it for Richard, who hit a high ball with heavy backspin behind the last defender to put Charlie clean through!

The winger raced clear of the hapless defender and finished off the move to send the stadium into a complete frenzy!

Our goal is scored by Ranger
Our goal is scored by Ranger
Our goal is scored by Ranger
Our goal is scored by Ranger

The fans sang their chant for Charlie and his dad repeatedly while the players gathered in front of them to celebrate. There surely was no way back now.

The referee waved every player back in their half before he whistled for the re-start, but once Connor kicked off he blew again to signal the end of the dramatic cup final.

Thames Ditton Football Club had won the FA Cup, their first ever major trophy!

The small village team that nobody had any expectations for had achieved the unthinkable. They had written their own chapter in the history of the oldest football competition in the world!

Richard raised his hands in the air to celebrate the moment of glory. He closed his eyes and enjoyed listening to the sound from jubilant fans round the stadium. It was like a dream. He had done it.

His whole footballing journey flashed back in his head. Memories of all the twists and turns throughout the years returned to make him appreciate what an achievement it was.

And a key part of that journey crashed into him and pushed him to the ground!

"We've made it Richie! We've made it!"

Richard opened his eyes and saw a tearfully overjoyed Layne on top of him. They looked at other, and smiled.

"Yes we have, baby. We have."

They got up and joined their teammates in front of their supports, as the familiar tune of "We Are the Champions" began.

We are the Dragons, my friends.

And we'll keep on fighting till the end.

We are the Dragons!

We are the Dragons!

No time for losers,

Cause we are the Dragons, of Ditton!

The fans belted out one chant after another and the players sang along to them. They lifted David in the air to their hoorays and thoroughly enjoyed their moment.

Soon the organisers advised the team to gather by the middle of the north stand for the trophy presentation. The Tyneside players had lined up to sportingly congratulate the Black Dragons before they went up to collect their runners-up medals. They had more than certainly contributed to the great final as it was only decided by the smallest of margins in the end. Richard had a hug with his old friend Hakim, who pretended to punch him in revenge for his last ditch tackle that stopped him from scoring what could have been the winning goal.

For the second season in a row David led the match day team up the famous 107 steps to access the Royal Box and presentation area. He specifically asked Tom to go last, which indicated that he would like his captain of the day to pick up the trophy. Gordon was relieved that his dismissal didn't ruin the day for the team and was only too happy for Tom to claim the glory he deserved.

Richard walked up the steps with Layne near the end of the line and received his winners medal from the President of the Football Association. They joined their triumphant teammates at the presentation area and the excitement reached fever stage as the jubilant Tom arrived.

"Remember the name, we are the Black Dragons!" he screamed as he lifted the prestigious trophy aloft.

"Fly, you Black Dragons!" the players responded with the club slogan.

They brought the trophy back on the pitch for more photographs and other squad members, many of whom deserved and would no doubt receive one of the forty winners medals provided by the FA, joined them for a parade in front of supporters in the other stands.

"Thank you for winning it for me boys!" said Thomas, who was there with his crutches.

The players danced to fans' singing of Andrés's favourite victory song, "Campeones, Campeones, Olé Olé Olé" on the field. The supporters saw videos of it from the season before and decided to initiate it now they had the chance.

The celebrations moved to the dressing room eventually, where glasses of champagne were already lined up waiting for the players.

"Alright boys, well... champions! How are you feeling?" David asked, to a massive roar from the players.

"What can I say? Everything I asked for, you've delivered. Defensively, offensively, everything. The sending off and penalty were tragic, unlucky Gordon, but you've recovered well. The goals were exquisite – Danny, Ryan, Charlie, all top-notch. Layne, Rich, great passes.

"You've defended with your lives out there, thank you. We always say 'we'll never be beaten on efforts', it was true today, and in fact, the whole season. You deserved your achievement!

"What do we do from here? Well the logistics team better start thinking about hotels and flights and all that, now that we are in EUROPE! Of course we need to aim higher than eighth next season in the Premier League too, we don't do second season syndrome here. But for now, we celebrate! See you back at the hotel later!"

Richard sat next to Layne and they shared a smile after having their bubbly drink.

"Fancy kissing a FA Cup winner?" Layne asked.

"Sure, but we'll need to find a room if you want more!" The pair had a quick peck on the lips before being dragged by Charlie for more pictures and videos. Players had been flooding social media with those, to the delights of their supporters around the world.

The team party back at the hotel in Richmond started at nine and the pair joined players and staffs for the celebration.

"You boys are never early for parties!" Tom welcomed them.

"Never mind, I'll make up for lost time," Layne said before going in to find his friends on the dance floor.

"Can I offer you a drink Rich?"

"I may just take it slow this year. I don't want more photos of me passing out online!"

The two picked up their beverages and joined Thomas and Danny for a chat.

"What a season we had Rich!" Thomas said. "Did you expect any of that?"

"I'm always confident that we would stay up, but anything else was a bonus," Richard said.

"Hey we're eighth in the toughest league in the world! You can just say we're good!" Tom said.

"Take nothing away but luck was on our side," Danny commented. "In other seasons fifty-four points could be as low as twelfth."

"And we didn't play many top teams in our cup run," Richard added.

"We can only beat what's in front of us!" Tom countered.

"That's true, but we shouldn't underestimate the challenges we have next season," Danny continued.

"Surely we'll be fine if we carry on playing the way we did?" Tom asked.

"Other teams will analyse our tactics to death over the summer. They'll find ways to counter every single strength we have," Richard explained. "We only need to drop a few points to fall into the relegation battle."

"That's what's behind the so-called second season syndrome," Danny said.

"Oh don't make it sound so frightening, what shall we do?" Tom asked.

"I'm sure David and the team have it all planned, like additional ways of playing and new signings with specific attributes to enable those. As players we just need to focus on learning them and maintaining our own conditions," Richard explained.

"I wonder who we are going to sign," Thomas said. "I hope they don't get another centre half!"

"Sorry but I think we need to. With the extra games in the Europa League we can't start the season with only three fit centre backs," Danny pointed out.

"We'll need reinforcements in midfield too. We're so much weaker if you're not playing," Richard said.

"Or indeed when one of you two is missing. No offense to Toby and Kasper, we need more experience there," Danny added.

"Oh let's worry about them later. Today is about celebrations and I have a piece of good news – Elle and I are now engaged!" Thomas proudly announced.

"Wow congratulations! When's the big day?" Tom asked.

"We're thinking the next summer break. There's a church in the Lake District that we really like so it'll probably be there."

"Well done mate!" Danny said.

Richard couldn't stop thinking about proposing to Layne after hearing what Thomas said. He had been contemplating whether Layne would prefer him doing it publicly or in private, and had the ring with him just in case. He naturally had a little smile on his face and it was picked up by his mates.

"What's that sweet little smile there for, Rich?" Tom asked.

"I bet someone is thinking about marriage too!" Thomas teased.

Richard's face went a little blushed and he made a shush gesture. His friends gave him a thumbs up in return and moved on.

"Are you going to move to a bigger place Bondi? The flat can't be good enough for the boys?" Tom asked.

"I'm not earning anywhere near you hot-shots! But yes we're looking to buy, maybe a small house near the schools," Thomas said.

"That'll be lovely! Layne can see the boys more often then!" Richard said.

"We'll probably be doing the same but nearer the station," Danny said.

"I thought you're happy living at the town centre?" Tom asked.

"Yes it's convenient and great for our commutes but we're getting a little too much attention these days," Danny explained.

"I guess that's inevitable for a Young Footballer of the Year nominee!" Tom said.

"Carla's going to be very busy with the estate agents then!" Richard said.

"You two millionaires are not buying another one, are you? Don't push up the price for the local area!" Thomas warned.

"No no no… there're currently no plans for more…" Richard was keen to clarify.

Before his friends quizzed him any further, David requested everyone to gather by the centre stage for his announcement. Richard found the very giddy Layne there and stood by him.

"Are you having fun, our FA Cup winning Black Dragons? It's time for our end of season awards, are you ready?" he said, to the cheers of the players.

"Similar to last year, the winner will need to down a drink up here. To make it easier for some, we'll make it a shot and not a pint this time!"

"Isn't that more lethal? You'd better find a spare sofa now!" Layne joked.

"First one up is most appearances. Danny did well to start forty matches, but someone else trumped him with forty-two overall, and it's... Nelson!"

"But don't worry Danny, you're our top scorer with fifteen!"

"Can Charlie also come up for providing fifteen assists too?"

The three players made their way up the stage, had a group hug with David and downed their drinks. They also forced the manager to take one and he happily obliged.

"For goal of the season, we have some decent contenders: Tom's counter attack against the champions, Ryan's debut screamer against Manchester and Layne's amazing volley in the quarter-final! Which one is your pick?"

Players shouted their favourites and David slowly raised his hands to calm them down.

"The result, decided by our trusted panel of experts, is... Layne's volley!"

"We want Moore! We want Moore! We want Moore!" the crowd chanted.

Layne ran up stage and performed his favourite celebration, which was forming a heart shape with his hands. He did it towards Richard and the crowd sent them lots of cheers and whistles.

"Thanks Mr Moore, off you go... We have a new category this year for individual performance of the season and it's a tough one. We have Danny's fight back against the Reds, Ryan's perfect hat trick against west London and Richard's triple free kick against his boyhood club!"

"Richie! Richie! Richie!" Layne was clearly way beyond his limit.

"And the panel's decision is... Richard and his free kicks!"

The super excited Layne gave Richard multiple kisses before letting him go on stage. He applauded his teammates and the staff members, gave David a hug before picking up the shot glass. He downed it in one go and felt the spiciness from the alcohol running up and down his throat. He thought about proposing to Layne at that moment but missed his chance as David moved on to the next, and final, award.

"Here we are with the last one, player's player of the year. I'll give you the final three: The first one is our top scorer and fans' player of the year, Danny Westwood! The second is our rocket boy, our guard of the bowling alley, our midfield conductor and destroyer, Richard Lucas! Finally, we have our dynamo, our inspiration and our, wait for it, deputy captain, Tom Nelson!"

"I voted for you!" Layne told Richard the obvious.

"Oh... I went for Tom..." Richard said embarrassingly.

"You're such a bad boyfriend! But I love you anyway!"

"And the answer is... Nelson!"

Super, Super Tom,

Super, Super Tom,

Super, Super Tom,

Super, Super Tommy Nelson

The crowd chanted Tom's name and he gladly returned to the stage to take his second shot.

"Right! You guys have a great night, don't forget we will meet up for the parade at 3pm tomorrow!"

The strong music resumed while David left the stage and players continued their party. Richard felt the effect of the drink and Layne helped him to a sofa to rest on.

"Feeling dizzy again?" he asked.

"I'll be fine. You go and have fun with the boys."

"No way! I'll take care of you, do you want some water?"

"Yes please baby."

"Hehe, sure!"

Layne quickly grabbed him a glass of water and he felt slightly better after having it.

"Do you want to head back to the room?" Layne asked.

"The party is only halfway in, we shouldn't."

"But I can't wait to have some private time with you," the young one said cheekily, with one of his cutest smiles.

"Oh…" Richard's face boiled up and he couldn't help but pulled Layne closer for a kiss.

One quickly became two and the pair enjoyed their moment.

"Maybe… maybe we should go…" Richard said after a little while.

"I'm glad you agree!"

The pair quietly sneaked back to their riverside room and promptly resumed where they left off.

"I'll never be bored of this," Richard said after another round of passionate kisses.

"Me neither. I love the way you smile when you are with me."

"And I like how you turn into a lovely boyfriend when we're alone."

"Hehe, I really want to take your clothes off now!"

"Oh… there's something… I want to tell you…"

"Can't it wait until later?"

"Err… no, I would like to say it now."

Looking at Richard's suddenly serious impression, Layne became a little nervous.

"What… are you going to say, Richie?"

"Okay baby… " Richard cleared his throat before he started.

"When I joined the club five years ago, all I wished to do was to become a professional footballer. I worked very hard and progressed well but there was something that I could never be completely open with anyone, and I was very lonely. Then you showed up with your lovely warm smile, gave me all your attention and showed me that I can actually live the life that I dare to imagine, with confidence and happiness. Every day was a dream with you – we had our ups and downs but you're always there for me. I really, really enjoyed the last four years, and I want it to carry on forever."

668

He then went down on one knee, took the engagement ring out, and said, with his eyes locked onto Layne's.

"Will you marry me, Layne?"

"Oh Richie..." Layne covered his face with his hands but Richard could see a tear or two on their way down.

"Will you let me be your husband?"

"Yes Richie! Yes!"

Layne crashed into Richard's arms with tears in free fall. Richard could feel his shaking body and wrapped his arms round his now fiancé tightly. His eyes were full of tears too, tears of joy.

"I promise to treasure you forever, baby."

"I'll love you for the rest of my life too, Richie."

"Do you want to try the ring on?"

"Wait," Layne wiped his tears with his hand before taking something out from his pocket.

"I... have bought you a ring too... Will... you marry me, Richie?"

"Oh this isn't fair, why aren't you on your knees too?"

"Hehe, okay..." Layne said before going down on one knee and repeated the question with a big smile. It was probably not his best looking one, but for Richard, it was surely the most beautiful.

"Yes I will, sweety."

The deeply in love young couple held onto each other again, before Layne coming up with an observation.

"Have we bought exactly the same ring?"

"I think we have!"

They laughed and put the rings onto each other's fourth finger. They fit perfectly.

"It looks great on you," Richard praised.

"It's beautiful, I love it very much!"

"Can I kiss you now, my fiancé?"

"You never needed permission, my fiancé!"

The pair merrily kissed again, and again, and again...

"That was the best one ever," said Layne after the exhausted pair eventually settled down in bed.

"I love it when you enjoy it this much," Richard responded with a gentle kiss on Layne's forehead.

"What's your most memorable moment with me?"

"Mm... it's hard to single one out, but I can never forget that night in Bournemouth. The way we kissed for the first time ever."

"Hehe, when you finally came out of your closet? I love our first Christmas together at my Bath home. Mum was still around then..."

"I'm sure she's happy with what we've become."

"Yes, I think she'd be delighted to see us getting married. Do you have any ideas on the wedding?"

"I haven't planned anything. What about you? Do you have a preference, for example, local or overseas?"

"I guess we can make a big holiday out of it? I wonder which countries we can go to?"

"We can check later but I've read that Spain and Portugal are fine."

"Oh I can't wait to show the ring to the boys tomorrow!"

"During the open-bus parade? That'll be a bit... oh well I guess it's fine, we really are engaged!"

"Do we need to buy wedding bands too?"

"Yes, we can get those together."

"I would like a simple one that goes well with this."

"Sure baby. We'll go to that big department store next week?"

"Thanks. Oh, do you want Nico to be our pianist at the wedding?"

"... Do you have to?"

"He offered it when he left for Italy, so I'd better ask. But before you get anxious again, he's dating a model now."

"Good for him... and us! I don't mind having a world class pianist for free!"

"Hehe, you're such a silly hubby."

"I love how you called me just now, my little hubby!"

"Okay, big hubby!"

The pair giggled into another snuggle, blissful that they would be spending the rest of their lives together, no matters what challenges lay in front of them.

Printed in Great Britain
by Amazon

16595473R00383